Praise for *The Stolen Crown*

"*The Stolen Crown* is a rich and riveting read, a jewel
in the crown of historical fiction."
—Brandy Purdy, author of *The Boleyn Wife* and
The Confession of Piers Gaveston

"The aftermath of the Wars of the Roses. A new King
with a secret Queen; love and tears, loyalty and turmoil. With a
single stroke, Susan Higginbotham transports her readers into a
vividly portrayed past, where the turbulent lives of her characters
become very real. Probably her best novel yet!"
—Helen Hollick, author of the Pendragon's Banner trilogy

"The Wars of the Roses come spectacularly to life in Susan
Higginbotham's compelling new novel about Kate Woodville,
sister to Queen Elizabeth of England. A sweeping tale of danger,
treachery, and love, *The Stolen Crown* is impossible to put down!"
—Bestselling author Michelle Moran, author of *Cleopatra's Daughter*

"A fascinating and compelling look at a tumultuous era. Susan
Higginbotham writes the perfect blend of historical fact and fiction."
—Elizabeth Kerri Mahon, creator of the Scandalous Women blog

"A tale of love, palace intrigue, and betrayal…Susan Higginbotham draws
the reader under her spell, her characters vivid and real: their voices, their
loves, their losses. She brings the dead to life."
—Christy English, author of *The Queen's Pawn*

The STOLEN Crown

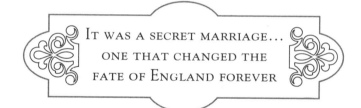

IT WAS A SECRET MARRIAGE...
ONE THAT CHANGED THE
FATE OF ENGLAND FOREVER

SUSAN HIGGINBOTHAM

sourcebooks
landmark

Published by Sourcebooks Landmark, an imprint of Sourcebooks, Inc.
P.O. Box 4410, Naperville, Illinois 60567-4410
(630) 961-3900
Fax: (630) 961-2168
www.sourcebooks.com

Library of Congress Cataloging-in-Publication Data

Higginbotham, Susan.
  The stolen crown : it was a secret marriage… one that changed the fate of England forever / Susan Higginbotham.
    p. cm.
  1. Woodville, Katherine, 1457 or 8-1497—Fiction. 2. Elizabeth, Queen, consort of Edward IV, King of England, 1437?-1492—Fiction. 3. Edward IV, King of England, 1442-1483—Fiction. 4. Great Britain—History—Edward IV, 1461-1483—Fiction. 5. Richard III, King of England, 1452-1485—Fiction. 6. Great Britain—History—Richard III, 1483-1485—Fiction. 7. Great Britain—History—Wars of the Roses, 1455-1485—Fiction. I. Title.
  PS3608.I364S76 2010   JUL 16 2010
  813'.6—dc22
                        2009039226

Printed and bound in the United States of America.
VP 10 9 8 7 6 5 4 3 2

To those who died in 1483

Characters

ALL THE NAMED CHARACTERS IN THIS NOVEL ARE BASED ON HISTORICAL figures. I have listed all of them below, except for a few, like some of Edward IV's daughters, who appear only fleetingly. I have also listed several historical figures, such as Eleanor Butler and Elizabeth Shore, who never make an appearance but who are mentioned by the other characters.

The House of York

Edward IV ("Ned"), King of England.

Elizabeth ("Bessie") Woodville, his queen.

Elizabeth ("Bess"), their eldest daughter, later queen to Henry VII.

Cecily, one of their younger daughters.

Edward, Prince of Wales, their eldest son. Later Edward V.

Richard, Duke of York, their younger son. Married to Anne Mowbray.

Cecily Neville, Duchess of York. Mother of Edward IV.

Anne, Duchess of Exeter, sister of Edward IV. Married to Henry Holland, Duke of Exeter, and to Thomas St. Leger.

Elizabeth, Duchess of Suffolk, sister of Edward IV. Married to John de la Pole, Duke of Suffolk.

George, Duke of Clarence, brother of Edward IV. Married to Isabel Neville, Duchess of Clarence.

Edward, Earl of Warwick, their son.

Margaret, Duchess of Burgundy, sister of Edward IV. Married to Charles, Duke of Burgundy.

Richard, Duke of Gloucester, brother of Edward IV. Later King Richard III. Married to Anne Neville, Duchess of Gloucester.

Edward, their son. Prince of Wales during Richard III's reign.

John, out-of-wedlock son of Richard, Duke of Gloucester.

Katherine, out-of-wedlock daughter of Richard, Duke of Gloucester.

The House of Lancaster

Henry VI, King of England.

Margaret of Anjou, his queen.

Edward of Lancaster, Prince of Wales, their son.

The Staffords

Henry ("Harry") Stafford, second Duke of Buckingham. Married to Kate Woodville, Duchess of Buckingham.

Anne Neville, Duchess of Buckingham, widow of Humphrey Stafford, first Duke of Buckingham. Later married to Walter Blount, Lord Mountjoy. Grandmother of Harry Stafford.

Margaret Beaufort, Countess of Stafford, widow of Humphrey Stafford, first son of Anne Neville and Humphrey Stafford. Mother of Harry Stafford.

Henry Stafford, second son of Anne Neville and Humphrey Stafford. Married to Margaret Beaufort, Countess of Richmond. Uncle of Harry Stafford.

John Stafford, Earl of Wiltshire, third son of Anne Neville and Humphrey Stafford. Uncle of Harry Stafford.

Joan, daughter of Anne Neville and Humphrey Stafford. Married to William Knyvet. Aunt of Harry Stafford.

Humphrey Stafford, younger brother of Harry Stafford.

Edward Stafford, later third Duke of Buckingham, son of Harry Stafford and Kate Woodville.

Henry ("Hal") Stafford, son of Harry Stafford and Kate Woodville.

Elizabeth Stafford, daughter of Harry Stafford and Kate Woodville.

Anne Stafford, daughter of Harry Stafford and Kate Woodville.

Humphrey Stafford, deceased son of Harry Stafford and Kate Woodville.

The Woodvilles

Richard Woodville, first Earl Rivers.

Jacquetta Woodville, Duchess of Bedford, his wife. Widow of John, Duke of Bedford, younger brother of Henry V.

Anthony Woodville, Lord Scales, later second Earl Rivers. Son of Richard and Jacquetta. Married to Elizabeth Scales and to Mary Fitzlewis.

Elizabeth ("Bessie") Woodville, queen to Edward IV. Daughter of Richard and Jacquetta. Previously married to John Grey.

Richard Woodville, later third Earl Rivers. Son of Richard and Jacquetta.

John Woodville, married to Katherine Neville, Duchess of Norfolk. Son of Richard and Jacquetta.

Jacquetta Woodville, married to John, Lord Strange. Daughter of Richard and Jacquetta.

Anne Woodville, married to William Bourchier. Daughter of Richard and Jacquetta.

Mary Woodville, married to William Herbert, later Earl of Pembroke. Daughter of Richard and Jacquetta.

Lionel Woodville, later Bishop of Salisbury. Son of Richard and Jacquetta.

Margaret Woodville, married to Thomas Fitzalan, Lord Maltravers, later Earl of Arundel. Daughter of Richard and Jacquetta.

Joan Woodville, married to Anthony Grey of Ruthin. Daughter of Richard and Jacquetta.

Edward Woodville. Son of Richard and Jacquetta.

Katherine ("Kate") Woodville, Duchess of Buckingham, married to Harry Stafford, Duke of Buckingham; Jasper Tudor, later Duke of Bedford; and Richard Wingfield. Daughter of Richard and Jacquetta.

Thomas Grey, later Marquess of Dorset. Son of Elizabeth Woodville by John Grey. Married to Anne Holland and to Cecily Bonville.

Richard Grey. Son of Elizabeth Woodville by John Gray.

The Nevilles

Richard Neville, Earl of Warwick ("the Kingmaker").

Anne Beauchamp, his wife, Countess of Warwick.

Isabel Neville, Duchess of Clarence, daughter of Richard Neville and Anne Beauchamp. Married to George, Duke of Clarence.

Anne Neville, Duchess of Gloucester, later queen to Richard III. Daughter of Richard Neville and Anne Beauchamp. Married to Edward of Lancaster, Prince of Wales, and to Richard, Duke of Gloucester, later King Richard III.

John Neville, Marquess of Montague, brother of Richard Neville.

George Neville, Archbishop of York, brother of Richard Neville.

The Tudors

Margaret Beaufort, Countess of Richmond, married to Edward Tudor, Earl of Richmond; Henry Stafford; and Thomas Stanley.

Henry Tudor, son of Margaret Beaufort and Edward Tudor. Later King Henry VII.

Jasper Tudor, brother-in-law of Margaret Beaufort and uncle of Henry Tudor. Later Duke of Bedford.

Others

Ralph Bannaster, retainer of Harry Stafford.

Edmund Beaufort, styled Duke of Somerset, maternal uncle of Harry Stafford.

Richard de la Bere, sheriff of Hereford.

Walter Blount, Lord Mountjoy, husband of Anne Neville, Duchess of Buckingham. Stepgrandfather of Harry Stafford.

Henry Bourchier, Earl of Essex. Relative of Harry Stafford.

Thomas Bourchier, Archbishop of Canterbury.

Robert Brackenbury, servant of Richard III.

Eleanor Butler, purported first wife of Edward IV. Sister of Elizabeth Talbot, Duchess of Norfolk.

William Catesby, official of Richard III.

William Caxton, printer.

Cecilia, attendant of Katherine Woodville.

Peter Courtenay, Bishop of Exeter.

Walter Devereux, Lord Ferrers, owner of the manor of Weobley.

William, Lord Hastings, courtier and friend of Edward IV.

John Howard, made Duke of Norfolk in 1483. Married to Margaret Howard.

Thomas Howard, made Earl of Surrey in 1483.

Richard Huddleston, servant of Richard III.

William Knyvet, uncle by marriage of Harry Stafford.

Francis, Viscount Lovell, courtier of Richard III.

John Morton, Bishop of Ely.

John Mowbray, Duke of Norfolk (died 1476). Married to Elizabeth Talbot, Duchess of Norfolk.

Anne Mowbray, their daughter. Wife to Edward IV's son Richard, Duke of York.

Thomas Nandyke, physician and astrologer of Harry Stafford.

John Nesfield, servant to Richard III. Custodian of Elizabeth and Katherine Woodville.

Katherine Neville, Duchess of Norfolk. Married to John Woodville.

Henry Percy, Earl of Northumberland.

Richard Ratcliffe, official of Richard III.

Thomas Rotherham, Archbishop of York.

Thomas St. Leger, lover and later husband of Anne, Duchess of Exeter.

Elizabeth Shore, mistress of Edward IV.

Thomas Stanley, third husband of Margaret Beaufort, Countess of Richmond.

Robert Stillington, Bishop of Bath and Wells.

George, Lord Strange, son of Thomas Stanley. Married to Joan, niece of Elizabeth and Kate Woodville.

Elizabeth Talbot, Duchess of Norfolk. Sister of Eleanor Butler and mother of Anne Mowbray.

Thomas Vaughan, chamberlain of Edward IV's son Edward, Prince of Wales.

The Vaughan family, residents of Tretower in Wales, unrelated to Thomas Vaughan.

John de Vere, Earl of Oxford.

Christopher Wellesbourne, servant of Richard III.

Richard Wingfield, servant of Kate Woodville.

"Now take heed what love may do, for love will not nor may not cast no fault nor peril in nothing."

—*Gregory's Chronicle*, on the marriage of Edward IV and Elizabeth Woodville

i

Harry: November 1, 1483

YOU MIGHT THINK THAT THE LAST NIGHT OF A CONDEMNED TRAITOR would be a rather solitary affair, but you would think wrong, for the last couple of hours have been bustling with people coming and going. In some ways I welcome the commotion; it keeps my mind from the object that lies hard by my lodgings here at the Blue Boar Inn in Salisbury. It is a scaffold, and I will be its first, and probably its last, occupant, for it has been built just for me. Such is the fate of a man who tries to take a king from his throne, and fails.

Yet I do wish that things were more peaceful so I could better gather my thoughts, for what I say in the next world about my life will determine whether I am saved or damned. The best way to explain myself, I suppose, is to start at the beginning.

༄

People who knew all of us say—or said, for there are few of them alive now—that I favor my mother more than my father. I will have to take their word for it, for he died just a month or so after I turned three. I remember a man who bounced me on his shoulders and held me on his lap when I saw him, which was not all that often, and I remember the scar on his right hand, which I would trace wonderingly because it made the hand so different from my mother's, soft and white, and my nurse's, plump and scarred by nothing worse than years of honest labor.

Father's scar was from the battle at St. Albans in May 1455. The battle had been a disastrous one for my family. My mother's father, Edmund Beaufort, Duke of Somerset, had died there, and his eldest son, Henry, had been hauled away insensible in a cart, more dead than alive. My paternal grandfather, Humphrey, had had his face slashed, and my father too had been badly injured. Worse, the battle had left the Duke of York the ruler of England in all but name, and my family had fought for the House of Lancaster.

All of this must have dispirited my parents, and I like to think I cheered them a little when I was born on the fourth day of September of that year and when I was named not Humphrey, the name my father and his father bore, but Henry, after the king for whom they had fought. I do hope indeed I cheered them, for in my eight-and-twenty years in this world I do not think I can say that I have done so for many people.

In the fall of 1458, the pestilence, which in those days still swept through England regularly, paid one of its dreaded visits. It did what the Yorkists had failed to do—kill my father. As I was now the heir to the dukedom of my grandfather, he and my grandmother wished to take custody of me. So to their care I went, once the pestilence had stopped its raging and it was considered safe for me to travel. I was not much upset at the change. The two mainstays of my existence at that time were my nurse and my puppy, and both went with me.

I came to know my grandfather somewhat better than I had my father, being more of an age now to observe what went on around me—and being doted on by my grandparents besides that. (Four of their seven sons had died young, my father had just died, and neither of my surviving uncles, Henry and John, had sons yet. I, therefore, was precious.) Grandfather, Humphrey Stafford, was a good man who tried to do what was best for England and to protect King Henry while trying to reach some sort of accord with the Duke of York. If only he had lived longer for me to profit by his example!

As I settled into my new life with my grandparents, Fortune's Wheel, which had been spinning back and forth with regularity, spun in the direction of Lancaster. As a result, not long before the Christmas of

1459, visitors arrived at my grandparents' Essex manor of Writtle: Cecily Neville, Duchess of York, and her three youngest children, Margaret, George, and Richard. Cecily was my grandmother's younger sister. Needless to say, she and my Lancastrian grandmother had not been on the warmest of terms as of late, and though we politely referred to her and her children as our guests, it was no social visit the Duchess of York was paying now. The Duke of York was in exile, and his wife had been placed in my grandmother's custody at the order of King Henry.

Since the youngest of the York children, Richard, has proven to be the death of me, I wish I could say there was a sense of doom from the first day of our meeting back at Writtle, but of course there wasn't. I was four at the time, just a month shy of being three years younger than Richard and nearly six years younger than George. My younger brother, Humphrey, who had been born shortly before my father died, was living with my mother. Thus, up until now there had been no other boys in the household except for pages, whose duties kept them to themselves. Naturally, I was delighted by this new company. I tagged along behind the York brothers, did my best to insinuate myself into their games, and tried with all my might to impress them. I am sure they regarded me as a thoroughgoing nuisance—and a Lancastrian nuisance at that. Probably I was an annoyance in another way as well. At the time, neither Richard nor George was a duke or a king's brother; they were simply two younger sons, far less important in the grand scheme of things than their father or their two older brothers, Edward and Edmund, both of whom were earls. Even at my young age, I, on the other hand, knew full well that I would be the next Duke of Buckingham, heir to one of the richest estates in the realm. I probably pointed this out more often than was strictly necessary.

Yes, I must have been completely insufferable.

Grandmother counted Queen Margaret among her dear friends and often said that the queen was only doing what was right, fighting for her husband's throne and that of her dear little son, Edward. She could not forbear from expressing this opinion to Cecily, who as Duchess of York held a view that was considerably to the contrary. Because of this, there was occasional tension in the household, but for the most part, the sisters rubbed along well enough. Both, after all, were worried for their husbands and sons, and both knew that their lives could be changed at a stroke of a battle ax.

For about seven months, we lived together in this fashion. Then, one day in July 1460, I was confined indoors with a bad cold, much to my disgust, for it was the first day in several that it had not rained. George and Richard were outdoors shooting at butts, and I deluded myself that I had improved my skill enough to give them at least a hint of competition. Some men came to see Grandmother on business, and she left the solar where the rest of us had gathered and was gone awhile. I was tossing a ball to my dog, and Cecily and her daughter Margaret were at their embroidery, when Richard and George rushed into the room as Cecily was critiquing Margaret's stitches. "Mother! Do you know what has happened?"

"Obviously not. George, when will you learn not to interrupt?"

"It is important, Mother. Truly. We heard it from the servants of the men who came here just now. Mad King Henry has been taken captive by the Earl of Warwick and Ned!"

"It was at a place called Northampton," put in Richard.

"It's a disaster for Lancaster, Mother! The men who were guarding that fool Henry's tent were killed by the Kentishmen. They didn't stand a chance. The Earl of Shrewsbury, Egremont, the Viscount Beaumont—and best of all, the Duke of Buckingham! Dead, all of them! The rats."

"George, you fool!" Margaret dropped her embroidery. "Harry—"

"Oh." George winced and looked at me. "Er, sorry."

"It's a lie!" I said. "You're just making that up to tease me." He often did things like that, and having grown up with no other children in the household until recently, I was particularly vulnerable to such tactics. Hopefully, I looked around for confirmation of my words.

Richard shook his head. "No, Harry. It's the truth."

I broke free of Margaret's consoling hand and ran to my grandmother's chamber. She was sitting in her cushioned window seat, sobbing. I had not known until then that people of my grandmother's age—she was nigh on fifty—cried. I had no need to ask her if what I had heard was true. When she saw me, she wrapped her arms around me and held me tight, but she did not stop weeping until my own sobs started. "Get your tears out now, Harry," Grandmother said, patting me on the back as I huddled against her shoulder. "Don't let that Yorkist brood of Cecily's see you cry. And then when you are done, I have something for you."

After a time, she rang a bell and whispered something into the ear of the page who responded. When he came back, he bore a small box.

Grandmother unlatched the box and showed me the coronet glittering inside it.

"Wear it proudly, my boy, in your grandfather's memory," she said, setting the golden coronet on my curling black hair as I brushed at my eyes. "You are now the second Duke of Buckingham."

Kate: September 1464

IT WAS ON A FINE SEPTEMBER MORNING IN 1464 THAT THE KING MARRIED my sister, although I couldn't tell a soul about it, and in truth I wasn't supposed to know myself.

I found out the secret when, just after dawn, my older sister kicked me in her sleep. As Joan was a compulsive kicker and I was well used to such awakenings, I normally would have gone back to sleep, but something made me sit up instead and listen. There appeared to be more life in our manor house at Grafton than usual, a sense of something extra going on besides the usual servants arising.

Disentangling my legs from my sister's—not only did she kick me, she encroached upon my half of the bed, though she claimed it was purely accidental—I climbed out of bed, took my night robe off its peg, draped it over my shoulders, tucked my favorite doll under my arm for company, and quietly made my way downstairs. Sure enough, there were sounds coming from the chapel—a highly unusual occurrence, for these days my family was in no position to keep its own chaplain. I pulled upon the heavy door.

Inside were a priest, my mother, two gentlewomen of my mother's acquaintance, a good-natured-looking man whom I guessed to be in his thirties, my sister Elizabeth, and a rather young man—the last two kneeling by the altar. It was obvious even to my six-year-old self that I had interrupted a wedding, but why on earth was my sister getting married at dawn, with none of the family present but Mother? And why was everyone—even the bride and groom—in everyday clothes? Why, the groom might have been going out for a day's hunting, so casually was he dressed.

As I stood there, at a loss for words and sensing that I had somehow done a Bad Thing, the groom turned and stood, making me gasp. He was tall—well over six feet—and dazzlingly handsome, with hair of a rich brown. Small, sallow, and of middling appearance, I was none of those things, and I averted my eyes as if caught gazing into the sun. "Well, now. Who is this young lady?"

"Katherine, sir," I managed.

"Kate," the groom said as I thrilled from my head to my toes. How did this man know that I loved to be called "Kate," only Mother insisted on the more dignified "Katherine"? He turned to my sister. "I've changed my mind, I'm afraid. *This* will be my new bride."

"She's a trifle young for you," said my sister a little tensely. (She was, I could not help but notice, several years older than the groom.)

"Oh, maybe a bit," the man conceded. He smiled. "Some other lucky man will have little Kate, then. Lady Kate? Can you keep a great secret?"

"You had better," my mother warned.

"I know Kate will," the man said reassuringly. He looked down—a long way down—straight into my eyes. "Kate, I am getting ready to marry your sister. But it is a great secret. No one can know until I announce it personally."

"Your family would not approve?" I ventured, as he was being so confiding.

"Indeed no."

"That is a pity."

"But they will come to understand in time." He cleared his throat and looked thoughtful for a moment, then appeared to make up his mind. "But there are other reasons why there are difficulties just now. I suppose you have not seen our King Edward yet, Kate?"

"No."

"Have you heard much of him?"

I was delighted by his question, for it gave me the opportunity to demonstrate what a good Yorkist I was, a great necessity in our family, since it was not so terribly long ago that Papa and my brothers Anthony and

Richard had fought for the House of Lancaster. Having gone over to what now all agreed heartily to be the right side, Papa had sternly informed us children that we should always speak well of the House of York. As with all of my father's advice, I had heeded it dutifully, but I seldom had the chance to put it into practice, for all of my brothers and sisters, being older and much wiser, were naturally much better Yorkists, and never made a mistake I could correct. "No," I admitted. "But I hear he is very brave. And very handsome."

The second man laughed, a sound that made the chapel echo. He was well over a decade older than the groom and less handsome, though his ruddy face was a pleasant one. "Ned, there's a fine courtier for you! Shall I?"

The younger man nodded, and the older man reached in a purse and drew out a fine gold chain, then handed it to me. (Later, I was to learn that he always kept one or two on his person, in case of emergencies.) "There's a reward for your loyalty, Lady Kate."

"Thank you," I said vacantly, staring at the chain. It was lovely, and even to my inexpert eyes looked frightfully expensive. Was my sister marrying a highwayman?

The younger man laughed at my expression. "You see, Kate, *I* am the king. And I have come here to marry your sister."

There were any number of dignified and proper responses I could have made to this announcement. I, of course, made none of them. My mouth gaped open, most unattractively I fear. "*You?*" I asked. "*Her?*"

"Me. Her." The king nodded. "She will make a lovely queen, don't you think?"

"Yes," I admitted feebly. Bessie was indeed lovely; sometimes I thought that she and my brother Anthony had taken so much beauty for themselves that there was not enough left for the other ten of us children, especially me.

"But you must keep this a secret, Kate, as I have said. You will promise?"

"On my life!"

"Good girl," the king said. He grinned. "Or I would be obliged to put you in my Tower as a lesson, you know."

My previous promise was empty compared to the one I made now. "I swear and hope to die if I break my promise," I vowed, kneeling and making the sign of the cross for good measure. I might have gone further and prostrated myself had Bessie not interrupted.

"Time passes. Ned, I know the child will not tell. Can we please resume the ceremony?"

∽

While my sister and the king are getting married, it seems a good time to explain what sort of family the king was marrying into.

My mother, Jacquetta of Luxembourg, was the daughter of the Count of St. Pol and the second wife of John, Duke of Bedford, brother to Henry V. My mother was but seventeen at the time of their marriage; the duke was in his forties. They had been married only two years when the duke fell ill and died, leaving Mama free to contract her scandalous marriage to my father—the son of the duke's chamberlain.

Mama could (and did, when roused) trace her ancestry to Charlemagne, but my father, Sir Richard Woodville, was a different matter altogether. He was no more than a knight when he and my mother wed, secretly and without the license of the king, the unfortunate sixth Henry, then a mere youth. The king could not let such a match pass without censure, and he promptly fined my parents a thousand pounds. But he got over it soon enough, and so completely that the marriage was the making of my father, a fact that he was candid enough to admit in the privacy of Grafton. In time my father was made a baron and a Knight of the Garter by King Henry. He and Mama were among those appointed to bring Henry's bride, Margaret of Anjou, from France for the couple's marriage, and my mother was soon on the best of terms with Margaret, then a girl of fifteen. When poor Henry went mad (or took ill, as good Lancastrians said) and the

Duke of York claimed the crown, Papa fought for Henry and for Margaret on the side of the House of Lancaster.

Then, in 1461, there was the dreadful battle of Towton. My father and my oldest brother, Anthony, were on the queen's side—by this time poor Henry was in such a state that no one thought of him as the person they were fighting for—and the queen lost the battle, horribly, on a blindingly snowy day. The Woodville men were captured, and the queen, the king, and their young son fled to Scotland. All seemed lost for the House of Lancaster, so when Father and Anthony were given the chance to make their peace with our new, young king, the fourth Edward, they took it gladly. So faithfully did my father discharge his new allegiance that within two years, he became a member of the king's council.

It was not all war and advancement with my parents since their marriage, however. There was the matter of begetting children—and that, my parents often said fondly, was a pursuit in which God had richly blessed them. Some died quite young, to everyone's sorrow, but by September of 1464 there were twelve of us living, seven girls and five boys, Anthony at seven-and-twenty being the oldest and me at six being the youngest.

I knew my parents worried about how they were going to provide for all of us when we grew older. My father's wealth came chiefly from my mother's dower lands, and because of England's reversals in France, Mother no longer enjoyed the revenues from her estates there. We were by no means poor, but she had to manage our household carefully. Yet as shabby as some of our everyday furnishings were, our house was full of beautiful objects from my mother's days as the wife of a king's son: sparkling gold cups, lushly illuminated manuscripts, my mother's coronet. They were too steeped in family history to be sold, but they hardly fit in with our modest existence at Grafton either. Still, my parents had managed to make matches for three of us: Bessie with Sir John Grey, Anthony with Elizabeth, Lady Scales, and Jacquetta with Lord Strange. They were good marriages, all agreed, and at six I was not much worried about whether a similarly suitable husband would be found for me when my time came. There were, after all, many sisters to get through before I became anyone's concern.

Poor Bessie, though, had not been married for long when her husband—just barely knighted, poor man—was killed in the second battle at St. Albans in 1461, leaving her with two boys, Thomas and Richard. Bessie's husband, though of good family, had not been rich, and my sister was left with a small income and a fear that her husband's family would take what was due to her sons. She came back to us at Grafton, and with us she had been living for the past three years. Lovely as my sister was, no one had offered for her since; I suppose in those uncertain days more than just beauty and virtue was needed to attract a man.

Until the king came along.

જી

When the ceremony ended, there were none of the usual festivities. The priest went to my sister's chamber—being widowed, Bessie had been given one to herself when she came back to Grafton—and blessed the bed, practically mumbling so as not to wake the rest of the household. Then we all left, leaving the king and Bessie to consummate their marriage, the king's friend to go for a ride ("A very long ride. Eh, Ned?" I'd heard him hiss to the king), and my mother and I (though I do not think she was anticipating my assistance) to figure out how to keep the secret from spreading through the household. Some contrivance was certainly necessary, as the king was going to have to emerge from my sister's chamber sooner or later, and at six feet tall and with his dazzling looks, he did not exactly blend into his surroundings. I was full of helpful suggestions—dressing up the king in Father's clothes, dressing up the king in Mother's clothes, dressing him up in a monk's habit, having him use a rope ladder to crawl out the window, drugging the entire household with a sleeping potion—but in the end, my mother settled for confiding in the most trustworthy of the servants and the eldest of my brothers and sisters, who found various ways to occupy the uninitiated outside the house. This solution rather disgusted me, for I was certain I could have obtained a monk's habit if someone had just given me the chance.

With this problem solved, though not as ingeniously as I would have preferred, the newlyweds tarried in my sister's chamber for several hours while the rest of us went around the daily business of the manor, keeping as well away from the bridal chamber as we could. I had to pass it a couple of times (I couldn't help it, truly) and found that the sounds within were pretty much of the sort that emanated from my parents' bedchamber on occasion, with the exception of a few feminine giggles. I wondered what the king was doing to provoke this reaction from my rather serious sister.

By noon, the king and his companion—William, Lord Hastings, I later learned—had ridden off, the king having first kissed Bessie very tenderly in the privacy of my mother's chamber, where he took his leave of us. My sister went back to her bedchamber to do whatever a commoner who had just secretly married a king did to pass the time, and I went outside, where I proposed to my nephews, who were nearer my own age than most of my brothers and sisters, that we play a game of getting married. They found the idea exceedingly dull and girl-like, and said so in no uncertain terms, so we played buck-hide instead, with I the hunter and they the bucks. It took me a while to find them, but I always succeeded.

৵

One of the advantages of having so many older brothers and sisters was that there was always someone I could find to give me whatever help I needed. If I was puzzled over my lesson, I went to Anthony if he was at Grafton or, most often, Lionel. If I needed to get through some difficult embroidery, I went to Mary. If I needed someone to get me out of trouble with Mama, I went to John. If I wanted a frog to put down someone's back (usually Joan's), I went to Edward.

If I wanted information, though, I went to Anne, who more than the rest of us had the confidence of my sister. So that night, after everyone had retired, I climbed out of the bed I shared with Joan and climbed into the bed that Anne had all to herself. "Kate! It's late."

"Please? When else can I ask you?" I didn't even need to tell her what I sought. She knew.

"Oh, all right." Anne sighed, purely for show. She loved being a fount of information. Meanwhile, several other heads poked out from behind bed curtains, for just as I relied upon Anne for information, my sisters had come to rely on me to ask the questions that they were too discreet to ask. "I suppose all of you know by now that Bessie got married today." Everyone nodded, to my disapproval, for this meant that someone had told the secret. I certainly had not. "But do you know who the groom is?" Joan and Margaret shook their heads. "Well, you'll think that this is madness when I say it, but it's not. Bessie has married the *king.*"

Joan and Margaret stared. "Are you joking?" Joan asked.

"She is not." I tossed my head. "I was at the wedding."

"What was a chit like you doing there?" That was Margaret.

"Keeping my eyes and ears open," I said grandly. Then I realized that I was upstaging poor Anne, whose pretty face had turned almost sour. "But I don't know how they met, or anything like that. I just know that they married today and it is a great secret until the king says it can be told. So how did it come about?"

Anne relaxed, relieved that I was not attempting to usurp her. "Well. You know that poor Bessie had had problems with the Greys about her lands." I nodded, for even I knew about this; it was a topic on which my sister (naturally enough) expounded a great deal. "Papa, of course, would have done what he could to aid her, being on the king's council, but the Greys are so very well connected, what with their ties to the king's family, and we are—not so very well connected. So she decided to go to Lord Hastings, the king's great friend, for help. He has land not far from here, you know."

"I met him this morning," I broke in grandly. "A charming man. Oh. Pardon me."

"Not far from here at all," Anne continued, a note of warning in her voice. "Anyway, he and Bessie agreed that one of her boys would marry one of Lord Hastings's daughters—although he doesn't have any yet. They were to share in the rents and profits of what could be recovered for the boys. That way, Bessie knew Hastings would help her to get what was due to her and to her sons. Wasn't that clever of Bessie?"

We nodded approvingly.

"So it might have ended there, but"—she looked at me and hesitated— "Lord Hastings is, er, a man with an eye for a pretty woman, they say, and so is the king. He, ah, sometimes introduces the king to women he thinks he might—like. And Hastings thought that the king might like Bessie. So when the king and Hastings went to Stony Stratford on business, he told Bessie that the king wanted to see her about the arrangement. And she came to him."

"And the king liked her," I surmised.

"Very much. But you see, the king likes a great many women. Anyway, he spoke with Bessie a very long time, and then he found an excuse to call her back to him the next day, and then he asked Bessie to be his mistress." The raptness of her audience overcame Anne's discretion, fortunately for me, for I could not have borne it had she fallen silent. "You know, to lie with him but not to be his wife. He told her that if she did, she could have anything she wanted for herself and for her family, and that she would be kept in the best of comfort."

I nodded sagely, though in truth I was shocked. I had seen some wicked women once at a fair, with tight, bright gowns and brighter cheeks and hair, and had been hustled past them by my brother John. Surely that was not what the king had had in mind for Bessie.

"But Bessie refused. She said that she had her boys' good names to protect and her own honor, along with that of Papa and Mama, and that she would be no man's mistress, not even if the man was her king. So the king shrugged and dismissed her rather coldly."

"This was way back in April. Then, just a few weeks ago, Hastings asked

the king for our nephew Tom's wardship and marriage, as part of the agree-
ment he'd made with Bessie. The king agreed and signed the document.
Then, just three days ago, Bessie got a note from the king, asking to see
her alone."

"After he tried to seduce her?" asked Mary. I made a mental note to find
out what "seduce" meant. Maybe Lionel could tell me.

"Well, she felt she had to. It might affect Tom's lands, after all, and he
wasn't asking for a meeting by night, so she felt safe. So she went and
waited by that old oak tree that people meet at around here, and then he
came galloping up and told her that he had been thinking about her all
summer and that he couldn't bear it any longer. And then he told her that
a queen should be virtuous, and a queen should be beautiful, and that she
was both, so why should she not be his queen? His advisers wouldn't like
it, but they would have to accept the idea or they could go hang. I believe
they must have kissed and so forth quite a long time"—Anne blushed—
"and then he gave her his ring as a token of his fidelity and told her to have
Mama find a priest and that they would marry the next morning—that is,
today. And so they did."

"That is the most splendid, romantic thing I have ever heard in my life,"
I murmured. I could hardly wait until the next morning to reenact the
scene with my dolls, though I was still somewhat unclear about the mistress and seducing part. Still, I could improvise quite well, and I certainly
understood the kissing part.

"I wonder when the king will announce it," said Mary.

Anne shrugged. "It will probably be a while. The Kingmaker won't
like it."

"The Kingmaker?" I asked. "I thought God made kings, just like the
rest of us."

Margaret rolled her eyes. The next frog Edward procured would be
for her.

Anne laughed. "The Kingmaker is Richard Neville, the Earl of Warwick.
He is immensely rich, and very popular among the people, and it was with

his support that King Edward gained the throne after his father, the Duke of York, was killed at Wakefield. Were it not for the Kingmaker, Henry might still be on the throne."

"So why would he not like the king marrying Bessie?"

"Because he would prefer him to marry another king's daughter, or at least a member of another king's family. Such marriages can be useful at times of war. Bessie can be of no good that way, being English. And there is the matter of a dowry as well. Kings like rich brides, and sometimes need them quite badly."

"But she is virtuous and beautiful," I said, deciding that no Kingmaker would be welcome among my dolls tomorrow. Edward and Bessie could do quite nicely all by themselves.

"That will have to be enough, because she certainly won't bring a dowry with her. Not fit for a king, anyway!" Anne laughed.

"I wonder what that will mean for us, once it is announced," said Margaret. "We will be the queen's sisters, after all. Shall we go to court?"

"Why not?" said Mary.

"Court," I murmured. "How wonderful that would be!" Then I yawned immensely, and Anne shook her head.

"Before you think of going to court, missy, you'd best think of going to bed."

⁓

As the days passed, the Queen of England continued her usual life at Grafton with the rest of us: tending her two sons, embroidering, even helping with the work of the household when necessary. When no servants were present, for not all had been let in on the secret, I rather enjoyed calling my sister "your grace" when possible. "Will your grace come to dinner now?" "Has your grace seen that shirt I was mending for Father?" But the charm of that began to wear thin, especially for Bessie, who more than once told me to stop my your-gracing and make myself scarce. She said it, though, in a suitably regal tone.

I might have wondered if the wedding had been a dream, but it was not that the king had forgotten about his bride. Every couple of days, a nondescript messenger on a nondescript horse would appear at Grafton with a royal letter for Bessie and usually a small gift—some trimmings, a purse, a top for the boys. Sometimes there were pretty presents for the rest of us as well; I still have a little brooch from that period.

Papa, meanwhile, had been visiting one of our other manors on business, unaware that he had acquired the king as a son-in-law. When he arrived home, Mama and Bessie quickly pulled him aside for a conference, from which he emerged looking like a man who had been struck by lightning. For the rest of his stay, he looked pleased and proud but also a little dazed. That first evening home, he asked, "Did I ever tell you younger children what happened at Sandwich?"

We were all sitting in the solar, one of the improvements my parents had made to Grafton while they still had the income from their French lands and when there were not quite so many of us children. Most of us shook our heads. "Well, Anthony and I were fighting for Lancaster at the time, back in 1460." My father looked vaguely apologetic before continuing. "We were planning to set sail for Guines, which the Duke of Somerset had taken, to help him take Calais. Instead the Yorkists took your mother and Anthony and me by surprise, in our beds, no less. So we were captured and hauled off to Calais. We had good weather, but it was about the longest trip I've ever made in my life, let me tell you, for I was a prisoner of York. When we arrived there, the Earl of Warwick and the Earl of March—that is, our present king—rated us mercilessly. They said that I was a lowborn knave's son who had been made by marriage and that Anthony as my son was no better."

"I could have scratched their eyes out!" Mama interrupted. "Such impudence. And I in my oldest nightshift!"

"I believe you would have scratched their eyes out, my dear, if they hadn't taken the precaution of shackling you. Anyway, they carried on like that for hours, or at least it felt like it, and as we were at sword point and badly outnumbered, there was nothing we could do but bear it with dignity. When the king appointed me to his council, he said nothing of the incident, and neither did I; better just let some things be, I've always said." He smiled wryly. "And now the man is my son-in-law? I am sorely tempted when I attend his council at Reading to remind him of our conversation."

"Do you think he'll announce it at Reading?" Anne asked.

"He left a letter assuring me that Bessie would receive all honors due her, but did not give specifics. Who knows? Do you, Bessie?"

Bessie held out her palms and shrugged. "He tells me he will announce it when the time is right."

"Whenever that is," muttered Margaret.

"It is an awkward situation for the king, my dears. When has such a thing happened before in England, a king marrying in secret and making his bride his queen?"

"Well," said my brother John cheerfully. "Someone had to be the first."

○○○

My sisters and I, including the queen, were sewing one morning in late September when we heard the sound of approaching horses. *Many* horses, I realized just as Bessie with a sharp intake of breath walked to the window. "It is true!" she breathed. She grabbed Anne, her usual confidante. "The king has told his council! The secret's out."

We all crowded to the window, where I saw that the days of our nondescript, single messenger had ended. A score of men were riding up on the finest horses to be seen in England, and no one who saw them could be in any doubt as to from whom they came, for the man in front bore what even I recognized as the king's standard: the lion of England and the lily of France. A gaggle of villagers had attached themselves to the contingent and trailed at a respectful distance behind them, doubtlessly hoping to pick up some gossip.

"Follow me."

We lined up behind Bessie obediently and filed into the hall, where the royal entourage had just arrived. My sister had barely cleared the doorway when the king's men went down upon their knees. "Rise?" she ventured after a moment or two. With growing confidence, she added, "What news do you bring?"

"Your grace, I bring word from the king. His grace has informed his council at Reading of his marriage. He wishes your grace to proceed to Reading so that your grace might be introduced to the council and to others of importance." Even in the midst of all these "your graces," Bessie looked down at her dress, which was far from new, with such a look of horror that the man came close to smiling as he guessed my sister's thoughts. "The king wishes to assure you that all necessary items of apparel are being prepared against your grace's arrival."

I longed to ask, "Can the rest of us come?" but hardly dared. My eyes, however, must have spoken for me, because the man added, "His grace will be pleased to see the queen's family at Reading also, but he asks that they return to Grafton afterward while lodgings are being prepared for them."

"Where?" asked the queen.

"It is not certain, your grace. The king intends to stay at Windsor after he leaves Reading, but he may choose quarters at Greenwich or Sheen for the family of your grace. For now."

"For now?" my mother asked.

"It is the king's intention that your daughters be wedded suitably, and soon, to men worthy of a queen's sister. Their residence at court may thus be only temporary."

I grabbed at one of my sisters' hands—any sister would do—to keep upon my feet. *Windsor*, spoken as we might say "Grafton." *Wedded suitably.* I had imagined this scene often enough, enacted some reasonable facsimile thereof with my dolls, but now that it was coming true, it was beyond belief. Nothing, I realized, would ever be the same for the Woodville family now. Nothing.

iii

September 1464 to May 1465

THE KINGMAKER, IT APPEARED, HAD GIVEN MUCH THOUGHT TO FINDING a suitable bride for the young king. It had been with the greatest satisfaction that he informed the king's council, meeting at Reading Abbey, that he was all set to travel abroad to negotiate for the hand of the French king's sister-in-law, Bona of Savoy ("a most beauteous lady," the Kingmaker noted with an appreciative smack of his lips). The Earl of Warwick was getting ready to elaborate, whether upon the proposed terms or upon the lady's charms no one shall ever know, when the king held up his hand for silence.

"I fear that there is an obstacle of my own making to this proposed match," he said quietly. "You have had my interests well at heart, and I commend you for it and shall remember it. But no marriage can take place, for the best reason in the world. The truth is, my lords, I am already married." He paused, but no one even attempted to speak. "To an Englishwoman. To a beautiful, seemly Englishwoman who will fulfill her role admirably. To the former Lady Elizabeth Grey, the daughter of Lord Rivers here."

According to my father, my informant, the Kingmaker's expression might have scared the dead out of their tombs. The king rose and beamed. "I suspect, my lords, you may wish to discuss this matter amongst yourselves more freely. I shall take myself off so that you can do so, and I shall send for my queen so that she may be received by you in the proper manner. Come, Lord Rivers, with me."

My father obeyed, but he had barely cleared the room before the

Kingmaker let forth a series of expletives, in both English and French. Even if I could bring myself to reproduce his words here, it would be impossible, for my father felt that they were far too vivid and descriptive to be shared with the family. There was more silence, either in awe of the earl's hitherto unknown verbal dexterity or in fear that the king would return, until Lord Hastings said mildly, "Now, now, my lord. I've seen her, and I can tell you that she's a lovely woman. And with two sons, she's fertile to boot."

⁓

"Which one is the Kingmaker?" I hissed to John as we rode toward Reading Abbey, me riding pillion behind John. For most of the trip to Reading, I'd been behind one of the king's men, but for the last stretch of the journey, I'd begged to ride behind John, who as ever had cheerfully obliged.

"Never seen him, you know. But I'd lay odds on the brown-haired man standing next to the king. He looks disgusted enough," said John.

As subtly as I could, which was probably not very subtly at all, I gazed at Warwick the Kingmaker, if indeed that was he, and felt a twinge of disappointment. Aside from his robes, which were obviously of great cost, he was an ordinary-looking man, neither tall nor short, handsome nor plain. Even his hair was the most unassuming type of brown. It did not help, of course, that he was standing next to my new brother-in-law, who was every bit as fine as I remembered.

We rode toward the rear of the queen's party, whose imminent arrival had evidently prompted the king and several other men to stand at the abbey entrance, waiting. As the rest of us drew rein, the king stepped forward and headed straight toward my sister's horse. As Warwick and a boy in his teens watched, both looking slightly greenish, Edward greeted my sister not as a king meeting his queen, but as a young man of twenty-two who had been eagerly awaiting his love. Not allowing a page to do the job, he assisted Bessie from her horse, embraced her, and kissed her soundly and quite at length for their being in a public place. "Welcome to Reading, my dear," he said, stepping back. For a moment I thought he was going to draw Bessie into another extended kiss, but he mastered himself and waved a hand that included all of the family. "And welcome, all!"

Warwick's eyes moved from Woodville to Woodville, quite evidently counting us and arriving at a figure he thought was too high. It was the boy, however, who said, "Quite a sizable family, Ned."

"As a matter of fact, George, there are some missing, I believe," said the king genially. He glanced around. "Who's not here?"

As this seemed to be a question anyone was free to answer, the impulse to be the one to provide this information to the king was irresistible to me. "My sister Jacquetta," I called out. "And my brother Anthony. We hope they will be here soon, though."

The king's smile grew even broader, and he walked to where I still sat my horse behind John. As effortlessly as if he were lifting a kitten, he swept me out of my seat, then swung me round as I squealed in delight. "This is my wife's chief rival for my affections," he said solemnly, after kissing me on the cheek and placing me on the ground before Warwick and George. "I am very glad to see you here, Kate."

George tried not to glare at me as I beamed toothily up at them. The Kingmaker managed, "A fine new sister-in-law indeed." He smiled. It looked like a painful process.

✍

It was a couple of days later, on Michaelmas, that the king's council and some sundry other men of importance gathered into Reading Abbey and awaited the formal presentation of my sister as England's queen. My mother and my second oldest sister, Jacquetta, Lady Strange, were to carry my sister's train, but the rest of us Woodvilles stood in a large knot in the transept with the others.

The Kingmaker and the king's brother, George, were to lead my sister into the abbey. By now I had learned that the king had a number of brothers and sisters, but several had died very young. The next oldest boy after Edward, Edmund, had died, aged seventeen, with the Duke of York at the battle of Wakefield. Remaining to the king were three sisters, Anne, Duchess of Exeter, Elizabeth, Duchess of Suffolk, and the Lady Margaret, who had yet to be married, and two brothers, George, Duke of Clarence, and Richard, Duke of Gloucester.

George, the only one of them present at Reading, was not quite fifteen at the time. Though his hair was lighter, he otherwise greatly resembled the king. He was tall and nicely built, having an exceptionally handsome face without the spottiness that marred so many faces of youths his age. Yet I did not find his looks as nearly as appealing as the king's, though I could not quite understand why. Still, he looked more agreeable than he had the day of our arrival, perhaps because he was aware of the fine figure he cut as silence was ordered and he and Warwick processed into the abbey, my sister between them.

I gasped as John lifted me onto his shoulders to get a better look. Lovely enough in everyday clothes, Bessie was stunning in the scarlet and gold robes, trimmed with ermine, that the king's tailor had hastened to make for her. The king, I supposed, must have given her the jewels that sparkled as she moved, for they were certainly not anything from my mother's collection, which I liked to sort through on rainy days. Were it not for the fact that her hair was concealed by her headdress, instead of being unbound, she might as well have been going to her coronation. She might have been born to be a queen, indeed, for she walked with her two escorts and her train-bearers as though she were perfectly accustomed to such pomp.

Bessie walked to the altar where the king stood. He stepped forward and took her hand as my mother and my sister gracefully swiveled backward with her train, which fortunately for them was a relatively short one. "I give to you your most gracious lady, my wife and consort, your Queen Elizabeth!"

༄

After that, any business of the council was strictly anticlimactic. Soon its members dispersed to their homes, as did we Woodvilles. The king and queen stayed at Reading for several weeks, with only a small company of servants. I knew there were hopes—in my family, at least, and presumably on the king's part—that my sister would emerge from this quiet time with an heir to the throne in her belly.

Before the council departed from Reading, however, the king, my father, and the Earl of Arundel had a conference. When it ended, my sister Margaret was betrothed to the earl's fourteen-year-old heir, Thomas Fitzalan. We had barely settled ourselves at Grafton before it was time to escort Margaret to Arundel Castle in Sussex, where she was to live with the earl's family until she and Thomas were a little older and were considered ready to consummate their marriage.

Perched up high above its surroundings and even more magnificent inside than it appeared from the outside, the castle was the grandest place in which any of us girls had been to date, and as the earl and his family were most hospitable, I was at liberty to wander around it undisturbed. I lost no time in climbing the winding stairs to the castle's highest turret, where I gazed down at the River Arun and the town below, imagining myself in the glorious days of the third King Edward, with some knight in shining armor racing across the terrain to save me. (From what he was supposed to be saving me was a matter on which I was vague, not to mention histori-cally somewhat confused.) When we left Margaret in her new home and returned to Grafton, it seemed unbearably small, even with fewer of us living there now.

I did not have too long to suffer, though, for in December we were on the move again, this time to Eltham Palace. It would not only be my first time at a royal palace, it would be the first time I met the king's family, other than Clarence, and I did not think he had boded all that well.

Our days at Eltham were formal, with the elaborate lengthy meals that I was used to, on a considerably smaller scale, from Grafton. In the evening, however, only the immediate family gathered in the king's chamber, some to play chess or other games, some to dice, some to dance, and some just to chatter, and it was then that I began to get a sense of who my new relations were.

Cecily, the king's mother, was pointedly absent from the gathering—I heard later that she had carried on dreadfully about her son's marriage to a commoner, and John swore that steam had been seen to rise from her hennin when she heard the news—but the king's brothers and youngest sister, Margaret, all had come for the festivities from Greenwich, where they spent most of their time. George, of course, I had met. Margaret was eighteen; old, I thought, to still be unmarried, especially since she was quite seemly in appearance, though very tall for a woman. If she had any misgivings about her brother's marriage, she kept them to herself and spoke quite amicably to the queen and the rest of us. Encouraged by her approachability, I always claimed the closest seat to her on informal occasions, when protocol did not forbid it. If she got tired of me doing this, she had the goodness never to say so.

Richard, Duke of Gloucester, twelve years old, was the youngest of the royal family. Unlike the king, George, and Margaret, he was of middling height, with just a fortunate inch or so saving him from being called short. He was darker than they were too, though far from ill-favored. As he was much quieter than his brother or George, though not at all melancholy, I paid little mind to him.

Edward's sister Elizabeth, the Duchess of Suffolk, and her husband the duke, John de la Pole, did not make much of an impression on my young mind either, though my mother had been godmother to Elizabeth twenty years before when she was born in Rouen. They were a quiet couple. My brother Lionel told me that the Duke of Suffolk was the great-grandson of the poet Geoffrey Chaucer, which impressed Lionel a great deal. I, however, stayed at a distance lest the poor duke, who in all fairness did not appear the least bit inclined to do so, fall into reciting verse to me.

By far the most interesting of the king's family (aside, of course, from the king himself) was his older sister, Anne, Duchess of Exeter. She had arrived at Eltham after Margaret, George, and Richard. Finding it strange that a duchess should be without a duke, I sidled up to the Lady Margaret at the earliest opportunity. "Where is the duke, my lady? The Duke of Exeter?"

"Oh, dear," said Margaret. "You mustn't mention that duke, you know."

"Why? Is he dead?"

"Worse. A Lancastrian." Margaret looked around to see if she could speak in safety, and finding that she could, continued, "Her husband is Henry Holland. My late father arranged their marriage when they were quite young, but they never suited, although they have a girl—another Anne, who is to marry Warwick's nephew."

"The Kingmaker? That Warwick?"

Margaret smiled. "Yes, that Warwick. Anyway, the Duke of Exeter was never loyal to my father, even though he was his son-in-law. He fought against him time after time, and Anne had no influence over him. He could have made his peace after Towton, as did all others with sense"— she glanced in my father's direction—"but he refused, and now he is in France with that virago Margaret of Anjou. Where we all hope they stay and rot."

"Of course. It must be hard for her. The Duchess of Exeter," I hastened to add, as Margaret's eyebrows shot up and she stiffened. I wondered if she had been named for the virago in more congenial times.

Margaret, evidently assured that I did not have latent Lancastrian tendencies, relaxed again. "Well, my brother has treated her well. She was granted her husband's forfeited estates, so she lives quite comfortably. And she has custody of the little Duke of Buckingham, who is very wealthy. I wonder that he is not here with her, in fact. Hush, now, here she comes."

I hardly needed the warning, as the Duchess of Exeter was a large lady, though of the sort who carried her avoirdupois grandly, and her entry into a room could not be readily missed. I moved to let the sisters sit side by side, but Margaret kindly steered me to a nearby stool. "We are all sisters now. Stay." As I settled down, respectfully silent but quite alert, she asked Anne, "So where are your charges?"

"They stayed behind. Humphrey is ailing."

"Poor Humphrey is always ailing. I am surprised, though, you chose not to bring Harry by himself. There has been talk, you know—"

"I know. But Humphrey never does well without Harry, and I shall not have it on my conscience that I caused the boy to sicken worse. And Harry wouldn't have gone with Humphrey ill, anyway. He's very protective of him. It's sweet to see, but quite sad too. That boy hasn't long for the world, even though I have the best physicians attending him. There's plenty of time for this other business, after all; Harry's but nine."

"So has a girl been chosen, by the by? There seem to be several likely choices."

"I cannot say. But I think the answer is close at hand."

"Ah."

"So, sister, how goes it with your marriage negotiations?"

But my favorite new relation was the Duchess of Norfolk, who was the king's aunt, being his mother's older sister. She was four-and-sixty and immensely rich, and Margaret told me in private after she came to know me a little better that her heirs had a running wager over whether she would ever die. More as an accessory than out of need, she used a cane, finely carved and richly bejeweled, and in speaking, she often used it to emphasize her points, sometimes even poking the listener when she wanted to be particularly emphatic. By this I do not mean that she was a harridan; her pokes were usually of the friendliest sort. I should know, as she took somewhat of a fancy to me—"my fellow Katherine" and "a bright-eyed creature," she called me—and I was often called upon to help her thread her needle or some similar task suited for the young and sharp-eyed.

John, my third oldest brother, though quite useless for such ladies' tasks, also got quite a few pokes with the cane that Christmas, being, like the duchess, quite fond of chess. Just after a few days at Eltham Palace, it had become generally accepted that a small table in the corner was reserved for them alone, and I often heard the duchess thumping her cane in satisfaction when she had made a good move or in warning when John was being too dilatory in making his.

It was nearly Twelfth Night when the king came in and waved for silence, rather to my disappointment, for I had been practicing some dance steps with my brother Richard, who, despite being the quietest male in the family, was the best dancer. Thanks to his skill, I was practically floating. As we came to a halt, Edward said, "I am pleased to say that there will be another wedding in the family. Within a couple of weeks, as a matter of fact."

We unmarried Woodville girls looked back and forth at each other. We shared the same suite of chambers at Eltham. Had one of us been keeping a secret from the others? It was something we frowned upon.

"Not I, brother, I hope?" asked Margaret. There was always some scheme afoot to marry her to someone, I knew. I suspected that she was in no hurry to leave England.

"No, my dear, don't you think I'd have the courtesy to tell you first? No. Our happy couple is my dear aunt, the Duchess of Norfolk, and young John here." He gestured over toward the chess table where my brother and the duchess had duly lifted their attention from the game. "Will you join me in congratulating them?"

"Have you lost your senses?" said George.

"No. Have you lost yours, speaking to your king like that?"

"Brother, it is diabolical! A man of how old—twenty?—and a lady in her sixties?"

"George—"

"It is obscene!" He looked around for the youngest female in the room, who much to my dismay turned out to be me, and pointed. "Why not put this girl in bed with a man of seventy, while you're at it?"

"How dare you speak of my young sister in bed with anyone, you blackguard?" demanded John.

"How dare you address me so when you are not even a knight?"

"That will soon be remedied, I hear," said John. "In the meantime, how are my marital affairs any of your concern? I am not in your wardship."

"No, because a ward must have an income, and you've none—a fine sort to marry a duchess, and my own aunt! Ned, don't you see the canker you've set loose? It's not bad enough that you marry a nobody just because she wouldn't spread her leg—"

The king lunged at George, and I truly think he might have murdered him then and there were it not for what happened next. The Duchess of Norfolk stepped between the brothers and rapped her cane against the floor with a mighty thud. Then she prodded George with it. "Silence, you fool!"

George stepped back. Breathing hard, so did the king.

"As my heirs know to their chagrin, I am in full possession of my faculties. I am marrying this young man under duress from no one and at no one's instigation except for his and mine," said the duchess. "Our motives are simple: I wish for congenial companionship in my old age and he wishes for a larger income. We have become friends over these past days, and we understand each other perfectly. Our marriage will provide us both with what we desire, which in neither case has anything to do with the bedchamber. So, Nephew George, you may rest your mind easy on that account. In fact, I suggest you retire and rest your body as well before you say something else you will come to regret."

George muttered something that sounded vaguely apologetic and left the chamber. My sister's lip was trembling. I had seen it do so from anger as well as from hurt, and I wondered which emotion was uppermost. The king put a hand on her shoulder. "George can be a fool sometimes, as you've seen," he said quietly. "I will speak to him further about his folly tomorrow. I suggest we retire for the evening, my dear." He waved breezily to the rest of us. "But the rest of you are free to stay and make merry."

None of us, however, felt like doing so.

∽

"Why, John? Why would you put us to shame?"

"Shame in marrying a rich widow, sister? I'm not exactly the first man to conceive such an idea, my dear."

The king was transacting some business, leaving the queen with her ladies, Mama, and some of her sisters to do needlework together. Along with the rest of the ladies, save for Mama, I moved off at a distance and made a great show of playing with my sister's dog by the hearth, hoping that my presence would not be remembered, as it too often was when conversations turned interesting.

"A rich widow forty years older than you!"

"Not to be ungallant, but it's five and forty, actually."

"What will people say? It would not be so bad if there were a possibility of children, but—"

"You heard the lady last night. It suits us both. And by 'people,' I suppose you mean the Earl of Warwick, not just the king's fool brother George?"

"John, do bear in mind that the earl is a powerful man, and that George is next in line to the throne. He cannot be dismissed so easily, not until I bear a son."

"Something you have had no difficulty doing in the past, and something the king has effected with others in the past too, if rumor informs me correctly. Ah, sister, don't look so distressed! You cannot believe that the king came to your bed a virgin."

I concentrated hard on making myself invisible, and evidently succeeded.

"John, I am in no mood for your jests today. I have found out but recently—" My sister bit her lip and fixed her eyes on her embroidery.

"Found out what, Bessie?"

Mama said, "The king has a mistress, it appears."

"The king has several, of varying degrees and complexion," John said bluntly. "Always has. Always will. Bessie, your husband is not the sort of man who can be faithful to a single woman. Some men simply aren't, you know. Face that, and treat it as a failing about which you can do nothing, and you will be far happier. They're not his queen. You are."

"That is what Mama tells me. But—"

"But what, sweetheart?"

"I am not with child, yet again. I have had evidence of it just this morning."

"Pshaw! You and the king have been together constantly only since late September. There's plenty of time. Now, let me tell you the conditions that the duchess has set upon my marriage with her, and that will make you smile. I am not to incur huge gaming debts. A gentlemanly amount is fine, but not *huge* ones. I am to spend time at my wife's household regularly, except in time of war, when I can be excused. My dogs are to stay out of her chamber. My harlots—the duchess flatters me by assuming I have harlots, though I don't—are to stay far away from any property that she owns. And I am not to wear my doublets too short, for it is a fashion of which she mightily disapproves and that she informs me makes any man appear to have a large arse."

"Did she really say *arse?*"

The queen and my mother looked stricken. "Katherine, do go work on your music. Immediately."

"Yes, your grace."

"Kate?"

"Yes, John?"

"She did say *arse*. Now run along."

༄

The Duchess of Norfolk and John were married not long after that, in the king's chapel at Westminster Palace. The duchess's heirs stayed far away from the ceremony, as did her nephews the Kingmaker and George, but those of us who attended enjoyed ourselves thoroughly—and John's doublet was not at all too short.

With this excitement over, the court was busy planning for my sister's coronation in May, while we unmarried Woodvilles settled into our living quarters at Greenwich, which the king had granted to my sister along with Sheen. Overlooking the Thames and a short barge ride to Westminster or Sheen, it well deserved its nickname of Placentia—House of Pleasure.

I had been resident at Greenwich Palace (which is precisely how I liked to say it in those days) for some time when, around Easter, the Duchess of Exeter was announced. She swept into the queen's chamber, followed by two boys who almost seemed lost behind her rustling, trailing skirts.

The boys knelt to the queen, who quickly bade them to rise, after which

I had the leisure to study them. I guessed the older to be about nine, the younger about seven. With their curling, dark, shoulder-length hair, large brown eyes, and finely etched facial features, it was obvious that they were brothers, but though neither boy could be called robust looking, it was painfully apparent that the younger boy was of delicate, if not outright sickly, health. His gentle face was too pale and had a pinched expression, and he seemed to need the help of the older boy to rise.

"Your grace, may I present the Duke of Buckingham, Henry Stafford," the Duchess of Exeter said. "And Lord Humphrey Stafford, his brother."

My sister smiled. "Welcome, boys, to your new home. I believe you shall like it well here."

New home? The boys, however, did not look surprised.

"Someone shall show you your chambers," the queen continued. Her eyes traveled to me. "And then my sister, Lady Katherine, will show you around the grounds if you like."

"Not Humphrey, your grace, if you please," said the Duke of Buckingham quickly. "He's tired from the barge and needs to rest."

Tired from the *barge*? I wondered in the arrogance of good health. "Harry, speak only when you are bidden," warned the Duchess of Exeter.

"But Humphrey's tired," said the small duke in a firm voice. There was something fierce in his face, which changed abruptly when he looked down at his brother. "Aren't you, Humphrey?"

"A bit," admitted Humphrey.

"Then he must be allowed to rest."

The Duchess of Exeter opened her mouth, probably to give the Duke of Buckingham another talking-to, but my sister said, "I quite understand, my dear. Go to your chamber and rest as long as you need, both of you. There will be plenty of time to get used to your new surroundings."

∽

"I told them I didn't need to have you show me around, but they said I should go anyway," said Harry a while later. "You see, I've been here before with the Duchess of Exeter. I probably know this place better than you do, actually."

As the youngest of twelve children I was well used to being told that other people knew things better than I did, so I merely shrugged and said, "Probably."

Harry Stafford looked somewhat perturbed by my lack of opposition. "But I suppose your sister wouldn't know that."

"My sister the *queen*," I reminded him loftily.

"Well, anyway, I've been to most of the royal palaces. I'm a ward of the king, you see, and I've been in the care of the Duchess of Exeter."

"I know. The duchess mentioned it when she was at court for Christmas." I felt that I had scored a point here, and being naturally magnanimous, I added, "I suppose you are a ward because your father is dead?" I had begun to understand how these things worked.

The boy nodded. "My father and my grandfather, the first duke. My father died a couple of years before Grandfather was killed at Northampton."

"How was he killed?"

"Why, in battle in 1460, of course. He was guarding King Henry's tent and some knaves killed him. He was outnumbered badly or he would have slain the cowards." The duke's eyes narrowed disdainfully, not at the knaves but at my ignorance. "Don't you know anything?"

"I can speak French."

"Well, so can I. Anyone can."

"But not like this." Thanks to my mother, I spoke French as easily as English and with no trace of an English accent. I launched into some prayers in my mother's tongue, at top speed—but not, I am afraid, with the proper reverence due to the words I was speaking—and saw to my satisfaction that I had left the boy far behind me, so fast and fluent was I.

"Well, that's not so much," he said when I finally stopped for air. "The French are our enemies, after all." He frowned. "You sound *too* French, I think."

Youngest as I might be, I could be pushed only so far. "I was born in

England, for your information. And the king says I have a lovely speaking voice; just you ask him! And what is it to you how I sound?"

"Because—"

I stomped off in high dudgeon before the Duke of Buckingham could finish his sentence.

◦◦

"What do you know about the Duke of Buckingham?" I asked Cecilia, my nurse, that evening as she braided my hair for the night.

"Little Duke Harry? Oh, my." Cecilia gave my half-formed braid an emphatic tug. "When he's of age, he'll be the richest person in England other than royalty, at least once the dowager Duchess of Buckingham dies and he gets her dower lands. Of course, he's close enough to royalty himself. A descendant of Thomas of Woodstock, the third King Edward's youngest son, and of his second oldest son John of Gaunt, if you please, through Katherine Swynford. John and Katherine had the Beaufort babes when he was married to someone else, mind you, but then they tidied things up right well after he was widowed by marrying themselves. So the duke has royal blood on both sides of the blanket. His Beaufort relations are Lancastrians through and through, and so were the young duke's Stafford father and grandfather. I don't know if little Harry has an opinion on the matter."

"Oh, I think he has an opinion on everything," I muttered.

"Eh? The young duke didn't make a good impression?"

"I thought he was very rude. How am I to know about Northampton, with so many battles to keep straight?" I sulked for a moment or two. "Is his mother alive?"

"Yes, but as the Buckingham heir, young Harry was taken to live with his grandparents when his father died. Then the king bought his wardship from his grandmother the Duchess of Buckingham, and he was put in the Duchess of Exeter's household to be raised, and now in the queen's to be raised. It's a great deal of shunting around for a boy his age, but such is the lot of the rich."

"Why'd they take the boys from the Duchess of Exeter's household and put them in my sister's?"

"My, you're full of questions, aren't you? Well, it's the only way to learn things, they say." Cecilia stepped back to admire her handiwork, as she always did. "Well, I've a notion, but as it's no more than that, I think I'd best keep it to myself for now."

"Why?"

"Because that's my notion."

✍

The next day I was told that my sister had a visitor of some importance, who particularly wished to see me. After some delay, during which more fuss had been made than usual about my clothing, I was sent to my sister's chamber. There sat a lady who, though somewhat younger, reminded me a bit in appearance of the Duchess of Norfolk. With her was my mother, newly arrived from Grafton, where she traveled to and from court from time to time.

"Hello, my dear," said Mama, giving me a kiss after I dropped a curtsey to them all. "This is the Duchess of Buckingham. We have known each other a very long time, since we were often at court together during the time of Margaret of Anjou. The Duchess of Buckingham is sister to the Duchess of York, the king's mother, and to the Duchess of Norfolk, John's wife."

Momentarily overwhelmed by all of these duchesses, I merely nodded, then remembered that I had been told by the Duchess of Norfolk that her father, Ralph Neville, the Earl of Westmorland, had sired nearly two dozen children, including the Kingmaker's late father, by his two wives. I wondered how he had kept their names all straight. Perhaps he couldn't, and had assigned one of his servants to this task exclusively.

"She's a little thing," said the Duchess of Buckingham. "Why, the title will be longer than the girl!"

"But very healthy. Katherine has hardly had a sick day in her life."

"That's certainly to be desired. Tell me, child. I hear that you met my grandson Harry yesterday. Did you like him?"

I was still indignant about being called too French, but I could hardly tell this to Harry's grandmother, especially as I was puzzling over this exchange between her and Mama. "Yes, your grace," I said in a rather flat tone.

"Good. It has been arranged that you are to marry him. The wedding will take place just before the queen's coronation. So you and I shall share a title. Duchess of Buckingham."

I rocked back on my heels.

Since coming to court I had learned a great deal about matters of precedence, and I knew that as Duchess of Buckingham, I would be one of the greatest ladies of the land. Only a few women, such as the queen and the king's sisters, would outrank me. Sakes alive, my own sisters—except for the queen—would have to give way to me! I would wear a gold circlet on my head. Save for one of the king's brothers, I could not have made a grander match in all of England.

And the young duke was rich. How many castles and manors would he have to call his own when he came of age? I would have my own household, my own servants, my own ladies. In time, I would surely have my own children, set to continue this grand lineage down through the generations.

I came out of my ducal ruminations to see that my mother was staring at me with amusement. "I don't believe our Kate has ever been so quiet for so long."

"I am most honored," I managed.

The Duchess of Buckingham—soon to be the dowager Duchess of Buckingham, I thought dreamily—chuckled and patted me on the head. "Mind you, child, one of my nephews won't be happy to hear about this. You might as well know."

"The Earl of Warwick?"

"My, she is a sharp little thing, isn't she?" The Duchess of Buckingham gave me another pat. "Yes. He has two girls of his own, you see, both of whom would have done quite nicely for Harry with all that they will inherit, and I daresay Warwick had hopes in that direction. But we women have decided that you will suit better, and the king has given the match his blessing. So that is that. Nephew Richard will just have to fume. And fume he shall, I've no doubt."

I was on the way to becoming a duchess, and I had made the Kingmaker angry. What more could a child of seven have accomplished in one day?

When I left my sister's chamber, I saw that my betrothed was waiting for me—a bit of a jolt, for in my excitement I had forgotten that Harry and I had not made a sterling impression on each other. "So they told you?"

"Yes. I hope I shall be English enough for you."

"I told Grandmother when she talked to me this morning that I thought you were too French," Harry said solemnly. "But she told me that I was being foolish, that when I was older I would be delighted with your French ways. She didn't say why. Anyway, she told me that it was either you or the Earl of Warwick's girls and that if I married one of them, he would probably insist that I go to the North and live with him—I wouldn't want to do that, my lands are in Wales and nearby, and a man should live on his own lands—and he would try to rule me as he tries to rule the king even when I came of age. She thought I'd enjoy marriage to you more. And she said that you would probably be a better bearer of children for me. The Earl of Warwick's countess has only had the two, and lost others, they say, and the Duchess of Bedford your lady mother has had so many healthy ones. So I said that I guessed that you would do, and Grandmother said that I was shaping up to be a man of sense after all."

"Oh," I said, my mood somewhat dampened.

"And better yet, Humphrey and I are to become Knights of the Bath soon after you and I marry, right before the coronation. We might have had to wait if I weren't going to be your husband. So I've decided that marrying you isn't such a bad thing as I thought at first."

"I am glad to hear that," I said hollowly, and continued walking toward my chambers.

My spirits, however, were usually pretty resilient back then—indeed, they still are today, I think—and I soon regained them in full force. As the days before my wedding passed, I played Duke and Duchess with my dolls, letting the least feminine looking of them stand in for the duke—not that I intended any disrespect toward my fiancé. Because their play consisted mainly in saying what my dolls usually said to each other, with the added novelty of them addressing each other as "your grace," I tired soon enough of this, after which I would count up the duchesses of England and never cease to find the figure gratifyingly low, even on the occasions when I realized I had missed one or two. There was the Duchess of York, the Duchess of Norfolk I knew, and the wives of her late son and her living grandson as well, the Duchess of Exeter, the Duchess of Suffolk, her mother-in-law the Dowager Duchess of Suffolk, Mama the Duchess of Bedford, and the Duchess of Buckingham. Eventually, I supposed, there would be a Duchess of Gloucester and a Duchess of Clarence. It was a select company indeed— and joining it would be me.

I soon had no need to while the hours away, for there was the matter of my wedding dress, not to mention the dress for my sister's coronation, in which I as duchess would get to take a prominent part. As a result, my sister's tailors were always coming and measuring me, or holding bits of cloth against me, and the days passed quickly.

John, hearing the news—he was my sister's Master of Horse and often around—visited one morning in my chamber immediately after the queen's tailor had finished one of his visits. As soon as I saw him, he fell to his knees, then prostrated himself. "My duchess, do have consideration on us poor lowly peasants from time to time, won't you?"

"Oh, John," I giggled. "Do get up."

He did, and cut me a low bow. "So, you have met young Buckingham, I presume? Does he suit?"

"He did not want to marry me, but he will not have to go to the North if he does, and his grandmother says I am likely to be a good breeder, and he will be knighted soon as well. So he is content."

John laughed. "The unappreciative puppy! I am to be made a Knight of the Bath with him. Shall I drown him in his for you?"

"No, John! No! I would not want to hurt him—and then I would be a widow."

"Very well, I'll keep my hands off the young fool. He's but a lad, after all. Someone older would be able to see your potential for beauty and be well content."

"Beauty?"

"Poppet, I am old enough to remember our sister Bessie when she was not so much older than you are now. You are the image of her then, skinniness and all. And now look at her. Buckingham has a treat in store for him, ill as he deserves it."

I pondered this possibility and found it incomprehensible. "Anyway, his grandmother is very kind to me. I like her, and she likes me, I think."

"Yes, and so does *my* duchess. Here is something from her for your wedding apparel. She wore it when she was a girl, I believe."

I gasped at the gold ring he held out to me. It was sized for a child and fit snugly on my right fourth finger when I slipped it on. "John, it is beautiful! I will write to her and thank her straightaway," I added, for my handwriting had improved immensely since I had joined the queen's household.

"She thought you might enjoy it."

"It is so kind of her," I said. My lip began to wobble, just as my sister's did when she began to lose her composure. "John, what if I can't be a good wife to him?"

"Kate?"

"I mean, what if I can't bear him children, or run a household, or do all I will have to do? They will send me back! We will all be in disgrace!"

John put his arms around me and let me cry upon the fine new doublet he was wearing. "Wedding nerves, even at your age, sweetheart," he said, patting my head. "Do you think our sister and our mother won't have taught you how to do all you need to know when you begin to live together as husband and wife? And as for children—goodness knows there are enough of us alive and thriving. The Lord has His own ways, I know, but I think His way with you will be more likely than not to give you children. You will do fine. We all will be fine."

"You really think it's just wedding nerves?"

"Yes. Even I had them. I was a bundle of nerves, let me tell you, before my wedding. Just ask my wife."

I began giggling.

"Now dry your eyes and let me take you riding in the fine fresh air, where you shall get away for a time from all of this pother. I'm not Bessie's Master of Horse for nothing, you know."

∽

Our wedding was a relatively quiet affair, most of the court's energy—and funds—going toward my sister's coronation to follow in a few days. Still, it was a grand occasion, and over thirty years later, I still remember it clearly.

What should I write of? My dress? I have worn finer ones since, I suppose, but I loved the exquisite little creation of blue and yellow silk that my sister's tailor finally completed the evening before I married Harry. I remember Harry's robes too: scarlet, worked with the golden knots that were the Stafford badge and that I learned early on could not be called "twisty little knots," as I called them by mistake a time or two, but "Stafford knots," if you please. Topping off the Stafford-knot-covered robe was the shining circlet of gold that Harry wore on his head as a mark of his dukedom. No doubt, as all the adults commented, the two of us made a charming little couple. And yet I do not want to write about dress.

The ceremony? My father and my oldest brother, Anthony, led me to the chapel door at Greenwich Palace, where the king and queen awaited us under a gold canopy. Harry was there before me, having been led to his place by George, Duke of Clarence, in rather better spirits since he had complained of John's marriage to his aunt. (Later, I realized that he himself wished to marry one of the Kingmaker's daughters and was quite pleased

that one of their prospective bridegrooms had been taken off the market.)
But yet I do not want to write about the ceremony, save perhaps for the
kiss Harry gave me at the appointed time. It was a little boy's kiss given to
a little girl, but there was a tenderness in it that I had not expected and that
I cannot think of to this very day without shedding a tear.

The feast afterward? It was a great feast, with the most amazing variety of
food I had seen to date, though it was to pale beside the coronation banquet
that I would attend in a few days. There was a great variety of wine, too,
and the king and Lord Hastings seemed to enjoy it particularly well, though
Harry and I of course got only a couple of watered-down sips as we sat in
our places of state. But it was not the food or the drink that I wish to write
about, but this:

It was a very long feast as well as a grand one, at least for us children.
Humphrey, Harry's brother, finally gave up staying awake as a hopeless
task and went to sleep with his head almost upon his plate, and I myself,
infected by his example, started to drift off. Too tired to think of what I
was doing, I let my head rest on Harry's shoulder and began to give myself
up to a long-needed sleep.

Laughter and exclamations came from the adults near us, and in my
half-dreaming state I sensed someone trying to pluck me out of my seat,
doubtless to carry me to bed where I belonged. But Harry held on to me
tightly as I opened my eyes to gaze around confusedly.

"Don't disturb her," he said in the same voice he had used when he had
spoken of Humphrey that first day I met him. "My wife is comfortable as
she is."

iv

May 1465 to February 1466

Though I am not old—eight-and-thirty now—I have seen my fair share of crownings. My sister Bessie was my first.

Because of our youth, Harry and I were to be carried on squires' shoulders during most of the procession—a subject Harry waxed indignant upon when we were told. "I'm too old for that! I stayed awake through our entire wedding, after all."

Humphrey, the sweetest-tempered lad I knew, sat back and watched his brother fume with his usual gentle expression. "But your wedding was much shorter than the coronation will be," he pointed out mildly.

"It seemed to take forever," my spouse muttered ungallantly.

Harry's anger somewhat cooled, however, as the day when he was to be made a Knight of the Bath approached. Humphrey was also being knighted, as were my sister Margaret's husband-to-be and my brothers Richard and John. My brother Anthony had been knighted some years before; Lionel was destined for the Church; and Edward, the youngest, would have to wait for his turn later, there being a great many young men and boys who were to be dubbed at the Tower.

Among them was a man of twenty-two, John de Vere, the Earl of Oxford. I felt very sorry for the young earl, who had gained his title in the saddest possible way several years before when his father and his older brother had both been beheaded on charges of plotting with Margaret of Anjou. King Edward had been very kind in allowing him to succeed to the earldom and to attend my sister's coronation, I thought, as there were rumors that he was not inclined to be loyal to the House of York. But he had married a sister of the Kingmaker, who was as good a Yorkist as could be, so that was a good sign.

Harry and Humphrey had been told many times what to expect at their knighting, and listening to them talk about it, I was rather relieved on the whole that I was a girl and would never have to go through such a ceremony. The bath on the evening before the knighting would be pleasant, I thought, if it were warm enough, and the blue ermine-trimmed robes one put on at the very end sounded magnificent. But the all-night vigil of prayer beforehand sounded cold and wearisome even for the most pious. All in all, I decided as I snuggled into my warm bed with Cecilia and my favorite doll the evening Harry and the others were to proceed into the chilly church, it was far more pleasant to be a Knight of the Bath's lady than a Knight of the Bath.

I probably slept no better that night than Harry, though. The next day, Friday, May 24, was the day my sister was to ride from Eltham Palace to the Tower, where as was the custom she would sleep before proceeding to Westminster. I was all agog; if my sister was a fraction as excited as I, she must not have slept a wink.

When at last the morning came, the king's aunts and sisters, my mother, a few other sundry duchesses, and myself were seated in several richly decorated litters, behind one in which Bessie rode in solitary splendor. We were to ride to London's great bridge, where the mayor and the alderman had prepared a show on which they had been working for months. At Shooters Hill, the fathers of the city, their scarlet robes ablaze against the usual grayness of the London sky, joined us.

Though my travels had mostly been by barge, John had taken me across the bridge once or twice. It had been a marvelous enough sight then; now I barely recognized it. The laundry poles that protruded from the houses that lined both sides of it had been festooned with banners, and the mud and muck on the path of the bridge had been obliterated by clean sand that seemed to momentarily confuse the horses. Stages had been erected every few feet. On them were men dressed as angels and saints, choirs of boys sweetly singing, and members of all of the guilds of London in their finest clothes. I could not see my sister's face as she took in all of this that had been planned for her, but I saw Mama next to me trying not to cry tears of pride. I squeezed her hand, and she smiled at me and squeezed back.

But, of course, the ceremonies were only beginning.

At the Tower, the newly made Knights of the Bath greeted us in their blue and silver robes, Harry as the highest ranking standing at the forefront of the group. John looked especially dashing in his robes, which later earned him an approving thunk of the cane from his wife, and my brother Richard looked quietly dignified in his. Harry at nine, I am afraid in retrospect, looked rather more quaint than manly in his knightly attire, especially as he was surrounded by grown and nearly grown men, but of course his grandmother told him that he was the height of mature masculinity, and he puffed up in a manner indicating that he believed her wholeheartedly. Humphrey, fortunately, was having a good day and looked almost the picture of health as he stood with his comrades, as proud as the rest of them.

I thought the new Earl of Oxford looked appealingly melancholy as he stood there with his fellow knights. (Much later in life, having had occasion to become friendly with the earl, John de Vere, I mentioned this to him. "Of course I looked melancholy," he replied. "I was a Lancastrian in a sea of Yorkists. How else could I look?")

On Saturday, the Knights of the Bath escorted my sister from the Tower to Westminster, we ladies following in our shared litters behind Bessie in her open litter as we wound our way through the city streets, lined with guild members. Bessie flashed her smile right and left, and so, for that matter, did I. I waved so much my wrist ached, and the Fishmongers and I gave each other such enthusiastic welcomes that when we had passed clear of them, Mama muttered through clenched teeth, "Child, it is not your coronation. Have you forgotten that?"

"But they like us so much, Mama!" I protested. Still, I tried to conduct myself with a little more dignity—for a few minutes, anyway. Then the joy of the occasion swept me up again, and even Mama and the dowager Duchess of Buckingham (whom I now called Grandmother Buckingham) lost some of their matronly reserve and began to dimple and wave as much as I.

At last, coronation morning, Sunday, May 26, arrived. The Earl of Warwick was not there, being in Burgundy on the king's affairs. (There was speculation that he might have absented himself on purpose, but I supposed that he was simply a very busy man.) The king's mother, the Duchess of York, had no business to excuse her own absence, as everyone well knew, and I felt sorry for Bessie's sake that she was being snubbed so. But the king's sisters Margaret and the Duchess of Suffolk were there, smiling and pleasant, and I soon forgot to care about Cecily Neville's absence. If she wished to miss the finest day in England, let her do so!

"Lord God, keep me from swooning," Bessie muttered that morning as my mother adjusted her robes for the millionth or so time. She was a vision—with her honey-colored hair falling unbound to her shoulders, her purple mantle, and a golden circlet upon her head—but a very nervous one. "Has anyone ever swooned during this, I wonder?"

"Now, now," my mother said.

My sister took a deep breath and took her place underneath a purple canopy borne by the four barons of the Cinque Ports. "I'm hot," she moaned. "I *will* faint."

Three people at once moved to fan my sister.

Meanwhile, I, clad in ermine and red velvet like the other duchesses and countesses, clambered on the shoulders of the squire who was to bear me. When I had settled myself safely, the squire—a strapping, handsome young man for whom any maiden over fourteen would have died for the privilege of being carried so—carefully arose. "Up we go, Duchess. No fingers around my eyes, please; I need to see where I am walking, you know. You're a light weight, I'm glad to say."

"And you are very strong," I said gallantly, staring around me. "It's better than being on horseback!"

My mother left off adjusting my sister's robes for a moment to fiddle with mine. From where we were, we could hear the sound of the Duke of Clarence, the Earl of Arundel, and the Duke of Norfolk riding through Westminster Hall on horseback, clearing a path through the onlookers so that my sister and the rest of us could pass safely through.

The Bishop of Salisbury and the Bishop of Durham took their places on either side of my sister, while the Abbot of Westminster listened for a signal from within the hall. "Time, your grace," he said at last, and took his place behind Bessie under the canopy. A trumpet sounded.

I do think my sister groaned. Then she took a scepter in each hand and a deep breath and began walking forward as Grandmother Buckingham lifted her train.

Never in my life had I imagined that so many people could crowd into Westminster Hall—not that I had had much occasion to consider the matter. I knew not whether to look at them or to look at the rafters of the hall above my head, which thanks to my squire I could see better than I ever had in my life. "Hold tight, my lady, and keep a sharp look-out," my squire hissed as the spectators pressed forward. "Some of them will try to grab at the ladies' gowns, for souvenirs."

I gasped and tightened my grip on the squire. As I did my little gold coronet drooped to one side a little, giving me what I suppose now must have been a rather jaunty air.

My gown and the other ladies' made it through Westminster Hall intact, though, and we arrived outside of Westminster Abbey unmolested. There waiting for us was the Archbishop of Canterbury, and surrounding him were so many other bishops and abbots that if the Lord Himself had suddenly appeared among them, I would not have been the least bit surprised. The Duke of Clarence, the Earl of Arundel, and the Duke of Norfolk had left their horses—which had been as splendidly attired as any human present—behind, and stood ready to lead the way into the abbey. With them, carried like me on the shoulders of a squire and looking far less pleased about it, was Harry. I caught his eye and smiled as Bessie stepped out of her shoes to walk upon the striped cloth spread for her to make her way to the high altar. He made a motion with his mouth that could have been a grimace or a hint of a smile.

I decided to take it as a smile.

Behind Harry, a group of earls and barons, my father and my brother Anthony among them, and the newly made Knights of the Bath led my sister inside the abbey, Grandmother Buckingham still holding her train for dear life. It must have been heavy, for she looked as nearly as grim as Harry had, but she rallied as the procession started up again. Behind her were my mother and the king's sisters Elizabeth and Margaret, and behind them was—me. Snaking in back of us was a group of other richly clad ladies, including a few of my sisters. I knew not to look for the king, for it was not the custom for him to attend, but I did think it sad that he was missing all of this splendor. Perhaps he had found a secret place to watch, I hoped.

Bessie at last reached the altar and knelt as the Archbishop of Canterbury began to read in Latin, words that were incomprehensible to me but which Harry appeared to be following quite well, an accomplishment of which I knew his tutor, Master Giles, would be duly proud. At least the effort had distracted Harry from the indignity of being carried, for he no longer looked sullen but attentive.

The archbishop paused in his Latin, and my sister prostrated herself gracefully (a feat I would not have thought possible to accomplish gracefully until my sister did it) upon the red velvet cushions. More Latin followed, then Bessie rose. I watched impatiently as her circlet was removed and she was anointed with oil on her head. Then her gown was opened at the lacings specially provided for that purpose so that she could be anointed on the breasts. I would have giggled or shivered or blushed if the archbishop had been touching me so, I was sure, but my sister took this all with perfect composure; no one could have guessed that she had been threatening to faint not at all long before. A ring was blessed and put on Bessie's finger.

All eyes turned to the jewel-encrusted crown that had been sparkling on the altar all this time. The archbishop blessed it—an endless process as far as I was concerned—and a coif was placed on my sister's pretty hair to keep safe the holy oil with which she had been anointed. Then, at last, the golden crown was placed on my sister's head, and she was led to her throne.

The squire who had carried me patiently on his back all this time looked up as one, then another, of my tears of pride splashed on his forehead. "Happy day, eh, Duchess?" he whispered.

"Oh, yes," I whispered back.

∽

Bessie's crown must have carried with it some special powers, for a few weeks later, as I was sewing in her outer chamber, the queen gasped and without a word of warning ran into her inner chamber, where we heard the unmistakable and very unroyal sound of retching. My sister Anne, who was one of her ladies in waiting, hastened to help her, while Mama sat smiling on her chair. "The third time in three days," she said when Bessie finally emerged, looking decidedly greenish. "Have you mentioned this to the king?"

"I would like to wait a month or two, Mama, just—just in case. But I am certain. I was just as miserable when I was carrying Tom and Richard."

I gasped. "You mean you are to have a baby? That I am to be an aunt?"

"You already are an aunt," Anne pointed out as Bessie nodded blearily.

"But this is different," I said. Tom was a couple of years older than I, Richard about the same age. They hardly counted as nephews. Besides, this would be a royal baby—perhaps even a king. I stared at the queen's belly in awe. "How long?"

"February, I think. But keep quiet, Kate! The king must hear it from me first, and no one else, and not until I am quite certain."

"I can't tell even Harry?" I pouted.

"No. He might tell Humphrey, and Humphrey keeps nothing to himself." I nodded gloomily. Telling anything to Humphrey was equivalent to passing an Act of Parliament.

"John?" He was a great secret-keeper, having never revealed the unfortunate accident that had befallen Mama's best hennin two years before when I sneaked it from her chamber to try it on. (How was I to know that my puppy would find it so irresistible?)

"Oh, all right. But tell him it is a secret."

"Now?"

"Oh, go. You'll be good for nothing if you don't."

Grinning, I raced down to the stables to find my brother.

∽

Bessie had not been mistaken. On February 11, 1466, at Westminster, she bore the king his first child—not the hoped-for son, but a fine girl, whom the king named after Bessie. I helped attend my sister during her confinement in her last days of pregnancy and during the childbirth itself— men were not allowed in the birthing room, so Bessie had needed as much help as she could get—and came out of the ordeal with the certainty that whatever exactly Harry would have to do to get me with child, it could well wait for another ten years.

Little Elizabeth's birth proved to be the impetus needed to get Cecily, Duchess of York, to court. I suppose like any other woman, she wanted to see her grandchild, no matter what she might feel about her daughter-in-law. The king, moreover, added a sweetener by asking her, along with my mother, to be one of her godparents.

All was being put in readiness for the christening of Bess, as she was called among the family, when the arrival of the Duchess of York was announced. She kissed the king, who was standing by the cradle admiring the dexterity and cunning with which Bess took a nap, as casually as if she had just seen him the previous day, and she greeted my sister as graciously as if Cecily had made the match between her and the king herself. The queen responded in kind, and the rest of us took our cue from her. It was as if we had known each other always, except that we didn't know each other at all, which would have made for some awkward moments had it not been for Bess choosing to awake at that moment and to commence howling at the top of her lungs. She was not a terribly attractive sight when she did this, and I decided that Harry could wait yet another five years before he begat any such creature on me.

Cecily nodded approvingly as two nurses nearly banged heads in their haste to comfort Bess. "She has her father's lungs," she said, turning to the king. "My, you would scream at the least provocation. And you had the finest nurse in all of Rouen."

I watched with interest as the quicker of the nurses picked up Bess and put her to her breast. Being the youngest of twelve, and of an age with or younger than my nephews, I had no experience in taking care of babies. With Bess quiet, she was considerably more appealing. I flicked out a finger and touched the fuzzy hair on her head. "It's so soft," I said reverently.

Cecily, wonder of wonders, looked at me and smiled. "One of your girls?" she asked my mother.

"Yes. The Duchess of Buckingham—Kate, that is—is my youngest."

"Ah, Harry Buckingham's wife. I remember him when he was a little lad." The Duchess of York's eyes took on a far-off look. "Much has changed since then."

By-and-by, it was time for the christening. The Duchess of York and Mama were little Elizabeth's godmothers; the Earl of Warwick—smiling and genial—was the godfather. His brother, George Neville, the Archbishop of York, officiated. I was not much given to thinking about such things then, but to older observers, the christening must have boded well: the king and his mother on good terms again, the Kingmaker content with his role and looking positively avuncular as he stood at the font with the king's firstborn child.

The older observers, of course, would have been dead wrong.

v

June 1468 to August 1468

I WAS JEALOUS. MARGARET, THE KING'S YOUNGEST SISTER, WAS GOING TO Burgundy to be married to its duke in July, and my brothers Anthony and John were to be in the wedding party accompanying her across the seas. I was not. "I could be of plenty of use," I told Harry and Humphrey, who were bearing all this with remarkable patience. "I could keep her gowns in order, and fetch things for her, and—"

"Kate, the king himself is staying here! So is almost everyone else in England. It's not as if you're the only one not going."

"Well, it feels that way," I said, and flounced off to heap a little guilt on John's shoulders.

I told my tale of woe to John as he sat studying my sister's stable accounts, but he only smiled. "Be reasonable, poppet. We all can't go."

"But you are going!"

"A lot of tiresome ceremonies, I'm sure."

"And jousting." John loved to joust.

"Well? It's not as if you can joust, after all."

"I ought to go! I am a duchess, after all. The youngest Duchess of Norfolk is going—and Harry's dukedom is far greater than the Duke of Norfolk's."

"Oh, the ducal nose is out of joint? That is the problem? Methinks your head has swollen a little, poppet."

I was silent. It was true that I did enjoy my position very much. Whenever there was a procession, I was near the front of the ladies, behind only the king's sisters, and I loved wearing my small, jeweled, golden coronet, which glittered so prettily on my sandy head, on those grand occasions. Perhaps I had also been a bit too forward lately in reminding my own sisters (all married now, but none higher than to earls' heirs) of my superior rank.

John was my favorite brother; I could never pretend otherwise. I loved him even better than my father, whom I had not seen as much when I was little. To have him looking disapprovingly at me was more than I could bear. "Am I that awful, John? Truly, I didn't mean to be!" My eyes began to well with tears.

"Kate! For God's sake, don't cry. Tone it down a little, is all I advise. We know you're a duchess, after all."

"All right, John. I will mend my ways, I promise." I tried to look as humble as I could. "I will go now and read my Book of Hours."

"Stay a while, sweetheart, before you turn too holy on us. We haven't talked lately." He patted the seat beside him, and I settled in happily. "I'll tell you, though, our family has put some noses out of joint lately. Truth be told, that's probably why of the family, only Anthony and I are accompanying the Lady Margaret abroad."

"How?"

"Well, with myself and you married so well, and all of the other girls married now—"

"But their husbands were happy to marry them! I know that some of them asked the king for the chance. Bessie said so."

"True, but people think what they want to think, and some want to think that the men were given no choice. And with other girls—though none as fair as the Woodvilles, I'll grant—going begging for matches, some are upset."

"Oh, you are speaking about Warwick's girls again, I wager! I don't see why they can't marry the king's brothers and be done with it."

"Me neither, but I'm the queen's Master of Horse, not the king's adviser. And when Bessie bought the Exeter girl's marriage from the duchess, it made things even worse with Warwick."

Warwick's nephew, young George Neville, had been expected to marry the Duchess of Exeter's little girl, Anne, who would inherit all of the Exeter estates. Then Bessie had bought the marriage for her own eldest son, Tom, for four thousand marks. They had had a lovely wedding at Greenwich, though not as lovely, I thought complacently, as my own. "Well? She paid a fair price for it, and the Duchess of Exeter was well content."

John shrugged. "True. But to Warwick it was just something else snatched from his hand. Then there is Father. His having been made an earl, and treasurer and constable of England—"

Papa had looked so pleased and so proud when he was girded with his earl's belt. Earl Rivers! "But why should he not be? He does his work well; I heard the king telling someone so."

"He deserves it. But for some it's a matter of too far, too fast. And the king has raised others as well, which doesn't suit the likes of Warwick. William Herbert, for instance. And now Warwick's in another huff because of this upcoming marriage of the Lady Margaret's. He wanted a match with France."

There was a lot, I realized, I was missing in my snug little cocoon at Greenwich.

⁂

After my talk with John, I made a conscientious effort to be rather less irritatingly grand, and I was duly rewarded by heaven (as I saw it) when I was allowed to travel in the entourage taking Margaret to the coast. The Earl of Warwick, again putting his displeasure aside (he did a lot of that in those days, I must admit), was one of the party. He rode beside Margaret, though, well away from my brothers.

Harry too went with us to Margate, from where the future Duchess of Burgundy set sail, not to return to England for many years. Humphrey stayed at Greenwich, for consumption, which had been clawing at him for years, had him firmly in its grip. The winter had been a bad one for him, and the milder conditions of spring and summer did nothing to restore him.

My sister called in the best physicians for him, but to no avail. The next person she sent for was Harry and Humphrey's mother, Margaret, Countess of Stafford.

Though the countess was my mother-in-law, I had never met her, for she never came to court. For one thing, she was a Beaufort, and the Beauforts were not in favor with the king. Harry's maternal grandfather, Edmund Beaufort, the first Duke of Somerset, had died at St. Albans. His sons had kept up the fight. For a time, Henry Beaufort, the eldest—whom my own father had served in his Lancastrian days—had appeared to accept King Edward, but he had turned traitor and had led troops against the king, leading to his execution four years before. The other sons, Edmund and John, had escaped and were living in Burgundy.

Their sister Margaret, Harry's mother, had remarried after Harry's father died and had a little girl, another Margaret. She did not live with her husband, Richard Darell, however, but in a convent, which I thought was a most peculiar place for a countess who was not a widow. Cecilia had once told me that there was something not quite right about her that made her live there instead of with her husband and child, but she had not elaborated. Harry seldom spoke of her, and when he did, he was so guarded that I knew instinctively not to bring the subject up on my own.

By the time the countess arrived at Greenwich, a few weeks after we had returned from Margate, Humphrey was beyond the reach of any physician. There was nothing for his mother and Grandmother Buckingham and Harry to do but sit in his chamber and wait. I joined them there on occasion, for Humphrey was my brother-in-law as well as my playmate, but I felt as if I were an intruder on the family's grief. So for the most part, I went around my daily business of learning to be a great lady, occasionally coming to Humphrey's outer chamber to wait for news.

The third or fourth day of this, I had no need to ask for news; I could hear Humphrey fighting for each breath even behind the heavy wooden door of his chamber, could see the priest and the physician rush in and know that it was the former and not the latter who was needed most. At last, the room was silent. Humphrey had given up the struggle. Then I heard another sound: Harry's sobs.

I rushed into the chamber and straight to Harry, who was kneeling by the bed, his face hidden in the coverlet. I barely noticed Humphrey, lying on the bed and holding a cross in his lifeless hands. "Harry! I'm so sorry."

He did not turn his head. "Go away."

"But Harry—" I touched him on the arm.

He did turn his head now, and shoved me away so hard that I nearly reeled onto the bed and into poor Humphrey. "Why couldn't it have been one of your brothers and sisters? There are so many of them, and just one of Humphrey! Or you? What do I need with a wife? It should have been one of you. Not my only brother!"

"Harry!" Grandmother Buckingham put down her handkerchief to stare at him in horror. "Kate—"

But I was already gone.

∽

I was sitting in my chamber embroidering—or rather, in my present mood, stabbing a needle through a poor defenseless square of cloth—and making a mental list of all of the things I hated about Henry Stafford, Duke of Buckingham, when someone knocked. "Come in," I said sullenly, regretting this interruption of my list. It was shaping up to be a long one.

Harry's mother entered, without the nuns who usually were by her side, and I realized as she did that I had never been alone with her during her visit. I had been looking for whatever was not quite right about her and had not yet seen it, for she was a pleasant-looking woman, dressed very plainly for a countess, though, and not much given to conversation. She was still a Lancastrian, though, and so good a Yorkist had I become, I wondered if I should check her for horns. "Katherine?"

She didn't even know I preferred "Kate." "Yes, my lady?"

"Harry did not mean what he said a while ago."

"It sounded to me as if he did," I said sulkily.

"When people are grieving they say foolish things sometimes. Harry loved Humphrey very much, you know." She brushed at her eyes and added, "Probably more than he loves me."

I wondered if she had meant me to hear that.

In a stronger voice, she said, "He was speaking out of shock, you see."

"But poor Humphrey was always sick. No one expected him to live long." Too late, I remembered that I was speaking to Humphrey's mother, who might not appreciate this sound common sense. "I beg your pardon, my lady."

"There is truth in what you say. I knew this day would come. But all of us hoped in a way too that it never would, and I think Harry hoped that more than any. So you see? He did not intend to hurt you just now. I know he will repent of what he said later. He was so fond of his broth—"

Her eyes began to fill with tears. I remembered that she had lost one brother to the headsman and had two others far away, whom she might never see again. Impulsively, I put my arms around her, Lancastrian or no. "I am so sorry about Humphrey, my lady. I liked him."

She cried a little, then touched my hair. "You are a good girl. Now I want you to do something for me. Will you go find Harry now, and keep him company? I think that will do him good."

"But he won't want me there. And I will probably say the wrong thing."

"I think just your being there will make him feel a little better. You needn't say much at all."

"Well, where is he?"

"I don't know. I thought you might."

"Oh, he is in his secret place, I suppose. I know where that is, though I'm not supposed to. Humphrey told me." I looked at his mother apologetically. "Humphrey never was any good at keeping secrets. Oh! I'm sorry, my lady. But he really wasn't. "

The countess almost smiled. "No, he wasn't, indeed." She pinched my cheek. "I think they did right to pick you as Harry's bride."

⁓

By the banks of the Thames a large tree had fallen years ago, providing a natural if not a particularly comfortable seat. Shrubbery grew unchecked around it, making the spot a secluded one. Harry and Humphrey, who both liked to fish, had dragged a wooden chest there in which they stored their tackle. It was a boys-only spot, Humphrey had told me even as he parted with his secret, and I had dutifully stayed away except to wander there sometimes when I knew the brothers were elsewhere. I had even sat there myself from time to time, but I failed to see the attraction of the place, and quickly had left to sit in my own favorite spot at Greenwich, underneath a large oak tree where a person who was obviously fond of the creature comforts of life had erected a bench that afforded an excellent view of the Thames. Perhaps Margaret of Anjou herself had put it up.

I Iaving arrived at the boys' lair, I pressed through the shrubbery. Sure enough, Harry was sitting on the fallen tree, a rod in his hand and a line dangling in the water. His thin face had a puffy look, and I suspected that he had been crying hard not long before my arrival.

"Go away."

I decided against telling Harry that his mother had sent me. "Greenwich is my sister's property. I can go where I please here as much as you can."

To my surprise, Harry conceded the point with a shrug. "Don't fall in, then," he offered as I gingerly made my way along the slippery bank.

"I won't."

I sat down on the tree, careful not to sit too close to Harry, and watched the Thames flow and the occasional boat pass as Harry sat in silence. No fish showed any interest in his line.

After a while, the sun and the silence soon made me drowsy. I closed my eyes, only to hear Harry's voice. "Kate? I'm leaving now. You'd best come with me. You shouldn't sit here all by yourself."

The remark struck me as absurd, but I did not argue. Dutifully standing up to leave, I watched as Harry stowed his fishing gear in the box, then carefully locked it. "Someday I could fish with you?" I suggested cautiously.

"You don't know how."

"Yes, I do. John taught—I mean, I do know how." I cursed myself for my gaffe in mentioning my superbly healthy brother. "I can bait a hook and cast a line, and I was very quiet just now, and did nothing to scare the fish. You saw that."

"Yes. Well, maybe someday. They weren't biting today, I guess you noticed."

"Yes, I did notice." I had also noticed when Harry pulled his line from the water that Harry had not even baited the hook, but I kept my counsel.

He walked up the slope and pushed through the brush, then turned and gave me his hand to help me. "Be careful." Then he said to the ground, "You're not bad company, for a girl."

It was, I knew, the equivalent to a heartfelt apology.

౿ఞ

Humphrey's body was taken to Pleshey to be buried next to that of his father. I had come to like Harry's mother, and when it came time for her to return to her convent, I felt sorry for her. As she and her nun companions made ready to leave, accompanied by only two manservants, I ventured to ask, "Will you come back soon to court, my lady? I am sure the king would be glad to have you."

She smiled at my naïveté. "Hardly, I fear. My brothers still work to overthrow your king, child."

"But surely you do not—"

"My allegiance is to the House of Lancaster, and always will be." My mouth dropped open, and the countess chucked me on the chin. "It shocks you, good little Yorkist that you are, and I am sorry for it. Never fear, I do not spy or plot; I am not even in communication with my brothers. It would endanger Harry and all whom I love. But I can pray, and I pray daily for the restoration of King Henry to the throne." I shuddered at such heresy, and Harry's mother smiled again. "Anyway, even if Edward wanted me at his court, it is an odious place to me. My Harry must stay there because he is a ward of the crown, and I would do nothing to interfere with his Stafford inheritance. But it is not a place I wish to be. Not while York sits on the throne."

She looked at Harry, who I think had been hoping that she would agree to extend her stay. Quietly, she said, "And there is another reason why I keep to myself. Has Harry told you?"

I shook my head.

"Mother—"

"Hush, Harry. The child is your wife, and should know." She turned toward me. "Several years ago, Kate, after the birth of my daughter, the demons came upon me, and I tried to do violence to myself—and to her. We were both saved, thank the Lord, but my husband decided that I should not live with him and her after that, and he was right. I lived with his mother for a time, and when she died, I moved to where I am now. The nuns take good care of me, and when my fits of melancholy come upon me, they tend me and bring me out of them with prayer. I fear Humphrey's death will bring another on."

She shuddered, and one nun gently touched her shoulder. "They have never been as bad since that first time, my lady."

"Yes. God has been merciful." She kissed me and then tightly hugged Harry, who had been staring at the ground. "You are growing into a man, Harry. I hear you will be moving to Westminster soon?"

"Yes. It is time I learned more of the arts of war, the king—Edward—says."

Margaret smiled. "Learn them well, and perhaps you can put them to use for Lancaster one day!" She shook her head. "No, I should not say that. Your loyalties are torn enough as it is. Be a true man and an honest one, York or Lancaster, and I shall be well satisfied."

She kissed Harry and let a man assist her onto a horse. After we had stopped waving good-bye and she was well out of sight, I said, "Harry—"

"Don't you ever tell anyone of what she said just now. Never."

"All right, Harry."

He stared after her a little while longer. "Let's go fishing," he said at last, and we turned away.

vi

Harry: January 1469 to March 1469

SOON AFTER MY GRANDFATHER WAS KILLED AT NORTHAMPTON IN 1460, Cecily of York and her children left us for London, where they waited for the Duke of York to join them from abroad. Warwick, though he had captured King Henry just as that creature George had said, made a great show of being his obedient subject, but no one was fooled, even less so after the Duke of York returned to Westminster and placed his hand upon the throne. His obvious intentions did not meet with the reception he wished, and war broke out anew. Within a matter of months, the Duke of York and his second son, Edmund, died in battle outside Wakefield, King Henry was a fugitive, Margaret of Anjou was traveling about desperately trying to raise troops, and the Duke of York's eldest son, Edward, the Earl of March, was on the throne as Edward IV. It was a confusing time to be an Englishman.

During all of this tumult, I had been left undisturbed in my grandmother's household, and my position did not change when the throne came to York. I was lucky, I realize now. The new king could have found some pretext to seize my grandfather's estates, depriving me of them, but he did not, nor did he prevent my dukedom from descending to me. No doubt it helped that my grandmother was aunt to both the king and the Kingmaker and sister to the king's mother. If Grandmother was not happy with the latest turn of events—and I am heartily sure that she was not—she wisely kept her opinions to herself.

I was lonely after the York children left us, and my grandmother, recognizing this, sent for my younger brother Humphrey to join me. Being so young, he was not ideal company at first, but once he reached an age where we could play together more readily, we became inseparable. Together we went to live with the king's sister in 1464, when the king purchased my wardship from my grandmother, and together we went to the queen's household the following year. I enjoyed the chance to be the older brother to Humphrey, and tried my best to shield him from any harm. When he died despite my best efforts, I was grief-stricken.

Fortunately, this sad time in my life was soon followed by a happier occasion: my turning thirteen. I continued to learn my lessons with my tutor Master Giles and the rest, but it was necessary that I spend more time learning the manly arts as well. Because this knowledge was quite beyond the queen's ken, I was moved to Westminster in the early part of 1469.

My cousin Richard—made the Duke of Gloucester after his brother was crowned king—was there as well. Until recently, he had been staying in the Earl of Warwick's household, learning the many lessons that mighty man could impart, but he at sixteen was, evidently, now considered old enough to take up some responsibilities for the king, which included helping occasionally with my own knightly training. This time, unlike those days at my grandparents' manor of Writtle, we became friends.

"Friends" is an understatement, however, for I loved him, as a matter of fact. Why wouldn't I? Richard was bright, charming, and confident; he was trusted by his brother the king; he had come through Warwick's schooling (so I heard from the other boys and young men at Westminster) with nothing but acclaim. I was thirteen, three years his junior, raised mostly in the company of women and of my beloved but frail younger brother. Quick in my studies, I knew little of the ways of men. Richard was everything I wanted to be.

I like to think that our friendship was not entirely one-sided. There was that three-year gap between us, to be sure, but I was no longer as insufferable as I had been when I was age four. I was not as nearly as important to the Duchess of Exeter and to the queen and king as I had been to my grandmother, and Humphrey's presence had made me more bearable as well. And I was not without winning qualities myself, I hope. Be that as it may, Richard must have had some regard for me, for we began to go out riding sometimes even when he was not required to give me instruction.

It was on one of those rides that Richard asked me, "How does it feel, being married?"

I was pleased that this was a matter about which Richard, for once, knew nothing. "Kate will make a good wife, I suppose. She's pretty and sweet."

"You don't mind that she came with no portion? From a family of nobodies?"

"The Duchess of Bedford isn't a nobody," I pointed out. "She was married to the fourth Henry's brother."

"*Was* is the operative word, Harry."

"But she's still a duchess. My grandmother is married now to Sir Walter Blount, Lord Mountjoy, and she's still a duchess. And they're our family now anyway—the Woodvilles, that is."

"If you say so. You could have married one of Warwick's girls, you know."

"Yes, Grandmother told me once." I frowned. "How did you know?"

"The earl told me. He said that he had hoped Isabel or Anne would have married you. What an estate that would have been! Your estates and half of the Countess of Warwick's Beauchamp and Despenser estates. Of course, the Warwick estates are entailed in the male line, so his nephew will inherit. Still, that would have been grand for you."

"Kate will be a beauty one day, I expect. And she's from good childbearing stock."

"So is many a peasant."

I did not much like this conversation, for I was genuinely fond of Kate. Low-born on her father's side she might well be, but she was certainly no peasant. "Well, I like her, and that's important too. What if I had married one of the Warwick girls and we didn't get along?"

"Oh, they're agreeable girls, and pretty too. I'll probably marry one of them, most likely Anne, as she's the younger. You would have gotten along. But if you didn't, it wouldn't matter if you didn't like her. You could pack her off to some manor and come back just long enough from time to time to beget a child upon her."

"I could do that with Kate. I will have sufficient estates." (It was time, I thought, I reminded Richard of this.) "And I don't want to pack her off! When she's old enough, I think I shall like her in my bed." I blushed as I touched upon a subject I thought about altogether too much lately, though not yet, of course, with little Kate as the object. (At the time, Margaret, Duchess of Burgundy, if you must know—and what harm can you knowing possibly do me now?—was the main occupant of my thoughts in that direction.)

"Oh, there are mistresses for that."

This was too much. "You're not going to tell me you have a mistress!"

"But I do. Soon I'll have a bastard, as a matter of fact."

"She's with child?"

"That's the way it works, old man."

I sat back in my saddle, amazed at the worldliness of the man—I could call him nothing but a man now—at my side. "How do you get one? A mistress?"

"Easy enough when you're a king's brother. Or even just an ordinary duke, maybe," he said kindly, to give me hope. "Women push themselves forward. It's just a matter of picking one who's the most fair and personable. I suppose you don't even have to pick just one, but more than one can get complicated, not to say expensive."

I nodded in what I hoped was a jaded manner. "Richard, when—I mean, can—"

He was good at guessing my thoughts back then. "You're a bit young, I think, to taste the pleasures of life. When you're older, there's some houses I can take you to."

"In Southwark," I said, eager to prove that I was not entirely ignorant.

"Yes, that's the place. I'll take you there when you're sixteen." He snorted. "If Ned hasn't already taken you by then."

⁂

During my thirteenth year, my mind was not always preoccupied with carnal matters. I spent a great deal of time thinking about my family—the family I'd been born into, not the one into which I'd married.

My Beaufort grandfather died in battle while I was still in my mother's womb, as I have said earlier, but he left behind three sons, my uncles. The eldest, Henry, the second Duke of Somerset, had been carried off half dead from the first battle of St. Albans, after which he had waged war against the House of York and the Earl of Warwick for years until finally making his peace with Edward. The king, at least, had been sincere in his desire for reconciliation; he'd hunted with my uncle, arranged a tournament in his honor, even done him the great honor of allowing him to sleep beside him. But Henry Beaufort had either been planning to rebel all along or undergone a change of heart. He soon fell back in with some of his old comrades, who rose against the king. It was a fateful choice. John Neville, the Kingmaker's younger brother, defeated the Duke of Somerset's troops at Hexham in 1464. My uncle and thirty others were executed straight-away. No one in the Duchess of Exeter's household, where I was living at the time, saw fit to tell me the news; I found out later when I heard some servants gossiping.

There were two other Beaufort uncles left to me after that: Edmund (who called himself the third Duke of Somerset, though the king said that he had no right to do so) and the youngest, John. They had fled abroad after the defeat at Hexham and were now living under the protection of Charles, the Duke of Burgundy—much to the irritation of Edward, whose sister Margaret was Charles's duchess.

I, of course, had never met any of these uncles, which gave them all a certain glamour to me. No one spoke to me of them, save for my mother when Humphrey died; it was as if I were not supposed to know that they existed. One day, Kate and I were playing at bowls in the queen's chambers when the king stormed in, muttering about Duke Charles sheltering the whoreson Edmund Beaufort, the Duke of Sowshit, and then he noticed me and hastily changed the subject, saving his rant for a more private time, I suppose. Fortunately, others were less circumspect than the king, and I picked up information about my Beaufort uncles here and there. I wondered if I looked like them or had any of their mannerisms.

My Stafford uncles were another matter. There were two of them, Henry and John, and both had made their peace with York. Owing to that, I saw them now and then, so neither, of course, interested me nearly as much as the Beauforts.

With half of my family for Lancaster and the other half for York, I naturally spent, as I said earlier, a lot of time thinking about the subject. My mind should have been made up for me, I suppose, as I was married to the queen's sister and was being raised at Edward's court. But it was not. Edward was affable enough to me back then, when he noticed me, and I adored Richard and tolerated George. But I was named for King Henry, and I could not forget that or my relatives who had died fighting for his cause.

King Henry had been in the Tower since 1465, having been a fugitive for months before finally being captured and taken there. I would look at the fortress when my travels brought me by it and wonder what it was like for a man who had been king since he was nine months old to be a prisoner there. Once or twice, I even wondered about getting permission to visit him. I said as much one day to Richard, who replied, "Are you daft, Harry? How much of a Lancastrian are you, anyway?"

"I was named after him, after all. And Grandmother Buckingham was godmother to his son. Grandfather presented his baby son to King Henry after Henry had been ill for all of that time."

Richard snorted. "Ill, Harry? Mad as midsummer, you mean. I'd not brag about that connection if I were you."

"I don't. I just get curious."

"Ned wonders about you, you know, with your Beaufort blood, whether it will out. And it doesn't help that you are always asking all and sundry about those uncles of yours."

I flushed. I thought I had been more subtle. "Well, what I am supposed to do? Pretend they don't exist, as does everyone else?"

"At the moment, that might be a good idea. Have you forgotten what happened last autumn to Poynings and Alford?"

I had not forgotten. Though you couldn't have guessed it from life at Greenwich or Sheen, Edward had never been all that secure on his throne. Each time one threat to it was removed, another popped up, and last year had been a particularly bad one. That summer, Thomas Cook, a rich draper who had been the mayor of London for a time, had been convicted of misprision of treason for not revealing a Lancastrian plot to kill the king. He'd been fined eight thousand marks, and he should have been grateful that was all that had happened to him; that same autumn, Henry Courtenay, Thomas Hungerford, and the Earl of Oxford had been arrested. The earl had gone free—it helped that he had wed Warwick's sister—but perhaps terrified of the fate that had claimed his father and his brother, he had implicated John Poynings and William Alford, servants of the Duke of Norfolk. When in Burgundy in the Duchess of Norfolk's train, they had taken the opportunity to communicate with my uncle Edmund Beaufort, who frequented the Duke of Burgundy's court. For that, Poynings and Alford had lost their heads in November. Other deaths had followed; it had been a fine season for London's executioners. "I suppose you're right. I shouldn't mention my Beaufort uncles."

"That would be wise indeed. Especially because, if you ask me, more treason will soon be afoot."

"Oh? I thought the king had taken care of his enemies."

"For the time being, but Ned's shortsighted. He doesn't realize how the Earl of Warwick and others detest his favorites. Your Woodville in-laws and that lot. Or if he does realize, he can't be bothered to worry about it."

"They're your in-laws too. And what have they done that's so offensive?"

"It's not so much what they've done as who they are. Upstarts. Warwick feels pushed aside, especially after the king made that alliance with Burgundy when Warwick was pressing for France. And Ned isn't as popular as he once was. His taxes have irritated people; trade isn't all that it could be. The laws aren't enforced properly; order isn't kept. Sometimes I think Ned's a little lazy, to be honest. If I were—" He stopped and looked me full in the face. "I've been speaking to you very frankly of Ned and his faults. Too frankly, really. Don't say anything of this conversation, Harry, will you?"

"Of course not," I said.

And I kept my promise. Only on one occasion have I ever been untrue to Richard.

vii

Kate: March 1469 to December 1469

IN 1467 BESSIE BORE THE KING ANOTHER DAUGHTER, MARY. IN MARCH of 1469, she gave birth to the king's third child—yet another daughter, named Cecily after the king's mother, who naturally was the baby's god-mother. If Edward was bothered by the lack of a son, he did not make it apparent, and we had another grand christening, with a festive churching a month later.

Not long after Bessie's churching in April, word arose of a rising up north. (I have never been to the North, by the way. I cannot say that I regret this.) It was led by someone who gave himself the absurd name of Robin Mend-All, and John Neville, who had recently been made Earl of Northumberland for his loyalty to the king, handily put it down.

Then yet another group of northern malcontents appeared. This group wished to restore Henry Percy, a youth who had been long imprisoned in the Tower, to his family's earldom—the earldom, in fact, that had been given to John Neville. Neville put this rising down as efficiently as the last, and beheaded the leader—who was yet another person calling himself Robin, this one Robin of Holderness—for good measure.

Then Robin Mend-All surfaced again in June.

The king decided that traveling to the North himself would be the best way to deal with the problem, but neither he nor anyone else saw any reason to rush. Instead, he went ahead with plans to go on a pilgrimage to Bury St. Edmunds and to Walsingham, then to make his way north.

My father and my brothers Anthony and John accompanied him, as did Richard, Duke of Gloucester.

Much as I had sulked when I could not accompany Margaret of York to Burgundy, Harry outdid me when he found that he was not to go on pilgrimage with the king, for he was a great admirer of the Duke of Gloucester and had also hoped to see a touch of battle up north. The king, however, was adamant. Harry was to stay with the queen, who herself was traveling to Fotheringhay Castle. In the king's absence, he reminded Harry, who better to escort the queen on her travels than a duke?

"Richard could get to fight. And I must travel with the queen and her mites!"

Needless to say, this speech was directed to me and not to the king. "They surely wouldn't let you fight yet. You're still only thirteen."

"But I could watch and learn, and help the men get into their armor. Instead, I'm stuck with a bunch of women!"

I tried to look sympathetic, but in truth I was delighted about our trip, and also pleased that Harry would be coming along. He had spent so much time at Westminster lately that I had not seen much of him. And when I did see him, all I heard about was Richard, Richard, Richard. Maybe a separation would mean that I wouldn't have to hear so much about the wonderful Duke of Gloucester, who, if Harry could be believed, combined the best qualities of Richard the Lionhearted, the Black Prince, and Henry V.

So to Fotheringhay Castle we went, with the queen's two oldest girls forming part of the company. It was pretty country, but somewhat dull compared to Greenwich with its proximity to London, so I was duly grateful when, at the end of June, the king and his entourage joined us. Papa was not with them, being off in our manor of Middleton raising troops, but John and Anthony were there. I greeted them with delight, but my joy was as nothing compared to the greeting Harry gave Richard.

"Have you seen the castle?" Richard asked later, when the royal party was all settled in and we were relaxing in a solar.

Seated beside Harry in a window seat, I assumed that I was included in the question. "Why, of course. It's been so quiet here, there's been nothing to do but explore."

Richard looked at me as if it were the castle laundress who had dared to join in on this conversation. "Well, I suppose that's true. Still, I was born here, you know. Harry, I've a fancy to see the chamber. Would you like to come along?"

Harry did not wait to answer, but got up straightaway, leaving me forlorn and alone in my window seat until John took Harry's place. "Where's our young buck off to?"

"The chamber where Richard was born," I muttered.

John laughed and patted me on the knee. "The holy shrine! That will have to do unless Harry can get to Bethlehem one day, I suppose."

"I don't understand what Harry sees in him," I said sulkily, after some snickering. "He's not nearly as fine as the king, I think."

"Hero worship. Common enough in lads his age; he'll grow out of it. Why, there's the one I worshipped when I was Buckingham's age," he added as our oldest brother walked over to lounge at our side.

I had always been rather in awe of Anthony myself. He was much more handsome than the rest of my brothers (though John's looks were the type that grew on one), and people still talked of the great joust Anthony had had with the Bastard of Burgundy not that long after Bessie married the king. Yet he was not merely a comely man and a splendid jouster. He was much more learned than anyone in our family, though Lionel, who was in his teens now and had entered the Church, showed some promise in that direction. Although all of us Woodvilles spoke excellent French thanks to Mama, Anthony could write and translate from it also, as easily as if it were his first language. He even wrote verses, though only his wife, Elizabeth Scales, saw most of them.

Perhaps because of all of these accomplishments, I had never been as close to Anthony as I was to John, or even as I was to my youngest and wildest brother, Edward. I looked up at him almost shyly as he stood beside us. "What's this?"

"We were discussing idol worship. Oh, not that kind, Anthony, don't look so perturbed! Harry Buckingham's for Gloucester, and mine for you, to be more exact."

"Yours for me? Why?"

"Merely because you do everything so well, and so much better than the rest of us."

"Oh? I seem to recall you distinguishing yourself in Burgundy. Prince of the Tournament, wasn't it? You put me quite to shame. I was proud of you. Still am."

For the first time in my life, I saw John at a loss for words. "Well, thank you," he muttered at last. "A lot of it was luck, I believe."

"Luck, against some of the finest jousters in Europe? I think skill was more likely."

With the king seeing some petitioners in the castle's great hall, and Gloucester reliving his youth with Harry in tow, there was none but us Woodvilles in the solar now. Perhaps eager to change the subject, John said so that my sister could hear, "Well, we've news of George. The wedding that he's not supposed to be making is proceeding along apace."

"Don't speak of that in front of Edward, John. It's one of the few subjects that turns him ill-tempered."

The Earl of Warwick had long wanted to marry his daughters to George and Richard (Harry having been taken), and George, now nineteen, had been eager to oblige with seventeen-year-old Isabel. The king, however, had forbidden the match, partly out of irritation at the earl's high-handedness in demanding it, partly because he wanted to give George to a foreign bride. Undeterred, the earl and George had pressed on with their plans (Isabel's point of view in all of this was unknown, of course), and rumor had it that the Pope had granted his dispensation a few months back.

"I won't, Bessie, trust me. But you have to admire the sheer gall of the man. It's to take place in Calais, they say, and Warwick's been inviting all and sundry to the wedding. No secret marriage here! Er, sorry, Bessie."

"Apology taken," my sister said sweetly.

"Why doesn't the king just lock up George?" I asked. "And Warwick?"

"It's an awkward situation," said Anthony. "Warwick's very popular with the people. At his house in London, they say, anyone who comes by at mealtime can walk away with all of the meat he can carry, which always wins friends. Same at his other residences. Up north, he's a positive hero."

"He can well afford all that largesse," said John. "For all that he complains about our marriages, he did well in that area himself, through a couple of lucky deaths that made his countess a great heiress. Of course, it helps that he's taken to piracy on occasion." John was quiet for a moment, then pulled a dreadful face.

"John! What's wrong?"

"My invitation! I've lost my invitation to the wedding!"

"Really?" I asked, for John looked so mournful.

"Of course not, poppet, I'm only being foolish. Do you think we Woodvilles would be invited to the marriage? Not even my wife has been invited, thanks to her folly in marrying me. So I'm deeply affected—though not as bad as Anthony. Just look at him. He's in a brown study."

"I had something else on my mind, actually. This rising by this Robin Mend-All—"

"Robin of Redesdale in formal company," added John.

"This rising by whatever you call the man. Sometimes I wonder if there's not a stronger hand behind it. A strong hand like Warwick's."

"What gives you that idea?"

"Nothing I can put my finger on. But coming at the same time of this marriage, which is such a blatant act of defiance of the king, something in it seems suspicious."

"Have you told the king of your suspicions?" asked Bessie.

"No. They're too vague as of yet. To tell the king without good grounds to support them would be to have him think that we are trying to estrange him further from Warwick. If this marriage takes place, all will likely become clear soon enough."

The king tarried at Fotheringhay for several days, awaiting men and supplies. We in the queen's household were rather busy, for we were preparing to go to Norwich, where the king had been received warmly in early June. So pleased had he been by the city's welcome, which appeared all the more gracious in contrast with the northern troubles, that he had pledged that his queen would visit.

We set out on our journey the same day that the king's party set out on its own way northward. "Do be careful," Bessie warned the men, having embraced her brothers and then been kissed good-bye by the king in a manner that made me sigh romantically and Harry roll his eyes.

"Don't worry," said Edward. "We'll take care of the wretches—if there are any of the churls left by the time we get there." He grinned and locked my sister into another long embrace.

Harry parted from Richard with such reluctance that I, having parted affectionately but calmly from my brother Anthony, rolled my own eyes. Then came time for me to embrace John, and I found that I could hardly bear to let him go. "There could be a battle!" I wailed, holding onto him stubbornly.

"The king is right, sweetheart. Don't worry." John pried me loose and smiled at me. "The king has many men. They'll make short work of our cocky friend Robin." I giggled at the pun, on which John had laid a great deal of emphasis so I would not miss it. "That's a good girl! Frankly, I think you're in for a rougher time than we are."

"How?"

"You'll have to listen to every man of any importance in Norwich giving a long-winded speech of welcome, that's why."

"Oh," I said gloomily.

John laughed and mounted his horse. "Picture them in their drawers, sweetheart. That's what I always do."

⁓

Despite a few speeches, which fortunately were not long enough for me to have to utilize John's advice, the citizens of Norwich put on a wonderful spectacle—even Harry was impressed, I think, although he wouldn't admit to it. The angel Gabriel himself greeted us, along with all twelve apostles, two patriarchs, and sixteen virgins. There were pageants, and singing by boys with voices so sweet they might have been angels themselves. All would have gone wonderfully had it not been for the drenching rain that started with barely a warning cloud, forcing the citizens to hustle Bessie and the rest of us to our lodgings at the Friars Preachers while the city fathers and the performers tried frantically to salvage the materials upon which they had bestowed so much time and effort.

We had been in Norwich for a day or so, and the rain had yet to let up, when one of Edward's messengers, grim-faced, came to see the queen in her modest lodgings. He and she conferred in low tones while her ladies stitched and Harry tried to teach me to play chess.

Even I could see that my sister was badly shaken when at last the messenger left. She waved us all over to her—even Harry and me.

"The Duke of Clarence and Isabel Neville have married," she said. "But that was expected, and is not the worst of it. The day after the wedding, Clarence and the Earl of Warwick issued a proclamation. They claim that England has fallen into a dreadful state, and they blame it all upon our family and the king's other friends. They name Papa, Anthony, and John. Even Mama. And the Earl of Pembroke, the Earl of Devon, and Lord Audley. They plan to cross to England, and then take an armed force to Canterbury to seek a remedy and reformation."

"Remedy?" asked Anne. "What type of remedy?"

"They do not say. But they compare the king to Edward II, Richard II, and the last Henry."

All three of them, deposed. And even I knew of the fates of the first two. I shuddered, and Harry in one of his bursts of protectiveness put his arm around me. "Maybe Kate should lea—"

"No!"

"There's not much more to tell anyway," said Bessie. "The king has sent Papa and Anthony and John away for their own safety. I do not want to frighten any of you, least of all Kate, but the king wished us to be aware of the situation. He still seems quite confident that all will be well, and he wishes us to stay in Norwich until we next hear from him. He is raising more men, and the Earls of Pembroke and Devon will be dealing with Robin of Redesdale."

"Robin of Redesdale?" Anthony's wife, Elizabeth Scales, one of my sister's ladies, asked. "Why not with Warwick and his followers?"

Bessie's hands trembled, and I wondered if she entirely shared the king's confidence.

"Because Anthony was right about Robin of Redesdale," she replied. "His real name is John Conyers. And he is Warwick's man."

✑

In early August, another messenger rode to us at Norwich, this time from William Hastings, the king's closest friend. He knelt before Bessie and said, "I can do no better than to put this plainly to you, your grace, and then explain. The king is Warwick's captive."

My sister has been called many things, most of them untrue, but none have ever dared to call her a weakling. She took this news and remained standing upright. "Explain."

"Has your grace heard the news from Edgecote?" Bessie shook her head. "Several days ago, Pembroke's and Devon's Welshmen engaged with the men of that Robin of Redesdale. There had been some sort of quarrel between Pembroke and Devon, and Devon's forces were slow to arrive. By the time they did, it was too late. Our men were outnumbered, and they were slaughtered. Devon escaped, but Pembroke and his brother were taken and beheaded on Warwick's orders the next day."

The Earl of Pembroke, William Herbert, was father-in-law to my sister Mary. I gasped as Bessie said, "For supporting their lawful king?"

"It is madness, your grace. The king was unaware of all this. He was at Nottingham during the battle, and had planned to join forces with Pembroke and Devon. At Northampton, he heard the news. My lord and the Duke of

Gloucester stayed with him, but most of the rest panicked and deserted him, the whoresons." The man stopped to excuse himself, but my sister waved her hand. "The king headed toward London. At Olney, he was arrested by the Archbishop of York, acting on his brother Warwick's orders."

"And Edward allowed this creature in a bishop's miter to take him captive? I cannot believe this!"

"The king had no real choice; I was there. The archbishop had troops with him; the king had almost none. He has been taken to Warwick Castle. My lord and the Duke of Gloucester were released and sent on their way. They have gone to London."

"Is there news of my father? My brothers?"

"None, your grace, at least that I have heard."

"We must go to London ourselves," Bessie said. She looked at the handful of servants who could fit into our cramped quarters at the Friars Preachers. They were standing still, mouths agape. "Well? It's time. Start packing. Anne, Elizabeth, go with my men and make our excuses to the mayor. Harry, look after Kate."

"I don't need looking after," I protested. But I didn't argue when Harry led me from the room, and though I was eleven years of age, that night I was more than happy to sleep with Cecilia's arms wrapped tightly around me. What would happen to all of us?

∽

When we arrived in London, we found that the council had voted to make the queen a gift of wine. Just in case, Anne said sardonically, we wanted to drown our sorrows.

Bessie had thought the Tower the safest place for us to go. The old King Henry, of course, was lodged there also, and we all wondered if we—or at least Bessie and Edward—would end up prisoners there as well. For what did Warwick intend to do? It was all we talked of at the Tower. Did he plan to rule through Edward as a figurehead, as had been tried before with Henry? Did he plan to put the Duke of Clarence in his place? Had he conceived of his own claim to the throne? No one knew, and the Kingmaker, at Warwick Castle with England's other captive king, was not saying, at least not in public. He summoned a Parliament to meet in September—at York, in the heartland of his own supporters. There, we supposed, he would show his hand.

We were still worrying and wondering over Warwick's plans for the king when, one hot day in mid-August, I saw Cecilia and my sister Anne walking toward me in the garden where I was sitting. I knew when Anne drew me close to her and put her arms around me that something was very, very wrong. "Kate," she said, "I have news. Very bad news. It concerns Father and John. They have been captured."

I began to shiver. "Are they safe?" I whispered.

Anne held me tighter, so much that it hurt. "Sweetheart, they are where no man can harm them. They are in the arms of the Savior now."

Father and John had not wanted to leave the king; they wanted to stay and fight for him. But Edward insisted. So for several weeks, dressed nondescriptly on equally nondescript mounts, they had been roaming the countryside, attended only by one man each, picking up what news they could. Hearing through that means of the defeat of William Herbert, Earl of Pembroke, at Edgecote, they had made their way to the environs of Chepstow, where they had had the misfortune of being recognized by one of Warwick's men. They had resisted their captors, but it was futile. They were far outnumbered. From Chepstow, they'd been taken to Coventry, where Warwick and George had ridden to order their deaths and to see them die.

In Coventry, they pleaded for each other's lives. Father said that John was a mere youth still and had done nothing wrong: why should he die? And John said that his father, a man in his sixties, had served the crown since he was in his teens: why should he die when he had been nothing but loyal to his king? But Warwick and Clarence would have none of it. They allowed them no trial. This pair of murderers gave my brother and my father time to confess their sins and to write their wills, and in that they congratulated themselves they were being most generous.

John went first on that evil day of August 12, 1469. He bore himself bravely and said he had lived as Edward's loyal subject and was dying as the same. My father had to watch as John died, as the headsman bungled the first stroke and had to take another. Then it came his turn. He prayed as he died and was still praying when they took his head.

I did not learn these details until much later, when I was a woman grown and could bear to hear them. At the time I first heard the news, I did not care how or where the deed had been done. I only knew that the men I loved best in the world—Father, and above all others, John, who had never harmed a soul in his life—were gone for good.

∞

With Father and John dead, we waited to hear the worst of Anthony or even the king. Beheading, we were certain, awaited one; death in a remote castle by some mysterious means the other. It was only a matter of time. Our fears were increased when news came that the Earl of Devon had been captured and killed.

All of England seemed to take the king's capture and these killings as a signal to go simultaneously mad. John Mowbray, Duke of Norfolk, began besieging the Paston family's castle of Caister. The Berkeleys and the Talbots were feuding; so were the Stanleys and the Harringtons. Some Londoners rioted in favor of the king, some in favor of Warwick, some simply for the sheer fun of rioting. There was even a rising in Hexhamshire by Sir Humphrey Neville, Warwick's cousin, in favor of the House of Lancaster.

Warwick tried, none too successfully, to control this violence, but he found the leisure to attend to other matters as well. In doing so, he helped distract my family from its misery somewhat, though this was surely not his intention.

He branded my mother a witch.

The accusation did not come directly from Warwick himself. As with

Robin of Redesdale, he acted through a proxy—in this case, one Thomas Wake, whose son had died fighting for Warwick at Edgecote. He produced a leaden image, broken in two, of a man in arms which Wake claimed was supposed to represent the Earl of Warwick. My mother was also reported to have produced leaden images of the king and queen, supposedly at the time the two were courting, and joined them together in an indecent manner.

If the earl and Wake thought that my mother, newly widowed and mourning the loss of John as well, would be too unstrung by grief to fight her accusers, they reckoned wrong. Mama sent an impassioned note to the mayor and aldermen of London, proclaiming her innocence and reminding them, not at all subtly, of the good services she and Grandmother Buckingham had performed for the city years before by interceding on its citizens' behalf with Margaret of Anjou, whose troops it was feared would wreak destruction upon them and their goods. The city officials agreed to assist her in putting her case before the king's council—which, of course, was essentially Warwick's council at the time—and Mama, who had been placed under guard by Thomas Wake, was allowed to travel to join us at the Tower.

I think some effort was made to keep the news of this latest family disaster from me, but it must have failed miserably. Already crying myself to sleep each night with thoughts of John and Papa, I now had the worry that Mama—as pious a lady as any I knew, though not ostentatious about it—would be found guilty of witchcraft. Would she be burned alive? Or would she merely be forced to walk barefoot through the streets and then be imprisoned for life, like Eleanor Cobham, the wife of Humphrey, Duke of Gloucester, had been, less than thirty years before? Would my remaining brothers be accused with her, and sentenced to the horrid death of a traitor? Would my sisters suffer? Would I?

Harry was no comfort to me during this time. It was not for lack of effort on his part—he tried to distract me in sundry ways, and he even shunned Richard's company on one or two occasions for my own—but his very status as my husband only added to my misery. I knew that my marriage to Harry had angered Warwick, and it was perfectly logical to my eleven-year-old self to deduce that had Harry not married me, Papa and John might still be alive and Mama would not be branded as a witch.

I was still in this unenviable state of mind when our fortunes shifted yet again. Charles, Duke of Burgundy, had used his considerable influence with the merchant classes in London to calm the situation there, but he was no friend to Warwick, who in the meantime was attempting to cope with Humphrey Neville's rising but was finding that no one would answer his call for troops, a kingmaker being a very different thing from a king. Only with Edward at liberty would men respond, so in September—all thoughts of holding a Parliament being put aside—the king was allowed to travel in due state to York and then to Pontefract, after which Humphrey Neville was duly caught and executed. Having let Edward out of his cage, the Earl of Warwick could hardly now put him in again, especially since the episode had reminded everyone that Edward could be quite effective when the occasion demanded it. The upshot was that in October, the king rode triumphantly back to London, surrounded by the cream of the nobility of England and the mayor and aldermen.

It was not a sight I saw, for with the kingdom having returned somewhat to normal, I had been sent from the Tower to pretty Greenwich. I had been listless and pale since the news came of my father's and my brother's deaths, and it was thought that there I might recover my spirits. With the king back in London, my sister and her daughters returned to the comfort of Greenwich as well, and soon the king had left Westminster to join us there for a family evening, as had been his wont. Only one thing had changed in Bessie's chamber since then: the window seat on which John had liked to perch was empty. No one dared sit in it.

We were all gathered there—all of us Woodvilles, that is, for John's widow, said to be feeling her age these days, was at one of her manors outside the city—when Edward came in. A few months ago, I would have run to him and embraced him, for I was a demonstrative child and Edward not one to stand on ceremony with his family. Now I curtseyed and returned to my seat, where I was working on the same piece of embroidery that had occupied my hands for weeks now. It was my only pastime then. It was deadly dull, a biblical scene instead of the bright flowers and cheerful birds I preferred, but it was complex enough to occupy my thoughts so I did not have to think of the picture that haunted my mind at all other times: my father and handsome, lively John, headless and lying tangled together in a heap of dirt near Coventry.

"Kate."

I blinked and realized that the king had been speaking to me. "Yes, your grace?"

"I asked how you had been occupying your time lately. It must have been dull for you at the Tower; I know you are fond of Greenwich."

"I have had this, your grace," I said, and looked at my embroidery. So did the king. All of a sudden, I saw what he saw: a hideous mishmash of stitches that would have shamed even my little niece the Lady Elizabeth had she produced them. "It's horrid," I said, clapping my hand to my mouth. "Isn't it?" Then my tears began falling fast.

The king hauled me to my feet. "Come. We need to have a talk."

⁂

"Bessie is very worried about you, Kate. She says you hardly eat or speak and want to do nothing but sit and attend to that needlework of yours."

"I do not mean to worry her. I am sorry, your grace."

"Stop calling me 'your grace.' We are brother and sister, are we not?" His voice was very gentle. "I know you are grieving for your father and for your brother. So am I, for they were good men. And I can understand your grief, for I have grieved for my father and my brother too, you know. My father was all I wanted to be, and my brother Edmund was my closest companion."

"Yes."

"I suspect it was easier for me than it is for you, for after they died I had no time to mourn; I had to carry on their fight."

"But no one is carrying on Papa and John's fight. They have been forgotten."

"Kate?"

I stared at the floor and felt my tears start to fall again. "They say the Earl of Warwick and the Duke of Clarence will be coming back to court soon, and that you shall forgive them."

"That is true. And what would you have me do to them?"

"Kill them, as they killed Papa and John."

I waited for lightning, or Edward, to strike me dead.

The king shook his head. "Do you know how it chills my blood to see a pretty child like yourself standing there saying that? It is not that easy. For one thing, George is my brother."

"But the Earl of Warwick isn't."

"No. But it is not as simple as that. The truth is, Kate, I couldn't kill him either, even if I could forget his years of service to me, which I cannot. It is not a good time for me or anyone else on my behalf to take vengeance, even though it might please some. I myself have little love for them; did you know that they have even spread rumors that I am a bastard? The offspring of my mother and some archer she fancied?" Edward stared off into space, his face hardening. "For George to slander his own mother so, and Warwick his aunt! But for now, I must work with them."

"But you are king!"

"A king, not God. We mortals must sometimes keep company we would prefer not to, I am afraid."

"But it is so hard to think of my father and John dead, and no one paying the price."

"My brother and my father are dead, too. Some paid the price for that, and yet it is still hard to think of their deaths. It will always be hard, Kate. I won't tell you otherwise. But your grief will ease with time; that I can tell you for certain. It will help, I think, if you will remember your father and John at their best and happiest, and keep that picture in your mind when you think of them." He plucked the embroidery out of my hand and threw it into the fire. "It will ease faster yet if you put aside things like this, which I know well give you no pleasure, and do things that bring you cheer. Your mourning should not keep you from going out riding, for instance. Has Harry been riding with you? I know you used to like going with him."

"He has been." I drew a breath. "But that is another thing. I cannot be married to Harry anymore. I want to take the veil."

For a moment, I thought Edward was going to laugh. Then he saw my face and drew me closer to him. "Sweetheart. Are you serious?"

"Yes. I want to have my marriage annulled and no longer be Duchess of Buckingham. I know it is one of the things that made the Earl of Warwick so angry, that I married Harry when one of his daughters could have. If I hadn't married him and become a duchess, perhaps Father and John would not have—" I could not bear to finish the sentence.

"Christ," Edward muttered. "Now I begin to understand this better yet." He released me and stepped back. "Kate, I will not lie to you. Your marriage did anger Warwick. But it was one thing, only one thing of many, and much of the problem is simply that Warwick could not control me forever as he would have liked to. You must not believe for a moment that you are responsible for his anger or that you could have prevented your father's and your brother's deaths. You will never be happy again if you let yourself think that."

"But if I take the veil, perhaps Mama will not be found to be a witch. She can say she gave me to God to please Him and that she is a good daughter of the Church."

"Sweetheart, the matter is before my council now, and there is not a man there who will find your mother a witch. That I can promise you. She has friends there and friends in London as well. She does not have to sacrifice you to the Church to prove that she is a pious woman. I am aware that she is."

"Then I can't take the veil?"

"I have seen you squirming in chapel many times, Kate. You would make a miserable nun indeed. No. You will make a much better duchess. If you truly wish to please God, you must moderate your grief. God likes moderation in all things, the priests tell me." He grinned. "Not that I always listen."

I could not help but smile.

"There's an improvement! Now there are three things I wish you to promise me before I send you back to Bessie's chamber. The first is that you will embroider me a handsome bluebird cushion for my chamber, to match the redbird you did a while back. A nice plump one that looks as if it is about to burst into song."

"I will!"

"I shall look forward to it. The second is that when Warwick and George return to court, you will face them proudly with your head held high. You have as much right as they to be here, and you are a far more pleasant sight at court than they are."

"I will do it."

"That's my Kate! The third is that when you go back to Bessie's chamber, you will sit in John's seat."

"John's seat!"

"You were his favorite sister. I can think of no one else he would like to see sitting in his favorite seat. I shall lead you to it."

"All right," I said.

Together the king and I went back to Bessie's chamber. With a slight prod from Edward, I took a breath and headed as nonchalantly as I could to the empty window seat and sat down. It was full of John's presence, and I was amazed at how comforted I felt by being there. When I dozed off a while later—for I had not been sleeping well lately, and the soothing music the king's musicians played soon had me nodding—it was if I were leaning against John's strong shoulder again.

∽

I did not stop mourning for Father and John after my talk with the king, but I took the king's advice and thought hard of the last time I had seen each of them and their last good-byes to me: my father's gently affectionate one, John's jovial one. It comforted me and made me more at peace.

It helped, too, that there was a bit of brightness in our lives that I had scarcely acknowledged at the time: Anthony was safe and sound. He had been imprisoned at Norwich, it turned out, but fortunately Warwick, finding by that time that his popularity was not as great as he had expected, had hesitated to issue the order to kill him. By October Anthony was back at court, with one difference: he was now the second Earl Rivers, and the king made a point of calling him by his new title. Perhaps because John's easier-going nature no longer stood between me and Anthony, I grew a little closer to him than I had been, and was less intimidated by him. Perhaps Anthony too, grieving like the rest of us, became a little less austere and a little more approachable.

By December, Warwick and Clarence were back at court as well, along with their wives and Warwick's younger daughter, Anne. Warwick had come into my sister's immediate presence only once, looking deadly uncomfortable, and had made his escape after a few inconsequential remarks. It was a different matter with the earl's wife and daughters. As these ladies were blameless of Father's and John's deaths, they could be safely sent to the queen, and it fell to them and to us Woodville women to exchange small talk and pleasantries as if nothing the least bit untoward had happened over the past few months. John, no doubt, would have found our predicament an amusing one.

I could not dislike any of the Warwick women, though I certainly tried at first. The Countess of Warwick and her daughters were each amiable and pretty, though in a delicate way that made me remember what Grandmother Buckingham had said about the girls not promising to be good breeders. None were the harridans I might have expected to belong to the Earl of Warwick or to George. Isabel, who was eighteen, tried to boss her thirteen-year-old sister, Anne, about in a manner that was all too familiar to me from my own childhood with six older sisters, and Anne resisted in a manner that was quite familiar to me as well.

The Countess of Warwick was of a rather anxious disposition, I thought, and she had a way of hovering over the Duchess of Clarence in a manner that seemed peculiar for a girl of Isabel's age. In a day or so, when the countess proudly displayed a baby blanket she was embroidering, the reason became clear: Isabel was with child. This fact, once learned, turned out to be a godsend to our awkward little company, for Bessie, as the mother of five, and the countess, as a mother of two and as an attendant at many a childbed, were more than happy to trade stories of childbirth and to heap Isabel with advice about how to conduct herself in the months to come and how to choose a good wet nurse for the baby. Isabel rolled her eyes when the older women were not looking, and Anne looked alternately bored and jealous that she was not the center of attention. I could not help liking them for that.

Only once did a chink in our female good fellowship appear, when in a rare departure from baby conversation, young Anne, undoubtedly with the best of intentions, inquired about Mama's health. I saw Bessie start to reply blandly, then give way to temptation. "She is doing well," my sister said sweetly. "For an accused witch, that is."

The countess blushed as I snickered into my embroidery, and Bessie then had the kindness to switch the conversation to which draper the ladies patronized.

Congenial as our relations were with the Warwick women, I was still grateful not to have to spend the Christmas festivities with them. My excuse came via an invitation for Harry and I to spend that time with Harry's uncle Henry Stafford and his very rich wife, Margaret Beaufort, Countess of Richmond. They had a home at Woking, and we were to stay in Guildford.

Harry always liked to talk about his Beaufort relations, and from him I had learned that the Countess of Richmond was his mother's first cousin, both ladies sharing the name of Margaret. The countess had been married first to Edmund Tudor, Earl of Richmond, a half brother of the sixth King Henry, whose widowed mother, Catherine of Valois, had made a scandalous secret marriage to a nobody named Owen Tudor. (Not even my own parents' marriage could match it.) Margaret Beaufort had borne Edmund a posthumous child, one Henry Tudor. Not long afterward, she had married Harry's uncle. Harry had seen the couple a few times, but they were strangers to me.

"Do you think they'll like me?" I asked Harry as we traveled to Guildford in high state. It was our first real journey together as duke and duchess, outside of travels with the king or queen, and Edward and Bessie had sent us off in grand style, surrounded by attendants from the household Harry now had at court.

"Why wouldn't they?"

I shrugged. The last few months had sapped my self-confidence a little. "I don't know."

Harry said kindly, "I don't see why they wouldn't. But ask the countess about her son, Henry Tudor, and you'll have made a friend for life. He's a ward like me. Henry was in William Herbert's care"—Harry hurried past these words as I winced, remembering this man who had died shortly before my father and my brother—"but Lord Ferrers, who's married to Herbert's sister, took him in after Herbert was killed."

"Murdered!"

"Murdered, then. The countess would like to see Henry restored to his lands and title, but there's not much chance of that, I think, with Jasper Tudor as his uncle."

"Jasper Tudor?"

"Lancastrian. He's King Henry's youngest half brother, and assisted the countess and her baby after the Earl of Richmond died. He raided Wales last year, but Lord Herbert defeated him. Jasper escaped to France. He's there now, no doubt up to something. The Countess of Richmond is very fond of him, because of his help with her and Henry Tudor, and King Edward knows it."

"So where's Henry Tudor now?" I asked, somewhat bored with the subject of Jasper Tudor.

"Weobley, with Lord Ferrers. The countess is trying to work out the details of his wardship now that Lord Ferrers is gone."

"Does she have other children?"

"No. She had Henry when she was only thirteen. They say the birth was a hard one and that she can't bear children now. So Henry is very important to her."

It was soon after this that I met the Countess of Richmond. She was a young woman, only twenty-six, but she bore herself with the authority of a woman twice that age, despite her very small stature—indeed, she was scarcely taller than my eleven-year-old self. Even in the high-waisted fashion of that day, it was apparent that her figure was that of a girl in her early teens. Having seen statuesque Bessie bear three babes, and all of the effort involved, I wondered how on earth tiny Margaret had survived her single ordeal. It was no wonder she was protective of her son.

Despite her undeveloped figure, Margaret was a handsome lady with sharp, expressive eyes, which she fixed upon me to intimidating effect. "Your wife is a pretty child, Harry," she announced. She made "pretty" sound as if it were my only asset. "Are they teaching you to look over household accounts, I hope? You will need to be useful as well as decorative when Harry comes into his estates."

"Of course, my lady," I said. I decided not to mention that the accounts were not my strong point. (Indeed, my eldest son will tell you they are still not.)

"I think I will never come into them," said Harry, more, I think, to rescue me from Margaret Beaufort's scrutiny than to register an actual complaint.

It worked, for Margaret Beaufort turned her eyes on Harry. "Don't be a fool, Harry. A fourteen-year-old lad out there in Wales with all of that land? Your tenants would take advantage of you, or eat you alive. I'm not sure which. Maybe both. You're best off waiting for your majority. Frankly, I think most young men would do well to wait until after their majority, and let the womenfolk manage for them. Now, tell me about this mummery between the Earl of Warwick and the king."

"You should come to court to see for yourself, Aunt," said Harry with a rare mischievousness in his tone. I realized with a pang of jealousy that brusque as Margaret Beaufort might be, she and Harry were evidently quite fond of each other.

The countess snorted. "I've had quite enough of the Yorks, thank you very much. When Warwick had control over the king I went to the Duke of Clarence's house in London to discuss the Earl of Richmond's situation."

"Her son Henry," Harry hissed, seeing my puzzled expression.

"My hearing is quite sharp, Harry. You have another thirty years or so before you can expect it to be otherwise. Yes, my son Henry, the Earl of Richmond, as I call him, and as he should be called. Well, as I was saying, I went to Clarence's place. He wasn't there, of course, he was in the North. Hiding under Warwick's wing, the young fool. But his man of business was there, which at first pleased me just as well, because I'd as soon deal with a man of mature years as with that puppy Clarence. But he gave me no assistance either." Her voice dropped to an approximation of a masculine one. "'All must wait until my lord the Duke of Clarence and the Earl of Warwick return to the city, my lady.' Bah! He could have at least been honest and said just the Earl of Warwick. Clarence hasn't a mind of his own; everyone knows that." She patted Harry on the cheek with affection. "You would have made him a better son-in-law."

I was beginning to wonder if I should take a walk somewhere, such an intruder did I feel. Then a genial-looking man entered the room unannounced and pecked Margaret on the cheek. I could only assume that such a liberty meant that he was Henry Stafford, her husband, and sure enough, I was right. He embraced his nephew Harry and then brought my hand to his lips. "The Duchess of Buckingham," he said gallantly. "And a lovely one she is."

I curtseyed. The Countess of Richmond looked at her husband fondly, then shook her head. "The worst thing about my jaunt to Clarence's is that it angered the king once he was released and found out about it. I don't know why—would not any mother do the same? But it did anger him. And now my husband's younger brother is to be Earl of Wiltshire, and my husband is to have nothing."

"You are a Beaufort, my dear," said Henry. "That's cause for suspicion enough in King Edward's mind. Hardly your fault. Don't fret about John's earldom. He deserves it well."

Margaret sighed. She looked at Harry again. "So, Harry, you never told us. How are matters between Warwick and the king?"

"They are friendly and were planning to celebrate Christmas in great fashion together. But—"

"But what? You notice things, Harry, always have, because you keep quiet while others chatter. But what?"

"I believe that they hate each other, and would destroy each other if they could."

"And I believe, boy, that you are probably right." Margaret Beaufort rose. "But come now! It is time we began the Christmas festivities ourselves."

viii

Harry: October 1470 to April 1471

THE RAPPROCHEMENT BETWEEN THE KING AND THE EARL OF WARWICK was doomed to failure, as even I had predicted.

All seemed to go smoothly at first, though. The king's council, Warwick among them, cleared the Duchess of Bedford of the charges against her, much to my wife's relief. (I for one had never believed there was anything in them; the only thing the poor duchess was guilty of was speaking English with a much too pronounced French accent and of breeding an eldest daughter who was too beautiful for anyone's good.) The king's oldest daughter, the Lady Elizabeth, was promised in marriage to Warwick's small nephew George, who stood to inherit the Warwick estates entailed in the male line. Little George was made the Duke of Bedford, and his father, John Neville, Earl of Northumberland, was made Marquess of Montagu, though he lost his Northumberland earldom when it was restored to the Percy family. That pleased at least some of the northerners, who had risen previously on the Percy heir's behalf, though there were whisperings that John Neville himself did not think much of the lands he was given in compensation for losing those attached to the Northumberland earldom. But John, who had never joined his brother the Kingmaker in intriguing against King Edward, made no complaint. The king himself, while devoting most of his time to putting his government back in order, did not neglect his marital duties or (so I heard) his extramarital affairs. England, in short, as the new year of 1470 came and went, appeared to be on the mend. I felt rather foolish for having told my elders at Guildford otherwise.

Then this tranquil state of affairs vanished almost overnight. An incident in Lincolnshire, seemingly a private quarrel involving one of the king's servants, turned into another uprising—led from behind the scenes, it turned out, by Warwick and Clarence. This time, there was no doubt of their intentions. They meant to depose Edward and place Clarence on the throne.

On this occasion, though, Edward, marching north, was far too wary to be trapped. Instead, it was Warwick and Clarence who ended up fleeing the country in April, their wives and Warwick's younger daughter, Anne, in tow. Aboard ship, the young Duchess of Clarence gave birth to a stillborn child, who had to be buried at sea. Nothing daunted by this, Warwick alternated between playing pirate in the Channel and negotiating with the French king, Louis, for his assistance. Soon, shocking news arrived in England: Warwick had formed an alliance with none other than Margaret of Anjou herself. Gone was the talk of putting Clarence on the throne. Instead, Henry VI would be restored and Edward, his son, would regain his position as rightful heir. He was also to get a bride: Anne, Warwick's daughter.

Soon there were new risings, coordinated from abroad by Warwick, who arrived back in England himself in September, accompanied by a sulky Clarence and a radiant Earl of Oxford and Jasper Tudor, delighted at this Lancastrian turn of affairs. Edward might have dealt with this yet, but then the unthinkable happened: John Neville, who'd been utterly loyal to King Edward, suddenly turned his coat and joined his brother the Kingmaker. Facing an attack he knew he could not win, Edward saw it was now his turn to jump on a ship. Together with the Duke of Gloucester, Anthony Woodville, Lord Hastings, and a handful of other stalwarts, Edward fled to Holland. Queen Elizabeth—heavily pregnant—took herself and her daughters to sanctuary at Westminster.

It was October 1470. Henry VI was back on the throne as King of England—and if you understood the twists and turns of fate that had returned him there, I probably have confused you.

King Henry's return to the throne came just weeks after my fifteenth birthday, and flush with this new manhood, I had outright refused to accompany Queen Elizabeth into sanctuary. The thought of being cooped up there was grim enough, but being shut in with three little girls, and probably a fourth girl on the way, was downright unbearable.

Rather to my disappointment, as I had wished for more of an argument, the queen acquiesced readily—not, I realize now, out of respect for my fifteen years but because she had no more desire to share close quarters with a bored boy of my age than I had to share lodgings with the queen's girls. Because my grandmother was staying at her house in Bread Street, as was her custom this time of year, it was arranged that I would go to her.

Kate insisted on going with me—a surprise, for I thought for sure she would want to stay and help with the baby, whose arrival was expected in a matter of weeks. But she said that it was her marital duty to accompany me. Perhaps Kate, loyal sister though she was, had also thought life in Bread Street preferable to life in sanctuary.

We had just settled into Bread Street in early October when Warwick made his grand entrance into London. I could not resist seeing this sight, and I took Kate along.

That was a mistake. I had been as glad as anyone else when Kate, who at first had slunk around like a little wraith following the deaths of her father and her brother, had begun to return to her former talkative self, but now I wished she had had a temporary relapse. No sooner did the first sign of Warwick's army appear than Kate decided it was time to speak her mind. "Wicked traitor!" she muttered. Then, evidently finding that she had made herself insufficiently clear, she raised her voice. "How can he live with himself, knowing that he betrayed his king? The real king. King Edward!" she added helpfully, in case anyone around us was in any doubt as to her loyalties.

We were not inconspicuous to begin with. As Duke and Duchess of Buckingham, we were probably the best-dressed couple within the confines of the city, even wearing everyday attire as we were. And Kate, who

was about twelve and a half, was no longer the skinny, sharp-faced little girl
I'd married. Like all of the Woodville sisters, she had developed early and
amply, and I realized that she had become quite pretty. So, too, did most
of the men standing around us, judging from the admiring glances they shot
her, even as she made remark after remark that would probably have got
anyone other than a lovely young girl thrown into Newgate.

"Kate, I told you. It's a complicated business."

Kate ignored the low tone I'd spoken in as a hint. "And poor King
Henry! I heard that when he was taken out of the Tower, he was in a
frightful state—all dirty and ill-clothed, without much idea of what was
happening. It is cruel to put him back on the throne. Cruel! Warwick just
seeks to use him."

"Kate, you must be more dis—"

"He should be ashamed of himself! All last year, when King Edward had
forgiven him—which he never should have—to be thinking of turning
traitor all along. What a blackguard! And look—there he is!"

Sure enough, there was the blackguard himself, the Earl of Warwick,
magnificent on his black charger. He acknowledged the cheers of the crowd,
managing neatly to look triumphant and benevolent at the same time (not
a mean feat—I have since tried it). Beside him rode the Duke of Clarence,
nodding condescendingly at the bystanders as if it had not yet occurred to
him that he was not a bit closer to the throne than he had ever been.

The shouting had even drowned out Kate's Yorkist rants. She tensed as
Warwick drew nearer, and for a horrid instant I feared that she would spit
on him. Instead, in that faintly French-accented voice of hers that carried
so nicely, she shouted piercingly, "Long live the King! King—"

As her husband, I could slap Kate, or I could kiss her. Having the
instincts of a gentleman, I kissed her, and kept kissing her until Warwick
rode serenely by, utterly unaware of this treason within feet of him. I probably kissed her longer than was strictly necessary. At last I pulled back, and I
saw with gratitude that I had reduced my wife to utter silence. "Let's go,"
I said as Kate stared at me.

"That was our first kiss since our wedding," Kate said finally as we left the throngs behind. "It was *hard*."

"Watch what you say in public, or I may have to give you another such," I said, realizing as I did that I had not put this as well as I could have.

⚉

The next few months were, I must admit, some of the best of my life. The queen had kept a close eye on me as her ward, and much to my chagrin, the king when I arrived in his household had turned out to be no better. Like many licentious men, he was a strict guardian. Under his regime, I'd had very little chance to wander about London unaccompanied. Now, as my elders were preoccupied with other matters besides my upbringing, I was virtually my own man. For the first time I enjoyed idling in taverns and gambling with the ample allowance my grandmother allowed me. I was not naturally dissolute, so my adventures were of the mildest sort, but it was nonetheless a heady time for me.

My pocket money was sufficient to take me into the best brothels of Southwark had I chosen to go there, but something made me turn back on the one or two occasions my feet (urged forth by another appendage) took me in that direction. Richard had promised to take me there when I was sixteen, and I felt that if I went now instead of waiting, I would almost be disloyal to him, living in Holland as he and his brother Edward were. In any case, I felt like a bit of a fool going on my own. What would I say? Would it be painfully obvious that I had never been with a woman before? What if I made an utter ass of myself? So I resisted temptation and waited for Richard's return, being confident that he would somehow make his way back to England. I missed him a great deal; it was the one blot on the sunshine of my days then.

In the meantime, in late October I was invited—if my aunt Margaret Beaufort's peremptory message could be deemed an invitation—to sup with her and my uncle. There, my aunt wrote, I would at last have the chance of beholding my cousin Henry Tudor, whom his faithful uncle Jasper had recently brought from Wales.

Kate frowned when I told her of the news. "Am I invited?"

"Of course. You are my wife."

"I don't know if I want to come. Your aunt didn't seem to care for me, and there will be so many Lancastrians there."

"You may have to start getting used to that," I said, not unkindly.

My aunt, however, was in such a transport of good spirits when we went for supper the next day that she even parted with a smile and an embrace for Kate. "Well! Things have changed since we last met, have they not, Harry?"

"Indeed they have."

"My son and Jasper will be here presently. Do you know, yesterday my son had an audience with the king? It went very well, I thought. Of course, King Henry is always kind; it is Warwick and Clarence with whom we must deal, though. I would like to see my Henry get his title and lands restored to him, but Clarence may be difficult. We shall see. Ah! There you are!"

My uncle Henry came in, along with a boy a little younger than myself—he was a couple of months shy of his fourteenth birthday—and a man of about forty. Kate's eyes widened at the pair, who could be no other than Henry and Jasper Tudor, but she greeted them politely enough. Then Jasper Tudor, whose father, after all, had managed to get himself into the bed of a queen, said something about English roses that made my wife blush rather prettily. For a man who'd spent most of his time on the run, he seemed quite at home.

While Jasper made inroads with Kate, I greeted my cousin. "What was the king like?"

"Not what I expected, but I wasn't sure what to expect. I was a little worried that he might be—well, you know."

"Mad," I agreed.

"He wasn't, not as you would think a madman would be, anyway. He didn't talk gibberish or anything. He knew Uncle Jasper perfectly well, and he knew who everyone around him was. But sometimes he would just stare off into space for a moment or so before he would remember that we were still there and continue with the conversation. And he said something very strange to me. Mother liked it, but I didn't know what to make of it."

"What?"

"He said I would be king someday."

"You? With his own son alive and well and getting ready to marry Warwick's daughter?"

Henry shrugged. "It sounded strange to me too, but that's what he said. He just said it in ordinary conversation, too, not as if he were a soothsayer or something." He glanced at his mother, who was talking to my uncle. Jasper Tudor was still charming Kate, it appeared. "Mother said we ought to keep it quiet, though. It's not the sort of thing one would want to get back to Queen Margaret, after all."

"I can see that," I said drily.

"I'd be quite content just to get my father's lands and my title back, and to see my uncle get his own lands restored to him. Mother?"

My aunt had suddenly started weeping. Uncle Henry instantly broke off the conversation he'd been having with Jasper Tudor and Kate. "Sweetheart? What is wrong?"

"Nothing." Margaret brushed at her eyes. "I am ashamed of myself. It is just so moving to me. To have so many whom I love in one place. It is what I have wanted for so long—" She began to sniffle again.

Henry Tudor looked mortified, as any lad of our age might, but Jasper Tudor stood and raised his cup, all of us having been sipping wine. "Of course, it is a cause for celebration! Let us raise our cups to our three Henrys—and to their lovely mothers and wives as well."

⁘

I never saw Henry or Jasper Tudor after that day. Soon they traveled with my aunt Margaret to her estate at Woking, then to her other lands, and by late November Jasper and Henry had returned to Wales, where

Jasper had business. I regretted this, for I had got on quite well with Henry Tudor.

Jasper Tudor was a different matter. Kate on the way home asked me what I had thought of him, and at fifteen I could only tell the truth, that I thought he had been far too flirtatious with her and that she had not sufficiently discouraged him.

Needless to say, Kate did not accept my remark in the constructive way it had been offered. "Flirt? He never flirted with me!"

"Then you're too young to know a flirtation when you see it."

"I know perfectly well what one looks like, Harry Stafford! He was merely kind to me—more so than your aunt, who always looks at me as if I were a fly in the room that she wishes she could—could—"

"Swat. She does nothing of the sort. She is very civil to you."

"I was going to say 'swat' if you had given me a blessed moment, Harry! And if you call saying that I am merely decorative civil, then I suppose she was civil. Why, she never asked about Bessie, and she will be brought to childbed any day, we expect."

"Did Jasper Tudor ask about her?"

"No, but he is a man. One doesn't expect men to ask about such things."

"So what did he ask you about, if he wasn't flirting and he wasn't discussing your sister's lying-in?"

"He asked if all of the Woodville girls were as pretty as I was," Kate allowed after a moment or two.

"No, no flirting there." I looked at the men escorting us, who were all making a show of not hearing this quarrel. Plainly, each and every one of them was enjoying it immensely.

"He didn't mean it like that. And he said other things as well. Like—like—"

"Like what?" I snapped, before I noticed that Kate's eyes were filling with tears. There is enough bad that can be said about me now, but it can never be said that I was so base as to enjoy seeing my wife weep. "For God's sake, don't cry. What?"

"He told me that he thought Warwick had behaved badly in killing John and Papa. He did say that! Do you call that flirting?"

"No, no, Kate. Here."

Kate blew her nose on my handkerchief almost triumphantly.

Just a few days later, on November 2—a date that meant nothing to me then but that has acquired a certain significance thirteen years later—Queen Elizabeth, meagerly attended in sanctuary, gave birth to a healthy baby boy, whom she defiantly named Edward.

Kate was as smug as if she'd delivered the baby herself. "I said it would be a boy," she announced. (I remembered her saying no such thing.) "Now the king is sure to come back and claim his throne!"

"You may well be right, child," my grandmother said.

Kate had to do most of her gloating that day by herself, however, for Grandmother and I were on our way to see the king—King Henry, that is. Grandmother, after much deliberating, had decided to pay her respects— she was, after all, the godmother of his son. "And as your grandfather died in his cause, Harry, I know he would like to meet you, too." It was decided that Kate, as Queen Elizabeth's sister, was best off staying at home, a decision to which Kate gladly acquiesced. I suspected that she would bat her blue eyes at some of the household men and coax them into taking her to see Elizabeth and the new baby in sanctuary, King Henry having chiv-alrously insisted that the deposed queen—if that be the proper phrase—be allowed to receive visitors.

As Grandmother and I rode by water to Westminster, we could hear a few church bells bravely pealing, celebrating the birth of little Edward. "What do you think, Grandmother? Do you think Edward will come back?"

"I don't doubt it for a moment." Grandmother sighed. "And then all this will begin all over again. My, but I'm feeling too old these days to live through much more of these men trying to push each other off the throne."

"What do you wish for, Grandmother?"

She shrugged. "I'm not partial to Warwick, nephew of mine that he is. He's not the king, and he forgets that. Young Edward—King Henry's Edward—is a proud, high-tempered lad, they say, and when he comes back to England, he's not going to be happy to be led around on a chain by Warwick as his poor father is. And I suspect that when Warwick's old enemies—your uncle Somerset and the rest—return, there will be more trouble. Warwick's made himself some strange bedfellows, and I for one don't know if one bed can hold them all." Grandmother gazed over the Thames. "If King Edward comes back, your uncle John will fight for him, I know. So will my husband. Your uncle Henry—I don't know. His wife Margaret is a strong-minded woman, and I know she would like to see him fight for King Henry, but your uncle can only be pushed so far before he balks. I suspect he will fight with the rest of the Staffords, and their loyalties are with Edward now."

"I am looking forward to seeing my Beaufort uncles," I confessed.

"I know you are, lad. And chances are they will soon be in arms against your Stafford uncles. You realize that, don't you?"

I nodded, and my grandmother gently ran her hand through my hair, reminding me of the day Grandfather had died. "Either way, you will suffer a loss, I fear. I do not envy you, Harry."

King Henry's chambers, where we soon arrived, were nothing like King Edward's. Whereas Edward's chambers had been bustling, with people scurrying back and forth and dogs roaming in and out, Henry's were quiet, with a clerk writing in a corner and a few guards standing silently by. Edward had sat smack in the middle of the room; Henry's great chair was in a corner. Henry, indeed, seemed to be an afterthought in the rooms, for they had been decorated to house Queen Elizabeth during her lying-in and still very much reflected the queen's quite feminine preference in colors and textures. I could even see her emblem, a gillyflower, here and there.

The king was a stooped man, with the prematurely old look of someone who had suffered greatly in his mind, yet he had a very pleasant voice. He even managed an air of gallantry when my grandmother was announced, though I doubt he would have known her had she not been named upon her entrance. "Ah, the Duchess of Buckingham. It seems like only yesterday that my lady and I were in company with you and your dear lord. A brave, loyal man. How I miss him."

"I too, your grace."

"And this is your grandson, the present duke. A fine-looking lad. Grow up to be like your grandfather, my boy."

"I will endeavor to do so, your grace."

"Good. But where is Margaret? She will never come, I fear. She is not ill?" He looked sharply around him, at no one in particular. "They would tell me if she were ill, would they not?"

"Of course they would, your grace," said Grandmother softly. "She is quite well, but I believe she has details to attend to before she leaves that have taken much of her time. No woman can move as quickly as a man likes, you know."

The king suddenly smiled, for a moment appearing entirely rational. "'Tis true. And we have a boy. I should like to see my boy again." He looked at me, and for a horrible moment I feared he had mistaken me for Edward of Lancaster. Instead, he said genially, "Perhaps you can come live in his household when he arrives. He would like that. Would you?"

"Indeed, your grace."

"Then it shall be arranged!" The king nodded before his face started to cloud again. "Henry... I saw another boy named Henry just a few days before. Do you know him, son?"

"Henry Tudor?" I ventured.

"Indeed. He shall be king, you know." King Henry nodded at me cheerfully. "I do not know how or even why, but I know it." He settled back into his chair, and I realized that this brief conversation had exhausted him. In a moment, he had begun to doze, and a servant led us off.

I was deeply affected by poor King Henry's plight at first, but as the days passed and our encounter became less vivid in my mind, my boyish callousness reasserted itself. I decided that if I ever saw Richard again—and however torn my loyalties were during this period, I always prayed for his safety and his prosperity—I would tell him about this madman's wild prophecy. It was something that would no doubt amuse him.

Christmas came and went, rather sadly for Kate, who had held ill-concealed hopes that some disaster might befall the Earl of Warwick and place Edward back on the throne. My grandmother, her husband Walter Blount, and I dined occasionally at Westminster, but we never had another private audience with King Henry, who made only the briefest of public appearances. Rumor had it that he wore the same blue gown he'd been wearing as a captive in the Tower and that he adamantly refused to change into something more suitable for a king, though his servants did manage to clean it while he was abed. It was certainly what he had been wearing when I saw him.

Rather to my excitement, my uncle Edmund Beaufort, the Duke of Somerset—at least, he styled himself so—returned to England at the end of January. I was eager to meet him, having never known my mother's kin except for my aunt Margaret, but events dictated otherwise, leaving Somerset no time to bother with a nephew in his teens who, as a ward, couldn't raise troops. For raising troops suddenly became of the utmost urgency. France was at war with Burgundy, and when Warwick sided with France, the Duke of Burgundy gave in to Edward's pleadings and lent his assistance. By mid-March, Edward was back in England, and armies were once again on the move in our country.

I too was on the move, in one respect. For two weeks after Edward landed, I was a prisoner in the Tower.

⸎

It was nothing personal, the soldiers at Grandmother's Bread Street house told Walter Blount, Grandmother's husband, as they tied his hands behind his back, then started on mine. But these were dangerous times, and the Earl of Warwick could not risk having potential enemies at large.

As Bread Street was hardly in a good state of defense and a dozen armed men had come to arrest us, we were not in the best position to argue. Instead, Blount, who in any case had never manifested more than resigned tolerance for Warwick's regime, nodded grimly. "But why the boy? He's no danger to Warwick." (Normally, I would have bristled at being called a boy, but I gave Blount credit for good intentions here.)

"He's old enough to fight if need be, and he's married to a Woodville and is in your care. That's enough, says my lord. No harm shall come to him."

I was not fearful—in fact, I was oddly excited, thinking that at last I would be sharing in some of the danger that Richard had faced. Kate was a different matter altogether. "You can't take Harry! He's done nothing. He's not even a good Yorkist. Harry, tell them you're not!" Kate grabbed the arms of the man who was attempting to tie me. "Let him go!"

"Kate, it's all right," I said, turning to comfort her and only further frustrating the efforts of my guard. "It's only temporary."

"You don't know that, do you? You know what that evil man did to my father and to John!" Kate threw herself on the back of the guard and began pummeling him with very little effect. The other guards looked at her open-mouthed, either reluctant to use force against a young girl or finding the scene too amusing to interrupt, I do not know.

My grandmother caught Kate by her dress and yanked her backward, then dealt her one smart slap on the face. "You are disgracing your title, girl, to carry on so. Stop it immediately or you shall be whipped."

Kate stared open-mouthed at my grandmother. I knew then that Grandmother herself must have been frightened for us, or she'd never have treated Kate so. I turned to Kate and took her into my arms—clumsily, not being accustomed to marital embraces. She was trembling, poor creature, from head to toe. "Kate. There is nothing to fear. I am sure of it."

"But—"

"You must be brave, Kate." I pulled her a little closer, and she rested her head against my doublet. I felt her tears fall on my chest as I awkwardly patted her back. "Promise me you will be."

"All right, Harry. I promise."

I released Kate, and she took her place beside my grandmother, who patted her on the shoulder and said in the usual kindly tone with which she addressed my wife, "Good girl."

"The lad speaks the truth," Walter Blount said jovially as my relieved guard resumed tying my hands. He scooted forward to kiss his own wife on the cheek, then smiled at Kate. "Nothing to fear. You ladies will be glad to have the house to yourselves for a while, I wager."

They led us off, our duchesses waving goodbye and even managing smiles as if we were on our way to a banquet instead of to a cell in the Tower. When we had passed out of sight of them, my guard shook his head. "Is your lady always like that, my lord?"

Being led away from my grandmother's house by armed men was beginning to give me pause. For the first time I considered the possibility that Warwick might indeed shut us up for life, or worse. I also realized, to my surprise, that nuisance as she was at times, I was beginning to miss Kate already. "Always like what, man?" I said coldly. "If you mean to ask if she is always loyal to those she loves and concerned about their welfare—yes, then she is always like that."

Sometimes, I am pleased to say, I have given my wife her due.

The Tower was already teeming with newly made prisoners when we arrived, including my uncle John Stafford, the Earl of Wiltshire. He owed his earldom to King Edward, and probably Warwick had remembered this fact. The three of us were put in a fairly comfortable chamber together, not far from that of my relatives the Bourchiers, whom we often met when allowed out for walks. It was quite a family gathering.

Our guards, we soon found, were rather more inclined to support Edward than Warwick, whose French alliance was not particularly popular, especially with those London merchants who traded with Burgundy. Not that the guards cared much for that; when it came down to it, they simply preferred the robust, free-spending, womanizing Edward to poor Henry.

He'd been a prisoner in the Tower for so long, the guards sometimes forgot he was back on the throne, one confessed to us. As a result, we had no difficulty getting news from our captors, and the first piece they brought us was impressive: the Duke of Clarence had assembled a large army—and marched it straight to his brother instead of to his father-in-law.

"Prostrated himself before King Edward, he did," said Henry Bourchier, the Earl of Essex, stroking his thickening beard—my elders' barbers had not accompanied them to the Tower—contentedly. "I'd have given much to see that sight. The king pulled the lad upright too soon, in my opinion. I'd had kept him on his knees a good long while, as they say Margaret of Anjou kept Warwick when he made his peace with her."

"Was the Duke of Gloucester there?" I asked. The Bourchiers' guards were considerably more informative than our own, we'd found.

"Oh, yes. All three brothers embraced."

"Very touching." Uncle John snorted. "I'd have been checking Clarence for knives if I were King Edward."

"What brought him back to the king?" (I meant King Edward; captivity at Warwick's command had turned me into a good Yorkist, though not perhaps as good as Kate would have liked.)

"Mainly his women. The Duchess of York, the Duchess of Exeter, and the Duchess of Burgundy all begged him to come back to the fold. I had a hand in it myself before I got shut up in here. We all reminded him of how much his brother had done for him—and how little Warwick was likely to do for him, now that he's got Beaufort and the rest of them to please, not to mention Margaret of Anjou. Poor Warwick had it much simpler last year."

"Where do you think they'll go, the king and his brothers?"

"Straight to London." He paused. "And I think we ought to be there to join them when they do."

ix

Kate: April 1471

With the Tower full of suspected Yorkists, the sanctuaries full of unmistakable Yorkists, and all but a handful of the most important Lancastrian leaders having left London to raise troops, London was an eerie place. Business went on as usual, but with a sense of just going through the motions while everyone was waiting to see what would happen next.

The Archbishop of York, George Neville, who was Warwick's younger brother, tried his best to raise some Lancastrian enthusiasm by parading poor mad King Henry through the streets, accompanied by the archbishop himself and by Ralph Butler, Lord Sudeley. As I had not seen Henry before, I begged Grandmother Buckingham for permission to see this show, and she consented immediately—probably as it got me out from underfoot for a while. Although I was trying to be brave, as a great lady should be, I found it rather hard. I could not resist the temptation to ask, three or four times a day, whether there had been news of Harry and the other prisoners.

Showing King Henry to the people was a mistake, as even I at thirteen saw. Harry had told me how oddly he had acted during their meeting, down to his prophecy that Margaret Beaufort's spotty-faced son would be crowned king, and the stress of recent days had evidently done nothing to help his state of mind. Stooped and bewildered-looking, he hardly seemed aware of the crowds around him as he sat his horse, and a small child next to me went so far as to whimper in fright at his strange appearance. He was wearing what I knew from Harry was his usual blue gown, an item at

which a draper standing near me clucked his tongue in disgust and muttered, "My dog wouldn't piss on it!"

Poor Henry had been a respectable horseman in his younger days, people
said, but having been a prisoner for so long, he appeared to have forgotten
how to manage even the gentle mare on which he rode. He clearly needed
the pages who were leading the animal along.

If a man with presence, like the Earl of Warwick on his black charger or
the Duke of Somerset, who was said to be of a handsome, dashing appearance, were with the king, it might have helped—it couldn't have hurt.
But the Archbishop of York, a plump man, however solemn and grand a
figure he might have cut in a church procession, looked simply silly on his
own horse, and Lord Sudeley, who had no doubt been a fine man in his
prime, was long, long past it. The attendants who came before and after this
unhappy trio looked as if they would rather be doing almost anything else
in the world, like shoveling out the royal garderobes.

The bystanders were polite. There was too much gentleness in Henry's
ravaged face for anyone to want to mock the king, but there was nothing in
it to inspire anyone either. Motherly-looking women here and there called,
"God bless you, your grace," but no one could manage a more enthusiastic
response than that.

When the procession disappeared from sight—heading, I was glad to
see, toward the bishop's palace at St. Paul's, where Henry was better off than
anywhere else and where poor Lord Sudeley could take a much needed nap—
there was a general sense of relief. I wended my way home with the pages
who had accompanied me. We were on Bread Street when one of my pages
suddenly grabbed my sleeve. "My lady! It's your lord, and Walter Blount!"

"Harry?" I stared. Sure enough, my husband was being ushered into his
grandmother's house. I hoisted up my skirts and raced down the street,
heedless of anyone unfortunate enough to be in my path. "Harry!" I threw
myself upon my husband and hugged him tight. Nearby, Walter Blount
was receiving similar attention from Grandmother Buckingham, normally
not a demonstrative woman. "You're safe!"

He kissed me gingerly. "Well, of course. I told you I would be."

I stepped back and dabbed at my eyes. "But how did you come here?"

"We escaped," said Harry laconically. I could have strangled him. Instead, I turned to the more communicative Walter Blount.

"The lad's right. We prisoners there overpowered our guards—with the help and connivance of some of our other guards—and took over the Tower. It's in the hands of York now."

"But how?"

"Coordination, Kate, coordination. The friendly guards had been smuggling us weapons for several days in advance, so we were well armed. As the others made their rounds, we seized them and locked them in our own cells. Bit by bit, we got farther and farther. Some guards who hadn't shown support for our cause before suddenly turned in our favor too. When that happened, the game was up for Lancaster." Walter Blount nodded at Harry. "Your husband's got a strong arm on him, lass. He knocked one of the blackguards senseless, though he was coming to himself when we left him."

Harry, despite his nonchalance, was visibly pleased at the compliment. I clapped my hands before adding piously, "I hope there was no bloodshed."

"No. There's a few whose heads will hurt, but they'll get over it." Harry grinned, a rare thing with him.

Walter Blount snorted. "We heard of that farce that took place just now—parading poor Henry about. It's no good, and George Neville knows it. Rumor has it that King Edward is encamped at St. Albans and will be entering London tomorrow. From what we heard coming over here, he'll not meet any resistance in London. The merchants for one will be more than glad to have him back—some so they can have their debts paid, some so the king can run up more debts. Henry hasn't been good for business, they say."

"Not in that blue gown," I said, giggling, and again felt quite ashamed of myself. By way of repentance, I said three extra Hail Marys that evening as I prayed—but I also prayed long and hard for Edward's safe coming into the city, having long been convinced that God was as good a Yorkist as I. He had just been testing us lately.

∽

I could hardly concentrate on anything the next day—Maundy Thursday—and neither could anyone else, not even Grandmother Buckingham. She squirmed through morning prayers almost as much as I. No one in the city could go about his business as usual, it seemed. By noon, we gave up trying and went to Bishopsgate, where it was considered most likely that the king would make his entrance. The guards at the gate had been sent home to dinner, and fresh ones had not been put in their place. Some men had been seen that morning wearing Warwick's badge of the ragged staff, but they had disappeared from the streets—gone back to hide in bed, the crowd at the gate jested.

The church bells of the city rang out one o'clock, then two o'clock. And then a roar came from outside the city gate, and I saw one of the finest spectacles I have ever seen in my life.

King Edward was on a splendid horse—a white one, if you please—and in the months that the people had not seen him, they had forgotten just how handsome he was. After poor King Henry's ride the day before, he could not have been more of a welcome sight. Soon the ground underneath him was a mass of blossoms, all of the women and girls in the crowd, including myself, having brought flowers to throw the king's way. They might have run up to the king had not he and his entourage—the king's brothers, my own brother Anthony, and Lord William Hastings among them—been flanked by the Flemish soldiers who had accompanied the king from abroad.

Edward rode on, smiling and waving and blowing a kiss to a particularly pretty woman now and then. Beside him was the eighteen-year-old Duke of Gloucester, whose smile and wave were somewhat stiffer than that of his older brother. The Duke of Clarence, who so recently had been allied with Lancaster, fixed a smile on his lips and kept it there, but stared straight

ahead, probably hoping that no one remembered that he had ridden into
the city not too many months ago under Warwick's banner. Lord Hastings
acted as his dearest friend, the king, did, and my brother Anthony, while
acknowledging the crowd, looked a tiny bit removed from his surroundings, as if his body was all there but his mind was not.

Even though Harry and I, as Duke and Duchess of Buckingham, had
been afforded a good vantage point from which to see the king, I doubted
he could see us and Harry's Stafford relations, so thick was the press of the
crowd and so protective the Flemings of the master they had been hired to
serve. But I hoped he could hear me. "Long live King Edward!" I shouted.
"Our rightful king!"

The bystanders near me took up the cry. "Long live King Edward! Our
rightful king!"

The cry carried the king to St. Paul's.

❧

At St. Paul's, the king and his entourage heard mass, after which—so
I heard from Anthony later—Edward went to the Bishop's Palace and
greeted the man whose occupancy of the throne had just ended for all
practical purposes. Henry, poor man, ignored Edward's proffered hand
and embraced him, saying, "My cousin of York, you are very welcome. I
believe that in your hands my life will not be in danger." Edward assured
Henry of his kind intentions, and then consigned him to the Tower.
Then he went to Westminster, where the Archbishop of Canterbury,
who had been imprisoned in the Tower with Harry and the others, hastily
recrowned him.

During all of this, Bessie and her children had remained in sanctuary,
and it was there the king next proceeded. In the interval, Harry and I had
arrived there ourselves.

As Edward walked into Bessie's lodgings, Bessie ran into his arms. They
kissed for what must have been a solid five minutes. Then Mama led in the
little girls. Bess, the oldest, hugged her father straightaway, but the younger

two required a little coaxing. Only when the king had won them over and jiggled them on his knee for a little while did Bessie nod at me.

I went into the other room and very carefully lifted little Edward out of his cradle. Then I carried him back into the chamber and placed him in his father's arms.

For the first time, and the last, I saw King Edward lose his composure altogether.

"My son and heir," he said in a cracking voice, taking the baby's fingers in his. "Bessie, you have given me the most precious treasure a woman can give a man. Everything I do from here forward will be for him—and for you, my love. The lady of my heart."

At that point the rest of us had the good sense to make ourselves scarce.

☙

By that evening the king had removed Bessie and his children to Baynard's Castle, where the king's mother lived. The Dukes of Clarence and Gloucester were there as well, as were Lord Hastings and my brother Anthony. As Harry was enjoying his reunion with Richard, and I with Anthony and Bessie and the children, we stayed at the Duchess of York's that evening, too.

After we heard divine service, the entire family gathered in the solar. It was almost as if we were at Greenwich again that night.

Life for the exiles, we discovered as they reminisced for us, had not been entirely without its pleasures. Anthony and even Edward described the wonderful manuscripts in the collection of Louis of Gruuthuse, who had been a generous host to the king and his followers. Even Lord Hastings— whose eye I had hitherto believed was attracted only to a pretty woman— rhapsodized over them. I must have shown my weariness of this topic in my face, for during a pause in Anthony's discourse, Lord Hastings looked at me and suddenly laughed. "Upon my word, my little duchess! If those masters who paint from the life were to see you now, they would have to depict you with a very sour face. What makes you frown so, your grace?"

"I have had so much of books lately," I admitted reluctantly. I looked apologetically at Harry, but he was deep in a conversation with Richard. "Grandmother Buckingham, you know, is a biblio—biblio—"

"Bibliophile?" suggested Anthony.

"Yes. A bibliophile like you and like the Duchess of Burgundy. When Harry was in the Tower, I would worry, and Grandmother Buckingham would tell me to read, so I would improve my mind and not fret about Harry so much. And I did—but I became so very tired of it, I do not want to be improved anymore!"

"Indeed, I do not believe you can be, in appearance at least," said Lord Hastings gallantly. I wondered how the ladies in the Low Countries had withstood his charm. Perhaps they had not, and a crop of bastards would soon result. "You have grown lovely since we saw you last, your grace. Harry will have to guard against poachers."

I blushed furiously.

Anthony rescued me. "Yet at the risk of boring Kate further, I must say there is someone that fascinates me. Have you ever seen one of these?"

He held up a book. It could not have looked more dull if it tried. We stared, trying to discern whatever quality in it appealed to my brother. Even Harry and Richard were drawn into the mystery.

"I know!" said Harry finally. "It's printed, isn't it?"

Anthony nodded and passed the book, which turned out to be in German, to him. "In Cologne. An Englishman I met in Bruges gave this to me. His name is William Caxton—he's a prominent merchant there—and he plans to start his own printing press in Cologne. I wish he would bring his venture here instead."

"But what good is it?" I asked. "The illuminators make such pretty books as it is."

"But they are slow to make. The printing press can produce many copies of the same book, you see. With this, anyone who wanted a book could simply go in a shop and buy it as other things are bought."

I frowned, not convinced at all that this was a good thing. The king laughed. "So Kate, my bibliophobe, what would you rather be doing than reading?"

"Playing ninepins," I confessed. "Riding. Dancing. None of which I have had any of lately." I heaved a martyred sigh.

The king grinned. "Soon, Kate, we shall have all the ninepins and riding and dancing you wish, God willing."

"After Easter, of course," the Duchess of York said severely.

"After Easter," conceded the king. He sighed. "And there are other matters we must attend to first, we men that is. Indeed, I fear you ladies must excuse us now, for we have matters of which we must talk. Warwick's army was not far behind ours."

✍

On Good Friday, men emerged from sanctuary and traveled from their estates in the country to join Edward's troops. Even Harry's uncle Henry Stafford joined, probably to the chagrin of his wife and to the great relief of Grandmother Buckingham. She had been much distressed by the prospect of her son John fighting against her son Henry.

The reinforcements came just in time. Late that afternoon, we learned that Warwick's men were at St. Albans. Doubtlessly they had hoped that the holy days would put Edward off his guard, but they had reckoned ill. The king had never forgotten that his own father had been killed just days after Christmas, during a supposed truce. So on the Saturday before Easter, the king and his army—Harry among them, for he had begged for the chance to fight—left London to face Warwick.

What would happen if Edward lost this battle? If he survived the fight, he would surely die on the block. Bessie and her little girls might end their days in a convent, her small son as a prisoner. And if… if Harry were to die, I would find myself a virgin widow.

I pulled a ribbon from my gown and handed it to Harry as the men said their last good-byes. "Wear this, please."

"Kate, it's not a tournament."

"I know that, Harry! Please. Wear it for luck."

"All right." He thought for a moment, then looked around as if afraid of being caught in what he was going to do next. Satisfied that no one was watching, he brushed his lips against mine, then pressed them cautiously a little closer.

A trumpet blared, and we jumped apart. It was the signal for the army to start moving. "Well," said Harry. "I'll see you soon, I guess."

I watched as all of the men I loved slowly passed and drew out of sight, and wondered if I would ever see them again. Then I saw one more familiar figure—King Henry, headed to the battle as Edward's hostage. Good Yorkist that I was, my heart still ached when I saw this man who had been king since he was nine months of age, seated in a litter and looking like a scared child.

And he was still wearing the same blue gown.

X

Harry: April 1471 to May 1471

WHEN EDWARD RETURNED TO LONDON, I BEGGED TO BE ALLOWED to fight, not so much for the House of York but for my Stafford and Bourchier relations. Our shared imprisonment had given me a sense of Yorkist solidarity that all my years as a royal ward had not. "You're but fifteen," said Edward dubiously. "You've not had that much training."

"Fifteen and a *half*."

"It's a strange age," Edward conceded. "Almost too young to fight, almost too old to sit back with the baggage carts. But when I was fifteen, I'd have wanted to fight, so I shall say yes. You will serve under Lord Mountjoy's banner."

Walter Blount did not appear to be very pleased when I told him the news; undoubtedly he dreaded bearing my youthful corpse back home to my grandmother. "For God's sake, obey my orders and don't do anything brash. There will be other battles."

I nodded, happily picturing the glory that would soon be mine.

⁓

On the night before Easter, we arrived at Barnet, near which Warwick's army was encamped. Lord Hastings was commanding our left wing, Richard the right, and Edward, with the dubious aid of Clarence, the center. Warwick commanded his reserve, his brother the Marquess of Montagu the center; on the right was the Earl of Oxford, who'd been made a Knight of the Bath alongside me but had long since fallen astray from King Edward's cause. On Warwick's left was the Duke of Exeter, who was married to my former guardian, Edward's eldest sister, but who had not cohabited with her in years. My uncle the Duke of Somerset was on the coast awaiting Margaret of Anjou, whose arrival had been expected for some days now. For that reason, Edward was eager to bring Warwick to battle before more troops arrived, Easter or no Easter. Already he was outnumbered by several thousand, we estimated from our spies.

All that night we heard the rumble of Warwick's artillery, firing at us noisily but futilely, for we were closer to the Lancastrians than they thought, and they were overshooting. We kept our own guns silent to avoid alerting them to the mistake, and we kept ourselves as silent as we could also. It was eerie. No one could sleep, not even me, though like most lads my age I had a great capacity for doing so. Instead, I sat in my stepgrandfather's tent and diced wordlessly with him and my Bourchier and Stafford relatives.

Easter announced itself not with an angel from heaven, but with a mist so thick that I could not imagine how we were to walk in it, much less fight in it. Edward, however, determined that we should fight in it. So at around five in the morning on April 14, 1471, I joined my first battle, fighting in the troops commanded by the king in the center.

I could hear arrows whizzing by me, the men near me breathing hard, the thud of bodies clashing and falling, but I could scarcely see beyond my own hand in the fog. Someone—I could only hope that it was a Lancastrian—suddenly hove in front of me, and we began fighting hand to hand, as all around us were fighting.

To my shock, the man went down, whether felled by my own mace or someone else's I shall never know. Before I could congratulate myself, another rose in his place. He laid me a blow that sent me reeling backward, but the force of someone pressing behind me kept me upright and allowed me to strike back.

Then something crashed against my helm, causing a pain that first blinded me, then invited me to sink into the darkness. After making one last attempt to swing my mace, I accepted the invitation.

To my great irritation, someone was jerking on my helm and sloshing water on my face. "Stop," I mumbled. I turned my head and found myself looking into the face of my uncle John.

"Well, you're alive, at least." He completed pulling off my helm, this time without protest from me, and gently touched my temple. I flinched and yelped. "Nasty-looking bruise, but that looks to be the worst of it. I wasn't so sure when I found you whether you'd wake again. You're lucky no one decided to finish you off after you fell."

I frowned groggily. Something was missing. There were voices around me, shouting orders to and fro, some groans here and there, and footsteps going back and forth, but there was no fighting. No mist, either; it had turned into a perfect April day. "Is it over, then?"

"Over for Warwick's men. Victory for us." He and my page helped me to a sitting position. "Easy there. Just wait until you get your bearings a little more before you try to stand. It was anyone's battle there for a while. Oxford's men routed Hastings's troops, but the fools decided to go toward London and loot to celebrate. Oxford finally got them back in order, but when they returned, they ran into Montagu's men instead of the king's. It was still damnably foggy, and the Marquess's men started attacking Oxford's. Oxford's men started screaming, 'Treason!' and that's when all started coming undone. Montagu was killed, and Warwick's men got spooked and began breaking rank. Oxford escaped, we think. No one knows what became of the Duke of Exeter. Warwick—"

My still muzzy head was having difficulty following this. Less out of rudeness than out of my dazed condition, I interrupted. "The Duke of Gloucester?"

"Slightly wounded. He made a fine name for himself today, the ones who could see him in the mist say."

Proud as I was to hear this about my friend, I could not help but contrast it with my own less glorious performance. The mighty Kingmaker had been defeated, and what would I tell my sons? That I had spent most of the battle lying unconscious on the field. Scowling, I touched my forehead, hoping for blood, and found none, only a pulpy welt. So I would likely not even have a scar to show off. Then I remembered the words my uncle had said when he first saw me conscious. "Who of our people died?"

John sighed and crossed himself. "Lord Mountjoy's eldest son was killed. So was Sir Humphrey Bourchier."

I winced. Hours ago, I'd been playing dice with these men. They'd lost at that game, too.

"Our Henry's alive, but badly wounded." John's good-humored voice cracked a bit. "I don't know if he'll recover. I'm going to look after him now that I know you're in no danger." My uncle helped me to my feet. "Try it now."

I was a trifle dizzy, but no worse, and I had my page to lean on. As I got my bearings back, I asked, "And what of Warwick?"

John pointed to the woods where Warwick's men had kept their horses and baggage. "You'll find him over there."

✎

Richard Neville, Earl of Warwick, the mightiest man in England, lay stripped of his armor, his underclothing dark with his own blood. I joined the Duke of Gloucester in staring down at the body.

"They say that once he realized all was up, he tried to reach his horse and flee, but he couldn't move fast enough. Some blackguards killed him, even though Ned had given orders that his life be spared." Richard pointed to the earl's hand, bare of the costly rings that usually adorned it. "They stripped him and cleared out before anyone knew what was happening, I suppose."

"You were in his care once," I said. "It must be hard seeing him so."

Richard flicked a hand toward the earl's body. "He brought it on himself. Ned gave him opportunities to make peace." He turned his dispassionate gaze from his dead guardian onto me and tapped his forehead. "I see you've seen some action."

I shrugged modestly, which wasn't hard under the circumstances. "A bit. You too," I added, noting that Richard's left arm was bandaged. "I heard that you distinguished yourself."

Richard gave his own modest shrug, which was certainly more honestly come by than mine.

"So what next?" It was the first chance I'd had to talk with Richard since Thursday. The second most important man in London, he'd been running around over the past couple of days, busy with war preparations, while I had been occupied mainly in staying out of everyone else's way.

"Capture the French bitch and her bastard-born whelp, I hope."

"You really think Edward of Lancaster's a bastard?"

Richard snorted. "Doesn't everyone? By your grandfather Edmund Beaufort, they say. Or at least he's the leading candidate." He grinned and suddenly clapped me on my shoulder, which I discovered, rather to my pleasure, was sorely bruised as well. Yet another war wound. "Oh, sorry, old man. I know you don't like to hear ill about your Beaufort relations. Though it's not such an ill thing to get a queen in one's bed, is it? Anyway, that's off in the future. As for the here and now, I think, Ned will be heading back to London shortly. Who knows? We might be back at the Tower in time to hear mass with my lady mother."

He was right. Before we began our triumphant ten-mile return to London, however, I stopped by the tent where the highest-ranking wounded, including Uncle Henry, had been moved. Uncle John was there by his cot; he and his older brother were close, like Humphrey and I would have been if he'd lived. "How goes he?" I asked.

"Drifting in and out."

I looked at my uncle, wounded so badly in a battle he'd never really wanted to fight. As I stood there awkwardly, thinking I might never see him alive again, Uncle Henry opened his eyes. "Harry? You'll send my love to Mother?"

"Yes. Of course."

He smiled. "And Margaret. Tell her I'll see her soon."

"Yes." In my most cheerful tone, I added, "I imagine she'll soon be sending people to see after you."

"Yes," said my uncle contentedly, his eyes starting to close again. "Margaret thinks of everything."

✐

The day after we arrived in London—"we" including our hostage the unfortunate King Henry, who had probably never been so glad to see his apartments in the Tower as he was that afternoon—a cart lumbered into the city bearing the bodies of the Earl of Warwick and John Neville, Marquess of Montagu. Edward planned to give them honorable burial at Bisham Abbey, the resting place of their father the Earl of Salisbury, but first he wanted all of London to have a look at them—partly to scotch rumors that they had survived Barnet, partly to remind everyone of the fate of rebels. So for two days, the brothers were to lie at St. Paul's, clad only in loincloths.

Kate wanted to see them. I rather doubted the wisdom of this; she'd not seen a dead person except for my brother Humphrey, and he in death had looked peaceful and sweet, nothing like these men with their ugly wounds. I didn't want to see them again myself; there were enough live men walking around London with cloths over their faces, concealing mutilated features. But Warwick had ordered the deaths of Kate's father and of her favorite brother, and I could understand her wish, unexpressed though it was, to gloat over his corpse.

Women, however, are strange creatures, I was quickly discovering. Kate took one look at the two brothers and began to cry. "It's so sad, Harry," she whispered. "Their feet are so sad."

"Their *feet*?"

"Well, look at them." I obeyed and saw nothing out of the ordinary, except that the Kingmaker's toes were less calloused than those of his brother, and certainly nothing that would bring tears to my own eyes. "Bare like that—they could be anyone, couldn't they? Peasants, even. *Anyone*. All the glory, all the titles—all come to nothing."

All this philosophy from my little wife was disconcerting. (Maybe she'd been paying better attention to Grandmother Buckingham's improving books than she let on.) "Well? Aren't you glad to see him come to nothing, after what he did to your family?"

Kate touched her favorite ring, given to her by her father. Her pretty blue eyes turned hard and tearless. "Yes. I am." She gave the Kingmaker one last glance before we turned away. "But it is still a sad sight to see."

                              ❧

As Kate and I were viewing the Kingmaker, word arrived in London that Margaret of Anjou, her son and her daughter-in-law in tow, had landed in England at last. She had, in fact, arrived on the morning of Barnet. Instead of turning tail when she received the news of Warwick's defeat and death, she had begun raising an army. It was led by my mother's brother, Edmund Beaufort, the Duke of Somerset. Leaving his queen and the rest of his family in the Tower, along with Kate and others, King Edward went out to confront Margaret's forces.

It would be tedious to recount the twists and turns Margaret's army and King Edward's followed over the next days. Suffice it to say that on May 4, 1471, they finally met in the town of Tewkesbury, not far from the town's fine abbey.

I can say no more of my performance at Tewkesbury than that I remained conscious throughout the battle this time. I was kept in the reserves by Walter Blount, who had probably made a promise to my grandmother to that effect after Uncle Henry had come so close to dying. By the time we joined the battle, it had pretty much been won by the House of York.

Under fire, the Duke of Somerset brought his men downhill into Edward's at the center, a maneuver that might have worked had he not been met not only by Edward's men, but by Richard's on his flank as well. Even then, as Somerset was pushed back uphill, there might have been hope had it not been for Edward's idea of stationing two hundred men at arms in a wood, where they would be able to come to his aid when they believed that the conditions warranted it. They chose this moment to advance, and what followed was a slaughter. When Edward's men were finished with Somerset's, they started on the Earl of Devon's, then on Edward of Lancaster's. By the time all was done, seventeen-year-old Edward of Lancaster lay dead on the battlefield, the last hope of Lancaster destroyed.

John Beaufort, the youngest of my mother's brothers, died not far beside the prince. The Duke of Somerset, along with a host of others, took sanctuary in Tewkesbury Abbey. King Edward would have hauled them all out at swordpoint straightaway had not the abbot, armed only with the sacrament, begged him to pardon them all. He did—but only for the time being. For on Monday, the intervening Sunday having given the men inside the abbey a reprieve, the king changed his mind and decided to force the Lancastrian leaders from sanctuary.

It was a heinous act, I thought then, and I still think it now. Swords drawn, a few dozen of the king's men barged into the abbey just after matins, while most of the men who had sought shelter, their arms cast aside, were still half dozing among the abbey's great columns. The abbot pleaded, the monks pleaded, some of Lancaster's men pleaded, but to no avail. Several men gathered up some swords and tried to fight; for their pains they were slain right there and then in this house of God, their blood polluting its aisles and staining the monuments that had rested there in peace up until now.

I tried to push my way inside the abbey, perhaps with some wild idea of trying to intervene myself, but I couldn't get through its great door; it was blocked by Edward's men. Instead I had to wait outside with the rest of the king's army and watch as one Lancastrian after another was dragged out in shackles past us, to the jeers of the Yorkist troops.

Then the last of the leaders was hauled out. I'd never seen my uncle Edmund Beaufort, save as a distant figure in armor, but I knew him instantly as he was hustled through the throng. His face, even when bloodied and covered with dirt and sweat, was unmistakably that of my mother's brother.

"What is to happen to them?" I asked my uncle John Stafford as he stood beside me.

"A trial, with the Dukes of Gloucester and Norfolk as their judges," he said quietly, not looking at me. "Harry—"

"And then?"

There was no need for the Earl of Wiltshire to answer my question; his face as he turned to look at me said it all. I ran to the king's tent, where he was giving instructions to Richard and the Duke of Norfolk, and more or less shoved my way past his guards. Edward stared at me, then waved away the guards who were belatedly trying to seize me. "It's always a pleasure to see you, my young cousin," he said genially. "But you might try asking next time."

"Your grace. Is my uncle Somerset to die?"

"Yes, unless he can explain away his presence on the battlefield against me two days ago."

"Then, your grace—please grant me a boon. Spare him."

The two dukes stared at me as I fell to my knees. From a height above me, the king said, "Are you mad, boy?"

"No! As his nephew, I want you to spare his life. And perhaps those of the others, too," I added generously.

"Rise, Harry."

I obeyed. With scarcely an effort, the king then shoved me down again, so I landed on my backside. I sat blinking at him.

"By God, someone should have done that earlier, you fool boy. Have you no idea what your damned Beaufort relations have cost this country, in men, in money, in time wasted? Have you no idea that I pardoned your beloved uncle Henry Somerset, only to be betrayed by him? I did more than that: I shared my bed with him, went hunting with him, even held jousts in his honor. In that traitor's honor! When men threatened his life in Northampton, I saved it. I should have let them slay him then and there. How did he reward it? By plotting against me!"

"But that was Henry. Not my uncle Edmund."

"'Not my uncle Edmund,'" the king mimicked. "Your uncle Edmund was scarcely better. I released him from my prisons when I pardoned Henry Beaufort, and what did Uncle Edmund Beaufort do? Smiled and grinned his thanks, then followed his eldest brother's lead and took off to join that she-wolf Margaret of Anjou the first chance he got. That bitch is still at large, need I remind you? Perhaps when I find her, I should set them up in their own household together, Harry, with a handsome annuity. Would you like that?"

"No! I just want you to spare him. For my mother's sake. He's the only brother she has left now." My own temper was beginning to rise. "What harm would it do you? You've always treated my mother unkindly, just because she's a Beaufort. You've never let me visit her, the whole time I've been in your wardship. I wouldn't have seen her the last time if Humphrey hadn't died. She and her husband haven't even been allowed to administer any of my lands. She's a countess but she might as well be a squire's wife, the way you treat her."

"I've treated your mother as I have because she's not only a Beaufort but half mad, Harry. Don't delude yourself."

"You hauled my uncle and the others out of sanctuary, with no right, after promising to honor it. You broke your word as a king and as a gentleman! Not only that, you've treated all of the Beauforts shabbily, and their kin! Aunt Margaret's son Henry has never been allowed his title or his lands, although he's nearly as good as a title to the throne as y—"

Edward was one of those men who did not raise his voice when he was angriest. "Get that brat out of my sight. Now."

Richard, who was stronger than he looked, grabbed me and more or less hauled me out of the king's tent. When we were at a safe distance, he grinned at me and said, "You don't know when to stop talking, do you, Harry? I don't think there's much of a future for you in Ned's diplomatic service after you started outlining that Henry Tudor's claim to the throne."

"I only wanted him to spare my uncle. He's part of my blood. Why did he explode at me?" I rubbed my backside. "I was respectful, at least at first."

Richard shrugged. "Aside from not liking to be told his business by a youth of fifteen, Ned doesn't much like executing people, never has. He'd rather be playing the jolly king. And he didn't like taking those men out of sanctuary; it goes against what piety he has. Maybe you made him think of things he'd rather not think."

I turned to Richard and placed both of my hands on his shoulders. "Richard. If that's the way he feels, perhaps you could persuade—"

"No. Harry, think. What would happen if your uncle was put in prison instead of being executed? More years of chaos, even if he didn't find a way to escape and stayed locked up, because men would still rise up on his behalf. Ned's decision is the best one."

"So you'll condemn him and the rest to death?"

"Yes. I'm sorry, Harry. Sometimes it's better for the safety of the realm as a whole that a few should die. And don't lie to yourself. They're grown men; they knew the risk that they were facing."

I was silent, knowing that there was no hope left.

"Harry? Is it true what he said about your mother?"

"I don't want to speak of it. Not now or ever."

"All right, Harry." Richard was kind enough to ignore the tears that were falling down my face. Then he said, "I need to get back. There's a little yet to be done before we're ready to try them. Would you like to see your uncle in the time being? I know that's not quite what you wanted, but—"

"How?" I swatted at my cheek. "Edward—I mean, the king—would never let me."

"But I can."

He led me to a tent and left me waiting outside while he spoke to someone within. In just a moment or two, he emerged. "Come on, Harry."

Inside the tent sat what remained of the cream of Margaret of Anjou's army—my uncle Edmund, Sir Hugh Courtenay, and Sir John Langstrother among them. My uncle was sitting between a couple of guards, evidently lost in his own thoughts. He was a young man, only in his early thirties, and good-looking; thanks to his long exile, he would die without ever having taken a wife. Rousing himself, he gave me a cold stare as I was led to where he sat. "So, a little Yorkist come to gloat. To what do I owe this pleasure?"

This was too much. "I'm your nephew, Harry, Duke of Buckingham, and I didn't come to gloat. I begged for your life, as a matter of fact, but the king wouldn't grant my wish. I came to see you for my mother's sake, because you're part of my family. But if you're going to be like that— well, then, go to hell. To hell with the king and the whole sorry lot of you." I cannot overemphasize the immense satisfaction that all of these consignments to the world below gave me, but as I turned on my heel, I did suspect that Richard at my age would have managed this business more eloquently.

"Wait. For God's sake, boy, wait. I'm not in the best of humors at the moment, you see. Make some allowances for circumstances. Come back, and we'll talk. Please, Harry?" He half smiled at me as I returned to stand warily beside him. "Not language that I expected to come out of a lad with such an angelic face."

I shrugged, hoping it made me look less angelic and more manly.

"You look like Meg, I see now."

Meg? It took me a moment to realize he was speaking of my mother. I'd never heard her called this; it belonged to a long-ago time when the Beauforts were flying high. "I suppose."

He gave a wry smile. "And you favor me, too. Though my face has become less angelic with the years. Along with the rest of me."

I had been schooled at court in the art of polite conversation and was fairly adept at it (despite the coarseness in which I had just engaged, which I assure you was not the doing of my tutors), but none of my training had prepared me for this encounter. Now that my uncle was speaking to me, what did one say to a man whose head would be off in a couple of hours? Especially to a man whom I had just cursed? My uncle, however, must have understood how I felt. "Sit. How old are you, Harry?"

"Fifteen."

"Did you fight here?"

I nodded. "Here and at Barnet." Something made me confess, "I didn't distinguish myself, though. I was in the reserves here and never did all that much. At Barnet I was knocked out and missed most of the battle."

"We all have our bad days, and you're very young," my uncle said kindly. "You'll improve. I suppose you're still a ward of the crown?"

"Yes, and I hate it. I want to live on my own lands so much, to be my own master. I've not seen any of my estates since I was little." It occurred to me that my uncle, who aside from his present circumstances had long ago lost his own inheritance through his family's attainder, might not find my plight especially moving. "I know that must sound like a trivial complaint to you."

"It's a quite natural one. What lad doesn't want to be out on his own? You're married, aren't you, to one of the Woodville girls?"

"Yes. Kate—Katherine."

"No use asking if she came with a dowry, then. Is she pretty, at least?"

"They say she is very fair."

"They? Surely at fifteen you have an opinion. What do you think?"

"I think so, too."

"Then that's all that matters. And Meg? How is she?"

"She's married again to Richard Darell and they have a daughter. I haven't seen her since my younger brother died. The king discourages contact between us, you see, because—"

"Because of her Beaufort brothers? I should think that obstacle will be soon removed entirely," my uncle said, with perfect composure.

"But there is another reason." My voice dropped to a whisper, and I found myself telling him what I had never told Richard, and never wanted to discuss with Kate. "There are times when the demons come upon my mother. Once she even tried to make away with herself and her young child."

My uncle sighed. "During her fits of melancholy?"

"Why, yes," I said.

"She had them even as a girl." He patted me on the shoulder. "I'm sorry, Harry."

"Do you think *I* could run mad?" I dared to ask him.

"You look sane enough to me, Harry, and your father and your Stafford grandfather were a level-headed pair." He grinned. "If you've anything to worry about in your Beaufort blood, it's foolhardiness. God knows there's a lot of that to spare."

We talked for a while longer—a little about my uncle's years in Burgundy, which he remembered with fondness, a little about my mother as a girl, but mostly about myself. I would not have monopolized the conversation in that manner, but it seemed to be how my uncle wanted it to go, so I deferred to his wishes. He asked me about mundane things—my studies, my knightly training, whether I wanted to go abroad, whether I liked music, whether I preferred hawking or hunting, the lands I would inherit, which castles I thought I would spend most of my time in. Not since Grandfather Buckingham died had any man bothered to talk to me thus, and I chattered on as if this were a perfectly normal talk between uncle and nephew. Not once did we speak of Lancaster or of York or of the battle that had been fought. When there was at last a pause in our conversation, I blurted, "Perhaps I should try again for your life. This time I'll grovel to the king. I'll offer him my lands, anything. I don't want you to die!"

My uncle laid an arm on my shoulders and pulled me closer to him. "You would beg in vain, Harry, even with the kind offer of your lands. Stay here instead. Your presence does me good."

We sat there talking quietly for a precious few more minutes. Then there was a clatter, and the king's men barged in. "All's ready. Come along, all of you."

I helped my uncle up—I had seen that he had a fresh wound in his leg that would make it difficult for him to stand without assistance—and supported him until he could get his balance. He thanked me, then slid a ring off his finger. "Wear that as a remembrance of me, and give Meg my love, if you can do so without grieving her too much."

Not trusting myself to speak without tears, I nodded.

"And when you come into your lands, I'd like you to have some masses said for my soul. You'll do that?"

"Every day," I managed.

Two of the king's men surrounded my uncle, and I stepped back reluctantly as they led him off. "Harry?"

"Uncle?"

"Meg ought to be proud of you. God keep you."

∽

The trial was purely a formality—not that anyone had expected anything different. Richard played his part in the show with becoming gravity, and moved through the proceedings as though he'd been doing it all of his life. My uncle sat through the business with a look of cool detachment on his face, which changed only to show a glint of relief when it was announced that the king would not exact the penalty of hanging, drawing, and quartering reserved for traitors.

So forgone had been the conclusion, the scaffold was ready and waiting at Tewkesbury's market cross when the dozen men were led out to execution—the first one I'd seen. It was something that a man was supposed to watch without flinching, and I managed it, not wanting to give anyone the satisfaction of seeing me betray any girlish emotion. The prisoners were beheaded in reverse rank; my uncle, as the head of the army, had to wait until all of his followers died. None of the condemned men made any speeches; a few prayed. The executioner held up each head as the deed was done but made little to-do about it. There wasn't much of an audience except for Edward's army and a cluster of townspeople.

My uncle was looking around for something as he waited his turn, and I knew it was me he sought. I moved my cap ever so slightly, until he saw me. Then he smiled faintly, knelt and placed his head on the block, and prayed. In a stroke, the male line of the House of Beaufort was extinct.

∽

After my uncle's execution, I slunk off, not wanting anyone's company. I wandered through the town of Tewkesbury, through the wooded areas around it, all the while paying very little attention to my surroundings. Finally I made my way back to the market cross by which my uncle had been executed just hours before. The scaffold had already been knocked apart. Its remnants, and the bloody ground surrounding it, were the only signs of what had happened there.

I stood there staring for a while. Then, heedless of the passersby, I fell to my knees and wept, until presently someone knelt beside me and put an arm around my shoulder.

"Easy, old man. Easy."

Much of what I did years later, I suspect, can be attributed to that one moment—that when Richard sat beside me and held me next to him as I cried my heart out. We must have presented quite a spectacle—two well-dressed young men smack in the middle of the marketplace, one bawling like a baby while the other supported him—but Richard paid it no mind. Only when I had exhausted my store of tears and lay almost limp against his shoulder did he raise me. "Come. Let's get some food and drink in you. You'll feel better."

Wiping my nose on my sleeve, I let Richard lead me away. We had walked in silence for a while, me still mostly leaning against him, when he said, "There will be no display of their heads, Harry. The king is going to pay for your Beaufort uncles to be buried with all due honor at the abbey."

I tried to gather together a little dignity. "How kind of him."

"Well, it is, considering the alternative, and they'll be in fine company, with all of the old Earls of Gloucester and our Clare ancestors. It is meant to be a mark of respect, Harry. Take it as such, is my advice."

I blew my nose. "I suppose I can understand what you said earlier about the king having no choice about my uncle Edmund. But I miss him."

Richard tried not to smile. "Miss him? Harry, you spent less than an hour with the man in your entire life."

"I know. But we got on well. I shall miss him all the same." I crossed myself, and Richard kindly followed suit.

We went into a tavern—after the shock of the battle, the merchants of Tewkesbury had rebounded nicely enough. Richard ordered us ales and meat pie. As we tucked into our food, which I found did indeed improve my spirits, I began to realize how much I had missed Richard during these past months. Even after he had returned to England, he'd hardly had a chance to speak to me, so busy was he with the king's affairs.

I took another deep drink of the ale. Perhaps in my famished state, it went to my head a bit, for I dared to ask Richard, "Now that the Lady Anne's a widow, are you thinking of marrying her?"

Richard looked surprised. "I did tell you that I would probably marry her, didn't I? You still remember that?"

"Yes, of course."

"Well, I'd like to. I don't think Ned can possibly object now that Warwick's dead. And, of course, if she'll have me."

"Why wouldn't she?"

He shrugged. "Edward of Lancaster died in fair battle, but at the hands of York. Women can bear a grudge. And she was set to become queen of England in her time. Duchess of Gloucester might seem a comedown after that."

"She'd be a fool not to have you, Richard, queen or no queen. Any woman would be a fool not to have you. She's not worth the having if she refuses you." I banged my knife to emphasize my point.

He grinned at me. "Christ, I'm fond of you, Harry. I wish to God that I'd had you instead of Clarence as a brother. Or maybe just as another brother. The younger brother I never had."

"Sometimes I think of you as the older brother I never had," I admitted, my cheeks burning in the dim light of the tavern.

"Really? Then…"

With a quick, graceful gesture, Richard flicked his knife across my finger, drawing blood, then did the same to his. "Hold it next to mine until they merge. There. *Loyaulte me lie.*"

"*Loyaulte me lie.*"

"We are brothers in blood, Harry. From henceforth we are all to each other. We help each other, support each other, uphold each other in our time of need. If it be necessary, we'll die for each other. Agreed?"

"Agreed."

Having carried out this solemn rite, we continued in a more common and far less solemn rite of brotherhood—drinking far into the evening. With what I know now was my usual poor head for drink, I was thoroughly intoxicated when we left the tavern, and even Richard was somewhat tipsy, as I had never before seen him. On the way to our respective tents, we encountered William Hastings heading toward his tent, accompanied by a busily dressed woman who very clearly was profiting from our stay at Tewkesbury. He nodded at us as we wound toward him, arm in arm. "Your graces. Good night to you."

"Shesh a beauty!" I announced approvingly for all of Tewkesbury to hear. Richard, laughing, clapped me on the back.

Hastings (dismally sober) looked at me and shook his head. "Do you need some assistance getting the Duke of Buckingham to his tent, perchance, your grace?"

"No. I'll have him sleep in mine tonight."

"Blood brothers mush share a bed," I explained. "Like the king and Henry Beaufort."

"Oh," said Hastings. "Then I do believe I'll leave you to it." He beat a very hasty retreat with his light of love.

In Richard's tent, I rolled into his ample camp bed without bothering to undress. The more sober Richard stripped to his shirt and washed his face before climbing into bed next to me and giving me a brotherly embrace. "Good night, brother."

"Good night, brother," I echoed, returning the embrace before the ale carried me off into a deep slumber.

☙

The next day, we set off for the North, where some supporters of King Henry were continuing to make trouble. On the way there, a messenger informed King Edward that Margaret of Anjou, her daughter-in-law Anne Neville, and two of the queen's ladies, the Countess of Devon and Katherine Vaux, had been found in hiding at another abbey. They had submitted to Edward's authority and craved his pardon.

Several days later, the ladies were brought to the king at Coventry. Though Anne and Katherine Vaux had each been made widows at Tewkesbury and the queen had lost her only son there, none had had the opportunity to have mourning clothes made, so they made a rather incongruous sight as they rode up to us under guard, dressed in subdued but still pretty colors and with carefully arranged headdresses—courtesy of the serving women who accompanied them. Their captors hadn't been unkind. Margaret of Anjou had been put in a chariot for security's sake, but the other three rode on the fine horses they'd brought with them from abroad. A wagon behind them carried six coffers of belongings: two for Margaret, two for Anne, and one each for the other ladies.

Margaret of Anjou made no move to leave her open chariot when it pulled up at Coventry. I thought at first it was the arrogance of a woman who had had people dancing attendance on her for years and hadn't adjusted yet to the change in circumstances. Then I realized that it was grief and shock that had rendered her impassive.

Katherine Vaux dismounted and stepped inside the chariot. I could hear her making coaxing noises. Then she emerged with the queen. I'd never seen her that I could recall; for most of my life she had been in exile. Now as she at last turned her face toward my direction I gasped at her beauty, ravaged even as it was by her recent anguish. My sister-in-law Elizabeth Woodville was lovely, but she had nothing of Margaret of Anjou's classical features.

She composed herself enough to sink to her knees in front of the king, her head touching the floor. Moonstruck, I would have loved to have pulled her up and comforted her, but even I had enough sense to realize that this would be a mistake. Edward let her rest in that position for longer than seemed chivalrous. Finally, he said, "Rise, madam. Have you anything to say for yourself?"

Margaret of Anjou began to say something, cleared her throat, and tried again. Finally, in a voice husky with sorrow, she said, "Your grace has a newborn babe. Would you not do anything to protect him, to keep the throne for him? I have done all for love of my own son. In doing so I have acted only as any loving parent in my position would act. But that is all gone. From henceforth I am yours to command. I ask only that you allow me to end my days in peace and dignity and that—"

"Not an only wish, after all, madam? Well. Go on."

"I ask that you extend your protection to the Lady Anne, and to my dear friends the Countess of Devon and Lady Vaux. They have been loyal wives and, in the case of the Lady Anne, a loyal daughter as well. I should be sorry to have them suffer for anyone else's actions, particularly the Lady Anne. She is but fifteen years of age."

She bowed her head again. "Rise," said Edward gruffly. The queen obeyed. "You have been troublesome, madam, but you need not fear for your person or for theirs. You and the countess and Lady Vaux will be taken to London and held in the Tower until suitable living arrangements can be found for you. The Lady Anne will be taken to join her sister, the Duchess of Clarence. My brother the Duke of Clarence shall be her guardian." He narrowed his eyes at the Lady Anne, who had been kneeling beside the queen. "Cousin, forgive a blunt question. Are you with child?"

The Lady Anne, Kingmaker's daughter that she was, narrowed her eyes right back at him. "I believe not. Is that the answer you wished, your grace?"

Beside me, I heard Richard make a half-suppressed whistle of admiration.

The king snapped, "It was." In a kinder tone, he said, "We stop here overnight. My men will find some suitable lodgings for you. In the meantime, perhaps a tent can be made available for you to— Oh, they can have your tent, Richard? Very thoughtful."

He walked away, visibly glad to be free of the female prisoners. It was a much more straightforward matter to deal with men, I supposed. You either executed them or you clapped them in prison; you didn't have to worry about the niceties.

Richard offered Anne his arm to lead her toward his tent. Since no one else was considerate enough to do so, and because I was longing to get closer to her, I took the opportunity to offer my own arm to Margaret of Anjou.

"Thank you. You are a kind young man, er—"

"Harry, Duke of Buckingham, your grace."

She turned her violet eyes on me, and I nearly swooned. "Is it so? Your father and his father were some of the truest friends I ever had. And your Beaufort grandfather and his sons—" I saw her fight back tears. "I fear your family has suffered much for my cause, young Harry."

"It was worth it for a lady such as yourself," I said fervently.

She clucked her tongue at my treasonous remarks, and I sensibly fell silent as I continued escorting her. Our progress was slow: either from grief or from the aftereffects of her journey in the none-too-comfortable cart, she moved like an arthritic old woman. "Harry, tell me something. Do you think I will be allowed to join my husband? He will be grieving sorely for our son."

I caught the word *our*, given just a hint of emphasis. Richard might be right about many things, but he was wrong about one thing: Margaret of Anjou's son was not my grandfather's by-blow, or anyone else's. "I don't know, your grace. I am not in much favor with the king, and cannot guess his temper that well."

She sighed as we reached the tent. "I fear—" She stopped herself and turned to me. "Thank you, Harry. I shall always remember your family in my prayers."

Then she kissed me on the cheek and slipped inside the tent. It was the only conversation I ever had with her.

⁓

With no male Nevilles to rally round and the Earl of Northumberland, Henry Percy, lending his support to King Edward, the rising in the North collapsed without our army ever having to leave Coventry. We cut short our northward journey and headed south, toward London.

Then news arrived that there was trouble in Kent and London from a die-hard known as the Bastard of Fauconberg, who was a nephew of Warwick. Having been denied admission to the city, he was attacking it. The mayor and aldermen of London wrote a frantic letter to the king, informing him that his queen and his children in the Tower stood in the gravest jeopardy. Edward sent an advance guard of fifteen hundred men to hasten to the city and began to hurry there himself. He could not get to London fast enough, as far as I was concerned. What might happen to a pretty young girl like Kate if those vengeful brutes penetrated the Tower?

My fears proved to be for naught, however, for good tidings soon arrived: the Londoners, led by the Earl of Essex and Anthony Woodville and encouraged by a thoroughly Yorkist mayor, had repelled Fauconberg, leaving us a quiet city to enter in all due magnificence on the twenty-first of May. I'd been restored to sufficient favor to ride with the other dukes: Gloucester, Clarence, Norfolk, and Suffolk. Much farther back in the grand procession was Margaret of Anjou, in the same open chariot she'd been in before. She sat upright between the Countess of Devon and Katherine Vaux, looking straight ahead and ignoring the stares and the occasional taunts of the crowd.

Kate, her face aglow, threw herself into my arms when the procession was over and we were all reunited at the Tower, having first attended a service of thanksgiving at St. Paul's. "Anthony was a hero!" she informed us after at last releasing me from her grip. She turned to her brother, who stood there with his usual kindly but abstracted look. "You were!"

"Many did their part, Kate. The Earl of Essex, Sir Ralph Josselyn, the citizens of London—"

"But Anthony did most of all," Kate insisted. She began telling us what we had heard already from messengers, but no one had the heart to stop her. "That Fauconberg man attacked London! It was a week ago today. His men tried to burn down the houses on the bridge, and they were attacking the city gates as well. It was worst at Aldgate, but the mayor and the sheriffs pushed them back to St. Botolph's. And then Anthony came from the postern gate here and began to fight them, with arrows and hand to hand." Kate was bouncing around now, happily slaying imaginary Lancastrians with her sword arm. "Finally the whoresons—oh, I beg pardon, Fauconberg's men—started to retreat. Anthony chased them to Mile End, and then to Stratford. He crushed them!"

"We are well proud of him and the rest," agreed the king, finally getting a word in edgewise. "And that includes you, Kate, for being brave."

Kate beamed as the conversation turned to other topics. As the king began a conversation with his queen and the rest of began our own private conversations, she said, "You look more manly somehow, Harry. Older, too."

"Well, I have aged a month," I said dashingly, but I thought as I looked in a glass in my chamber at the Tower that night that I was more manly. I'd fought in two battles, stood up to the king, acquired a blood brother, and been kissed by a queen, all in a matter of weeks. Perhaps fifteen wasn't such an awkward age after all, I thought that night before falling into a sound sleep, having first prayed for the souls of my uncle Edmund Beaufort and all of my other dead relations.

The next morning, I woke to a pounding at my door and the shrieks of my wife. Had the Bastard of Fauconberg resumed the fight? Beating my page to the door, I sprang up and undid the latch, heedless of the fact that I was clad only in my shirt.

Kate did not even notice. "He's dead, Harry! Dead!"

"Who?"

"That dear sweet man, King Henry. They found him dead in his chamber here late last night." She wiped her eyes. "I saw him once or twice, when he was taking some fresh air. He always smiled at me, and I always smiled back. Once I gave him some flowers I picked from the garden, and he thanked me so very kindly. What harm was there in it, after all, if it brightened his life a little?"

"What did he die of?" I asked, knowing full well the answer as I saw Margaret of Anjou in my mind's eye, saying, "I fear—"

"Some say his heart was broken when he heard of the death of his son. But—" Kate swallowed. "But others say he was helped to his death, and I—I think so, too. I know my history, Harry."

So did I.

October 1471

W ITH EDWARD BACK SECURELY ON THE THRONE, LIFE BEGAN TO
return to normal—much to my disgust. I was restored to my royal
guardians and resumed my old routine of studies, waiting on my elders at
table, and knightly training, as if I'd never seen a battle.

I complained about this vigorously and often to Richard, when I saw
him. This wasn't frequently, for he had more responsibilities now and
was often up north, having been granted Warwick's castles of Middleham,
Sheriff Hutton, and Penrith and many of the offices he had held as well.
Richard wasn't terribly sympathetic, however, as he had problems of his
own: George wanted all of the Warwick estates.

Warwick's countess had taken sanctuary at Beaulieu Abbey upon landing
in England and learning that her husband had died that same day at Barnet.
She was an heiress in her own right, to the Beauchamps and the Despensers,
and should have been allowed to keep those lands after Warwick's death,
along with jointure and dower, but no one except the countess herself
was concerned much about her claims, even though she was passing her
days at Beaulieu writing every woman of any importance in the kingdom
about her rights. Kate got one such letter; even the king's eldest daughter,
Elizabeth, was the puzzled recipient of one. The letters probably made the
countess's dreary days in sanctuary go more quickly, but they otherwise
served no purpose. The only question in anyone's mind was whether the
Duke of Clarence, by dint of being married to Isabel, would get the entire
Warwick inheritance, or whether Anne would get a share. And Richard,

having made it clear that he wanted to marry Anne, was determined that he and Anne got a share.

The summer had come and gone without this quarrel being resolved when I heard sad news: my uncle Henry Stafford had died on October 4, just a month after my sixteenth birthday. I was not surprised, for he had never been of the strongest health and had suffered deeply from the effects of his wounds at Barnet. It was a dismal time for his widow, my aunt Margaret. Even after Tewkesbury, her brother-in-law Jasper Tudor had stubbornly continued to resist Edward, but he had at last given up the fight and fled to Brittany with Margaret's son Henry. First, however, Jasper Tudor had executed a Welshman, Roger Vaughan, who had been sent by Edward to capture him and who had evidently had a hand in the execution of Jasper's father years before. I add this only because Roger Vaughan's death was to have unexpected consequences much, much later; at the time, Roger Vaughan's fate meant nothing to me. I only felt sorry for my aunt Margaret, a widow whose only child was an exile.

Then the king summoned me to his chamber. Our relationship had been polite since the day he ordered my uncle's execution, but rather stiff, which in all fairness was more my fault than the king's, for he had been kindly enough disposed to me now that my Lancastrian relations were safely dead and buried. He'd even allowed me to spend a few days visiting my mother.

Upon my entry, I bowed deeply, knowing full well that it irritated Edward, who with family was inclined to be far less formal. "Your grace," I said in my best courtier's manner.

"We were sorry to hear of your uncle Henry Stafford's death, Harry."

"Thank you."

"You are sixteen. Time, perhaps, for you to have a bit more freedom. Certain of his lands reverted to you, as your grandfather's heir, upon his death. It is our intention to let you enter upon them."

I stared, too stunned by this good news to keep up my formality. "Really?"

The king shot me an amused glance. "Really. Mind you, these things take time to settle, so don't pack your belongings tonight. And lest you be wondering, you are still a ward of the crown. Your grandfather's estates will remain in our hands until a more suitable time."

"And my Bohun lands?" I ventured.

Edward's face changed. "*Your* Bohun lands?"

"The Stafford properties that came into the crown's hands with the marriage of my ancestor Mary de Bohun to the fourth Henry. With the sixth Henry now deceased and without heirs—"

"We are quite aware of the origin of the claim, Harry. Whether it is as strong as you seem to believe is another matter entirely. It is not an issue we are disposed to decide today, if ever."

"Yes, your grace."

"Who has been speaking of those lands to you, anyway?" He frowned. "Your mother?"

"No, your grace," I said truthfully. My mother, in her grief at losing the last two of her brothers, hardly cared about her own chamber at the convent, much less the Bohun lands. It was Aunt Margaret who had reminded me of my claim to them. "It is common family knowledge."

"Hmph," said Edward. "Well, you may be excused now."

෴

When Richard came back to court from the North a few days later, I lost no time in acquainting him with my good fortune. "I shall have land of my own now! Of course, I was sorry about my uncle Henry," I added piously, though I confess I hadn't given my poor uncle, of whom I had been fond, a second thought since Edward gave me the news. "I also mentioned the Bohun inheritance to him. You know about that? It was probably premature to raise the subject, but I think now that at least it's been broached, he might—"

"For God's sake, Harry! Stop yammering about your lands. You'll be rich soon enough, if you don't goad someone into stabbing you out of sheer boredom first."

"Richard? I—"

"Anne's missing."

"Missing?"

"He echoes, too," Richard told the wall.

"Ech— Richard, I beg your pardon. I just don't understand. Wasn't she staying with George?"

"Supposedly." Richard took a turn around the room, then took a deep breath. Having composed himself, he said, "Edward gave me permission to ask for her hand in marriage. I've not raised the topic in so many words with her, because it seems from what she's let drop that she did have some regard for that bastard whelp of Margaret's who was her first husband." I started to protest Margaret of Anjou's virtue and thought better of it. "Don't worry, I've not called him that to her face. But she's an intelligent wench, more so than most, and I think she realizes that I'm the best match for her. She doesn't want to see George get all of the Warwick lands any more than I do.

"So when I arrived in London today, I stopped by George's place. I'd brought some gifts from the North; Anne rather prefers it up there, I gather. I figured it was about time to start making my intentions more clear. But when I asked to see her, as I've done before, I was told that she was no longer living there. No one would tell me where she'd gone. The worst of it is, I'm not sure if anyone there could tell me. I tried bribery, threats—everything. All I got was the same reply. The Lady Anne was not staying there, and where she had gone they did not know and could not venture to say."

"George wouldn't tell you?"

"I wasn't admitted to his presence. That alone tells me he has something to hide."

"Jesus," I whispered. "Do you suspect—" I could not bear to finish the sentence.

Richard shook his head. "I don't believe he's murdered her, if that's what you mean. He's genuinely fond of Isabel; he'd not harm her sister.

What I do believe is that he's poisoned her mind against me somehow, or convinced her that she'd be best off taking the veil. That's what worries me most, actually. She's stubborn; if she determines on a course of action, she'll stick to it."

I thought of the times at court I'd seen Isabel and Anne, during that almost comical period when Edward and Warwick were trying to pretend all was well. The Warwick girls were pretty, with finery befitting their father's wealth that they plainly enjoyed showing off. I couldn't imagine either of these heiresses settling for a nun's habit. Richard must have read my skepticism, for he said, "Don't underestimate George's smooth tongue when he cares to exercise it. And remember, Anne doesn't know me that well. She was off in someone else's household most of the time that I stayed in Warwick's. George can tell her every sin I've committed, real or imagined, and she might just believe him."

"We have to find what's become of her, then."

"We?"

"We are blood brothers, are we not?"

"Harry, there was a great deal of ale as well as blood between us that night." I must have looked shattered, for Richard hastened to add, "Well, yes, we are. But how can you help? You're not a confidante of George. And"—Richard hesitated—"frankly, Harry, you can run off at the mouth sometimes. I'd prefer to keep the inquiries discreet."

"I see." I stood. "Well, then you must excuse me. I'm off to my nursery."

"Harry!" But I was long gone.

⁂

When my anger cooled, I realized that Richard was quite right. I did let my tongue run away with me sometimes, as I had at Tewkesbury and about the Bohun inheritance. I still had much to learn about the world, I began to realize. All the more reason, I decided, that I should prove my worth to Richard by finding Anne. But how?

George and I were on civil terms, and could chat idly on the few occasions when we were thrown in each other's company at court, but I didn't like him. I'd not liked him since that day he'd so triumphantly announced the death of my grandfather, a man worth a dozen of the Duke of Clarence. Even making allowances for George's youth at the time, I couldn't like him.

I doubted, however, whether he thought enough about the matter to like or to dislike me. Six years younger than he, I was probably quite insignificant in his eyes. And did he know that I was good friends with Richard? I had no idea. I tended to think not, though he had to know we talked together. But that in itself meant nothing. After all, we were all cousins, all dukes, and all (more or less) on Edward's side. There was no reason why we shouldn't talk together. No reason, either, why I shouldn't pay a visit to my cousin the Duke of Clarence—except that I never had. Would it not look strange if I did now? I needed an excuse.

Then, that same evening at supper at court, two men got into a brawl, one that was quickly broken up but which left both men with impressive-looking bruises. As I watched them being hauled away to cool their tempers in a cell for the evening, I suddenly had my inspiration. Now I just needed to put my plan into action.

✍

"The Duke of Buckingham, your grace."

George stared at me as I limped into his chamber, clothes torn and dirty, leaning on my page. "Harry? What the hell happened to you?"

I stared shamefacedly at the floor. "A brawl," I muttered.

"Well, I hope you didn't get the worst of it."

"I did." I hoped my page, still supporting me, was keeping a straight face. At my command, it was he who had roughed me up an hour or so before, and he had set about his duties with more enthusiasm than seemed quite proper. In his zeal, he'd knocked me rather hard on the cheek, which ached intensely. "Your grace, I was hoping you would do me a favor."

"Not avenge you, if that's what you're thinking," George said affably.

"No. It's just—well, you know how it is at court. Everyone knows everyone else's business. If I came back there as I look now, I'd be the talk of the place, and that would be humiliating. Since, as you say, I got the worst of it. And besides—"

"Out with it, Harry."

"The king keeps us wards under close watch, as you've probably heard. And—well, I would hate for him to know what happened. If he found out, I'd probably never be allowed out on my own until I was one-and-twenty." That was no lie; the king did guard us closely. "I was hoping that I could wait here and clean up while my page went and fetched me some fresh clothes. Then when I come back, nothing will look so amiss, and if the king asks where I was, I can say I was with you. He can't object to that."

"Ah, but what about your cheek, Harry? Quite a bruise you have coming up there." He tapped it hard, and I winced.

"I tripped in the dark."

"Clever boy." Clarence showed me a set of dazzlingly white teeth. "All right, you can stop here for a while. But tell me. What was a pretty lad like you brawling about? Because I just can't picture it."

I gave the floor another piercing gaze. "A woman," I admitted.

"A woman! And you a married man, Harry!" Clarence snorted. "Don't tell me you're on the way to siring a bastard too, like my upstanding brother Richard." He rang for a servant. "Wine, man!" Then he snorted again. "Not one bastard, mind you, but another on the way! And the hypocrite turns his fastidious little nose up at Ned's escapades."

Richard had another bastard on the way? It was the first I'd heard of it. Remembering that Clarence himself had a reputation as a faithful husband, I hastened to give my own disapproving snort at Richard's hypocrisy.

"So, what's her name?"

"Er—Molly." I hoped George didn't ask for more intimate details, for I'd yet to lose my virginity, except in my imagination. "She has black hair and green eyes. A real beauty. With lovely breasts," I added for good measure. (There was no reason to stint myself, surely.)

"Best keep her far away, Harry. Ned won't like to hear of you keeping company with the likes of Molly when you've got your pretty Kate waiting for you. Now, that's a beauty, Woodville or no. If I were you, she'd have been in my bed by now."

"She's still very young," I said in my most urbane manner as the servant brought our wine. Here, I knew, was where the hardest part of the evening lay.

George could drink prodigiously. He wasn't a habitual drunkard by any means, though his drinking would get worse (and sloppier) later. Most of the time he drank in moderation. But when he chose to, he could drink vast quantities of wine, and he would be drinking long after the last of his companions was in a stupor on the hearth. Richard had witnessed these episodes two or three times and had told me that George scarcely seemed drunk, except for his speech being much less guarded. I could only hope that this would be a drinking night, and that I would be able to keep my faculties intact sufficiently to lead him onto the subject of Anne.

It didn't work out that way.

George liked sweet malmsey wine, so that was what we drank that night; to this day, the thought of the stuff makes me queasy. I didn't try to keep up with him; that surely would have killed me. He drank twice as much as I did, and never showed it.

Nor did he talk of Anne. We talked about every subject under the sun—he turned out to be able to discourse well on almost any topic—and I think we even recited the prologue to *The Canterbury Tales* together at one point, for reasons that mercifully escape me now. We talked of Isabel; we talked of the Countess of Warwick; we talked of Margaret of Anjou; we talked of my wife; we talked of Cleopatra, even—but no Anne.

Finally, the wine having overcome my discretion, I hazarded, "How is the Lady Anne? Is she grieving the loss of her husband?"

"She is well."

"I thought I might pay my respects to her—and your lady wife—before I left." By this point in the evening I could manage this longish sentence, and the ones before it, only by speaking very slowly. I hiccupped once, then twice for good measure.

George chuckled. "I don't think either lady would welcome seeing you at present, Harry."

"But I truly hoped to see them. They're so"—I searched vainly for a gallant remark but could not find one in the mists fogging up my brain— "pretty. Couldn't I at least see Anne and just gaze upon her?"

Clarence's smile faded and he put down his wine cup. "You want to see Anne," he said. "Well, she's not here to see. Why, you're not surprised to hear that, are you? You little snake! Richard sent you, did he not?"

"No! I came myself." The wine was beginning to make me queasy. "But not to spy…" I felt myself slumping to my left.

George yanked me up. He was a tall man, not quite as tall as the king but still impressive, and I thought he might try to kill me. He certainly could have without much effort, especially in my condition. Perhaps it was the very lack of challenge I presented that dissuaded him, for he stared in my face for a moment or two, then grinned and released me. "Well, since you took the trouble to come here, I'll tell you what my man told Richard. I don't know where the lass is. And I'll do you one better for your pains by telling you this: I don't care a damn." He shoved me into the arms of my page. "Take your idiot master home, boy. Use the river landing if you please. He looks green. Don't let him puke on those fresh clothes you dressed him in; it's a sad waste of fine fabric."

We were making our way to the landing, my feet growing more unsteady with each step I took, when the servant who had been given the task of seeing us out—one who had been in and out of Clarence's chamber earlier in the evening, and who I realized later had been paying unusually close attention to our conversation—whispered, "Your grace? If you are indeed a friend of the Lady Anne, I have tidings for her of you."

"I am," I said faintly.

"She is in the habit of a cook maid, at a tavern in Fleet Street."

"*What?*"

"It is true, your grace. There's no time to explain; I must be back." He handed a slip of paper to me, then thought better of it and gave it to my page. "Here is the address."

Late as it was when our waterman finally deposited us at Westminster—more or less hauling me out of the boat by my collar—I insisted on being brought to Richard's chambers, with a vociferousness that carried the day against the common sense of my page. Richard's servants would have kept me out, but I protested so vigorously, and so loudly, that I at last heard Richard say wearily, "Let him in. God know what he wants, but it had better be good."

"It ish!" I promised as my page supported me into Richard's bedchamber.

Richard stared at me. "Harry?"

"I've found her! Anne! She's in a cook shop! In Fleet Street." I held out my hand with a flourish, having forgotten that it was my servant who had the precious paper. "Address!"

"Harry, you're drunk."

"That's where she *ish*!"

Richard sighed. "Harry, how did you come by this er—information?"

"Clarence's man." Wobbling out of range of my page's grasp, I teetered dangerously to one side, then to another, and caught hold of a bedpost after only one or two misses. "Visited his house. We drank together," I added in a confidential tone.

"Well, I can believe that much."

"It's the truth, Ricshard. She's a kitchen maid! In Street Fleet!" To better demonstrate my credibility (clearly my words were not doing the job), I let go of my friendly bedpost to wave my hand in emphasis. Somehow I ended up in an undignified heap on the floor. "I wist you would believe me," I said lugubriously from my new station.

"Shall I take him to his chamber, your grace?" my page asked as I tried to remember how to rise to my feet. It was a question that suddenly required a lot of thought.

"No. He's too far gone; you'd probably have to drag him. I'll keep him here with me. You go and explain that he took slightly ill and he's staying here overnight. God knows, he will be ill, so there's no lie there." Richard helped me to my feet as my page scurried off. "Easy now, Harry. Let's get you undressed and into bed."

"Cook shop," I repeated with a drunkard's stubbornness. "Anne."

"All right, Harry. If you say so. I'll check in the morning."

I pointed in what I thought was the direction of my page and touched my own nose, which I couldn't have managed otherwise. Staring at my finger in surprise for a moment, I finally added, "Has address."

Shaking his head, Richard propped me against the bed and began undressing me. Whether it was the strangely erotic sensation of being undressed by hands other than my page's, or whether it was my complete and utter intoxication, or whether there was some longing in me that I had never dared to acknowledge, or all three, I do not know, but when Richard had stripped me of my clothes and more or less pushed me into his bed, I put out my hands and drew his face to mine, then kissed him full on the lips, with a passionate abandon of which I would not have guessed myself capable at age sixteen. "I love you," I whispered.

To Richard's everlasting credit, he did not slam me across the face or laugh. He pulled away from my grasp and pushed my hands down upon my chest, gently. "You're very drunk, Harry," he said quietly. "I'd best sleep elsewhere tonight, I think."

"No. Stay."

"Go to sleep, Harry. I'll wait here while you do."

Had he done the unthinkable and acted upon my kiss, I hardly know how I could have managed to play my part; I am not sure I even knew exactly what that would entail. Too inebriated to form further words of protest, I closed my eyes and did not open them until late in the morning, when my page obligingly held back my hair as I retched into the basin he had wisely provided for me. Twice I repeated this inglorious act before falling into a deep sleep, from which I did not awake until late in the afternoon. My head was pounding, half from the effects of drink, half from the awful memories of my behavior with Richard. Hoping that some time the previous evening I might have caught some plague that would carry me off without delay and with a minimum of fuss, I buried my face in the pillow and turned against the wall.

Then I heard Richard's voice and felt him shake my shoulder. "Awake, old man?" I whimpered some sort of answer. "Good! You were right! I have found her."

"Did you doubt me?" I asked miserably, still with my back to him.

"Of course. Addled as your brain was last night, your own mother would have doubted you. Your own confessor! But you told me true. *In vino veritas*, eh? I've brought Anne out and taken her to sanctuary. St. Martin's. They've pleasant quarters for a lady. She'll stay there until she and I marry."

"Did you find her well?" I asked, less out of concern than a desire to forestall the moment when we would come to my unspeakable act the night before. Painfully, I rolled over to look at Richard.

"Yes. She's Warwick's daughter, all right; she was telling them how to run the kitchen! What a manager! They won't be sorry to see her go, I'm sure. I will make good use of her talents on my own estates. Damn George had her convinced I'd personally slain her husband as he was fleeing so that I could get her estates, instead of him dying in fair battle."

"But why was she in the cook shop?" I asked foggily.

"It's owned by a family that's connected with one of George's servants. George and he arranged for Anne to board there until George could quietly move her to one of his estates to escape my wicked clutches while Anne pondered whether she wanted to take the veil." He saw my puzzled look. "I know, it's somewhat lacking as a plan, isn't it? Did George really think everyone would just forget about the girl after a couple of months? Even Anne admitted that it had its shortcomings. But she said she couldn't stand to marry the man who'd killed her husband in cold blood. Fortunately, we got that straightened out. I told her I had witnesses—and I do—to prove that I did no such thing and that Clarence was not exactly a disinterested party. Wenches! You never know what they are going to get into their heads, even the intelligent ones." He chuckled and then looked at me sympathetically. "Speaking of heads, how's yours, Harry?"

"It would be kind of you if you chopped it off."

"You'll feel better by tomorrow. Sooner if you're lucky. But what possessed you to drink with George? And why is your cheek bruised?" He touched it gently. "Did he assault you?"

I longed to prove myself to you. To serve you, I almost said. I shrugged. "No, he didn't assault me. It's a long story. I just wanted to help you find her, that's all."

"Well, you did that, even though I told you not to, and I'm grateful. But don't try to keep up with George again, old man, whatever you do."

"I won't." I started the painful process of getting out of bed, then remembered my state of undress and decided to stay put. "Where's my page?"

"I sent him out for a while. There's something I wanted to talk about."

"Richard, I—"

Richard looked out the window. "You've not been with a woman yet, have you, Harry?"

"No. Kate's too young to risk getting with child just yet."

"I wasn't thinking of your wife. Do you remember I promised to take you to some houses I knew when you turned sixteen?"

"Yes."

"Well, it's time, I think. Your wife will need a man with some experience when the day comes. You're sixteen, right?"

"I just had my birthday in September," I said, a little hurt that Richard had not remembered the date.

"Well, then, you need to go to Southwark with me. I'd say tonight, but I think you'll have more enjoyment if you wait until tomorrow. The wares there are best sampled with a clear head. Anyway, I need to stop by and see how Anne's faring."

"All right. Tomorrow."

"Good. I'll call in your page for you." He turned away from the window and smiled at me. "Thank you again for helping me find Anne. I won't forget it."

∽

I will leave the details of my visit to Southwark to the imagination, as my experience was probably no different than that of any other youth my age. Richard, much amused by the story of my visit to George that I told him when I was feeling more myself, made a great point of trying to find a whore named Molly, but the only Molly we found in the fine establishment Richard patronized was a rather tall, large lady whose Amazonian presence might have intimidated even the king or William Hastings, never mind a novice like myself. Instead, we settled on Sally, a comely lass of around twenty who appeared to specialize in initiating nervous young gentlemen.

I enjoyed myself with Sally. I even returned to see her from time to time, though not perhaps as much as another youth my age might have done, for I soon discovered in myself a certain fastidiousness that shrank from enjoying women who had been palmed by so many others. It was much sweeter to think of chaste Kate, who would be all mine and no other man's when the time came. There was something else, too, that I might well admit now that I never could admit then: that the odd feeling that Richard—and no other man but Richard—had stirred in me never quite left.

I suppose, at this point, it never will.

xii

Kate: May 1472 to January 1473

With Harry waiting impatiently to enter onto his late uncle's estates—there had been a delay in proving the will that delayed the assignment of the lands—I itched to be away from my sister's household and to be the mistress of my own establishment. I knew how to run a household—in theory, at least. I could dance gracefully, sing, play the lute, and embroider. I could make gracious small talk for hours on end in English, if called upon, and I could do the same in French—much better than many others, thanks to Mama. I knew the uses of various herbs, and I could dress a wound if need be. At fourteen, in short, I knew all I could possibly know, and I was eager to demonstrate this once and for all.

My longing increased when Mama died in May 1472. She had been ailing quietly for some time, so her death was not a surprise, though we all mourned her deeply. I prayed for her several times a day, liking to think that she would soon be out of Purgatory and reunited with my father and John, who surely had not tarried long there before landing duly in Paradise. But her death made me even more acutely aware that my childhood had drawn to a close, and that it was time to leave childish things far behind.

There was something else: I wanted to share a bed with Harry.

The bawdiness of my brother-in-law's court has been greatly exaggerated. It was true that Edward had mistresses—sometimes more than one at any given time, especially if Bessie was in the late stages of pregnancy and was unavailable to him. But he conducted his amours discreetly; his mistresses were not seen at court, and he would not have welcomed them there to mingle with Bessie and his daughters. We in the queen's household were expected to behave with propriety, and even the boys at court, as Harry had often complained, were kept on rather a short leash. It was, in short, a decorous place for young people. Yet I had become well aware of what went on between men and women, and I wanted nothing more than to have it happen between me and my husband. Not being a wanton, I thought of the act with no other man; my daydreams and my night dreams were all of Harry.

Harry and I had married so young and so long ago, the details as to when we were to consummate our relationship had been left very vague, all depending, I gathered, on how soon I physically matured. The word "fifteen" had been mentioned now and then, but when I considered the matter one evening as Cecilia was undressing me, I looked at my full hips and breasts and decided that this was a purely arbitrary figure and that fourteen was just as good. How much difference, after all, would a few months make? This, I decided, would surely be Mama's sensible position on the question if she were alive.

I had high hopes that summer of 1472, for there were two family weddings at that time. The first nuptials, in June, were of Harry's aunt Margaret Beaufort to Thomas Stanley, the king's steward. As she was nearly thirty and he nearly forty, and she had been married twice before and he once before, with a large brood of children to show for it, it was not a terribly romantic wedding, but I hoped against hope that it might give Harry ideas. It did not, a circumstance for which I blamed Margaret Beaufort. Though her wedding dress was obviously expensive, it struck me as old-fashioned, and indeed, the bride looked rather prim and grim throughout the whole proceeding. I suspect that she found Stanley tolerable enough but would have preferred to live the pious life of a wealthy widow had she not thought that this marriage might somehow serve her young, exiled son.

The next wedding, between the Duke of Gloucester and Anne Neville, which took place just weeks later, was more promising, especially as the bride was only a couple of years older than myself. Accordingly, I dressed myself as alluringly for the festivities as I could, even coaxing Cecilia to dab a tiny bit of rouge on my cheeks and to let me wear a tad more scent than usual.

I felt quite confident when we were finished. Poor, sweet John had been overly kind in his prediction that I would match my sister in looks, but I knew I was by no means unattractive. My scattered freckles were so small that only a man kissing me could notice them, and then wouldn't he have his eyes shut anyway? My hair was sandy, but indisputably on the safe side of blond, my eyes were bright and blue, and my features were regular. I had wide, red lips, covering white teeth. My bosom, though not magnificent, was more than adequate. I was neither too thin nor too wide, and although I was on the short side, there was no harm in that, as it would have been a dreadful thing had I towered over Harry. Any false modesty I might have possessed had been destroyed some time ago by Lord Hastings, a known connoisseur of women who had often cast his approving eye in my direction as of late. I knew that his admiration was harmless, as he was not the sort of man to toy with a married lady who was also the queen's sister, and I took some comfort in his appreciative glances.

The Gloucester wedding was a stately one though not an elaborate one, the newlyweds having wished to get it over with quickly so that Richard could attend to his affairs in the North, in which he was greatly interested. The bride's mother did not attend, being still in sanctuary in Beaulieu Abbey, but the Duchess of York made one of her rare appearances, along with the Duchess of Exeter (minus her imprisoned Lancastrian husband) and the Duchess of Suffolk (with her faithfully Yorkist husband). Anne's sister, the Duchess of Clarence, was there too, of course, as was the Duke of Clarence, who played his role in the proceedings with a martyred air, it having been his hope, Harry said, that Anne would take the veil and that he would get all of the Warwick lands for himself.

Harry was an especially honored guest at the wedding. Evidently he had done Richard some service in finding Anne, who had been hidden away by George for a time, and this was confirmed when I noticed that George reserved some of his most sullen looks for my husband. But with the king himself at the wedding, along with the queen and a couple of the older royal daughters, he could do no more than sulk and glare.

By the end of the evening, I was sulking and glaring nearly as much as George. Harry paid my finery no attention whatsoever. We danced together, once or twice, but we might have been sister and brother as we moved together palm to palm. His only concession to our married state was to escort me to my chamber, where he gave me the most formal of good-night kisses and left. With him gone, I relieved my frustration in the only way I knew how: by dashing an expensive container of scent across the room.

Cecilia, who fortunately had been out of harm's way, stared. "Good Lord, girl, what is the matter?"

"I shall never be Harry's true wife! All of this was for naught." I yanked at a hand cloth and began removing my spot of rouge. "I might as well be old and dried up. He'll never lie with me."

"Child, you are still very young."

"But I'm ready now! And I'm not getting any younger. Why, I'm fourteen, for heaven's sake!"

Cecilia repressed a smile. "Oh, I think it'll be a while before you're past your prime, my lady. And Harry is young too, you must remember. Not all men are like the king, you know, who they say was seducing ladies when he was younger than you. Some men start later."

"The Duke of Gloucester has two bastards already, and he's but nineteen."

"Aye? You want Harry to sire some bastards, then?"

"No, of course not." I scowled at Cecilia. "I want him to sire children on me, and don't tell me I'm too young. The Countess of Richmond, that Margaret Beaufort—"

"Had a child when she was barely thirteen, and it almost killed her. Her husband should have waited."

"I'm more developed than she ever was." I pouted as Cecilia, having removed my hennin, began to pull pins out of my hair until it finally fell around my waist. Thick and slightly curling, it was a fine sight for a man's eyes, I privately thought, one that I wondered if Harry would never see. "Cecilia, do you think he could be what they call a—a sodomite?" The very word made me blanch.

"No, child. I think you just need to give him time. When the hour is right, he will come to you."

"If I'm not dead by then," I groused. "And buried."

❦

At Windsor Castle that autumn, the court gathered to welcome Louis of Gruuthuse, who had sheltered the king during much of his exile. In gratitude, the king had planned a round of festivities, which would culminate in Louis being made the Earl of Winchester.

As we women waited for Louis to be brought to meet the queen in her chambers, the Duchess of Exeter and I played at ninepins. It is a game for which I have always had a gift, and I was trouncing my opponent handily.

The duchess didn't seem to mind, for she was much preoccupied by other matters. "Ned has finally agreed to help me get my annulment," she announced as a servant set up my pins again. "Soon, the Lord willing, I shall be shed of that man."

I nodded sympathetically, though I secretly felt a little pity for the Duke of Exeter. A servant of his had found him stripped of his armor, lying half dead on the field at Barnet. The man had taken his master to a surgeon, then smuggled him into sanctuary at Westminster, but the king had removed him from there and confined him in the Tower, where he was said to live a comfortable but very dull existence.

The duchess read my mind. "If he'd switched his allegiance to the House of York like any sensible person, now he'd be in a world of difference, wouldn't he?" Her ball sailed past the patiently waiting ninepins, and I shook my head in disbelief. Little Bess, my niece, could do better than that. "But no. He had to stay true to Lancaster. All well and good, his loyalty, but there comes a time when it becomes stupidity. Though I'm not sure York would have had him anyway. The man could quarrel with a tree."

My ball slammed into the pins, producing a gratifying sound of crashing ivory as I tried to think of a suitable reply. It was a sign of my maturing appearance, I supposed, that the duchess was bothering to speak to me of such adult matters. I finally managed, "Shall you remarry, my lady?"

This was a much less innocent question than it might appear, and actually almost an impertinent one, it being common knowledge that the duchess had long had a lover, Thomas St. Leger. He was only a knight in the king's household, though—hardly a suitable husband for a king's sister. Belatedly, I hoped the duchess did not take offense. Anne, however, merely smiled archly. "The king has promised I may marry as I wish, provided it is to a man who has been loyal to him, and my choice shall produce no worries on that score." She rolled her ball again and gasped as it grazed two pins, knocking both down. "Now, will you look at that! How about you, my dear? My old charge, your husband, has just turned seventeen, if I recall correctly. Are plans being made for you to live with him?"

"I wish!"

"Aye?" The duchess glanced at me appraisingly. "Have you bedded with him yet? You look of a condition to do so."

"I certainly am. But I have not," I added mournfully.

"I suppose the queen won't allow it until you're older."

"She has not forbidden it. Neither has the king."

"I see."

"It is Harry," I confessed, lowering my voice, though it was hardly necessary in the noise of the room. The queen and some of her ladies were playing at tables, and another group was dancing to a lively tune. "I have encouraged him in every way possible, but nothing happens. I contrive to stand in dark corners with him, perfume myself, dress my best—and nothing! Is it something in me, do you think? Is my breath sour?" I exhaled for the duchess's benefit.

"No, not at all."

"Then what is it, do you think?"

"You are hardly speaking to an authority on the subject of marriage, child. The Duke of Exeter and I bedded together just long enough for him to sire my girl, and no more. It was not until later that I realized that the act need not be unpleasant—but I speak too frankly. My husband and I did not suit, plain and simple, in or out of bed. Yours is a different situation, I think. Shyness, maybe. Harry never was a very forward lad when he was living in my household, at least around women. He is fond of you, isn't he?"

"Like a sister," I grumbled. I stared at the ninepins thoughtfully. "But he does treat me like a wife in one way at least. He doesn't like it when men flirt with me. He got angry back when that Jasper Tudor did, or at least Harry said he did. I think he was just being pleasant."

"Then perhaps what he needs is a reminder that you are not his sister."

The door to Bessie's chamber swung open and the king, unannounced, strode inside, followed by Louis of Gruuthuse and a crowd of courtiers, including Harry. "Is not this a splendid sight?" Edward shouted to his guest over the din. "The fairest ladies of England at their play."

"There can be none more pleasant."

I puffed out my chest and hoped that Harry found it a pleasant sight, too.

⁂

Six-year-old Bess, the king's eldest daughter, had been dressed in her prettiest clothes for Louis of Gruuthuse's visit, and her dancing master had been just as hard at work as her tailor. The evening before, after Louis arrived at the queen's chamber, she had danced with her tall father, to the delight of all of the onlookers. Tonight Harry partnered her. Being much shorter than the king—as most men were—Harry was rather better suited for her. He was a good partner, leading little Bess around gracefully and amending his pace to hers.

The king, never one to sit and watch others dance, led my brother Anthony's wife to the area that had been cleared for the dance, and soon others were following suit.

"May I?"

"Why, of course, Lord Hastings," I said.

From the moment Lord Hastings led me out to dance, I knew something was very odd. He never directed any of his remarks to my face, but to my bosom, which I admit was as much in evidence as it could be without going beyond the pale of respectability. He touched me much more often than was necessary to the dance, and his hands lingered where they had brushed. I was utterly baffled, for Lord Hastings, though his glance might linger on a woman, was never other than perfectly correct in his outward conduct.

The Duchess of Exeter, partnered by the discreet Thomas St. Leger, brushed against me heavily. When I glanced over, irritated at her clumsiness, she gave me a wink. Light dawned.

Never in my life have I entered into a conspiracy so gladly as I did on that day—with one notable, later exception. I bestowed my best smiles upon Lord Hastings. I threw my shoulders back so that my bosom was even more prominent. I made arch conversation and laughed.

And all the while, Harry danced studiously with the Lady Elizabeth.

William Hastings shook his head as I looked over to Harry to see some sign of a reaction. "It's not working, is it?"

"No," I muttered.

"Then perhaps, my lady, more drastic measures are called for." And with that, Lord Hastings gave my rear a mighty pinch.

"Lord Hastings!" I squawked. I slapped him across the face as hard as I could. "How dare you!"

I had not even had a chance to pull my hand back when Harry was at my side, eyes ablaze. "What mean you by this? Did you take liberties with my wife, you blackguard?"

Lord Hastings was the soul of contrite sheepishness. "My lord, I know not what came over me. Forgive me, your grace. And especially you, my lady." He bowed and reached for my hand, but before he could bring it to his lips, Harry was dragging me out of the room and to my chamber.

"Out!" he yelled to Cecilia, who lost no time in obeying. He shoved me onto a stool. "What were you doing to lead that creature on?"

"Nothing," I said sullenly. "I was merely enjoying the dance and the company." The Duchess of Exeter's and Lord Hastings's plan, if it could be dignified as such, plainly had not worked.

"Hastings doesn't usually do that sort of thing uninvited. You must have done something." He eyed me coldly. "You dress too provocatively, I've noticed."

"I dress like every other lady at court." I dabbed at the tears that were beginning to fall down my face. "I put on my prettiest gowns for you, and you pay no mind. I spend hours on my headdress, and you pay no mind. I might as well be old and covered with warts. I might as well be shut away in a nunnery." I snatched off my towering, sharply pointed hennin—perhaps one of the most idiotic contraptions women have ever been known to put on their heads, and a fashion that I have had the pleasure to outlive—and stamped on it with my foot. "Why don't you send me to one? It can't be worse than this."

Harry stared. "You've been dressing like a harlot for *me*?"

"I have not been dressing like a harlot, and yes, I have been doing it for you." To stop my tears, I retrieved my hennin and started to make a great production of securing it back on my head, but such a task seemed impossible without the help of Cecilia. "But no more, as it has been a wasted effort." I returned to my work on my hennin.

"Stop. Don't put that thing back on." Harry touched my hair, cautiously. "Can you take it down?"

"I suppose." I began yanking out pins willy-nilly, and very shortly my hair hung to my waist. "All done," I said, since Harry seemed at a loss for words.

"It's beautiful," he finally said. "I always wanted to see it hanging down loose."

"All you had to do was ask," I said softly. My heart was thumping. Even more softly, I asked, "Would you like to see more of me, Harry?"

After what seemed an eternity, he nodded. I pulled off garment after garment until I finally stood in front of Harry dressed only in my stockings and shift, and then after a deep breath I undid my garters. As my stockings fell to the floor, I untied my shift and let it slither after them.

Harry stood transfixed. I did not drop my eyes but stared at him boldly. What did I have to be ashamed of? I was his lawful wife, and I was coming to him a virgin, which was more than Harry could probably say. "Do you like what you see, my lord?"

"Yes." Harry took me in his arms and kissed me, cautiously at first, then with more fervor. He drew back. "You're shivering. Are you frightened?"

"I'm *c-cold.*"

Harry led me to my bed. I climbed under the covers and huddled under them, too grateful for the warmth for the moment to wonder if Harry would follow me inside. Then after a few minutes Harry, bare as I was, parted the bed curtains, then lay beside me and took me into his arms.

Goodness knows who will be reading this, so I shall only say that our first loving was sweet, if a bit clumsy, and that when I was at last a true wife to Harry, I was as happy as any girl in England. We lay drowsing together afterward, and I had nearly dozed off against Harry's chest when Harry whispered, "Kate? I must confess something to you. I—" He swallowed. "I am—not as experienced as you might think I am, being a man. I have been with women—one woman, actually—only a few times. There's a lot I don't know."

"Well, there's much more that I don't know," I said lightly.

"You're so French in some ways, and— I was afraid I'd not please you. I kept meaning to come to you. Then I'd lose my nerve."

"You did please me." I spoke the truth, though I see now what a bumbling, fumbling pair we had been that first time. "It did hurt," I admitted. "But they say it doesn't the next time. Is that true?"

Harry did not reply, but pulled me closer against him.

Years later, vile men would tell stories of how my husband had detested me and our marriage, so much so that his resentment caused him to bring down a king. I would remember our first night together then; I often wondered whether Harry did also. But that was in the future. For now, Harry and I tried out our new pastime one more time that night before falling asleep in each other's arms, truly husband and wife at last.

∽

To my immense delight, there was not a soul in Windsor Castle who did not know the next morning that Harry and I had consummated our marriage. Cecilia, finally arriving back in my chamber after Harry had left it (following our third essay into the marital act), glanced at my sheets and said, grinning, "My, someone's been busy." At dinner, Lord Hastings nodded at me with a distinct look of accomplishment, and the king, passing me, pinched my cheek and said, "Why, you little minx! Seducing young Harry!"

Sore from my deflowering, I still managed to strut, instead of to merely walk, that day. In my sister's chamber, the Duchess of Exeter made a few heavy jokes about my having been ridden hard, though only out of the hearing of Bessie, who said nothing about my new state. Only when we were in comparative solitude did she say, "You should have waited."

"You're not going to lecture me about the hazards of getting a child, surely," I protested. "Not with seven of your own."

"No. You're sturdy enough, I daresay. But if you had waited, we could have had your bed blessed. A proper ceremony, and a feast."

I smiled, then kissed Bessie. "I didn't want a ceremony or a feast. Just Harry."

∽

With Harry seventeen and the two of us now bedding together, we hoped daily that the king might hand over Harry's Stafford lands to him. Then Harry and I could have our own households, our own servants, and—most important—our own bedchamber.

Having discovered the joys of each other's body, we were shameless those days in our lust, which we indulged every time Harry could get away from the king's household and visit me, usually at Greenwich. Sometimes he managed to stay the night, but most of the time we dallied in the after-noon in my own chamber. Our skill had grown as our shyness with each other had rapidly decreased. I had been unaware that there were so many variations on how the sexual act could be performed, and Harry, though less naïve, confessed to me that he'd felt too foolish to experiment widely on Sally, the whore he'd visited before we consummated our marriage. There was no need for Sally now; we had each other.

If I could only get with child! I thought. The king would be bound to give Harry his lands—my sister, who had been supporting me and my servants in her household for years, would hardly want to be paying for a wet nurse as well. We would be free. But my monthly course came as promptly and as annoyingly as ever.

In December a very sad thing happened, one that at last got my thoughts out of the bedchamber: Bessie's newest baby, Margaret, died. She was only eight months old. It was the first such loss Bessie had experienced, and coming just months after Mama's death, it made her very quiet for a few weeks. The king himself was more subdued than usual. It was a much less lively Christmas than the festive one we'd had the year before, and I thought it boded ill for the new year.

Instead, just after the beginning of January, the king called Harry and me into his chamber. "A belated New Year's present for you, Harry," he said, and handed him a parchment. "For Kate, too."

Harry turned pale as he read, and I squealed.

The king was allowing Harry to enter into his grandfather's inheritance.

xiii

Harry: January 1473 to December 1475

H OW OLD IS THIS CASTLE, SIR WALTER?" ASKED KATE.
Sir Walter Devereux had been custodian of Brecon Castle for the past couple of years, and had traveled from his home at Weobley to help us get installed in what would be our chief residence. He handed over the keys to me wistfully, as if sending his child out into the world. "Old," he said succinctly, and launched into an account of its history since Norman times.

I listened only to be polite, for since I had learned to read I had perused the chronicles eagerly, alert for any mention of the lands that would some-day be mine. There was not anything Sir Walter could say that was new to me. In any case, Sir Walter's intended audience was Kate, off whom his gaze seldom moved. I'd begun to get used to the way men's eyes lingered on my wife; what man in his senses could do otherwise than contemplate her? I didn't care so much now, for I knew that I was the only man she looked at the way she had looked at me the night when we had consummated our marriage.

Even now, thinking of her standing before me unclothed that evening made me blush and my blood run hot. To hide the state I'd put myself into, I turned toward a window and gazed at the valley and the River Usk below, keeping a polite ear turned toward Sir Walter.

My journey to my new lands was the first time I had ever seen Wales as an adult. It was a beautiful country, but all wild and strange to me, and I wondered how I would get on with my tenants. I had been told by everyone—or at least by Grandmother, Aunt Margaret, and the king—that

I and my men would have to be firm with them; otherwise, at seventeen, I would be taken advantage of mercilessly.

Sir Walter was well into the saga of the Braose family, a thoroughly unpleasant lot. I was relieved to hear him move on to my Bohun ancestors, who were considerably worthier in my estimation. The king hadn't seen fit to give my share of their great inheritance, but I hoped that it lay in my future. For once, I'd kept a discreet silence about the matter.

"No one died here, did they, Sir Walter? I mean, I know people did die here—but not unpleasantly, did they?"

Sir Walter pondered. "Well, there's been some attacks from time to time through the years, but all very long ago, I believe." He smiled. "All omens appear to be good for the two of you. You make a fine young couple."

I turned away from the window and took Kate's hand. She squeezed it in a way that I had learned held a great deal of promise. Something must have showed on our faces, for Sir Walter coughed and said, "I believe I must be heading back to Weobley now."

"Do take some refreshment first," said Kate in her best lady-of-the-castle voice. She must have been practicing.

"No. The two of you have traveled far and will want to rest by your-selves, I am sure."

We did indeed want to be by ourselves, but not to rest. When Sir Walter had been seen out with all due form, Kate and I adjourned without any discussion to my bedchamber. Furnishings had been sent up before our arrival, and my magnificent new bed sat patiently waiting for us. Gallantly lifting Kate over the threshold, I set her down on the bed and began kissing her, then pushing her backward and her skirts upward. "Harry! Let me at least undress first."

Her laughing protest carried no conviction whatsoever, and was quite inconsistent with the actions of her own hands. "Next time," I promised.

Afterward, now lying decorously side by side under the covers, we stared up at the canopy over our heads. It still was difficult to take in the fact that we were no longer dependents in others' households, but the master and mistress of our own domains. "Whom shall we invite to stay with us first, Harry?"

"My mother." It'd been a dream of mine for so long to entertain her in the style to which she ought to have become accustomed. "I saw a chamber that I want to have made ready for her. She'll like the view over the castle gardens."

"I should like to see her again; she was very pleasant. And I would like to have my brothers and sisters visit."

Not all at once, I secretly hoped. "Of course. And my aunt Margaret—oh, come now, she's not the harridan you think. And Grandmother, if she's up to traveling. And Richard, too."

"Oh, yes, Richard."

I had noticed that my wife had never taken all that kindly to my friend. For that matter, I did not think that my friend had ever taken all that kindly to my wife. Perhaps there were just too many years between them. "He'd come with Anne, of course. You like Anne."

"Oh, yes. It will be good to see her again."

There could have been more enthusiasm here, but I did not press the matter, especially since Kate was pressing another matter altogether. "Harlot," I whispered as she covered my mouth with hers, her sandy hair tickling my chest.

What I can say? We were young, and it was an exceedingly commodious bed.

❧

My mother did come to visit a few months later. She had been much affected by her brothers' death at Tewkesbury, and I thought that she had faded a great deal since I had last seen her, but the trip to Brecon and the sight of my riches seemed to do her good. She admired the chamber we had had refurbished for her, although she scolded me for running up a debt in doing it—which indeed I had, and I was glad of it, for it was pleasant for both of us, I think, to have Mother scolding me like anyone else's mother. I also had put in a generous order with the draper, and Kate's tailor stayed hard at work turning the material into new robes for my mother. I wanted her to look like the countess she was, even if she did spend her days in a convent.

The nuns who kept my mother told me that despite her grief, she had not had any of her struggles with her demons over the last year, and I thought because of that, I might have her to stay with me permanently. Kate, whose sweet nature was never so sweet as when she spoke to my mother, heartily joined in my invitation. But Mother refused. She felt more safe from the demons at the convent than in any other place, she told us, and after life there for so long she was ill fitted for life in a great household, preferring as she did to take her meals in private and to pass her days helping the nuns with their good works and praying for my father and for her many Beaufort dead. Reluctantly, then, I let her go. It was a pleasant visit nonetheless, and I thank God that we had that happy time together, for the next year, she caught a fever and was dead in a couple of days.

I was a little pensive myself after Mother left, but soon Kate and I had a new distraction, for we had received word that Richard had business with the king in Shrewsbury, where he was staying at the time, and would be glad to visit Brecon.

Poor Kate had to put up with a lot from me at this time. Mother had seen everything and pronounced it good, but I noticed that she did not pay much attention to her surroundings. Richard was a different matter, and I wanted everything to be perfect for his visit down to the little bells on my fool's cap.

"I don't see why we are making so much fuss," grumbled Kate after I had made my latest inspection tour and found things still sadly wanting. "It's not as if the king were coming. And if the king were coming, it wouldn't be half so bad, for he would just enjoy himself. Why can't Richard be as easy to please?"

"His household is said to be very well organized," I said stiffly. "Perhaps you could profit from the example. You are a little lacking in that, you know."

Kate said a few things in French that were spoken too quickly and eloquently for me to grasp, which was probably just as well. That night she shut me out of her bedchamber, from which I was usually barred only when she was having her monthly course.

But on the day Richard was due to arrive, everything was in order—minstrels in tune, old rushes replaced with new, adequate plate for all, servants functioning perfectly. Not a minute too soon, for just minutes after I had ascertained all of these things, the Gloucester horses were spotted at a distance.

Richard having brought Anne along, as I had hoped, the ladies went after supper to Kate's chamber, while Richard and I decided to ride off our meal. "I suppose you've heard about Ned's and George's children," he said.

I nodded. Just three days apart, the Duchess of Clarence had given birth at Farley Castle to a girl, Margaret, and the queen had given birth at Shrewsbury to her second son, Richard. We had sent a gold cup in honor of little Richard, a silver one in honor of little Margaret. Without thinking, I said, "I suppose it's your turn next."

"I won't be obliging this year. Anne had a miscarriage a couple of months ago."

I winced. "I—"

"Don't say she's still young, or that we're likely to have more, or that it's God's will."

All were true, though. I said quietly, "I wasn't going to say any of those things. Only to offer my sympathy. Kate hasn't conceived either," I offered as a consolation. "With her being one of twelve, I thought we'd have a child well under way by now. But she's shown no sign of quickening with one. Her old nurse Cecilia thinks she might need a year or two."

Richard raised his eyebrows. "You're bedding with her? I thought for sure the queen would make you wait until she was a safer age. Twenty, perhaps."

"She doesn't meddle in that sort of thing. In any case, Kate didn't want to wait. She seduced me, you might say."

Richard snorted as I smiled dreamily, remembering not that night but the one just past. Kate and I had made up our quarrel over the management of our household in the most satisfactory way possible. "You certainly seem content with yourself these days."

"I'd be more so if you were happier. What ails you? You've been irritable since you arrived here." I frowned. "Is it the food? My servants? We tried to make everything right."

For the first time since his arrival, Richard laughed. "For God's sake, Harry, don't start turning anyone out of doors. Your food and your people are fine. I have been irritable, you're right. More George, I suppose. It's what I came to see Ned about."

"He's still not satisfied with his share of the Warwick lands?"

Richard nodded. "Anne's been wanting to have her mother out of sanctuary, so I finally gave in and asked Ned for permission to bring her out. He'd have soon let her stay there for life, I think—he doesn't trust any of the family after Warwick betrayed him. Not even Anne, really. But I told him that we would make sure the countess didn't get up to trouble, and he finally agreed. Anyway, George took it very badly. He decided that I'd brought the countess out as a means to having Ned give her all of her land back, so that she could convey it all to me. Why he just didn't offer to bring her out himself first is beyond me, but you know how George's mind works. Or maybe you don't, having been spared him as a brother. This is what you get from trying to please your wife, Harry. Remember that when your pretty Kate bats those Woodville eyes at you."

"So what is the king going to do about it?"

"Placate him, as he always does, I suppose. And what's worse, I think George is turning traitor again."

"How?"

"Plotting with Oxford."

Whatever you could say about the Earl of Oxford—and the king had plenty to say about him, none of which need be repeated in polite company—he was not one to give up easily. After Barnet and Tewkesbury, a different man might have either resigned himself to life in exile or thrown himself on the king's mercy, but Oxford had doggedly continued to harass Edward. Just last year, he had been plotting with the Archbishop of York, who was the last of the Kingmaker's brothers and who had been sent a prisoner to Hammes Castle for his pains. With French help, Oxford had attacked Calais several times, and he had managed to land in Essex in the spring. He had been repelled, but completely unbowed, had turned to piracy and was said to be quite successful at it. Secretly, probably for my uncle Edmund's sake, I rather admired the man, though it was a sentiment I naturally kept to myself. "Are you sure?"

"Of course I'm not sure. If I were, I'd make certain Ned knew of the details." Richard shook his head. "All I have is suspicions." He brightened. "At least Oxford's old mother can't send him any aid. Did I tell you I've acquired her lands?"

"How?"

"Got the old lady to sign them over to me, last Christmas as a matter of fact. Ned had sent her to live in London, in a convent there. Stratford le Bow. With her son up to no good, he wanted to keep a close eye on her. I told her that she was the mother of a traitor and that she could either sign them over to me, for a fair consideration, or I'd get them some other way and she'd get nothing. She's a reasonable enough lady and agreed to sign them over to me, though not without putting up a bit of a fuss. I had to threaten to take her to Middleham. What is it about some people that the thought of going to the North scares them so?" Richard pitched his voice to resemble an old lady's quavering tones. "'To Middleham, my lord? In all this great frost and snow? I would surely die!' So I saved her from a fate worse than death, to hear her tell it."

"Was that quite necessary? The woman must be in her sixties. She can't be in the best of health."

"Now you sound like Ned, Harry. Not everyone is an eldest son like you; some of us have to expand our holdings by other means. It's not that she got such a bad bargain; I agreed to pay her an annuity of five hundred marks, to pay her debts, and to promote her youngest son who's studying at Cambridge. Odd place for the Earl of Oxford's brother to be studying, by-the-by. And in any case, what's good for me is good for the realm, for with the countess in the convent, where were her revenues going to go? Straight to her pirate son and his brothers, or to Louis over in France. I'll put them to much better use than any of them, I'll wager. Not that I have them yet. Her feoffees are dragging their heels; I've had to go to Chancery to get them to turn them over. I'll win, but it's another irritation I don't need."

I absently stroked my horse's mane, not knowing what to say. Richard's behavior with the Countess of Oxford struck me as less than chivalrous, and not quite worthy of him. For all that the old lady's son was a traitor, she was an old lady.

"Well, I do intend to uphold my share of the bargain," Richard said irritably.

"Yes, of course." I decided to change the subject. Waving around me, I said, "Have you spent much time in these parts?"

"Not all that much. Have you trouble keeping order?"

"A bit," I admitted. "Everyone does here, though. That's one reason why the king's moved the Prince of Wales' household to Ludlow. Well, of course, you know that. You're on the council, right?"

"Nominally. I have a man who attends it." He frowned. "But you're not on the council, are you? Why not, with all your holdings here?"

It was a question that had occurred to me also, though only fleetingly. "I suppose because of my age."

"You're almost eighteen. I was commanding armies when I was eighteen, Harry."

"The king has appointed me to some commissions here," I said lamely.

"That's hardly the same, though, is it? You need to keep a lookout, old man, that he doesn't shut you out." He waved a hand as if to indicate the landscape through which we were riding, all of which belonged to me. It was a thought that still made me giddy at times. "Don't let yourself get complacent here in Wales. It's easy enough to do when you're far from court."

"I won't," I promised. For a few moments, I brooded on my not being a member of the prince's council. Then I brightened. "We have fine minstrels, Richard. Just wait until they play for us tonight."

∽

I didn't forget Richard's words to me about the council, but a rumor soon reached Brecon that when there came a vacancy in the Order of the Garter, I would be elected to it. This was far more appealing to me at eighteen than sitting on the council of a small boy, albeit a very important small boy, so when the rumors proved to be true, I forgot for the time being all about the matter of the council.

In anticipation of this great occasion, I applied to the College of Arms to be allowed to use the undifferentiated arms of my great-grandfather, Thomas of Woodstock, the youngest son of Edward III. My grandmother, visiting us in the spring of 1474, shook her head when I showed her a copy of the decision in my favor. "I'd not remind the king of your royal ancestry, Harry."

"Why? He's got two sons now, and two brothers as well. I'm no threat to him."

"Still and all, there's no need to provoke him." She sighed. Last year, her youngest son, my uncle John, who'd helped tend me after I was injured at Barnet, had died, survived by a little son. He and I were the only male Staffords now. "I've not got any Stafford men to spare, Harry."

"That's why I wanted to bear Thomas of Woodstock's arms. To pay tribute to them. Nothing more." I was sorry to see that age seemed to be turning the Dowager Duchess of Buckingham into a somewhat nervous old lady. I smiled at her with all of the superior wisdom of my eighteen years. "Grandmother, it won't bother him in the slightest."

And it didn't seem so, either, for I was indeed elected a Garter knight. My only regret was that my mother was not alive to see me in my Garter robes, my new arms duly mounted in my stall at the Chapel of St. George at Windsor Castle. I wore gowns over my doublet as seldom as possible so that the world could all the better admire the jeweled garter that rested under my left knee. Kate was ecstatic the first time she saw me in it, and what happened after the first time she took it off me was indescribably pleasant.

To cap it off, we were heading toward war again with France, a prospect that all of us younger men regarded with delight. After years of fighting each other with nothing to show for it, it was time for us Englishmen to fill our castles with French booty and to gain some glory.

I spent the late months of 1474 and early 1475 raising troops, as did virtually every other man of quality in England. When in April I arrived at Barham Downs in Kent, riding at the head of more than four hundred men wearing the Stafford knot, I could not have been happier. Only Richard and George (for the time being, not quarreling with each other over their lands) had done better.

By July we had landed in Calais, where we tarried awhile, awaiting the arrival of our ally the Duke of Burgundy. It was not the duke who first appeared, however, but his duchess, of whom I'd been quite enamored as a boy. She had not worn well, I thought with great disappointment. Like her mother Cecily of York, she had become overly pious, though she unbent somewhat at the sight of the Duke of Clarence, always her favorite brother. Margaret and the Duke of Burgundy had no children, which was not surprising since it was said that his martial activities preoccupied him so that the two of them were hardly in each other's company. Looking at her, still pretty but too prim, I compared her smugly to my delicious Kate and congratulated myself on my good fortune.

After Margaret left Calais, her husband arrived—without the army we all had expected. There were some who were ready to give up the campaign then and there, including, I suspected later, the king himself. But Charles, though he had come without men, had not come without plans. He suggested breezily that the English forces conquer Normandy and then move into Champagne. There they would be met by the Duke of Burgundy himself and his men, fresh, as the plan went, from conquering Lorraine. In Rheims, Edward would be duly crowned as the King of France. It seemed like a reasonable enough plan, particularly the crowning part, for which the king was rumored to have brought a magnificent garment along just in case. So by July 18, our army was marching at last, led by the King of England and the Duke of Burgundy.

The best that can be said about the days that followed was that we spent two nights encamped at Agincourt, where our forefathers had fought so nobly. From there, it was all downhill. King Louis of France, having at last learned of our whereabouts, began moving toward Compiègne. Our ally the Duke of Burgundy would not let our army into any of his towns, much to the disgust of some of the common soldiers, some of whom began raiding as far off as Noyon and who got killed by King Louis's men for their trouble. The Count of St. Pol having promised to deliver St. Quentin into English hands, yet another group went there, only to be greeted by a cannon blast that killed several more men. In a drenching rain, the miserable party marched back to St. Christ-sur-Somme, where we had an excellent view of the gates of Péronne, shut as firmly against as the rest of the Duke of Burgundy's towns.

I can recount all of these circumstances jadedly enough now, yet at the time I saw them only as minor annoyances. I was ready for war and glory, and was convinced that soon all would fall into place and we would be soundly defeating the French. I actually daydreamed, as I sat in my tent at St. Christ-sur-Somme, of which French castles I might beg of the king. I'd heard of several that would suit me perfectly.

Then on August 12, the Duke of Burgundy left us to join his own forces. The king called his captains to the little wooden house, covered in leather, that had been made for the king's lodgings and could be hauled from place to place. "Louis has made it known to me that he wishes to treat for peace," he said. "His real quarrel is with the Duke of Burgundy, not England, and he is offering to make terms."

I snorted with laughter. Terms! Plainly the man was worried.

"It could be worth our while," Edward continued, glancing in my direction with the trace of a frown, for no one else had made a sound. For the first time, I realized that Edward was putting on weight. "His envoy was vague, but it appears that Louis is prepared to pay quite generously for a treaty. And having been dealing with Burgundy lately and seen the results, I'm ready to listen to his terms. In short, I will be sending a delegation to treat with him. We shall draw up our proposals tonight."

"Edward?" asked Richard. "You truly mean this?"

"Brother, I know this is not to your taste, but it's best for us. We've seen how useful an ally Burgundy is; he appears with no men, and he won't let us into his towns. We saw how mighty the Count of St. Pol was. What can we expect if this continues? More of the same. I've had my doubts from the start, and they've only been confirmed. Don't worry, England shan't be the worse for this." He smiled charmingly. "We won't be bought cheaply, rest assured."

"But, brother—"

"But you will be bought."

"Ah," said Edward. His smile was thin. "Young Harry."

Richard opened his mouth, then closed it as I stood, so angry I was trembling. The greatest army that England had ever sent abroad, by all accounts, had been amassed for this venture, and what was it coming to? "All of this preparation, will it go for nothing? Why, we could win this. We have the men, the determination, the equipment—everything! It's true it might look grim now, but it has before. Think of Crécy, of Agincourt. All we need is the will, the will and the leadership."

Edward said politely, "Oh? Tell me, Harry, about your vast military experience, if you please. Tell all of us."

The men around me were looking at this exchange with interest, caught, no doubt, by the novelty of seeing a man digging his own grave. Anyone with an ounce of common sense, which has never been my constant companion, would have stopped then and there. But I was only getting started. "Of course I don't have vast military experience, and I never will, because you're going to sell us out! To sell yourself! It's prostitution, that's what it is. We'll be no better than those strumpets parked outside our camp. No better than common whores."

"Holy sh—" whispered Richard, and William Hastings stared studiously at his rings.

"We'll never achieve the glory of England as it once was at this rate," I said, not unwisely changing tack. "We'll be the laughingstock of Europe if we enter into a treaty, and what makes you think the French will honor it? And we'll be letting down the Duke of Burgundy. Your own brother-in-law," I added helpfully, in case the king had somehow forgotten this fact. "I know he hasn't been entirely reliable, but what makes you think Louis will be any better? All we'll do is alienate Burgundy; we'll gain nothing." It was time for a breath. "England's honor will be tarnished because of this, don't you realize? Yours most of all. Why, if you enter into this treaty, you'll be disgracing your forebears, and disgracing yourself most of all. You won't be fit to be remembered alongside the third Edward and the fifth Henry. Please! Don't do this to yourself, to us, to England! Don't treat with Louis. Fight him. That's what we all came here for, wasn't it?"

"Have you finished?"

"Yes." After a beat, I added submissively, "Your grace."

"Good. I've borne with your ranting and your slanders because you're my kinsman and you're young, though your time for giving that excuse is beginning to run out, don't you think? But my patience has reached its limit. Tomorrow morning we'll be sending men to treat with Louis. I think it'd be best for all concerned if you were gone by then."

"Gone?"

"I mean packed and headed back to England. Take yourself out of my sight now and do your best to keep yourself there. I'll give you until dawn to break camp. Oh, and your men will be joining you. You can regale them on the way home with tales of Agincourt and Crécy."

I stood and walked out. It was the loneliest walk I'd taken since that time I'd begged for my uncle's life at Tewkesbury, but this time, Richard didn't follow me. No one did. No one spoke to me that entire miserable night as my men and I prepared to leave. I was utterly alone.

∽

The less said about my journey back to England, the better. My men were baffled by our sudden departure and sullen about missing the action they still hoped would transpire.

Once in Calais, I had to borrow money to pay our expenses home and to pay the men. I was already heavily in debt, both from setting up my household and from this present expedition. Revenues from my Welsh estates were always difficult to collect, and I'd been at considerable expense to equip my men properly. I had hoped that this trip would be the making of my fortune.

Having beggared myself, I then had to wait around while I scrambled to find ships to take us all home. If there was any bright spot to this, it was that while we were idling in Calais, the news reached us that the treaty had been signed at Picquigny near Amiens—so at least my men could no longer silently accuse me of having blighted their prospects. There was another bright spot: when I at last rode into the courtyard of Brecon Castle, Kate, bless her, greeted me as joyously and as sweetly as if I'd come home laden with glory and booty.

By early September, our men began coming home from Calais. With them came the news of the terms of the treaty, which made more lips than mine curl in disgust. Edward had been bought off with a promise of fifteen thousand pounds within fifteen days of the signing, with an additional ten thousand pounds each year for the rest of his life. Ample pensions were to be given to Lord Hastings and to a number of others, and the king's oldest daughter, Elizabeth, was betrothed to the Dauphin Charles. Richard, I'd heard, had refused to be present when the treaty was signed, and was not among those getting pensions, but even he had not escaped unsullied: he'd visited Louis at Amiens and had received fine horses and plate.

Some disgruntled soldiers had not returned with the rest of the army, but had taken service with the Duke of Burgundy, who was rumored to have been so angry at Edward's conduct that he'd torn his Garter into pieces with his teeth. (I'd settled for slamming mine against the side of my pavilion.)

Another man would never return: my kinsman Henry Holland, the attainted Duke of Exeter. The king had released him from the Tower with the promise that if he conducted himself well on the French expedition, he would be restored to some of his lands. Instead he drowned on the voyage home, a victim of one of the wine-soaked brawls that had broken out between the soldiers again and again since the French treaty. I had hardly known the duke, but the pity of his life—he'd spent much of his adulthood as a prisoner or an exile, and had been deprived of his daughter and his spouse before meeting his lonely end at sea—added to my melancholy that autumn of 1475. It was with trepidation, then, that one day around Christmastide, I looked up from my accounts (a gloomy enough sight) to find Kate standing over me. "Harry. I have some news for you."

"The tenants are revolting?"

"Don't be so silly. Here. Feel." I put my hand on her belly, and my eyes widened as I realized from its roundness what a less oblivious and more experienced husband would have guessed weeks ago. "I wanted to be absolutely sure before I told you. I am with child, Harry."

xiv

May 1476 to February 1478

IT WAS IN EARLY MAY OF 1476 THAT I NEARLY DRAGGED GRANDMOTHER out of her antelope-and-Stafford-knot-covered chariot as it lumbered into the courtyard of Brecon Castle. "Harry, patience! My bones are older than yours." She and her ladies (utterly ignored by me) adjusted her dress as I danced a little jig of impatience. "I gather Kate has begun her labor?"

A blood-curdling scream answered her question. She cocked her head and listened dispassionately. When a second scream followed, accompanied by words that I was unaware were in Kate's vocabulary, Grandmother nodded approvingly. "A woman who can scream and curse like that isn't weak, Harry, and it's when they get weak during birth that you have to worry. As I said when the marriage was arranged, the girl's mother was a good breeder, and she probably will be too." She glanced around at Brecon Castle. "You've made some improvements here, it appears."

"Never mind the improvements. Go to Kate. Now."

One of Grandmother's older ladies chuckled, and I gave her a freezing look.

The castle was already full of women. My aunt Joan, Grandmother's only living daughter, had arrived the day before, and several of Kate's sisters—I never could quite keep them all straight—were here also. The queen had sent her own midwife, who, according to reports coming out of Kate's chamber, was feuding with the local midwife. (I could only hope that they didn't come to blows in the middle of the delivery.) But it was Grandmother I wanted by Kate's side, though as she disappeared behind the door of the birthing chamber, I wished she were by mine as well.

William Knyvet, Aunt Joan's husband, was the only male guest at Brecon Castle. He clucked at me sympathetically as I returned to my chamber. "Perhaps a game of tennis to pass the time?" I'd had a court installed so that my expected son could play, and Knyvet, who'd never tried the game, had been admiring it wistfully since his arrival.

"Perhaps," I said, and kept my seat in front of the fireplace, the best place at Brecon Castle by which to brood, I'd found.

Six hours later, I heard a cry from poor Kate that shook the foundations of the castle, then a piercing wail, followed by a bang on my chamber door. Grandmother, looking wrung out, but not as wrung out as I from sitting and waiting, smiled and patted me on the shoulder. "You have a lovely little girl, Harry. Kate is tired, but well. They will clean them and bring the baby to you shortly."

Girl? It was not quite what I had expected. But presently the local midwife, trailed by the wet nurse Kate had engaged, came into the room (it was kind, I supposed, for the royal midwife to let her have the honor) and with Grandmother's assistance, put my daughter into my arms.

Like all good subjects, we had never been in doubt what to name our first child: Edward for a boy, Elizabeth for a girl. I held little Elizabeth gingerly, scared to death that I might drop her, and cautiously kissed her on the forehead. Men begat these tiny creatures daily, in and out of wedlock, yet I could still scarcely believe that I had managed this feat myself. I wondered whom she would favor, Kate or me. I could have kept holding my child forever and smiling foolishly at her, except that after a few minutes she started whimpering and the wet nurse instantly reached for her.

Grandmother smiled as I reluctantly gave up my precious burden, having first whispered, "Papa's pretty little love," in a voice that I hoped no one else had heard.

"I was going to tell you not to let Kate see your disappointment over her being a girl. But I don't think I need to now, do I?"

I shook my head and watched, enthralled, as the wet nurse settled on a stool with Elizabeth. After worshipfully watching my daughter make her first acquaintance with the breast, I went upstairs to see my wife.

Kate lay dozing in her great bed, her eyes ringed with dark circles. She had been laboring for four-and twenty hours, at least. Her sister Anne, whom I knew better than the other Woodville sisters because she was married to the Earl of Essex's son, sat by the bed, embroidering. I'd not expected to see my wife looking so peaked. "Is she going to recover?"

"She's not ill. Just exhausted, and a little inclined toward being tearful. Some women get that way after childbirth. I wish Mother were here for her, poor lamb."

Anne gave her place to me and I sat there looking at my wife, now the mother of my child. At my command, my page went on an errand, and when he returned, I took the bracelet he had brought from my chambers, where it had been stored up for several weeks, and fastened it onto Kate's wrist. She opened her eyes then. "Harry? What is this?" She lifted her wrist, and sapphires sparkled. "It's beautiful."

"It's a gift of thanks for giving me such a beautiful daughter."

"Harry..." Her eyes filled with tears. "I wish I had borne you a son."

"Why? Elizabeth is lovely. She's sweet. Just like her mother." I kissed her. "Go back to sleep, and when you wake, the three of us—we and Elizabeth, that is—will sit a while together. And we'll have your favorite dishes brought to you and plan your churching and what you'll wear. I want you to look more beautiful than ever for it."

She smiled wanly and obediently closed her eyes. Lying still on her back, pale from her recent ordeal, she looked like a lovely corpse, and my blood chilled. *Don't die*, I thought, and I must have said the words, for Kate opened her eyes. "Don't be silly, Harry," she murmured before falling asleep again. "I'm fine. Just very tired."

I prayed fervently that she was right.

⁂

God was merciful. Kate did indeed quickly regain her strength, and by the time she was churched a month later looked as fit and hearty as she had ever been—except that now she had a bit of extra padding on her hips, which after consideration I decided suited her wonderfully. We were equally blessed in that Elizabeth was a healthy baby, suckling vigorously and growing rapidly. To my council I became an utter bore on the topic of her many perfections. Soon, Kate's ordeal and my fears long forgotten, we began hoping for another child.

There was more pleasant news that spring, for Richard's return from France a month or so after my own had had the same effect on Anne that mine had had on Kate. Anne gave birth at around the same time Kate was having her churching. Their son—naturally named Edward—was a fine lad, quite worthy, I thought, of marriage to my Elizabeth.

There was a cloud upon my happiness, though, for what I had dreaded in France had come to pass: there was no place for me at Edward's court. It was a subtle snub, for outwardly, things were as normal. I'd been sent a silver cup from the king when Elizabeth was born, and the queen and Kate were on good as terms as ever. But when the king set up commissions, I was not on them, and I played no role in the council of the Prince of Wales, even though his household at Ludlow was not all that far from Brecon.

I had sent the king a letter of apology after he returned to England. It took me hours to compose: to grovel, but not to grovel so much as to sound insincere, proved to be no easy matter. The king sent me a genial reply that must have been dashed off in a couple of minutes by one of his most junior clerks. All was forgiven, and I would be welcome at court any time I chose to come there. But as I finished reading the letter, I realized belatedly that it wasn't the king's forgiveness that I needed, it was his trust, and that, I feared, I had lost for good—if I with my Beaufort connections and my own royal blood had ever had it in the first place.

I tried to pretend that this did not bother me, and a reasonable voice in my head advised me to let it be for the time being and let time prove my reliability to the king. Instead, I turned my attention to my own affairs, which indeed needed some ordering. First on my priorities was more aggressively pursuing the revenues owed me.

By nature I am not hard-dealing or cold, though it seems that I have acquired a reputation among my tenants for both. I wanted to be a good lord, and I truly tried to be. But I was in debt and could not afford to be overly indulgent, especially now that I had a daughter who would need to be attended properly and married well. And I have to say that I was not entirely at fault; my estates having been comparatively neglected during my minority by some of the people who had the running of them, my tenants had grown accustomed to thinking that this relaxed state of affairs would continue. Perhaps they would not have minded so much if I had had royal plums to hand out, but being in little favor at court, I had none.

But my problems would soon be as nothing compared to the Duke of Clarence's.

Unlike me and the more restrained Richard, George had not remonstrated with Edward about the French peace, but I doubt he could have been happy with it. The king had not trusted him with any major responsibility since his antics with the Kingmaker, and George had probably hoped to prove his ability in the French war. If he was disappointed, though, he kept his thoughts to himself. Like me in 1476, he turned his attention to his own affairs.

Then, at the end of the year, his duchess died, followed on New Year's Day by his infant son.

Whatever else his faults, George had been a good husband, faithful to Isabel even in circumstances like our French expedition when the most uxorious man might have felt justified in taking some pleasure on the side. She in turn had been a good wife to him, even to the point, common rumor had it, of having played the chief role in persuading him to abandon her own father's doomed cause for Edward's. With her gone, George was cast adrift. He began to drink more wine than was good for him, men who did business for both of us told me. At the same time, he was now an eligible widower, and when he was not being maudlin on the subject of poor Isabel, he was weighing up the possibilities of a dazzling new match.

For this we had the Duke of Burgundy, Clarence's brother-in-law, to thank, for just a few days into the new year of 1477, Burgundy was killed in battle, leaving behind as his heiress Mary, his daughter from an earlier marriage. The Duchess of Burgundy could think of no better thing for her stepdaughter to do than to marry George, her favorite brother. If that wasn't enough, the Scottish king, James III, proposed that George should marry James's sister.

Edward thwarted both matches.

It wasn't hard to see why. Either marriage could offer George an excellent chance for mischief-making, and George had openly rebelled against Edward twice and was suspected of having engaged in more treason on the sly. The Burgundian marriage would have also irritated Louis of France and the Archduke of Hapsburg, Mary's betrothed. But all of these practical objections were lost on George, as I suppose they would have been lost on me if I had been in his position.

He didn't take the disappointment well. George's tongue began to run away from him, making me look almost discreet in comparison. To anyone on his vast lands who would listen, he raked up the old rumor, started back in the day by his late father-in-law, that the king was a bastard, sired by a commoner in a moment of weakness on the Duchess of York's part. No one seriously believed it that I ever heard of—it was hard enough, frankly, to imagine the pious and austere duchess in bed with her own husband, much less with some obscure churl—but the rumors spread, as rumors will when people run out of other things to gossip about. If those idiot rumors were the worst of it, though, Edward might have shrugged them off, for George talking was something not all that harmful. George acting was another thing altogether, and in April of 1476, he acted about as badly as a man could act.

He hung one of his duchess's ladies.

Following Isabel's death, Ankarette Twynho, an older lady in receipt of a modest pension for her services, had returned to her family in Somerset, where one day, out of the blue, Clarence's men came and dragged her out of her home. It was not until the poor woman arrived at Warwick—the heart of Clarence country—that she found out the charges against her:

poisoning the duchess. To cap matters off, a local man, John Thursby, was accused of poisoning Isabel's infant son. In a matter of three hours, both were tried and convicted by a jury that was plainly too scared of Clarence to return any other verdict other than guilty. They were dragged to the gallows straightaway.

One of Ankarette's relations did business for me as well as Clarence, and he said that Isabel and her babe had been ailing since the birth. And what, after all, would either of the defendants have to gain by poisoning either of them? Whether this ever occurred to George, I do not know, just as I do not know whether George ever believed the truth of his accusations. Perhaps it was simply a matter of wanting to believe them. I suppose George had to find someone in corporeal form to blame; one couldn't hale God to Warwick and hang Him high.

But the play was not yet finished, for during that same mad spring, an Oxford astronomer, John Stacy, was accused of using his arts to bring about the king's death. His confession, extracted by means that were said to have been none too gentle, implicated Thomas Blake, another Oxford astronomer, and—more sensationally—Thomas Burdett, a member of George's household. A commission was formed to try them—needless to say, I was not on it, which for once I was happy about—and it found all three guilty. After they were convicted, they were hung at Tyburn.

Burdett and Stacy had maintained their innocence to the end; whether they were or not is beyond me to say. Their heads had been perching on London Bridge for but a day or so when the Duke of Clarence stormed into the king's council chamber at Westminster, dragging a preacher with him. The man—the same man who had proclaimed the sixth Henry's claim to the throne back in the fall of 1470—was made to read out Burdett's gallows-side protestation of innocence. Then Clarence, having made his point, swept out of the room, leaving the council agape.

It was Clarence's last great scene, and Edward's last straw. By late June, George, Duke of Clarence, was a prisoner in the Tower.

~ৎ৵৲~

One thing Edward could not be accused of with regard to Clarence was summary justice. He remained shut up, with all the comforts due to a king's brother, but shut up all of the same, while the king dithered for the next few months about what to do with him.

Meanwhile, in November 1477 I came to London, where the seven-year-old Prince of Wales, paying a visit to his father's court, was to host a great dinner and take homage from the various lords of the land. It promised to be a busy couple of months, for a royal wedding was in store: that of Richard, Duke of York, to little Anne Mowbray, who was heiress to the deceased John Mowbray, Duke of Norfolk. She was a rich little girl, or would be once the elderly but still spry dowager Duchess of Norfolk, who had been married to Kate's brother John, died and finally freed up her dower lands. Edward spared no expense for the wedding, which he decided should took place the following January, to coincide with Parliament.

"How's your wife?" Richard asked me as we settled ourselves in for a companionable evening at Baynard's Castle, one of the Duchess of York's homes. Richard was staying there while in London; I'd borrowed Grandmother's Bread Street residence. Our goods had scarcely been unpacked when I'd decided to pay a visit to Richard. "Is she here in London?"

"Yes. She's with child again, did I tell you? We expect the baby around February."

"I'm surprised you didn't leave her in Wales."

"She's in good health, and she wanted to come to the wedding. We figured she might as well come up now instead of having to travel later when she's heavier with child. I suppose Anne's here?"

"No. I wish she had come, but she didn't want to leave our son. She frets too much over him when she's away from him, although he's been of good health. She's become worse about it since her sister died." He took a sip of wine.

"So, tell me. Is the king going to bring George to trial?"

"Most likely. It looks as if he's going to be the main business at Parliament. Edward's been assembling quite the case against him."

"What do you think will happen to him?"

"Execution."

He spoke as casually as if we were speaking of slaughtering a pig. "Are you serious, man? Do you think the king would put his own brother to death?"

Richard shrugged. "He's been rather more than your ordinary nuisance, don't you think? Aside from hanging his servants on a whim, he's been spreading rumors about the king's bastardy, associating with the likes of Burdett and Stacy... There's even talk that he was behind that Earl of Oxford imposter last summer."

The Earl of Oxford's luck had finally run out. The earl was safely locked up in Hammes Castle near Calais, but the summer before, a person claiming to be him had been stirring up unrest in Cambridgeshire and Huntingdonshire. "The king could simply keep George locked up."

"Yes. But it's safer to put him to silence. Of course, our mother will likely have a go at talking him out of it, but my money's not on her. Edward the king will prevail over Edward the son and brother."

༄

The Prince of Wales's feast a few days later in November was the first great dinner the seven-year-old had ever hosted. Though his father the king was fairly informal in private, he liked a great deal of pomp and circumstance in public, and the dinner was accordingly a rather stiff affair. It was made even more so by everyone being on his best behavior for the child host, a dire necessity, for the king guarded the virtue of his son most strictly, leaving nothing to chance. I knew from Kate that Edward had drawn up a series of ordinances sternly prohibiting swearers, brawlers, backbiters, and gamblers from coming into the young boy's presence at Ludlow, and ribald words were absolutely forbidden. The ordinances might have been drawn up by the ghost of the late Henry VI.

After a performance by a decorous juggler, followed by some stately tunes, it was time for those of us who held lands of the prince to give him homage as he perched in a great chair with his four-year-old brother, Richard, Duke of York, seated nearby. We lined up to pay our respects.

The Duke of Gloucester, naturally, went first. Young Edward watched Richard solemnly as, bareheaded and with his belt ungirded, he knelt, put his hands between those of the prince, spoke the words of homage, and kissed him on the cheek. "We thank you that you do this so humbly," Edward said.

With Clarence in the Tower, I was next. I placed my hands between the prince's. They were fine and delicate, and I could not help but think of the son I hoped that Kate was carrying in her belly. "I become your liege man of life and limb and truth and earthly honors, bearing to you against all men that love, move, or die, so help me God and the Holy Dame."

A lot of trouble and grief for a lot of people could have been averted then and there if the Lord had sent a convenient bolt of lightning to strike Richard and me dead at that moment. He did not, and so I move on.

*

William Caxton, an old acquaintance from Anthony Woodville's days in Bruges, had returned to England the year before and set up a printing press at Westminster, where his maiden production had been the first printed version of *The Canterbury Tales*. I was curious to see his shop, and Kate in particular had a good reason for wanting to go there: Anthony had translated a book from the French, *The Dictes and Sayings of the Philosophers*, and Caxton had printed it that November. It was released in the middle of that month, and naturally, we went to buy a copy.

The release was quite a family occasion: except for the queen, most of Anthony's brothers and sisters, and some of their spouses and children, were crowded into Caxton's shop when we arrived. I could hardly see for Woodvilles, but from the little I could tell, Caxton's shop was a pleasing sight: the tables piled high with books, some printed by Caxton here in London, others imported from Caxton abroad.

Anthony, the man of the hour, stood in the middle of all of this, clutching a copy of *The Dictes* like a proud parent. "I came across this when I was on pilgrimage to Santiago," he explained when one of his sisters asked. Plainly, he did not need much encouragement to expand. "It was given to me by a fellow pilgrim. I've always cherished it, and I thought it would be an excellent work to translate for the Prince of Wales. He knows much French already, but this way he can enjoy the entire work now, and so can the members of his household."

Edward Woodville, who was a couple of years older than Kate, picked up a copy and began reading. "'A Wiseman ought to beware how he weds a fair woman, for every man will desire to have her love and so they will seek their pleasures to the hurt and displeasure of her husband.'" He grinned at Kate and me. "My lord of Buckingham must take care."

"For shame, Edward!" Kate said, looking quite pleased with the implied compliment, though.

"Aye, but Lord Rivers did have a care for the sensibilities of the ladies," said William Caxton. He nodded toward Kate and her sisters. "The philosopher Socrates, as you may be aware, has some rather uncomplimentary and ungallant things to say about your sex. But Lord Rivers left them out."

"And you put them back in," said Edward. He read, "'I find that my said Lord hath left out certain and divers conclusions touching women. Whereof I marvel that my Lord hath not written them, ne what hath moved him so to do, ne what cause he had at that time; but I suppose that some fair lady hath desired him to leave it out of his book; or else he was amorous on some noble lady, for whose love he would not set it in his book.' Anthony! You rascal!"

Anthony snorted. He seemed to be enjoying himself thoroughly.

⁂

Soon after the new year began, I received a summons to the king. I obeyed it dutifully and not without a little dread, given my history to date with him.

I need not have worried. With money rolling in from France, the Duke of Clarence unable to make any trouble, and the Duke of York about to marry the richest little girl in England, Edward was in fine spirits these days.

"Good to see you, cousin," he said as if our meetings had always been the height of good fellowship. "I've a job for you, Harry."

My spirits soared. A diplomatic assignment, perhaps? Well, no. But a place on his son's council? That was certainly a possibility. "I'm happy to serve you, your grace," I said modestly.

"Good. We'll need you and my brother Richard for the wedding. He'll lead the bride to the feast on one side, you on the other. It'll be a charming sight, don't you think?"

"Charming indeed," I said in a voice as hollow as the honor I was receiving.

❧

Richard raised his eyebrows when I told him later about my audience with the king. "Don't you find that insulting, Harry? You should be on the king's council, or the Prince of Wales's council. Or both. Not relegated to escorting little girls to their weddings."

"Well, I'm better off than George." I shrugged. "What can I do about it? France put an end to any hopes I had in that direction."

"Has it ever occurred to you that it's more than France? Granted, you made a fool of yourself there, but it's been over two years. Ned usually doesn't hold grudges that long."

"So I'm the lucky exception. Anyway, I'm used to it. Almost."

"He should be including you instead of those low-born relations of his wife."

"Who include my own wife, incidentally."

"Your wife's not the problem, it's the men. Anthony's not so bad; at least he has some learning, even if he trifles it away on tournaments. I've never understood the point of them. But the others! The Marquess of Dorset's a fool; if he didn't have the queen for a mother, he'd be rotting on some obscure manor somewhere. His brother Richard Grey's a puppy. And yet the king can find room for them in his government, but not for you, the third greatest duke in the land. The second, if we take George out of consideration, and we probably should." He stared at me thoughtfully for a while. "Perhaps I should have a word with Ned."

"Richard, please. Don't."

"Why?"

"Kate once offered to do the same thing with the queen for me. It would humiliate me, that's why, having my relations pleading my case. I wouldn't want to think that the king brought me back into favor just to humor you or Kate. I'll have another chance to prove my worth to the king, I'm sure of it. Let me handle it myself. If that means sitting quietly and behaving myself for another two years, or longer, I shall. At least I'll have earned my way back by my own efforts."

"Very well, then."

"But I do appreciate the offer. It means a great deal to me. For a while—" I decided not to complete my sentence and say that for a while, when France had made me a laughingstock in the court, I thought that Richard had lost interest in our friendship. Instead, I said brightly, "So. Which side of the little bride shall I take?"

༄

Kate and I at ages seven and nine had been a young enough married couple, but the Duke of York and his bride, aged four and five, made our wedding appear to be an elderly affair indeed. They got through the long ceremony with a minimum of squirming and looking about, but they were clearly at the end of their tethers toward the end. Only when it came time for the wedding feast, and the promise of sweetmeats, did the newlyweds' faces brighten. I heard the groom announce, "I'm hungry, Mama!" and even the bride, the elder and the more dignified of the pair, would have rushed headlong to her place of honor had not Richard and I each had hold of one of her hands.

I did my duty at the feast unexceptionably, and was rewarded with the further honor of being asked to carry the Marquess of Dorset's helmet at the tournament that was to take place within a few days. As I had not been planning to joust myself—it was not my forte, and even if it had been, Kate's pregnancy would have deterred me for fear of having an accident that might upset her and take our coming child—I graciously agreed, though remembering Richard's contemptuous words about Dorset, I could have done without the privilege. For my acquiescence I received a royal smile, which I tried to tell myself might lead to some duties of some real substance.

Kate was at the feast as well, seated next to the bride's mother, the widowed Duchess of Norfolk, Elizabeth Talbot. My wife was too great with child to join in the dancing and merriment that followed, and left the celebration early. When I came back to Bread Street late in the afternoon, exhausted from playing the good courtier, she was lying on the bed in our chamber, dozing with an open book—*The Canterbury Tales* from Caxton's shop—spread next to her belly. As soon as I came in, she pushed aside the book and stretched like a contented cat stuffed with kittens. "Harry? Did I miss anything interesting?"

I clambered onto the bed next to her and patted the belly that I hoped this time contained a son, though I loved my little Elizabeth dearly. "No. Oh, I should say that the bride's mother was rather tipsy and began telling me all about the bargain the king struck with her for the marriage. She was quite pleased with her negotiating skills."

Kate sniffed. "I thought her a shrew when I sat beside her this morning. Scratch, Harry? Please?" I obeyed as Kate turned on her side. She sighed happily as I began to move my fingers over her back. "Anyway, I think the Duchess of Norfolk should take more care around wine. Do you know, she told me at the banquet that her sister had a dalliance with the king."

"Eleanor?" I'd not thought of Eleanor Butler in years, though she and her sister the Duchess of Norfolk were relations of mine through the Bourchiers. The widow of Thomas Sudeley, she had died back in the late 1460s, still quite young. I'd never met her that I could recall. "When?"

"A year or so before he married Bessie, and after Lady Eleanor was widowed. The Duchess of Norfolk didn't know that much, really. She just said that her sister had succumbed to the king's charms and that after a few months he got bored and moved on. The way they say he often does with his lemans. Of course, one can't call Lady Eleanor a leman, but—"

"If it's true, she's certainly a cut above his usual choice of woman." Too late, I realized that this could be taken the wrong way by the queen's sister. "I mean—"

My wife kicked me. "Edward even spoke of marriage, but the duchess didn't say why it never took place. The king wandered by, so she stopped talking. I'm certainly glad they didn't marry, because then you and I would never have married, I suppose. Harry? You don't regret marrying me, do you, instead of someone like Warwick's girls?"

Kate when she was breeding was a moody creature, I'd discovered, apt to change emotions in a heartbeat; in the middle of this short utterance, she'd turned almost tearful. "Of course not, sweetheart." I kissed her on her cheek and patted her belly. "I'm very thankful you're my wife. Don't talk nonsense."

She sighed and lay quietly against me. I was thinking that she had drifted off when she said, "I have been thinking, perhaps it would be better if I went back to Wales. Then our next child would be born at Brecon, and we would not have to worry about traveling with him—or her—from London in winter."

"I like the idea, but are you sure you can travel safely?"

"I will have plenty of attendants, and I do not think my time is that near yet. Even traveling slowly, I think I will have time to spare."

I did want my son, if I were to be blessed with one, to be born at Brecon. "All right, but I just hope to God that you're right about the timing. I wouldn't want the babe to be born in a manger, even if it sufficed for our Lord. Brecon is better."

Kate laughed and rolled over—a cumbersome process—to face me. "In all honesty, Harry, there is another reason I wish to go back to Wales. This business with the Duke of Clarence saddens me."

"Why? You've no love for him, I'm sure."

"No. But I hate to see the king being forced into the position that he has been placed. He will be executed, don't you think? It is sad to have to execute one's brother for the good of the kingdom, especially with the Duchess of York living. And then the Duchess of Norfolk said the most unkind thing to me at table today."

"What?"

"She said, 'I suppose the king will do the queen's and your family's bidding, and put his brother to silence.' Harry, it is not our bidding! None of us like him after Papa and John's deaths, but we did not force Clarence to murder that poor harmless old woman. We did not cause him to spread those rumors about the king being a bastard. We did not make him associate with that dreadful Stacy person. We did not entice him into plotting with the Earl of Oxford. My poor sister can't force Edward to give up his mistresses, much as she would like to. How can people think she could force him to execute his own brother?"

"There, there." Kate had begun to cry. "I think you're right about leaving," I said, stroking her hair, which she had taken down for her rest in bed. "People are always saying malicious things at court, and you shouldn't take them to heart. But I think you would be happier at Brecon, far away from all of this nonsense. Still, you must send me word of your health every day. Promise?"

⁂

Parliament—the first in three years, for Edward was not partial to them—opened the next morning with a suitably ominous sermon by the Bishop of Rotherham, who expanded on no uncertain terms on the text, "The king does not carry the sword without cause." There were a few days of the usual parliamentary petitions, important to those who brought them but of little interest to the rest of the human race, then an interlude for a tournament, at which I dutifully performed my ceremonial duty of carrying Dorset's helmet. In this I must have pleased the king, for I was named as a trier of petitions from Gascony, all other places overseas, and the Channel Islands. It was, as I wrote Kate in my daily letter to her, an improvement.

All this time, the seat normally occupied by George, Duke of Clarence was a vacant, silent reminder of why we were all there. Toward the end of January, he at last was brought in for his trial. Edward had a long list of charges against him. George had accused the king of falsely putting Burdett to death and of resorting to necromancy. He had claimed that the king was a bastard. He had accused the king of taking his livelihood from him and of intending his destruction. Queen Margaret had promised him the crown if Henry VI's line failed—old business, surely, for Margaret, a shadow of the fiery queen of my youth, had been sent back to France as part of the French treaty. He planned to send his son and heir abroad to win support, bringing a false child to Warwick Castle in his place. He planned to raise war against the king within England and made men promise to be ready at an hour's notice. In short, he had shown himself to be incorrigible, and to pardon him would endanger the realm. Sundry witnesses were introduced, who largely echoed the king's accusations.

George answered, but to little effect. He offered only to prove his case through personal combat with the king, a proposition that might have met with approval in King Arthur's court but fell flat in the year 1478.

Preordained as its conclusion was, all of this took time. January had passed into February, and February was six days old when a messenger from Brecon Castle accosted me just as I was about to depart for Westminster. "I come from the duchess, my lord. She is doing well."

"No letter?"

"No, my lord. She told me to tell you that she was too busy." The man finally cracked a smile. "Three days ago she bore your grace a fine boy."

⟡

I sent messengers to anyone with whom I had even a nodding acquaintance. I even started to send one to my grandmother—recalling just before the messenger departed that she had gone to stay at Brecon with Kate and therefore hardly needed to be told of her great-grandson's arrival.

My good news had preceded me to Parliament, and both the king and Richard were waiting with their congratulations when I arrived there. "You'll be wanting to go to Wales, I know," said Edward, in a kindly tone I'd not heard from him in years. He hesitated. "But there is one service I require of you first."

I had a brand-new son, and the king had chosen this time of all others to finally discover my merits. But I was in too jovial a mood to quibble. "Yes, your grace?"

"Parliament will vote on the Duke of Clarence's fate today," the king said as matter-of-factly as if speaking of a distant acquaintance. "I've no doubt he will be convicted. A high steward must be appointed to pronounce his fate. Normally, my brother Richard would be called upon, but in this situation it is a bit awkward, as you can see. So you will be appointed steward of England in order to pronounce the sentence."

I gulped. Though the sentence—and I had no doubt what it would be— would not be of my own ordaining, it was still a daunting task to proclaim that a king's brother must die. Following hard upon the heels of the birth of my son, it also seemed ill-timed and even ill-omened. Yet it was my place and duty, as Duke of Buckingham, to serve as steward, and the bad had to be taken with the good. "Very well," I said.

"Good. All will be in readiness by tomorrow morning. You can leave immediately afterward to see your son and that pretty wife of yours." I waited to be dismissed, but the king showed no sign of letting me go. "Cantref Selyf," he said after a pause.

"Your grace?"

"Cantref Selyf shall be yours. I'll have the papers drawn presently. Run along so we can get this business over with and you back to Wales by tomorrow."

Cantref Selyf was part of the Bohun inheritance, which I'd not dared to mention to the king in years. Who knew what would come next? I bowed my thanks. As I left (practically skipping), I heard Richard saying, "Now for me, Ned. My son's to be Earl of Salisbury, right?"

Clarence's title. "Why, of course," the king said as I stepped out of hearing range.

Not surprisingly, the Duke of Clarence was found guilty that afternoon. He had never put up much of a defense, though he had spoken eloquently (and lengthily) enough—perhaps he had none to put up. The very next morning, I took my seat as steward of England and pronounced the sentence: death, by a method of the duke's own choosing.

George didn't blink when I spoke the words. I half expected him to repeat his offer to prove his innocence by combat, but instead he simply said, when invited to speak, "I have no choice but to accept this sentence. Pray for me, my lords." Then he was led away.

I watched, thinking of the boy who'd run into the solar at Writtle to gleefully announce my grandfather's death, and felt no pity. God forgive me.

Kate had had much less trouble giving birth to Edward, our new son, than to our firstborn, and she looked lovely and serene when I arrived at Brecon several days later. Her chamber was sparkling with plate we'd been sent as christening gifts, to which I added a golden cup, courtesy of the king. It was the red-faced creature who the nurse put in my arms, however, that occupied my attention entirely. "He's in good health?" I asked for about the sixth time or so since I'd come home.

"Perfect, Harry," Kate said for the sixth time also.

Elizabeth, having caught wind of my homecoming—she'd been napping in her nursery when I arrived—toddled into Kate's chamber and bristled at the sight of her new brother and me. "Baby go!"

"No, Elizabeth, he's here to stay, but it's your turn to visit Papa. Come sit here. I've brought a new doll for you. All the way from London."

Elizabeth climbed into my lap and gave the offending baby, whom Kate had taken from me, a triumphant glare. I cuddled her and gave her the new doll, which looked as much like Elizabeth as a doll could look. It was, I know now, the happiest day of my life.

Kate did not ask about the Duke of Clarence, and I did not tell her—for all I knew, the sentence might have been carried out by now. That was a topic for another time and for another place. There was no room in this chamber at Brecon Castle, where I sat with my fine new son and my lovely little girl and my beautiful wife, for the ghost of George.

∽

I was wrong, though: George still walked the earth, or at least the small portion of it that was the Tower. "Ned's dithering," Richard told me when I reluctantly returned to Westminster. "At this rate, George will outlive all of us."

"Why does he delay?"

"Conscience, I suppose—it's not been known to trouble Ned much, but it makes an unwanted appearance now and then."

"I suppose your mother is pleading with him also."

"No—she is just praying. Mother doesn't waste time with ordinary mortals when she can speak to her Maker. I supped with her yesterday, and she said, 'What will be, will be. The Lord will determine his fate.'"

The Lord finally acted in the person of the Speaker of the Commons, William Allington, who with a delegation asked that the sentence be carried out. Probably the king had been hoping that someone would do just that, for several days later, on February 18, the Duke of Clarence was dead.

George's execution was a strictly private affair, out of consideration for the Duchess of York more than anyone else. She spent a long time with George before his death; so did Richard. I asked him what their last encounter had been like, and he shrugged. "Damned awkward. But he was in a suitably pious frame of mind, getting all in order, so it wasn't as bad as I expected. He spent a lot of time enumerating his debts; Ned has agreed to pay them. Oh, and your in-laws did nicely too. George asked that lands be alienated to Anthony Woodville to recompense him for the injuries to his parents."

"I hardly think that my wife would count that as recompense." Kate still was quiet and pensive on the anniversary of her father's and her brother John's deaths. "So how did they do it? I suppose they beheaded him?"

"Now here you have to give George credit for imagination. He asked to be drowned in a barrel of wine. And by God, that's how they did it. They gave him a little sleeping draught with his last meal, and when he dozed off, they dumped him headfirst into a barrel of malmsey and held him."

Clarence's feet sticking up in the air out of a barrel made such an absurd picture in my mind, I did something truly unforgivable. I smiled, or at least I twitched my mouth upward. Richard stared at me, and then he smiled himself.

"Come on, old man," he said, lifting the cup he was holding. "Let's get good and soused in memory of Brother Clarence."

And we did.

As the night wore on and both of us had some difficulty remaining upright, we flopped in front of the fireplace and lay there side by side with our feet propped up, sometimes getting our cups to our mouths, sometimes sloshing them over the rushes. "I remember when you called my brother a whore," Richard reminisced. For once, he was far drunker than I was.

"Not that again."

"You should have seen his face."

"I did see his face."

"But you were right, Harry. He was a whore. And you know what? We're whores, too."

"How?"

"How are we whores? Hear, Harry, how we hath been whores."

"*Hic, haec, hoc,*" I intoned. Master Giles, the tutor of my youth, would not have been pleased.

Richard gathered together his dignity. "The Duke of Bedford."

The Duke of Bedford, a boy in his teens, was John Neville's son. He had some lands from his mother's inheritance, but the rich Neville inheritance, which by rights should have been his as it was entailed in the male line, had gone to Richard after John Neville, the Marquess of Montagu, had died at Barnet. I rubbed my forehead, which I found helped to clear my brain. "Parliament ruled that he wasn't able to support the dignity of his dukedom anymore. Right?"

"It did, because Ned knew I wanted it to do so. He didn't want me to make a fuss about Brother George, you see. So now thanks to Ned, young Neville can't come to Parliament to complain about his inheritance, can he? He won't even inherit his father's barony. Oh, and Ned gave me other things as well. The earldom of Salisbury for my boy, some better lands—anything to keep me happy. And I am. I'm a happy whore, Harry. And so are you, because he gave you Cantref Selyf. Part of your Bohun inheritance, right?"

"Someone had to pronounce sentence on George. It could have been anyone."

"But it was you, old man, wasn't it?"

"All right, then. I'm a whore." I raised my cup and managed to get it to glance against Richard's. "To us whores."

"To Ned."

"And to George."

"Rest in peace, brother." Richard raised his cup high in the air, then let it fall with a crash. "Christ, Harry, what have I done? I could have saved him if I'd begged Ned for his life. Could have if—"

He staggered to his feet and kicked his cup into the fireplace. "If I'd wanted to," he finished.

⸎

Two days later, George's body, borne on a black-draped hearse, began making its way to Tewkesbury Abbey, where his wife had been buried. That same day, Richard got a license to found colleges at Barnard and Middleham Castles.

⸎

The next five years can be disposed of quickly. Kate bore me three more children: two sons, Henry and Humphrey, and one daughter, Anne. Poor

Humphrey, like his namesake my own brother, was frail. He never thrived, but still it broke our hearts when he died in our arms.

Grandmother died in 1480, full of years. I wish she had lived long enough to see her little namesake, and I wish she had lived long enough to give me the wisdom of her counsel when I needed it most—but I anticipate myself. With her death and the release of the lands she'd held in dower, I became truly rich, second only to the king himself and Richard.

With my newfound wealth, I thought that my influence at court might grow accordingly, but of course I was wrong. It took me a long time to realize it, but the king was not hostile toward me. He probably even liked me well enough—after all, I'd not insulted him in years—but there was no place in his grand scheme of things for me. There did not have to be, for England was at peace. Trouble-making George was dead. The Earl of Oxford was locked up tight in Hamnes Castle. Margaret of Anjou, poor lady, was dead; her most valuable possessions—her hunting pack—having gone to Louis of France. Jasper Tudor, that aging Lancastrian, and his nephew Henry were exiled in Brittany and would probably die as old men there. The Scots caused their usual trouble but were handily subdued by Richard. Everything was working in perfect harmony. Why disturb the balance? Why take a chance on an untried young man like myself, with a history of saying the wrong thing? As 1483 approached, I could almost see the king's point.

Almost.

XV

January 1483 to May 1483

WAR WAS IN THE AIR AGAIN IN 1483, WHEN EDWARD CALLED A Parliament. There had been a to-do between Burgundy and France, which ended in the Treaty of Arras in December 1482. Poor Elizabeth, Edward's eldest daughter, had been the chief sufferer by it. As part of the Treaty of Picquigny, she'd been affianced to the Dauphin of France, and Edward had even insisted that she be addressed as Madame la Dauphine, a title that for a while had tied many a good English courtier's tongue into knots. But now that her title finally slid off everyone's lips with ease, it was no more, for the Dauphin was to marry Margaret of Austria, daughter to Burgundy's regent, and poor Elizabeth was back to "the Lady Elizabeth."

"I was right all along," I told Richard breezily as we supped that evening, having arrived in London for Parliament. "I knew Picquigny would never last. And Edward even lost his pension! So, do you think we'll be going to war with France?"

"You'd like to think so, wouldn't you, Harry? Don't get your hopes up."

"I'm not the fool I was at nineteen, if that's what you think," I said. "I know it could all come to naught. But he did wage a war in Scotland."

"No. I waged it for him while he sat back in England and amused himself with Mistress Shore."

Elizabeth Shore was a London mercer's wife who had caught the king's eye some years back. With help from the king, it was generally supposed, she had had her marriage annulled on the ground of impotency (her husband's, needless to say). Since then, she had lived in a comfortable house in London, where she was said to divide her time between entertaining the king and doing good works for the poor. Buxom and cheerful, she was the sort of harlot whom even men who did not like harlots liked. I smiled. "There are worse things."

Richard, however, was one of the rare holdouts against Mistress Shore's charms. "The creature's got even the Marquess of Dorset panting after her."

"I hope for his sake he isn't trying to poach on the king's territory."

"He's stupid enough to try, even though it irks William Hastings as much as the king." Dorset was married to Hastings's stepdaughter. Though Dorset was not a model of fidelity, he certainly could not be accused of avoiding his wife's bed; I'd long since lost count of their offspring. My household had practically a standing order to send a christening cup to Dorset each year. "Two enemies for the price of one. The man's an utter fool. How the queen produced him is beyond me, for she has some sense."

I felt like a boy asking the next question, but I could not stop myself from asking it. I said quietly, "But fool or no fool, Dorset served on your Scottish campaign. So did Edward Woodville; you even made him a banneret. I wasn't asked to go. Why, Richard?"

Richard sighed. "I thought you would ask that sooner or later. Harry, I had no choice with Dorset; the king thinks he should work for his keep, and he has the peculiar idea that he's capable of it. And Edward Woodville is capable. Foolhardy sometimes, but at least he gives his men a fighting spirit."

"But that doesn't answer my question."

"Harry, between my troops and those of Northumberland and Thomas Stanley, there were quite enough of us when Dorset and Woodville were added in; we didn't need you as well. Besides, you've not much presence in the North. It wasn't your fight. And—" He hesitated.

"And?"

"You've no experience in battle, Harry, save for that little bit at Barnet and Tewkesbury. You've never led men in a fight. The Scots would have made a dog's breakfast of you and of your men. Frankly, you would have been a liability."

"I see."

"You've other abilities, of course."

"Oh? Catching rats, mayhap?" I took a sip of ale. "Well. Let's change the subject."

"Harry, you shock me. I thought you would have swept everything off the table in anger."

"No. I'm not the fool I was at nineteen, as I said earlier. You're right. I lack military experience. Why should I be angry when you spoke the truth?"

Inside, of course, I was hurt. But I was seven-and-twenty, and it was time to stop playing the fool.

Richard continued to look at me quizzically for a moment or two, unconvinced of my calmness. Finally, he shrugged and said, "I think Hastings was rather hoping that Dorset might get at the wrong end of a Scottish sword. Aside from Dorset's wenching about under his stepfather's nose, they just rub along together the wrong way. Of course, Hastings isn't fond of Anthony Woodville, either. Too different, and Hastings has always suspected Anthony of slandering him to the king after Hastings replaced Anthony as Captain of Calais. Is the feeling mutual, do you know?"

I shook my head. "Kate and I visit Ludlow once in a while, but Anthony and I are not confidants. I don't know of anyone who is, really. Not even Kate, who can talk to anyone. He's perfectly friendly, but he's always at a remove, it seems. Fortunately it doesn't seem to have rubbed off on the Prince of Wales. He's intelligent, but he likes horses and dogs more than the contemplative life, though he's certainly fond of his uncle Anthony."

"Is it true that Rivers wears a hairshirt? Ned said something of the sort once."

"I don't know. He's never shared a bath with me for me to see him strip, and if there's a hairshirt, I'd just as soon not have the privilege. For his wife's sake, I hope he's abjured it for the time being." Anthony had recently remarried. I sometimes felt sorry for his young bride, who seemed almost an afterthought to her husband's duties as the prince's governor.

"Well, he wasn't wearing one when he fathered his bastard daughter, I suppose."

"Neither were you," I said sweetly. "Or your bastard son."

Richard grinned at me. "Touché."

"How do the two of them fare?"

"Both John and Katherine are thriving. They're at Middleham now with my son Edward. Anne put up a bit of a fuss about them coming, but she gave in soon enough. She's become quite fond of Katherine in particular, as I knew she would, not having a daughter of her own. And they're good company for Edward; even Anne says so now, especially as they're likely to be the only brother and sister he has. Anne's not conceived in years."

"I'm sorry, Richard."

"That's what I get for marrying an heiress, I suppose. Have you ever noticed that either women are heiresses or they're good breeders, but almost never both? Like your wife. No dowry, but five children, one after an—Christ, Harry, I'm sorry. I forgot you lost Humphrey just a short while ago."

"Even with four healthy children left, I still mourn him."

"I know, old man. Forgive me."

He touched my hand gently. After we had both concentrated on our food for a while, he said, "Well, let me tell you what our cloth merchants have begged Parliament to enact. No one below the estate of lord is to wear any gown or cloak unless it covers his genitals and buttocks while he is standing upright. A beneficial piece of legislation, no doubt, but who wants to be the fellow who has to check?"

"Not me," I said, my good humor restored.

⁂

Though Edward as king could have worn his gown or cloak as short as he pleased, I found myself thinking with some gratitude that he had not exercised this prerogative, for the last couple of years had not been kind to him—or he had not been kind to himself. He was still a good-looking man, but he'd added to the extra weight he already carried back at the time of the Treaty of Picquigny. Going to war would have done his physique wonders. Yet he still cut an impressive figure, dressed in robes that surpassed in magnificence anything that had been seen in England, and he dealt with his Parliament as briskly and as efficiently as he ever had.

Therefore, I received the shock of my life when, back at Brecon in April, I was riding back from an afternoon of hunting when I saw my wife and some of my men riding toward me at a fast pace. I galloped to meet them. "Kate? Are the children well?"

"Yes. It is the king." She stared at me as though not believing the words that came out of her own mouth. "He's dead, Harry."

"Dead?" Edward was just under one and forty. For all that he was no longer the fine-looking man he'd been in his youth, he'd never had a day of ill health.

"He caught a chill. For a while it looked as if he were shaking it off, and everyone thought he would recover—but then he suddenly took ill again and failed rapidly. Harry, it is so sad! The king had faults—I never liked his spending time with harlots—but who does not? And he did love Bessie truly, for all that; she told me he never had an unkind or hasty word to say to her in his life. He was kind to all of us Woodvilles, never making us feel unwelcome like some did. I am so sorry for Bessie!"

"I'm sad to hear about it too," I said, and crossed myself.

My thoughts—God curse me for them—were anything but the kind, though. I did pity my wife, who aside from her sympathy for the queen was probably half in love with the king, as most women seemed to be; I even pitied the queen and the king's children. But I knew this: with the king gone, my own time had come.

Young Edward—I would have to think of him as King Edward now, I realized with a jolt—was but twelve years of age. There would have to be a protectorate, and there was no better choice for protector than the old king's brother—Richard. My friend, who had so often commented on my exclusion from anything of real importance. With Richard guiding the king, I would no longer be a nonentity; I would be a man of importance, like my grandfather the first duke. And I would make the most of my new responsibility, so by the time the king came of age, I would be indispensable to him. Why, he might even give me my share of the Bohun inheritance— if Richard didn't give it to me before that.

It was the beginning of a brand-new life for me—and for my children, for that matter. I would leave a legacy of not only land but also power to my own Edward. There might even be an earldom for my younger son, great marriages for my daughters. And Kate, though she might not appreciate her good fortune now, would enjoy it with the rest of us. It was a pity, I'd often thought, for her beauty to be wasted on our estates in Wales when she could be shining at court.

Richard's court, in all but name.

I hoped I wasn't smiling as I took Kate's hand. "I'm sorry, sweetheart; I know you were fond of him. I shall miss him, too."

⁂

The king had died on April 9, not too long after midnight. For much of the day, he had been displayed naked from the waist up at Westminster, where various church and city dignitaries had dutifully filed by to view his body—probably not, I thought rather disrespectfully, the most pleasing sight in the world, seeing as the king had carried so much of his weight in his belly. From there he had been taken to the chapel to lie in more dignified state.

That was the news that the king's messenger brought us before he took some refreshment and rode on to his next destination. Just a few hours later, a second messenger arrived. He came from Lord Hastings. God rest his soul.

I liked Hastings, though we were dead opposites in personality and years separated us. For those very reasons, though, we weren't close, so I was surprised when the messenger handed me a letter. "Your grace, my lord wishes you to read this in privacy." He hesitated. "Out of the company of the duchess."

"Why?"

"Your grace, it will be apparent from the letter."

I shrugged and broke the seal. It was addressed to both me and to Richard, and appeared to have been dictated hurriedly. Hastings was convinced that if the Duke of Gloucester did not bring men with him to London in sufficient numbers, the queen's relatives, especially the Marquess of Dorset, would take the rule of the realm into their own hands, excluding the deserving, such as Gloucester and me. Already the king's councilors who were there in London had set a date for the coronation, and when it had been urged that this decision wait until Gloucester had arrived, the arrogant young fool, as Hastings told it, had replied, "We are so important that even without the king's uncle we can make and enforce these decisions." The only way the disaster of a Dorset rule could be avoided, Hastings had concluded, was for Gloucester and me to bring a strong force with us. The queen, Hastings added, had seen reason and had asked her brother Earl Rivers, who would be escorting the young king to London, to limit his escort to two thousand men. If he did not, Hastings was fully prepared to take ship to Calais, where he would have no difficulty raising a force to thwart Dorset's fool ambitions if necessary.

I put down the letter with a frown. Did Dorset really think that he could take Richard's rightful role from him? Edward would have certainly wanted him to guide his young son through his early years of kingship, and as the man who'd soundly defeated the Scots, the man who was virtually king in the North, there was no better man suited for the task. No wonder Hastings was threatening to take off for Calais! Dorset, whose only talent was in the begetting of children, would be bad enough merely as a member of the king's council. As its leader, he would be sheer disaster. Given the choice between him and Louis of France running the government, many an Englishman might wish for Louis.

Clearly, this fool had to be stopped.

I sent Hastings's messenger back with assurances that I understood the import of Hastings's news and would assist Richard in every way possible. To Richard, I sent a letter assuring him of the same. I was apprehensive about what might happen next, yet oddly exhilarated. Here, at last, was what it felt like to be of importance!

In a few days, I heard from Richard, not in the form of a letter but from the mouth of his messenger, who told me that Richard had arranged to meet the king and Anthony Woodville on their way to London. Would I join them?

Of course I would.

Richard told me that Anne was staying behind for the time being, though she would likely join him later, and I decided to have Kate do the same. Kate didn't object; she liked Brecon and our estate in Gloucestershire, Thornbury, particularly well and had our children and her ladies to keep her company. "What a fine sight all of your men make," she said fondly as they all assembled to begin our journey. "So many Stafford knots!"

"And Richard will be bringing even more men with the badge of the white boar."

"Northerners," said Kate, wrinkling her pretty southern nose. "You'll give my sister my love when you see her, Harry? And my brother Anthony?"

"Of course."

I hugged my children—all of them doubly precious to me since poor Humphrey's early death—and gave Kate one last, long embrace. She'd been too grieved at the old king's death to show any enthusiasm for my advances over the last few days, but finally, the night before, we'd given each other a proper farewell. Perhaps, I prayed, she'd soon quicken with child again. Between Humphrey and the king and my elderly great-uncle, the Earl of Essex, there'd been too much death lately among us; we needed a respite.

Little did I know.

Waiting for me at Northampton were Richard and Anthony—but not the king. Anthony explained that as the day had been fine, he had decided to ride on to Stony Stratford and lodge there, leaving more room at Northampton for our own followers. Tomorrow, he proposed, we could leave at first light and meet the king, then make the journey to London together. It was agreeable to Richard and me.

That little matter of business being done, it was a convivial evening, and Anthony being older and better traveled than either of us—far better traveled than me—the conversation eventually meandered toward his adventures abroad. We'd traveled around Italy with Anthony, jousted a bit, and been waylaid by bandits when Anthony smothered his second or third yawn in an hour. "Time to retire," he said sheepishly. "For me, at least."

Richard waited until Anthony's small band of attendants was lost from sight. Then he said to one of his men, "Stand by the door. Let no one pass. Station others outside the windows."

"Richard?"

"Harry, we must talk."

"We must?" Truth was, I'd been tempted to follow my brother-in-law off to bed. I stifled my own yawn. "About what?"

"Anthony Woodville is plotting against me—and you too, perhaps. He means to rid one, or both of us, of our lives."

That woke me up. I stared at Richard. "What?"

"My men have intelligence that some of his men, dressed as common bandits, mean to stage an attack on the three of us as we move to Stony Stratford the next morning. I will be killed; probably you as well. It will be passed off in London as a tragic accident."

"Why?"

"Why do you think? To prevent me from serving as protector. To keep the Woodvilles in control during the king's minority."

"Anthony would do that? Richard, I don't believe—"

"You doubt me?"

"No. Not you. But perhaps your spies—"

"My spies are first rate. Think, Harry! Anthony's no innocent beneath that hairshirt, if he's wearing one. For all these years he's been the most important man in the king's household, had the virtual ruling of Wales—at your cost, I might add. Do you think he's keen to give all that up? If he can eliminate me, and perhaps you—he may not think you're an obstacle, being married to his sister and shut out of power for so long—then he has a few years yet to run the country. To run the country with a king who's thought of him like a father and will give him anything he wants."

"But—"

"Don't you know that he just recently requested a copy of the patent Ned gave him to raise troops in Wales?"

"I heard something of that. I assumed it was in readiness to fight the French or the Scots. Or in case there was trouble in Wales."

"You assume too readily, Harry. The man's a danger."

I put my head in my hands, thinking. Anthony a killer? I found it hard to believe, but the truth was, as I had told Richard a few months ago, I didn't know Anthony all that well; I'd sometimes wondered if anyone did. There might be things going through his head of which I'd never dreamed.

But Richard I did know. We'd been friends since I was thirteen. He'd comforted me after Tewkesbury, overlooked that foolish drunken kiss I'd given him, taken me to my first brothel. I loved him like a brother, at the very least. And we were—as I recalled now—brothers in arms. He'd supported me when I needed it. Now he needed my support.

I lifted my head. "So what do we do next?"

◦◦◦

"The two of you are stark raving mad. Mad!"

"Shackle him," I told the guards. It was dawn. Overnight, Richard's men and mine had blocked every road out of Northampton and put a guard around Anthony's chamber. My men with drawn swords were the first sight his page saw when he poked his tousled head out of the door.

"I don't understand. Is this a peculiar joke of yours? If so, it's gone too far. Plotting against the two of you? Is that what you said? Harry, all I want is what the two of you want! To get the king crowned and to get back to business. There's trouble with the French, trouble with the Scots—we need to get a council in place to deal with all of this."

"There will be a council, don't you fear. But you won't be on it."

"Harry, I'll have a chance to clear my name, I hope, and you'll see, I've done nothing but my duty to the king, to the Duke of Gloucester, and to the kingdom. There's no plot. Listen to me!"

"We need to get moving."

"Harry! You're fond of Kate, I know. For her sake, won't you believe me?"

"Oh, I forgot. Kate sends you her love. Though that was before she knew you planned to make her a widow."

"A widow? You're well and truly mad! Why on earth would I want to kill you? What harm have you ever done to anyone?"

I stared past Anthony Woodville and thought of what Richard had said to me as we talked late into the night. "Has it never occurred to you that there was something more than your outburst in France that's shut you out all of these years? Ned could have put you on the prince's council; the worst that could have happened was that you'd blunder and then he could give that shrug of his and replace you. No, Harry, there was someone else who found it convenient to have you stay an outcast, and that someone was Anthony Woodville. He wanted to keep you as obscure as possible so he could build up his own power in Wales. God only knows what rot he's talked to Ned about you all of these years."

"As he did with Hastings," I had said slowly. "After he was replaced in Calais."

Richard had nodded solemnly. "Precisely. But now that Ned's gone, mere slander's not going to work for him any longer, is it? He has to find another solution."

Anthony's guards had him all trussed up now. My brother-in-law's voice changed again. "By all that is holy, Harry Stafford, I swear it! There is no goddamned plot!!"

I turned on my heel and walked away.

ے

"But why did you arrest them? My father chose these men to serve me. He would not put evil counselors in my household. And Richard Grey is my own brother!" The young king stared at Richard and me.

I am not proud of how we seized Richard Grey, the king's half brother, and Thomas Vaughan, the king's aged chamberlain. We arrived at Stony Stratford, asked to see them in private, and then gave a signal for our own men to rush in and shackle them. It was done to prevent bloodshed, and also to spare the king the sight of witnessing their arrest, but knowing what I know now, I wish the men at least had had the chance to put up a fight.

"You must trust us, your grace," said Richard in a mild voice. From the time of our arrival, he and I had been perfectly respectful to the twelve-year-old king. "There are plots afoot that threaten not only my safety and that of the Duke of Buckingham, but of perhaps your own person as well. These two men, I fear, are implicated deeply in them."

"I don't believe you. And who are you to arrest my men, anyway? Who gave you authority to do so?"

This was not going to be easy. Richard himself looked a little nonplussed. We'd expected more of a boy, less of a king. "Your grace, your late father, my dearest brother, wished for me to be your protector. I know not what you might have been told by those bearing false witness, but that is the truth. It was his dying wish that I assist your grace in governing until you come of age—"

"You weren't even there when he died!"

"—and I intend to carry out that trust."

"Indeed, your grace," I put in, "before he came to Northampton, the Duke of Gloucester went to York and swore fealty to you, and had his followers do the same."

The king flicked his hand as if swatting away a fly—his mother's gesture.

Richard went on, "Your father knew that I have governed the North for him well and wisely. He would not have put you in my charge if he did not think I would discharge my duties to the best of my ability and in a manner best calculated to bring to you the most profit and honor. I have the additional advantage of being popular with the people, which can only redound to your advantage."

"My father picked good men for my household. I have seen nothing evil in them."

"You are inexperienced in the ways of the world, your grace, and have had little opportunity for comparison."

Edward drew himself up taller, looking more like his father than ever. "And what will my mother the queen have to say about this?"

"You show your youth by such a question," I said. "Women have no business to govern kingdoms. You must not put your faith in your mother, not as an adviser anyway. You must trust to the nobles of the realm, and most particularly in your uncle the Duke of Gloucester."

The king gave me a mulish look, then dropped into a window seat and scowled. Something else in his face made me regret what I'd just said. I had two sons of my own; I'd not want them to be in a situation like this, with all of their familiar advisers under arrest and two uncles they barely knew telling them to trust them. I sat beside Edward and said in a more gentle tone, "Your grace, we really are acting for your own good, though it may not seem so now."

The king ignored me. "Are we leaving?" he demanded. "Or staying here?"

We both looked to Richard for an answer. "We'll return to Northampton once I take care of a few things here. It shouldn't take very long."

"Where are you taking Uncle Anthony? And my brother Richard and Sir Thomas?"

"To the North," said Richard. "They shall be comfortably housed."

"Can I say good-bye to them?"

I was glad this was Richard's decision to make. He made it swiftly. "No."

We left Stony Stratford that same morning, the king's household and his escort, leaderless and dumbstruck, having obeyed Richard's orders to disband. A few attendants had been allowed to stay, though, and they trailed uncertainly behind us as we made our way toward Northampton, the king, mounted on his favorite horse, riding between Richard and myself. Just the act of doing something appeared to have lifted his spirits a bit.

Richard did his best to encourage this brighter state of mind. We took a little detour to the spot where the battle of Northampton had been fought—a gloomy place for me, as Grandfather had fallen there, but the site of one of King Edward's early triumphs in his days as Earl of March. I suspected that Edward had not been quite as key to the victory as Richard told his son—that credit would probably be due to the treacherous Lord Grey of Ruthin, who'd chosen that day to switch sides—but I dutifully played along. When we reached our lodgings in Northampton, our small sovereign was in reasonably good spirits.

We stayed in Northampton through the next day, Richard wanting to hear some news from London before we made our entry there. Meanwhile, he found the king some business to do, starting with perfecting his royal signature. "You wouldn't want to blot it, after all, and force your poor clerks to write what you are signing all over again, now would you?"

"I've already practiced it," the king confessed, in a sheepish tone that made me smile. "I'll show you."

I handed him a quill and spread a sheet of parchment in front of him. Without hesitation, the king inscribed a neat "Edwardus Quintus" on the paper—evidently, he had indeed been practicing. Richard nodded approvingly. "Have you ever seen mine? Here." He wrote, "Richard Gloucester," and for good measure added, "*Loyaulte me lie.*"

"You too, Uncle Harry."

I signed "Harry Buckingham," followed by "*Souvente me souvene.*" "'Remember me often,'" I explained.

The king frowned. "I know what it means, Uncle." He shook his head. "*That*'s your signature?"

It was, I admit, an elaborate one with several flourishes, almost whimsical, but it was legible. Richard pulled the parchment to him and started laughing. "For God's sake, Harry. Signing a few documents a day with that would wear a man out. And what's that little touch here? It doesn't mean anything, Harry. It's an utter waste." He squinted. "Or maybe they're supposed to be little spectacles here?"

"I like my signature. I devised it when I was about the king's age."

"It shows. And what an absurd motto, Harry. 'Remember me often!' What are people supposed to remember? Could be your valiant deeds, but could also be that you owe them money. I'd change it if I were you."

"I'll consider it," I said huffily as the king snickered with Richard as if they were old friends. You would have thought it was my idea to take Anthony Woodville and the rest into custody.

⁂

News came from London just before nightfall in the form of Francis Lovell, who had been made a viscount by the fourth Edward a few months ago. He was one or two years younger than me. I'd seen him from time to time but didn't know him well, and was chagrined to find that he and Richard appeared to be on the best of terms. Evidently Lovell had served under Richard in the Scottish expedition from which I'd been excluded.

"Things have been wild in London," Lovell said, settling down in Richard's chamber. "First, Edward Woodville has taken to sea, supposedly to fight the French."

There had been French raiders pestering the coast since the old king's death, I knew. Richard asked, "With permission?"

"With the council's permission, but considering… He should have waited for you. But it gets better. As soon as the news of what happened to Rivers, Grey, and Vaughan came, the queen dashed into sanctuary."

"Sanctuary? Why, for God's sake?"

"She's putting it out that you have ill designs on the entire Woodville family. And God knows, they're scattering like rats. Edward Woodville's out to sea. Dorset is with the queen in sanctuary. Though not before he tried to raise an army. Couldn't do it. The council received your letters, Richard, and is glad you're in control. Hastings is positively glowing."

"Where's the Bishop of Salisbury?" Lionel Woodville had achieved a bishopric the year before. "And Richard Woodville?"

"Oxford, as far as I know, for the bishop. And as for Richard, who knows? He's never done much more than potter on his estates. One hopes he'll keep doing that."

I frowned. Not for the first time, it occurred to me to wonder what Kate would think when she heard that I'd arrested her brother and her nephew. It wasn't a thought upon which I liked to dwell. Richard, however, was grinning. Lovell said dryly, "You don't seem too concerned."

"I'm not. This proves that they're guilty as hell. I've already told the council of the plots against us. This just buttresses our claims. It couldn't be better."

"But you're not going to tarry here much longer, are you?"

"No. Tomorrow we're leaving here. With all our men we'll be moving slowly, but we should get into London the day after next."

"The fourth of May. That was the day the council set for the king's coronation."

"It's going to have to wait, then. We'll tell the king that more time is needed to make it a grand affair—and that's true enough."

"Is the boy in good spirits?"

"The king," corrected Richard. "His moods come and go. He has a chaplain he's fond of. Tomorrow we're going to appoint him to a church. That should keep him happy for a while. And then when he enters London as king, there will be a grand show, of course. If he's not reassured by all of that, then I don't know what will."

"Has he asked you what you plan to do with his uncle and the rest?"

"Many times. I tell him that it's for the council to decide."

"And what when he finds that his mother is in sanctuary?"

Richard yawned. "We'll deal with that when he finds out." He stood. "Anyway, it's time to pay your respects now. Bow deeply. His grace gets touchy when you don't."

❧

The king could not have wished for more ceremony than he received when the three of us, accompanied by five hundred men of Richard's retinue and mine, rode into London on May 4. We had sent cartloads of arms belonging to the Woodvilles—rounded up, Richard told me, by his spies—ahead of us as proof of the plot, but they had not made much of an impression, we later heard. All wanted only to see the new king.

As we approached the city at Hornsey, we were greeted by a flood of scarlet and murrey—the mayor and the aldermen clad in the former, the hundreds of men from the city guilds clad in the latter. Richard and I, garbed in mourning, looked downright gloomy next to them. The king was smiling, though, and he kept on his smile as the mayor launched into a long speech of welcome. Only when he had finished and the procession began to wind its unwieldy way toward Bishopsgate did Edward say, "My uncle Anthony should have been here! And my brother Richard and dear old Vaughan! When do you intend to release them?"

"When I am satisfied that they pose no threat to me," said Richard. "Or to your grace."

Edward stared sullenly at his horse's mane for a moment. Then he lifted his head and resumed smiling at the guildsmen.

❧

There is nothing so exhausting as ceremony, particularly royal ceremony.

By the time the king had been settled at the Bishop of London's palace and all of the necessary forms had been gone through, I could have crawled into a corner and slept for hours, and so, I suspect, could Richard.

At the palace, however, was William Hastings, and he was too elated to be tired. "The power in the right hands, and with no more blood than would have been spilled from a pricked finger!" he said after we had described the events at Stony Stratford and Northampton to him. "Though I really didn't think that the Woodvilles would go as far as to try to assassinate you. An ambush, you say?"

"Yes, and we've the weapons to prove it. Four cartloads of weapons stored up outside the city."

"Yet hadn't those been stored there long ago for the Scottish campaign? But your intelligence is no doubt superior to mine. The king looked well, considering. Poor lad, all this must be a shock to him. We must get his brother to him; he's a merry lad and will be good company. If the queen had had more sense than to scamper into sanctuary with him... But all will come right. You'll find the council most amenable to your serving as protector, your grace."

"So Lovell said."

"Those letters from you were very reassuring to the council. Which, I presume, my lord of Buckingham will be joining now?"

"Indeed," said Richard. "Harry's been invaluable to me."

I smiled.

"And there shall be offices for Harry as well, very soon."

I gulped. All those years in outer darkness...

Hastings just barely raised his eyebrows. Perhaps he was wondering about the speed of my ascent, and wondering if something might come his way as well, but he was too polished to say anything other than, "Well deserved, I'm sure."

"Shall you stay for supper with us?" I stammered.

"I must decline, your graces, as I have a previous engagement. Mistress Shore has asked me to sup with her tonight. Indeed, I should be setting out now."

He took his leave, a decided spring in his step. Richard shook his head after he was gone. "Taking over that Shore wench, and Ned dead for less than a month. The old rooster."

xvi

May 1483 to June 1483

Once the ceremony of the king's entry into London was over, the council—including me—set busily to work. We scheduled the king's coronation for June 22, and it was I who suggested that his lodgings be moved to the Tower. It was a sensible enough suggestion; there were comfortable royal apartments there, room enough for both the king and his brother when the queen came to her senses and saw fit to let him leave sanctuary.

Rivers, Grey, and Vaughan were all still in prison: Rivers at Sheriff Hutton, Grey at Middleham, and Vaughan at Pontefract. Richard was all for executing them, and requested that the council authorize him doing so. But the council would not agree without more definite proof of a plot. Richard's own word was good enough for me, but I didn't gainsay the council on this point. I'd already written Kate to tell her the news, and I'd received a furious letter in her own hand, then another letter in the same hand a day later, this one begging me to use my influence to see that the three men were shown mercy.

I frowned at the second letter with irritation. Kate was a grown woman, who'd not taken it all that amiss when the late king executed his own brother. Did she really expect Richard to show mercy to the men who had plotted against his own life—and perhaps mine? But yet these were her blood relations; I couldn't expect her not to be angry. So I was glad to write to her and say that they were still in prison, but that nothing had been decided and that there was an excellent chance that in time—perhaps when the king was a man grown and they could cause him or Richard little trouble— they might go free again.

I believed that, Kate. I truly did.

∽

In the meantime, Richard more than kept his word to grant me offices. I was made chief justice and chamberlain of North and South Wales, and constable and steward of so many castles, I could not tell you all of them now, less than six months later.

From nobody to virtual king of Wales was a dazzling change, and I would be a liar if I told you that it did not go to my head. I careened around town with a large escort, spent huge sums of money, and slapped Stafford knots on any man who would stand still long enough to allow it. Yet I did attend to my new duties conscientiously, as all of us on the king's council did. I wanted to be worthy of the trust Richard had placed in me—and perhaps I also wanted to show the dead king how ill-advised he had been not to place such trust in me.

As for the living king, despite the initial signs of a thaw he had exhibited, he had not really warmed to Richard or me—that, I knew, would not happen, if ever, until the day came that Rivers, Grey, and Vaughan were released. Maybe not even then. Hastings, however, was not at the same disadvantage we were, and as he had sons and wards not far from the king's age, he made considerable inroads in Edward's confidence. One day, he requested permission to take the king hunting, a proposition to which Richard agreed, though somewhat reluctantly.

"You've not rewarded him much," I said after Hastings had made his amicable way out of the door.

"Should I relieve you of some of your offices?"

"Well, no. But simply reappointing him as Master of the Mint didn't seem that generous to me."

Richard shrugged. "He's a decent fellow. But he's Ned's boon companion, not mine." He drummed his fingers on the table at which we sat. "I wonder if I should have allowed Hastings to take the king hunting. He's been pressing in council to release Rivers and his ilk, you know, and the king's bound to ask him about it. I've a mind to recall my permission."

"I wouldn't. You'll only make more of an enemy of the king than he is already to you. And to me."

"Enemy?"

"I'm not overstating it, Richard. The boy hates us for those arrests. Before Northampton, when I saw him at Ludlow, he would talk to me readily, laugh. All has changed."

"You're right, I suppose. I did right to have the council extend my powers as protector beyond the coronation, until he's of age."

"But after that? You're Duke of Gloucester. Not a title without ill omens. You know the history as well as I. My forebear Thomas of Woodstock, Duke of Gloucester, was murdered on orders of Richard II. Humphrey, Duke of Gloucester, died suspiciously during the sixth Henry's reign."

"You speak of ill omens, and yet you tell me to allow the boy to go off alone with Hastings?"

"Yes. You don't want the boy growing up with a grudge against you. He's no fool, no more than his father ever was. So you need to gain his confidence. Do more than let him go hunting. Free his Woodville kin, Richard. My wife would thank you for it also. You can keep a close eye on them, limit their landholdings and power, to ensure there's no trouble."

"I don't know. Maybe I should just start by taking him hunting, like Hastings did."

"You could do Hastings one better by taking him to a brothel."

"That's more Hastings's department." For the first time, Richard smiled. "He's made a conquest of that Shore woman, I hear. He spends every night with her; it's convenient that his wife hasn't arrived in London yet."

"Dorset in sanctuary must be going mad with envy."

"Sometimes I wonder, Harry, who corrupted whom: Hastings, my brother, or my brother, Hastings?"

"It's surely a toss-up."

"Well, Ned has Hastings beat by sheer numbers, not to mention variety. Tavern wenches, shopkeepers, merchant's wives, gentry—they've all been well represented in my brother's bed. A miniature parliament in skirts, you might say, except for the nobility."

"Well, there was the Earl of Shrewsbury's daughter, Eleanor Butler." I chuckled. "Kate told me some choice gossip about that years ago."

"Oh?" Richard yawned.

"Yes. According to the Duchess of Norfolk—Lady Eleanor's sister, that is, not the old dowager—Edward went so far as to promise marriage to her if she would succumb. Or maybe she simply succumbed without the inducement. It's all hazy now—Richard?"

Richard's face had gone white. "What the hell did you just say?"

"The Duchess of Norfolk said—"

"I heard you, I heard you. For God's sake, Harry, how could you have kept this to yourself?"

"What was to report? That Edward had made yet another conquest? And the lady was long dead when I heard about it."

"Christ, Harry, don't you see? If he promised her marriage and they had sexual intercourse, there was a marriage! This could change the whole succession! Don't you see? If there was a marriage between those two, there was no valid marriage between the king and that Woodville woman. That means—"

"Young Edward is a bastard. All of the king's children are bastards. Leaving Clarence's son next in the line for the throne."

"No. Clarence was attainted. So leaving—"

"You."

We sat there staring at each other for a few minutes. Then Richard shoved his chair back. "We have to find out the truth. Now. Starting with the Duchess of Norfolk."

"The king took advantage of my sister," said the Duchess of Norfolk. We had been so fortunate as to find her at hand in London, where she'd traveled to attend the upcoming coronation. "She was widowed and vulnerable, and he young and handsome, so she was an easy mark for him. It didn't take long for her to fall into his bed."

"But did he promise her marriage beforehand?" Richard asked.

"She didn't care to speak of the matter, not to me at least. Perhaps to her confessor. But I can tell you this: my sister was a lady of the highest principles. She would never have allowed him into her bed by any other means."

"But he reneged on his promise."

"Yes. The Woodville woman turned his head, with a little help from that witch her mother. I wouldn't be surprised if the daughter wasn't dabbling in the black arts as well, but that's for another day."

"She never tried to hold him to his promise?" I asked.

"Well, what choice did she have? He was the king, not some ordinary knight, after all. And she had her pride. Who would want to be queen under such circumstances, with the king being forced by the papal courts to acknowledge the marriage? No, she stayed silent, and so did I, except on the occasion you know of." She chuckled ruefully. "Heady wine the king had at that wedding celebration. I always assumed that the marriage of my daughter to the Duke of York was some sort of recompense, though goodness knows the king also had his eye on my daughter's Norfolk inheritance." The duchess sighed, for little Anne Mowbray had died just a few years after her magnificent wedding to the Duke of York. "I would be pleased to at last see my sister's good name vindicated."

"And perhaps you shall, my lady," said Richard, rising. "Perhaps you shall."

✑

"Well," said Richard as we left the duchess. "We have it."

"But do we? Lady Butler never said straight out to the duchess that there was a promise of marriage, or gave her any details. Can we really be sure that there was a promise? Do we really have enough evidence to put this before a court?"

"You're in a questioning mood today, Harry."

"I'm just trying to look at things sensibly—for a change." I smiled, but Richard did not. "The king could charm many a virtuous woman out of her shift. The duchess just might not want to admit that her sister could fall so easily. I think we should speak to others—like Hastings."

"Very well. You speak to Hastings. I shall make my own inquires."

⌘

Like Edward his friend, Lord Hastings had become an admirer of all things Burgundian during his enforced stay there, and his private chamber in his London home was a tribute to that duchy, with paintings on the walls and gorgeously illuminated manuscripts spread out on tables for all to admire. I duly did so, then told him of the rumor I'd heard and the need to inquire into it.

"Lady Butler? Now that's a name I haven't heard in a while."

"But you did hear of her before from the king?"

"Why, of course—just as I heard of many another in those days. Think of it, your grace. A young man loses his father and his brother, the person he respects most in the world and the person he loves most in the world, on the same day. Just three months later, he gains the crown. There's the pain of how it was gained, but there's also the pleasure, in knowing that everything he dreams of can suddenly be his. Women are ready to fall into his arms with but a smile. What young man's head wouldn't be turned by all that? What young man wouldn't be profligate in such circumstances?"

"I was not condemning the king."

"No. You think I'm digressing. I'm not. Eleanor Butler was a pretty young woman, though a few years the king's senior—with all that he had been through at a young age, he rather liked his women a little older. The two of them met in the usual way, when she came to him to have her dower rights sped along. He took a fancy to her, and her to him, I daresay, and very soon, they were bedfellows. I know; I helped them meet privately now and then; out of the glare of her family and the court."

"But did he promise her marriage?"

Hastings snorted. "To use an old cliché, why buy the cow when you can get the milk for free? And Lady Butler was most willing to be milked. Not that it's a reflection on her virtue. There was only one woman who held out against Ned, or at least only one about whom he cared, and you know what happened to her. He made her his queen."

"But couldn't he have made her the promise, just to inveigle her into his bed?"

"Ned didn't break his promises. And why make one to begin with? She was a lovely woman, but he didn't love her, no more than he did the others he meddled with at the time. If she refused him, there were others who wouldn't. He wasn't in love with her; he wasn't ready to love anyone at that time. It wasn't until several years later, when the novelty of being able to bed anyone he wanted had worn off a little, that he fell in love, and that woman he married. He was willing to incur the anger of everyone around him for her. Not for Lady Butler, even though she would have been a better match for him in terms of rank."

"And what happened to the king and Lady Butler?"

"She was too proud to be his mistress openly, and he got tired of all of the secrecy involved, especially where there were others who could satisfy him as well or better without all of the to-and-fro required with her. My apologies for my bluntness; I mean no disrespect to the memory of the lady, who was a kinswoman of yours if I'm not mistaken. She was proud, as I say, and I believe she came to regret the affair also. It just ran its course in the end. He found others, and she decided to devote herself to religion. Ned drove more than one lady into the arms of the Church, you know. I hope the Lord remembers that." Hastings sighed. "Christ, I miss him."

"His likes will never be seen again in England," I said.

"Hm. Gloucester's not seriously thinking there's anything to this promise of marriage business, is there? For I can tell you, Ned loved those boys of his. If there were anything amiss that would threaten the succession, he would have paid the Pope a pretty sum to get it put smooth. He would have done—and did—a lot more than that. Clarence died because Ned didn't want him to menace his son's throne one day."

"He's simply doing his duty to investigate a rumor he has heard. He too is concerned for the king's security."

"Well, I'll be glad when the lad is crowned. For Ned's sake. Maybe that will get the queen to come out of sanctuary, too. The sooner that nonsense is all finished, the better."

Hastings walked me to my waiting barge. As it pulled away, another barge pulled into view, close enough for me to recognize Thomas Rotherham, Archbishop of York, and John Morton, Bishop of Ely. Evidently they were coming to visit Hastings.

Odd, I thought. Why not just meet at Westminster?

☙

As I walked into Richard's inner chamber at Westminster, I hoped that he had not set his heart on becoming king, for it seemed to me that if anyone knew the truth about King Edward and Lady Butler, it would have been Hastings. Richard, however, hardly blinked when I told him of our conversation. "I expected as much."

"Richard?"

"Harry, if there is one thing you can say about Hastings, he was devoted to Ned. He'd do anything for him, including lying for him, and he naturally wants to see Ned's son safe on the throne. Commendable, but an incentive to lie. So if he says there was no contract of marriage between him and Lady Butler, it's almost a guarantee that there was one."

"But what if he simply happened to be telling the truth?"

"How did he act when you asked the question? Surprised?"

"Well, no. But hearing that a wench had entangled herself with Edward wouldn't come as a surprise to him."

"Especially not if he'd prepared a story beforehand, knowing that the time was coming for him to be questioned about it. Now on the other hand, we have the Duchess of Norfolk. What would she gain by lying? Nothing. The story makes her sister look like a simpleton, and there aren't any offspring to gain the throne by its telling. No, Harry, I think we have to give the duchess precedence over the lord, in both rank and truth. And knowing that, and guessing what Hastings would say, I've been speaking to a bishop."

"Bishop Morton?"

"Why, no. What brought him to mind?"

"I saw him at Hastings's house. Him and the Archbishop of York."

Richard frowned, then shrugged. "Well, in any case, I've been speaking to the Bishop of Bath and Wells. Stillington has a fine mind."

"Speaking to him about what?"

"Why, this marriage between the old king and Lady Butler, of course. Or shall I call her the uncrowned queen?" Richard yawned. "No, that's too time-consuming. Let's stick with 'Lady Butler,' shall we? She's not in a position to mind, poor lady."

"But the only word we have is her sister's! And she wasn't unequivocal."

"No, there are other circumstances to support it. Look at my brother George. Why do you think he was killed?"

"Because he executed Annette Twynho for no good reason. Because he was dabbling in treason well before he became of age, with Oxford and the like. Because he spread those rumors that Edward was a bastard. Because—"

"Because he knew the truth about the king and Lady Butler."

"How?"

"Who knows? Maybe someone babbled it to him. Maybe even Ned did in a misguided moment. But why else kill him? Annette Twynho's death was an outrage, but it wasn't a threat to Ned. As for the other reasons, the House of Lancaster wasn't exactly flourishing at the time. And no sane person would believe that my mother was an adulteress."

I could not help smiling. "You're certainly right about that."

"So there's only one reason that I can think of that would explain why

Ned executed George: George knew something that would threaten the succession. And this was it. Don't think it's just my opinion; Stillington thinks there might be something to it also. Harry? You're looking green."

"You mean to take the crown," I said. "You want it. Don't you?"

Richard nodded slowly. "Yes. I do."

"Even if it means taking it from your nephew?"

"I'm not even convinced it belongs to him. And if it does? Harry, you know your history. Richard II and Henry VI were child kings, and look what happened. Disaster after disaster, crisis after crisis."

"But they had poor advisers, men who were interested in their own gain. Here you would be in charge, and you would rule wisely."

"Yes, for a few years. And then what would happen when the king came into his majority? All my good work would be undone; all wasted with a few strokes of a whelp's pen. With me being king, England could be great from the very start, and could go from triumph to triumph. We'd win back the lands in France that Henry VI lost, for one thing; we'd be bringing Edward III's dream to fruition. You hated that Treaty of Picquigny; so did I. Why, Louis has been laughing up his long nose at us ever since. Do you want more of that?"

"But—"

"It wouldn't just be France. The people of the North love me, and with good reason; I've served them well. Why couldn't all of the people grow to love me? They wouldn't love me because of my cockmanship, like they did Ned; they'd love me for what I did for them. I'd give them good government, better laws, peace and tranquility. Trade would flourish, because we'd open new markets. Now, Ned's boy is a clever boy, I'll grant you that, but he's a boy. By the time he got on his feet as king, assuming that he stood upon his own legs and wasn't guided by his mother's people, precious years could be lost. There are so many things we could be doing now, now and for years to come. We would make this little island the envy of the world."

He draped an arm around my shoulders.

"I'm telling you all this because I know I can trust you more than any other man in the world. You've never failed me; you've always wanted to serve me. Will you help me in this? If you say no, I'll manage, but I'd like to share this glory that is to come with you."

"All right," I said. "I'll help you."

Richard embraced me hard and held me there for a long time. Finally he released me, and burst out laughing.

"Just think, Harry. All this is due to one man's inability to keep his cock in his drawers."

∽

We set to the work of claiming the crown—I never thought of it as usurping, not then—that very afternoon. First on the agenda was Richard's sending to York for armed men. They were needed, he wrote, to protect us against the queen, her kin, and her affinity, who were intending to murder the two of us and all of the old royal blood.

"The queen plotting against us?" I asked skeptically. "She's in sanctuary. How can she plot?"

"Dorset's still there. Besides, if she's not plotting now, she will be when the news of the marriage with Lady Butler comes out. In any case, we're going to need the troops, and this will get them here as soon as any other means."

Without protesting further, I watched as Richard put his seal to the letter.

Quietly, we set about finding other witnesses to the relationship between Edward and Lady Butler, for although we were counting on Edward's notoriety with the female sex to carry a great deal of weight, we wanted something more substantial than the Duchess of Norfolk's sisterly assurances of the lady's virtue. But nothing was forthcoming, so we consulted with Bishop Stillington and William Catesby, a lawyer whom Richard had recently made Chancellor of the Earldom of March, and decided that other grounds should be put forth. "The oldest lawyer's trick in the book," explained William Catesby. "Throw enough muck against the wall, and hope that some of it sticks."

"I should hardly call this muck," protested Bishop Stillington. He was a former chancellor of the fourth Edward's, and had spent several months in the Tower after Clarence's execution. No one, not even Richard, who had been back in the North at the time, was quite sure why, but I had always assumed he'd made a careless comment about the high-handed manner in which George's trial had been handled. He'd not stayed on Edward's bad side for long: the following year, he'd been sent to treat with the Bishop of Elne, King Louis's ambassador.

"Don't mind me, your grace. I simply tell it as it is."

I knew William Catesby well, which was not to say that I liked him, but he was certainly competent. He'd acted as one of my estate agents for several years and was a man of talent and energy. His chief patron was Hastings, though, and it had been through Hastings that he had come to my attention. I was used to his plain speaking, as he liked to call it, but poor Stillington looked discomfited, even more so when Catesby said, "Well, your grace. Give us some muck."

"I hardly—Well, for one thing, the king's marriage to Elizabeth Woodville was made without the knowledge and assent of the lords of the land."

Richard frowned.

"Not the firmest ground on which to rest a case, I know. More to the point, it was made privately and secretly, in a private chamber, a profane place, with no banns."

Richard smiled, then frowned again. "Of course, the Butler marriage was secret too."

Catesby put in. "Let us think back to Warwick's time, gentlemen. Was it not put about that the Duchess of Bedford procured the marriage of her daughter to the king by sorcery and witchcraft?"

"She was acquitted," I said.

"By a council controlled by the king. How could it help but acquit her, his mother-in-law? Another council, not intimidated by the king, might have reached a very different result. And is it not odd, you think, that the Duke of Bedford—only in his forties—died so soon after marrying his young duchess, and that she married that obscure squire Woodville so soon afterward?"

Richard grinned. "What think you, Harry? Was your mother-in-law a witch?"

"I hardly knew her." Some residue of decency made me add, "But no, I don't believe she was. She was a pious woman, but just very French. Bedford was in failing health and was under immense strain at the time of his death; his cares aged him, they say. It's no wonder that his widow looked for a lusty young man afterward."

"Nonetheless, it may bear looking into," Richard said. "Well. Go on."

Stillington said, "There is the question of jurisdiction, your grace. Strictly speaking, the matter of the precontract should be raised in the Church courts, but the resolution might not be a speedy one—and the verdict would not be sure by any means, I fear. If it were brought in Parliament on the grounds of public notoriety, however—"

"Look into that for me, Bishop." Richard stood and stretched. "I think we've done a good day's work."

Thus dismissed, Stillington hurried off, but Catesby lingered. Seeing him do so, I, of course, did also. "Well, Catesby? What think you? Do we have a case?" Richard asked.

"With your troops from the North, you won't need one," said Catesby. "Not much of one, anyway. Londoners are scared to death of anyone from up there. Just the knowledge that armed northerners are on the way will throw them into a panic here. They're a soft lot when it doesn't involve commerce. No, I think you have another problem on your hands, your grace."

"Oh?"

"Hastings. When the news of the marriage hits the council, he's going to do anything in his power to keep that boy on the throne. Including calling on his followers. Who are numerous, here and in Calais. Plainly speaking, your grace, he could destroy you."

Richard looked at me. "You mentioned that Morton and Rotherham paid him a visit the other day."

"Yes. It could have been nothing."

"It could have been treason." He twisted the dagger he wore at his side. "Well. Something else to look into."

∽

John Morton, Bishop of Ely, was a plump man who always made sure that refreshment was on hand for our council meetings. At the last meeting, his servant had brought in wafers so good I'd taken a couple with me when I left to tide me over later between dinner and supper. On Friday, June 13, a bowl of fat, glistening strawberries greeted us as Hastings, Catesby, Morton, Rotherham, Thomas Stanley, Richard, and I filed into the council chamber at the Tower at around nine. The rest of the council was meeting at Westminster, for greater efficiency, Richard had decided.

The berries disappeared quickly. "You must have more brought to us, Bishop," said Richard affably. "Delicious!"

"There are plenty more where those came from," said Morton proudly. "They are flavorful, aren't they? My gardener outdid himself this year, truly."

"Then have some more brought, please. And it would be kind to share them with those meeting at Westminster, don't you think?"

Inwardly, I heaved a sigh of relief. Since yesterday, I'd felt uneasy, worrying about Richard and Hastings. But if Richard was sitting chatting about strawberries, there clearly couldn't be anything amiss, not now.

Morton's manservant went out to fetch the strawberries, and we spoke for a while about the situation with Edward Woodville, who had taken his fleet to Southampton. There Richard had sent men to seize him, but Woodville, learning of his brother Anthony's arrest, had managed to escape. Reports had it that he had landed safely in Brittany—along with some ten thousand pounds in gold that he had seized from another ship, as forfeit to the crown, while at Southampton. We were all bewailing this loss when Richard excused himself to answer nature's call.

"I do hope it wasn't the strawberries," Hastings said. He popped another one into his mouth.

"Never," said Morton touchily. "To the contrary, they are most healthful."

The door swung open, and Richard marched in.

It was if another being had taken possession of his body. His eyes glowed with anger, and he even looked taller somehow, so rigid he was. "My lords," he said. "What would you do if you discovered treason in your midst?"

The answer seemed to be an obvious one, so much so that we all simply sat there staring. But Richard clearly expected an answer, so Hastings finally said, in a light tone, after gulping his strawberry, "Why, arrest the traitor, of course."

"Correct, Lord Hastings. Then, come! Arrest the traitor."

A dozen armed men sprang into the room and seized Hastings. "What the devil is this?" he sputtered as they tied his arms and legs. "Gloucester, have you gone mad?"

"You will deny you have been plotting against me, and Buckingham, and all of the blood royal?"

"Deny it? Hell, yes! I was the one who urged you to take on the protectorate, have you forgotten that? What ails you?"

Morton stood. "My lord protector, there is the gravest misunderstanding here!"

"Yes, there is—in trusting you! Arrest him too. And Rotherham."

Morton and Rotherham stared at each other as men grabbed them from behind. Then Rotherham thudded to the floor in a dead faint.

Hastings jerked in my direction. "Buckingham! You tell him. We've done nothing treasonous. Nothing—" His face suddenly changed. "Christ," he said softly. "This is about that business you saw me about the other day, isn't it? That Eleanor Butler strumpet?" Hastings's face was ashen. "This whoreson Gloucester means to take the crown for himself!"

"Take him out! I'll have his head. Now!"

"No block," the youngest of Richard's guards squeaked.

"Improvise!"

Hastings was fighting now, trying to break free of his bonds. "You'll not take the crown from Edward's boy, not while I've breath in my body! Someone let me near him. I'll kill him! I'll kill him!" They jerked him backward, began to drag him out of the room as Richard watched impassively. "For God's sake, Ned! Forgive me! I thought it best for the boy that Gloucester take over. I only wanted the best for him. Never in my life did I think—" Hastings's voice broke into a sob, and then strengthened again as his heels cleared the threshold. "A curse on you, Gloucester, and Buckingham as well! A curse on you, and upon your sons!"

"Take Morton and Rotherham to cells here," Richard commanded. "Let Hastings have a priest if he can stop babbling long enough to confess."

"Good work," said Catesby. He nodded and put the last of Morton's strawberries in his mouth.

Richard sank into a chair and bit his nails. I sat rigid in mine.

A quarter of an hour later, two of Richard's men appeared, carrying a sack. Without saying anything, one of them pulled an object out of it.

I looked upon the head of Lord William Hastings, Edward IV's best friend, who'd whored with him, shared exile with him, fought with him, triumphed with him. Then I vomited on my shoes.

xvii

Kate: April 1483 to June 1483

HOW CAN I DESCRIBE THE MONTHS AFTER THE FOURTH KING EDWARD died? It was as if the world went topsy-turvy, not once but over and over again.

I mourned the late king for days. I knew his faults, as a man and as a king. I deplored his killing of the sixth Henry, his unfaithfulness to my sister, his refusal to give poor Harry the responsibilities due the Duke of Buckingham, but I also loved the man who had honored my sister in every way except for faithfulness of his body, who had comforted me after John's and Papa's deaths, who had made me a duchess at age seven. I mourned his death doubly because no one had expected it. True, the king had not cut the fine figure he had as a youth—but dead, at age forty?

And then came the news that my brother Anthony, my nephew Richard Grey, and the young king's chamberlain, Thomas Vaughan, were under arrest. Anthony, one of the most learned men in England, who'd served the House of York for over twenty years. Richard, who had tamed his wild ways and was turning out to be an excellent administrator in Wales—the king had told us so. Old Thomas Vaughan, who had carried the infant Edward around at court as proudly and as lovingly as if he had been his own son. And they had been arrested at the orders of that creature Gloucester—and at those of my own husband.

I had never liked Gloucester, but my dislike for him had been strictly personal, based on the supercilious way in which he'd always treated me. Yet I had known him for a loyal man, faithful to his brother the king.

But how loyal could a man be who arrested men appointed by the late king himself?

Then came the news that my sister was in sanctuary, my nieces and nephews with her, my brothers there or in hiding. The king's coronation had been postponed, and Gloucester had made himself protector.

I could not sit in Wales waiting to hear what happened next. Though Harry had told me he would send for me when the time had come to go to London for the coronation festivities, I decided not to wait. Harry might not like it, but I was coming to join him in London.

∽

To my dismay, as my men drew close to London, they learned that the Duchess of Gloucester was making the same journey as I and that our paths would inevitably join soon. As she took precedence over me, it would have been the height of impropriety not to acknowledge her, so when I settled down—irony of ironies—in Northampton where she was also staying, I dutifully sent my respects and was duly invited to dine with her.

What do two duchesses speak of, when their husbands are allies and when one duchess's husband has sent the other duchess's relations to prison? We spoke of our children, naturally. She described her little Edward's education and knightly training with great pride, and I described my little Edward's education and knightly training with equally great pride—leaving out my younger son and my two girls so as to not seem that I was rubbing in the fact that I had four children to her one. When that topic was worn to death, we discussed what we were planning to wear to the coronation of yet another little Edward, being very careful to compliment the other's appearance a few times as we did so. We discussed the shortcomings of a few of our staff. We discussed our flower gardens and our herb gardens. In short, we discussed everything except for what was uppermost in our minds.

Only after we were parting for the evening did I dare to ask, "My lady, has your lord given you any indication of what is going on in London? What on earth does it all mean?"

The Duchess of Gloucester shook her head. "We shall soon find out, I daresay."

✂

As expected, Harry's greeting was not an enthusiastic one. "What in the world are you doing here? I said I would send for you."

"And when would that have been? Christmastide? Harry, what is going on? Why are my relations in prison? Why is my sister staying in sanctuary?"

"Your relations are in prison because they were plotting against Richard. They might have been plotting against me as well. Your sister's in sanctuary because she was involved in the plot and is afraid to leave."

"Harry, I cannot believe that."

"I don't expect you to," Harry said with the air of one reasoning with someone either very young or very stupid. "Now, how are the children?"

"They are well." I was not to be deterred. "What proof does this Richard of yours have of a plot?"

"The Duke of Gloucester has his spies, and he displayed cartloads of weapons stockpiled by your kin. Kate, I'm sorry, but it's their own folly that brought them to this. Not mine, not Richard's. But I am certain that Richard will be merciful. As for your sister, she's free to come out when-ever she sees fit to grace us with her presence. We are prepared to swear an oath as to her safety if she has any fears, which she shouldn't have."

"Can I see her?"

"No. Being allowed to see her family as normal can only encourage her to stay there. But I'm sure she'll see reason soon." Harry's hand suddenly landed on my breast, and he pulled me close to him. "Now that you're here, I must admit that I've missed you," he said coaxingly.

"I've had a long journey, Harry. I'm tir—"

Harry only pulled me against him more tightly, and I deemed it best to let him have his own way. But it was like lying with a stranger, at least for me, and as passively as I lay under Harry as he completed his business, it probably was for him, too.

This was on the fifth of June. For a few days afterward, I did believe that all might come right. Preparations were being made for the coronation, I saw, and while there seemed no prospect of having Anthony and the rest released, there was no reason to think that any worse might befall them either.

Then, on June 13, William Hastings was beheaded, and the world was no longer topsy-turvy. It had gone stark raving mad.

xviii

Harry: June 1483

"WHY? WHY?"

"Harry, I had no choice. The man was plotting against me. You heard Catesby."

"Couldn't you have imprisoned him, like you did the Woodvilles?"

"No. He was too popular, too dangerous."

"He cursed us and our sons."

"Harry, I've heard watermen do the same for people who short them on their price. It hasn't cut down on water traffic that I've seen."

"Has the king heard of this? He may have seen it, for Christ's sake!"

"No. I had him taken elsewhere. But he will hear of it in due time, from me personally. So will the entire city, for I've drawn up a proclamation explaining the treason. Harry, you can't turn soft on me. The man knew what he was doing, the risks involved. And I shall be generous with his widow. She is, after all, Anne's aunt." Lady Hastings was a sister of the Kingmaker. "She shall get her dower, and Hastings won't be attainted, which is certainly better than he deserves. Why, I'll even honor Hastings's wish to be buried at Windsor in a tomb next to Ned's. They can whore together for all eternity."

I sighed.

"In the meantime, we have other things to worry about. Dorset has escaped from sanctuary. Probably with the help of that strumpet Mistress Shore, whom I've placed under arrest. And with that, it's high time we brought the Duke of York out of it to stay with his brother."

We had a long council meeting the next day, and it was decided to send the Archbishop of Canterbury, Thomas Bourchier, and a delegation to Westminster to reason with the queen. The archbishop—my grandfather's half brother—did not take to the task enthusiastically. He was seventy-two years of age and had largely retired from public life until we'd written to him back in May, ordering him to take custody of the Tower and its treasure.

The archbishop did not know of the Eleanor Butler business. Only a handful of us knew; indeed, those who had met at Westminster on the day of Hastings's death had been busy working out the details of the coronation.

The human mind can perform majestic acrobatics, and mine was proving particularly adept at this art. I did not think of myself as dishonest as I joined Richard in arguing that the Duke of York should be freed from sanctuary so that he might take part in his older brother's crowning. In the back of my mind I was still thinking that Richard might decide that his case was too weak or that something might come to light that made his case so strong that there could be no question that Edward was indeed a bastard, in which case we could have no qualms about taking him from his throne. In the meantime, I persuaded myself, there was no shame in going forward as if there would indeed be a coronation on June 22.

So on June 16, a flotilla sailed from the Tower to Westminster, bearing the archbishop and a load of soldiers. We had supplied him with any number of points to raise in argument against the queen. Her refusal to release the boy was inciting the hatred of the people against the nobles of the land, making it difficult for them to govern and making England a laughingstock among nations. The Duke of York, having committed no crime, and being of tender years, had no right or need to take sanctuary. The sanctuary was rife with criminals of the worst sort, with whom it was highly improper for the boy to consort. The king was in need of company of his own age and station.

It was hours before the archbishop returned to Westminster Hall, where I awaited him. The queen, no fool, had met him argument for argument, even in the face of all of the soldiers flanking him. Only when the archbishop, exhausted as she was, pledged that no harm would come to the boy, and begged her to let him go voluntarily lest sanctuary be broken and the Lord's house dishonored, did she finally agree to relinquish her son. The armed men lurking behind the bishop no doubt influenced her decision as well.

So the Duke of York stood in front of me, holding the archbishop's hand. "Sanctuary was *dull*," he said chirpily as I conducted him to the Star Chamber where Richard awaited him. "Nobody but Mama and the girls there. I shall enjoy seeing Edward. Has it been dull for him?"

"Indeed, I think it has, your grace."

"When he's crowned it won't be so dull, I imagine. Is it ever dull, being king, do you think, Uncle Harry?"

"I suppose anything could get dull occasionally."

"That's when having a lot of minstrels comes in handy, I suppose. Or mistresses."

"*Mistresses?*"

"Well, something like that. One day I heard Papa saying that he had three mistresses. One was the merriest, one was the wiliest, and one the holiest in the realm. I suppose they must be a very special sort of minstrel."

"No doubt," I said, grateful that we had reached the Star Chamber.

∾

The next day, Richard ordered that the coronation would be postponed again—until November 9.

There would be no more postponements, everyone had started to realize. There would be no coronation. Not for Edward.

We'd stopped trying to improve our case about Eleanor Butler—Catesby had been right. With Hastings's death, and rumors that troops from the North would be pouring into the city, we didn't need much of a case. We could have put a crown on the city rat-catcher and called him a king, and the Londoners probably would have accepted him—sullenly, but without a fight. They remembered what Margaret of Anjou's unchecked northerners had done to the countryside, and they had visions of their own shops in flames, their sons beaten to a pulp, their wives and daughters despoiled, their own heads lined up in neat rows on London Bridge. They weren't visions that we did anything to discourage, even as we had to smile at the impossible numbers of troops the Londoners were conjuring up in their heads. Twenty thousand was one of the more modest estimates I heard.

"After I've ruled for a while, the people of the South will realize I don't have horns and a tail," said Richard. "In the meantime, it won't hurt to let them think I might be in league with the devil."

"While keeping the Church on your side, too," I reminded him. The next day, Sunday, June 22, preachers throughout London were to give sermons on the subject of the king's bastardy.

"Well, old man, no one said that this was going to be easy." Richard laughed, then shook his head. "Harry, there's something I must tell you."

"You've changed your mind."

"No. Yesterday I sent orders out to Sheriff Hutton, Middleham, and Pontefract. Rivers and the rest of them are to be executed at Pontefract."

"Richard!"

"I know you didn't want it done, Harry, so I didn't consult you. That way, you'll have a clear conscience."

It wasn't clear at all, though. "Wasn't there some way you could have let them live?"

"Yes, and spend my entire reign fretting about them plotting against me. No, Harry, it's best to show my claws at first. When things are settled, I can show mercy. That's where Ned made his mistake. At the beginning of his reign he was merciful to scoundrels like your Beaufort kinsmen—sorry, old man, but it's true—and it came back to haunt him. If he'd been ruthless from the start we might have been spared a lot of bloodshed."

He gave the papers he was riffling through a great thump and left the room, leaving me with nothing but my conscience for company.

I knew Kate mourned the loss of her brother John and her father to this day; for as long as we had been living together, I'd seen her making her way in silence to our chapel every August 12.

But Kate's father and John Woodville hadn't been traitors. Anthony and the rest were.

Then where is the proof? Kate's voice asked me. *Where is Richard's proof?*

In the end, it was bad enough facing Kate's voice inside my head without facing Kate herself. I stayed at Westminster that night, and for the next couple of nights after that. Besides, I had a speech to draft, the most important speech I would ever give in my life. It was the one in which I was to urge the leading men of the city to offer Richard the crown—the stage having been set with the Sunday sermons.

Writing it would be a hell of a lot easier than trying to figure out how to tell Kate that her brother was doomed to die.

❧

The sermons went well. As hoped, they put everyone in London in a thoughtful mood, and gave them the rest of Sunday and all of Monday to recall the old king's sexual proclivities. They were, after all, better known to Londoners than anyone, Edward having had a pronounced liking for merchants' wives and daughters, as they were not so lowborn to be disagreeable to the senses and not so highborn as to be a nuisance. There were even hints in the speeches that the old king himself was a bastard—not a text of my making or of Richard's, to do us justice, but a holdover from the Warwick days slipped in by the overenthusiastic Ralph Shaa, who'd not much cared for the old king. Warwick's house full of meat, free to anyone who asked, and his slanders about the king were well remembered, it seemed.

With the sermons out of the way, I set myself to practicing my speech in any spare moment I had—sometimes with my pages as my audience, sometimes with Catesby as an audience, sometimes with only the ravens flapping outside my chamber window as an audience. I was not entirely a novice at such things. As a boy, I had been given some training in rhetoric. I'd done well, my tutor always said. Though by nature I was reserved and rather quiet, I knew my voice was pleasing, and I could project it well so as to be heard—there had been no difficulty in hearing me at Clarence's trial, the last time I'd had to make a pronouncement to a large audience. But I was still a bundle of nerves, because this speech had to be perfect. On it rested Richard's future, and mine as well. For if anything happened to arrest the momentum in which London was moving, our lives would not be worth the purchase when young Edward came of age.

On Tuesday I proceeded to the Guildhall, where the mayor and the leading men had been summoned. There, I reiterated the story—what there was of it—of the precontract between Edward and Eleanor Butler. For good measure, I dropped vague hints that Edward might have been involved in marriage negotiations abroad before his secret marriage to Elizabeth Woodville—quite possibly, I reasoned, there could have been a betrothal that had never been revealed to us in England. Then I moved on to the subject of Richard's virtues.

I wish Richard had been there to hear me. Men afterward told me that it was an eloquent speech, uttered with an angelic countenance, and who am I to gainsay them? I spoke of Richard's years of faithful service to his brother, who, I hinted, was not entirely worthy of such dogged devotion. I spoke of his bravery at Barnet and Tewkesbury and about his triumph over the Scots. I spoke of his piety, his generosity to the Church, his munificence to the poor. I spoke of how the North had come to love him, a child of the South, and how when the South saw more of him, they would soon do the same. By the time I finished, I was choking with tears, so convinced had I become myself that the country could not flourish without Richard. When I at last finished, I cried out, "And now, gentlemen, will you take this good man as your king?"

There was a silence, which continued for an agonizing moment too long before a group of my men, primed for such an eventuality, shouted, "Yea! Yea!" Then, much to my relief, the mayor and the rest joined in, their voices firm if not enthusiastic. It was not the rapt acceptance I had hoped for, but it was enough.

On Wednesday Stillington, aided by Catesby, put the final touches on the petition we were to present to Richard, urging him to take the throne. On Thursday the lords of the land, spiritual and temporal, rode to Baynard's Castle, the Duchess of York's London home, where Richard was staying. I was at the head of the procession.

That day, June 26, 1483, is a blur to me now. I remember kneeling before Richard with the petition, tears streaming down my face, and I remember Richard raising me, then telling the assembly that yes, he would take on the duty of kingship for the sake of the realm. I remember riding from Baynard's Castle to Westminster, where Richard, putting on royal robes with my assistance, and taking the scepter handed to him, sat in the marble chair at the King's Bench. I remember Richard's speech—one that put my effort to shame—in which he said that he would administer the law without delay or favor and that he would pardon those who had offended against him. (Did I think, then, of Anthony Woodville, Richard Grey, and Thomas Vaughan, lying in a common grave at Pontefract Castle since the day before, having been given but a show of a trial? Probably not.) I remember John Fogge, an elderly cousin of the queen who had taken sanctuary at Westminster, being brought out to Richard, who took his hand in friendship. I remember processing into the abbey, where Richard took Edward the Confessor's scepter in his hand, and then another procession back to the city, and a procession to St. Paul's. I remember a great joy, and yet underneath it all a great sadness, at the thought that my dearest friend now belonged not only to me and a few others, but to all of England.

Was my great sadness a foreknowledge of what was to come? I think not; I have not the gift of prophecy.

At last I remember processing back to Baynard's Castle. There Richard shooed the others out of his chamber. When we were alone, he smiled. "We've changed history, my friend," he said.

I nodded, wondering if people who changed history always felt a little

seasick afterward. Seasick, and drunk with fatigue as well. "So it seems." I
yawned before I could even cover my mouth. "My apolo—"

Richard laughed. "Poor Harry, you're about to fall over, aren't you? So
I am I, I'm not ashamed to say." He nodded toward the inner chamber.
"You shall have the privilege of sharing my bed tonight. The first person
to be so honored by me as king."

"No Anne?"

He shrugged. "She didn't help me to the crown. You did." I made as
if to take his robes off, and he shook his head. "No. We must do this in
proper form. Boys!"

A group of pages hastened in and began the work of preparing the king's
bed and undressing us, a ceremony that no doubt would later become more
elaborate in the days to come. On this night, however, the task was accomplished briskly. When all had departed and we lay side by side, Richard
said, "Do you think I'll make a good king?"

"If I didn't, why did I tell half of London you would? You'll be the best
king England could ever have, Richard."

Richard smiled in the light of the cresset lamp that burned over us.
"Thank you." His voice dropped a note. "I couldn't have had a better
friend than you in all of this." He leaned over and kissed my cheek, lightly.
"I love you, Harry."

Those were, I realized as Richard rolled over in preparation for sleep, the
four words I'd been longing to hear since I was thirteen years of age.

xix

Kate: June 1483 to July 1483

HARRY TRIED TO JUSTIFY WILLIAM HASTINGS'S DEATH TO ME. HE SPOKE vaguely of secret meetings, plots, fears for his and Richard's life. I believed none of it. No one did, really, especially when, just days later, Richard and Harry began to put it out that Edward had been precontracted to Eleanor Butler.

I remembered, faintly, the Duchess of Norfolk tipsily babbling about a romance that her sister had had with the king. I remembered, also faintly, mentioning it to Harry. But a marriage? I could not believe it. Surely if there had been the slightest hint of such a thing, Edward, a loving father and a proud Yorkist, would have done all that he could to protect the crown for his son. He'd obtained papal dispensations for his sister the Duchess of Exeter to annul her marriage to the poor Duke of Exeter on the flimsiest of grounds. He'd helped his mistress Elizabeth Shore annul her marriage to her supposedly impotent husband. Why for the sake of his sons could he not have done the same for himself, if there were such a marriage in his past? I even asked this of Harry, in the early days when I could still hold a conversation with him, but he merely shrugged. The best minds of the Church, he said, were looking into the matter. It was not a woman's business to meddle.

In the meantime, other rumors swirled, put in motion by the king and his creatures. There was the vile old one that the Duchess of York had committed adultery and that her son the late king was the bastard offspring of their relationship. There was the vile new one that my sister Bessie had taken the royal treasury into sanctuary with her—the amount of her haul grew daily, so that within a week or so the late king (and therefore my sister with her purloined goods) had become as rich as Croesus. Within another week, my brother Edward and my nephew Dorset, and then all of us Woodvilles, shared in the loot.

Mama was a witch, so was Bessie. The ladies of our family gathered each All Hallows' Eve with our familiars and cast spells over anyone who had slighted us recently. Poor Lionel, who had become the Bishop of Salisbury just the year before, did unspeakable things with the Host. Edward had turned pirate. Even my brother Richard, who had no taste for public life and who was happiest on his manors deep in the country, was said to be lusting after the crown.

During those miserable days, I hardly saw Harry. I did, however, beg him to spare my brother's life, and those of Richard Grey and Vaughan, for I knew that with Hastings's death, their own lives hung by the weakest of threads. I got back a reply that any petitioner would get: my request would be considered.

Then, the day after Richard, Duke of Gloucester, became the King of England, the news arrived that Anthony, Richard Grey, and Thomas Vaughan had been beheaded at Pontefract. Harry had not told me; I learned it when the news was cried out by Gloucester's heralds.

༝

"I'm sorry, Kate. I know you're upset."

Upset, as if three men's deaths were no more than a spoiled bolt of fabric or an overcooked piece of meat. "You knew all along he planned to kill them."

"I did not! Kate, you have to understand, they were plotting against Richard—and even me as well. They wanted to destroy us. Richard had to order their deaths. It wasn't a decision he made lightly."

"They wanted to take my nephew to London and crown him, as his father wished! You and Gloucester swore your allegiance to the boy!"

"That was when we believed that he was the rightful heir to the throne. Kate, you're hardly unbiased, being Elizabeth Woodville's sister."

"And you're unbiased, being Gloucester's friend?"

"I told him of the story about Eleanor Butler—the story you told me— and the Duchess of Norfolk confirmed it, as best she could. The king did nothing to influence her. If she had denied it, we would not be having this conversation."

I gave up, realizing what a hopelessly circular conversation this would turn into. Harry would justify anything his idol, Richard, did. "I have asked my tailor to have mourning robes made for me. I trust you will at least allow me to wear them, and for me to have masses said for my brother's soul, and those of the rest?"

"Well, of course," said Harry. He touched my face, and for a moment I almost recognized the remnants of my husband in what had become Richard's creature. "I am sorry, Kate, truly. Perhaps Anthony felt that he was acting for the best. It is—unfortunate that he's gone."

"Yes. But I still have three other brothers, don't I? We Woodvilles are so very expendable."

Harry shifted on his feet uncomfortably. "I am sorry for your brother's death, sincerely, whether you think it or not. But now there is something else I must say to you. I am afraid you will not be allowed to take part in the coronation as one of the queen's attendants. It would be very awkward— your being a Woodville, you see, and so bitter toward the king."

"Indeed. There is no telling what I might do, lawless wretch that I am." I inspected my sleeve. "Yes, I could fit a dagger right here, and stab Gloucester when he walks by."

"I am sure, though, that in time, you will be welcome at Richard's court, as of course, will our children." I closed my eyes, sick at the very thought of my darlings at that man's court. Harry continued, "But for now, I think it best that you stay away."

"But it is such a pity. I had already planned my robes, with matching ones for my familiar. It would have been quite charming."

"Kate, those rumors. I didn't st—"

"Go to the devil, Harry." I turned away, then looked back over my shoulder. "But you already have, haven't you?"

⤸

There is nothing quite like being in a city preparing day and night for something in which you can take no part, and that you pray every night the Lord will work a miracle to prevent. A day or so after this last exchange, Harry returned to his quarters at Westminster in order to superintend the preparations for the coronation, of which he had the ordering. Though many of his servants had followed him there, others remained by necessity in our Bread Street home, and I watched with amusement in those days as the poor things scurried around, frantically doing their part to ensure that all was ready for July 6, the date that had been set for the crowning. For, as I was fond of saying to anyone who would listen, time was of no object to the usurper.

My own servants did nothing to assist Harry's in the days that followed. Indeed, they hindered them in what small ways they could, while I smiled blandly. I am half—but only half—ashamed to say that I thoroughly enjoyed the difficulties we caused them.

But despite the lack of cooperation from the distaff side of Harry's household and my fervent, unanswered prayers—evidently even the Lord himself had been corrupted by Gloucester—the preparations went ahead on schedule. Poor Harry was more efficient than the fourth Edward had ever realized, it appeared. So when it was apparent that the coronation was inevitable, I gave in to the lure of curiosity and decided to watch the procession from the Tower to Westminster that would take place the day before the crowning. After all, Harry had not said that I could not do that, and it might be my only chance to see what the devil looked like in his royal robes.

In my scheme I found a willing accomplice: my page, Richard Wingfield, a boy of around thirteen whom I had long suspected of harboring a bad case of calf love, with myself as the object. At an old-clothes market he procured me suitably shabby garments, with what turned out to be a resident colony of fleas, which made me itch for days afterward. "You look terrible, my lady," he said approvingly as we footed it toward Cheapside.

"And so do you," I said. We looked like the perfect laboring brother and sister, honest poor folk come to get a glimpse of royalty. Perhaps we might even catch some coins the king's servants threw our way.

As a duchess I was ill accustomed to the press of the crowds around me, for someone had always been there to clear the way to let my party pass. Without Richard Wingfield's help, I would have given up early on. But he, the eleventh of twelve living sons, was well used to pushing his way about, and through his judicious use of elbows and his yanking me through spots where I would never have dreamed I could fit, we at last arrived at a fair vantage point. Had Harry looked straight at me at that moment—my feet aching and blistered, my head covering awry and my hair tangled underneath it, my face smudged with the grime that seemed peculiar to London, my skirt stained with substances that I decided would not bear close analysis—I doubt he would have recognized me as his wife.

We had arrived there early, so we had a long wait. Richard manfully guarded our precious places so that none could press in front of us and obstruct our view. At last, however, the sound of a moving procession reached our ears.

Richard protected me from the push of the people behind us as I watched impatiently, shifting on my uncomfortable pattens, while the first wave of the procession—various lords, knights, aldermen, royal heralds, and royal officials—made its way past us at a stately pace. I knew many of the men, at least by sight, from Edward's court. Some of the older ones had been present for my sister's coronation. Maybe those two squires who had borne Harry and me on that day were in this procession too, wearing the new king's badge with that cruel white boar, while I stood in my stinking old clothes gazing at them. It was unreal.

At last the mayor of London came into view. After him came John Howard, a rich lord in his late fifties whom I had always thought a man of honor. Yet he had sided with Richard throughout the last few weeks, never raising a word in favor of my nephew the young king, never blinking, it was said, when Hastings was murdered. In return he had been made the Duke of Norfolk, there being no more Mowbrays of the male line to inherit that title. His son Thomas Howard—riding next to him bearing the king's sword—had been made the Earl of Surrey. *Bought and sold, both of you*, I thought.

And on the other side of Surrey rode a man I knew very well. Nearby, a woman clucked her tongue. "Fine-looking man, the Duke of Buckingham. Wouldn't I like to warm his bed."

I instinctively moved to slap her for her impertinence, then fortunately stopped myself.

Not a man who smiled easily, Harry on this occasion was beaming, turning his head graciously from side to side as he moved past the onlookers. My neighbor was right: he did look handsome in his blue velvet robe, embroidered with golden, burning carts, and for an aching moment I desired him myself. He was on his finest palfrey, a chestnut that matched my own favorite steed. In better days, before the world went mad, we'd ridden them side by side.

I could not brood long on this, though, for just behind the sword of state, underneath a canopy carried by four knights, rode the devil himself, a vision in purple.

He must have practiced the expression he wore. It wouldn't do, after all, to look too terribly happy about having snatched the crown from a twelve-year-old boy, one whom he had sworn to protect. So instead of a smile, like Harry, he'd plastered a look of benevolence onto his face, mixed with humility.

I wore a dinner knife at my waist. I could have bolted into the road and stabbed Gloucester in the thigh; perhaps I could have even swung upon his horse and thrust my blade into his chest or, better yet, into the neck below that odious visage. But I would have been killed in the doing of it, even if I had the strength to force my knife in deep enough, and I could not bring myself to make that suicidal gesture. Instead, I contented myself with fixing upon him a look of utter hatred, hoping against hope that looks could, occasionally at least, kill.

They could not.

Presently the queen's procession came into view. It was a spectacle that occasioned more interest than that of the king, for he'd been a familiar sight around London for the past few days, clattering around town with Harry and their hordes of retainers, whereas hardly anyone outside of the North had seen the queen since she had married Gloucester.

As was the custom for a queen about to be crowned, Anne, clad in white cloth of gold and seated in a richly draped litter, wore her hair loose. I had thought when I saw her at Northampton that she looked a bit peaked, but with her golden hair falling past her shoulders, framing her face, she appeared to be a few years younger than she was, which flattered her. If she had any misgivings about the way her husband had reached the throne, they didn't show. No doubt Warwick the Kingmaker, if he had managed somehow to wrangle his way into Paradise, was mighty pleased with the twists of fortune that made his daughter a queen after all.

Richard Wingfield suddenly squeezed my hand. I did not think it overfamiliarity, for I knew he sought to comfort me. The duchesses were coming.

There were six in England at the time, including myself, but only four were in the procession: the Duchess of Suffolk, who was the old King Edward's sister (King Richard's too, of course, but I did not like to think of that), and three Duchesses of Norfolk. I sighed inwardly as Katherine Neville, my brother John's widow, came closer. Among the tales put out by Richard's creatures was that she'd been forced to share John's bed, even though she was eighty and had cried pitifully at the thought. In a couple of weeks, she'd probably be a hundred and forced at knifepoint to lie with my brother, I thought bitterly. I fingered the rosary that hung from my belt.

At least John would soon be joined in Paradise by Anthony. Perhaps he was there even now, being idolized by John once more. It brought a slight smile to my face.

Beside John's widow sat Elizabeth Talbot, whose sister Eleanor Edward had supposedly married before Bessie. Did she care how much trouble her careless words had caused? Was she pleased at their effect? Next to them sat the newest Duchess of Norfolk, John Howard's wife. Margaret Howard had been a duchess for only a couple of weeks and still looked bedazzled by her elevation. I knew the feeling; it had worn off only recently.

But where was the Duchess of York, the king's own mother? It was true that she was an aged lady, close to seventy, but she was a good fifteen years younger than her sister Katherine Neville, who was wrinkled and fragile now but still looked alert. Berkhamsted was not terribly far from London; surely the Duchess of York could have made it to the city in time for the coronation, traveling in easy stages. Had she not considered her son's coronation an important enough event to drag her from her religious devotions even for just a few days? Or—I hoped—had her son's means of acceding to the throne appalled her?

The women beside me were counting up duchesses too. "No Duchess of York."

"Too old, maybe."

"Well, after what they said about the old king being a bastard!"

"Plenty of Duchesses of Norfolk, ain't they? But where's the Duchess of Buckingham?"

"That's her."

"No, you bird-brain, that's the Duchess of Suffolk."

"'Tis odd that she's not here, then. They say that the Duke of Buckingham had the arranging of all of this."

"So where's his duchess?"

The loudest of the women dropped her voice. "I don't know, but they say he was forced to marry her when he was just a wee lad. By the old queen, of course. Dragged the poor little mite kicking and screaming to the altar, they say. He's hated the whole lot of the Woodvilles ever since, and all their kin."

"Is his duchess old?"

"Now, I don't know that, but they say she's not much to look at."

"Oh, she is old—at least a dozen years older than the poor duke. Starved for a man, they say, by the time they married him off to her. They forced the lad to lie with her to satisfy her devilish lusts, though he was not even in his teens."

"Witches, those Woodville wenches, all of them."

"Well, *I* heard that she was young, but that she's an idiot. Her keepers take her to the Duke of Buckingham once a month or so, so he can try to beget a child upon her. They hold her down for him. And when she does quicken, her keepers mind her until she pops out a babe. So she's good for that much, at least."

"Poor man. It's a sad life for one so handsome, and so rich. I thought he looked melancholy, with all of his finery and burning carts."

"A reason we should all be grateful for the station to which the Lord has called us."

I stared fixedly at the procession, thinking that doing so would stop me from trembling with rage. Then a young male voice spoke loudly beside me.

"I have seen the Duchess of Buckingham through my master's business with the duke. She is only five-and-twenty, younger than the duke, and she is not an idiot. Not by any means. And as for her person—she is most seemly. Some think her as beautiful as an angel. And I agree with them."

Someday I would have to find a way to show my gratitude toward Richard Wingfield.

"Well, if you say so, young man," said the senior of the goodwives. "But why isn't this angel of yours here with the other duchesses? Can you tell me that, Master Know-All?"

Richard hesitated. Then he shrugged. "Because the Duke of Buckingham has nothing but rags between his ears. That is why."

✑

Even if I could have contrived to view the coronation itself the next day, I had no stomach to try. I had seen, and heard, enough.

It was four or five days later, when the post-coronation festivities had finally ceased, that Harry returned to Bread Street. We greeted each other civilly before Harry closeted himself with his chamberlain. After a polite supper and some music, we retired to our separate chambers.

Cecilia was taking down my hair when Harry stormed in, scattering her and my other ladies. When they were gone, he said, "You were watching the procession. Without my permission."

So someone in our household had turned traitor. It hardly mattered who. "Well, what of it? I was told not to participate, and I did not. I was not told that I could not be a spectator like anyone else in London."

"How do I know you were not recognized? It would be humiliating for me if you were."

"I took great care to disguise myself. I have the flea bites to prove it."

For a moment Harry looked almost admiring. Then he snapped, "That's no better. You're not used to wandering around London unaccompanied; what if some churl had ravished you? Or found out who you were and held you for ransom?"

My, Harry had a wild imagination when he worked at it. "As a Woodville, my ransom would have been cheap, surely? But in any case, I had a protector."

Harry frowned. "Who?"

"I shall not say. It is past, and he discharged his duty well and faithfully. There is no vice, after all, in protecting a lady."

"You needn't. It was that impudent Wingfield boy, wasn't it? The one who always makes sheep's eyes at you."

"So what if he does? It is a far sight better than hearing that I am a dozen years your senior, an idiot, or sore disfigured, or all three, and that I ravished you when you were a small boy, all of which is gossip making the rounds."

Harry wrinkled his nose. "What vile rumors."

"You think them so? Only because you and that creature Gloucester weren't clever enough to start them yourselves, I suppose."

"Who?"

"You heard me. That creature Gloucester."

"You will address my friend the king properly."

"I will address your friend the usurper as I please. He is a whoreson, a devil's spawn. A murd—"

"Silence! I've put up with much of your insolence since you came to London—without my permission also—knowing of your grief. But no more! You shall do my bidding and speak of the king with respect."

"He deserves no respect." I snorted. "A brave man, to take a throne from a boy!"

"He was entitled to it, as I have told you time and time again! I am warning you, you shall give him respect, just as you shall give me the respect due to a husband and to your better!"

"My better?"

"Yes, your better! I'm of the blood royal; you're the daughter of a Frenchwoman who married above herself and who then degraded herself by marrying a handsome nobody who took her fancy. He brought nothing to their marriage, just like you brought nothing to ours when it was pushed upon me. No royal blood, no prestige, no dowry—nothing." He snorted. "Nothing but your Woodville cunt. That's all you and your sisters ever had to offer, wasn't it? By God, it ought to be on your family's coat of arms!"

I started to slap him, but he grabbed my arm, so instead I spat in his face. He gasped, then with one sure blow knocked me against the bed, onto which I clambered instinctively, like a pursued animal seeking higher ground. "So that's your game?" he said softly. "Well, for once you'll do as I say!"

Harry was on the bed with me now, his hands on my shoulders. "Harry! No! Please!"

He pushed me onto my back and pinned me underneath him, slapping me hard when I tried to resist. Dazed and winded as I was, I still protested and struggled, but it only aroused him. It was over quickly—though I would not have said that at the time—and when he had spent himself he also seemed to have exhausted whatever demon had possessed him as well. I willed myself not to cry as he lay shuddering on top of me. "Are you all right?" he finally asked.

"What do you think?"

"Kate—"

I managed to extricate myself from beneath him and sat up. He had held me so tightly my arms ached, and I knew I was bleeding where he had forced himself into me. I had never known that the sexual act—or Harry—could hurt so badly. I caught my breath. "Our marriage and my Woodville cunt, as you so graciously put it, have brought you four beautiful, healthy children, Harry. Five if the Lord had not taken poor Humphrey. You might remember Edward and the rest of them if you choose to free yourself from me. I suppose you can find grounds for an annulment if you work at it." Any one of my remarks might have merited another blow, but I no longer cared. "One of the king's creatures can advise you, I am sure. Who knows? Perhaps I was precontracted to one of our grooms at Grafton."

"Kate, I—"

"Please. Leave."

To my surprise, he did.

When he was gone, I huddled, fully clothed, on my bed, too miserable to move. After a few minutes a knock came, and Richard Wingfield came in at my barely audible response. He was holding an all-night of bread and ale—a redundancy since one had been brought earlier—and his hands were shaking as he set it down. "Thank you, Richard."

He nodded and turned toward the door. Then he swung around. "My lady! I can't leave without saying anything. I heard— Did he hurt you?"

"I am fine. Go to bed. I shall soon be doing so myself."

"I wish I could kill him for you. I do."

"That would create more problems than it would solve." Believing that I had not been as firm as the situation might require, and not fancying myself in the role of Henry II and Harry in that of Thomas Becket, I added sternly, "There will be no killing, Richard. These things happen among married people on occasion. You will understand when you are older and married."

"But I don't see how he can treat you like this. You're so pretty, and so sweet. If you were my wife—"

"Now, Richard. I am a Woodville, and that is a liability at the moment, so perhaps it is just as well that I am not your wife." I smiled at my page. If I were the witch the king's creatures said we Woodvilles were, I thought, I would use all of my powers to make Harry a youth again such as the one before me now, guileless and kind. "There is one thing you can do for me."

"Only tell me what."

"Tell my chamberlain that I wish to be gone from here tomorrow as soon as possible. I think Brecon is the best place for me at the moment." There was no place for me in Gloucester's and Harry's England, that was for certain. "And tell my ladies that they may return to my chamber. And, Richard—tell them that I do not wish to discuss what took place tonight. Not now or ever."

Richard looked disappointed, probably because I had not ordered him to slay anyone, but he nodded, kissed my hand, and left. My ladies— Harry's spy, perhaps, among them—appeared almost instantly, then helped me into my nightshift and without comment sponged off the area around where Harry had hurt me so. I went to bed positively reeking of rosewater, but it did nothing to make my dreams—the few I had, for I scarcely slept—rose-colored.

The next morning, I made my impending departure no secret from Harry. How could I have? Everything I owned, everyone who waited on me, was under his control. Indeed, he could have ordered me to stay, and the law would have bound me to obey him, but to my relief, he raised no objection. Instead he treated our parting as the perfectly routine desire of a mother to see her children, though by this time there was probably not a soul in the household who had not learned of his shouted words to me the evening before and of what had followed. It suited me well enough to acquiesce in this pretense of normality. "Soon I'll be sending Bishop Morton to Brecon," he informed me as I got ready to step into my Stafford-knot-adorned chariot, surrounded by an even larger entourage than usual. Harry might despise me as a parvenu, but he evidently had no intention of losing face by letting me travel in less than ducal style. "He is to be lodged as befits his office, of course."

"Of course," I said coldly. How did he expect me to lodge an imprisoned bishop? In a dungeon?

"Give the children my love. I will be there soon once my business here is finished."

I nodded, and Harry bent and pecked me on the cheek, then the lips—for show, I thought scornfully as I let him hand me into the chariot. When we were safely out of sight, I brushed with my finger at the place where his lips had been.

Beside me, Cecilia snorted as she heard the driver crack his whip. "I'm not to discuss a certain matter, I know, but I'll say this much. Do you know what the driver told me?"

"What?"

"That he wanted to use that whip of his on someone else we all know. And that there's not a man in the household—your lord's as well as yours—who doesn't feel the same way."

I smiled.

⟡

A couple of weeks after I had settled back down at Brecon, Bishop Morton arrived, as promised, with an entourage that belied the fact that he was a prisoner. Harry had every reason to have an uneasy conscience, but at least it could not be said that he mistreated a man of the Church.

Though the record-keeping aspect of running my household had never been my outstanding point, I was quite capable of making my guests, willing and otherwise, comfortable. After I had given the bishop some time to settle in and have some refreshment, I went to his chamber.

Bishop Morton smiled at me as I entered.

"I came to make sure that you had everything you needed."

"Indeed, yes." He gestured toward a chess set that I had provided, complete with its own table. "It was kind of you to think of this. Do you play?"

"No." It was yet another one of my many failings; I'd never enjoyed the game and had forgotten most of the little I'd learned about it from Harry. "I prefer more frivolous pastimes, I fear. Such as cards."

"Really, my lady? I confess to a weakness for them myself. Perhaps when you have a spare moment we can have a game." He patted a stack of fresh parchment approvingly. "And you have been thoughtful enough to provide writing materials too, I see. I shall quite forget I am in prison, with such consideration. You see to everything, my lady."

My eyes filled with tears. It was a novelty for me to receive a compliment from a grown man these days. Bishop Morton missed nothing. "I have grieved you somehow, your grace. I beg your pardon."

"It is not that," I said. "It is Harry."

In moments I was spilling out the whole miserable saga, sans Harry's forcing himself on me. "I am certain he will annul our marriage," I concluded. "Richard will have thoroughly convinced him that he can do better. Perhaps he will marry abroad, or there is even that bastard daughter of Richard's. I would not be surprised. And then what will become of me and the children?"

"Surely your husband would not bastardize his children?"

"Who knows? Perhaps Richard has even convinced Harry that they are another man's. They are not," I added hastily. "I have never been with any man but Harry. Not even in my thoughts. But what does the truth matter now, in Richard's England? I have been friendly with other men; it is my nature. Richard can twist that into any slander he likes, just as I am certain he twisted King Edward's dalliance with that Eleanor Butler woman into a precontract. If Richard says I lay with some dead man like poor William Hastings, how can I possibly disprove it? If my ladies testified that I have spent every night with them that I have not spent with Harry, Richard would say that they have been suborned by me. The children have my coloring more than Harry's, too, which makes it even easier. And—"

"Dear lady! Your worries may be all for naught. I have heard your husband speak with pride of his children. *His* children. The worst you fear may never happen."

"No, and then I will merely have to live out my life with a man who despises me and my kindred." I shook my head. "And I feel scarcely different about him. It has all gone so wrong, Bishop Morton, and so suddenly. I don't understand it. I have been a good wife to Harry; I have my failings, but don't we all? Yet Harry was kind to me up until recently—and to my family. At least, he never spoke ill of us. But now he is entirely under the spell of—that hellspawn." I sighed, then came to myself. "I have been rattling on about myself, your grace, and I apologize. Your lot is worse than mine. I am merely a miserable wife; you are a prisoner. Tell me; we are alone, and your secret is safe with me. Was there a plot against Richard?"

"Upon my word, no. Hastings believed until the last minute that Gloucester's motives were honorable. We did meet to discuss some concerns we had—among them, I must say, that your husband was being given too much power too quickly, given his inexperience and his past impetuosity. Hastings was also, I think, feeling neglected in terms of offices and the like. But he was willing to wait until the young king was crowned and to see how the situation developed."

"You were right about Harry, I fear. I will tell you: I believe that Hastings was killed because he knew there had been no marriage with Eleanor Butler and could give evidence to that effect. Harry would tell me that was women's imaginings."

"If so, my lady, I am unmanned, for I have imagined the same thing. And I will do you one better by suggesting that the Archbishop of York and I were arrested to get us safely out of the way in case Hastings had spoken of the matter to us. Were we not men of the Church, I do not doubt that we would be dead as well."

We sat there staring at each other mournfully for a while. "What news is there from London?"

"Gloucester has left on a royal progress so that his subjects may get to know him better."

I snorted. "They might find they know him as well as they want to. Is there news of my sister and her children?"

"I have picked up little, but it appears that there have been no attempts by Gloucester to force Queen Elizabeth—I may call her that in her sister's company, I hope—from sanctuary, as some feared he might do. The boys—"

He stopped. I crossed myself and said, "There is a piece of the True Cross in this place, passed down from Harry's Clare ancestors. I will swear an oath upon it that if you have a secret to tell me about the boys, it shall stay with me."

"There is no need, Duchess. Your honesty shines upon your countenance. There is a plan, led by some of the old king's faithful servants, to free them from the Tower, then to take them abroad where they can be kept in safety until young Edward can be restored to his rightful throne. Through some of my household with contacts in the Tower I have lent what support I can—mainly money."

"Oh, that it might succeed!"

"I hope so, my lady. I pray so. For I fear that if it does not, I shall have no need to pray for the welfare of the boys, as I do daily. I shall be praying instead for the welfare of their souls."

XX

Harry: July 1483 to August 1483

WITH MY NEW OFFICES, I HAD BEEN GIVEN MAGNIFICENT CHAMBERS at Westminster that were, if not quite fit for a king, certainly fit for a kingmaker. One had to get through several outer chambers, and the suitable complement of servants, before one could even get to see me. I had hung my walls with rich tapestries and covered the floor with rugs from the East, and there was not a silver cup in sight—everything was gold. It was the sort of room that I had dreamed of during all of those years of obscurity in Wales.

It was certainly not a setting that was conducive to misery—and yet, just a few days after Richard's coronation, a triumph of good order and high ceremony, I was utterly miserable.

The night before, I'd lost my temper with Kate. I had had every right to; her recent insolence and disobedience were more than any husband, not henpecked, could be expected to endure. But I had gone too far; I had known that even then. I'd insulted her lineage and made her sound little better than a peasant and a whore. And when she had spat straight into my face, I had struck her, then forced myself upon her. It had been as if some other man had inhabited my body, for though I'd been annoyed with Kate many times over the years, I'd never hurt her. Not in that way. It was against every rule of chivalry I had ever been taught.

I'd only wanted her to show some respect to me, and to Richard. Then I could take her to court again; then Richard would see how gracious and lovely she could be, Woodville that she was. She in turn would see him for the good man he was, despite the hard measures he had had to take. We would be reconciled, and then we could lie together—not as we had the night before, but as lovers—and we could make another child. One whose presence would perhaps ease our grief over our little Humphrey, who had died in my arms one cold November night at Brecon, though we had prayed so hard for the Lord to spare him.

I suddenly shivered, warm as the July day was, for I could not help thinking about my living sons, Edward and Hal. Hastings had cursed Richard and me, and our sons. Richard had said that it was an impotent curse, but...

I shook my head and reached for an apple on my table. I was half-famished and exhausted, that was all. I'd been keeping later hours than usual lately, and I hadn't slept well last night or eaten this morning. I'd felt too ill to eat or sleep, for I could see and think of nothing but Kate's terrified eyes as I went down upon her—

"Why the long face, Harry?"

I blinked. There might be many chambers one had to go through to reach me, but they were not an obstacle for the king. "Kate left for Brecon this morning."

"Oh." Richard looked thoughtful for a while. "Tell me, old man. Have you ever considered annulling the marriage? You really could do better, you know."

I dropped the apple. "Are you mad, Rich—your grace?" And yet Kate had said the same to me the night before. "I would never do that to Kate. And how could I? I've been married to her for eighteen years. We've had five children!"

He shrugged. "You were children yourselves when the Woodville wench palmed her off on you. And rather slow to consummate it. You could say you were forced to consummate it." He smiled. "After all, you once told me that it was the girl who seduced you, instead of the other way around." I flushed, wishing I'd not shared this story with Richard. "Her mother was a witch, so is that sister of hers, I'll wager. Who knows? Perhaps your bride knew some tricks of the trade."

"It was nothing like that." I thought of my first night with Kate, her luscious body at last in my arms, her eager yet suddenly shy face as I taught her the little I knew about the act of love. There had been no sorcery there, just a lovely girl with desires of her own.

"Are you even sure she was a virgin? You weren't the most experienced swordsman at the time, were you?"

"I am very sure." For the first time in my life, I found myself becoming angry at Richard. To calm myself, I added, "Besides, have you forgotten our children? I'm fond of them. Why would I bastardize them?"

Another shrug. "I'm fond of my bastards, too. Treat them as I will mine. Marry them well and put them in high positions. Why, one of your bastards could marry one of my bastards, you know."

For a moment I actually gave this some consideration before coming to my senses. "Richard, I have no bastards! They are my lawful children, from my lawful wife, and all will stay that way."

Richard sighed. "Well, I tried. But in any case, you won't need to marry well."

"Richard?"

"I'm granting you your Bohun inheritance. It will have to be approved by Parliament, but I'm sure that won't be a problem."

I was dizzy with shock. All these years, I had hoped for this—but never in my wildest dreams had I thought it would simply be handed to me like the apple on my plate. "How can I possibly thank you?"

Richard shrugged again. "You've earned it, Harry. It's a small token of my gratitude." He turned to go. "I've some people to see before I leave on progress. I spotted your aunt Margaret out there, by the by. Shall I have your men send her in, or tell them to shoo her away? She'll want to inveigle you about that son of hers, no doubt, and you look peaked. The Countess of Richmond should be taken on a full night's sleep and with a full belly, I think."

I grinned at him. "I'll hazard it."

Even before Richard became king, my aunt had been after him—through me—to allow her son to return to England and take up some of his inheritance. I had broached the subject to Richard, as the countess was, after all, kin to me and the only Beaufort relation I had left. But Richard had been less than receptive.

"Your brother was on the verge of letting Henry Tudor come back," I had reminded him. "With some of his lands, and some of the estates of his grandmother, the late Duchess of Somerset."

"Yet another reason Ned was a blockhead. For one thing, who would come back? Not only the man himself, but that Jasper Tudor. Why not invite the Earl of Oxford back as well? It'd be the House of Lancaster's grand reunion. No, Harry, sorry. Your aunt Margaret is going to have to do without her heart's desire. She got to carry Anne's train at the coronation. That will have to suffice."

I didn't have the heart—or the stomach—to tell this outright to my aunt, however. One angry woman in my life was enough.

In very few minutes, Margaret was in my chamber, which she gave an approving glance—I'd been in rather more modest quarters when we last spoke together. "Well. Your mother would be very proud to see you now, Harry."

"I hope so, Aunt. I wish she had lived to see this."

"Yes. It is sad that she didn't. It is also sad when a son has a living mother, but is unable to see her."

I could not help smiling. "You do come to a point quickly, Aunt Margaret."

"Don't I? Yes, people have always said I don't shilly-shally. Well? Has the king come to a decision?"

"He is—uncertain, but I hope to persuade him."

Aunt Margaret frowned. "Why, what obstacle could there be?"

"Not so much your son—who, after all, no one in England has seen since he reached manhood—but his companions. Mainly Jasper Tudor, I believe."

"Jasper Tudor is no fool. He knows the cause of Lancaster is dead and will not try to resurrect it."

"You seem well informed of his state of mind."

My aunt was not in the least abashed. "Well, why not? He is with my son, and a mother ought to stay in contact with her son by whatever means presents itself. Tell the king, if you please, that I am ready to stop fighting this war if he is. I only want my son back, and I want him in a position to receive his inheritance when I am gone. And I have another proposal, also. Let my son marry the Lady Elizabeth, or whatever we call the poor girl these days."

"I am not certain he would look favorably on that, Aunt."

The countess flicked her wrist in irritation. "How can he object? The girl is a bastard—or at least they say." (My aunt uttered this addendum in so sweet a tone no one could have found it treasonous.) "That being the case, how can there be any harm in allowing her to marry my son? It could be argued that my son was too good for her, actually."

"I suspect that you might say that about any young lady, Aunt."

Aunt Margaret snorted. "How well you know me, Harry. Do continue to press my case with the king, I pray."

"I shall."

"There is another matter, not a personal one. The old king's boys. What is to become of them?"

I saw no harm in telling her. "I believe the king intends to move them to one of his castles in the North. Why?"

"There is gossip about them. They have not been seen lately, and the people are concerned about their future. The king needs to reassure his subjects that they are being treated kindly. Their father was a popular man in London, after all. This is not the North, where hardly a soul has laid eyes on the boys. Here, they remain of importance. The king is deluding himself if he thinks otherwise."

It was a shame, I thought, not for the first time, that my aunt had been born a woman. A little stiffly, though, as she *had* been born a woman and was meddling outside her sphere, I said, "I am certain he realizes the importance of seeing to their safety and comfort, and will do so."

"For their sake, I hope so." My aunt's face took on a wistful expression.

"They are but boys, Harry. Remember your own lads when you think of them."

∞

I had not wanted to tell my aunt, but a few days after the coronation, the boys' old attendants, from Edward's personal physician, Dr. Argentine, on down, had been replaced with ones of Richard's choosing. It was a reasonable step to take, for the boys were no longer a king and a royal duke, but merely royal by-blows, and there was no need to keep their former entourage intact, especially an entourage inclined to be bitter about the blighting of their own prospects. The boys were also kept largely in their rooms, a necessity these days because ever since Richard had been declared king, there had been hints here and there of plans to take them overseas to start another court in exile. As if we hadn't had enough of that in poor Margaret of Anjou's day.

Still, Aunt Margaret's words sent a twinge of guilt through me. I'd not seen the boys ever since the Eleanor Butler business was made public, and they were my kinsmen through the king as well as my nephews by marriage. It was only right that I pay them a visit, little as I relished the prospect of dealing with two sullen young boys.

"Welcome to our prison," Edward greeted me as I was ushered in.

"It's not a prison, Edward."

"Oh? We've not been allowed outside for days now; our servants have all been sent away; and my brother Richard Grey and my uncle Anthony and faithful old Thomas Vaughan are dead. And Hastings, who treated me with respect, is dead. So what do you call it, dear uncle? The Parthenon?"

I blinked. Anthony had had this boy reading widely indeed. But now Richard—lively, merry Richard—broke in. "You lied to me, Uncle! You told me that I was to attend my brother's coronation, when you meant all along to depose him and take away my own title! Isn't that true?"

"No," I said hopelessly, knowing that it probably was, even if I hadn't admitted it at the time. "Boys, you must realize this: your father's marriage to your mother was invalid. It was being investigated when I took you here, Richard, that is true. But it was an investigation done in good faith. You must understand that."

"Dr. Argentine said that a church court should have investigated it, and that my uncle didn't have one do so because he knew there was nothing in it. That it was all lies that he made up."

"Bishop Stillington investigated it, Richard, and he is learned in the law. The lords of the land accepted it as true. I am sorry, boys." I waited, expecting another rejoinder, but got only two sullen stares.

I took the opportunity of the boys' silence to look around their chamber. It was large and comfortably furnished, and connected to a chamber that was equally pleasant looking, but both had mere slits for windows, and the boys had a pasty look. Clearly, they needed to be taken north soon. There, little known, they could safely be given more freedom. "As for your quarters here, I know it is getting wearisome," I resumed. "It is for your own protection, though you might not believe it. But it won't be like this forever, I can promise you that. Soon you shall be taken north to live, I believe. It is not a bad place, you know. The king's own son lives there. So does his natural son, the Lord Bastard, John."

"Maybe we won't have to move north," muttered Richard. "Maybe we might get to live someplace el—"

Edward put a warning hand on his brother's shoulder.

"What did he mean?" I asked sharply.

"Nothing. He's just talking nonsense."

I looked back at Richard, but he had plainly decided to clam up. Something was going on. "Is there anything the two of you want, in the meantime? Some more books? Some games?"

"We have all of that. Until our dear uncle Richard decides that we're not even fit to have that much."

Richard's lip wobbled. He looked, I realized, a great deal like his mother and my Kate. "I just want out of here. I hate it here, Uncle."

"I know you do," I said, more gently than before. I touched his shoulder, and he didn't resist my comfort. "I promise you, Richard, I will see that you and your brother are soon out of here. I am in favor with the king, and I shall use my position to help you. But you must trust me—and not others who you might be convinced are working in your interests, when they are working in their own."

"Why trust you?" asked the former king. "You put us here."

A few days after this, one of the Tower guards came to its new constable, Sir Robert Brackenbury, and told him that there was a treasonous scheme afoot. The plan was to set fires across the city, then, during the confusion, to snatch the boys out of the Tower and spirit them abroad. The wardrober of the Tower, Stephen Ireland, was one of the ringleaders. Some of the boys' old attendants had also been implicated. All in all, about fifty men were involved.

I hastily wrote to Richard about what Brackenbury had learned and arranged for the arrests of the men involved. Then, my business in London being over, I left the city myself. I would meet Richard on his progress and then go to Wales, where there was much work to be done, thanks to the offices with which Richard had entrusted me. I was glad to be going. London in late summer was oppressive, whereas my Welsh estates, particularly Brecon, were at their loveliest that time of year. So was my Kate.

As I rode toward the Midlands, surrounded by a veritable mob of attendants, I pondered a new idea. Why not take Edward's boys to stay at Brecon? It was as well fortified as any of Richard's northern castles, and Wales was a familiar place to Edward at least. My sons, four and five years of age, would enjoy their cousins' company. Besides, growing up in the North along with Richard's son, the boys would never be able to forget the contrast between his status as heir to the throne and theirs as heirs to nothing. In Wales they could grow used to their changed position and gradually learn to accept it. And Kate would be the kindest of aunts to them.

So enamored was I with my new plan that as soon as I reached Gloucester, where Richard's party had arrived, I raised it the moment the king and I were alone.

⤜⤛

"No."

"Richard? I don't understand. They would be kept at my expense, of course—"

"Expense has nothing to do with it."

"Then why? I've more retainers than I can keep count of now, you know, with so many of Hastings's men joining my household. God knows, they need more to do; they'd keep the boys as secure as they would be up north. You can trust me."

"I know I can." He walked to the window and stared out of it before abruptly turning round again. "You let me know very quickly about that business in London."

"Well, of course," I said, baffled by his strange manner.

"And I sent two men to London. The first went to the chancellor, ordering him to commence the prosecution of the conspirators. The second went to the Tower with a verbal order to the boys' servants. It was carried out yesterday."

"An order for what? Richard, you're speaking in riddles."

"I shall be plain, then. Harry, the boys are dead. At my order."

I thought for a moment that I was going to vomit or to faint, but I managed to do neither. Hastings. Rivers. Grey. Vaughan. And now his own nephews. *My* own nephews. "How?" I managed.

"Smothering," said Richard easily. We could have been talking of killing rats. "They were asleep—had been given a little something to make them sleep more deeply. They didn't feel a thing, I'm sure of it. They went to bed happy. They had a message that they would be leaving the Tower the next day and would be heading north, as promised. Their things were all packed and ready to go, in fact." He shrugged and pointed upward. "Well,

of course they were heading north, in a manner of speaking. The cooks
made them their fav—"

"Tell me no more about it." I sank down upon a stool.

"For God's sake, Harry, don't stare at me like Christ and all of his saints
rolled into one! It was necessary for the safety of the realm. If there was
another way, I'd have taken it, but there was no other. Not once I learned
of that plot. We foiled this one, but what of the next one, and the one after
that, and the one after that? There will be peace in England now that they're
gone, just as there was when we did away with poor old King Henry."

"We?"

"Why, Ned and I, of course. It was Ned's order, but I did the deed. I
had to; Ned didn't trust anyone else to carry it out without talking. Just
a pillow over his face when he was fast asleep. He was a sound sleeper; it
couldn't have been easier. He was half dead anyway; had been for months.
Years. He'd probably have thanked me if he'd had a chance, the poor holy
fool. You never guessed?"

"No."

"And what came out of it? Years of peace. We can make something even
better of this, Harry, you and I. It will be a golden age, the age my brother
was too lazy to let come to fruition."

"A golden age," I echoed. An age founded on a lie—I could no longer
gainsay it—and steeped in blood. As if this was just a routine matter of
business we were discussing, I asked, "Will you display their bodies?"

He shook his head. "I considered it, but no. They were handsome lads,
not worn-out wrecks like old Henry. Seeing them dead would upset the
people. As it is, people will at first think they've just been secreted away,
and by the time they figure out the truth, they won't care anymore, because
England will be so strong and prosperous they won't want to care. After all,
who cares about Arthur of Brittany, whom King John put to death?"

"Who cared for King John?"

"John was a fool; he alienated the people. I'll win them over. They love
me in the North. Why can't they learn to love me elsewhere? Already I've

pleased them on this progress by refusing to take their money." He chuck-led. "Ned would have had bagfuls of it by now. Not to mention siring the odd bastard or two along the way." When I didn't chuckle in return, Richard said more stiffly, "I can assure you, it's not a decision I relished making. But it's for the best of all, in the long run."

"Sometimes it's better for the safety of the realm as a whole that a few should die," I recited.

"Well, precisely. I won't lie and say I slept well after giving the order, but it had to be done." He poured some wine, then proffered the cup to me. I shook my head and he drank from the cup himself. "I'm glad I've unburdened myself to you, Harry. I hadn't been looking forward to telling you, after I told Anne. I had to; she kept asking me when the boys were coming north." He smiled, very slightly. "All of this could have been avoided if everyone hadn't been so uncommonly anxious to take them out of the Tower."

"What did Anne say?" I asked for the sake of saying something.

"What do you expect? She's a woman. She wept and carried on and said that God would have his revenge on me, that I'd doomed the entire House of York. Oh, she also said that if my father had known what I would do, he would have had the midwife strangle me when I came out of my mother's womb." Richard winced. "One thing you can say about my wife; she's not shy in expressing her opinions when the occasion suits. I let her huff and storm for a while, and then I reminded her that those boys would be a threat to our own son's crown and that they had to be eliminated because of that. That calmed her a bit, and I think after that she began to see reason. Or she will, given a little time. Women will forgive a great deal when you tell them it's for the good of their children, especially when it also happens to be the truth."

"And God? Will He forgive you?"

Richard sighed. "I suppose the Lord might be even less understanding than Anne, but when my time comes He will weigh the good to the entire nation against the harm to the two boys; I'm sure of it. What sort of life would it have been for the poor lads, anyway? I never would have felt safe having them at large; they would have had to be prisoners always in deed if not in name. Even at your Welsh paradise of Brecon, Harry."

I could hardly bear to ask my next question. "There was no plot by Anthony Woodville and the rest. Or by William Hastings. Was there?"

For a passing moment, I saw what I had never seen before in Richard's face when he looked at me: contempt. Then he shrugged. "Not that I could verify. There would have been if they had been allowed to live. Some chances aren't worth taking."

"The precontract?"

"Come now, Harry! You heard the evidence as well as I. It's damn shabby. But all it takes is a promise of marriage, followed by sexual intercourse. It certainly could have happened. I wouldn't underestimate Ned's determination when he was rutting. Hell, he could have secretly married half of the female population of England before he got around to Eleanor Butler. Edward's real queen could be one of my mother's laundresses for all I know."

"Did you plan to take the throne all along? Back at Northampton?"

"Lord, Harry, you'd think you had me on the witness stand! The possibility did occur to me, but back then all I really wanted to do was to clear the queen's nuisance relations out of the way. What real choice did I have? It would have been nothing but struggles between me and them as long as Edward was a child, and what would that have accomplished? We'd have been at arms against each other in the end. I didn't need that again. Neither did England. Sooner or later, one side was going to be vanquished, and it sure as hell wasn't going to be mine." He smiled at me. "Actually, it was you, with your dire warnings about the fates of the dukes of Gloucester, and your information about Eleanor Butler, who finally decided the issue for me. So you truly have been a kingmaker, Harry. Who would have thought it back all those years ago at Writtle?" Richard laughed. "Did I ever tell you what a snotty-nosed brat you were at the time?" He put his hand on his hip and his nose in the air and squeaked, "'I am Harry, and one day I will be the second Duke of Buckingham!' Thank God you improved with age."

"Indeed," I managed.

"Now, there are some others waiting for me, Lovell said. I'd best see them; we'll be off early tomorrow. You don't mind, old man, if I leave you alone after your journey?"

"No." I forced a smile and rose off the stool. "I'm stiff from riding, anyway. I need to stretch my legs before the sun sets."

✑

I'd had my conversation with Richard alone, with a couple of my men waiting outside his chamber for me. I ordered them off and wandered around the streets of Gloucester, scarcely knowing or caring where I went.

Two young boys were dead, after I had promised them they could trust me. True, the killings hadn't been my idea. None of the deaths had been. But I'd not done anything in defense of the victims. Instead I had helped place Richard on the throne. If I had protested, refused to give him my support, King Edward's sons might still be alive today.

There was no more despicable crime than infanticide. And my hands were hardly cleaner than Richard's. From the day those boys' attendants were withdrawn and their confinement became closer, I should have known what fate awaited them. Anyone who knew his history would have known. Edward II, Richard II, Henry VI—all had died when they lost their thrones.

But the boys were children. Who would have thought that he would put them to death?

Everyone. The men who had staked their lives upon getting them out of the Tower. The men whom I had passed in the streets on occasion, pointing to that fortress and whispering, tears streaming down their faces. Aunt Margaret. The boys themselves. Only I, foolish I, had willed myself blind to their danger.

What if I had resisted Richard's quest for the throne or sided with my wife's relations? Probably Richard would have disposed of me as easily as the others, with some regret, perhaps, but without hesitation. But the thought that I would resist had probably never crossed his mind. He knew me, and the love that had made me abandon all honor, much better than I did myself.

I had wandered to the quay. The sun had long since set, and under the cover of the darkness it would be easy enough to throw myself into the Severn and disappear from the world forever. Indeed for several hopeless moments I stood there contemplating just that. But then sense took hold. My children would already have to live down the association of the Stafford name with infanticide—and regicide. How could I shame it more by staining it with my own self-destruction?

I turned and made my way back to St. Peter's Abbey, where the king and his nobles were staying. Instead of going straight to my lodgings in the priory, I knocked at the Cemetery Gate, where the pilgrims entered. If the monk who opened the door thought there anything odd about my appearance, as there surely must have been in my state of mind, he said nothing. "Take me to the tomb of King Edward, please. I should like to stay there alone for a while."

"Yes, your grace."

King Edward II was an ancestor of mine, and Richard's too of course, and it was his deposition following his disastrous reign that had set the stage for so much misery to come by showing men that it was not all that hard, after all, to get rid of an unwanted king. He had suffered a horrid, unspeakable death at Berkeley Castle. As a young boy in the queen's household, I'd snickered about the means—a red-hot poker shoved into his fundament. Every lad my age had made a nervous jest about the subject. Yet in his time poor Edward had been thought a saint by some, and it was the offerings of his pilgrims that had made the abbey the fine place it was today. Even today, some still came to this tomb and prayed.

I stood next to the tomb and gazed at the king's alabaster face. It was his love—some said a wicked and unnatural love—for his friends that had brought him down. He had clung to them when to forsake them would have been to save himself. This, then, was a man who could understand the love I bore for Richard, the love that until this day had proven steadfast against all other considerations.

"I didn't think he would do it, your grace," I said softly as the alabaster face with its sweetly sad look stared impassively at the tomb's canopy. "How could I? I loved him. I *still* love him."

Then I leaned my head against the tomb and wept until sheer weakness sent me to my knees. Once upon them, I sent prayer after prayer to the skies.

ॐ

Richard and I were both up early the next morning, and we met as if all were normal. He chatted about his recent visit to Magdalen College at Oxford, and twitted me about my own Stafford family's distinct preference for Cambridge. Mostly, though, we spoke of business, chiefly concerning my duties in Wales.

"So you're off for Brecon," Richard said finally as I started to take my leave of him. "I can't persuade you to venture north on my progress with me, just for a few days? Not even to see whether the northerners truly have tails, as all of you southerners seem to think?"

"I'll take your word for it." I managed a ghost of a grin.

He walked with me to the abbey entrance, where all my men had gathered, and embraced me as I prepared to mount my horse. "God keep you on your progress, Richard," I said as we embraced in farewell. I held him more tightly than was my wont; did I know then that we would never meet again? "I shall write soon of events in Wales."

"God keep you, Harry." He smiled and said into my ear, "It was for the best, old man. Remember that."

"I will."

I longed, as I proceeded to Wales, to have someone beside me to whom I could unburden myself about what I'd learned the night before. But for all of the men who surrounded me, there was not a single one of them in which I could confide such a terrible secret and seek the counsel I so desperately needed. I had no close friends, I realized with a jolt—except for Richard.

The gods of old could not have played a better joke on a man if they had tried.

xxi

Kate: August 1483 to October 1483

WHILE I MOURNED MY BROTHER AND MY NEPHEW AND FRETTED ABOUT my own future, my children, of course, were happily oblivious to all. They knew only that due to a puzzling turn of events that no adult could explain adequately, there was a new king on the throne and that their papa was a very important man now. Their only complaint was that he was not in Brecon with them, and when in early August a man brought news that Harry was expected shortly, their happiness was complete. For the children adored Harry, and much as I was schooling myself to despise him, I could not gainsay that he had always been a loving father. I could only hope that Richard would not poison even that.

Everything had to be perfect for Papa's arrival, seven-year-old Elizabeth sternly informed the household, me included. Edward at five was not much less commanding. When word came that Harry was just a few miles away, he stared at my gown as if it were made of rags. "You're wearing that?"

It was less than a year old, and as expensive as anything else in my wardrobe. "Yes."

"But it's not Papa's favorite! You should wear his favorite." Edward screwed up his face in deep thought. "He likes you best in your light blue gown. The one with the pretty golden birds on it."

Edward was right. It was for that very reason that this gown had not seen the light of day this summer. But how could I tell a small boy that it no longer mattered what I wore for his father? "All right. I shall put on the one with the birds."

"And not that hennin either," Elizabeth chimed in. She plucked it out of my lady's very hands. "The one with the gold trim around the edges looks so much better. And it matches the birds," she added firmly.

Just minutes after I was dressed to my eldest children's satisfaction, I heard the sound of horses. Bracing myself, I went down with the children and the rest of the household to await my husband's arrival. Even Bishop Morton was there, standing dutifully at attention.

Four-year-old Hal pumped my hand. "I see him! There's Papa!"

"I saw him first!" protested Elizabeth, who was a little short-sighted but hated to admit it.

"*I* did," said Edward, in a voice that indicated that as he was the heir, the matter was as good as settled.

"Me!" piped up three-year-old Anne. "I saw him too."

For the sake of the children, I plastered a smile onto my face. "I think you all saw him at the same time."

Elizabeth suddenly grabbed my free hand, "Mama, he looks ill."

That was putting it mildly, I realized. He looked ghastly. Had there been illness recently in London? I wondered. It would not have been surprising; even without the devil sitting on the throne, the place was at its most unpleasant in summer.

Harry dismounted from his horse, far too slowly for a man not quite eight-and-twenty. The children swarmed around him while I stood politely nearby.

At last, Harry rose from the children's level and kissed me on the cheek as I tried not to recoil. Quietly, he said, "Kate. I must see you alone. I will send for you when I am ready."

My blood froze within me, but I said calmly, "Yes, my lord."

"You're wearing my favorite dress."

"Edward forced me."

"Sit down, Kate."

I obeyed, and decided I would go down fighting. "If you have called me here to tell me you are annulling our marriage, I promise you I shall not let you make a beggar of me or the children. I have relations in Luxembourg to protect me, you know." I didn't even know most of their names. "And—"

"Kate! It's not that. It's nothing to do with the two of us. Not in that way." He drew a breath, then another one. Finally, he said, in a voice so low I had to strain to hear him, "King Edward's boys are dead."

I heard the news with a strange sort of calmness. "How?" I asked unnecessarily.

"Murdered."

I forced myself to ask, "At your order?"

"No. I am innocent of that, at least. The king's order. I knew nothing about it until it was too late. But I should have guessed."

"Yes."

He looked down into my face for the first time. "You're not surprised."

"No. Bishop Morton feared for their lives, he told me. And I never expected anything good from Gloucester once he arrested my kinsmen."

"I did. Try to believe me, Kate. I did. I never thought him capable of shedding the blood of infants." He fiddled with the dagger at his side, a gesture he'd copied from Richard years ago. "Yet there is more. You were right about your brother and the rest, and about Hastings. They were innocent."

"The precontract?"

"A lie, most likely. No one shall ever probably know the truth but Edward and Eleanor Butler. And perhaps William Hastings. At the very least, there's not enough evidence to say that there was one."

We were silent for a time. Then I asked detachedly, "What shall you do?"

"I don't know. I have been asking myself that since I left Richard at Gloucester." He gazed out the window. "I tell myself that he can do no worse than he has done, that with this deed—no, these deeds—done and over with, he will be a good and just king. He might be, Kate. He is not a cruel man by nature."

I chose not to argue the point. "What of my nieces?"

"I don't believe he would harm women or girls. But I cannot be sure. I am sure of nothing now."

"Have you spoken to your confessor of this?"

"No. You are my first confessor, Kate." He sank on the bench beside me and put his arm around my rigid shoulders. His voice cracked as he said, "Try to forgive me. I have wronged you so much, but that seems the least of my sins now."

We sat there in mute misery. Finally, I drew back. "You need counsel, Harry, wiser counsel than I can give. There is someone here who can give you such, if you will heed it."

"Who?"

"Bishop Morton."

√

"Amen."

We all maintained a moment of respectful silence for the poor boys who had died in the Tower. Then Bishop Morton raised his head. "So, your grace. What do you intend to do?"

"Kate asked me the same question. I still don't know. He might do naught but good from now on."

"Or he might do more evil, your grace. Six people have died, two of them children. And more, God help them, will die for their role in this failed plot to rescue the poor lads."

"Yes." Harry stared into space. "I just don't know what I can do. Put someone in his place? The young Earl of Warwick has a better claim to the throne than he. But he's a child—and the son of Clarence, for whom no one mourned overmuch. No one even advocated on his behalf when Richard seized the crown. Would people fight for him?"

"There is yourself."

"Me?" Harry smiled tiredly. "Do you know, I actually thought of that while riding here? My claim to the throne isn't a poor one. But no. I

would inherit all of Richard's enemies, and none of his friends. And—"
He shook his head sadly. "I'd not make a good king. These last few
months have taught me that. And besides, what joy could I take from
a throne that came to me through the deaths of innocents? No. I don't
want it."

"Then allow me to suggest another candidate. Henry Tudor."

"That spotty boy?" I said involuntarily.

Bishop Morton smiled at me. "He is surely neither a boy nor spotty now,
my lady."

"I know; it is just how I remember him. But king?"

"His claim is not a remote one. Through John of Gaunt—"

"But it is a bastard one," said Harry. "And no one knows anything of him,
save his mother, who is hardly impartial. I met him myself only briefly."

The bishop spread his hands wide. "What can I say, your grace?
Desperate times call for desperate measures. I do not believe that the
people would accept you as king, as you yourself say, and the Earl of
Warwick is under the disadvantage of youth." He nibbled at a sweet cake
I had set out; I had learned that the bishop appreciated good food. "You
might protest that I am attempting to restore the House of Lancaster,
which I supported for many years. I can only tell you that I have served
the House of York faithfully since the battle of Tewkesbury, and that the
late King Edward was well pleased with my services. It was through his
own good offices that I was made Bishop of Ely. Were his son on the
throne, I would have gladly continued to serve the House of York. It
comes down not to Lancaster or York, but to this: with the poor boys
gone, what is left is a choice between this unknown Welshman and the
murderer Gloucester."

Harry shook his head. "For all that Richard has done, he is my friend,
and I don't know if I can bring myself to betray him," he said softly. "I
must mull this over, Bishop."

⁓

That night, Harry came to my bedchamber. Instinctively, I gathered the covers around me protectively. He sighed. "Might I lie beside you? Just to sleep?"

"I suppose."

He crawled in beside me and touched my unresponsive hand, then rolled over on his side. Much later, long after the time we both should have been sleeping, I heard the sounds of sobbing. I lay there rigid, staring at the canopy. Then the sobs at last stopped, and we both fell asleep.

✺

Though the plan to rescue the boys from the Tower had failed, and its four leaders had been hung, England was at last arising from the stupor into which she had sunk in the days before Richard's coronation. From Harry, I heard that plans were being made to smuggle my nieces out of sanctuary. Alas, Gloucester learned of the plan from a spy, and men were sent to guard Westminster Abbey so that it looked, so I was told later, like a foreign city under siege. But with that plan foiled, others sprang up in its place. Soon Harry was appointed by Richard to investigate treasons in London, Surrey, Sussex, Kent, Middlesex, Oxfordshire, Berkshire, Essex, and Hertfordshire. The plans were to smuggle the poor boys out of the Tower, for besides Richard and the men who had done his bidding, only Harry, Bishop Morton, and I knew that they were dead.

During this time, Harry acted as Richard's trusted servant, carrying out his orders with an alacrity and ability that made me wonder how differently things might have turned out if the late King Edward had shown him more favor. Yet he continued to closet himself with Bishop Morton daily, and I knew that he was struggling with the question of whether to remain loyal to Richard. For once I restrained myself and said nothing, thinking that my womanly meddling might produce an effect opposite from that I most desired.

Meanwhile, unwelcoming as I had been on his first night home, Harry continued to come to my bed at night. We slept as close to our respective edges as possible at first, but each evening we moved a little closer and exchanged warmer good-nights, and one night in mid-September, perhaps out of sheer loneliness more than anything else, we found ourselves in each other's arms again. Harry let me initiate each stage of the lovemaking that followed. When it was over, I was at last ready to share the knowledge I'd had for some days. I put his hand on my belly. "Harry," I said quietly. "I am with child again."

"Sweetheart! But when—" Harry buried his face in my neck. "Christ," he whispered. "Kate, try to forgive me for the pain I caused you that night."

"I have. I goaded you into it, perhaps."

He shook his head. "What I said and did was inexcusable." He rolled on his back. "But I loved him so much. It hurt me when you spoke ill of him as if you spoke against my very self, and I lost all reason." He caressed my belly again. "I can't believe it. It is a mercy that something good came out of that miserable night."

"A mercy, and more than that, perhaps. Harry, this cannot go on, your being half Richard's man and half the good man I married. Let our babe be a sign to you. Will you join the fight against the king?"

The world seemed to stop as I waited for Harry's answer. It was short and simple. "Yes." He took my hand. "I shall join forces with the rebels—the very men I have been investigating for Richard. And I'll write and invite Henry Tudor to take the throne."

⁂

The news that Harry set in motion the next morning—that the old king's sons had been murdered at the command of King Richard, their own uncle—was the final spark the rebellion needed to take fire.

Men started galloping to and from Brecon, bearing news of a new arrival to our cause each day. Men from the fourth Edward's household joined. My brother Lionel, the Bishop of Salisbury, joined. My brother Richard—his modest landholdings seized by Gloucester solely because he was a Woodville—joined. The husband of my brother Anthony's bastard daughter joined. The late Duchess of Exeter's husband, Thomas St Leger, joined. Lionel and Richard, a home-loving man who I knew would have rather been doing anything besides raising men in revolt, joined because of what had been done to our brother Anthony and our nephew Richard Grey. Some joined because of the land or the positions the king had taken from them. Yet others—many others—joined for the love of their old master, Edward IV, and for their anger at what had been done to his young boys.

Margaret Beaufort joined too—or, to put it more aptly, she connected her own conspiracy with ours. Angry that Richard had ignored her requests to bring her son safely home to England, she had been involved with the failed plot to free the boys from the Tower. Her half brother had already had his lands seized for his suspected role in the plot. When she learned from Harry of what had been done to the lads in the Tower, she became the heart and soul of the rebellion in London.

Margaret had a physician, Lewis Caerleon, who also served my sister. As my sister was indeed ailing, he was able to pass freely into sanctuary, despite the guards that questioned everyone coming or going. It was he who broke the news to Bessie that her boys were dead, and at whose hands. It was he who also carried another proposal: that Bessie salvage the wreck of our family's fortunes by allowing her eldest daughter to marry Henry Tudor: a joining of the houses of York and Lancaster for once and for all. From their union, Caerleon told her, would result a son who would blend the best of the two houses.

So we plotted, and we prayed, as King Richard continued on his progress, making a show of refusing any monetary gifts that were offered to him and smiling benevolently upon the poor who were all but shoved into his path so that he could make a show of giving alms to them.

At Brecon, I was the one doing most of the praying, for Bishop Morton was enjoying himself much too thoroughly to spend much time on his knees. Instead, he helped Harry, dashing off letters and conferring with messengers late into the night and in general moving about like a man half his age. Harry needed the help, for though he had never swerved from his purpose once he committed to overthrowing his dear friend, I knew that it pained him deeply and that it took its toll on his body as well as on his peace of mind.

In early October, the letter that Harry had been dreading for days arrived. It was a curt note from Richard ordering him to join him at Pontefract. I had seen other letters from Richard, full of friendly affection; this bore none. "He knows?" I said, leaning over Harry's shoulder.

"He knows." Harry turned to the clerk nearby. "Tell him that I suffer from an infirmity of stomach, and cannot accede to his request."

He sighed, and I wrapped my arms around him gently, for I knew that he was indeed sick at heart. "Soon this will all be over, Harry."

"For one of us," Harry said.

⁂

On a crisp, pleasant October day, Harry's troops were finally ready to march east from Brecon.

My boys and I were among them. The plan was for the three of us to cross the Severn with Harry's men, then settle at Thornbury in Gloucestershire; Harry had feared that if we were left in Wales, we might be taken hostage by one of Richard's followers. The girls too were to have gone, but at the last minute, little Anne fell ill with a bad cold. She was a delicate creature at that time, and Harry and I, still nursing our grief for our dead son Humphrey, did not wish to risk the journey. So we left her and Elizabeth there, well attended. "We can send for them soon," Harry reassured me. Clearly, he was trying to reassure himself as well. "It won't be long, and no one shall bother a pair of little girls. You as a Woodville, and the boys as my heir and his brother, are more at risk."

I nodded sensibly, stifling my misgivings. I had no knowledge of these things, but it did occasionally occur to me that our plan might be called a foolhardy one. A man with almost no experience was leading an army against a man who had defeated the Scots and helped to scatter Margaret of Anjou's hopes to the winds. He was to be aided by a near stranger from Brittany with no service as a soldier whatsoever. And even I, woman that

I was, could look at Harry's troops and realize that they had no heart for this battle. Richard, Henry Tudor, the Earl of Warwick, King Arthur—it mattered not to them who was king. There was little glory to be won in a civil war, and there would be precious little booty to come out of this one. These men were here only out of duty, and grudgingly given duty at that.

"Papa! It all looks so glorious!" Elizabeth nodded at the banners with Stafford knots flapping in the breeze. "And you look so fine in your armor."

For the first time in days, Harry smiled. He lifted Elizabeth in the air and twirled her around, just like King Edward had me that long-ago day at Reading. "It looks all the better because you helped polish it, sweetheart."

"I wish I could come with you and Mama and the boys."

"And I do too. But you must take care of Anne. She would be lonely without you. And when she feels better, you must help make sure that she minds Nurse and doesn't catch cold again."

"Oh, I will," Elizabeth said in a tone that made me as a fellow youngest sister feel rather sorry for poor Anne.

Harry pointed to the uppermost turret of Brecon Castle. "Now come. You must go to the top of the castle and wave your handkerchief at me as we depart. It is what all fair maidens do."

"I shall!" said Elizabeth. She kissed me hastily, gave Harry another hug, then scampered off.

Shortly, we saw a white handkerchief fluttering from the castle. Only then did Harry's army begin to march. As we set off, I said one last prayer, short and simple: *God help us.*

Instead, He sent the rains.

&

Never before, or since, have I seen rain and wind like that which came that October of 1483. The winds whipped the Stafford banners out of their bearers' hands, blowing them into the faces of the men who rode behind them. The rains came through the sides of the chariot, soaking me and the boys to the skin. Even the very act of breathing made us swallow drops of water. To complete our misery, the chariot began to list to one side, then jolted to a halt. A wheel was stuck in the mud.

Harry got me and the boys on horses, the boys riding pillion, and we resumed our slow progress, the horses slogging through the mire. Finally, I saw the faint outlines of a manor house. I had traveled this road many a time, but such were the rain and wind that I had lost all track of my surroundings "Where are we?"

"Weobley," said Harry. He looked around at the weary men and horses surrounding us. "We'll stop here for the night."

∞

Walter Devereux, Lord Ferrers, who had welcomed us to Brecon Castle so many years before, stared at the soaked crew inside his great hall. "I have heard of this mad scheme of yours, your grace. As your senior by many years, I take the liberty of speaking frankly to you. I beg you, abandon it and make your peace with the king. Nothing good can come of this."

"It is not a good thing to remove a usurper and a child-murderer from the throne? I have heard of the murders from his own lips, sir."

"You will throw the country back into civil war."

Harry shook his head, spraying water as he did. "This discussion boots nothing. My wife and sons are sodden through. Give them and my party lodgings. It is all I ask."

"Aye, and how could I refuse, with an army at your back? But as my daughter-in-law is your wife's niece"—Cecily, standing in the hall gaping at our mud-splattered appearance, was my sister Anne's daughter—"I would have agreed to shelter her in any case."

Harry smiled his thanks. "You sheltered Henry Tudor once, too." He had been in the care of Walter's sister years before.

"Yes, and that is another reason I don't attempt to throw you out of my home. Perhaps if you stay here, I can talk some sense into you."

"Or we might be able to convert you to our cause," put in a waterlogged but smiling Bishop Morton. I was beginning to learn that it took a great deal to demoralize him.

"I doubt it," said Sir Walter with a sigh. "Come. Let me get the lot of you before a fire."

∽

Instead of ceasing, the storm was only worse the next day. Harry sent out men, who returned the next day in a bedraggled state to tell him that the Severn was flooded. There was no hope of crossing it. Until we could, Harry's army would not be able to join with the rebels in the West Country.

For days upon days it rained. The flooding was so bad in spots that people claimed later to have seen babes in their cradles floating down the Severn amid the remains of their washed-out houses.

Each day more of Harry's soldiers—billeted wherever they could beg or command a place to lay their heads, as no one could make camp—deserted. I could hardly blame them. Harry went out daily to speak with them— sometimes ordering them to stay, sometimes begging them—but to no avail. Soon we were down to a couple of dozen men.

Then on the sixth day of our stay one of our servants from Brecon arrived, not wearing any sort of badge to identify himself. "My lord. I bear bad news. Brecon has been overrun and plundered."

Harry went white. "Where are my daughters?"

"At Tretower."

Tretower was the home of the Vaughan family, who had been longtime retainers of the Staffords. I clutched at Harry. "You mean the Vaughans took them into their care?"

"No, my lady. Not in that sense. It was the filthy Vaughans who overran the castle. They had a swarm of men with them—far outnumbering the garrison at the castle—who'd been promised spoils. Gloucester had spies in the neighborhood, you see, my lord, and they knew exactly when to make their move. Within hours of your departure, they marched on Brecon.

We tried to defend it, but there were just too many of them. Some of the garrison are dead."

I crossed myself. Harry looked numb. "Go on," he managed.

"Once they made it in, they had the decency to bring the young ladies out—they were screaming and crying, but not hurt. Their attendants were taken with them."

"Anne had a cold," I said. "Elizabeth has nightmares sometimes. Harry, we must return to them!"

"My lady, you can't. Brecon was sacked. Looted, and all of my lord's papers burned. All of the land around it was laid waste—at least as much as they could before the rains started. And now you could not go there if you tried. The Vaughans and their creatures, acting on Gloucester's orders, have blocked the roads leading to and out of Brecon. Everyone who goes is being watched. I have been days trying to get here myself, and they nearly caught me once or twice."

"But I don't understand," I said. "What did we ever do to the Vaughans? They have never had trouble with Harry that I can recall."

"I asked one of their followers myself. He cuffed me for my impertinence, but he'd been at your wine and answered readily enough. Jasper Tudor executed the Vaughans' father back in '71, my lady, and they are at last exacting what revenge that they can. That is why."

The year 1471, when I was still a child and Harry only a lad of fifteen. And my little girls were in the hands of these men. I laid my head on Harry's shoulder and wept.

Bishop Morton, uncharacteristically grim-faced, had been standing listening to all of this in silence. Over my sobs, he said, "It's all up here, my lord. You can't get over the Severn, and you can't go back to Wales, and you've not enough men to fight."

"And, my lord, you can tarry here no longer." Lord Ferrers's voice was apologetic but firm. "It is treason to be sheltering you, and I can no longer put myself and my family at risk. Your lady, of course, is a different matter, as are the children. I'll not turn them out. But the men must go."

"Then we shall be gone tonight," said Harry calmly. He turned to Richard de la Bere, Sheriff of Hereford. "But there is one last favor I wish to ask of you."

"Anything, my lord," said Richard gently.

"Take my eldest son and convey him from here, secretly. You understand the necessity for this, Kate? If I am—gone—he might be the target of the king's wrath. I cannot risk that."

I was still sobbing for my girls, but I nodded a mute assent.

"Hal shall stay with you, Kate. I do not think his danger is as great."

I nodded again.

"The boy had best be disguised in coarse clothing when he is conveyed from here," said Bishop Morton. "You too, my lord. As well as myself. We shall all be out of your hair soon, Lord Ferrers."

"I am very sorry, your grace."

"There is always another day," said the bishop, so brightly that for a brief moment I forgot my girls and contemplated strangling him. "Well, what are we waiting for? Let us find some clothes and go."

⁊

In our chamber, Harry prepared to dress himself in the second-worst set of clothes that could be found at Weobley—Bishop Morton having gallantly put on the worst, which smelled not at all faintly of pig. We had sent our attendants out and were spending these last moments alone. As I helped him out of his own clothes, he shook his head. "Nothing's gone right with this, Kate, and I've put us all in danger. Forgive me."

"I should be asking for your forgiveness, Harry. I encouraged you to rebel."

"Yes. But I couldn't have lived with myself if I hadn't."

"It may still go well, Harry. Henry Tudor may be able to join the rebels. Richard's army may not be able to control the rising in the South."

He sighed. "I hope so. Kate, if it doesn't go well and I end up an exile, we may not see each other for years. Or—"

"Don't say it, Harry. Don't even think it."

He pulled me against him and we embraced each other for a long time. All of the remaining bitterness that had been between us in those last few months melted as we stood there together, our tears blending.

Finally, we pulled apart. As I wiped my eyes, Harry said, "I want you to keep something safe for me, sweetheart. Lift your skirts."

I obeyed. Harry unstrapped his jeweled garter from his calf and gently strapped it on my own. "Do you remember? When I was eighteen and received this, I checked every hour to make sure it was still there."

"I remember. I shall take good care of it."

He smiled sadly. "It was Richard who first strapped it on me, did you know that? But it is where it belongs now, on the being that I love the best in all the world." He pulled on a pair of dingy hose, then the rest of his garments, and put his arm around me. "Come, sweetheart. Let me take my leave of the boys."

✑

"I am to go away soon too," bragged Edward as Hal stared sulkily at the floor.

"You must be good and mind what Sir Richard tells you. And Hal, you will have much to do as well, taking care of your mother, so don't look so surly. But now, boys, let me have a word with each of you."

He bent and spoke at length to one son, then to the other as Sir Walter stood uncomfortably by. I wondered if he was having second thoughts about evicting his houseguest. But Harry looked strangely calm when he stood. "Good-bye, Sir Walter. I thank you for your kindness to my family."

"God be with you, your grace, if not with your cause." He hesitated. "There's still time to reconsider."

Harry smiled and shook his head, then embraced me. We clung together for a short time as Bishop Morton called out his cheery farewells to our reluctant host.

Then Harry and the other men disappeared into the darkness.

xxii

Harry: October 1483 to November 2, 1483

JOHN RUSSELL, BISHOP OF LINCOLN, HAD A SAYING WHENEVER DETAILS were too unpleasant to be elaborated upon: "Why enlarge?" It had become a catchphrase among the king's councilors, I had discovered when I at last became one, and one that could send them off in gales of laughter when used at the right moment.

And now I am eight-and-twenty, in the prime of life and the peak of good health, and I shall be dead within hours. Why enlarge? But I suppose I must.

⚭

My few followers—Bishop Morton, my physician and astrologer, Thomas Nandyke, my uncle by marriage, Thomas Knyvet, and a few others—each took a separate path when we left Weobley. Our plans were to await the outcome of the rebellion in the South and then, if necessary, to flee abroad. I chose to go north, then head east toward the coast and take ship if the rebellion proved a failure.

I had not told even Kate where I was going, thinking it best that she knew as little as possible should she fall into the king's hands. Already he, through the Vaughans, had my daughters under his control... I put the thought from my mind, for it could only paralyze me. I had to keep moving.

I had a retainer, Ralph Bannaster, who had a good-sized house near Wem, not far from Shrewsbury. I didn't know the man that well, but I had favored him in the past and knew his family to have long been loyal to the Staffords. So it was his house to which I made my way under cover of darkness. I went by foot, as a man in my shabby garments riding a fine horse would have been too conspicuous. Besides, a horse would be just one more encumbrance.

The rain had subsided to a drizzle, just enough to make my journey a miserable and cold one. It was a distance of about seventy miles between Weobley and Wem. I did most of my walking at night; during the day, I hid where I could and slept.

On a day near the end of October, I entered Shrewsbury. It was a bustling place, and in my disguise I felt safe walking through it openly in broad daylight. In the market square some placards had been posted, and it was there that I read, with the strangest sort of feeling, that a reward of a thousand pounds was being offered for my capture. "Lucky man, to catch the duke," a man beside me said.

"Lucky, indeed," I agreed. It then occurred to me that I did not look the sort of man who could read, and I hastened to get lost in the throng and out of Shrewsbury.

The weather had turned dry and crisp—precisely the type of weather I could have used at Weobley—and within three hours I was at Ralph Bannaster's manor. It took me some considerable time to be admitted to him, as I would not reveal my identity to anyone else in his household, but once I finally stood before him, I was surprised at the warmth of his greeting. I had fully expected to have to use the gold I had secreted on my person as a bribe.

"Stay as long as you need, your grace," he said kindly. "Now, come and lie down for a time. You must be exhausted. I'll have some food brought to you." He shook his head. "You look like two miles of bad road."

"More like seventy," I said, smiling. It was good to hear some friendly words.

Bannaster led me to his own chamber and sat me down before the fire. I had not realized until then how worn out and cold I was, and when a pallet was brought out for me, I wanted nothing but to settle down into it and sleep my life away. I hardly wanted the wine or food that was served to me, but Bannaster insisted. "Take some refreshment, your grace, or you'll be weak when you awake."

In my exhausted state this made a good deal of sense to me. I sipped the wine and felt it go to my head at once. Bannaster took the cup from my fingers as I yawned and curled up on my pallet. "Want—sleep," I mumbled.

My host draped a blanket over me and settled a pillow under my head. "Sweet dreams, your grace," he said as I mumbled my thanks.

∽

There was someone standing over me, but I refused to let this interfere with the dream I was having about Kate, who was stripping to her shift and smiling at me all the while. I pushed my head deeper into the pillow and gathered the blanket around me more tightly. It was chilly; the fire had gone out.

"Come, your grace. Your little game is up."

I rolled on my back and stared up irritably. There were a dozen men, all armed, surrounding me. "I don't understand," I said sleepily.

"Aye? You're under arrest, for high treason. Now do you understand, my lord of Buckingham? It doesn't get much plainer than that."

And then I recognized the speaker: Thomas Mytton, the sheriff of Shropshire. I sat up and looked around. At the edge of the circle of men was Ralph Bannaster, staring at his feet. "You betrayed me," I said. "Why?"

Ralph shrugged. "What do you expect a man to do when a thousand pounds walks inside his home and plants itself at his hearth? You made it too easy."

"That's what you think," I said, rising to my feet and reaching for the dagger that hung at my side. But it had been taken from me while I slept. No matter; I had some pride left in me. I lunged at Ralph and landed a blow on his jaw, then tried to break away from the sheriff and his men and run for my life.

It was a futile gesture, of course; there were too many of them. In a matter of minutes I was shackled and led outside.

∞

It all goes downhill from here. Wrapped in the rusty black cloak I'd been wearing for days, I was taken to Shrewsbury and held prisoner there, and on All Hallow's Eve two of Richard's men, James Tyrell and Christopher Wellesbourne, came to conduct me south, where Richard and his army had gathered. We moved quickly: today is the first of November, and I am in a guarded room at the Blue Boar Inn in Salisbury.

It could be worse, I told the guards when I saw the place. It could be the White Boar Inn.

Rather late in life, I seem to be developing a sense of humor.

∞

Hastings, Rivers, Grey, and Vaughan, all innocent men, died without trial or with only the mockery of one. I, guilty as charged, receive one, after a fashion at least. As Constable of England, it would be my job to conduct this trial, and I indeed suggest saving some time by doing this—a joke that falls flat with my guards. It might appeal more to Richard's sense of humor, I think.

Well, perhaps not under the circumstances.

In lieu of my own services, Ralph Ashton conducts the trial. It is a short one, and the only thing in doubt is whether I shall die the traitor's death of hanging, drawing, and quartering or the nobleman's death of beheading. Nobility wins out, and I whisper a prayer of thanksgiving, for it is hard enough to contemplate being cut open while still alive, and harder yet to think of my wife and children learning that I died such a death.

After that, I am taken back to my room at the Blue Boar Inn, outside of which construction of my scaffold is proceeding apace. The workmen, though busy, nonetheless find leisure to converse and joke among themselves, which strikes me as less than tactful under the circumstances, but no doubt they are delighted at the chance of earning some unexpected wages. I hope they are suitably grateful to me.

I have assumed that these last hours would hang heavy, but I find much to do. First there is my will to write. As an attainted traitor I will have no possessions to leave, but I can list my debts in the hope that Richard sees fit to pay my creditors, and I can make some bequests for the good of my soul with the hope that he may honor them. The debts take the better part of the afternoon to list; my life has not been an inexpensive one.

Then there is Kate. I specify a jointure of a thousand marks for her, as was promised upon our marriage. It will be enough to keep her comfortable and, I hope, to attract a good husband for her, for my sweet Kate is not the stuff of which vowesses are made. I wonder what sort of man she will marry; whoever it is, I know, will serve her better than I have in the past few months.

I sigh and go on writing. When one of my guards returns, I ask, "Did the king return an answer?"

"He'll not see you. You should know that by now."

I have been begging since my arrival at Salisbury to see Richard, who is in the city, though he was not present at my trial. Not to plead for my life—I know that is beyond hope—but to plead for the well-being of my wife and children. I would remind him that although I betrayed him, I served him faithfully in the past and loved him dearly, and I would tell him how well it would become him to treat a traitor's wife and children kindly and allow them to prosper. I would remind him of the times that he was kind to me when no one else was, as at that miserable day at Tewkesbury when my uncle was executed, and I would beg him on my knees to remember that and to repeat it.

I would spend the rest of the afternoon on my knees before him, if it suited him, if I could die with my mind at ease about Kate and the children. But it appears that I shall never get the chance.

∽

The landlord of the Blue Boar offers to make me a last meal. I hesitate at first, remembering the false hospitality shown to me by Ralph Bannaster. But there is nothing to gain from drugging me now, I realize, so I ask for chops and ale, Bannaster having put me off wine for life, or the little I have left of it.

My last meal is delivered, and is delicious. Perhaps my cause had a sympathizer at the Blue Boar. I think to myself that the next time I am in Salisbury, I must make a point of stopping at this inn.

Well, no.

Each time the door of my chamber bangs open, I perk up, hoping against hope that it is a message from Richard, but it never is. This time, it is Francis Lovell, with a run-down of what I may expect tomorrow. I will be shaven and shriven, in that order, which relieves me, for I am vain enough to want to go to my death looking my best, and I desperately want to make my last confession. I will be given a clean shirt and hose, which is also soothing. At around ten I will be led to the scaffold, where I may make a short speech if I please. "Nothing treasonous, mind you, or you'll be put to silence more roughly than you might like."

"I know. I might be about to lose my head but I haven't lost my mind."

Lovell snorts, almost in laughter, and starts to leave. Then he turns. "Why did you do it, Buckingham? He gave you everything. Was there some mean office, some half acre of land he omitted that made you rebel?"

I long to tell him that it wasn't greed, it was the boys. But what if he is asking Richard's question? "Allow me to see Richard, just for a few moments, and I will tell him all. I would like to do so, in fact."

"Nice try, Harry. He won't see scum like you. He has better things to do. Like taking a piss. Or a crap."

Doomed men are hard to insult, I am finding. "If he changes his mind, I'll be here."

Lovell slams the door and thumps down the stairs.

⁓

I should have asked Lovell where my body will be taken; in my will, I requested burial with my parents and brother at Pleshey, but I doubt that my wish will be honored; most likely the king will hand me over to the Grey Friars. Pleshey makes me think of my poor mother, who lost all of her kinsmen to the ax or to battle, and I am grateful that she did not live to see my death as well.

The guards inside my chamber being occupied in a game of dice in the corner, I practice my last speech under my breath. It shall be a short, simple one: a warning for others to profit by my example, a plea for forgiveness, and a plea for mercy toward Kate and the children. Yet even as there is little to remember, I worry that my nerves will overcome me and that I may omit or repeat something. I would not want to look foolish.

It is a foolish thing, I grant you, for a man whose severed head is about to be held up by the hair for all of Salisbury to gawk upon to worry about looking a fool in public, but there you have it. And I hope they remember the clean shirt as well.

∽

There are two schools of thought, I suppose, about whether one should sleep before one's execution. The first group reasons that one is about to sleep for eternity, so why bother? The second is that one should get a good night's rest before doing anything of importance, including dying. I turn out to belong to the latter, for when my scaffold is complete and the streets of Salisbury fall silent, I decide to lie down for the night.

In another part of Salisbury, Richard might be doing the same. Or is he going to stay awake? He might; he once loved me as a brother, or at least he said he did, so perhaps his mind is too troubled to sleep. I shall never know, I suppose.

My guards curtly agree that I can retire. The shackles on my feet jangling, I kneel beside my bed and curl my fingers around an inexpensive rosary, the only personal possession that was not taken from me when my captors searched me. I tell the beads and pray for the dead: those whose deaths of which I was guiltless and those whose deaths for which I must share the blame. Then I pray for the living. When I am done with my prayers and am lying in my last earthly bed, blankets pulled tightly around me to keep out the cold, I fall fast asleep and do not wake until dawn.

∽

Lovell spoke true: just as the barber leaves and I pull a clean shirt over my head, a priest enters. There is no need to repeat what I tell him; you have heard it all. I am forgiven my sins, and for the first time (and the last time) in my life, that knowledge moves me to tears.

And at last, men come into my chamber and bind my hands tightly behind my back. Trussed securely, I am led out of my chamber and to the scaffold.

On this Sunday, All Souls' Day, there is a good-sized crowd in the marketplace of Salisbury; after all, one doesn't see a duke die every day. From the scaffold I can see Lovell and many other of Richard's men, but there is no sign of Richard himself. Strangely, that no longer bothers me. All is out of my hands now. I must trust to the Lord's mercy.

I make my speech. I don't falter, just like I did not falter that day at the Guildhall, but today I speak to a better purpose. When I am finished, I kneel and place my head on the block. Like the scaffold, it is spanking new, and the pigeons, I am pleased to see, have left it alone. I turn my mind to higher matters and begin repeating my prayers.

There is a blow, and some shouting, and then a long, long darkness. Then there is a burst of light, and a man is standing beside me. "Well, Harry," he says, grinning at me in welcome. "You certainly did make a fine mess of things, didn't you?"

"I can't argue with that," I say sheepishly.

My uncle Edmund Beaufort laughs kindly. "Come. We've all been waiting for you," he says as he links my arm in his and leads me to kneel before my Savior.

xxiii

Kate: October 1483 to January 1484

THE DAY AFTER HARRY LEFT, RICHARD DE LA BERE, ACCOMPANIED BY Harry's uncle by marriage, William Knyvet, took little Edward away to Sir Richard's manor at Kinnersley. Dressed in the shabby little coat his father had had made for him, he looked at me tolerantly as I fluttered over him and kissed him again and again. "It's *fine*, Mama."

Sir Richard, dressed as shabbily as his charge, finally parted us by lifting my son in his arms. "Don't worry, my lady. We'll do all we can to conceal his identity." He glanced at Edward, who was fair-haired like myself but otherwise, with his delicate face, could have been his father as a small lad. "If worst comes to worst, we can dress him as a lass."

Edward's face scrunched up into a look of utter disgust. "A *girl*? I don't want—"

"Hush, Edward. Sir Richard and Sir William know best, and you will do as they tell you. Think of it as a great adventure."

Edward grumbled and submitted reluctantly when I gave him one last kiss.

With our party at Weobley down to me, Cecilia, a couple of other ladies, and Hal and his nurse, I kept mostly to my chamber. Sir Walter was not unfriendly—to the contrary, with Harry gone, he was quite gracious—but I felt keenly my awkward position here, as a fugitive's wife who did not dare go to one of her own homes to stay. Knowing that there had been risings scheduled all over the south of England and that Henry Tudor was set to invade, I could only hope that even without Harry, King Richard would be overthrown and I would be welcoming Harry home soon—from wherever he was.

That was my hope. Always I have had the power to hope—whether that be a good thing or bad, you may decide. So a few days into November, when Sir Walter came to my chamber and said he wished to speak to me about a serious matter, I hoped, even though nothing in his face encouraged it. "Richard is defeated?"

"No."

"Harry has escaped abroad?"

"No."

"He is still in England?"

"No. My lady, please hear me out. It is grim news for you. Your husband was taken prisoner near Wem. He was brought to Salisbury and tried for treason. The sentence was carried out on All Souls' Day."

I blinked. "You mean Harry is—" I could not get the word out. Sir Walter nodded. "But he loved the king!"

"He rose against him, my lady."

"But he never meant to harm him! And what of our children?" Sir Walter blinked and I rushed on. "They love Harry; they need him! The king can't take him away from them just like that. He can't! There is some mistake. There has—"

My knees gave way and I sank to the ground dizzily with my hands over my face, willing myself not to be sick or to swoon. When the world finally stopped spinning, Sir Walter was gone and Cecilia was supporting me. "Let me put you to bed, my lady."

"No!" I wrenched away. "We must get out of here. Now."

❦

An hour or so later, I walked into Weobley's great hall, trailed by Cecilia and by Hal and his nurse. Sir Walter stared at my traveling clothes. "Where in the name of God are you going?"

"To sanctuary."

"Which one?"

"I don't know. I will come across one, I am sure. Now let me pass. I thank you for your hospitality. I know we have imposed upon you greatly."

Sir Walter stopped me with a hand. "You are going nowhere," he said quietly. "I have sent word to the king that you are here and that we shall await his orders as to what you are to do next."

"The king— You cannot—"

"I have emphasized your innocence in all of this. You have nothing to fear from him, your grace."

"But I am not innocent. And you cannot keep me here!" I tried to push him out of my way.

Sir Walter grabbed my wrists. "My lady, even if I did not know my responsibility to the king, I would not let you leave here today. The weather's foul, you haven't men to escort you even if you knew where you were going, and it will be dark shortly. And there is the matter of your condition too."

I flushed. Evidently someone attending me had been talking.

Cecilia—crying, though I could not fathom why, since I was perfectly collected—touched me on the arm. "He is right. Please. Let me take you back to your chamber." She looked apologetically at me, then at Sir Walter. "My lady is not at all well, my lord. She's fevered, poor creature, can you see? I tried—"

"Yes, of course, woman. I see." Sir Walter began to steer me in the direction from which I had came. "You're going to get in bed and rest, your grace. My wife and daughter-in-law will tend you themselves. We'll have no more nonsense about leaving."

"All of you traitors! Let me pass!" I tried to yank away from Sir Walter. Then I dropped to my knees as a gush of blood poured down my thighs and onto the rushes.

Ignoring the mess, Sir Walter scooped me up into his arms and carried me to my chamber. Poor man. I was screaming the entire way.

∽

I had nothing to complain of as to my treatment at Sir Walter's hands after I lost Harry's child—quite the opposite. His own physician attended me in the dangerously high fever that followed, and when I resisted with all my might my caretakers' efforts to remove Harry's garter from my calf, Sir Walter himself thought of the clever expedient of strapping it to my arm, where I could look at it all I liked. For the benefit of my addled self he made a point of charging everyone who came into my presence that it would be certain death if they took it from me. He had them bring Hal to my chamber door so I could hear his voice—at my worst point I was convinced he had been taken to Salisbury to die on Harry's block—and he tried, I later heard, to have my daughters brought from Tretower as a comfort to me but was refused by the Vaughans, who said they would do nothing without an order from the king. By the time their reply arrived, I was well out of danger and entirely rational, and I was sitting up and taking a little bit of food. When two knights arrived from the king to take me into custody a couple of weeks later, I was quite restored to my usual state of health.

Sir Walter helped me down the stairs as I left my chamber at Weobley for the last time. "If you don't feel you're strong enough to travel yet, your grace, I can explain to the king. I am certain that he will understand."

"No. The sooner I find out what is in store for me the better. It cannot be worse than what I am imagining."

He grasped my hand. "There is nothing to dread, my lady. The king will be merciful, I am sure. Why, you know that he allowed Lord Hastings's widow her jointure, and did not attaint him after his death. That was chivalrous of him."

It would have been even more chivalrous, I thought, not to have killed Hastings in the first place. But there seemed no point in arguing, so I just shrugged.

Sir Walter, however, was wearing the expression that I knew by now meant unpleasant news. "I do not know if you are acquainted with the men who are to take you to the king. Sir Richard Huddleston is married to Queen Anne's bastard sister, Margaret."

"Yes, I've heard of him and her."

"Sir Christopher Wellesbourne was one of the men who escorted the late duke from Shrewsbury to Salisbury, your grace. He has also been attempting to find your eldest son."

"Has he asked you about his whereabouts?"

"Yes. I know nothing."

I gave Sir Walter's hand a grateful squeeze and went to meet my escorts.

Waiting in the great hall with them were Hal, all bundled up in warm clothes like myself, and Cecilia and Hal's nursemaid, who by my own decision were staying behind until I learned of my status. It might have been a reprise of the day when I in my distraction had tried to flee to sanctuary, except that we were in mourning attire now and that I was no longer carrying Harry's child. Only one thing was unchanged: I had no idea of what the future might hold for me, and I found that I did not much want to think about it.

Sir Walter released my arm. "This is the Duchess of Buckingham, sirs."

I glared at my captors, whose own expressions made it clear that they could think of better things they could be doing than escorting a traitor's wife and a small boy nearly two hundred miles to London. In this friendly manner, we proceeded out to the courtyard.

Waiting for me there was a litter that would have shamed my servants to be seen in. "That contraption is the crown's now, you know," explained Sir Christopher when I suggested that the chariot I had traveled in from Brecon, having been dragged out of the mud and taken to Weobley once the rains stopped, could be used instead. "All of your husband's goods are forfeit."

I looked back toward the stables, thinking of our horses, each one of which Harry and I and the children had named. "I suppose our horses are the crown's too now?"

"Down to the saddle and harness." He glanced at the jeweled clasp on my cloak, a gift from Harry following the birth of my son Hal. "Technically, all your frippery is the crown's, if you get right down to it. But I suppose you might be allowed a trinket or two."

I blinked back my tears and turned to Sir Walter. "I am sorry to have brought so much inconvenience upon you, my lord. You have been very kind to Hal and me." I looked down at my mourning robes, made at Sir Walter's expense while I was ill. At least they were mine, I supposed. "I am sorry I cannot repay you for having these made."

"It is not expected, your grace."

"At least I can spare one of these." I stood on my tiptoes and gave Sir Walter a peck on the cheek. It was mostly his wife and my niece who had tended me in my illness, and they had been gentle and attentive, but it was Sir Walter who had sat beside me and tried to comfort me that terrible night when, my fever gone and my sense of reality fully intact, I had at last broken down and cried for Harry and our lost child, my weeping so violent that I doubled over on my bed and pounded the mattress with my fists until my knuckles bled. Sir Walter had been like a father to me on that occasion, and I would sorely miss him.

He smiled and helped me into the litter. "Why, I don't believe I've ever been kissed by a duchess before. Thank you, your grace." He turned to Sir Christopher and Sir Richard. "Take good care of my lady. I shall be up for Parliament soon, and I will be asking about her welfare. I will want to hear that she was well treated."

As the litter began jolting along, I waved good-bye to Sir Walter and his family, then patted my calf where Harry's garter was safely back in its place. "Give me courage, love," I whispered, so softly that only the dead could hear. "I shall need it where I am going."

◊

"Good Lord, does the boy have to piss again?"

"You cannot expect a boy of four to have the control of a grown man," I said as our litter lurched to a stop. It gave me some gratification that traveling with a small boy with a small bladder was proving to be a rather trying task for my custodians. Sir Christopher reluctantly handed me out of the litter, and I just as reluctantly accepted his assistance, then helped Hal out. "He has been very patient, I think. Go here, Hal."

Hal lifted his black skirts with one hand and took hold of his small member with the other, then aimed toward a likely looking tree and did a fairly good job of hitting the mark. He crowed with delight and I clapped, then tried to look refined. "Almost as good as Papa can," Hal said with satisfaction.

My lip wobbled just as I had seen my sister's do. "Almost," I said, rearranging Hal's clothing. "Just keep practicing." I began to move off toward a large bush. "I shall return presently."

"Woman, where the devil are you going?"

"I have been quite patient myself, Sir Christopher. Trust me; I shall not prolong the experience. I have been used to the luxury of a portable close-stool."

✍

We stopped not only to make water, of course, but for refreshment and sleep, and it was at the inn at which we stopped for the night, where I sat picking at my food while the men talked around me as though I were invisible, that I learned that Harry's rebellion had been completely crushed. Thomas St. Leger, the king's own brother in law, had been beheaded at Exeter, as had several others. Henry Tudor, delayed in the Channel by bad weather, had dropped anchor near Dorset a day or so after Harry's death. Suspicious of the effusive greetings he received from the men on shore, he had recognized them for Richard's creatures and had pushed back out to sea. No one was certain of the whereabouts of my brothers Lionel or Richard, or my nephew Dorset, or Bishop Morton, but it was thought that they were either in sanctuary or abroad.

So all was lost, and Harry had died in vain. Richard would be stronger than ever. As Hal dozed against me, I pushed away my food uneaten and huddled over my cup of ale. In the dim light, no one saw the tears that dropped into it.

That night in our chamber, I lay down with Hal until I saw that he was sound asleep. Then I drew a cloak around me and cracked the door, guarded by two of Sir Christopher and Sir Richard's men. "Please let me see Sir Christopher."

My escorts stared at me in horror as I was led into their chamber. Fortunately, both were still dressed.

"I am not here to try to seduce either of you," I said wearily. "Trust me, it is the furthest thing from my mind. Sir Christopher, you saw my husband in his last hours. All I want is to know about them—and with Hal by my side I cannot ask at any other time. Do me that one kindness, and I will ask for nothing more."

Sir Christopher coughed. "My lady, it is a delicate—"

"My father, two of my brothers, and my nephew Richard all lost their heads as well as Harry. It is a subject I am as familiar with as anyone in England, I daresay. Do you think I will faint, or scream, if I hear about another such death? I will not, I give my word. I only want to know. It is unbearable not to. Why, no one has even told me where his body lies."

"Very well." Sir Christopher pointed me to the room's stool and began his tale as Sir Richard disappeared into the confines of the room's large bed. From time to time as Sir Christopher spoke, I saw garments being thrown out from behind the bed curtains. "The duke sought shelter with a Ralph Bannaster, who turned him in out of fear or for the money—I don't know which. Bannaster brought the sheriff and his men there while the duke was sleeping. He put up a fight when they took him, they say, but by the time we got him at Salisbury, he wasn't any trouble at all. He seemed resigned to his fate, and didn't say much of anything. Unlike some parties I can think of, we made good time traveling with him." Sir Christopher paused so that I could reflect on my husband's better example as a captive. "On the day after All Hallow's Eve we brought him to the Blue Boar Inn at Salisbury. I didn't see him after that, but he had a quick trial and spent the rest of the time in his chamber at the inn, where they let him write his will. Very quiet he was, so his guards told us, although they say he kept begging to see the king. The king refused, of course—no need to see the likes of him. The next morning I saw him as they led him out. He bore himself well and didn't show any fear, I will give him that. He had asked to be shriven before he died, and the king did grant him that one request, so I suppose his mind was at peace."

"Where did it take place?"

"The marketplace, on a scaffold built just for him. It was a fair-size crowd." Sir Christopher paused again, as if expecting me to be pleased about Harry's ability to attract spectators, and seeing my lack of gratification, went on. "He walked up the scaffold, then spoke for the first time. His voice didn't shake, but then, he didn't speak all that long. He asked that the king show mercy to his wife and children." Sir Christopher nodded at me in case I was so dim as to miss this reference to myself. "Then he begged forgiveness for betraying his king. I thought that was only proper."

"He was referring to the fifth Edward. The rightful king."

Sir Christopher looked at me with the all-patient look of a man who had long ago decided that women were fools and was constantly having his opinion reconfirmed. "Oh, no, my lady, I'm certain he was referring to our King Richard. Why, you weren't even there! Anyway, after the duke asked for forgiveness, he said that he deserved his death as a sinner. Then he laid his head on the block. He started praying and was still praying when—well, you know. It was done with one stroke, quick and clean. The head was brought to King Richard for him to see that the deed was done, and then the Grey Friars took him away, head and all, in a cart, to their abbey in Salisbury. The king gave them a little something for their trouble in burying him." He nodded at me sternly. "He could have displayed the head, you know. You can consider yourself a lucky woman that he did not."

"I could not possibly be luckier," I agreed. I felt a twinge of guilt for my sarcasm, but it had apparently gone over Sir Christopher's head. I rose to my feet slowly. I was only twenty-five, but I felt twenty years older than that. "Thank you for humoring me, Sir Christopher."

"Not so quickly, my lady. I have humored you. Perhaps you can humor me. You must know that I have been looking for your eldest son, at the king's order. Where is he?"

"I do not know," I said truthfully. "And I shall anticipate you by saying that if I did, I would not tell you."

Sir Christopher shook his head. "There's no need for secrecy. The king wants only to round up all of the duke's family to prevent further rebellion."

"As my son is but five, I think it is safe to say he shall not be inciting a rebellion, wherever he is." I gathered myself to my full height, which was not at all impressive. "My children are all I have left now, Sir Christopher. I shall not put my boy in the king's hands without knowing what he intends to do with him."

"Very well." He whistled and the guards came to lead me back to my chamber. "We'll be leaving at dawn tomorrow. Have yourself and your other boy ready by then."

"Sir Christopher?"

"Yes, wo—your grace?"

"If you will let Hal and I ride on horseback, I daresay our journey to London will be much quicker than in that dreadful litter."

"Amen to that," said Sir Richard's voice behind the bed curtains.

Back in my chamber, I heard the sounds of muffled sobs. I hastened to the bed and held Hal as he cried on my shoulder. "Mama. I thought you had gone away too like Papa."

"I had a headache and needed some fresh air, that is all. I am sorry to have frightened you. Come. Lie back down and we'll go to sleep together."

"I want Papa."

When King Richard took my husband's head, had he thought of the four-year-old boy who would be weeping into his pillow? But of course he had not. No one ever thought of such things. I stroked Hal's hair, so like his father's, and held him tighter. "I know you do. I want him too. But it cannot be. You know what I told you. He fell very, very ill while he was traveling and is with God now, helping to watch over us."

"I want Brecon. I want Edward and the girls."

So did I. "I know, but they must stay where they are for now, and we must go to London. It is a very interesting place." I decided not to bring up the fact that we were prisoners of the crown now. Enough was enough for one night. "Why, your brother and sisters have never seen it. You will be the very first." I kissed Hal on the forehead. "You must get to sleep now. We will be up early tomorrow."

To my surprise, he nodded and lay quietly against me. Soon he was asleep. It was I who spent a sleepless night, wondering what life could possibly hold for us now.

To my gratification, Sir Christopher and Sir Richard allowed Hal and me to ride on horseback the next day, albeit not on our own horse, but each of us on a pillion behind a squire. With that, we made better time, aided by the weather, which could not have been better for our journey to the king. We did not get even a drop of rain. Thinking of the weather that had shut us in at Weobley, I was beginning to have a very dim opinion of the Lord's sense of humor.

Several nights and several inns later, we were at Westminster. I was stiff and chilled when I was helped off my horse, but it was not for that reason that I could barely walk. Sir Christopher said gruffly, "Courage, Duchess. You've shown it so far. The king won't harm a lady. Why, the Countess of Richmond was involved in the scheme as deep as the devil himself, and she's suffered naught but being given into the custody of her own husband."

"Poor man," muttered Sir Richard.

I was briskly steered to the king's presence chamber, at a pace so sharp that I was unable to take much notice of my surroundings other than to notice a general prevalence of white boars, snorting and pawing on every surface imaginable. There were other supplicants waiting to see the king or, failing that, one of his officials, but Sir Richard and Sir Christopher went to the guards and said a quick word. In just a moment, I was in the presence of the man I hated more than any being on earth, before and since. Pushing Hal down with me, I sank to the floor in an obeisance.

The king looked at me. With my eyes cast to the floor, I could not see his gaze, but I felt its hostility. Whatever contempt he had had for me earlier, when I was merely an upstart Woodville, must have paled for what he felt for me now, not only a Woodville but the wife of his betrayer as well.

Beside me, little Hal sneaked his head up to stare in awe at the king—the first one he'd seen, I realized. Somehow it had not occurred to me on our journey that I should have given him some pointers in royal etiquette, and I could only hope that nothing would inspire my son, who since Harry's death had shown a tendency to turn chatty around men near his father's age, to tell the king about his and Harry's pissing contests. Hal had finally managed to lure Sir Christopher into one, I had observed on one occasion before hastily averting my eyes. (Lack of endowment, I had discovered, was not the explanation for Sir Christopher's occasionally sour temper.)

"Is that the king?" Hal whispered.

"Yes," I hissed, grateful that Hal had not picked up on any of the less flattering appellations I had for our sovereign. "Hush."

"Leave us," Richard said to Sir Richard and Sir Christopher. "Take the boy away too."

"Take him away? Where?" Forgetting myself and looking at the king, I clutched at Hal.

I saw then in the king's face the very faintest hint of shame for what he had done to those two other children. In a matter of seconds, however, the king had resumed his impassive gaze. "They may take the boy to get some refreshment," he said icily. "He will be brought back to you when we are done."

"Oh." I relaxed my grip on my son's arm. "Mind your manners," I hissed as Sir Richard and Sir Christopher led Hal away.

"Rise."

I obeyed, trembling.

"Lady Buckingham, you are the widow of the most untrue creature living."

"Harry loved you, your grace. It broke his heart to rebel against your grace."

"His broken heart is nothing to us. He is lucky we did not choose to rip it out of him while it was still beating. Were it not for his being our close kinsman, we would have done so. Enough about him, though. He shall rot in a hell of his own making, we hope. Have you anything to say for yourself?"

"I heartily beg your forgiveness," I said, deciding that this was the only safe reply. I considered kneeling again for good measure but decided against it.

"You were privy to your husband's schemes?" I hesitated. "Lying will boot you nothing."

"Yes, your grace."

"You encouraged them?"

"Yes, your grace."

"You aided them?"

"Yes, your grace."

The king scowled. "We do not kill women," he informed me. "Otherwise…"

Just children and innocent men, I thought. Involuntarily, I gave my neck a pat for reassurance. I thought of inserting another plea for forgiveness but decided to keep silent until I was addressed again.

"We cannot have you at large at this time," Richard said finally. "Your husband showed himself as untrustworthy as a man can be, and we have no reason to think you better. So what shall we do with you?"

"I thought I could stay with one of my sisters," I ventured. "Anne, Margaret, and Joan still live."

Evidently, however, the king's question had been purely rhetorical. "So you can send messages and plot with your brothers? You'll go where we say." I looked as meek as possible. "You and your son will be lodged at the Abbey of the Minoresses for now, and must remain inside its walls. Behave yourself, and you will be allowed to go where you will in due course. Don't behave yourself, and you will find yourself in the Tower instead."

At least, I reflected as Hal and I were placed onto the barge that would take us to the Minories, as it was called, I knew now where I stood with the king.

✑

Our chambers at the Minories, located conveniently near the Tower so that I could all the better contemplate the price of not behaving myself, were by no means uncomfortable. The convent had been patronized by generations of great ladies, some of whom liked to travel between their lodgings here and their great estates in the countryside, and our rooms had all of the luxuries I was used to, with the added benefit of not having Sir Christopher and Sir Richard snoring in the next room. The king had made a small allowance for our board, and my sisters Anne, Margaret, and Joan, having learned of my whereabouts, soon sent me gifts and money. Were it not for the absence of my girls and Edward, I could have settled into a sort of resigned numbness.

As it was, however, I passed the December days by praying for Harry's soul, by answering Hal's questions about our present state, which came at a rate of about twenty per hour, by doing needlework, and by sending petitions to the queen begging to be allowed to see her. Queens were supposed to intercede with their husbands for their subjects, and if my sister was any indication, they enjoyed doing this. I decided that it was time Queen Anne got some more practice at it.

In seeking a royal audience, I proved more successful than had Harry, for after a week or so of pleading, I was brought to the queen in her suite at the royal apartments at the Tower. After she bade me rise, she studied me. "You look very thin, my lady. I do hope you and your son are getting all you need to eat at the Minories?"

"Yes, your grace." I decided not to waste the queen's time and to make my request straightaway, especially since the queen had allowed me such a good opening. "My meals are ample, as is the king's allowance, but I am not eating well, your grace, because I am anxious. My young daughters, as your grace might know, are at Tretower in the care of the Vaughan family."

"I do know that. I have made a point of inquiring after them, and have been assured that they want for nothing and are in good health."

"That might be, your grace, but I fear for them, irrational as that might be, and I miss them deeply."

"The king tells me you have actively secreted your elder son from him."

"I carried out my husband's wishes, your grace. He was a wanted man, and he was terrified that our son might fall into the hands of men less generous and merciful than his grace the king." (Even today, I congratulate myself on that turn of phrase.) I dropped to my knees. "Your grace, in the name of the Virgin Mother, might I humbly ask that you be my advocate with the king in this matter? My petition is that all of my children be reunited and be returned to my custody, without punishment for those who have sheltered Edward." My voice began to shake. "Please, your grace, as a mother, you must understand. My heart bleeds for them every day. I have already lost my little Humphrey and—and after Harry died I lost the child that I carried in my womb. Without the four remaining to me I have nothing I wish to live for. *Nothing.*"

I had rehearsed the first half of my speech, but not the latter; it came straight from the heart. I began sobbing violently.

Women seeing other women crying are either moved or hardened, I have found; there is seldom any in between. Fortunately for me, Queen Anne was of the former type. She stooped and put her arm around my shoulder as I bawled. "I know well what it is to be the child of a rebel, and I know well how it is to miss a child," she said when I finally quieted. "I shall put your petition to the king. As he is a loving father, I believe he will look upon it with favor."

"Thank you, your grace."

"Sit and have some refreshment and compose yourself, Lady Buckingham, before you return to your lodgings."

I obeyed and asked the queen about the Prince of Wales, a subject, I soon found, on which she was inexhaustible. He was not in London with his parents, I knew, but at Middleham in the North. As the queen chattered on about her son's intelligence, precociousness, and charm, I wondered whether he had remained at Middleham for reasons of state, as had been the case with the fourth Edward's heir being sent to

Ludlow, or whether his health kept him from traveling long distances, but it was not a question I could presume to ask. As if sensing it, Anne said, "I do wish my Ned could be with us this Christmastide; he loves the festivities. But his father does not believe he should hazard the journey to London, for he is a bit delicate. Next year, we trust, will be different. He only needs to get through this growing spell he is having, I think."

"I pray for his robust health," I said. To give myself due credit, I did wish the best for the little boy.

Anne rose, and I knew she would shortly be dismissing me. I was sorry to have our encounter come to an end, for the other ladies at the Minories kept a distance from me because of my husband's treason, and I had not many opportunities for conversation these days. Impulsively, I asked, "Your grace, do you ever wonder what would have happened if you had married my husband?"

The queen looked shocked. "Whatever do you mean?"

"I was told as a child that your grace's father would have liked to marry your grace or the Duchess of Clarence to my husband, had not my sister arranged for him to marry me." I smiled ruefully. "It would have all turned out quite differently had your grace done so, would it not have?"

"Differently indeed," said Queen Anne. Her voice turned brisk. "I will lend you a Book of Hours, my lady. That will help you keep your thoughts better occupied."

⁓

A few days later, I had my reply: the king, remembering that it was the season of the birth of our Lord and a time in which Christians should show clemency to their fellow Christians, had granted the queen's request. Messages, at the king's expense, were sent to Tretower and to Kinnersley, Sir Richard de la Bere's residence. Early in January, Edward and the girls, escorted by Sir Richard himself, stood before me.

I burst out weeping for joy and tried to embrace them all at once. When

I had finally hugged them all to my temporary satisfaction, I turned to take a second look at all of them. "Edward? Good Lord, you did dress him as a girl!"

Sir Richard grinned. "Aye, we wondered when you'd notice." Edward's eyebrows had been plucked to thin lines and his forehead shaven bare. The hair had just begun to grow back. "When the king's men came looking for the boy—which happened almost as soon we left Weobley—we decided the only way to keep him safe was to disguise him as a lass. My daughters' governess—who is to be my wife—made him into the perfect little gentlewoman. She dressed him in my older girl's clothes and shaved his forehead and plucked his eyebrows—my, what a howling there was that day! I don't know how you ladies bear it. His own father, God rest his soul, wouldn't have recognized him. But the boy was brave and played his part well, even when the king's men were within a foot or two of him. He bore his womanhood like a man, you might say." Richard smiled and tousled Edward's hair. Then he glanced around. "My lady, might I see you alone?"

I nodded and led him to an adjoining chamber. Sir Richard said in a low tone, "My lady, I have taken the liberty of telling the children of their father's death, though not of its cause. When I fetched the young ladies from Tretower, you see, I learned that they were expecting his return any day. Lady Elizabeth was praying for it as much as an hour on end. It broke my heart to see that."

I looked though the door at Elizabeth, who stood to herself clutching her doll, and my own heart broke, too. Sir Richard continued, "I did it as gently as I could, and I told them only that he had fallen ill and died suddenly. All three cried a great deal at the time, but I think the eldest lass took it harder than the rest. Pray forgive me, my lady, if I presumed."

"There is nothing to forgive. I am grateful for all of the kindness you have shown." What if Harry had taken refuge with this loyal man at Kinnersley, I wondered, instead of going to that scoundrel's at Wem?

Perhaps he would still be alive. Disguised or exiled, but still alive. I pushed the thought from my mind. "How could the Vaughans be so cruel, to let them hope like that?"

"I don't know whether it was cruelty or whether they didn't want to break the news to them. Guilt, perhaps, as your husband had favored the Vaughans and they repaid him so treacherously. They didn't treat the young ladies ill, from what I could tell—they brought them away before they laid the insides of Brecon waste, and the Vaughan women seemed kindly enough disposed to them. But just in taking them, the whoresons did frighten the little lasses. Lady Elizabeth has nightmares about being snatched out of Brecon, her attendants tell me."

I wiped at my eye as a series of thumps and footsteps announced the arrival of more people and goods into our rooms. The king had allowed several servants to accompany the children, but there was an unexpected face among them that made me blink. "The Wingfield boy?"

Sir Richard followed my eye. "Another liberty of mine, your grace. The lad begged to be allowed to join you when he heard you were here. I found it hard to say no, as his older brother may be attainted for supporting your husband and the rest of the brood may suffer as well, but I can take him back with me if you wish. I know there's not much need for a page here."

"No, leave him with me." I smiled. "I am very glad to have him here. Aside from the fact that he is dear to me, he will be good company for my sons. Sir Richard, will you be attainted?"

He shook his head. "I was under suspicion for a short time, but it appears that I am forgiven and will be left alone."

"We can thank the queen for that, and I shall. What of Sir William Knyvet?"

"Being your husband's uncle by marriage, I doubt he will escape attainder. They say nearly a hundred will be attainted at Parliament. But they are lucky; that is all that will probably happen to them. Several of the king's yeomen were hung here in London."

I crossed myself in memory of the poor men. "So all was for naught."

"Don't be so sure of that, my lady. The day after the duke—God rest his soul—died, Henry Tudor was proclaimed king at Bodmin by the men there. And many men have joined him in his exile. Men have got the idea of deposing Richard in their minds, and he may find it more difficult than he expects to get it out."

"We shall see," I said dubiously.

༄

After we had arranged our lodgings to accommodate all of the newcomers, I took Edward aside and asked if he wanted to speak about his father. He shook his head vigorously and instead launched into an account of his adventures with Sir Richard de la Bere and his wife-to-be. I decided not to press the matter, knowing that he would mourn his father in his own fashion and in his own time. Besides, Sir Richard said he had wept. Perhaps he had cried his fill of tears already.

Anne was quieter than usual, but Hal's company seemed to do her good, as her company did Hal. Soon they were bickering as of old.

Elizabeth was a different matter. She helped us rearrange our quarters but said nothing, not even to boss her younger brothers and sister. When the others went outside to explore their surroundings, she remained sitting in a window seat, staring into space. "Don't you want to go with the others? You must have had a long and dreary ride here, and will want to move about a little, surely. It will be growing dark soon."

"N-No."

This stutter was new also. Even when Elizabeth was just a toddler, her speech had been remarkably clear. "Well, good. There is something I want to give you in private."

Elizabeth gasped as I took an object from a coffer and handed it to her. "P-papa's garter?"

"Yes. Before he left, he gave it to me and told me that you should have it if he could not come back."

"But w-won't Edward want it?"

"Edward is a boy. He will have his own garter when he becomes a man," I said firmly, though the possibility of this seemed slim to nil. "Your papa wanted his most special lady in the world to have this, and you were his most special lady. Anne, too," I added hastily. "But she could not take care of this properly as you will."

Elizabeth lovingly stroked the garter as I held her close to me. "Mama? The V-Vaughans said that Papa was a traitor. That is a b-bad man, is it not?"

I mentally heaped yet another curse upon the Vaughans. "Your papa was not a bad man. You must never believe that. He thought he was doing the right thing for England, and I believe that he was." I ran my hand through my daughter's curls. "But we must not say that here, or we will not get to leave. Do you understand?"

"Yes, Mama." Elizabeth was quiet for a long time. Then she said, "I m-miss him, Mama."

"I know you do, sweetheart. I miss him, too." I paused before saying, "And I know what it is like to lose a father, for when I was not so much older than you, my own papa died, and so did my dear brother John."

Elizabeth looked startled, as do all children when realizing that their parents were once young. "Were you sad? D-did you cry?"

"Yes. All the time. But a very wise man, the old King Edward, told me something I shall never forget. He told me to remember them at their best, and to keep that picture in my mind, and that it would ease me. And it did. It still does today. Oh, you mustn't think that it will cure your grief. It won't. Only time does. But it will make it easier to bear."

I fell silent, realizing that I needed to take my own advice. I'd eaten little lately and spent much of the time when Hal was asleep brooding about Harry and nursing my hatred for Gloucester. But now that my children were here, we could heal together, I hoped.

That night, my girls and I shared a bed, while everyone else doubled or tripled up as well. I watched as Elizabeth settled Harry's garter carefully under her pillow and said a prayer. She frowned as Anne, lying between us, squirmed. "It's too c-crowded in here," Elizabeth said.

I smiled to hear the sweet sound of my daughter grumbling again. It was true, what had been spacious accommodations had suddenly turned quite cramped, but I shook my head. "To me it can never seem so," I said. "Not now that we are finally together again."

xxiv

March 1484 to August 1485

O N THE FIRST DAY OF MARCH, WILLIAM CATESBY, ONE OF THE KING'S chief councilors, paid a visit to me. I greeted him less than warmly, for he had been the speaker at the Parliament that had just met. There, word had reached me, my sister's marriage to the king had been declared void on the grounds that the king had been precontracted to Eleanor Butler, that the marriage had been made without the consent or knowledge of the lords of the land, that it had been conducted in a private and profane place without banns, and—the accusation that I sincerely hoped would follow Richard to the gates of hell—that it had been procured by witchcraft and sorcery on the part of my mother and my sister.

"I come here with an offer for you from the king," Catesby informed me after I shooed all of the children outside to play. "Today, your sister Lady Grey agreed to leave sanctuary, along with her daughters." I blinked before remembering that "Lady Grey" was the new official title for Bessie, who could no longer be called queen thanks to Richard. "The king has provided a pension for her and has promised to provide for each of her daughters, and he has also pledged to marry the girls to gentleman born and to give them each a portion."

"Why would they need portions if my sister can work her magic to find them husbands, Master Catesby?"

Catesby scowled at me. "They shall be living under the supervision of John Nesfield, one of the king's squires of the body, at Hertford Castle, where he is constable. The king is proposing to allow you and your children to join them there. You will be allowed a generous pension of two hundred marks a year, at the king's pleasure"—Catesby gave an emphasis to the last phrase—"from the issues of your husband's former property of Tonbridge."

"That hardly seems generous to me, Master Catesby, as I was given to understand some time ago that my jointure would be a thousand marks. Harry made a will, did he not?"

"He did, but he died a traitor. The king has nonetheless arranged to have his debts paid out of the revenues of some of his lands. I am among those who have custody of them for that purpose."

I wondered if Harry's creditors would ever see any of their debts paid. "I do know a little of the law, Master Catesby. Even though Harry was attainted, I am entitled to jointure, am I not?"

"You'll get what the king allows you to get, my lady, which is the two hundred marks he is offering you."

"With all due respect, Master Catesby, I don't see how this is an offer. I may live at Hertford Castle under the eye of one of the king's creatures, with a modest sum to live upon, one that is much less than my jointure, or I may rot as a virtual prisoner here. An offer implies some bargaining power on my part; I have none."

"You have a lawyer's mind, my lady."

"No. I am not devious enough."

Catesby flushed, and I wondered if I had been unnecessarily rude. "Whatever you think of me, or my profession, or of the king, I'd take his offer, as I choose to call it. As I said, he's promised to provide marriage portions for the old king's daughters, and as your girls are his kinswomen, he might someday do the same for them, provided that you've stayed out of trouble. And he might eventually be willing to grant your eldest boy some of his father's forfeited land, and help establish the younger boy in a profession. Perhaps even the law." Catesby smiled archly at me. "One never knows."

"True."

"There might even be the possibility of a second husband for you, my lady. No more dukes, I daresay, but you're still young, and would be quite pretty with some more meat on your bones. The king might put a knight in your way, or even a lord."

"We can leave my bones out of this conversation, Master Catesby, if you please, and a marriage to a man of that creature's choosing does not enthrall me nearly as much as you might think. But I will accept this offer, as you call it, for my children's sake."

"Good. Though I normally approve of plain speaking, as you know, I would suggest that as part of your good behavior, you refer to the king as 'his grace' or even simply 'the king' instead of 'that creature,' by the way."

"Point taken, Master Catesby."

"And who knows? Perhaps if the right man comes along, the king might even allow you your jointure." He shrugged. "Or part of it, anyway."

∽

Bessie and her five girls were already settled into Hertford Castle when I and my brood joined them. My sister and I had not seen each other for many months, and we had a long, tearful reunion while our nine children got acquainted with each other. Finally, Bessie stood back. Taking her prerogative as the ex-queen and as my elder sister, she said, "Kate, you look horrid."

I shrugged. Catesby had been right about me needing more meat on my bones. But Bessie looked far worse than I; the last year had aged her a decade. Seeing that Nesfield was occupied with directing my servants and belongings to the suite of rooms that had been set aside for us, I took her hand. "Bessie—the boys…"

She said quietly, "I have come to terms with it. There is nothing more to be done. I tell myself that God must have had some reason to take those innocent children."

"Bessie, please believe me. Harry did not know what Richard's intentions were. I have heard him weeping himself to sleep, from regret for what Richard did. He was guilty of much, but not that."

"I know, Kate. And he has paid dearly for what he did do. I have forgiven him." She sighed as I watched my eight-year-old Elizabeth gazing worshipfully at my sister's eighteen-year-old Bess. "I still wake at night, though, thinking it has all been a terrible dream. Who could have thought it? Ned loved Richard, trusted him, denied him nothing. He died thinking that the kingdom would be in the best possible hands until our dear son came of age. And in less than twelve weeks—"

"I shall never understand it myself." I glanced around to make sure no one was within earshot. "I have heard rumors that at Christmas, Henry Tudor took a great vow at Rennes that he would marry your Bess."

My sister nodded. "I heard it too—we had a friend or two among the monks who reported such news to us. I believe that is why Richard offered us such comparatively generous terms. He is hoping to gain the hearts of the people to stave off future trouble, and being kind to us is one such way. The people were fond of Ned, and they are fond of the girls for his sake." Bessie smiled for the first time since my arrival. "I will tell you, though, whatever his motives, I was happy to accept his offer, for the girls—especially Bess and Cecily—were miserable in sanctuary. The king has sent them material for new dresses, and they are ecstatic. The queen has even offered to have them stay with her when they return from their travels." The court was headed north again.

"They wish to go? But surely they know about the boys?"

"They do. But they are young and eager to have some pleasure again; they have convinced themselves that some underling overstepped his authority and that Richard told your husband that he was responsible because he was ashamed to admit that he had so badly lost control over the situation. Their story gets more elaborate and their uncle saintlier each day." Bessie shook her head. "I cannot blame them at their age for wanting to think what they want to think, and for wanting to be where they can meet eligible men. After all, you and I were married and mothers at Bess's age."

"You don't fear for them in Richard's court?"

"No. They are girls, which is their best protection. It would be suicidal for Richard to harm them. Besides, he took a public oath that they will be in surety of their lives and that he will not imprison them in the Tower or any other prison. And the queen is kind—"

A loud quarrel had erupted between Bess and fifteen-year-old Cecily, who moments before had been chatting with every semblance of amicability. My sister laughed. "Wait until your girls reach their age, Kate! No, if they come to stay at Richard's court, I think it is Richard who may be getting more than what he bargained for."

∾

The next few weeks at Hertford were pleasant ones, so much so that at times it was easy to forget that we were living under supervision and that our futures depended on the whim of the king. Though our correspondence—mostly to and from our sisters—had to be read by Nesfield, and we were accompanied by his men whenever we ventured off the castle grounds, our freedom was not otherwise restricted. My boys took up fishing in the River Lea, and Nesfield allowed them the use of a horse. The girls and I planted a little flower garden together. My sister and I taught our younger children their letters and worked on everyone's French conversation, and the castle chaplain proved willing enough to instruct the boys in Latin. My Elizabeth slowly lost her stutter, and in the Hertfordshire air all of us women began to bloom and fill out again.

We had all gone for a long walk one sunny April day when we returned to find a grim-faced Nesfield waiting for us. "The Prince of Wales has died at Middleham, following a short illness. The king and queen are said to be half mad with grief."

I am not a woman to rejoice in the death of an eight-year-old boy. Neither was my sister. We crossed ourselves and even shed some tears for the sake of the poor child and his bereaved mother. But as we filed silently into our chambers and made ourselves seemly to attend chapel to pray for the lad's soul, I knew that my sister was thinking the same thing I was. Richard had killed to take the throne.

Now, at last, the Lord had exacted a price.

In November, the bereft king and queen settled at Westminster, and it was then that the long-awaited invitation for Bess and Cecily arrived at Hertford. They left in the midst of a fine quarrel, this one over whom Uncle Richard would find a husband for first. "I am the oldest," said Bess, tossing her head. "Why would our uncle arrange your marriage before mine?"

"He might if he finds someone closer to my age than to yours first."

"Yours can wait."

Cecily narrowed her eyes, which I had learned was a sign of danger. "True," she said sweetly. "After all, you're almost nineteen. You'll be leading apes into hell if you don't get married soon. Maybe our uncle—"

Bess found a stray strand of Cecily's hair and yanked it as hard as she could before my sister leapt into the fray. Dealing them each a smart slap on the cheek, she said, "If the two of you act like hoydens and speak like fishwives, neither of you will find a husband, not through your uncle or through anyone else!" She shook her head. "I've a mind to tell the king that you are unfit to be at court."

"No, Mama, please!"

"We will be good!"

"Very well," said Bessie. She shook her head as the girls departed at last, amicable at least until they moved out of earshot. "I do think court is the best place for them," she said gloomily. "Here with no society but each other and the garrison they have lost all of their manners and graces of which their father was so proud. As I fear we all shall."

I glanced down at my skirts, muddy from my riding with the boys, and could not muster an argument.

Bess and I heard sad news just a couple of weeks later: our brother Lionel died at Beaulieu Abbey, where he had been in sanctuary since Harry's rebellion. We had but two brothers left now: Richard, in sanctuary himself, and Edward, living in exile with Henry Tudor. I often wondered if I would ever see them again.

Then, in December, we heard news of our brother Edward from an unexpected source: the king. Through a proclamation in which Edward, the Bishop of Exeter, my nephew Dorset, and Jasper Tudor were denounced as rebels and traitors, I learned that the exiles had moved with Henry Tudor into France, where they had been taken under the protection of the government. Somehow even the long-imprisoned Earl of Oxford had ended up a free man and had joined what seemed to be a rival court to Richard's.

I pondered the subject of the proclamation as I lay in bed one night in mid-December. Barely over a year ago, Richard had crushed his opposition and taken my husband's head. Now he was plainly expecting another invasion—and this one backed by the might of England's greatest enemy.

That summer, William Collingbourne had pinned a rhyme on the door of St. Paul's:

> The Cat, the Rat and Lovell our Dog
> Rule all England under a Hog.

The rhyme referred to Richard Ratcliffe, who'd supervised Anthony's execution, and to Catesby and Francis Lovell. Richard had not found it amusing. Still less amusing had he found the fact that Collingbourne had been attempting to send a message to Henry Tudor to invade England on October 18, a date that too neatly coincided with the rebellion of the year before. Poor Collingbourne—who had once served Richard's own mother—had been hung, drawn, and quartered on Tower Hill just a couple of days earlier this December. The crowd had not jeered but stood silent, mourning, as Collingbourne managed his last words, "Oh, Lord Jesus, yet more trouble," in the instant that his entrails were ripped from his belly. I shuddered to think of the death of that brave man.

And yet men kept on plotting against Richard, inside and outside of England. There was hope yet that this king might fall.

I smiled. "Yet more trouble indeed, Gloucester," I whispered. Then I turned over and fell into a sweet sleep.

∽

A week from Christmastide, an invitation arrived from the king for Bessie and me to join the festivities at court. Lest we be tempted to plead the time-honored woman's excuse of having nothing to wear, it was accompanied by bolts of fine fabric from the queen, in subdued but attractive colors appropriate for us in our widowhood.

I must admit that I did not even consider refusing, even if such a refusal would not have been wildly impolitic in my position as a royal pensioner. Though I said a treasonous little prayer each night that Henry Tudor—or anyone—would overthrow Richard, I was not entirely sure on which side the Lord's sympathies lay. Therefore, if ingratiating myself with Richard meant that someday Edward would be restored to his father's title and lands, that Hal would find a wealthy bride, and that my girls would make good marriages, I was willing to plaster on a smile for the king, and this was a good opportunity to do it. In addition to that, I was curious to see his court.

Richard was not impolite to Bessie and me at these festivities. Indeed he rather suavely complimented each of us, as well as our other sisters, who had also been invited. As far as we were concerned, and probably the king too, the gallantries couldn't have been over fast enough.

Bessie and I, a former queen and a disgraced duchess, were not the only curiosities at court. After my nephew Dorset had fled from sanctuary, Elizabeth Shore, accused of aiding him and concealing his goods, had been locked up in Ludgate prison, where, everyone had assumed, she would end her days. Instead, she had had the extraordinary luck of attracting Thomas Lymon, the king's solicitor, who instead of merely dallying with her in her cell had proposed marriage to her. The king after some grumbling had, in his new mode of benevolence, granted permission for the couple to marry. A beaming Lymon had brought his new bride to the festivities, where she sat demurely with the wives of other officials, looking as staid and as prim as if she'd never been a king's mistress.

There was only one lady who shone at the Christmas court, however, and that was my niece Bess. Now that she was out of the everyday clothing she had worn with us at Hertford, I realized for the first time that she was a beautiful girl. Like Queen Anne, she was tall and fair complexioned, but the resemblance ended there, for the queen, despite her bright smile, showed every sign of her recent bereavement, whereas Bess was flitting around the court as if she did not have a care in the world. It was more than that, though, I realized as I studied the two of them together. The queen, always pale, looked downright wan, as if she were not only grieving but ailing.

"They say that if the queen dies, the king will marry Bess in a trice," my sister Margaret, Lady Maltravers, said to me in a low voice as we sat in my chamber together that night. Margaret's husband, Thomas Fitzalan, the son of the elderly Earl of Arundel, was on good, though not intimate, terms with the king, and because of that I was allowed to talk freely with my sister. Fortunately Lord Maltravers did not stint in his duty of bringing his wife gossip from court.

"Marry her? But she's his niece! And he declared her a bastard!"

"They are saying that a dispensation might be got for enough gold. And what's her bastardy to him when she can give him a son? The poor queen's quite beyond that, it seems. Even in her prime she brought only one babe into being, and that was years ago. And you saw her tonight. She's not long for this world. Anyone with eyes can see that."

I crossed myself. "The king might need a son, but there are surely other women who could do that just as well."

"True, but what better way to make peace with those who loved the old king than by marrying his daughter? And it would foil Henry Tudor's hopes, too. Not to mention satisfying the king's lusts. He can't take his eyes off the girl. For all he rails against his enemies as adulterers in those proclamations of his, he's got a prick of his own, and it's given him two bastards already."

"What do his advisers say?"

"Tom says they are appalled. They don't think the people would stand for it, especially the northerners, who would consider it an affront to the queen's memory. But what can the king's advisers say, with the queen still alive? They can only hope that if he becomes a widow, Richard will act like a man of sense and look abroad for a wife."

"Poor Bess. And poor Anne." I snorted. "And poor Richard, if this marriage goes through. How will he live down the shame of having a Woodville for a mother-in-law? Not to mention a passel of Woodville aunts." I made my voice even lower. We were alone, but one never knew at Richard's court. "Has there been news of Edward?"

Margaret shook her head. "No, but they say the king is desperate to win men back to him. I suppose you have heard about the Earl of Oxford."

"Something of him. Didn't he escape from Hammes Castle?"

"Not escaped. The constable, Thomas Blount, turned against Richard. Abandoned his post and took Oxford and the garrison with him straight to Henry Tudor. That was a sore blow to the king, they say, for Oxford has known battle and is still popular in Essex. Anyway, Tom says that the king has asked him to make overtures to our brother Richard, to see if he will pledge good behavior in exchange for a pardon, and I believe he is going to ask Bessie to invite her own Tom to come home."

"What could possibly induce Bessie to agree to that?" I asked.

"Love," said Margaret flatly, and I realized how stupid my question had been. She sighed. "Remember, he is the only son she has left now."

꧁

The next evening, Anne and Bess appeared in matching robes. It was a common enough honor—I had had such garments made for myself and my own ladies to wear at festivities—but Anne and Bess wore masks, so that it was hard to tell them apart except when they stood together. Then the differences in their appearance became cruelly apparent, for Anne was thin where Bess was nicely rounded, and Bess's cheeks bloomed where Anne's were deathly pale.

Richard, however, appeared to be completely baffled about which woman was queen and which was bastard niece. Challenged by his fool after a round of dancing with both ladies to kiss his consort, he spent a long time looking at one, then the other, until the fool finally suggested that the court help him by yelling out each lady's name. Yet though far more people yelled that the lady on his left was his queen, he kissed the lady on the right first. Only when both ladies swept off their masks did he realize his mistake and bestow his kiss on his left.

Nearby me, John Russell, Bishop of Lincoln, shook his head. "Frivolous! Shameful!" he muttered under his breath. "The queen ailing, and the prince dead just eight months before!"

Shameful? It struck me more as sad, for the gaiety of this court had something very forced about it. Except for Bess and Cecily and some other young people, everyone here would have rather been somewhere else—Bessie and I with our children at Hertford Castle; the courtiers in the privacy of their own homes, where they did not have to watch every word they said; the queen in the comfort of her chamber, where she could mourn her young son and not have to pretend she enjoyed cavorting next to a girl of eighteen; probably even the king among his loyal subjects in the North, where no one whispered behind his back or prayed nightly for his destruction. Even the fool had the appearance of a man whose mind and heart were elsewhere.

If I hadn't hated Richard so, I could almost have felt sorry for him.

⚬⁓⚬

The next morning, the day before we were to depart for Hertford, Bessie and I were summoned to the queen. Anne looked tired from her exertions of the evening before, and her eyes had an unnatural glitter that reminded me uncomfortably of Harry's younger brother in the last months of his life. Yet she was not giving in to her illness meekly: she had been dressed with great care and looked every inch a queen.

"I have called you here at the king's request to discuss a delicate matter," Anne said after we had given our condolences for the loss of her son and she had asked us about the welfare of our own children. "Perhaps you have heard something of it already. The king wishes your brother Richard to accept his pardon, and he wishes the Marquess of Dorset to abandon Henry Tudor's cause and to return to England. If the marquess does so, the king will publicly extend his hand in friendship to him and allow him to return to his wife and children. The king hopes that you will encourage your brother and the marquess to accept these kind offers."

Bessie hesitated. "Your grace, I must speak frankly in order to discuss this matter. May I?" The queen nodded. "His grace has treated my daughters well and honorably, as promised. I am grateful, and I know Bess and Cecily are happy here. But my son the Marquess of Dorset is a different matter. He is a man grown, and he has conspired against the king. Worse, my son Richard Grey died at the king's orders for a crime that he never committed, whatever the king might have believed at the time or might believe now. As for my other boys—" My sister paused, then plunged ahead. "I make no accusations, but your grace must know what is said, and no one has given me any reason to believe that what I have heard is false. Can I trust his grace to allow my son Tom his freedom if he returns? Can I trust his grace with my son's life?"

"I will do you the honor of speaking frankly too, my lady. My husband—" Anne began coughing. "What a nuisance," she said brightly when she ceased, pressing a handkerchief to her mouth. I thought I detected a spot of red on it when she brought it down again. "My husband has done much good," she resumed. "It was his intent when he became king to see that the laws were administered more fairly, and he has done much toward that in the short time he has been king. He has taken steps to make juries less corrupt, and he has made it easier for men to get bail. He has even set up a means by which poor men can get legal redress. And that is not all that he has done. He has set up a Council of the North, which is much needed now that he is no longer resident there. He has abolished benevolences and protected English merchants."

"I do wish Edward had given more thought to such matters," Bessie admitted. "But—"

Anne raised a hand to cut off my sister's speech. "But despite the good my husband has done, and that he intends to do in the future, the Lord is displeased." The queen looked directly into Bessie's eyes. "I need not tell you, of all people, why. He has shown his displeasure by taking our only son. The king has felt this blow deeply. So have I." The queen's face shadowed, but she went on calmly, "He will not risk the wrath of God further by pledging to pardon your only son and then betraying his promise. That is provided, of course, that your son solemnly swears off Henry Tudor's cause and pledges to be his faithful subject, and that he keeps his own word."

"I will give the matter serious consideration, your grace, and will have my answer for the king shortly."

"Good." Anne rose to dismiss us, only to have another long fit of coughing. "Do think hard upon what I have asked you to do," she said quietly after catching her breath. "The king does mean well. The dead cannot be brought to life, not on this earth, but justice can be done for the living. Let my husband do the good he intends for our country—and for your own family. He needs to do it. It may save his soul."

✍

"I have agreed to write to Tom," Bessie said to me later that evening.

"I trust the queen, and believe that she was sincere. But can you truly trust the king?"

"I would not have said so a year ago, but I believe I can now." She saw my look. "You are thinking of when I delivered my little Richard to him."

"Yes," I said gently.

"Believe me, I never will cease to relive that moment. If only I had refused!"

"I do not think you could have refused for long, with the might of Gloucester and the rest against you. After all, you handed him over to the Archbishop of Canterbury. What man could you have trusted more?"

"I know." My sister brushed at her eyes. "Poor old man, he meant well, I know; he was duped, too. But Richard is not the man he was just months ago. He knows now that he cannot trifle with the lives of others and go unpunished."

Bessie sighed and studied her wedding band. I broke her reverie by saying, "Our brother Richard?"

"I am to write to him, too. I have even been told that my letters to them need not be read by John Nesfield." She gave me an arch look. "That will disappoint you."

I smirked. Though Nesfield and his deputies were not unkind to us, I resented having my perfectly innocuous correspondence read and for that reason always penned my missives in a tiny, cramped handwriting that bedeviled our nearsighted custodian and that made my wrist hurt afterward. "It saves on paper," I had explained sweetly when Nesfield complained to me. "Parchment is dear, and I am a royal pensioner of limited means."

"And the king told me when I gave him my answer that he will soon arrange a marriage for Cecily, too," my sister said. "He is considering young Ralph Scrope. They are of an age."

Poor Bess, I thought, married after her younger sister just as predicted. "Did he say anything about a marriage for Bess?"

Bessie looked around her swiftly and dropped her voice. "I believe he is deliberately keeping her single for now."

"Do you think it possible that he could marry her if, God forbid, the queen dies? Could she bear to make such a marriage?"

"She likes him, she tells me. He has been very kind to her. So has the queen, but I fear he has made more of an impression."

I knew all too well from Harry's case that Richard could make an impression on one's heart, even when he didn't try. And perhaps with Bess he was trying. My sister went on, "You saw how he has treated her during our stay here—it has been that way since the very start. Showering her with pretty clothes, dancing with her, putting her in a place of precedence. Cecily too, but not nearly so much as Bess." Bessie shook her head.

"Indeed, she is more spoiled by him than she was at her father's court, I fear. Because this king can look at her as a woman, and Bess is all woman. I see her eyes wandering; she needs a husband. I regret every day that the French marriage never came through."

"What of Henry Tudor?"

"What of him? I have prayed that his cause would succeed, as I know you have also, and our prayers have not been answered thus far. Perhaps it is not meant to be." Bessie rose and kissed me on the cheek in good-night. "I do not like the fact that King Richard sits on the throne. But I cannot ignore the possibility that he may be on it for as long as I live, and I must consider the future of those children who remain with that in mind. I cannot make them hostages to an eventuality that may never take place."

"But I will keep praying for it."

Bessie smiled at me. "In truth," she admitted, "so will I."

⁓

It was the day after the ides of March, and my daughters and I were working in our garden when I noticed the sky blackening, but not the type of blackening that meant a storm was coming on. Instead, the sun was being blotted out, bit by bit.

I stood transfixed, unsure of whether to run for my life, drop down to my knees and pray, or simply stare at this horrifying yet strangely alluring sight. Then Richard Wingfield, who had been shooting at butts with my sons nearby, hurried up beside me. "'Tis an eclipse of the sun, I think," he said in an awe-stricken voice. "Thomas Nandyke told me of such things, your grace."

"But what does that mean? Will the sun come back?"

"Yes. They have happened before, he said. Sit down, my lady."

I shakily did as I was bidden, clutching the children close to me and trembling as Richard Wingfield and a few other brave souls stood around and pointed. Soon we were plunged into utter blackness. Someone screamed (I am not at all sure it was not me), but just as I was expecting the devil himself to rise up, a chink of light appeared and slowly dilated. Soon the sun was shining down on us in Hertfordshire as brightly as if it had never left.

"We may never see one of those again, your grace," said Richard proudly. He helped me to my feet. "Some say they are a bad omen, but I thought it a marvel."

I stared at the sky nervously, thinking that marvelous as such a sight might be, I would be well content to have seen it just once.

Later that evening, we were sitting in the solar my sister and I shared when one of the guards came in, his face pale. "Queen Anne is dead," he said. "She died almost at the same time the sun was blotted from the sky."

&

We learned later that the queen had died of consumption, having deteriorated rapidly after the Christmas festivities. Richard, it was said, had hastened her demise by refusing to share her bed, although in all fairness to him, a king with no heir could hardly risk the contagion from her illness.

We at Hertford were not invited to the funeral, although I daresay we would have mourned as sincerely as anyone else there, for the queen had been kind to us. Instead we had to rely on the account of Bess. She wrote to us that the Duchess of Suffolk, Richard's only sister left in England, had served as the chief mourner—it being the custom, of course, for a king not to attend his consort's funeral—and that Bess herself had followed the queen's hearse along with Anne's ladies in waiting. The queen had been buried with great ceremony at Westminster Abbey.

And then came the question of what would happen to Bess. The queen's household would soon be broken up, once her ladies and damsels and servants went back to their families or found new positions. Bess could hardly stay at court with her widowed uncle—a widowed uncle who was rumored to lust after her. Would she stay with Richard's mother or the Duchess of Suffolk, or would she be sent back to Hertford? We had no idea, for no letter from Bess came after the one she sent about the funeral.

It was plain that something was going on in London, but what? Nesfield was annoyingly circumspect, as were all of his underlings.

I was sitting in the solar one rainy day just after Easter, pondering the question of how to get some information, when I saw my daughter Elizabeth poring over a book. And there I had my solution.

◌

"I am requesting permission to visit William Caxton's shop," I said, batting my eyes at Nesfield in hopes that I still retained some feminine wiles. "My oldest daughter is a great reader of romances, and I confess, Master Nesfield, I am rather fond of them myself. And I would also like to acquire a good history for my sons," I added primly.

"Women and their romances," Nesfield said indulgently. "Well, I see no harm in it. But who shall escort you, and where shall you stay?"

"With your permission, I shall take Richard Wingfield with me. He is acquainted with London, and he has relations there who can put us up for an evening. We shall be gone no more than two days."

Nesfield hesitated. I dared not bat my eyes again. There was such a thing as being too blatant, and I did not want to flirt my way into this man's bed.

"Oh, very well," he said after a long interval. "But to Caxton's, and to the lodgings young Wingfield shall tell me of, and to nowhere else. Understand, my lady? I am trusting you."

"I shall not abuse your trust. Thank you."

Now I just had to hope that William Caxton would remember that my brother Anthony had been his first and greatest patron in England. And that when I asked him for news, he had some to give.

◌

I proved lucky on both counts.

"Your brother was a fine man, Duchess," William said, crossing himself in his shop at the sign of the Red Pale. He sighed. "The mirror of chivalry." He hesitated. "At the risk of causing you pain, where does his body lie?"

"Somewhere at Pontefract Castle, I believe, with that of my nephew Richard Grey. I suppose there is no monument, and doubtless will never be."

"I beg your pardon. I have caused you pain. But, my lady, you are wrong about there being no monument." He picked up a copy of *The Dictes and Sayings of the Philosophers* and spread it open tenderly. "This is it, along with the other books he translated for my press. They will be passed from generation to generation and live on, long after we all have turned to dust."

I pulled the book to me and read:

> *Whereas it is so that, every humayn creature by the sufferaunce of our Lord God is born and ordeyned to be subject and thralled unto the storms of fortune, and so in divers and many sundry wayes man is perplexed with worldly adversities, of the which, I, Antoine Wydeville, Erle Ryuersj Lord Scales, &c. have largely and in many different manner, have had my parte, and of him releived by the infinite grace and goodness of our said Lord, through the means of the mediation of mercy, which grace evidently to know and understood hath compelled me to set aparte all ingratitude, and droofe me by reson and conscience as far as my wretchedness would suffice to give therefore singular lovynges and thankes, and exhorted me to dispose my recovered lyf to his service, in following his lawes and commandements, and in satisfaction and recompense of mine iniquities and fawtes before donn, to seke and execute the workes that might be most acceptable to hym...*

Had Anthony recalled these words as he awaited his turn to die at Pontefract? I brushed at my eyes. "My own copy was left at Brecon Castle. I doubt I shall ever see it again."

"But there you have the beauty of printing, my lady. You shall take one with you when you leave here today, as my gift in memory of that fine man, your brother." I smiled my gratitude. "Now, what brings you here, my lady?" He himself smiled. "Earl Rivers once told me that you were not a great reader, so you will forgive me if I think you might have other business with me."

"You are quite right, Master Caxton. I do wish to purchase some books—my children, you will be pleased to hear, are more appreciative of the written word than I—but I also want some information. What are they saying of my niece Elizabeth?"

"Why, you've not heard?" I shook my head, and Caxton said, "They do isolate you, don't they? It is notorious in the city, my lady. Well, then, this is what happened: immediately before Easter, the king called many lords and the mayor and aldermen and most of the merchants here—including myself—into St. John's Hospital and claimed that it had never entered his mind to marry the young lady. He declared that he was not glad of the queen's death and that he was in fact grieving for her. He charged the people not to speak of such things, and ordered that anyone who does be seized and taken before him."

"The king had to say that?"

"Aye." He shook his head. "The graybeards there said that they had never seen anything like it. A king having to stand in front of the people and deny that he lusted after his niece!"

I tried in vain to picture any other king—even wicked John or the second Edward with his favorites—having to make such a speech. Caxton continued, "It was felt necessary, I'm told, because the king's advisers told him that if the northerners thought he had caused the queen's death so that he could marry his niece, they would turn against him, and they are the chief friends that he has. Indeed, the king had to out-and-out deny poisoning his queen."

"*Poisoning* her?"

"I can't believe that even of him, but that's the gossip that's been going around, your grace. Many believe it, after the young king and his brother disappeared." He crossed himself. "If things were different, people might have excused this as a lonely man making a fool of himself over a pretty lass, and indulged him. But as it stands—"

"He has dug a hole for himself," I said with satisfaction.

"Aye," said Caxton. He gently closed *The Dictes and Sayings of the*

Philosophers and handed it to me. "In confidence, my lady, I hope it turns into his grave."

❧

We finally heard from Bess after I returned to Hertford, having visited only where I promised Nesfield that I would visit and having arrived home well within the scheduled hour, dutifully bearing several printed books as well as Caxton's gift to me. Bess and Cecily, who was to wait a year before consummating her marriage, were to be sent to Sheriff Hutton, where the Duke of Clarence's son and daughter resided. Uncle Richard, Bess wrote grumpily, had promised to try to marry her to the Portuguese heir, but who wanted to go to Portugal? It was *so* unfair that she had to leave court because of some stupid gossip.

Meanwhile my brother Richard had made his peace with the king and had been pardoned his life in exchange for a hefty bond, although he had not been restored to his estates and had to live with one of the king's men, just as Bessie and I had to live under the supervision of Nesfield. Though we had heard that my nephew Dorset would accept Richard's hand of peace, Dorset himself had yet to appear in England. Whether he had changed his mind or whether he had not been able to get out of France, we did not know.

The king had more to deal with than the gossip that still circulated about him and the death of the queen: Henry Tudor, with the backing of the French, was all set to invade. As my own brother Edward was expected to be with him, Nesfield had been less than forthcoming about this, but when the king began to issue proclamations against Henry Tudor and his followers, it could hardly be kept secret.

"A ragtag army they say that Tudor has collected," Nesfield informed us before he at last set off in August to join the king at Leicester, word having arrived that Henry Tudor had landed in Wales. "Most of them Frenchies, and mercenary Frenchies at that. And some motley Scots as well, plus a few hundred English traitors and some Welsh scum that he's picked up along the way. A scurvy lot indeed. Whereas our king has the cream of the nobility assisting him. The Duke of Norfolk, the Earl of Surrey, the Earl of Northumberland—"

"The Stanleys?" I asked. Thomas Stanley, after all, was Henry Tudor's stepfather, although the men had never met. Harry had hoped that he would join his own rebellion.

Nesfield scowled. "They'll turn up if they know what's good for them. Lord Strange is in Richard's custody to ensure their good behavior." Lord Strange, Thomas Stanley's son, was married to Joan, the only daughter of my long-dead sister Jacquetta. Our custodian put a hand to his throat. "For if they don't turn up, the king will have Lord Strange's head."

Bessie and I shuddered, and Nesfield turned jauntily on his heel. "Behave yourselves, ladies. Until the Tudor scum is vanquished, I have given orders that you be kept close. I trust you understand the necessity." He nodded toward a pair of his sulky deputies, whose expressions made it clear that they were unhappy at the prospect of missing battle in order to guard two Woodville women and their collection of children. "Don't worry. It won't be long before we'll be back."

"Under the circumstances, we can hardly wish you Godspeed," my sister said. "But we will pray that God will lead the proper side to victory."

"I'm sure he will," said Nesfield affably. "After all, the North loves the king, and they say that the Lord is a Yorkshireman."

⁓

God's regional affinities aside, I did not dare hope for much from Henry Tudor's invasion. That he was ashore was an improvement over 1483, but Nesfield's reports, which I had no reason to doubt, made it appear that he would be sorely outnumbered if battle were joined. And if my brother Edward—singled out for special attention in the king's latest proclamation, along with Henry himself, his uncle Jasper, the Earl of Oxford, and the Bishop of Exeter—were captured instead of falling in battle, beheading was the very best that he could expect. I thought of my youngest, wildest brother suffering the fate of poor William Collingbourne, and I shivered in the August sun.

My worries were for myself as well. If Henry Tudor were vanquished, what need would a triumphant Richard have to court the favor of the people, especially if he married a foreign princess and had the backing of her country? He would be able to do as he pleased with us remaining Woodvilles and with the old king's daughters. And what might happen to my sons, bearing as they did a claim to the throne not far after Richard's? The older they got, the more dangerous they would grow in Richard's mind, especially if he were unable to sire an heir to replace the son who had died the year before.

I shivered again. Suddenly these last few months of my life seemed almost carefree.

∽

No matter what the state of my mind, my garden had to be weeded. I got down upon my knees one afternoon near the end of August and yanked at the latest crop, trying to focus my thoughts on matters horticultural. Bessie, who did not share my taste for the physical aspect of gardening, sat on a bench nearby, trying to train her own thoughts on the altar cloth she was embroidering.

From our vantage point, we could see some men riding over the moat and to the guardhouse, but what of that? A lot of local business took place at this castle, and the men did not seem agitated. I went back to my weeds, and Bessie back to her stitches.

Just a moment later a trumpet sounded, emitting blast after insistent blast, summoning everyone inside the castle to the gatehouse. Bessie and I followed the procession slowly, dreading the tidings that lay there. Then Bessie froze and pointed. "Mother of God! Can it be?"

Side by side on good horses, waiting at the gatehouse, were two men whose surcoats bore the Woodville arms.

I yanked my sister forward, forgetting that she had twenty years on me, and together we ran through the gates and to our brothers Richard and

Edward. They saw us and scrambled down from their horses. Crying out incoherent greetings, all four of us came together, laughing and sobbing in each other's arms.

Then the children joined us.

"Uncle Edward! Uncle Richard!"

"Was there a battle?"

"Are you prisoners?"

"Did you escape?"

"Are you free?"

"Where is the king?"

"What has happened?"

"Where have you been?"

"Did you bring me anything?"

"Can I ride your horse?"

My brother Edward pulled free at last.

"Oh, there was a battle all right," he said, grinning. "Trumpet!" It sounded obediently, and a dead silence fell as my brother hopped back into his saddle to make himself better heard. "People! Two days ago, Richard, Duke of Gloucester, usurper and murderer of innocents, late calling himself king of England, was slain in Leicestershire. Long life to your new king. King Henry!"

I have taken all of the bad news in my life standing upright, but my consciousness proved unequal to these very different tidings. "King Henry!" I shouted obediently. Then I slumped to the ground in a dead faint.

But Bessie had swooned first. Queen and older sister that she was, she had first right, I suppose.

August 1485 to October 1485

Hⁿ ow? How did Henry win the battle?"

Edward grinned. "God's favor, of course. And a little help from the Stanleys." He looked around the solar. "Do you want to hear the story?"

"No. We want to hear how the autumn crops look," I snapped.

My brother grinned again. "I missed you too, Kate." He shook his head. "You looked so sweet there lying on the ground just now. So docile."

"So quiet," agreed Richard.

"Go on!"

Edward laughed and rearranged the nieces on each knee, and Richard, sitting with another pair of nieces, followed suit. "Well, if you insist. The first thing of any importance, for our purposes, is that two days before the battle, a certain Sir Richard joined us." He nodded at his older brother.

"I took Gloucester's pardon only because I hoped the two of you might benefit," Richard said. "But when I realized that I was expected to be fighting for Gloucester—against Edward—I couldn't stomach it. Even if Edward wasn't my only living brother, I wouldn't bear arms against him— not even if Gloucester were worth doing it for. So I followed my orders and marched with Richard's army, but I was determined to desert and fight on Edward's side, or die trying. Fortunately, I got an opportunity to slip off under cover of darkness, and I took it. So did many others, those last couple of nights."

"What a sight it was, awakening the next morning with my brother standing over me!" said Edward. He grinned ruefully. "It almost made up for the fact that no one could find poor King Henry. Never let the king know I told you this, but he got separated from his men the evening before and was wandering around in the dark, lost as a man can be. We were wondering how we could go to battle with no leader when Henry rode in the next morning, saying that he had been meeting with some secret friends. Fortunately, that same day he actually did meet with some secret friends— the Stanleys. They promised they'd join him when they safely could, but with Lord Strange being Richard's hostage, they had to be cautious.

"That night, the twenty-first, we camped near Atherton, and we knew that the time for battle was coming, for Gloucester's men were encamped nearby. Even with those who had joined us after we crossed into England, Gloucester's side had the advantage, both in ground and men, but our spies told us an encouraging piece of news the next morning: Gloucester had slept badly. He didn't sleep much, and when he did, he had nightmares. Some say that the ghosts of those he'd murdered visited him. He said before battle that if he won, he would utterly destroy all who had fought against him. No ransoms, no mercy.

"Well, that was daunting to hear, and seeing his men all lined up on a hill, outnumbering us three to one at our best guess, was even more daunting. But King Henry gave the order to march, and so we did.

"As promised, the Stanleys were out there on the field, in force, but they neither helped nor hindered either side. That in itself was a fearsome sight, because we couldn't be sure of whether Gloucester had suborned them in the meantime, and they could have slaughtered us if they had chosen to do so. We learned later that Gloucester was furious when he realized what was happening, and that he ordered the execution of Lord Strange, who'd been dragged along just in case such a situation arose. But there was too much going on, and fortunately for our niece Joan, Lord Strange was forgotten about and will be coming safely home to her.

"Then the Duke of Norfolk's men smashed into the Earl of Oxford's troops. Poor Oxford has never stopped regretting what happened at Barnet, you know, when he lost control of his men and they had to be rounded up and taken back to the field, only to fight against their fellow Lancastrians. Well, he redeemed himself at last. His men drew around their standard and gave no ground. Worse for Gloucester, they began to drive Norfolk's men back against themselves. Norfolk was killed." Edward took a long draught of ale. "A pity that such a noble man died in such an ignoble cause. Richard, you take over. You can tell it as well as I can, if not better."

My oldest living brother smiled modestly and cleared his throat. "Norfolk's death must have been a blow to Gloucester—if he knew about it. Norfolk was the oldest and most experienced man in his command. If Gloucester did know, maybe that's why he did what he did next. Depending on your point of view, it was either extremely brave or extremely foolhardy."

"Or both," put in Edward.

"Or both, as I was about to say." Richard, usually the most serious of men, suddenly grinned. "Bessie, do you remember how he used to do this when he was little, never losing his chance to get a word in? I've missed it. Anyway, at this point Richard, with just a few followers, charges pell-mell down the hill. He'd spotted King Henry's standard and must have hoped he could finish Henry himself off there and then. I'll anticipate Edward by saying that he almost did."

"We were there in the thick of it, Richard and I," interrupted Edward.

"So we were. Sisters, just picture a fully armored knight, followed by more, careening toward you downhill at full gallop. It was the last sight poor William Brandon, King Henry's standard bearer, ever saw. Pity. Brandon was a brave man.

"We were holding our ground as best we could, and fighting back, but it wasn't looking good. Richard was almost within striking distance of King Henry. And that's when the Stanleys finally moved in—for us. They swept in and began to pick off Gloucester's men. And then they reached Gloucester himself."

Bessie and I had joined hands and were barely breathing by now.

"He didn't last long after that, needless to say—men in all directions were trying to take him down, some for glory, some out of pure hatred. I'll give him credit, he fought like a tiger—not that he had much choice, for he couldn't escape even if he'd wanted to, and if he was taken alive, he'd be facing the block. So it behooved him to go out with a good fight. At last he died—but not before Edward and I had stricken some blows upon him for the sake of Anthony and your sons, Bessie. Not the most chivalrous thing we've done, perhaps, as he was outnumbered, but it was satisfying."

"I thank you," my sister said quietly. "What happened to his body?"

"Stripped naked, flung across a horse like a slaughtered animal, and taken to the Grey Friars at Leicester for display. Some thought that as a king, he should have received more dignified treatment, but others thought that given his crimes and the way he attained the throne—"

"He deserved what he got," I finished firmly, thinking of all the good men and the innocent boys who had perished at the order of Gloucester. "Who else died?"

"Catesby was captured, and will probably be executed, I heard before I left. Sir Richard Ratcliffe died in battle, so did Sir Robert Brackenbury. Your man here, Nesfield, died. And Walter, Lord Ferrers."

"His death I am very, very sorry for," I said, and crossed myself. "He was a fine man."

We were quiet for a while, reflecting on those decent men who had given their lives for both sides, and upon those who had suffered before this battle for their loyalty to my nephews and to the memory of Edward IV. I was silent too for Harry, who'd died trying to bring about this day.

Finally, Bessie said dryly, "Now that our prayers have been answered, I realize I know almost nothing about King Henry. You must have come to know him well in exile, Edward. What sort of man is he?"

Edward considered. "He's shrewd, he's fond of gambling—goodness knows this enterprise was a gamble—and he has a certain sense of humor. He's ordered that the common soldiers who fought for Richard be allowed to return home safely, and I believe that aside from Catesby, he'll be merciful to those of a higher rank who supported Richard. He'll rule with a firm hand, I suspect, being wary from all those years in exile, but time will have to tell. In the meantime, he's not Richard. That will have to suffice for now."

"Amen to that," I muttered.

"What of Tom?" Bessie asked.

"He will be returning home soon. He tried to get back to England when Gloucester offered his pardon—against my advice, I might add—but Henry's men caught up with him and persuaded him, rather emphatically, to stay. Anyway, he was left behind in France as a surety for the money that the French loaned to our enterprise. I'm sure the French will be pleasantly surprised to find that they don't have to keep him; they didn't have a great deal of hope for our cause, I fear. And here is something else to look forward to: a wedding. King Henry means to marry Bess, as promised. Men have been sent to Sheriff Hutton to fetch her and Cecily to London, where the king will be arriving shortly. And men have been sent to fetch their lovely mother and aunts to London, too. Can you guess who they are?"

I smiled. "And the king's mother? I suppose men have been sent to fetch her?"

"To escort her," said Richard. He grinned. "No one *fetches* the Countess of Richmond. Not even the new king himself."

ᕲᕲ

I had been in London several days when I received a message from Margaret Beaufort to attend her at the Bishop of London's palace, where our new king, just recently arrived in the city himself, was staying.

Naturally, I obeyed, albeit with not a great deal of enthusiasm. It had been some years since I had seen Margaret Beaufort, except for an occasional superficial encounter at court, and I wondered whether she still considered me a useless, decorative object.

To my surprise, the king's mother—looking none the worse for wear for her nearly two years of house arrest—surprised me by greeting me with a hearty embrace. "I am very, very sorry that your late husband did not live to see this day," she said, more quietly than usual. "He was a fine young man. His sacrifice will not be forgotten. Nor shall yours."

"Thank you, my lady." I felt tears sting at my eyes at this unexpected kindness. No adult, not even my sisters, not even my brothers, ever spoke to me of Harry, even now that it was safe to do so. Their intentions were probably good, but it hurt me deeply, for it was as if the man to whom I had been married for over eighteen years and borne five children had never existed. This short eulogy was the first mention I could remember hearing of him in months. "I still miss him terribly."

"Of course you do," Margaret said in her more normal tone of voice as I showed signs of giving way to my emotions. "But you have your whole life ahead of you. You are but young." She squinted at me—the countess was short-sighted—approvingly. "And still very fair."

"Thank you," I said, thoroughly nonplussed.

"My son the king wishes to see you."

I cannot possibly convey the sense of utter satisfaction with which Margaret Beaufort said those first four words.

In the chamber where the king was staying, I sank to a deep curtsey until Henry, in a pleasant voice with more than a tinge of a French accent, bade me to rise. I had seen him briefly on the day he had entered the city—no borrowed rags for me that time, for I had watched the procession from the comfort of a viewing platform hastily set up for myself and other honored ladies—but I had not been close enough to study him well. Now I saw that at eight and twenty, he had a lean physique and fair hair. His blue eyes, set in a mobile face, were bright, without the rather piercing quality of his mother's. All in all, he was an attractive man, I was pleased to note for my niece Bess's sake. "It has been many years since we have seen you, my lady," Henry said, taking my hand. "Time has been kind."

"Thank you, your grace."

"Were you aware that your husband had made a will, in which he set you a jointure?"

"Yes, your grace. William Catesby told me of it."

The king smiled. "The late Master Catesby was rather taken with you, it seems. Did you know that you were mentioned in his will? No? Well, how could you have? He left a hundred pounds to you, to provide for your children and to help pay the late duke's debts and to see his will executed."

Poor Catesby; he might have been a good man in better company. I sighed, thinking of the waste.

"Well, my lady, you shall receive the jointure that you should have received upon the late duke's death. And we also wish to assure you that your husband's good services to us will not be forgotten. His attainder, along with those of the many others who were unjustly condemned by the late usurper, will be reversed at the next Parliament, which we will be calling soon. Your son Edward will be restored to his father's dukedom and to his lands."

"Thank you," I murmured. I could not help but feel a little dizzy as all we had lost was handed back. King Henry saw my reaction. "Be seated, my lady. Ah, thank you, uncle."

A man who had unobtrusively entered the room had pulled a stool for me. Now that I got a better look at him, I recognized him as Jasper Tudor. "Thank you, my lord," I echoed.

"My pleasure," said Jasper Tudor.

"We understand that you speak excellent French, my lady."

"It was my mother's native tongue, of course, and we learned it from her," I said half apologetically, remembering my small husband's reaction all those years ago.

"Of course." The king suddenly switched to French. "We rather like speaking it ourselves, don't we, uncle?"

"*Oui*," agreed Jasper Tudor firmly. He smiled at me and reverted to English. "It was my mother's tongue, too, of course. Queen Catherine." He crossed himself, and we all followed suit. "Were you named for her, perchance, my lady?"

"No, my lord. Saint Katherine is my patron."

"A fine saint," said Margaret Beaufort firmly.

I was beginning to find all of this approval bewildering. So wrapped up was I in my puzzlement that I nearly missed the next remark of the king's mother. "As you may know, Duchess, my brother-in-law Jasper has never married."

I almost said, "That is a pity," until I thought about it. Perhaps it was not to be thought a pity, but a conscious choice? "Ah," I said, in a vague tone that I hoped covered any eventuality.

"He has not had the settled life that lends itself to marriage, you see." So perhaps it was a pity, I surmised. "When my dear husband died, Jasper took up his fight for the cause of the sixth Henry, his half brother, and in his service of that cause, he was forced into long years of exile, as was my son the king. It was not a disinclination for the married state that kept him single, but his situation."

"And now that has changed," the king put in. "So that—"

"If you please, I can handle this," interrupted Jasper Tudor. He stepped toward me and lifted my hand. "I am asking you, my lady, to do me the honor of becoming my wife."

I sat there, stunned. I should not have been surprised, I suppose—more often than not, young widows did remarry, especially young widows with handsome jointures—but still, I had not seen this coming, especially in the presence of the new king himself. As the moments passed without my returning an answer, Margaret Beaufort cast upon me her familiar look of disapproval. "Perhaps the king's uncle, and Queen Catherine's son, does not suit you, your ladyship?"

"It is not that," I said. "It was unexpected."

"Well, then? Might we have an answer?"

"Might I see my prospective groom alone? And then I can give *him* my answer?"

Margaret sputtered, but her son looked amused. "Of course, my lady." He nodded to Jasper Tudor. "We will leave you to court in private. There is business to see to elsewhere in any case."

"Well, my lady?"

"I shall marry you. How could I refuse you, with my children and I dependent upon the good will of the king, and he himself urging the match? I simply wished to give my answer without the Countess of Richmond boring her eyes into me."

Jasper smiled. "The countess is a managing woman. Having been apart from her for so long, I had forgotten precisely how much that was true." He took my hand. "But, my lady, I do not wish you to feel that you are compelled to marry me. The king will treat you and your children justly, for their late father's sake and for honor's sake, whatever your answer."

"That may be, but if life has taught me nothing else, it is to be cautious around kings. I cannot risk finding out otherwise. I will marry you." Something amused in his expression made me add, "So do not think of withdrawing your offer."

"I shall not, for you are very fair."

"Flatterer."

He smiled and lifted my chin gently. "You know, my dear, when the king told me that I should find a wife, it was you I thought of immediately, for I remembered when I first saw you. Even then I thought you would be a lovely woman when you came of age. And Margaret confirmed it."

I snorted. "My jointure had nothing to do with your decision?"

"Of course it did. You are wealthy as well as young and lovely. You can hardly expect a rational man to ignore that. And to add to your appeal, you are closely allied with the House of York. The king is eager to see the houses united. So, dear lady, you hardly stand a chance of remaining single, unless you take a vow of chastity, and that would be a tragic waste."

I smiled. "King Edward's daughter betrothed to a Tudor, and now his sister-in-law to another one? The poor man must be spinning in his grave."

"No doubt. And I think he would be rather jealous of me, too."

"Why?"

"Because of what I am going to do now."

He drew me against him, whereupon I soon found that this man could kiss life into a statue. "Goodness," I managed weakly when it was over. Then I startled myself by anticipating and indeed almost initiating the next kiss. It was every bit as satisfying as the first, and led to more intimate contact, thereby confirming every joke made about lusty widows. But I had badly missed being in a man's arms, more than I realized, and this man knew a woman's body well indeed.

In the midst of a complicated embrace we heard Margaret Beaufort's voice at the door. "Jasper?"

"Bother," muttered Jasper, and I snickered a little breathlessly. "I shall be with you presently, Margaret," my betrothed called. Then he led me out a back door to his bedchamber, where in less time than I care to admit we were lying together in his bed, our clothes marking the trail of our progress to it.

I do hope Margaret Beaufort didn't spend too much time waiting for Jasper that day.

∽

While Jasper and I were thusly improving our acquaintance, things were bustling around me. Bishop Morton, chirpier than ever, returned from exile, along with my nephew Dorset. The king had set his coronation date, and with it flowed the inevitable ceremonies and rewards. Thomas Stanley was made Earl of Derby. My older son, Edward, was made a Knight of the Bath—and I freely admit that I wept when I saw him in his garments and thought of the day my nine-year-old husband had received the same honor. Jasper Tudor was made Duke of Bedford.

And in the midst of all these events, I married Jasper and became the Duchess of Bedford. It was the title my mother had borne through her first marriage, and for weeks afterward I started when I heard myself heralded, expecting Mama to be right beside me. Perhaps in spirit, she was.

∽

Yet in all of this flurry and ceremony, I did not forget my Harry. Just a few days after my marriage to Jasper Tudor, I traveled to Salisbury, where my brother Lionel had been bishop for such a short time and where my husband had died. With me came my children.

We passed by the Blue Boar Inn, where poor Harry had spent his last night on earth. I asked to be shown the room where he had stayed, but it was occupied, and although the friendly innkeeper would have allowed me to look inside anyway, I decided to let it be. It was enough to stand at the last earthly doorway through which Harry had passed on his way to the scaffold, enough to gaze at the spire of Salisbury Cathedral where his own eyes must have wandered in his last moments. Then we walked on to the Grey Friars Abbey, where Harry lay at rest. I remembered that the Grey Friars at Leicester had taken Gloucester's body, and wondered, as ever, at the Lord's strange sense of irony.

The abbot himself greeted us. "I shall lead you to his grave straightaway, your grace. But first, this was found pinned inside of his shirt when we buried him. It was addressed to your ladyship."

He handed me a folded, but unsealed, sheet of paper. I felt a weak-kneed sensation as I recognized Harry's handwriting on the outside: *For my duchess.* I thanked the abbot, who moved away. Then I unfolded the letter.

There is no one here to whom I can entrust this letter, for I can expect no kindness from the king's guards. I believe that the monks of Grey Friars will take my body when all is done. I can only hope, Kate, that they will find this paper then and that you will be the one who reads it.

I have been faithful to you since we consummated our marriage. I make no boast of this, for there is little else that can be said good of me as a husband. Were it not for whom I leave behind, I would be glad of my death, which I have deserved.

Until the darkness fell, I could see from my window the scaffold that I am to die upon. I have been rehearsing in my mind my walk toward it. For your sake and our children's I shall be brave and approach it composedly and quietly. Better men than myself, like Hastings and your brother Anthony, have made that final walk and for much less cause; I can do no more than to emulate them.

I love you, Kate, and I love the children you have brought me. I cannot write of them more—if I do, I will break down, and I have tried to be courageous. Give my love to them. May all of you prosper.

Harry

"What did he say?" Elizabeth demanded as I stood there, tears streaming down my face.

"That he loved all of us," I said, wiping my eyes. "Come. Let us see your father's grave."

Harry's grave, in an obscure, dingy corner, was covered only by an unmarked slab. Now that I had the means, I would have to provide a suitable monument, though what would be suitable for a man who had helped to destroy so many I held dear, and whom I still loved deeply nonetheless, was something that would surely baffle even the most skilled mason.

"Harry," I whispered. I dropped to my knees, along with the children, and together we prayed for his soul. And then we wept, I not only for my husband, but for all of those who had lost their lives in these past two years, including Queen Anne and her young son. I even shed a tear or two for Richard—for Harry's sake.

When we had cried our fill, we carefully spread a cloth of gold over the slab, then decorated it with the bright red and white roses the children had carried in with them. Elizabeth laid hers down last. "Mama, you won't forget Papa, will you, now that you've remarried?"

I put her hand on her shoulder. "Never," I promised my children. "I will always be your papa's duchess."

Epilogue

June 1492 to January 1496

I WAS THE YOUNGEST OF TWELVE, AND BY 1492, I WAS THE LAST OF THE Woodville children left on this earth. It was a strange feeling.

My sisters Anne, Margaret, and Joan and my brother Richard drifted off peacefully in their beds, attended by priests and surrounded by their families and servants, but poor Edward was killed in 1488 at St. Aubin-du-Cormier, fighting for the Duke of Brittany in what proved to be a lost cause against the French. He died a Knight of the Garter, having been raised to that honor by King Henry just months before his death.

After the rest died, there remained but two of us—myself and Bessie, whose marriage to the king had raised our family so high and brought us so much sorrow. And on June 8, 1492, Bessie died at Bermondsey Abbey, to which she had retired in 1487 with the active encouragement of King Henry, who was not at all displeased at the revenue this saved him.

I did not go to the funeral; the news reached me too late for me to travel to the ceremonies. My oldest daughter, Elizabeth—now one of Queen Bess's attendants—went in my stead. On Whit Sunday, two days after her death, Bessie was conveyed by water to Windsor, where her husband the king rested. She was attended by the prior of Charterhouse at Sheen, by her chaplain, and by Grace, a bastard daughter of the king whom Bessie had reared in her household. My sister was buried without pomp, in accordance with her wishes for simplicity. On Wednesday the requiem mass was held, attended by her only surviving son, Tom, and his wife, Bessie's daughters Anne, Katherine, and Bridget, my own daughter and several other nieces, and a few others. The queen did not attend, having just been confined with her fourth pregnancy. Neither did the king nor his mother.

"King Henry should have come," my daughter said indignantly. Aged sixteen now, she had grown tall and very fair; Harry would have been proud. "And his mother! It was disrespectful of her not to do so."

"Come, you know that the king is busy with the French," I said. We had fallen out with our allies of 1485, partly because of their reception of a young man, one Perkin Warbeck, who claimed to be the younger of Bessie's murdered sons. Henry was planning an invasion. "And the Countess of Richmond probably fancied herself needed by the queen's side," I added dryly. Bess had borne the king three children already: Arthur, Margaret, and, just a year before, little Henry. Margaret Beaufort had been present at each confinement and birth, sending the royal midwives into a state of distraction with her determination that everything be done according to plan. Bess, usually rather gracious toward her mother-in-law, had once muttered that Margaret would have probably been present at the conception of the royal children if King Henry had been willing.

"Yes, that is the excuse she gave," said Elizabeth. "But I think she was being rude regardless. And the torches! They were old! I know it was supposed to be simple, but there could at least have been new torches."

As Elizabeth fumed some more about my sister's funeral, I listened absently, unable to share her indignation. Shabby as her burial might have been in some respects, my sister had been laid to rest beside the king as his lawful wife and his queen, not as the concubine Gloucester would have had the world believe her to be, and she had been buried as a pious Christian, not as the witch Gloucester had branded her so many years ago. And that, I thought, was really all that mattered.

"You got the last word, Bessie," I said softly as I lit a candle for her that evening. "God keep you, my sweet sister."

∽

On December 21, 1495, I became a widow for the second time. Jasper, whose health had been failing, caught a chill and died, aged five-and-sixty.

I sorely missed him. I cannot say that Jasper and I loved each other passionately—he had been too long accustomed to bachelorhood to truly know quite what to do with a wife outside of bed, and my heart remained in Harry's keeping—but we got on well together, and until the last few months of his life we freely enjoyed the pleasures of each other's bodies.

"Shall you marry again, Aunt Kate?" asked one of my nephew Dorset's many daughters one day, as my ladies and I prepared to go out riding with Richard Wingfield as our escort. He was still in my household and had been knighted by Jasper not long before his death.

I shrugged. "As I am eight-and-thirty and past my prime, I suppose not, unless the king and his mother find some use for me as a bride." I snickered. "Besides, Perkin Warbeck has been taken." Much to King Henry's disgust, the pretender had been moving from court to court in the last few years and after an ignominious attempt to invade England had landed in Scotland, where King James IV, either because he believed in the young man or because he knew it would annoy our king, had not only greeted him warmly, but married him to James's kinswoman, Lady Katherine Gordon.

"The fool will regret the day he was born if he ever falls into King Henry's hands," Richard said. "But you are not past your prime, my lady, if I may be so bold as to say so."

It was rather bold, but Richard had been in my household for so long that I allowed him considerable license. I blushed modestly and said a little wistfully, "Well, too old to bear children, probably." I had never quickened with child during my marriage to Jasper, and I rather missed my own children, all of whom were at court. Perhaps it was time I left Thornbury in Gloucestershire, where I was staying, and paid a visit to London where I could see some of them, as well as my niece the queen and her family. I was especially fond of lively little Henry, now the Duke of York.

"I think I shall go to London soon," I said, following my thoughts instead of the conversation. "I need a change from here."

✍

"My lady, may I see you privately?"

I had never seen Richard Wingfield look so peculiar, or speak so formally. "Of course, Sir Richard," I said, falling into formality myself. "I hope there is not bad news from one of your brothers or sisters?" I said when we were alone. I could think of no other news that would turn the man so pale.

"No, my lady. They are well." He forestalled my next question. "There is nothing amiss with your kindred either, my lady."

"Then speak, Richard, and as a friend. We have been friends for many years. What troubles you? I shall be only too glad to help you if I can. You know that."

"My lady—" He bit his lip.

"Richard! It cannot be so bad. Perhaps you wish to leave my service now that the Duke of Bedford has died?" I asked, a little hurt. "I shall miss you greatly, but in the household of a great lord, I must admit that it is true that you will find better opportunities than in the household of a wid—"

"No! My lady, it is not that at all. I never want to leave you. In fact, I wish to marry you."

I stared.

"Hear me out, please." There was no need for him to say this. I was stricken dumb. "I love you. I have loved you since I was a boy in your household. When you married the Duke of Bedford, I was wretched." He swallowed. "I even hoped when Gloucester fell that you would never get your jointure, so that when I got older you would turn to me as your protector and I could marry you then. Forgive me, my lady, for hoping that. I was but a boy."

"Of course," I said blankly.

"Will you consider my suit? I know I am far your inferior in rank. I know I have no wealth or great position. I know it will displease the king and others—" He swallowed. "I know many things against the match, but I also know I love you dearly, and I do not care about those things. Please, my lady—Kate. Be my wife."

He dropped to his knees, and I stared down at him, amazed. I had suspected Richard Wingfield as a boy of loving me, but now? I had watched him grow into a man—a handsome one, I realized for the first time—and never guessed his secret. He had been honorable to keep it for so long, especially in those last weeks when Jasper had been sick and crotchety and I vulnerable to temptation. A woman could do far worse than to marry such a man.

Yet if I married Richard Wingfield, the court gossips would ridicule me as a pathetic, aging woman hoodwinked by a younger man obviously interested only in my wealth. My sons, especially Edward (who resembled his father more every day), would be scandalized. My daughters would titter as only daughters can. The king, who no doubt wished to keep me and my jointure in reserve for some exigency, would be furious. His mother would be disgusted. Clearly there was only one sensible answer I could give.

But since when had a Woodville made a conventional match? My father, a mere knight, had married a duchess. My brother John had married a duchess forty years his senior. I had married a duke. My sister had married a king. I owed my very existence to an unequal match. It was practically a family tradition—and thus, it was all the better that I, the last of the Woodvilles, uphold it.

I sat down beside Richard Wingfield and touched his face. "I would be honored to be your wife."

In reply he kissed me gently, then passionately as I gave myself up to the pure pleasure of his embrace.

You can probably guess the rest.

Author's Note

Katherine Woodville married Richard Wingfield by February 24, 1496, without royal license. Less than fourteen months later, on May 18, 1497, she died. The cause of her death, which occurred when she was about thirty-nine, is unknown. It is tempting to wonder if she died from a late-life pregnancy; however, there is no record of her having children by Wingfield. Richard Wingfield remarried and went on to have a distinguished career as a diplomat in Henry VIII's service. While on an embassy to Charles V, he fell ill in Toledo and died on July 22, 1525. In his will, he asked that masses be said for the soul of his "singular good Lady Dame Katherine."

Henry VII died in 1509, having outlived his queen, who died in 1503, nine days after giving birth to a short-lived girl. Their first son, Arthur, died in 1502; their only other surviving son, of course, became Henry VIII. Margaret Beaufort died just two months after her beloved son, but lived long enough to see the coronation of her grandson Henry VIII and his new bride, Catherine of Aragon.

Edward Stafford, third Duke of Buckingham, fared far less well under Henry VIII than did his stepfather Richard Wingfield. Buckingham's royal blood and pride in his lineage, Henry VIII's notorious difficulties in siring a male heir, and Buckingham's poor relations with Thomas Wolsey ultimately led to accusations that Buckingham himself aimed at the throne. On May 17, 1521, he was executed on Tower Hill. Edward had married Alianore Percy, the eldest daughter of the Duke of Northumberland, and had four children.

Henry Stafford, Katherine's younger son, was made Earl of Wiltshire by Henry VIII. He married Cecily Bonville, the widow of Katherine's nephew Dorset. Having managed to avoid Henry VIII's displeasure after the execution of Edward Stafford, Henry Stafford died on April 6, 1523, without heirs. Cecily, nineteen years Henry's senior and the mother of fifteen children by Dorset, outlived Henry.

Elizabeth Stafford married Robert Radcliffe, Lord Fitzwalter, in 1505, and died before May 11, 1532, having borne her husband at least four children. Her eldest son, Henry Radcliffe, second Earl of Sussex, was active in bringing Mary I to the throne.

In 1500 Anne Stafford married Sir Walter Herbert, the illegitimate son of William Herbert, Earl of Pembroke, who had been executed in 1469 by Warwick. Following her first husband's death, Anne married George, Lord Hastings, who later became Earl of Huntingdon. Hastings was a grandson of the Lord Hastings murdered by Richard III. The couple had eight children. Anne survived her second husband, who died in 1544.

The date of Edward IV's marriage to Elizabeth Woodville is usually given as May 1, 1464, but as both Michael Hicks and David Baldwin have pointed out, there is some reason to suppose that the May 1 date found in some chronicles may owe more to its romantic associations than to historical fact. Hicks notes that on August 10, 1464, William Hastings was granted the wardship of Elizabeth's son Thomas Grey—an odd grant to make if Edward had married Elizabeth months before. Furthermore, as Hicks also points out, Edward IV granted the county of Chester to his brother the Duke of Clarence on August 30, 1464, apparently in recognition of Clarence's status as the king's heir apparent. Such a grant would seem unlikely if Edward IV had married Elizabeth Woodville, who could be expected to give him an heir. David Baldwin has also noted that in the late summer of 1464, Edward IV was staying at Penley, halfway between London and Grafton; he was also staying there in early September 1464. Hence, I have departed from tradition and placed the couple's wedding in early September, several weeks before it was announced at Reading.

There is no proof that Richard, Duke of Gloucester, killed Henry VI, though Warkworth's Chronicle pointedly notes his presence at the Tower at the time of the imprisoned king's death. If Gloucester did indeed carry out the murder, it almost certainly would have been at the orders of Edward IV. The story that Henry VI predicted that young Henry Tudor would wear the crown appears in Vergil; though it can be regarded with a certain skepticism, it was too apt a topic of conversation for young Henry Tudor and young Buckingham to be left out.

All of the named characters in this novel actually lived, although in many cases, such as the lesser known Woodville siblings, their personalities are lost to us. One of the most elusive figures is Henry Stafford, Duke of Buckingham (who signed himself as "Harry," which he spelled "Harre"). We know little of him as a man, and what is conjectured about his personality depends largely on the reason assigned for his rebellion in 1483—a probably insolvable mystery. Most of Buckingham's records were destroyed in 1483 when the Vaughans (not connected to the Thomas Vaughan executed by Richard III) raided Brecon Castle and in a later raid on the castle by Welsh rebels in 1485–86. Harry is recorded as being present at various public events—for example, the coronation of Elizabeth Woodville, the procession of Edward IV into London following his victory at Tewkesbury, the welcoming of Louis of Gruuthuse to England, the wedding of the Duke of York to little Anne Mowbray—but almost nothing is known about his private life. He and Richard, Duke of Gloucester, would have had numerous opportunities to encounter each other before 1483, but whether they were close friends is unknown.

What is certain is that once he came of age, Harry was an outsider at court, who held none of the high offices that a man of his rank, wealth, and royal connections might have expected to receive. It has been suggested variously that Edward IV disliked or distrusted Harry, that Edward IV was wary of Harry's royal descent, that the king was cautious about giving too much power to the higher nobility, that Harry was inept or even mentally unstable, or that the Woodvilles contrived to squeeze Harry out of office. Both Michael Jones (in *Richard III: A Medieval Kingship*, edited by John Gillingham) and C. S. L. Davies (in the *Oxford Dictionary of National Biography*) have speculated that the anticlimactic French expedition of 1475 might have had something to do with Harry's alienation from the king, hence my scene where Harry remonstrates with Edward over the proposed treaty. Though the scene is fictional, Harry is recorded without explanation as having "returned home" from the expedition prematurely. He was not among the men who enjoyed pensions from Louis following the Treaty of Picquigny, about which Richard, Duke of Gloucester and unspecified English "men of quality" were said to be unhappy.

As noted by Michael Hicks in his biography of George, Duke of Clarence, Harry took supper with his uncle Henry Stafford, husband to Margaret Beaufort, on October 28, 1470. On that occasion he might well have encountered his kinsman Henry Tudor, who had met with Henry VI the previous day, according to a record cited by Michael Jones and Malcolm Underwood. Harry's presence at Barnet and Tewkesbury is not recorded, though a report written by an observer, Gerhard von Wesel, indicates that he was among the men arrested by Warwick's government in the spring of 1471. I have invented the incident where Harry begs Edward IV to spare his uncle Somerset's life, but Harry was in Edward IV's triumphant procession to London after the battle of Tewkesbury and might well have been at Tewkesbury to witness his uncle's death.

Harry's mother, Margaret Beaufort, Countess of Stafford, is a curiously obscure figure for a woman of her rank. Even her death date is uncertain, though we know that her second husband, Richard Darell, remarried in 1481. A record of a lawsuit shows that in 1463, Darell boarded Margaret with his mother, to whom he paid a certain sum each week for the countess's "diets" before Darell's mother died in 1464. From that entry the editor of *The Collections for a History of Staffordshire* has surmised that Margaret was an "imbecile," and it does sound as if Margaret was being made the responsibility of her mother-in-law rather than staying with her as an ordinary guest. Whether Margaret was actually incapacitated, mentally or physically, is not clear from this one record, but as there is a recorded instance where an insane widow, that of the rebel James Tuchet, was placed in her mother-in-law's care, it seems likely this might have been the situation with Margaret.

As is most often the case with medieval women, little is known about Katherine Woodville's life and personal qualities. Katherine and Harry were indeed carried on squires' shoulders during Elizabeth Woodville's coronation, and Katherine is recorded as sitting beside the Duchess of Norfolk at the feast following the Duke of York's wedding. The Duchess of Buckingham was conspicuously absent from Richard III's coronation ceremonies and was not among the noblewomen who received robes on that occasion, but whether she was barred from attending or refused to attend is unknown.

It is generally assumed that the Buckinghams' marriage was a miserable one, but that assumption is largely based upon one remark: Dominic Mancini, an Italian observer visiting England during the fateful summer of 1483, wrote that Buckingham detested the Woodvilles "for, when he was younger, he had been forced to marry the queen's sister, whom he scorned to wed on account of her humble origin." With no axe to grind on behalf of either Richard or his enemies, Mancini is one of the main and most valuable contemporary sources for the events of 1483. Nonetheless, his remarks about Buckingham's attitude toward the Woodvilles and Katherine are likely to be heavily colored by the gossip he was hearing in 1483, and must be read with that caveat in mind. Buckingham certainly cooperated with Katherine's brothers during the rebellion of 1483, and he took Katherine with him to Weobley before making his fatal flight to Wem. There is no evidence that his relations with the Woodvilles before Edward IV's death were hostile.

Part of the belief that Harry was unhappy in his marriage from the beginning lies in a misapprehension of Katherine's age that has been perpetuated by a number of modern authors, most of them partisans of Richard III. These writers depict Katherine as being much older than her young husband, thereby giving the impression that she was a sexually frustrated spinster pawned off by the vile Woodvilles on the hapless little Harry. One Ricardian novel even depicts the twenty-something Katherine as sexually molesting the twelve-year-old Harry! Primary sources, however, including a postmortem inquisition of Richard Woodville, the contemporary description of Elizabeth Woodville's coronation, and Elizabeth's household records, all indicate that Katherine was a child at the time she married Harry and as such had no more say in the marriage than did her husband. According to the postmortem inquisition, her birthdate was about 1458, making her about three years younger than Harry, who was born on September 4, 1455.

An account by Elizabeth de la Bere found among Edward Stafford's family papers indicates that Katherine was brought to the king from Weobley following her husband's execution and that Edward himself was dressed as a little girl and hidden from Richard III's officials during this time. It is sometimes said by modern writers that Katherine joined her sister Elizabeth in sanctuary at Westminster following her husband's death, but I have not seen any documentation or citation to support this claim. In December 1483, however, Richard III allowed Katherine to bring her children and servants to London; whether she was living on her own, imprisoned, or living under supervision in London at the time is unknown. It seems most likely that after she was brought from Weobley, she was boarded at a convent, a genteel way of confining troublesome ladies, but her whereabouts after December 1483 through the remainder of Richard's reign are unrecorded.

Elizabeth Woodville left sanctuary in March 1484. She was placed under the supervision of Nesfield, who was the constable of Hertford Castle. As there is no record of where Elizabeth stayed after she left sanctuary, I took the liberty of placing both her and her sister Katherine at Hertford, a location that was convenient for both the ladies and for my own purposes.

Richard III publicly pledged to provide for Elizabeth Woodville and her daughters if they would come out of sanctuary; interestingly, he also swore that they would be in surety of their lives and would not be imprisoned in the Tower or in any other place. Richard also was obliged to publicly deny poisoning his queen and planning to marry his niece.

William Catesby did indeed leave Katherine a bequest of a hundred pounds in his will "to help herr children and that she will se my lordes dettes paid and his will executed." The 1485 Act of Parliament assigning Katherine a jointure of a thousand marks also refers to Buckingham's will, which apparently has not survived.

Harry Buckingham's burial place is uncertain. The *Chronicle of the Grey Friars of London* states that he was buried at the Grey Friars in Salisbury, but other writers claim that a tomb at the Church of St. Peter in Britford was erected in his memory, although there is some question about whether it contains any remains. To complicate matters further, in 1838, renovations at the Saracen's Head Inn in Salisbury, on the site where the Blue Boar Inn stood, uncovered a headless skeleton that was also missing its right arm. The skeleton underwent an extremely unscientific examination by the locals, with the inn's landlord measuring a rib against his own and concluding that the deceased was of "large dimensions," before the remains were knocked around and merged in with the surrounding clay. Nineteenth-century antiquarians suggested that these could have been the remains of Harry. Colorful as this story is, I opted for Grey Friars, which was in accordance with Richard III's general habit of allowing his enemies an honorable burial. Whatever the location of Harry's body, Harry's ghost is said to haunt the Debenhams department store in Salisbury, which stands on the site of the Blue Boar Inn. Katherine's burial place is unknown.

The quotations from *The Dictes and Sayings of the Philosophers*, translated by Anthony Woodville, are taken from William Caxton's original edition, a facsimile of which is available through the Internet Archive. In connection with Caxton, I should mention that when Katherine refers to reading "romances," she is referring not to what we call "bodice rippers" but to a broad variety of narratives dealing with such themes as adventure, love, chivalry, and honor.

Edward IV's most famous paramour, Mistress Shore, bore the first name of "Elizabeth"; it was not until the late sixteenth century that she was christened "Jane" by a dramatist, Thomas Heywood. I have accordingly called her by her given name, Elizabeth Shore.

There are three great mysteries surrounding this period of history: Was Edward IV secretly married to Eleanor Butler? What happened to the princes in the Tower? Why did Buckingham rebel against Richard? Pages upon pages have been devoted to each of these subjects, and one can do no better than to read the sources—both those favorable and unfavorable to Richard III—and decide for oneself, as I have. There are a few comments I would like to make about my own choices, however.

I have not overlooked the story that Bishop Stillington himself offici-ated at the marriage of Edward IV and Eleanor Butler; rather, I have rejected it. Only one source, the Burgundian chronicler Philippe de Commines, states that Stillington presided at the ceremony; no English chronicler makes such a claim. A yearbook entry in 1488, on the other hand, states that Stillington drafted the petition urging Richard to take the crown, while Eustace Chapuys, ambassador to Henry VIII's court, wrote to Charles V in 1534 that Richard III "declared by definitive sentence of the bishop of Bath [Stillington] that the daughters of King Edward were bastards." Both the yearbook entry and Chapuys's comment suggest that Stillington played the role not of a witness to the marriage but of Richard's mouthpiece.

Stillington was arrested in 1478, following the execution of Clarence, and Paul Murray Kendall and other defenders of Richard have taken this as evidence that Stillington had told Clarence of the precontract. But Stillington spent only a brief time in the Tower and continued to serve Edward IV after his release. He was even sent in 1479 to treat with a French ambassador. To me it beggars belief that Edward, knowing that Stillington was in possession of information that could threaten the succession, would allow him to see the light of day, much less be placed in a position where he could gossip to the French.

Henry VII himself arrested Stillington after the battle of Bosworth. Yet Stillington was again imprisoned only briefly, and was pardoned that November. Only in 1487, when Stillington lent his support to a rebellion against Henry, was he imprisoned once more. Even then, he spent some time at his episcopal manor of Dogmerfeld in 1489 and 1491 before dying in the spring of 1491, aged eighty or so. This relatively lax treatment of Stillington suggests that although Henry VII might have regarded him as a political enemy, he did not regard him as possessing dangerous information.

What happened to Edward V and his brother, the Duke of York? No trace of them exists after the summer of 1483, and contemporary rumor, never denied by the king, accused Richard and/or Harry of their murders. It has been said in Richard's defense that he had no motive to kill his nephews, having declared them to be bastards, but this holds true only if bastardy was regarded as being an insurmountable barrier to kingship, which does not seem to have been the case, and if the allegations of the precontract were widely accepted. Mancini and the Crowland chronicler, the main sources for this period, were skeptical of the allegations, as were the men who died trying to restore Edward V to the throne just weeks after Richard was crowned. It has also been said that Richard's failure to exhibit the boys' bodies is proof that he did not kill his brother's sons, but Richard, already facing suspicion from his new subjects, might well have chosen not to risk outraging the public with such a display. Most telling of his guilt, however, is the fact that he never produced the boys alive after they disappeared into the Tower, even when doing so would have aided his reputation and hurt Henry Tudor's cause.

As for Harry Buckingham, I do not think he can be ruled out as a suspect in the princes' deaths (assuming, of course, that they were murdered), although I believe him innocent. If he did indeed have a hand in the deaths, it was most likely in collusion with Richard. Only if he himself aspired to the throne could he gain more from arranging their deaths on his own than he had already gained through Richard. While the possibility that he fancied himself king cannot be discounted entirely, it is notable that neither

Richard's proclamations against him nor Buckingham's attainder mentions such an ambition. It is also significant that Henry VII, a famously wary man, allowed Buckingham's son Edward to recover his dukedom and his lands, something that he might not have risked had he believed that Edward's father was aiming at the crown in 1483.

This brings us to the final question: why did Buckingham rebel? No one knows, though one possibility mentioned by Tudor chroniclers—that Richard denied him his coveted Bohun lands—has been long since discounted by evidence to the contrary. Besides royal ambition, various other scenarios—that Harry was mentally unstable, that he was pathologically greedy, that he had some sort of falling-out with Richard III, or that he joined the rebellion to avoid reprisals should it succeed—have been put forth. Yet it may well be, as the Crowland chronicler wrote, that Harry was simply "repentant of what had been done" and that it was his conscience that ultimately led to his destruction. In the end we shall probably never know what was in Buckingham's mind in 1483—but one wonders what, if Richard had granted his former ally the audience he sought before his execution, Harry would have said to the king.

Further Reading

C. A. J. Armstrong, trans., *The Usurpation of Richard the Third*. (Dominic Mancini) Oxford, Clarendon Press, 1969.

David Baldwin, *Elizabeth Woodville: Mother of the Princes in the Tower*. Gloucestershire: Sutton, 2004 (paperback edition).

Mary Clive, *This Son of York: A Biography of Edward IV*. New York: Knopf, 1974.

Anne Crawford, *The Yorkists: The History of a Dynasty*. London and New York: Hambledon, 2007.

Louise Gill, *Richard III and Buckingham's Rebellion*. Gloucestershire: Sutton, 2000.

John Gillingham, *The Wars of the Roses*. Baton Rouge: Louisiana State University Press, 1981.

John Gillingham, ed., *Richard III: A Medieval Kingship*. New York: St. Martin's Press, 1993.

Ralph Griffiths and Roger S. Thomas, *The Making of the Tudor Dynasty*. Gloucestershire: Wrens Park, 1998.

P. W. Hammond, *The Battles of Barnet and Tewkesbury*. New York: St. Martin's 1993.

Barbara J. Harris, *Edward Stafford: Third Duke of Buckingham, 1478–1521*. Stanford: Stanford University Press, 1986.

Michael Hicks, *Edward V: The Prince in the Tower*. Gloucestershire: Tempus, 2003.

Michael Hicks, *False, Fleeting, Perjur'd Clarence: George, Duke of Clarence 1449–78*. Gloucester: Sutton, 1980.

Rosemary Horrox, *Richard III: A Study in Service*. Cambridge: Cambridge University Press, 1991.

Michael K. Jones and Malcolm G. Underwood, *The King's Mother: Lady Margaret Beaufort, Countess of Richmond and Derby*. Cambridge: Cambridge University Press, 1995.

J. L. Laynesmith, *The Last Medieval Queens*. Oxford: Oxford University Press, 2005 (paperback edition).

Arlene Okerlund, *Elizabeth: England's Slandered Queen*. Gloucestershire: Tempus, 2006 (paperback edition).

A. J. Pollard, *Richard III and the Princes in the Tower*. Gloucestershire: Sutton, 2002 (paperback reprint).

Nicholas Pronay and John Cox, eds., *The Crowland Chronicle Continuations: 1459–1486*. London: Richard III and Yorkist History Trust, 1986.

Carole Rawcliffe, *The Staffords, Earls of Stafford and Dukes of Buckingham 1394–1521*. Cambridge: Cambridge University Press, 1978.

Charles Ross, *Edward IV*. New Haven and London: Yale University Press, 1997.

Charles Ross, *Richard III*. Berkeley and Los Angeles: University of California Press, 1981.

Cora Scofield, *The Life and Reign of Edward IV*. London: Longmans, Green and Co., 1923 (2 volumes).

Acknowledgments

IN WRITING THIS NOVEL I WAS GREATLY AIDED BY THE RESOURCES OF the Richard III Society, the publications and programs of which are invaluable for anyone doing research into this time period. I would especially like to thank the former research librarian of the Society's American branch, Brad Verity, who provided invaluable genealogical information on the Woodville siblings to me. I have also profited greatly from online discussions with Society members, who have graciously tolerated my own views of Richard, which in many cases are quite opposed to their own.

Thanks must also go to Sara Kase, my editor at Sourcebooks, whose eye has been invaluable, and to my newfound agent, Nicholas Croce.

As ever, my main thanks go to my family. My parents, Charles and Barbara Higginbotham, have been a constant encouragement to me. My children, Thad Coomes and Bethany Coomes, have borne graciously my obsession with the Wars of the Roses. My husband, Don Coomes, has patiently tolerated the encroachment of two bookshelves stuffed with Wars of the Roses materials into the marital bedroom. I cannot think of better people to spend my life with than these.

Finally, I must repair omissions in my previous acknowledgments by mentioning other family members. My cats, Ginny, Stripes, and Onslow, have diligently kept my reading chair and my computer chair warm for me when I am not sitting in them. Boswell, my cairn terrier, standing guard by the sliding glass door in the kitchen, has protected my workspace against countless invasions by local squirrels, rabbits, and deer, all undoubtedly on a relentless quest to sabotage my hard drive. He has earned all of the many treats he has received during the writing of this novel.

Reading Group Guide

1. Lord Hastings tells Harry that Edward married the only woman who refused to go to bed with him. Do you think Edward married Bessie out of pure lust? Or do you think he picked her because he respected her denial of him?

2. Harry is named after the king for whom his family fought, rather than after his father and grandfather. What does this say about loyalty in the fifteenth century?

3. Harry supports several of Richard's heinous actions because he loves his friend. Do you sympathize with Harry or do you think he should have seen the fault in Richard's actions?

4. Like most major events throughout history, a tiny spark can incite a fire. Do you think this marriage between Bessie and Edward is responsible for all the warring? Or was it the excuse needed to justify a grab for the throne?

5. Kate is married to Harry when she is just seven years old and he is ten. Although they dislike one another at first, their love seems to blossom as they grow older. What makes their relationship so much stronger than those of other members of the court, who seem to merely tolerate their spouses?

6. John marries a woman forty-five years his senior in order to increase his wealth. His wife, on the other hand, marries him in order to have a companion. Are these motivations acceptable for marriage? Is marriage just a deal to be made for the betterment of both parties?

7. The morning after Harry and Kate consummate their marriage, Kate is pleased to learn that the entire court knows. Cecilia remarks about the bed sheets, King Edward jokingly calls her a minx, and the Duchess of Exeter teases her about being ridden. How did you feel about the court discussing Harry and Kate's sex life so openly? How would such behavior be taken today?

8. When Richard finally tells Harry that he loves him, Harry realizes that he has been waiting for those words of validation for fourteen years. Does Richard really love Harry? Or does he just use Harry's love to manipulate him into doing his bidding?

9. Harry violently rapes his wife after she insults Richard and spits in Harry's face. Months later, after he has repented of all his wrongdoings, she forgives him. Would you be able to forgive in such a situation?

10. Unlike his brother George, who openly rebels against Edward's reign, Richard waits until Edward is dead to reach for the throne. First he becomes protectorate of the young king, but he quickly broadens his horizons to aim for the kingship for himself. Which brother do you think is worse—openly rebellious George or patiently power-hungry Richard?

11. Harry is distraught when his only brother dies of consumption. Kate also loses all her brothers by the time Henry Tudor takes the throne. How important are sibling relationships in this novel? Are they more or less important than spousal relationships?

12. Harry and Kate both brag about their high social standings when they are young children, when neither of them has done anything to deserve his or her title. How would you feel living in a time period when your name and your family history are the predominant factors in your chance for success? Are there times today when family name plays a large role in social standing?

13. The public's loyalty constantly sways as king after king is forced off the throne. With all the upheaval and treason, is loyalty represented as a good quality to have? Or does loyalty bring danger as power shifts from king to king?

14. Richard tells Harry that "Edward the king will prevail over Edward the son and brother" when Edward is forced to execute George for his treason. Would you be able to make this same decision if you were in Edward's shoes? Would you choose to protect your kingdom over your brother?

15. Harry is easily duped by Richard because he loves him and trusts him. He doesn't see that he's committing treason and usurping the rightful king. How would you have responded in that situation? Have you ever been led astray because of your love for someone?

16. Kate dislikes Richard from the moment Harry starts raving about how wonderful he is. Is this dislike a result of jealousy? Or does Kate see the latent danger in Richard?

17. After reading the first chapter of this novel, we know that Harry is going to die. Later we learn that Kate is telling her story twelve years after Harry tells his, meaning that Harry is already dead. How did this knowledge affect the way you read the novel?

18. When Harry is beheaded, he meets Uncle Edmund in the afterlife. Why do you think Harry meets Uncle Edmund, a man he barely knew, rather than his mother or his beloved brother Humphrey?

19. Several characters in *The Stolen Crown* experience losses of those close to them: Harry, with the death of his brother and the loss of his friendship with Richard; Bessie, with the murder of her two sons and the death of her husband; Kate, with the murder of her father, brothers, and husband. Who do you think suffers the greatest loss in this novel?

20. *The Stolen Crown* begins with a secret—the wedding between Bessie and Edward. It seems everyone has a secret to keep from someone else—suspicions of treason and knowledge of the whereabouts of others. Do you think some of the loss and tragedy could have been avoided if everyone were more open with their information?

About the Author

S USAN HIGGINBOTHAM LIVES WITH HER family in North Carolina and has worked as an attorney and as an editor. Her first two historical novels, *The Traitor's Wife* and *Hugh and Bess*, were republished by Sourcebooks in 2009; *The Traitor's Wife* won the gold medal for historical/military fiction in the 2008 Independent Publisher Book Awards. More about Susan's novels and the historical background to them can be found on her website, www.susanhigginbotham.com, and on her blog, Medieval Woman.

Tim Broyer

Also Available

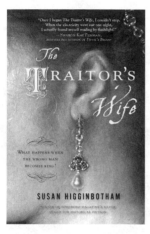

THE TRAITOR'S WIFE

978-1-4022-1787-6 • $14.99 U.S./$15.99 CAN

It is an age where passion reigns and treachery runs as thick as blood. Young Eleanor has two men in her life: her uncle King Edward II, and her husband Hugh le Despenser, a mere knight but the newfound favorite of the king. She has no desire to meddle in royal affairs—she wishes for a serene, simple life with her family. But as political unrest sweeps the land, Eleanor, sharply intelligent yet blindly naïve, becomes the only woman each man can trust.

Fiercely devoted to both her husband and her king, Eleanor holds the secret that could destroy all of England—and discovers the choices no woman should have to make.

HUGH AND BESS

978-1-4022-1527-8 • $14.99 U.S./$18.99 CAN/£7.99 UK

Amid her dreams of a wealthy, handsome man who would sweep her off her feet, young Bess de Montacute never thought she would end up with the son and grandson of disgraced traitors. How could she ever be happy with a man with such a vile past?

Hugh le Despenser, struggling to reestablish his family's good name, cannot refuse the king's proposition that he marry an earl's daughter. But even though the marriage is a beneficial alliance, Hugh is in love with another…

Far apart in age and haunted by the past, can Hugh and Bess somehow make their marriage work?

To

Jayme and Alex

for the love and joy that

fuel my life

CONTENTS

FOREWORD

Want to have more joy and contentment in your life? All the scientific studies of happiness, longevity, and mental and medical health point to one factor: the strength of your relationships with others. In *Wired to Connect*, psychiatrist Amy Banks, M.D., provides an innovative and user-friendly summary of the extensive research on the neuroscience of relationships and offers readers practical ways to use this knowledge to retrain their brains for healthier, more rewarding relationships. What's in this for you? Simply put, you can intentionally transform your life by improving how you connect with others. Relationships are not simply the "icing on the cake" for a life well lived. *Relationships are the cake.*

After decades of studying how culture shapes our relationships as well as working as a psychiatrist in clinical practice, Amy Banks has brilliantly created what she calls the C.A.R.E. system, which can help improve the four ways we "click" with one another: how *calm* we feel around others, are *accepted* by others, *resonate* with the inner states of others, and are *energized* by these connections. Using the C.A.R.E. system as it is described in this book, readers can target the neural pathways that need fine-tuning so that the quality of their relationships increases. With an understanding of how our brains truly work we can intentionally change how we live our lives!

I love this book! It is beautifully written, engaging, and inspiring.

Want more happiness? Want to live longer? Want to be healthier in mind and body? Then learning these four ways to click into more meaningful and rewarding relationships is your passport to achieving these goals. Let Amy Banks be your guide to a better life of love and laughter. Enjoy!

—DANIEL J. SIEGEL, M.D.

Chapter 1

BOUNDARIES ARE OVERRATED

A New Way of Looking at Relationships

B oundaries are overrated.

If you want healthier, more mature relationships; if you want to stop repeating old patterns that cause you pain; if you are tired of feeling emotionally disconnected from the people you spend your time with; if you want to grow your inner life, you can begin by questioning the idea that there is a clear, crisp line between you and the people you interact with most frequently.

People who talk a lot about boundaries tend to make statements like these:

"It shouldn't matter what other people do and say to you, not if you have a strong sense of self."

"How do parents know they've been successful? When their children no longer need them."

"Best friends and true romance are for the young. As you get older, you naturally grow apart from other people."

"You shouldn't need other people to complete you."

"You wouldn't have so many problems if you would just stand on your own two feet."

The message is clear: it's not "healthy" to need other people—and whatever you do, don't let yourself be infected by other peoples' feelings, thoughts, and emotions. The statements above are intended to have an emotional effect on you. You may notice that they sound just a *teensy* bit judgmental and shaming. I know they make me uncomfortable; when I read them, I feel like I'm standing in a harsh white spotlight with someone pointing a finger at me, intoning *You're pretty messed up, missy, and it's all your fault.*

The ideal of complete psychological independence is one that was very big with mental health professionals in much of the twentieth century, and it still has our culture by the throat. So even if those statements about boundaries carry a sting, they also probably sound familiar to you, or even self-evident. Obvious!

So I couldn't possibly be suggesting that they're untrue. I couldn't possibly say that it can be good to be dependent, or that our mental health is unavoidably affected by the people we share our lives with, or that we achieve emotional growth when we are profoundly connected to others instead of when we are apart from them.

That's exactly what I'm saying.

This book is going to show you a different way of thinking about your emotional needs and what it means to be a healthy, mature adult. A new field of scientific study, one I call *relational neuroscience*, has shown us that there is hardwiring throughout our brains and bodies designed to help us engage in satisfying emotional connection with others. This hardwiring includes four primary neural pathways that are featured in this book. Relational neuroscience has also shown that when we are cut off from others, these neural pathways suffer. The result is a neurological cascade that can result in chronic irritability and anger, depression, addiction, and chronic physical illness. We are just not as healthy when we try to stand on our own, and that's because the human brain is built to operate within a network of caring human relationships. How do we reach our personal and professional potential? By being warmly, safely connected to partners, friends, coworkers, and family. Only then do our neural pathways get the stimulation they need to make our brains calmer, more tolerant, more resonant, and more productive.

The good news for those of us whose relationships don't always feel so warm or safe: it is possible to heal and strengthen those four neural pathways that are weakened when you don't have strong connections. Relationships and your brain form a virtuous circle, so by strengthening your neural pathways for connection, you will also make it easier to build the healthy relationships that are essential for your psychological and physical health.

For many people, the news about the importance of relationships began with a 1998 study at the University of Parma in Italy, a study that proved how deeply connected we are to one another, right down to our neurons.

Your Feelings, My Brain

It was one of those lucky scientific mistakes, an unexpected observation that could have easily gone unnoticed if it hadn't been for an astute researcher. When Giacomo Rizzolatti, a neurophysicist at the University of Parma, and his research team began their now-famous experiment, they were not intending to explore how human beings interact. In fact, they were not even studying people. The Italian researchers were mapping a small area, known as *F5*, in the brains of the macaque monkey. At this point in neurological research, it was already well known that the F5 neurons fire when a monkey reaches his arm and hand away from his body to grasp an object.

One routine day in the lab, a researcher observed something unprecedented. The researcher was standing in the line of sight of a monkey whose F5 cells had been implanted with micro-sized electrodes. As the researcher reached out to grasp an object, the electrodes placed on the monkey's F5 area activated.

Remember: it was known that the F5 neurons activate when a monkey moves his arm to grasp something.

Then think about this: the monkey was not moving *his* arm; he was simply watching as the *researcher's* arm moved.

This seemed impossible. At the time of this observation, scientists believed that the nerve cells for action were separate and distinct from the nerve cells for sensory observations. Sensory neurons picked up information from the outside world; motor neurons were devoted to acting. So when the F5 area, known for its link to physical action, lit up in the brain of a monkey who was only *watching* action in someone else, it was a clear violation of this known divide. It was as if the brain of the monkey and the brain of the researcher were somehow synchronized. Even more unsettling, it was as if their brains overlapped, as if the researcher's physical movement existed inside the monkey.[1]

As Rizzolatti and other neuroscientists pursued this odd observation, they found that human brains also demonstrate this mirroring effect. In other words, you understand me by performing an act of internal mimicry—by letting some of my actions and feelings into your head. Ask a friend to briskly rub her hands together as you watch. Chances are that as her hands become warm from the friction, your hands will start to feel warm, too. In the aftermath of the monkey experiment, it was hypothesized that our brains contain mirror neurons, nerve cells that are dedicated to the task of imitating others. Most scientists no longer feel that specific mirror neurons exist; instead, there is a brainwide mirroring system whose tasks are shared by a number of regions and pathways. The imitating effect—the reason your hands warm up when your friend rubs hers together—happens because neural circuits throughout your brain are copying what you hear and see. Nerves in your frontal and prefrontal cortex (the same ones that are activated when you plan to rub your own hands together and then execute that plan) begin to fire. At the same time, neurons in your somatosensory cortex, which is the area of the brain responsible for bodily sensations, activate and send you messages of friction and warmth. Deep inside your brain, *your* hands are rubbing themselves together—even if your hands don't actually move.

Actually, the process goes far beyond the mere reflection of another person's actions. Your mirroring system is made up of neurons that can "see" or "hear" what someone else is doing. The system then recruits neurons from other areas of the brain to provide you with input not just about sensations and actions but about emotions, too. This input lets you have a comprehensive, detailed imitation of what the other person is experiencing. That's why you can almost instantly pick up on the emotion of another person. If you watch as I rub my hands together, your brain might read the excitement on my face as I demonstrate how the mirroring system works—and *you* may feel some of that excitement. If you've ever "caught" a smile that you spotted on the face of a complete stranger, or if the silent tension of your partner has caused your own heart to race, you've experienced the effects of the mirroring system. This emotional contagion is caused by a neural pathway that can, in effect, take in another person's feelings and replicate them squarely inside you.

When I ask groups of people to try the hand-rubbing experiment, there are usually two sets of reactions. Some people are amazed, as if they've just watched themselves pull a rabbit out of a hat. Their neurological connection with others feels like magic. But other people immediately say, "This is creepy!"

I get it. When you've been taught all your life that your mind is its own little castle, one that's surrounded by a thick, high wall that's designed to keep your thoughts and feelings in and everyone else's out, it can be unsettling to learn about the power of the mirroring system. And in fact, the discovery of our mirroring ability challenges some traditional assumptions about how our brains and bodies are wired. Vittorio Gallese, a neurophysiologist in the Parma lab, described the role of the mirroring system in human interactions this way: "The neural mechanism is involuntary, with it we don't have to think about what other people are doing or feeling, we simply know."[2] Marco Iacoboni, a professor of psychiatry at UCLA, takes it one step further in his book *Mirroring People*. He says that the mirroring system helps us in "understanding our existential condition and our involvement with others. [It shows] that we are not alone, but are biologically wired and evolutionarily designed to be deeply interconnected with one another."[3]

When you and I interact, an impression of the interaction is left on my nervous system. I literally carry my contact with you around inside me, as a neuronal imprint. The next time you hear someone say, "Don't let other people affect how you feel," remember the mirroring system. Because we don't really have a choice. For good or for bad, other people affect us, and we are not as separate from one another as psychologists once thought.

Maturity Has a New Meaning

When I say that boundaries are overrated, I don't mean that there are absolutely no boundaries, or that all of humanity is just one big, undifferentiated, brownish-beige lump. Nor am I suggesting that anyone give up her or his own distinct personality for the sake of fitting in with a cozy, companionable group. No therapist I know believes that it's healthy to abandon your beliefs, preferences, and quirks for the sake of a smoothly running—and bland—larger whole.

For decades, in fact, psychology moved in the other direction, in the belief that the only path to human growth was traveled via emotional separation. According to separation-individuation theory, which was most energetically advanced by Margaret Mahler in the 1970s, we all begin our work of separation in the first six or seven months of life, when we start to realize that our caregiver is a person distinct from ourselves. Separation-individuation theory holds that the rest of life is a variation on this discovery. In the *practicing* stage of human development, we supposedly practice separation by crawling or toddling away from our mothers and then returning to their arms. In the *object constancy* stage, we develop the capacity to hold an abstract image of Mom in our minds, meaning that we are secure enough to venture farther and farther away from her, thus developing our independence. As school-aged children, we become more aggressive in an attempt to move forward with our individual desires. In adolescence, we move further away from our parents by developing a sexual identity and pairing off with our peers. Adulthood? It's a constant process of refining our ability to stand on our own, soothe our own distress, and solve our own problems. With each stage, the boundary between the self and other people grows stronger, more solid. Separation-individuation theory has been written about in thousands of books and dissertations, but here's a micro-summary: in order to grow, we must step farther and farther away from others. The fully mature person may enjoy other people but doesn't really *need* them. He is defined by the firm boundaries between himself and other people, and within those boundaries he is a self-sufficient being.

Even before the mirroring system came on the scene, and before relational neuroscience began to turn up additional evidence for the biological basis of human connectedness, some in the field wondered whether the separation model had gone too far. In the 1970s, a forward-looking group of Boston mental health experts—psychiatrist Jean Baker Miller and psychologists Judith V. Jordan, Irene Stiver, and Janet Surrey—noticed that their patients weren't suffering from poor boundaries. They weren't suffering from a lack of personal independence from others. What they suffered from was a lack of healthy human connection. As Judith Jordan notes, "The Separate Self model has wrongly suggested that we are intrinsically motivated to build firmer boundaries, gain power over other people in order to establish safety, and compete with others for scarce resources. Mutuality helps us see that human beings thrive in relationships in which both people are growing and contributing to good connection."[4]

When you look at relationships this way, it's possible to take the stages of development according to separation-individuation theory and cast them in a warmer light. When an infant crawls away from her mother, she's not trying to separate from humanity. Instead, the baby is expanding her relational world; she's moving toward *more* connections, toward the big world and the people who populate that world, before scooting back to enjoy her relationship with her mother. A toddler who learns object constancy isn't building the ability to get away from Mom; by developing a mental image of her mother, she's able to carry Mom with her wherever she goes. She's learning a skill necessary for sustaining relationships over distance and time. As school-aged children interact with their peers and make mistakes, they learn how to manage relationships. Teenagers expand their relational worlds even further; they negotiate sexual relationships, and they have to learn how to become part of a group without succumbing to peer pressure. This reinterpretation of developmental growth has an overarching theme: human beings don't mature by separating. Instead, they grow toward a greater and greater relational complexity. This approach to human development has a name: *relational-cultural theory*, or RCT. As a young psychiatrist, I found that RCT was more effective than any other theory, including separation-individuation, in helping people heal and helping them grow. I've spent twenty years applying RCT to the problems of my patients and the disconnected world they—and we—live in.

Separation theory and RCT have a few ideas in common: to be healthy, you have to know who you are; what your feelings and thoughts are; that other people have thoughts and feelings, too; and you have to be able to differentiate yourself within a relationship. But in separation theory, you're learning all this in order to eventually walk away. You can still forge bonds and be part of a community if you want to, but your role as an adult has to be earned by your ability to tough things out on your own. This is a psychology that emphasizes a defensive stance, because you're always defining and protecting your boundaries. You're wary of being invaded by other people's emotions and problems. In fact, this is how Freud saw the condition of being alive: "For the living organism protection against stimuli is almost a more important task than reception of stimuli."⁵ It's sad, isn't it? In separation theory, there is always a wall between you and other people.

In RCT, there are no walls between people. Good relationships are the rich soil in which people grow and bloom. A good relationship with your parents helps you feel safe enough to approach other people and make a connection with them. A good relationship with your peers helps you try out who you are, practice your skills of empathy, and learn communication. As your skills for relationship grow, so does your desire for more relationship.

Relational-cultural theory doesn't imagine people as defined by boundaries; it sees relationships as more like a magician's linking rings. The rings are a set, but they are not stuck in a rigid configuration. They can move far apart and they can move closer together. And they can—this is the magic part—temporarily interconnect and overlap, just as they do when you watch someone rub his hands together and feel the warmth in your own. Or when you sometimes feel like you're in another person's skin, finishing their sentences or feeling their sadness. There's flexibility and movement in this definition of relationship. You come together, experiencing each other; and then you move away again so that you can absorb what you've learned. Relationships are a dynamic process of experiencing, learning, and integrating your knowledge so that you are able to see both yourself and the other person more deeply and more clearly.

Jean Baker Miller liked to talk about "growth-fostering relationships," a wonderfully descriptive term that suggests just the right idea: relationships aren't an end in themselves. Although a relationship can be a safe harbor, it is never just that. It also helps you grow. A good relationship helps you and the other person develop clarity about yourselves; promotes your self-worth; makes you more productive at your work; and it gives you an appetite for more relationships. In Baker Miller's language, a growth-fostering relationship brings more "zest" to everything you do. When you're in a growth-fostering relationship, you're not being belittled or silenced, and you're not hiding from the things that bother you. A growth-fostering relationship is the opposite of having to put up walls and fortify the battlements. Instead, you are constantly reaching out to others and stretching toward greater maturity.

So for years before the mirroring study, I was using Relational-Cultural Theory, or RCT, to help my patients. Instead of giving struggling young people the standard advice to "separate from your parents and stop depending on them for emotional support," we looked for ways they could stay connected to their families of origin while building their adult lives. Instead of telling people with explosive anger or chronic irresponsibility that they had to learn to self-regulate, we picked their relationships that felt the most durable—and worked on new emotional skills in an atmosphere that made it safer and easier to take risks. Sometimes I saw patients who were barely hanging on, whose relational worlds were limited to one or two abusive connections. In these cases, we worked together to find ways to detach from unhealthy relationships and—gently, slowly—grow relationships that held more potential for acceptance and warmth. From these starting points, we'd continue the work that would allow them to grow, expand, connect, heal, and move forward. I grew, too, refusing to maintain a cool distance in the therapy room. Whereas a separation-individuation therapist would see it as her job to help her patients stand on their own, I forged real relationships with my clients. I shared my own worries and feelings and expanded my emotional repertoire. Within the relationship, the patient grew—and so did I. That's how RCT works. As one client said, "Relational therapy differed from my previous therapy, which was about me as an individual with no real connection to the therapist. In relational therapy, we worked together. The therapist went out of her way to make an emotional bond with me. I saw and felt her concern and caring."

Healthy Relationships = Healthy Body

From a clinical perspective—my private laboratory—this approach was working. I wasn't alone, either; my colleagues at the Jean Baker Miller Training Institute at the Wellesley Centers for Women were doing the same thing, with similar good results. Patients who came to us as chronic "hard cases"—the kind who are transferred from therapist to therapist and never seem to improve—blossomed. They became more able to derive gratification from real give-and-take relationships. Stressed-out people became calmer; the rejected became more trusting; the abusive developed empathy; and people who had emotionally flatlined became more energetic.

On a case-by-case basis, we had enough proof for our approach to keep going. Every day we saw people developing through and toward relationships, instead of away from them.

But we also were bolstered by the stunning evidence about the health benefits of relationships. This evidence could fill an entire book—and in his book *Love and Survival: The Scientific Basis for the Healing Power of Intimacy*, the trailblazing cardiologist Dean Ornish does amass hundreds of pages of studies and thinking about the subject. Here are just a few of the highlights:

- Researchers in North Carolina measured the effect of social support on 331 men and women, sixty-five years of age and older. After controlling for known risk factors like age, sex, race, economic status, diet, physical health status, stressful life events, and cigarette smoking, the researchers found that those who perceived their social support to be impaired had a *340 percent* higher rate of premature death than those who felt their social support was good.[6]

- A Yale University study looked at the coronary angiographs of 119 men and 40 women. (A coronary angiograph shows whether and to what extent your coronary arteries are blocked.) The patients who reported more "feelings of being loved" had far fewer blockages than those who didn't. The patients who felt loved had fewer blockages even than the patients who had busy social circles but who didn't feel particularly nurtured or supported. These findings held true even after the researchers accounted for genetic predisposition to heart disease and environmental risk factors like age, hostility, smoking, diet, and exercise.[7]

- In a long-term study that began in the 1940s, male medical students at Johns Hopkins filled out a questionnaire that assessed how close they felt to their parents. There were 1,100 students who participated in the study, all of them healthy at the time they completed the questionnaire. In a remarkable feat of logistics, the students were tracked down fifty years later. The students who had developed cancer in the intervening years were less likely to have had close relationships with their parents than students who did not have cancer. Interestingly, a poor relationship between the male student and his father was the strongest predictor of cancer. Again, these findings were independent of other known risks for cancer.[8]

- In the 1950s, Harvard students (all healthy, all men) were interviewed about the warmth and closeness of their mothers and fathers. They were also asked to describe their parents. Thirty-five years later, when the students were middle-aged, 29 percent who had good parental relationships and described their parents in positive terms had developed illnesses. But

95 percent of students who had poor relationships with their parents and who described their mothers and fathers in negative terms had become sick.[9]

Let these studies sink in for a moment. Better cardiovascular health. Fewer cases of cancer. Better health in midlife. And 340 percent fewer premature deaths from all causes. Here was clear evidence that the perception of having healthy human connection is critical not just for emotional health but physical health as well. When I was a child, the government was worried about curious kids who were drinking household chemicals and accidentally poisoning themselves. To address the problem, they distributed acid-green stickers decorated with the face of Mr. Yuk, who displayed a theatrically sick expression. Parents placed these stickers on dangerous chemicals throughout the house to send a clear warning message to their children who were too young to read. I've often thought we need a similarly strong message for adults about the poison of disconnection. Why don't medical waiting rooms offer pamphlets marked with a skull and crossbones, with the words *Social isolation can kill you* in stark letters underneath? The evidence for the claim is certainly there. Maybe a clear message like that would temper our compulsive need to stand on our own two feet.

The C.A.R.E. Plan

At the time Jean Baker Miller and her colleagues at Wellesley were forming their theories about human development, there was no technology available to see what was happening in the brain when it was either isolated or connected. Like everyone else at the time, the group had to work from their external observations. But then, in the 1990s, technology made brain study more possible. With advanced scanning technologies that allowed scientists to see the brain functioning in real time, and with discoveries such as learning that the brain can grow new cells even in old age, new findings about brain activity and new fields of research emerged. By the year 2000, neuroscientists were eagerly studying the brain's activity within the context of relationships. What they've found since then has taken relational-cultural therapy's work and extended it. The new science is completely upending the old ideas about separation and individuation.

Relational neuroscience has been showing that people cannot reach their full potential unless they are in healthy connection with others. Take the mirroring system. It needs relational input to stay in shape. So you need to really "see" other people (in the emotional sense that you understand and honor their feelings) *and* be "seen" in order to keep the mirroring system functioning well; without that input, it's harder to perceive other people accurately and to feel close to them. There are other neural pathways, too, that are nurtured when we are in good relationships. Other systems use the input from healthy relationships to help tell our brains to turn off the stress response, to think clearly, and to feel pleasure without resorting to damaging or addictive behavior. (The next chapter describes the scientific findings in more detail.)

It's important to stay humbled by the knowledge of how much we still don't know about the brain and relationships. As always, we can only work with the best knowledge available. But the knowledge we *do* have has provided me with a way of talking to my patients about how relationships are vehicles for our growth and our healing. It helps people really "get" why relationships are so crucial to feeling happier, to managing their stress, to feeling less angry, to stop eating or shopping or drinking compulsively, or to make other changes. It's also provided the framework for a plan that blends relational psychology and neuroscience to help patients make those changes.

Remember when I said that good relationships help people feel calmer, more tolerant, more resonant, and more productive? Each of these four benefits of a healthy relationship is directly related to a specific neural pathway. These pathways help you feel:

Calm. A feeling of calm is regulated in part by a pathway of the autonomic nervous system called the *smart vagus*. When you're feeling stressed, your primitive brain wants to kick in—and when the primitive brain is in charge, it tends to make decisions that are bad news for relationships. When you have strong relationships, the smart vagus can modulate the stress response and keep the primitive brain from taking over. You're healthier, can think more clearly, and you're more likely to solve problems through creative thinking instead of exploding in anger or running away. But when you're isolated from other people, your smart vagus can suffer from what neuroscientists call *poor tone*. This means that your primitive brain is more likely to call the shots. In the short term, this leads to relationship problems. Over time, you can expect chronic stress, illness, depression, and big-time irritability.

Accepted. A sense of belonging flows from a well-functioning dorsal anterior cingulate cortex, or dACC. The role of the dorsal anterior cingulate cortex is featured in SPOT, or *social pain overlap theory*, in which scientists show that being left out hurts—physically. Unfortunately, a person who suffers frequent exclusion can develop a dorsal anterior cingulate cortex that is highly reactive to social pain, leaving him or her to sense rejection even when other people are welcoming. Have you ever known someone who snaps at you when you say something mild and friendly like, "Hey, you look a little tired today. Are you all right?" Then you know someone who may be suffering from an overactive dorsal anterior cingulate cortex.

Resonant. Resonance with other people—the feeling among friends who "get" each other—is facilitated by the mirroring system. As I've described, other people's experiences are imprinted onto our nervous system in a very literal way. When your mirroring pathways are weak, it's hard to read other people or even to send out signals that allow other people to accurately read *you*.

Energetic. Energy is a benefit of the relational brain's dopamine reward system. In the beginning—whenever that was—human beings were created with a clever, life-enhancing mechanism that exists to this day. When we're engaged in healthy, growth-promoting activities, we are rewarded with a hit of dopamine that sweeps through the body's reward circuitry, producing a wave of euphoria and energy. Dopamine's feel-good effects are the carrot on the stick for healthy behavior: water, healthy nutrition, sex, and human relationships all stimulate dopamine. It was such a simple and ingenious plan . . . until casinos, malls, and opium dens came along. Sigh. When people don't get enough pleasure from healthy relationships, they may turn to less healthy sources like addictive shopping, drugs, or compulsive sex to get their dopamine hits. And when they do this enough, they can rewire their brains so that the dopamine pathways are no longer connected to relationships. Even when they're in a good relationship, some people just can't get real enjoyment from it.

Calm. Accepted. Resonant. Energetic.

Each of these four pathways is a feedback loop. Supply the loop with good relationships, and most of the time, the pathway will become stronger. Strengthen the pathway, and your relationships become more rewarding. There are plenty of places in each loop to step in and boost the entire system.

This book describes what I call the C.A.R.E. program,

named after the four benefits of a healthy relationship. The C.A.R.E. program is the book version of work I've been doing with clients for fifteen years. It can help heal some of the neural damage that isolation or chronic emotional disconnection can cause. It can also help you form healthy, thriving connections—whether you need a new perspective on one particularly sticky relationship or whether you describe yourself as "just not good with people" and want a major relational overhaul. This program has also helped successfully address the symptoms that extend past the immediate pain of disconnection, including addictions, stress, anxiety, anger problems, and more.

In the first part of this book, I'll describe in detail the neuroscience of relationships, including the role of each of the four neural pathways. I'll also show you how the brain can make itself over, in ways that can be positive or negative. Depending on your emotional connections, your brain can either suffer the damage of rejection and isolation—or enjoy the healing benefits of growth-fostering relationships.

If a lack of healthy connection is a problem for you, at first the solution might seem to be simple: go out and make some friends. But of course it's *not* that simple, not in a society that underplays the importance of close relationships and overplays the need to be independent, judgmental, and separate. It is most certainly not simple if you have suffered neurological damage from chronic disconnection. In the second and very practical section of this book, the C.A.R.E. program

will help you use psychological and relational neuroscience—
together—to melt away unwanted neural pathways and create new ones that make it easier to forge healthy connections.
You'll take a relationship inventory that reveals which of your
neural pathways for connection are receiving good support,
and which need shoring up. You'll also discover which of your
relationships hold the most potential for growth. If you have
relationships that are damaging your C.A.R.E. neural pathways and making it harder for you to connect, you'll learn
that, too. These insights can help you heal the physical and
emotional damage from disconnection and help you make relationships that really click.

   With this information in hand, you can customize the
C.A.R.E. program to your needs. The C.A.R.E. plan is laid out
across four chapters, with one chapter for each of the neural
pathways. You can work through the entire plan, or you can
use the steps on an as-needed basis to target your neural pathways with specific treatments and exercises. Some of those
treatments can be done alone; a few require a prescription or
a specialist; and others you undertake within the context of
your safest relationships. In general, though, the C.A.R.E.
plan is a series of simple actions that strengthen your ability
to connect at all levels, from the cellular to the behavioral. At
the end of the program you will have relationships—some old
ones and maybe some new ones—that feel calmer, safer, more
zestful, and more mutual. It's time to start tearing down walls,
and time to start healing your brain.

Chapter 2

THE FOUR NEURAL PATHWAYS
FOR HEALTHY RELATIONSHIPS

A culture telling you that you need to separate from others and be independent above all else is selling you an ancient script. Not one that's based on the brain as it is, but the brain as it *was*.

Years ago, when my children were young, they were given a kit for raising a frog from a tadpole. With much positive anticipation, we set up the frog habitat in the kitchen and ordered a tadpole we dubbed Uncle Milty. Uncle Milty's home was just beside the breakfast preparation area. Each morning, as I made breakfast for my kids, we would peek into the small container of water to see if Uncle Milty had sprouted his frog legs yet. Weeks went by. Milty's head and torso grew bigger and bigger, but . . . no legs. In our household, we talk a lot about the importance of relationships for good health and development, so it was natural for everyone to speculate: was it possible that Milty was not becoming a frog because he was alone in his habitat? Like human babies who fail to thrive because they are not held, was Milty failing to grow legs because he didn't have another amphibian to cuddle with? Without relationships, would he remain an immature, unsatisfied tadpole? No. Our family was trying to analyze Milty as if he had a human brain. But he didn't. He had a reptile brain.

Reptiles and amphibians have brains that, basically, haven't evolved in about five hundred million years. The reptile brain doesn't need relationships. It doesn't require connection with others for physical development. The reptile brain is all about bare-knuckled survival, about breathing, eating, reproducing, fighting, and hotfooting it away from anything that might want to eat it. Uncle Milty never did develop legs (the poor guy couldn't hotfoot away from anything), but he was probably the victim of a genetic mutation, not loneliness— because the reptile brain doesn't get lonely. It doesn't care about anyone else. It doesn't need anyone else. It's the very model of separation and rugged independence.

We humans still possess the primitive reptile brain; it's what we call our *brain stem*. But the brain stem is just one structure within a human brain that has evolved far beyond the reptile brain to be much larger, more complicated, and more advanced. The human brain is different from the reptile brain in a zillion ways, but the one I'm most concerned with here is that, over millennia, the human brain has evolved away from reptilian independence. For example, reptiles don't have neural equipment that causes them to feel pain if they are left out of a social group . . . but you and I do. Reptiles don't possess a nerve that uses signals from welcoming facial expressions to modulate stress . . . but you and I do. Reptiles don't need to know that other reptiles really "get" them . . . but we do. Reptiles don't get a surge of a motivating neurochemicals when they're in the company of others. . . . but . . . you get the picture.

Uncle Milty didn't need or want friends to be a fully developed frog, but our brains are different. To us, healthy connection is central. The old reptile script of surviving on your own, of not needing others to help you develop and grow, is life threatening to mammals. It is life threatening to you. Fortunately, it is possible to write a new script, one that's more in tune with the reality of our human brains. Humans have developed a deep need to connect with others, and we're constantly learning more about the neurobiology that underpins our need for good relationships. This chapter will describe some of that neurobiology.

No single area of the brain exclusively regulates relationships; this is a function that appears to be integrated across many parts of the human nervous system. Although there's always a danger of oversimplification when it comes to describing neurobiology, I find it helpful to think about our human brain's need for connection in terms of the four major neural C.A.R.E. pathways I described in the last chapter. When you are in healthy relationships with others, your brain sends messages that help you feel:

Calm (this pathway is governed by the smart vagus
  nerve)
Accepted (ruled by the dorsal anterior cingulate
  cortex, or dACC)
Resonant (the mirroring system)
Energetic (the dopamine reward system)

The health and strength of these pathways are influenced
by early childhood relationships, and then these pathways are
reshaped continually throughout our lives, again in the context of our relationships. That's right: our relationships sculpt
our brains. The quality of our relationships helps determine
our ability to feel motivated, to remain coolheaded in a crisis,
and to perceive other people's social signals with accuracy.
This is exciting news; it means that even if our C.A.R.E. pathways aren't working very well, we can learn to leverage the
power of relationships to heal and change them. And we can
think differently about how we raise the next generation, so
that our children and grandchildren possess fully functioning
systems for connectedness.

C Is for Calm: The Smart Vagus

I'll begin with a story about Brooke, a client of mine. I'm bet-
ting that her story will sound familiar. Maybe you've lived it.
  After a stretch of unemployment, Brooke was delighted
to land a job just before the winter holidays. But she was

anguished, too, because her new employer was throwing her annual holiday party on the Friday of Brooke's first week of work. As the week progressed, Brooke was increasingly torn between the desire to make a good impression on her coworkers and her dread of socializing in a large, unfamiliar group. She imagined awkward conversations with colleagues she barely knew; the humiliating feeling of her sweaty hand in another's dry palm; the uncomfortable but liberating moment when a conversation partner declares that it is time to mingle with other people. Brooke resigned herself to an evening of stress and faking it for the sake of her career. Her only hope for escape was a sudden natural disaster or an open bar serving very large glasses of white wine.

The night of the party, Brooke entered the hotel lobby and immediately felt like an outsider. Everywhere she turned, small groups of people huddled together, talking. A few of the people seemed to be looking in her direction and smirking. *Get over yourself,* Brooke thought, *no one is laughing at you.* But she stood off to the side for nearly thirty minutes, sipping her wine and looking around in vain for a face that appeared even a little bit friendly.

Rescue arrived in the form of her coworker Pete, who greeted Brooke warmly and wished her happy holidays. Almost immediately, Brooke began to relax. She and Pete had met a few days earlier at an office lunch meeting. During a break in the meeting, she discovered they shared a similar sense of humor and an unusual hobby: fly-fishing. At the party, they picked up where they had left off at the meeting, swapping stories about streams that were off the beaten track and debating the best fly for catching a striped bass. The rest of the party went smoothly. Pete brought two of their colleagues into the discussion and Brooke introduced herself to a few more. Maybe it was the wine, Brooke remarked to herself, but the group seemed to become much friendlier and more open as the night went on.

It wasn't the wine. (Brooke had drunk very little.) Thanks to complex forces in Brooke's life, a pathway in her nervous system was unable to accurately read and respond to the people she saw when she entered the party. Instead of seeing welcoming faces, she saw mockery. Even when she tried to talk herself into seeing things differently (*Get over yourself, Brooke; no one is laughing at you*), she was nearly overpowered by a feeling of jeopardy, a feeling that no one wanted her around. But as she talked with her new friend Pete, that pathway in her nervous system, the smart vagus, started to do its job. Not only could Brooke relax, she was better able to transmit and receive social cues. She could show friendliness. She could *see* it on the faces of others.

The human central nervous system is the control center for the electrical activity that drives your thoughts and actions. It contains an essential subsystem: the *autonomic* (think automatic) *nervous system*, which is designed to help you quickly respond to threats or stress. The autonomic nervous system is at work 24/7, humming along below the level of your conscious awareness. It runs throughout your entire body, innervating muscles, organ systems, and glands. We used to think that our autonomic nervous system was a lot like Uncle Milty's, with only two major parts:

The *sympathetic nervous system*, which is responsible
for the famous fight-or-flight response.
The *parasympathetic nervous system*, which leads to the
freeze response.

In other words, scientists believed that when you feel surprised or threatened, your body automatically responds in one of two ways: either your sympathetic nervous system revs up, providing you with the energy and focus needed to fight or flee; or your parasympathetic nervous system activates, slowing your body processes down so that you freeze and play dead. According to most introductory biology and psychology courses, whether you fight, flee, or freeze is largely dependent on the extent of the threat and on your ability to man up to it. If the threat seems potentially survivable and you are large and strong, you face the threat head-on. If you face that same threat but are small and weak, it is better to turn and run as fast as you can. Those are the choices in the sympathetic nervous system's fight-or-flight response. In the face of a severe, life-threatening situation, you might do what the baby rabbit I found on my porch last spring did. The bunny, which had been dropped there by one of my cats as a special "gift" to me, looked dead. But it was actually in the midst of a full-blown freeze response, in which the parasympathetic nervous system exerts a slowing down or calming effect. The body and brain begin to shut down; they literally go numb. Ideally, this reaction causes the predator to lose interest and turn away, but if the predator keeps attacking, the freeze response creates protection from the tremendous pain and stress. This is where the expression "playing dead" comes from, but the freeze reaction is anything but play and is not under conscious control. This shutting down of bodily functions is so effective that one-quarter of the animals playing dead actually die. (Fortunately, when I separated the bunny from its predators for a few hours, the parasympathetic stimulation stopped and the bunny hopped away.) Obviously, this potentially lethal response is the last line of defense for any animal, including humans.

These reactions of the sympathetic and parasympathetic nervous systems, collectively named the "fight, flight, or freeze" responses, have been socially and scientifically accepted as the truth of how human beings respond to stress since they were identified by physiologist Walter Cannon in the early 1900s. But times are changing. Researchers are taking another look at the stress response in humans, and they are showing that "fight, flight, or freeze" is an incomplete list of the body's menu of options.

One of those researchers is Stephen Porges, the director emeritus of the Brain-Body Center of the College of Medicine at the University of Illinois–Chicago. His paradigm-breaking studies are what first identified a third branch of the autonomic nervous system: the smart vagus. The smart vagus is an evolutionarily newer pathway than the sympathetic or parasympathetic nervous systems. While amphibians, reptiles, and fish have the older responses, only mammals have a smart vagus in addition to the first two.

From an evolutionary perspective, the appearance of the smart vagus went hand in hand with the appearance of mammals and their increased social complexity and interdependence. Until the evolution of mammals, the world was populated by creatures that are less dependent on one another for survival. For them, the sympathetic fight-or-flight response and the parasympathetic freeze response are adequate to help them cope with the world. Have you ever wondered why turtles lay piles of eggs and fish release large clumps of roe? The primary reason for producing a large number of offspring is to increase the odds that any one of them will survive to reproduce. Young turtles, fish, and many other nonmammalian creatures have no psychological or physical need to be cuddled and fed by a parent; they leave the nest to fend for themselves immediately after birth. They are born with a complete set of instincts for hunting, eating, and hiding. They've got everything they need to survive in their habitats . . . except size. Unfortunately, in their turtle-eat-fish world, size matters. A lot. The only hope for the ultimate survival of these premammalian species is to mass-produce young and to hope that a few escape predation and survive into adulthood to reproduce. Though it has worked for millennia, it is not a particularly efficient system for the propagation of a species.

Mammals are different. Our reproduction efforts are more

efficient, in the sense that we produce fewer children, and those children have better odds of survival. One of the hallmarks of this system is a mammal baby's dependence on others for growth and development. A baby not only needs food and water, but also cuddling, cooing, and other stimulating contact with adults in order to grow and thrive. While turtles, fish, and frogs are born with instincts to manage the world on their own, mammals are born with a complete set of instincts to reach out to others. If you watch a newborn baby closely, you can see some of these instincts at work. The rooting reflex keeps an infant's neck and mouth turned toward the mother, searching for a breast for comfort and food; the Moro reflex causes an infant's arms to reach out, as if in a hug, when they are being put down. These instincts are vitally important, because a newborn mammal is not able to survive on his own without the help of a parent or older group member to care for him.

It appears that as mammals evolved and life on Earth became more socially complex, there was a need—or perhaps the opportunity—to use social connections as a way to moderate stress. Thus you and I have a smart vagus, a nerve that arises from the tenth cranial nerve at the base of the skull and heads north, where it links with some of the muscles of facial expression, speech, swallowing, and hearing. (Yes, hearing involves muscles—tiny ones—in your inner ear.) When you get input from other people's faces and voices telling you that these people are safe, the smart vagus sends a message to the sympathetic and parasympathetic nervous systems, telling them to turn off. In effect, the smart vagus says, "I'm with friends and everything is going to be okay. You don't need to fight, flee, or freeze right now." The smart vagus is one reason we feel less stress when we're around people we trust.

When you feel safe, the smart vagus also lets your muscles do the motor work that's necessary for engaging with the people around you. Your eyelids and eyebrows lift, so that your face becomes more open. The muscles of your inner ear tense, preparing you to hear the conversation. Without thinking about it, you look directly into the eyes of the people you're talking with. Your expression is animated, accurately reflecting your emotional response to the situation. This is a nerve that works to sustain social relationships, letting you send and receive emotional information that brings you closer to others and helps you feel calmer. Now *that's* smart.

In an ideal relational world, your autonomic nervous system automatically reads the environment and responds by activating the smart vagus when you are safe, the sympathetic nervous system when you are in danger, and the parasympathetic nervous system when your life is being threatened. But when your smart vagus isn't working well, you're less able to accurately interpret other people's intentions. Without the smart vagus doing its job, you can't see or hear other people as well, and you're at risk of misinterpreting their expressions. You don't make eye contact as easily, and your own facial expression becomes flatter, which increases the chances that you'll be seen as hostile or uncaring. Imagine how other people respond to your face when it looks closed off or angry.

If the smart vagus feels that other people are unsafe, it automatically shuts down.

It stops sending inhibitory messages to the sympathetic and parasympathetic nervous systems, allowing them to let loose with a stress response. If you're actually in danger, those stress responses are useful. But if you are around safe people *whom your nervous system has misread as unsafe*, imagine how problematic the feelings of the fight-or-flight response become. You get the familiar feelings of stress: elevated heart rate, sweaty palms, dry mouth, and fuzzy brain. You might not actually hit someone, but you may start an argument. Or you might perform the social equivalent of flight. (Have you ever zoned out during an uncomfortable conversation?) A parasympathetic freeze response is usually reserved for seriously life-threatening events, but in rare cases people who have experienced significant trauma at the hands of others can experience a partial shutdown in social situations. This goes way beyond a case of jitters; these folks literally can't speak or move.

In the case of Brooke, her smart vagus was off duty and her sympathetic nervous system was up and running as she entered the office party. Few people relish the idea of going to a cocktail party where they don't know a soul, but Brooke suffered from more than garden-variety butterflies. Brooke had a genetic tendency toward an overreactive stress response. In fact, both her mother and her mother's mother were anxious worriers who often preferred small, intimate groups to large crowds. These adults, however, were also capable of showing Brooke love and support. Both of these forces—anxiety and love—informed the way Brooke's autonomic nervous system responded to interpersonal interactions. She didn't have what neuroscientists call *good vagal tone*. Her smart vagus didn't always work as well as it should have, making it harder for her to navigate social situations. She tended to feel threatened by people she didn't know well, even when their intentions were friendly or neutral. And so, after spending a week in dread of the event, and without a friend's comforting presence, she was unable to read the smiling faces of the people around her as welcoming. To Brooke, those faces looked mocking and unreceptive. Her smart vagus, unable to sense that the environment was safe, failed to send a calming message to the sympathetic nervous system. Brooke didn't actually flee the party, but she did hide on the sidelines.

Brooke was unable to accurately read the expressions of strangers, but fortunately for her, her smart vagus wasn't completely broken. It was still able to respond to the presence of a friend. When Pete arrived and wished Brooke happy holidays, the vibrations from his kind, familiar voice traveled through space into her ear, moving the minuscule muscles that stimulated her smart vagus nerve. Almost immediately, she felt a wave of relief. Without thinking, her eyes scanned his smiling face and she responded with a delighted grin. As the muscles around her mouth and eyes tightened, they, too, stimulated her smart vagus. Instantaneously, the smart vagus sent an inhibitory message to both her sympathetic and parasympathetic nervous systems. She no longer had the urge to flee. She was safely in a conversation with Pete about fly-fishing. Not coincidentally, the other partygoers started to look friendlier—and she looked more receptive to them.

All in all, Brooke's social anxiety was fairly moderate. A friendly interaction could interrupt its loop. There are people who have it much worse. These are people with seriously poor vagal tone, sometimes because of genetic misfortune, but more often because their nervous system was shaped by an environment that was chronically threatening.

The human nervous system is shaped from infancy. A baby's life is full of routine stressors—hunger, sleepiness, wet diapers, sudden noises—that signal discomfort or danger and stimulate her sympathetic nervous system. Ideally, when a baby cries in distress, her caregivers respond supportively. They change her diaper, offer milk, or hold the baby tightly and rock her from side to side. This attuned adult–child relationship causes the baby's brain to release neurochemicals, like serotonin and endogenous opioids, that lessen the feeling of the threat. The baby's fear is soothed. Not only does the baby learn to associate her caregiver with safety, the experience helps her smart vagus become better connected with the parts of her brain that recognize safe faces, safe smells, safe noises, and so on. The multiple senses associated with a healthy relationship are eventually coded into the baby's nervous system. The regulatory pathway between the smart vagus and the sympathetic nervous system grows stronger and stronger. The result: human connection can now modulate the baby's stress response. The sympathetic and parasympathetic nervous systems can be soothed, or completely turned off, when the baby is in the presence of caring family and friends. The baby's sympathetic and parasympathetic nervous systems learn *not* to fire unless there is a real threat. The baby grows up with the ability to accurately distinguish between danger and safety, and she wants to seek out healthy human relationships.

This process of strengthening the smart vagus is one that continues throughout a child's life, into adulthood. If you have a terrible week at work, you may realize that you'll feel better if you have dinner with a friend Friday night. At the restaurant, you share the trials of the week, and your friend is appalled on your behalf. Your friend shares her own hard news: her mother has been diagnosed with a chronic illness. You cry together and laugh together, and at the end of the evening, you part ways. Not only do you feel better, the stimulation to your smart vagus has given it a fine tuning. Every time you share and receive comfort, your smart vagus becomes faster and more efficient at sending its chemical signals.

But what happens when the smart vagus develops within chaotic, disconnected, frightening circumstances? When a baby is repeatedly exposed to distress and is not soothed, her sympathetic nervous system is constantly stimulated. Her smart vagus doesn't learn to associate human relationships with comfort and safety. Her brain doesn't learn that there are times when the stress response can be turned off. She grows up hyperalert to danger, unable to relax even when she is safe, unable to enjoy other people even when their intentions are kind.

Infancy is the most significant time for brain development, but believe me: in a chronically dangerous environment, the smart vagus of an older child or adult will suffer.

If you are in constant danger because of a scary home situation, a violent neighborhood, or a war, your brain has a rational response—stay on high alert. Your sympathetic nervous system will flip to the On position, and depending on the intensity and consistency of the threat, it may more or less stay there. Your heart will race; your lungs will expand to take in more oxygen; and the blood vessels in your arms and limbs will dilate so more blood can flow through them. This way, you'll be prepared to fight or flee whenever the danger presents itself. If things are really bad, your parasympathetic nervous system might be preparing to bring on a freeze. But your body's nervous system is designed to respond to threats in short spurts, not twenty-four hours a day. Under extreme, chronic stress your body begins to break down. There's a greater risk of heart disease, illness, insomnia, depression . . . the list goes on. In fact, cortisol, the very chemical your body unleashes to counter the stress response, will damage brain cells needed for memory when it's released for too long.

The near-constant activation of the stress response is like exercise for your fight, flight, or freeze pathways. They become stronger and faster. At the same time, your smart vagus doesn't get the opportunity for a good workout. Eventually it will lose its good tone and become weak—leaving you with a loud and hypersensitive set of stress responses that perceives other people as basically dangerous and unkind, no matter what the reality. That's a tragedy, because we are built to use safe relationships as a way of reducing stress. Without this ability, we may look more independent, but in reality we are weaker and sicker. Happily, there are plenty of ways to improve the tone of your smart vagus. Later in the book, I'll describe these methods in detail.

A Is for Accepted: The Dorsal Anterior Cingulate Cortex

In 2003, three scientists at UCLA invited a series of volunteers to participate in an online game of catch called Cyberball.[1] The volunteer would arrive at the lab and, from inside a functional MRI scanner, begin playing the game. Things would start amicably enough, with the volunteer and researchers tossing the "ball" back and forth. So far, so good. But as things went on, the volunteer was gradually excluded from the game. No one explained to the volunteer why he or she wasn't receiving the ball anymore. No one even acknowledged that anything odd was going on. Eventually, the subject was completely left out as the other players tossed the ball among themselves.

Compared to other forms of social exclusion, like being beaten up on a playground or being snubbed because you look different from everyone else, getting inexplicably dropped from a game of Cyberball is pretty tame. But the researchers, Naomi Eisenberger and Matthew Lieberman, discovered that even this mild degree of social exclusion activated a specific part of the brain, the dorsal anterior cingulate cortex.

The dorsal anterior cingulate cortex, or dACC, is a small strip of the brain deep in the frontal cortex and part of a complex alarm system that—until this experiment—was primarily known for picking up the distress of physical pain. Walk into the corner of the kitchen table? The dACC activates. Catch your fingers in a drawer? That's your dACC, howling *Make this horrible feeling stop.*

So it was a surprise when the dACC lit up in response, not to being kicked or pinched, but to being left out. Remember, the volunteers weren't experiencing any physical harm. They were simply being excluded. The more emotionally distressed the volunteer was by the exclusion, the more activated the dACC became. The study's conclusion: to our brains, the pain of social rejection is the same as the pain from a physical injury or illness. That our major alarm system fires as a result of both physical pain and social pain is a measure of how important it is for us to be included—and how damaging it is to feel left out.

In our tough, hypercompetitive, gut-it-out culture, it is standard practice for some therapists to treat the pain of rejection or loneliness by encouraging the patient to become more emotionally independent. But when health professionals hear about this study that links social pain with physical pain, they tend to rethink this strategy. That's because the helping professions know to take physical pain seriously. Chronic physical pain is known to have significant medical consequences: it engages the stress response and causes depression, anxiety, and physical health problems. Imagine a person in extreme physical pain who visits an emergency room for help. Doctors might disagree about the best course of action, but most would try to treat both the pain itself as well as the underlying cause. No true medical professional would ever dream of dismissing this person's distress by saying, "We're going to reparent you so that you're less needy." After Cyberball, it seems incredibly cruel to do the same to someone who is suffering from social pain. Instead, it makes more sense to honor the pain and to help the person make healthy connections—because belonging to a group is, for all of us, more than one of life's fun perks. It's a biological requirement.

To understand why the dACC lights up when we're left out, let's look a little more closely at what we know about physical pain. In an interesting job share, your nerves register pain's noxious physical sensation, while your dACC registers how distressed you are by that sensation. The dACC is like a fire alarm that goes off when it senses smoke, warning you to get out of a burning house—except that this alarm goes off when you feel pain, telling you that you've got to do something about an injury. Without this alarm, you might not care enough to stop your hike through the woods and notice that your ankle hurts. Without that information, you might not see the blood that's gushing from a cut, and then you wouldn't know to stanch the flowing blood or to clean the wound. In other words, suffering from the sensation of pain gives you information that helps you preserve your physical well-being and even your life. On rare occasions, when a person has severe chronic pain whose underlying cause cannot be cured, a neurosurgeon may perform a cingulotomy, which is the surgical removal of the portion of the dACC associated with the distress of pain. What is so remarkable about this surgery is that afterward, the person still feels the physical sensation of pain but no longer feels bothered by it. Having a cingulotomy is like disconnecting your wailing smoke detector: you still have pain, but without the distress alarm, you might not have the impetus to seek out the source of the pain and stop it.

The fact that this same area of the dACC also registers the stress of social disconnection was revelatory to scientists, but I imagine our cave-people ancestors would find this discovery a no-brainer. Feeling distress from social pain was a way to alert them to the terribly risky condition of being alone. In a group, they could share information about food sources or team up to fight a mammoth. Alone, they were at high risk of starvation or being gored. And consider the experiment performed in the 1950s by the American psychologist Harry Harlow, who presented baby monkeys with two mother surrogates: a bare wire surrogate that provided food, or a surrogate that did not offer food but was covered with a soft cloth. The monkeys preferred the soft surrogate. For primates—and that includes you and me—there is a powerful

internal drive toward physical closeness, and it's more powerful than our drive for food. That biological need for connection is expressed, partly, in the behavior of the dACC.

When we respect our need for connection, we know to
pay attention to the distress call of the dACC. When we feel
isolated or excluded, we should be able to say, "This feels
awful. I need to do something about this!"—and then apply
our energies to the problem. We can reach out to dependable
friends. Where necessary, we can mend relational rifts or reconnect after long, sometimes awkward separations. We can
let our discomfort propel us to figure out why we're not included in the group, and then either change our behavior or
change the company we seek.

But when we adhere to the idea that it's healthier to be
separate and independent, we have a different reaction to the
brain's distress signal. Instead of listening to it, we try to
suppress it. We say, "I'm an idiot for feeling this way! I'm a
grown person; I shouldn't need anyone!" or "I'll just grin and
bear it." This is like hearing your smoke detector go off and
saying, "Well, I guess I just have to get used to that horrible
sound." You ignore the *cause* of the alarm. Meanwhile, your
house smolders.

I worry about what's happening to our brains in a world
that does not put a priority on connection. As humans, we are
blessed and cursed with the ability to form abstract thoughts
and an enormous capacity to remember past events. These
two characteristics of the human brain can enhance our enjoyment of life. You use these capacities when you conjure up

a fantasy about the date you are about to go on; or when you imagine an afternoon laughing by the pool with your best friends; or when you anticipate a loving reunion with your family after a long business trip away from home. Of course, you never really know how any interaction with another person will go. Essentially, you're making stuff up all the time, based on your past experiences.

The problem comes when you live in a culture that doesn't support healthy relationships or teach people how to make strong connections. Anyone who has a history of repeated social exclusion will use those painful experiences as a template for imagining the future. You expect more exclusion, and you will probably interpret your social encounters according to this expectation. The more you're left out, the more the experience of being left out is knitted into your neural pathways. Instead of anticipating happy reunions and pleasant social events, you tend to assume that you'll be rejected. And when *this* is the case, your dACC is almost always at least a little bit activated. This is especially problematic when people experience rejection and abuse in childhood, a time when their brains are creating their initial pathways for relationship. They live with an alarm system that is constantly ringing. The nerve pathway that is supposed to help them stay connected becomes a nerve pathway that keeps them frightened and apart.

One of my favorite movies, *Good Will Hunting*, illustrates how past relationships can create an overactive dACC. The lead character, Will, was born and raised in gritty South

Boston. Will is an Einstein-level math genius working as a janitor in the hallowed halls of MIT during the day and hanging out with his townie buddies in the evening. He meets a Harvard girl, Skylar, at a local bar, and charms her with his intellect, humor, and good looks. As their relationship gets more intimate, Skylar tries to deepen their commitment—and Will flips out. He rages at her, yelling while revealing his childhood history of neglect and abuse. (I'll go out on a limb here and suggest that screaming is rarely an effective way to communicate vulnerability.) At the peak of his outburst, Will lifts up his shirt and reveals a long red scar on his torso where one of his foster parents had stabbed him. It's clear that by exposing the physical evidence of his deepest wounds, Will is not inviting Skylar to be closer to him; he's aggressively trying to scare her away for good. He caps the scene by telling Skylar that he doesn't love her and storming out of the room.

You might know someone like Will; you might even be someone like Will. His relational template—which can also be called his controlling image, because of the way it significantly controls his adult life—was formed early and reinforced repeatedly by severe beatings, frequent abandonment, neglect, and poverty. For all of us, early environments are the shapers of our young neural pathways, including the distress meter, the dACC. For Will, and for many other survivors of severe abuse or neglect, the dACC has linked intimacy with the threat of abandonment and physical pain. This is the brain's equivalent of a DEFCON 1 scenario. In response, your ability to think gets tossed like nonessential personnel while your brain unleashes its most potent weapon: a cascade of terror and survival instincts. When that happens, a person trying to get closer is indistinguishable from a person moving in for the kill.

Traumatized people are not the only ones with overactive dACCs. Milder experiences with rejection also have lingering effects. Even if you had an ideally loving childhood and rejection-free adolescence, you're still living in a culture that measures success by how little you need other people and by whether you've battled your way to the top. Sure, we *know* that we're supposed to be nice to other people, and that everyone matters. But we still socialize around hierarchy and stratification. Children very early on learn their ABCs—but they also pick up from the adults around them that it's vital to sort the smartest from the dumbest and the fastest from the slowest, to know which kids are shipped from the inner city to the suburbs for a better education and which kids can walk to the same school from their very large house. In our culture, extreme competitiveness is at the core of child rearing and brain building. I'm not disparaging normal, healthy competition here. (Put me on a basketball court, and I will *take you down* . . . but then we'll go out afterward for cake.) I'm talking about the kind of competition that is really judgmental, the kind that becomes the basis for deciding who is worthy of love and acceptance, the kind that has everyone worrying that it's only a matter of time before they're voted off the island.

In a competitive, judgmental, unaccepting environment,

everyone's relational templates are distorted, and everyone's dACC is reactive to some degree. You can see the proof in the adults who have an exaggerated need to control the in-crowd at work or social activities. These people may act like they are kings or queens of the hill, but the harder they try to make sure they are "in" by leaving others out, the more anxious they become about being pushed out of the "in" group. If these folks weren't so afraid of candor, they would tell you that being on the bottom of the pile is so excruciating that they will avoid it at all costs—but being alone at the top is pretty destructive, too.

At the other extreme is the person who moves seamlessly into the outsider role, with no expectation of being welcome or included in any group. The first kind of person carries the weight of rage; the other carries the weight of shame. Both emotions go hand in hand with feeling unworthy of inclusion in the larger human community. And both are the cause and result of social exclusion—and an overactive dACC.

R Is for Resonant: The Mirroring System

Resonance is the deep nonverbal connection between our bodies and brains that allows our hands to feel warm when another person rubs his together, or to sense a friend's sorrow even before she tells you about it. It's the sense of "getting" another person, of instinctively knowing him. The neural basis for resonance is what Rizzolatti and his team first stumbled on to when they discovered that a monkey's brain internally mimicked the action of a researcher lifting his arm.

The mirroring system that creates resonance is the third C.A.R.E. pathway, and its story becomes even more fantastic when you consider the role it plays in understanding what another person is saying. The next time you have ten minutes, a clean pencil, and a nearby friend, try this experiment. It was designed by Paula Niedenthal, of the Niedenthal Emotions Laboratory at the University of Wisconsin–Madison, to highlight the important role of the mirroring system in understanding each other.[2]

Sit comfortably across from each other and think of a detailed, emotional story. The first listener should place a pencil or pen horizontally in his mouth and keep it there while the speaker tells his story. Once the story is told, switch roles.

Did either of you notice a difference in listening while the pen engaged the muscles of your mouth? I use this exercise with workshop participants, and I hear a similar set of responses every time. The first few comments usually focus on how ridiculous and distracted the speakers felt as they tried to communicate with someone who has a pen in his mouth. When pushed to think about the content of what they heard when they were listeners, the reaction is usually unanimous— it is more difficult to understand what is being said when the muscles in your face are busy holding the pen. For most of us, this is a strange and unexpected response. After all, the pen was not stuck in your ears. What in the world is going on here?

Stephen Wilson was a research student at UCLA when he began studying the connection between speaking and listening, using functional brain imaging to see the brain in action. He discovered that the exact same part of the brain was activated when his research subjects were listening as when they were speaking.[3] In another study looking at the overlap between speaking and listening, the German neurologist Ingo Meister used another new technique called *transcranial magnetic stimulation* to effectively turn off the speech center of a person's brain. He found that when the motor neurons controlling speech are turned off, people have difficulty understanding what they are hearing.[4] Apparently, when in conversation, internally mirroring the other person's speech is essential to understanding it.

So what happens when your face is really paralyzed? Let's say rather than placing a pencil in your mouth to disable your ability to make expressions, you have a condition that prohibits you from moving the muscles of your face. People born with Moebius syndrome, a rare disorder that affects the cranial nerves, present researchers with an opportunity to explore this question in real life. People with Moebius syndrome live with a frozen face and are found to have a more difficult time communicating their emotions to other people. Given how much we count on facial expressions in showing our feelings to others, this is no big shock. What has been surprising to researchers is that Moebius syndrome also makes it more difficult to read other people's emotions. Just as holding a pencil between your teeth keeps your brain from mimicking another person's speech, paralysis of the facial muscles prevents people with Moebius syndrome from internally copying other people. Because this mimicking is key to understanding what a person is hearing, victims of this disorder have a much more difficult time understanding other people. People who get Botox treatments for facial wrinkles also have a harder time reading others.[5] Because injections of Botox temporarily paralyze the muscles, they aren't able to perform internal mimicking in the same the way they are used to.

Your brain mirrors far more than other people's movements. After the Rizzolatti monkey study, a number of studies showed that the mirroring system works on a profound level. If you see another person experiencing pain, your brain mimics the experience. When you watch another person smile or frown, both of your brains will activate in the same regions as that person's, although your brain activity won't be as intense. Your mirror system activates even when another person simply gives a hint that he is about to do something. If, say, you're in line at Starbucks and the man in front of you begins to move his arm, you may simply "know" that he is about to point to a slice of lemon cake—even though he's not actually pointing yet—and that's because your brain is copying the experience and using that information to read his actions and emotions, and anticipate what he might do. And other people are doing the same with you.

The mirroring system appears to be a crucial element in the complex act of empathy. Once your mirror system registers information about what another person is doing or the feeling she is expressing, that information passes through the insula, a small strip of tissue that lies deep within the brain and helps attach content to feeling states. The mirroring experience becomes a feeling you have in connection with another person's feeling.

Of course, there's a limit. We don't copy every action we witness in another person, or feel every single thing that everyone else around us is feeling. That would be exhausting and paralyzing. A world of unfiltered emotions would be a nightmare! Fortunately, for most of us, biology has, again, saved the day by creating a *super mirroring system* as an integral part of the grand design to read others.

The super mirroring system acts like the brakes on an idling car. These days, cars with automatic transmissions have a baseline level of movement when you pull up to a stoplight. If all you do is take your foot off the gas, the car moves forward. If you want to keep the car from moving, you have to put your foot on the brake. Likewise, the classical mirroring system is constantly picking up the feelings and actions of people around you—and sometimes you need to put a brake on that activity and keep yourself in a more neutral state. That's when the super mirroring system steps in. Thanks to the super mirroring system, if you see someone crying, you do not necessarily break out in sobs; if you see someone reaching for the coffee shop pastry, your arm does not have to reach out, too.

Marco Iacoboni, the UCLA psychiatrist and author, believes that the super mirroring system has a regulatory, inhibitory impact on our classical mirroring system so that we do not physically act out every action or feeling we see in others. In collaboration with Itzhak Fried, a researcher whose studies of epilepsy involved placing electrodes on individual brain cells, Iacoboni is beginning to map the super mirroring system in the frontal lobe of the brain. Whether or not you actually enact a movement or simply know that another has made the same movement is dependent on how the two systems—the classical mirroring system and super mirroring system—interact. The classical mirroring system fires both when you move your arm and when you watch someone across the room move his arm. The inhibitory, super mirroring system is more active when you watch someone move his arm, however, and less active when you are moving your arm.

My experience with a client, Jessica, shows how both systems work together to bring about an empathic response. Jessica texted me the night before her therapy appointment to tell me that her boyfriend of one year, the man she thought she would marry—the man *everyone* thought she would marry— had broken up with her. Ray had been unusually distant for about two weeks, but Jessica figured that with the holidays coming up and with his family in town, he was simply busy and less available. She tried to reassure herself that things would be back to normal once the New Year started. They met up for what Jessica thought would be an ordinary dinner, and he broke up with her on the spot. The text read simply: *Ray just broke up with me. I am devastated!*

When I saw her in my waiting room the next morning,

my mirroring system was immediately activated. As my eyes registered her red, sad-looking eyes and the downward turn of her mouth, neurons in my prefrontal cortex were stimulated so that internally my own state mimicked her misery. Nerve cells in my somatosensory cortex re-created the state of having itchy, puffy, crying-all-night eyes. As my insula relayed the information to my own visceral system, I felt a tightening in my stomach and a heaviness in my chest. This empathetic experience of Jessica's pain happened in an instant.

Fortunately, my super mirroring system (a therapist's best friend) was also activated, enabling me to have a taste of what my client was feeling—but *just* a taste. As Jessica sat and wept, head in her hands, I felt a tear well up in my own eye, but I never got close to sobbing myself. This ability to modulate is crucial to maintaining healthy connections. Think about it. If we were all simply mimicking everything all the time, there would be a single feeling that traveled through humanity in a gigantic wave. Thankfully, that doesn't happen.

When the mirroring system fires in empathic response, it is not an exact duplicate of another person's experience, nor is it a complete merger of feelings. Jessica's sadness, however, was strong enough and clear enough for us to be joined through an empathic connection. Just as a fish knows how to turn in unison with the rest of its school, Jessica and I instinctively knew how to move closer together in this magical, mutual moment. It's not just emotional; it's biological, down to our nerve cells. Physically, emotionally, and neurologically, we were in sync. It was a reminder to both of us that, as human beings, we are never alone in the world.

Unfortunately, the separation-individuation model of human development doesn't leave a lot of space for thinking about the mirroring system and warm, connected closeness. It was not too long ago that mental health providers were taught that empathy did not belong in the therapy hour. The idea was that empathy was a contagion that would distort the real work of therapy—which was, supposedly, helping a person identify mental blocks preventing him from "standing on his own two feet." Now many therapists identify empathy as *the* most important ingredient in a healthy healing relationship. But you still see the old attitude in the idea that we're not supposed to need other people to share in our happiness or heartache, or that healthy individuals should be able to avoid "catching" other people's feelings. You certainly see it in our competitive day-to-day environment, in which we tend to view other people as adversaries, not potential friends, and everyone is under near-constant stress. In our ideal of success, you are admired for your ability to do what is necessary without considering the impact on others. To unwind from the tension, people play violent video games or watch violent television shows.

This environment actively undermines the natural physiology of connection. In a competitive, visually violent world, you're exposed to so much pain that the only way to thrive is to ignore the signals that your mirroring system sends you about other people's feelings, actions, and intentions. It's true that mirroring activities happen involuntarily, but it's possible to consciously reject the signals that other people send you. Over time, it's even possible to develop the capacity to dissociate from your own body, which is a bigger version of paralyzing your facial muscles by holding a pencil in your mouth—it makes it harder for you to decode the feelings of others. When you are disconnected from your body, you also miss out on the sensations that signal your own feeling states. Years ago, I treated a woman who had been physically abused as a child. Over the years, she learned to decouple her bodily messages from her thoughts, as a way to protect herself from feeling pain. She had so effectively ignored her basic body signals for so long, however, that as an adult, she had no idea what it felt like to be hungry. That slight ache you feel in the sternum when you wake up in the morning? You and I know this to be hunger—but my client barely registered the feeling. When she *did* notice the feeling, she thought it was a stomachache. As a result, she rarely ate in the mornings, and the rest of the day she barely ate enough to keep herself going. She had to relearn how to focus on her body in order to understand messages that she should have read instinctively.

Whenever an uncomfortable empathic message—like pain—comes through, you can choose to withdraw from it. Do this often enough, and your mirroring system takes a hit. Because the mirroring system is made of nerve cells throughout your brain, especially in the areas that govern action, sensation, and feeling, the system can thrive only when it's used repeatedly. As you'll see in the next chapter, complex neural pathways are made stronger by being "wired together"—by being stimulated over and over. It's this wiring together of different brain regions that forms the 3-dimensional experience of another person's world. It makes the information you get clearer and more complex, which means that the empathic response you feel is more likely to be in tune with what the person is actually feeling. Without frequent stimulation, the pathways between the neurons become weaker and less able to carry signals. Our complex mirror nerve system needs to be stimulated in order for us to maintain this gift of reading each other.

Is it inevitable that we will lose our ability to communicate and read one another as we interact increasingly through technology? I don't think so, but it is necessary to educate children and adults about the essential role of the mirroring system in our human interactions and teach them how to keep this part of their nervous systems robust. As I sit typing this chapter in Panera, I see and hear groups engaged in good old-fashioned conversation. Elderly men and women are gathered at a large table, laughing, talking, drinking coffee, eating muffins—and stimulating their mirroring system. Another group of coworkers is discussing a work project, two of them huddled over their computers. They are typing ideas, talking, laughing, drinking coffee—and stimulating their mirroring systems. My kids are now at school. In a typical day, they might be working in small groups in science lab and learning how to divvy up tasks and to cooperate in writing a report; sitting at lunch acting goofy with their friends; or asking teachers for help—in all these interactions, they are stimulating their mirroring systems. These human interactions are as ubiquitous as Apple products these days. What shapes us is not so much the devices we use, but the culture in which the device is placed. If, as a society, we value human connection as the center of our lives, and if we understand the need to stimulate our mirroring systems to maintain our ability to read others and to cooperate in groups, then the electronic world will follow.

E Is for Energetic: The Dopamine Reward System

On the fourth relational pathway, we meet up with dopamine, a neurotransmitter that makes our lives feel more gratifying. Like many of our neurotransmitters, dopamine plays a different role in our brains and bodies depending on which neural pathway it is traveling. The dopamine pathway that is most directly connected to relationships is the one that is involved in our brain's reward system. This pathway, known as the *mesolimbic pathway*, starts in the brain stem. It then sends projections to the amygdala, which is involved in feelings and emotions, and travels through the thalamus, which acts like a kind of relay station. The mesolimbic pathway ends in the orbitomedial prefrontal cortex, where some of the decision-making process takes place. The pathway then loops back to the brain stem and modulates the production of dopamine.

When dopamine is stimulated in this pathway, you feel good. Remember Jean Baker Miller's description of growth-fostering relationships as "zestful"? Dopamine gives you that zest; it can feel like a shot of warm, glowing, motivating energy. This is a system whose purpose is to reward healthy, growth-promoting activities—like eating well, having sex, and being in a good relationship—with a supply of dopamine that makes us feel great. The resulting feelings of elation make us want to participate in more of those healthy activities. It encourages the human population to do what's good for us.

It's a brilliant setup, but only when it works the way it's supposed to. In an ideal world, you're born with a brain that pairs human contact and dopamine. And then, in your first months and years, your early relationships are so rewarding and healthy that your dopamine system learns to connect relationships even more tightly with feeling good. In one study, the more dopamine receptors in the striatum (part of the forebrain), the better your social status and social support.[6] More dopamine, more interconnection.

But what happens to this pathway when a baby or child does not experience snuggly, supportive relationships? What happens to children who are raised to be fiercely "independent" above all else? To children raised to believe that counting on others throughout life makes them weak and vulnerable? In these children, relationships become disconnected from the dopamine reward system. Seen from the brain's perspective, this is a logical protective step: if relationships are threatening or seen as unhealthy, they should not be paired up with a rewarding boost of dopamine. These children become adults who simply don't get much pleasure from relationships. Instead of becoming energized by friendships—even good ones—they are drained and depleted by the interaction.

When the dopamine system is disconnected from healthy relationships, the brain looks for other ways to feel good—so it seeks out other ways to stimulate the dopamine system. Those "other ways" are familiar to all of us: overeating, drug and alcohol abuse, compulsive sex, shopping, risk-taking activities, gambling.

This is why you may have heard either dopamine or the mesolimbic pathway getting a bad rap. Recently it's been discovered that all drugs of addiction—and in fact all addictions, whether or not they're drug-based—stimulate the mesolimbic pathway and release dopamine. The more this pathway is repeatedly stimulated by a particular drug or activity, the more robust the addiction gets.

It's important to understand how a pathway that's meant in part to encourage healthy human connection can get hijacked to create drug addictions. Addictive drugs, such as cocaine, heroin, and marijuana, have a two-pronged attack on the central nervous system. A drug's first action on the body is unique to that drug. Cocaine produces its euphoria and grandiosity by stimulating the release of a large amount of the naturally occurring neurotransmitter norepinephrine. Heroin, on the other hand, works by imitating the effects of the body's naturally occurring opioids.

While the initial high a drug causes is compelling, it is the second action of addictive drugs, the stimulation of the dopamine reward system, that ultimately leads to addiction. With repeated use of a drug, the body adapts by either producing less dopamine or down-regulating its receptors. When this happens, you get less of a "hit," or reward, from the drug. Over time, tolerance develops so you need more of the drug to produce the same high. This double whammy of an altered mental state and stimulation of the dopamine reward system serves as the perfect storm for addiction.

Substance abuse may be the most well-known addiction, but it certainly is not alone. In reality, any activity done so repetitively that it gets in the way of other meaningful activities in life is an addiction. In a perversion of the dopamine pathway's original purpose, your brain learns to pair dopamine with activities that are incredibly *un*healthy. When the powerful chemistry of addiction sets in, humans are no different from rats in a lab that obsessively press a lever to receive stimulants even as they are starving to death. Producing dopamine trumps all other life-sustaining activities.

The science of addiction is specific and devastating. But in a way, we all seek out dopamine. We *all* live from one dopamine hit to another, and it's natural for us to want to feel good. What matters is the source of the dopamine. It can be as life affirming as drinking water or cuddling a newborn baby—or it can be as destructive as a drug addiction. But every single one of us craves dopamine. It is simply the nature of human physiology and the behavior of the dopamine reward system.

When we are under pressure to be highly separate, intensely independent individuals, we are at risk for cutting ourselves off from one of the primary healthy sources of dopamine. But it is possible to rewire your brain so that it can get more pleasure out of relationships—to crave human contact instead of unhealthy substitutes. The key, as Louis Cozolino writes in *The Neuroscience of Human Relationships*, is to understand that "healing involves reconnecting our dopamine reward system to relationships."[7] With practice and an understanding of how the dopamine system works, you can teach your brain to stop searching for dopamine in all the wrong places—and that the easiest way to feel better is to reach out to another safe human being.

The science is clear. Social disconnection stimulates our brain's pain pathways and our stress response systems, making it more likely we'll seek out unhealthy sources of dopamine. We also miss out on the richness of human experience, of the empathic connections that are intricately tied to the depth and breadth of feeling and emotion.

But there is plenty that you can do to nourish your neurological pathways for connection. If they are damaged, you can start to heal them. If they are neglected, you can cultivate them. And if they are stressed, you can soothe them. In the next chapter, I'll describe the science that is teaching us how to change our brains for the better.

Chapter 3

THE THREE RULES
OF BRAIN CHANGE

By now it should be clear that we are not as psychologically independent and separate as we've been led to believe. For better or worse, relationships reach deep inside our brains to shape how we feel, think, and react.

Ideally, our relationships are healthy and help us feel great—Calm, Accepted, Resonant, and Energetic. So great, in fact, that we crave *more* relationships, and we knit together a network of people who help us mature into even greater relational complexity. If that doesn't sound like you, well . . . welcome to the club, my friend. In a world that dismisses our biological need for warm, human connection, most of us have suffered through some pretty bad relationships or felt the chill of isolation. That means our brains have suffered, too. Instead of feeling Calm, Accepted, Resonant, and Energetic, you might feel any or all of the opposite: irritable, rejected, bewildered, and tired. You might even have the sense that you're just not good with people, or that you weren't built to enjoy relationships.

There is another perspective that needs to shift, and this is the idea that a history of difficult relationships can be traced to a fixed, unchangeable flaw in our personalities.

This is untrue. Both our genes and the environment will, over the years, write particular relational patterns into the brain—but they are not necessarily written onto our souls. It can be helpful to see these problems as nothing more than electrical impulses that, instead of following the four C.A.R.E. pathways for healthy relationships, go off track. With understanding and effort and support, it is possible to redirect those wayward impulses. We can shrink undesirable neural pathways that undermine our relationships and strengthen other pathways that are more beneficial. We can even grow neural connections that are completely new. These new or healthier pathways can help us do what we are designed to do: enjoy satisfying relationships in which we can grow.

Neurology Does a 180

Sally, a client who initially came to me because she had developed a habit of lying to her boyfriends, is a good example of how an adult can learn to change her brain, and how relationships are a vital part of that change.

My mother used to say to my siblings and me, "Why lie? The truth is far more interesting." This was not the case with Sally. Real life was almost never as interesting as her lies. If Sally didn't feel like going out on a Saturday night, she'd tell her boyfriend that she was going on a weekend trip . . . to London. If she was running late for a date, she'd say that her tires had been slashed. There were other kinds of lies, too: if Sally's boyfriend liked action movies, Sally—who preferred foreign films—would pretend to like them, too. Did Sally want to help her boyfriend finance a car? Let him move in without paying rent? Of course she did!

Flexibility is essential to relationships, perhaps especially romantic relationships. We have to be able to imagine each other's experiences of life and compassionately negotiate our different needs. But Sally was a relational contortionist who twisted herself like a pretzel to fit the desires of whatever man she happened to be dating. She wanted men to feel that she could perfectly suit their needs—that she would never be disagreeable, would never be late, and would never want to do anything different from what her boyfriend wanted to do. Sally's lies weren't just lies; they were her strategy for staying connected in her romantic relationships. They were also a source of dopamine, the neurotransmitter that creates a sense of pleasurable energy. When she told a whopper, she felt a rush of excitement—would she get caught this time?—as well as anticipation of tenderness from her boyfriend as he heard of her latest tragedy or her willingness to support his plans. But Sally's romances came to a predictable end: within a few months, she'd told so many lies and hidden so much of herself that the relationship was unsustainable. Sally came to me because she wanted to stop this pattern. But after more than a decade of advanced lying, could she change?

Common methods of addressing a problem like Sally's include the "you need to have more self-control" school of thought, which draws on the old separation-individuation model. The general idea is that Sally has to get a grip on herself and stop doing things that undermine her relationships. If she feels the impulse to lie, she should simply ignore that impulse, even if she has to white-knuckle her way through it until the temptation passes. There is some wisdom here, because self-control is an essential element of change. But this approach doesn't account for the complex role of relationships in Sally's problem, or the way that lying had become wired to the dopamine reward system in her brain. The self-control approach also doesn't take advantage of neurological methods of brain change. (For example, the neurochemicals produced by healthy relationships can help melt pathways for bad habits and solidify new pathways that are more desirable.) Not to mention that the self-control approach leads to a classically depressing circle: if Sally feels that the measure of her maturity is the ability to stand alone and control herself, she will feel like a childish failure if she gives in to temptation and tells a lie. Then she'll seek comfort in her most reliable source of dopamine—namely, telling some really impressive lies in order to elicit excitement and love.

Then again, some therapists might try to help Sally break her lying habit by looking at her present and past relationships. A psychodynamic therapist would probably try to understand her family history, for example, and talk about how Sally's parents had never accepted the true, real Sally—they'd preferred the false version she'd learned to present to them. There would likely be a lot of discussion about how she tended to choose boyfriends who were a little *too* comfortable having a woman meet all their needs. Most of all, there would be a big dose of understanding acceptance. These are wonderful qualities to bring into a healing, therapeutic relationship. However, they are not always enough to bring about brain change, and even when they are, that change can be a long time coming. Although I suspected that Sally's lying was connected to the nature of her past and present relationships, I worried that traditional talk therapy would not be enough to help her dig out of this entrenched habit.

Why are we stuck with only these two options—self-control and therapeutic acceptance—for changing habits and relational patterns? One reason is that most people, even therapists, aren't aware of the neuroscience of connection. Another reason is that for centuries, the brain was seen as fixed and unchangeable. Yet there is overwhelming evidence that the brain can change—that it is, in fact, always changing.

Your Brain Is Alive

Until recently, scientists could not actually see the brain or measure its components. Tucked away neatly inside the skull, its nature has been hidden. Scientists who were unable to witness the brain in action have struggled over the centuries to create models and theories to explain its enormous capacity. The brain has been compared to a chest of drawers with many discrete compartments; to a filing cabinet with folders that can be opened and closed; to the Wizard of Oz, controlling the city from behind his curtain; and to a supercomputer, endlessly performing operations along its circuits. All these analogies are to essentially inorganic, mechanical objects. These objects aren't alive. They don't grow and they don't change.

For the most part, scientists believed the same thing about the human brain, with one exception: childhood. It was believed that childhood was the only time that the brain could grow and adapt. A child soaks up signals from the internal and external environment and—for better or worse—the child's brain adapts to that environment. In a case that Antonio Battro documents in his book *Half a Brain Is Enough: The Story of Nico,* doctors removed the right lobe of a boy's brain in an attempt to treat his seizures. Despite Nico's loss of crucial brain tissue, he developed virtually without deficits. He developed not just the kind of functions associated with the left side of the brain, but musical and mathematical abilities as well—even though those functions are usually controlled by the brain's right side. Battro explains that the traditional explanation for how the boy's brain could compensate when half of it had been removed was that a child's brain is still developing during childhood.[1]

The old belief was that this kind of extreme compensation for a brain deficit or injury was possible—though rare—only while a child is still growing. As a child moves into puberty, scientists believed, the brain becomes fixed in place and no outside pressure can reshape it. No more growth, no more adaptation. At that point, if something from the outer world does damage the brain, that damage is mostly irreparable. To take a psychological example, children who grow up with unattuned, uninterested caregivers develop brains that result in behavior patterns reflecting hopelessness. According to the old model of brain development, such a child's only hope is early, caring intervention to reshape the brain. Without it, the child's emotional fate is sealed. Other physical and emotional traumas could carve their signatures into the young brain, too.

In an extension of the brain-as-hardware metaphor, it was also believed that the brain's destiny was to break down. Little by little, as it took the hits that befell it over the course of a normal lifetime, the brain's components would rust and short out. Or it could suffer a spectacular crash, with large parts of the brain going dark as the result of an accident, infection, or stroke. In this view, cells in the central nervous system are like pieces in a set of antique china; if you break one, there is nothing to do but sweep up the broken pieces and carry on as best you can with whatever is left intact.

No one believed that brain cells might be able to repair themselves or regenerate, or develop new connections among themselves. This depressing neurological "fact" had serious consequences for people who had injuries or illnesses that affected the brain. Until about fifteen years ago, it was standard for rehabilitation hospitals to aggressively treat people in the first few weeks or months after their injury, but once the brain swelling subsided and improvement plateaued, it was believed that nothing more could be done. Rehabilitation meant learning how to compensate for whatever deficits you'd developed. If you injured your visual cortex (the part of the brain usually associated with vision), it meant you had cortical blindness, period. If you lost function of your left arm, that arm would forever hang limp. Rehab therapists would teach you how to get around without seeing or how to get your groceries through the front door while using only your right arm. And if you had difficult relationships as a child, it was assumed that these relationships left an indelible scar on your capacity to connect.

Fortunately, this view of the brain can be now placed in the medical-history archives, filed away with other outdated ideas like bloodletting and black bile (the "humour" that Hippocrates thought caused cancer and other illnesses). Although the brain still needs protection, and I don't recommend knocking it around, your brain is not quite the fixed, fragile object we once thought it was. As you'll see throughout the book, you can use the rules of brain change to solve problems, repair your C.A.R.E pathways, and strengthen your relationships.

Brain Change Rule Number 1: Use It or Lose It

A friend of mine developed tinnitus, a disorder in which your nerves "hear" a sound that is not there. She described the sound as a high-pitched noise that stayed in the background during the day, when she was distracted by work or her kids. When she lay down to sleep at night, however, the noise seemed to get louder. With fewer other sounds to compete with the noise, nighttime became a nightmare. After a few months she was chronically sleep deprived; eventually, she was depressed. Then her doctor told her about a new treatment, one that would use a principle called *competitive neuroplasticity* to weaken the area of her cortex that was producing the phantom sound. The treatment was time intensive: for a couple of hours a day, the doctor had my friend listen to music she loved but from which the pitch that matched the ringing sound was deleted. After the treatments, her tinnitus was dramatically reduced and no longer interfered with her ability to sleep at night. Slowly, her life regained its old, normal hectic form.

If you'd had tinnitus several years ago, you would have

been told that it was untreatable. It was in 1997 that a surge of discoveries about the brain began, discoveries that led straight to this treatment for tinnitus, along with therapies for other disorders that originate in the nervous system. These are treatments that let us rewrite our brain pathways. They are becoming more familiar in certain settings, especially the rehabilitation hospital and the occupational therapist's office. In other settings, including the psychotherapy office, they are not familiar enough. When your relational pathways aren't working in the way you'd like them to, it is possible to change them.

The watershed event in 1997 was a study by Peter Eriksson, a Swedish neuroscientist who proved that the adult human brain can grow new neurons. Until then, it was thought that the adult brain was like hair on a balding scalp: although it was natural to lose neurons as you aged, and not necessarily a sign of disease, you could never grow new ones. Eriksson's discovery had many implications, but one of its greatest effects was to throw open a door onto a new field of research. This field is called *neuroplasticity*; the idea is that the adult brain can be remolded and reshaped, much the way a soft plastic polymer can be pulled and pushed into shape. Suddenly, the hardware metaphors for the brain no longer fit the known facts. The brain is not fixed. It is more versatile and more resilient than anyone ever guessed. It is more alive.

Neural pathways are constantly responding to their environment. When you stimulate a brain pathway repeatedly, it grows stronger. It grows more myelin, allowing electrical impulses to travel faster along its length. More branches develop, making the path wider. (Seen through a microscope, a well-traveled neural pathway has so many branches that it looks wild and bushy, like Einstein's hair.) Brain pathways also compete with one another for space, so as you use a particular pathway more and more frequently, other pathways die off. This leaves fewer alternative pathways for the brain's electrical impulses to travel. Instead of dispersing themselves along several different smaller paths, more impulses run together along the well-traveled one.

But if neurons are starved of stimuli for long enough and if your brain does not sense a demand for their use, they can wither away. If you could look at the brain of a person who's lost the use of a body part to amputation or paralysis, you'd see that the brain's "map" no longer features roads and pathways for that part. The area those pathways used to travel is not empty, however. It is grown over by other, nearby pathways that are taking advantage of the abandoned real estate.

This is why the tinnitus treatment works. The competitive sound forces the patient off the old pathway so that it's not used so repetitively; it also encourages a new, alternative pathway to grow. Rehabilitation specialists harness the use-it-or-lose-it rule with new protocols for stroke victims. Instead of merely teaching them how to compensate for lost function, they also will stimulate the neural pathways for the disabled body part by working it over and over.

The "use it or lose it" rule is also at work when people get stuck in relational patterns. You can see this when a long-married couple has "forgotten" how to talk about their problems without bickering and sniping: the neural pathways for these habits have, over the course of their marriage, become hardened and inflexible. Or when a woman always shows up with a date who drinks too much. For a person like this, there is probably a psychological tug of familiarity at work—maybe her parents had similar attributes—but there is a neurological factor, too. A neural track was laid down in her brain in childhood, creating a template that associates important relationships with alcohol. As she follows that template as an adult, and continues to follow it, she wears a neurological groove, replaying one set of preferences and behaviors over and over, until the alternative paths weaken from disuse. You also see "use it or lose it" when someone undergoes what looks like a significant change of temperament. A quiet person moves to a big city and becomes bolder; a selfish person undergoes a hardship and becomes more empathic. The changed circumstances force changes in the brain pathways.

Sally, my client who lied to her boyfriends, had a fast, strong neural pathway for lying that had been reinforced over years of repetition. Our work together would run in the same direction as the therapy for tinnitus. We wanted to intentionally weaken the path of her habit. At the same time, we'd stimulate some alternative pathways—relational ones—in the hope that they'd grow strong enough to compete with the old one.

Brain Change Rule Number 2: Neurons That Fire Together, Wire Together

The second rule of brain change is **Neurons that fire together, wire together.** Like people, neurons are stronger in groups. When neurons that are close to each other repeatedly fire at the same time, they will eventually link up and form part of a neural network or pathway. A neuron is made up of a nucleus, axons, and dendrites. Axons send messages toward other neurons, and dendrites receive other neurons' messages. It's as if axons and dendrites reach out from separate neurons and hold hands. (Their handholding is done across a gap called a *synapse*, into which neurotransmitters release chemical messengers that are passed from neuron to neuron.) In an immature nervous system, this handholding looks clean and simple. You can imagine that Neuron A holds hands with Neuron B, which holds hands with Neuron C—sort of like children playing a game of Red Rover. But with stimulation and the passage of time, neurons grow more axons and dendrites. They reach out to hold hands with many neurons, forming complex neural networks.

The direction that these pathways take, and their degree of complexity, is based partly on the DNA of the individual neurons. But the new field of epigenetics tells us that the expression of DNA is profoundly affected by the stimulation your neurons receive from the environment. DNA aside, your neurons and neural pathways are also directly shaped by environmental triggers. Consider the track that leads from the motor cortex of the brain to the right index finger. We're all born with this track. As a child who is studying piano repeatedly stimulates that track, it grows stronger, with more axons and dendrites—that's the "use it or lose it" rule in effect. But those axons and dendrites don't simply wave around with nothing to do. They reach out and hold hands with other neurons; in "neurospeak," they recruit neurons from nearby pathways. Brain scans of concert pianists show that the neural networks for their fingers are richly interconnected; the axons and dendrites of the relevant neurons have grown together so tightly that the whole hand operates as one unified part, rather than as five separate fingers plus palm and wrist. This interconnectedness results from the repeated stimulation of the different parts of the hand at the same time. Over the years, the hand's neural network recruits even more neurons into its pathway. The nerve cells themselves will be slightly larger because they have each grown so many branches, but a thicker pathway also results from the pathway finding more and more friends, all joining into this neural network. If a pathway like this is used often enough, it will actually take up *less* physical space in the brain. This isn't because the pathway is weaker. It's because the pathway has become incredibly streamlined, and efficient, sort of like a flabby body that gets leaner as it grows stronger.

In Sally, this rule of brain change—neurons that fire together, wire together—has created a complex, strong pathway for habitual lying. When she told a lie, she felt thrilled, like a kid on a roller coaster. Also, her boyfriend would become more understanding and sympathetic in response to the lie, and Sally felt comforted. All these feelings were recruited into a neural pathway that also became linked to lying. (More about neurons and dopamine, the feel-good neurotransmitter, in a moment.) Sally's brain was like a pianist's, except that instead of recruiting neurons into the pathways for her hand, it was the pathways for lying, excitement, love, and comfort that had become so rich and interconnected.

I wanted Sally's brain to change which neurons were wiring together and firing together. This would be a little like asking a pianist to become a lacrosse player; in effect, Sally would learn to let one set of pathways wither while building up a completely different set.

Brain Change Rule Number 3: Repetition, Repetition, Dopamine

Almost twenty years ago, I attended the first conference on the neurobiology of post-traumatic stress disorder (PTSD), held in New York. I was on a steep learning curve regarding issues of trauma and abuse and was thrilled to hear many of the leading researchers in the field present their piece of the neurobiological puzzle. The results were fascinating. People suffering from post-traumatic stress disorder were found to have a dysregulated hypothalamic-pituitary-adrenal axis, too much amygdala activation, too much norepinephrine stimulation, and not enough cortisol production. I'll spare you the rest of the terminology, but suffice it to say that the sum total of these alterations in brain chemistry is a very reactive, irritable person.

We all wanted to help people with PTSD, but at the time, treatments for the disorder were poorly understood and difficult to implement. One research group stuck out, however, because their treatment was working. Edna Foa, a clinician and researcher from the University of Pennsylvania, was getting better than usual results in a group treatment designed for women who had a history of abuse, even when compared to other therapists who were using group treatments. Conference attendees were puzzled by the results. At one point, someone mentioned that Edna was an "unusual woman"—apparently this was code for a warm relational style that was very different from the standard detached application of treatment protocols. But no one (including me) went as far as to say that the relationships she was forming with clients or that the patients formed with one another in group therapy may have been a factor both in the research and in the success of her standardized treatment.

I can look back now and see that in Edna's program, the therapeutic and group relationship was likely a direct contributor to her success. The chemistry of healthy relationships enhances your ability to change your old patterns. Change is a form of new learning, and learning, at the microscopic level, is about making new neurons. We're making new synaptic connections, too: when we learn, axons and dendrites are reaching out to different neurons. The structure of the brain is being altered.

It's almost impossible for this neurological change to take place when you're feeling cut off from others. Isolation is a stressful state for both your body and brain, especially when you sense that you're being rejected or judged; your body reads it as a dangerous situation. It prepares you to answer the question, "How am I going to survive the next few hours?" As the sympathetic nervous system shifts into high gear, adrenaline races through your body, diverting energy to the large muscles in your arms and legs and helping your heart and lungs provide the oxygen that will fuel your body's fight-or-flight response. At these times, your body doesn't have the interest in or energy for building new synaptic connections for learning. It's simply busy saving itself.

When you are in healthy connection, your physiology is soothed, and you have a higher capacity for learning. Although you need a small amount of "good stress" to arouse your nervous system and give you a little boost of energy (think of how a skilled coach can put just enough pressure on you—but not too much—to help you play at your highest level), you can't effectively grow new synaptic connections unless you feel basically safe. Healthy relationships release a full cascade of chemicals that ease the way for learning. These include serotonin, which in certain areas of the brain has a calming effect, and norepinephrine, which has a focusing effect in small quantities. Oxytocin in particular appears to propel both relationships and learning. When you're in love or when you become a new parent, oxytocin floods the body; in a literal sense, it makes you want to reach out to another person, to hold and touch them. In his book *The Brain That Changes Itself,* psychiatrist Norman Doidge describes the theory that oxytocin encourages brain change by melting away some existing brain pathways so that you have room for new ones.[2] Again, this comes back to relationships—it allows us to change our old ways so that we can prepare for a different kind of life, one with a new partner or child. Oxytocin is released, although in smaller quantities, by friendships and other warm connections. If you want your brain to build a new pathway, you can speed along the process by enlisting oxytocin.

The neurochemical with the strongest capacity to encourage brain change may be dopamine, which is also released by growth-fostering relationships. I've already mentioned the dopamine reward system, which is so compelling that it creates addictions when dopamine pathways are connected to the wrong activities. By supplying your brain with a hit of dopamine from healthy relationships, you create a powerful connection between the activity you want to encourage and the body's natural cravings. You're offering the brain a reward for reshaping itself. Neuroscientist Martha Burns tells teachers to think of dopamine as the brain's "Save button," because when dopamine is paired with learning, the neural pathways associated with that new information are solidified and retained.[3]

For all these reasons, a healthy human relationship can be

the biggest asset you have when you are trying to change. At the same time, a healthy relationship without repetitive stimulation of a new pathway may not be able to effectively compete for brain space with existing unwanted neural pathways and their troublesome behaviors. This is why a third rule for brain change, whether you are in therapy or trying to change without professional support, is clear: repetition, repetition, dopamine.

Putting the Three Rules into Action

A visual may help illustrate how to put the three rules of brain change to work. One of our recent winters in New England was a bear, with more snowstorms than I can remember since my childhood in Maine. During the third major snowstorm in a single week, my friend's car became stuck at the end of our driveway, the back two wheels spinning helplessly on a patch of ice. Each time she stepped on the gas pedal, my friend's wheels spun faster and faster. The pathway transformed from a slick of ice atop the snow's surface to a deepening icy groove. The more she revved the engine, the deeper the car went, and the more stuck it became. This is what happens with habits and relational patterns. They may start as a small nuisance, but as the action is repeated over and over again, the neural pathway bulks up. The habit becomes entrenched.

When my friend's car was stuck, she needed a new pathway. The tires needed to land on a different section of the driveway that was not on the patch of ice. To free the car, I created a different pathway by packing salt and sand down into the deep groove. The wheels found some traction on this new surface. The car lurched onto the clean side of the driveway, and she was able to drive away.

Changing your brain and your old habits requires a similar shift, away from a neural pathway that is undermining your health to a more desirable pathway that stimulates both dopamine (to help solidify new habits) and healthy interpersonal connection (to stimulate the connected brain, decreasing stress and isolation and improving learning). Some people like to imagine that they are setting physical roadblocks down on the unwanted neural pathway, to block the impulse from traveling through. Other people like to imagine that they are lifting up the impulse that is originating in their brain and redirecting it to another pathway, one that's more pleasant. These images are an oversimplification of what happens in the brain, but this is an instance when simplicity has an advantage. When you feel yourself careening off into a bad habit, you might find that the habit's pull is so forceful that it's hard to remember what you need to do to change. But if you have a strong, clear image in mind, you are more likely to coax your mind into behaving differently.

Let's go back to Sally, who needed to decide on roadblocks she might set up to divert her from lying to her boyfriend.

There was no right or wrong answer, I explained. The first roadblock could be whatever allowed her to pause, for even a second, when she felt the temptation to lie. I encouraged her to be unafraid of taking very small steps, which are less overwhelming and easier to make than sweeping changes.

I had another recommendation to make. Many people come to define themselves by their bad habits or their failures; being able to recognize the bad habit as something apart from themselves is an important first step and can serve as a roadblock. Sally was able to set up a small roadblock on her lying pathway simply by recognizing the desire to lie as a way to change her physiology and make her feel better in the relationship. Her lies and the resulting knot of relational difficulties did not have to define her. Other people have set up similar roadblocks by saying things to themselves like "that's just my crazy thinking" or "this is just my body telling me that it's craving dopamine."

When she paused and labeled the urge to lie as simply a bad habit and an ineffective way to feel closer in a romantic relationship, Sally was able to remember that she was more than the habit that had frustrated her for years. This left her the mental flexibility to call up other, more important images of herself as a successful professional, a culturally sophisticated adult, and a caring person. These were positive, rich relational images of good connections. By changing her focus, Sally literally changed the stimulation to her brain. The pause also allowed Sally to gradually recognize that the impulse to lie wasn't really an impulse. It actually began much more gradually, when she was feeling lonely and starting to look forward to being with her boyfriend and feeling special, cared for. Her old relational templates did not allow her to linger in this state of positive anticipation, however. Almost immediately, she was flung into an intense fear of abandonment—a fear that her boyfriend wouldn't like her if he knew how she felt. This fear inevitably led to a lie designed to keep him sympathetic and interested. Sally began to label those thoughts as a part of her habit and could see how these thoughts had been recruited into the lying pathway she now wanted to starve.

As she got better at identifying the thoughts that preceded the lying, she worked on picking her mind up and off its groove—and then moving it to a more positive neural pathway. When she was alone and craving connection, she'd try imagining a time when she'd felt authentically connected with her boyfriend. If this didn't work, she might call him and say honestly that she missed him or that she felt low. Over time, she was also able to describe some of her lying behavior to a friend; they agreed that if Sally felt like lying, she would text the friend and tell her about it. One day Sally found herself conjuring up an old memory of a high school boyfriend who had adored her, no lying necessary. Each of these activities served as roadblocks *and* exercised healthier relational pathways. Although these pathways were withered from disuse, they were like desert plants that lie dormant but come back to life when they are given just a little water. When she engaged in these more positive actions, she felt the jolt of pleasure, the surge of dopamine.

Sally was not able to hold on to a positive image or activity every time she had the urge to lie, especially at the beginning of her attempt to change. Sometimes she ended up telling her boyfriend about how her grandmother had died, or how she had been mugged during her last trip abroad (all lies, including the trip). But as she practiced the skills for more honest relationships, this pathway strengthened, and it became easier to reroute her thoughts in its direction.

I want to stress that Sally had a long path ahead of her. It is not easy to change a very old habit, especially when you have as little experience with healthy relationships as Sally did. But it is definitely possible, especially if you have at least one safe relationship that will support you and your work. Unsurprisingly, Sally eventually broke up with her old boyfriend. I was worried when, within just a few weeks, she began dating someone new. Early in the relationship, a warning sign flashed. Sally moved into a new apartment, and he brought her a housewarming gift: a bottle of his favorite barbeque sauce to keep in her refrigerator. Sally and I talked about how confusing it was to receive a "gift" that was about him, not *her*. The next week, she explained to her new boyfriend that she appreciated the gift, but that she didn't like barbeque sauce herself. We cheered this small success— because, actually, it wasn't small. It was one of the first times she'd ever risked being honest this early in a relationship. To her surprise, her boyfriend did not mind that she had different tastes in condiments. Sally expressed her amazement to her friend, who had grown closer to her, and the friend reinforced the idea that a healthy relationship can tolerate different opinions and ideas. The combination of this safe friendship, along with regularly *not* lying, were literally rewiring Sally's brain for honest connection.

The takeaway message from this section of the book? Your brain can change, and most important for our purposes, your brain can change its patterns of relating to people. You can teach your new brain to be Calmer, more Accepting, more Resonant, and more Energetic—to bolster all four pathways that relate to growth-fostering relationships. That work begins with the book's next section: the C.A.R.E. program.

Chapter 4

THE C.A.R.E.
RELATIONAL ASSESSMENT

U p until now, we've talked about the underpinnings of relational neuroscience. Now it's time to launch that knowledge into practical use. This half of the book is about how to
use the C.A.R.E. plan so that both your brain and your relationships are healthier.

Remember, the C.A.R.E. program consists of four parts.
Each part represents a neural pathway for connection, and
each of those pathways represents an aspect of relationships.
When those pathways are up and running smoothly, you feel:

- **C**alm (via the smart vagus nerve)
- **A**ccepted (thanks to the dorsal anterior cingulate
  cortex)

- **R**esonant (mirroring system)
- **E**nergetic (dopamine reward pathway)

The four chapters that follow are full of suggestions and exercises for strengthening each pathway. You'll get the most benefit if you follow the entire program, but I often mix up the order of the steps to reflect a client's needs. You can do the same. A few people find that they need to focus on just one or two neural pathways instead of all four, and that's fine, too.

However, *everyone* needs to begin with the C.A.R.E. relational assessment, a tool you'll find in this chapter. Performing this assessment is like putting on 3-D glasses at the movies: it helps you see your relationships and your mind in a fuller dimension. I guarantee you'll have at least one aha moment in this chapter. Most people have more than one.

The C.A.R.E. relational assessment helps you discover:
- which of your relationships are most actively shaping your brain;
- what kind of neurological shaping is taking place inside you;
- relational patterns that may have been invisible until now;
- how to engage the C.A.R.E. plan so that you can get right to work on the neural pathways that need the most healing.

As you work on the assessment, expect insight. Expect a little discomfort; that's normal whenever you take time for honest reflection. Most of all, expect to finish this chapter with a plan for a more connected, more satisfying set of relationships. The work begins right here.

If You Skipped the Science Chapters . . .

You're fine. I happen to love the science behind relationships, but if that's just not your thing, you can begin here. Inside this chapter you'll find everything you need to know to get going, including bite-sized summaries of the four neural pathways that form the foundation for the C.A.R.E. plan.

How to Perform Your Relational Assessment

Do this exercise when you have about fifteen to twenty minutes of uninterrupted quiet time. It involves these five steps, which I'll describe in more detail on the following pages:

Step One: Identify your brain-shaping relationships
Step Two: Complete the C.A.R.E. Relational
    Assessment Chart
Step Three: Sort your relationships into safety groups

Step Four: Evaluate your C.A.R.E. pathways

Step Five: Optimize the C.A.R.E. program

Step One: Identify Your Brain-Shaping Relationships

Relationships shape your neural pathways, so let's figure out which ones are doing most of the relational shaping inside your brain. Later, you'll see *how* they are shaping it.

When I began using relational assessments, I would tell people to perform the assessment based on the most important relationships in their lives. Then I realized that when we think of the people who are most important to us, it's instinct to pick out just one or two of the highest-quality relationships. Yet those relationships aren't necessarily the ones that have the most effect on us. In reality, most people have a much wider network of acquaintances who leave a mark on their relational templates. And the more time you spend with someone—no matter whether the relationship is good, bad, strained, or workaday—the more it shapes your brain.

To get a more complete idea of the relationships that affect you, make a list of the adults you spend the most time with. By "time," I mean two things. One is *face time*: the people you see most often during the week. These can include friends and family, but don't be surprised if the names that pop up are people you may not feel all that close to: coworkers, neighbors, carpool partners, parents of your kids' friends, and the acquaintances you're always running into at the hardware store. I also want you to list the people who take up your *mental time*. These are the people who, for good or bad, are under your skin. You spend time thinking about them, worrying about them, writing loving e-mails to them, or feeling annoyed with them. Don't make the mistake of writing down only the names of the people you like the best!

Everyone is different when it comes to relationships, so don't worry about how many people are on your list. For instance, I am a person with many acquaintances but only a few very close friends. Some would call me an introvert. When I did this exercise, my list had seven people on it. In contrast, my best friend could easily jot down more names than I have items on my weekly grocery list. He has so many people in his world that a really complete list would take multiple sheets of paper. He is an extrovert for sure.

Now put those names in order of how much total time—whether it's face time or mental time—you spend with that person. The person you spend the most time with should be at the top of the list; the person you have the least contact with should be at the bottom. Put stars by the first five people on the list. These are the relationships that most dramatically influence your brain.

This exercise is already pretty interesting, isn't it?

Turn to the relational assessment chart on page 96. Now take the five starred names and, going from the first to the fifth, write in the name of each person across the top of the chart in the spaces provided.

A note: people who have been traumatized in their relationships often equate human interaction with pain. They may be so terrified of other people—or so turned off by them—that they see no alternative to their isolation. If this sounds like you and you are not able to think of any current relationships, think about relationships in the past that have been important to you, or about a pet that you have been able to love and trust. Remember, one goal of this program is for you to learn skills that will gently and safely expand your relational world. As long as you have a brain, you can change and connect.

Why Aren't Children on the Relational Assessment Chart?

Relationships with children are important. But healthy adults don't depend on children for their emotional needs, so kids don't appear on the relational chart. If you spend most of your time with children, you need to be sure that you have time and contact with supportive adults. This is doubly true for parents who are in a difficult relationship with a child—for example, a teen going through a turbulent adolescence—because the stress can and will impact your brain.

Step Two: Complete the C.A.R.E. Relational
Assessment Chart

The C.A.R.E. Relational Assessment Chart makes twenty statements about relationships. For each of the five relationships you've written across the top, evaluate how frequently each of these statements is true, using this 1-to-5 scale:

1 = none or never

2 = rarely or minimal

3 = some of the time

4 = more often than not; medium high

5 = usually; very high

Try not to overthink this process; go with your gut. If you are struggling to come up with an accurate response to some of the statements, you can "try on" the relationship. Here's how: recall a recent interaction with the person, or create a mental image of a typical exchange between the two of you. Pay attention not just to the narrative that emerges in your mind but also to the feelings that arise in your body. Each relationship is coded within you as a complex mind/body image; that's why you have to listen to your body (in some cases, this is your gut in a literal sense) as well as to your brain when you are deciding how to rank each statement.

The C.A.R.E. Relational Assessment Chart

Answer the questions on a 1-to-5 scale: 1=None or never 2=Rarely or minimal 3=Some of the time 4=More often than not; medium high 5=Usually; very high	#1	#2	#3	#4	#5	Total Statement Score	C.A.R.E. Code
1. I trust this person with my feelings.							Calm
2. This person trusts me with his feelings.							Calm
3. I feel safe being in conflict with this person.							Calm
4. This person treats me with respect.							Calm
5. In this relationship, I feel calm.							Calm Accepted
6. I can count on this person to help me out in an emergency.							Calm Accepted
7. In this relationship, it's safe to acknowledge our differences.							Calm Accepted
8. When I am with this person, I feel a sense of belonging.							Accepted
9. Despite our different roles, we treat each other as equals.							Accepted

Answer the questions on a 1-to-5 scale:	#1	#2	#3	#4	#5	Total Statement Score	C.A.R.E. Code
10. I feel valued in this relationship.							Accepted
11. There is give and take in this relationship.							Accepted
12. This person is able to sense how I feel.							Resonant
13. I am able to sense how this person feels.							Resonant
14. With this person I have more clarity about who I am.							Resonant
15. I feel that we "get" each other.							Resonant
16. I am able to see that my feelings impact this person.							Resonant
17. This relationship helps me be more productive in my life.							Energetic
18. I enjoy the time I spend with this person.							Energetic
19. Laughter is a part of this relationship.							Energetic
20. In this relationship, I feel more energetic.							Energetic
Safety Group Score							

In a moment, I'll give you some tools for analyzing the chart. Most people, though, find that they have some immediate reactions, even before they do any kind of analysis. Take a minute to think about your own reactions now. Do you notice any patterns? Surprises?

The chart is a representation of the relationships that literally shape your brain. Remember the second rule of brain change:

Neurons that fire together, wire together.

This means that the more time you spend in a relationship, regardless of whether it is mutual or abusive, the more that relationship is actively shaping your central nervous system. Do you spend lots of time in relationships that you ranked with ones and twos? Your brain may be shifting to a state of chronic disconnection to protect you from the pain. On the other hand, if you spend most of your time in relationships marked by fours and fives, then your connected brain—your smart vagus nerve, your dorsal anterior cingulate cortex, your mirroring system, and your dopamine reward pathway—is being programmed to expect healthy relationships and to thrive in them. You are supporting your capacity to find joy and comfort in the context of the human community.

If your relationships score mostly in the low numbers, does this mean that you are bad at relationships? Absolutely not. Everyone spends some time in difficult relationships, and sometimes we are thrown into them through no choice of our own. Your challenge is to learn which relationships can be grown so that they are stronger and more supportive, and which ones you may eventually need to put aside. You'll also make it possible to create rewarding new relationships. Finally, you can learn how to inoculate yourself against very stressful relationships, such as those at work, that you may not be able to leave and cannot change.

At this point, don't write off any of your relationships unless you are clearly being abused. Instead, read on. You'll use the assessment to determine which steps of the C.A.R.E. program to use first. The C.A.R.E. program can help you lay down the neural circuitry that makes it easier to have growth-fostering relationships. Here's to a relational world ranked four and above.

Step Three: Sort Your Relationships into Safety Groups

As you go through the C.A.R.E. program, you'll perform exercises that are designed to improve your neural pathways for connection. You can do many of these on your own, but some of them ask you to practice new methods of interaction with another person. I promise that I won't ask you to try anything that feels too bizarre or too frightening; I firmly believe that baby steps are the best way to get where you want to go. But even when the steps are small, relationship changes make most of us feel uncomfortably vulnerable. Why? One reason is that most of us are wired to fear difference and change. Another is that our culture makes it really hard to be vulnerable; it doesn't teach the skills that can make relational change easier on everyone.

You can improve your chances of having a good experience with change if you take these small risks within relationships that are already fairly sturdy and flexible. Here, you'll sort your relationships into safety groups so that you can see which give you the room to try out new ways of relating.

Return to your relational assessment chart and add up the column of twenty numbers under each relationship. The maximum total score per relationship is 100 points (20 questions × high score of 5).

Using the following scale, sort your relationships according to these three safety groups:

HIGH SAFETY: 75 POINTS OR MORE

Relationships in this category are quite sturdy, with many 4s and 5s. A relationship in this group is a relatively safe place to try out new relational skills or to discuss concrete ways to support each other.

MODERATE SAFETY: 60–74 POINTS

These relationships are usually not the first place to turn when you need to express a difficult emotion or when you want to try out a relational skill that doesn't feel comfortable yet. Wait until you have more practice, and then you can try applying these skills to improve the relationship. In some cases, you may decide that you are willing to take the risk of letting the person know that you are open to making things better between the two of you. You may find that if the other person has more information about how to relate differently, he or she can meet you halfway.

LOW SAFETY: 0–59 POINTS

With their many 1s and 2s, relationships that are low in safety cannot tolerate much vulnerability or conflict. It's not wise to try new relational skills within this group, at least not right away, even if the people in this group are family members or longtime friends you feel you ought to be able to trust.

If a relationship is, frankly, abusive—emotionally, physically, or sexually—it is important for you to get help from an outside source (physician, therapist or counselor, religious leader, domestic violence specialist) to think of ways of extricating yourself from the relationship.

But some relationships in the low-safety category aren't abusive, just problematic. Often, bad relationships are bad because they are shaped by "power-over" dynamics, in which one person is dominant and the other is subordinate. You may be able to reset those dynamics, but this process will be much easier if you work on other, less risky relationships first.

Now that your safety groups are complete, do you see some of your relationships in a different way? If you need some time to absorb this new perspective, take it. Just remember that the goal of this exercise is not to search for the people who have done you wrong, and it's not to blame your parents for the ways they raised you. The goal is definitely not to make you feel bad about the current state of your relationships. So go ahead and note any discomfort you might be having, but come back. Even if all your relationships are low in safety, you'll learn more about how to improve your support system.

If you've made the rare discovery that each of your five relationships is in the safest group, please follow these instructions: put this book down, live your life, and call me. I could use some uncomplicated friends!

Step Four: Evaluate Your C.A.R.E. Pathways

Here, you'll use the assessment to gather information about your neural pathways for connection. Once you know more about your neural pathways, you'll have an entirely new understanding of your relationships. You'll see why some of them are rewarding and what makes others so difficult. Better still, you can use this information to customize the C.A.R.E. program to your needs. Most people who complete this step feel more positive about their innate ability to connect *and* the potential to make their relational network much stronger.

Remember, these are the four C.A.R.E. pathways:

Calm, promoted by the smart vagus nerve

Accepted, via the dorsal anterior cingulate cortex

Resonant, from the mirroring system

Energetic, from the dopamine reward pathways

Go back to the assessment chart that you've completed. For each of the twenty statements, add up the five numbers that appear across the row. Record that total under the heading "Total Statement Score." The maximum score for each statement is 25 (a maximum high score of 5 × 5 different relationships). These totals will help you identify the strength of the four major neural pathways for connection.

Calm: The Smart Vagus

The smart vagus is a nerve that transmits signals to decrease stress. It's also connected to your sense of relationships. Whenever you see a good friend, the smart vagus normally sends out soothing messages to your autonomic nervous system, telling your whole body to relax. But the smart vagus can get confused. You can be born with a genetic tendency to have poor vagal tone, meaning that it fails to send appropriate messages. Very stressful situations in childhood, or later in life, can also cause poor vagal tone. You may feel more threatened or anxious in social settings, and you may find it hard to trust people.

To assess the functioning of your smart vagus, add the total scores for all the statements whose C.A.R.E. Code includes the word "Calm." This includes statements one through seven. The maximum score for the smart vagus category is 175 (seven statements, each with a possible high scores of 25).

A Calm score of 135 to 175 indicates that you have good vagal tone. Your smart vagus is able to take in the messages from your primary relationships and translate them into calming, relaxing signals. You have relationships that help you manage the stress of everyday life.

If your Calm score is between 100 and 134, you feel stressed out and anxious more often than you'd like to. This tension may be the natural result of relationships that feel somewhat risky; these stimulate an appropriate response from your sympathetic nervous system. Or you may suffer from poor vagal tone, in which case you may currently have some good relationships—but your smart vagus can't send the stress-relieving messages that it's supposed to. You'll definitely want to investigate further, which you can do in the Calm part of the program.

A Calm score below 100 means that your relationships often feel unsafe; they frequently add to the stress in your life rather than diminish it. This could reflect significant problems in the quality of your current relationships. If those relationships are unsafe and unresponsive, you won't get the benefit of the smart vagus, and your stress-response system will be continually activated. A low score here could also be an indicator of a genetic tendency toward poor vagal tone or of past abusive relationships that blocked your smart vagus's ability to function. No matter what the cause, poor vagal tone leaves your nervous system reactive, always primed for the next attack. When a relationship feels chronically unsafe, it's often the case that neither your vagal tone nor your relationship is working well.

Accepted: The Dorsal Anterior Cingulate Cortex

The dorsal anterior cingulate cortex registers both physical and emotional pain. When you feel left out, it sends out a distress signal. Repeated experiences of feeling socially excluded can stress your dACC and lock it into a Fire position. When this happens, you feel all the pain of being socially excluded— even when people are trying to welcome you into their lives. To assess your dACC functioning, add the Total Statement Scores for lines five through eleven—these are all the statements with the C.A.R.E. Code that includes the word "Accepted." The maximum score is 175 (seven statements with a possible score of 25 each).

An Accepted score of 135 to 175 indicates that your dACC is well tuned. You tend to feel safe and unthreatened in your relationships, but when you are being excluded, your dACC sends a message of pain and distress. You benefit from a helpful signal that lets you know when to trust people and when something is wrong.

If your Accepted score is between 100 and 134, your emotional alarm system is somewhat reactive. You may often feel left out or as though you do not belong. Even when you spend time with others, you may have an underlying sense of loneliness. The Accepted part of the C.A.R.E. program can help you determine whether you are truly being left out and, if so, can help you take steps toward more supportive relationships. It can also tell you if a reactive dACC is sending you mistaken signals that leave you feeling unsafe and under attack even when people would like to be friendly with you. That same step can help you calm your dACC to give you more accurate feedback.

An Accepted score below 100 indicates that your relational alarm system is being chronically stimulated. This overactive system probably results from past or current destructive relationships—but it is also distorting the way you see *all* your relationships, even the ones that have the potential for warmth and mutual support.

Resonant: The Mirroring System

The mirroring system allows you to read other people's actions, intentions, and feelings with accuracy. When the mirroring system is working well, you feel a sense of resonance with others. When your mirroring system fails, you may feel that there's a wall between you and everyone else.

To assess the functioning of your mirroring system, add

the Total Statement Scores for lines twelve through sixteen. These are all the lines whose C.A.R.E. Code says "Resonant." The maximum score is 125 (five questions, each with a possible high score of 25).

A Resonant score between 95 and 125 reveals that your mirroring system is functioning well. Your relationships feel emotionally easy; you and your friends don't have to spend a lot of time explaining yourselves to each other. You understand most other people, and you feel that the people close to you can "see" who you truly are.

A Resonant score between 70 and 94 shows that you sometimes find other people confusing. Occasionally, important people in your life don't seem to "get" you, and in turn, you misread people's intentions or reactions more often than you would like. The exercises in the Resonant portion of the C.A.R.E. program can help activate and clarify your mirroring system.

If your Resonant score is below 70, you probably think of other people as baffling. You may find yourself shaking your head in bewilderment at friends and colleagues, saying, "I just don't understand you!" Some people with low Resonant scores get into trouble because they are overly suspicious; others are guileless, naively assuming that everyone around them always has sterling intentions. And *you* are misunderstood as well: when you try to be kind, you get accused of being sneaky or invasive. Or maybe you give off signals of romantic interest that you'd never intended. You find feelings uncomfortable and overwhelming. If this sounds like you, go directly to the Resonant step of the program, where you can more fully assess the activity of your mirroring system. You'll also discover ways to make subtle distinctions among different kinds of feelings—both yours and other people's.

Energetic: The Dopamine Reward Pathways

Dopamine is the pleasure neurotransmitter. Ideally, your dopamine reward pathways are linked up with healthy relationships, so connecting with other people stimulates feelings of energy and motivation. But when your relational world leaves you drained, paralyzed, and unhappy, you may find yourself seeking dopamine from other sources. You get your dopamine hits from food, alcohol, drugs, meaningless sex, or other addictive behaviors. One way to tackle bad habits and addictions is to rewire your dopamine pathways so that you get pleasure from your best relationships instead of your worst vices.

To determine your Energetic score, add the Total Statement Scores for statements 17 through 20. These are the statements whose C.A.R.E. Code is "Energetic." The total maximum Energetic score is 100 (four questions with 25 maximum points per question).

If your Energetic score is between 75 and 100, your dopamine pathways are plugged directly into relationships. You have good connections with other people, and those connections naturally supply you with more energy, more motivation, and more ability to act on behalf of yourself and your friends.

An Energetic score between 55 and 74 indicates that your relationships can sometimes feel unrewarding. You may have one or two relationships that you are truly enthusiastic about, but the others leave you feeling neutral and not so jazzed up. It's a good bet that you often turn to food, alcohol, or another source of dopamine as your consolation prize. Practicing the exercises in the program's Energetic step will help you redirect dopamine stimulation away from addictions (including "soft" ones, such as eating and shopping) and back toward healthy connections, significantly brightening your life.

A dopamine score of 54 or below reveals that the relationships in your life are draining. You may long for at least one close friendship, but you would rather be alone than participate in relationships that are unrewarding. You may rely on addictive, repetitive behaviors, such as substances or shopping, to give yourself a lift.

Step Five: Optimize the C.A.R.E. Program

You've got your chart, your scores, and your results. Now what? Be honest about where you're weak and where you're strong. Then decide how you'll work the steps of the C.A.R.E. program. Will you do them in order, or switch them around? Do all the steps, or select just a few?

I'm going to show you how three of my clients used their results for a clearer understanding of their relationships and to customize their C.A.R.E. program.

Jennifer: From Despair to Clarity

One of the most powerful benefits of the relational assessment is that it helps you put a name on what's bothering you. Then you can take concrete steps toward solutions.

This is exactly what happened to Jennifer, who called me for an appointment after a devastating week. She and her on-again-off-again boyfriend, Jakob, had an explosive fight after Jennifer playfully criticized the suit he wore to a friend's wedding. At the same time, Jennifer's sister, Claire, was giving her the silent treatment. Although Jennifer recognized this as a ploy often used within the family to punish certain behaviors, Jennifer was not sure what she had done to make her sister mad. Fearing that she simply "sucked" at relationships, she turned to the only place she knew of for help: the Internet. She Googled the word "relationship" and the Jean Baker Miller Training Institute appeared.

One week later, Jennifer was sitting nervously in my office, friendly and polite but making little eye contact with me. She described the fight with Jakob and explained that the two of them had repaired the rift in their usual way: a few days after the fight, Jakob texted Jennifer and called her a judgmental snob. Jennifer, feeling she deserved it, simply took the hit. They moved on quickly from there, making plans to go out with a small group of friends Friday night. They were talking again, but the interaction did little to deepen the trust between the two of them.

Jennifer predicted that the tension with her sister would be resolved in a similarly unsatisfying way. It had been a week since Claire's silent treatment had begun, and, Jennifer told me, she expected it to last exactly one week longer. The punishment for almost any infraction in her family, from speaking too bluntly to breaking a piece of heirloom china, was two weeks of being quietly shunned by the offended party. When the two-week period was over, the coldness thawed, and the relationship resumed as if nothing had happened.

Jennifer unflinchingly and, I thought, honestly offered detail after detail of her relational life, but she was frustrated that she couldn't assemble these details into a coherent picture. With no better way to understand her relationship problems, she fell back on the simple but depressing idea that she was bad with people.

At this point, I invited Jennifer to complete a relational assessment, explaining that labeling herself with the shorthand "bad with people" wasn't going to get her very far toward her goal of feeling better. I wanted both of us to have a clearer sense of the relationships that were currently shaping her brain and body.

Jennifer was drawn to this exercise. Her mind was naturally analytic—in fact, she was often accused of overthinking things by those closest to her—and she liked the idea of bringing more precision to her thoughts. She began by making a list of the people she saw during a typical week. Her list included her mother and sister; Jim, a coworker who occupied the cubicle next to hers; her boss, Frank; and her sort-of boyfriend, Jakob.

I asked Jennifer to sit quietly and to visualize a few interactions with each of these people, and to pay close attention to what she felt. Then she completed the assessment.

JENNIFER'S SAFETY GROUPS

High Safety: No one

Moderate Safety: Jakob and Claire

Low Safety: Mom, Jim, Frank

Jennifer's first response to seeing her relational safety groups was to say, "This proves I suck at relationships!"

I countered with an important truth: no one person "sucks" at relationships. Bad relationships are always formed by at least two people. You cannot be in a bad relationship alone! We agreed to replace her self-deprecating statements with one that was more accurate: the relationships that dominated Jennifer's life were disappointingly nonmutual.

From there, we took a closer look at Jennifer's relational safety groups. With two of her relationships in the moderate category and three posing a high risk, it was obvious that she had no safe, mutual relationships. This was not a shock to Jennifer. She had already told me that she really didn't trust

Jennifer's C.A.R.E. Relational Assessment Chart

Answer the questions on a 1-to-5 scale: 1=None or never 2=Rarely or minimal 3=Some of the time 4=More often than not; medium high 5=Usually; very high	#1 Jim	#2 Frank	#3 Claire	#4 Jakob	#5 Mom	Total Statement Score	C.A.R.E. Code
1. I trust this person with my feelings.	1	1	2	3	2	9	Calm
2. This person trusts me with his feelings.	2	1	3	4	3	13	Calm
3. I feel safe being in conflict with this person.	2	1	2	2	2	9	Calm
4. This person treats me with respect.	3	1	3	3	2	12	Calm
5. In this relationship, I feel calm.	2	1	3	4	3	13	Calm Accepted
6. I can count on this person to help me out in an emergency.	2	1	3	3	3	12	Calm Accepted
7. In this relationship, it's safe to acknowledge our differences.	2	1	3	4	2	12	Calm Accepted
8. When I am with this person, I feel a sense of belonging.	2	1	3	3	3	12	Accepted
9. Despite our different roles, we treat each other as equals.	2	1	4	4	2	13	Accepted

Answer the questions on a 1-to-5 scale:	#1 Jim	#2 Frank	#3 Claire	#4 Jakob	#5 Mom	Total Statement Score	C.A.R.E. Code
10. I feel valued in this relationship.	2	1	4	4	3	**14**	Accepted
11. There is give and take in this relationship.	1	1	3	3	2	**10**	Accepted
12. This person is able to sense how I feel.	2	1	3	3	2	**11**	Resonant
13. I am able to sense how this person feels.	3	1	4	3	3	**14**	Resonant
14. With this person I have more clarity about who I am.	2	1	3	3	2	**11**	Resonant
15. I feel that we "get" each other.	2	1	3	4	2	**12**	Resonant
16. I am able to see that my feelings impact this person.	2	1	3	3	2	**11**	Resonant
17. This relationship helps me be more productive in my life.	2	1	3	3	2	**11**	Energetic
18. I enjoy the time I spend with this person.	2	1	4	4	3	**14**	Energetic
19. Laughter is a part of this relationship.	2	1	3	3	3	**12**	Energetic
20. In this relationship, I feel more energetic.	2	1	3	4	2	**12**	Energetic
Safety Group Score	**40**	**20**	**62**	**67**	**48**		

anyone and that if she was to be successful in life she would have to do it all on her own. But Jennifer did have a few surprises coming. She wouldn't have thought of her relationship with her mother as particularly low in safety. She loved her mother. But after some thought, she came up with a more complex portrayal of the relationship. She recognized that it felt close but also rigid, without much room for either of them to make a misstep.

The very low scores for Jim and Frank came almost as a relief. They explained the sense of dread Jennifer felt every morning as she got ready for work at a small software company. She had to physically harden herself for an environment with an unsmiling, critical boss who openly pitted workers against one another in what seemed like a sadistic attempt to increase productivity. As we looked at her overall score for Frank, it was clear to both of us that this work relationship was emotionally abusive. Her relationship with Jim was only a little better. Although Jim was not in a position of power over Jennifer, he was generally quiet and dismissive of her.

Even at this early stage of our work together, before she had even finished interpreting her relational assessment, Jennifer had a new way of describing at least one aspect of her troubles: her relational world at work was stimulating stress pathways in her brain and body. This explained why she felt a slight but constant agitated buzz in her body throughout the week. Up until now, Jennifer had thought this feeling was just another sign that she was odd or not meant for normal human interaction.

I asked Jennifer to imagine that the five people on her chart took up all her relational time and then to determine the percentage of time she spent with each person. This is a useful imaginative exercise that makes patterns and trends more obvious. Jennifer's percentages looked like this:

Person	Percentage of Relational Time
Jim	30
Frank	30
Claire	15
Jakob	15
Mom	10

This breakdown made it clear to Jennifer that she spent 70 percent of her time (with Jim, Frank, and her mother) in relationships that felt unsafe and, in one case, fairly abusive. Spending that kind of time in difficult relationships can bring the rest of your relational world down, because they can adjust your template of what "normal" looks like. You can forget what respect and warmth feel like. You can forget that you even *want* to be treated well.

From a relational standpoint, a job change would be ideal for Jennifer—the sooner, the better. But she felt that quitting her job would be a stupid move. She visibly deflated as she realized that she knew of no other companies that were hiring.

"Is there *anyone* at work you can relate to?" I asked. I explained that even if Jennifer couldn't leave Frank and Jim behind, she could dilute the impact of those bad relationships by reducing the percentage of time she spent in them.

Jennifer immediately shook her head, but then she paused. There was a new hire, Emily. They had met briefly the week before, and Jennifer had liked her energy. Her spirits lifted a little as she thought about asking Emily to lunch and seeing if they could form an informal support network. We also speculated about whether there was potential to improve things with Jim. Was he merely responding to the threatening office environment in the same way Jennifer had, by shutting down and retreating to his cubicle? Would he, like Jennifer, appreciate an opportunity for safe connection?

At this point Jim was still a question mark, but Jennifer decided she would spend a moment each day making contact, saying hello, and asking how he was doing—in a professional way, just to see if there was any softening of his demeanor.

Of all Jennifer's relationships, the ones with her sister and her boyfriend were clearly the most mutually supportive. As Jennifer reflected on these two relationships, she felt that she was most able to be herself with Jakob. This thought came as a revelation, because they'd never had a long stretch of dating without fighting. Yet she felt more comfortable around Jakob than she did with most other people. He seemed to trust her, and she liked that feeling. A cycle of fighting and then breaking up is often a sign that something is awry in a relationship. Jennifer, however, was surrounded by people who couldn't tolerate relational differences—when a problem occurred, they moved to disconnect from her. With Jakob, at least she had a relationship with some flexibility, in which both parties could disagree, move away, and then come back together to engage in relational repair. We decided that this relationship was the one that could most easily tolerate some stretching and growing. When the C.A.R.E. program identified exercises that could help Jennifer expand her relational skills, she'd practice them with Jakob.

Jennifer's C.A.R.E. Pathways
Calm: **80 (low)**
Accepted: **86 (low)**
Resonant: **59 (low)**
Energetic: **49 (low)**

When we looked at her C.A.R.E. neural pathway scores, it was clear that Jennifer needed major work in all areas. Having an abusive relationship in your life, like the one with her boss, Frank, leaves lasting imprints on your central nervous system. Those changes make it harder for you to trust and feel safe with others. As we talked about this, Jennifer was reminded of her grandfather. Although he died when Jennifer was five years old, she remembered that he was a difficult man, nasty and critical of everyone around him. Were there traces of this relational style that ran throughout her family life? It seemed possible that Jennifer's neural pathways had been influenced by challenging relationships from the very beginning, although this was a matter we'd investigate more fully at a later date.

All of Jennifer's neural pathways were taxed. Her Calm score likely signified a weak smart vagus nerve, one that was easily overrun by the sympathetic nervous system's stress response. Given her low Accepted score, her dACC alarm system was likely to be highly sensitive, contributing to that unpleasant "buzz" she carried in her body. And no doubt from her Resonant numbers, Jennifer's mirroring system had taken a series of blows from the frequent periods of silent treatment her family had used to control her behavior. This was clear from her low scores and from her ongoing difficulty in making eye contact, a classic strategy for preventing connection.

Of the four neural pathways, Jennifer's dopamine system was the hardest to read. Her overall score was low at 49, but her very low scores with the two men at work were throwing off the decent scores she had with her sister and Jakob. Despite the number, there was clear evidence that Jennifer could enjoy herself in some relationships. And she did not appear to rely heavily on external sources of dopamine. She had no addiction, not even a mild one, to alcohol, drugs, shopping, food, or the like.

Overall, Jennifer's relational map indicated that she would benefit most by doing the whole program. The exercises in each step would help soothe and strengthen her connection pathways; she would also get plenty of education about what a healthy relationship looks and feels like. I also wanted Jennifer to think about a long-term solution to her work problem. As Jennifer developed a taste for mutual relationships, and as she left behind her self-concept as a person doomed to isolation, I was hopeful that she'd find it easier to network her way into a new job. At the very least, perhaps she could protect herself from the worst of Frank's behavior.

Dottie: A Simple Solution to Work Stress

Dottie, a college professor and activist, was neither a wall-flower nor a bully. Confident, composed, and witty, she was able to speak her mind in a variety of circumstances. Out of curiosity, she attended a workshop I was teaching, and when she took a look at the C.A.R.E. assessment, she thought: *Interesting, but why bother? I already know I have a strong support system.*

Dottie began the assessment anyway, quickly and easily jotting down the names of her live-in boyfriend, friends, family members, and close colleagues. But when I explained that the list should include anyone she spent a good deal of time with, her eyes widened. Her relational scales had just tipped significantly. Two of the people she saw most often were the two people who caused her the most grief. One of these people was Ken, the head of her academic department and a man she had to see on a daily basis. Throughout the years, their relationship had grown heavy with tension. Although they were mostly civil to each other, sometimes that tension broke through in faculty meetings or yearly evaluations. The other person Dottie added to her assessment was a senior colleague, Cynthia, who treated Dottie in a bossy, condescending way.

Dottie's C.A.R.E. Relational Assessment Chart

Answer the questions on a 1-to-5 scale: 1=None or never 2=Rarely or minimal 3=Some of the time 4=More often than not; medium high 5=Usually; very high	#1 Luca	#2 Ken	#3 Cynthia	#4 Lisa	#5 Kim	Total Statement Score	C.A.R.E. Code
1. I trust this person with my feelings.	4	2	2	4	5	17	Calm
2. This person trusts me with his feelings.	4	2	2	4	5	17	Calm
3. I feel safe being in conflict with this person.	4	2	3	4	5	18	Calm
4. This person treats me with respect.	5	2	3	4	5	19	Calm
5. In this relationship, I feel calm.	5	2	2	4	4	17	Calm Accepted
6. I can count on this person to help me out in an emergency.	5	3	3	5	5	21	Calm Accepted
7. In this relationship, it's safe to acknowledge our differences.	5	3	3	4	5	20	Calm Accepted
8. When I am with this person, I feel a sense of belonging.	5	2	2	5	5	19	Accepted
9. Despite our different roles, we treat each other as equals.	5	2	3	4	5	19	Accepted

Answer the questions on a 1-to-5 scale:	#1 Luca	#2 Ken	#3 Cynthia	#4 Lisa	#5 Kim	Total Statement Score	C.A.R.E. Code
10. I feel valued in this relationship.	5	3	3	5	5	21	Accepted
11. There is give and take in this relationship.	5	2	2	4	5	18	Accepted
12. This person is able to sense how I feel.	4	2	2	4	4	16	Resonant
13. I am able to sense how this person feels.	4	2	3	5	4	18	Resonant
14. With this person I have more clarity about who I am.	5	3	1	4	5	18	Resonant
15. I feel that we "get" each other.	5	2	2	4	5	18	Resonant
16. I am able to see that my feelings impact this person.	4	2	2	4	5	17	Resonant
17. This relationship helps me be more productive in my life.	5	2	2	4	5	18	Energetic
18. I enjoy the time I spend with this person.	5	2	2	4	5	18	Energetic
19. Laughter is a part of this relationship.	5	2	2	5	5	19	Energetic
20. In this relationship, I feel more energetic.	5	2	2	5	5	19	Energetic
Safety Group Score	94	44	46	86	97		

DOTTIE'S SAFETY GROUPS

High Safety: Luca, Lisa, Kim
Moderate Safety: No one
Low Safety: Ken and Cynthia

Dottie's C.A.R.E. Pathways
Calm: **129 (moderate)**
Accepted: **135 (high)**
Resonant: **87 (moderate)**
Energetic: **74 (moderate)**

When we looked over her assessment, it was clear that Dottie's initial instinct had been correct: she did have a strong support system of largely mutual relationships. Although her scores for her C.A.R.E. pathways were in the middling range, it was obvious that the mostly high scores in her good relationships were pulled down by her two difficult colleagues. In a situation like this, it's tempting to say, "Oh, well, the numbers don't really reflect the reality. This lady has some annoying colleagues, but who doesn't? She's basically fine."

Not quite. Recall the first two rules of brain change:

1. Use it or lose it.
2. Neurons that wire together, fire together.

These tell us that the brain is influenced and sculpted by what it is most exposed to, and the relationships that were sculpting Dottie's brain on a daily basis were the ones that felt the least mutual, least safe, and most stressful. Instead of trying to work *with* Dottie, her colleagues Ken and Cynthia were constantly trying to establish power *over* her. Even with a lifetime of good relationships behind her, these two difficult relationships could powerfully affect Dottie's thinking and feelings. Although she had thick skin and didn't take her co-workers' power moves personally, Dottie felt distracted and extra tired when she had to "put up" with them. She was more likely to go home and isolate herself—and maybe eat a little more ice cream than was good for her—instead of spending her free time with her boyfriend or her friends. As we talked, Dottie realized that this isolation was making things worse: the percentage of relational time she spent with her difficult colleagues was increasing.

Unlike Jennifer, Dottie did not need to do a major overhaul of her relational world, but she did need to target the two relationships that had so much negative power. She drew up a two-step plan. Dottie knew that she couldn't change her relationship with her coworkers—she'd already tried—so she decided that they would occupy a lower ranking on the list of people she spent time with. She'd do this by increasing the time she spent in mutually supportive relationships; in essence, she'd move those good relationships up on the list. This was a pledge that was going to be difficult to honor. She thought of times when she'd been too busy to return friends' calls or hadn't followed through on plans to meet up. The thought of letting negative relationships shape her brain, however, was all the prompting she needed to put a few lunch dates on the calendar. She also realized that she was not using one of her most obvious sources of growth and support: her partner, Luca. After her long workdays, Dottie had been content to tuck away into her study at night, feeling the relief of not having to interact with anyone. By the time they went to bed, she and Luca had often not spoken more than a few sleepy sentences to each other. She explained to Luca what she'd learned from the seminar and they made an effort to spend more connected time together at the end of the day— not just venting their problems, but savoring each other's company. Finally, Dottie concluded that she could benefit from the strategies in the Calm step to help her get through the inevitable meetings with her challenging colleagues. She also decided to try a few ideas in the Energetic step to keep her from turning to sweets when she needed a dopamine boost after a hard day.

A couple of weeks after Dottie returned to work, she sent me a note. Her two-pronged plan was already helping: she was feeling more energetic and had noticed a reduction in her daily stress level.

Rufus: Addicted to Energy

Rufus saw himself as an ordinary guy with a big problem. He'd graduated the year before from a local community college and found a job within three months at a biotech company. He liked his job, but to him, a job was just a way to make money and pay his bills. It was not a passion and never would be. He was a guy who was comfortable living an anonymous life—again, this is how Rufus described himself to me—without major highs and lows, a guy who did not stir extreme reactions in anyone. He was part of the background, blending into the fabric of life. He looked forward to weekends and hanging out with some of his buddies, drinking a few beers and watching whatever game was on television. He dated occasionally, but no one had swept him off his feet.

Three years ago, when Rufus was eighteen, he discovered Internet porn. He was online looking over his next picks for his fantasy football team when a pop-up screen appeared in front of him featuring a provocative picture of a young woman. He wasn't sure why he clicked through. In retrospect, he thought he might have just been bored. What Rufus discovered going through this portal was a virtual world he never knew existed. He had heard his friends describe images they'd seen online, but he'd always assumed they were making up most of the details.

That night Rufus stayed up until four a.m. roaming from one porn site to another, each one giving him a little hit of energy. This was a new feeling for him, very different from his predictable, mellow life. He was not even sure he liked this feeling at first. It was unfamiliar and uncomfortable. But he returned to the site the next night, and the next.

Very quickly, Rufus was spending hours every night browsing for new and different porn sites. He shared this new world with no one and figured the only drawback was that he was getting less sleep at night. After three months of staying up late and dragging himself to work in the mornings, he realized he was hooked and tried to cut back, but was simply unable to. It was as if the websites had taken over his brain and body. Rufus came to my office when he found himself unable to resist sneaking peeks at work during lunch or whenever he felt bored. Before he was caught using his work computer for porn, he said, he wanted to get control of himself.

I explained that although we would clearly have to address the big problem of porn, addictions rarely happen in isolation. We'd use the C.A.R.E. assessment to create a more complete picture of his world. When I asked Rufus to come up with the five people he spent most of his time with, he quickly mentioned his card-playing buddies, Drew and Kevin. Rufus loved his mother and sister, Angela, and usually had some contact with them during the week, so they were listed. But after that it was slim pickings. I needed to prompt him about work relationships, and he did not seem to think of his colleagues as people with whom he had relationships. They were simply people at work. Then he came up with Wendy, who sat in the cubicle kitty-corner from his. Although Rufus was surrounded by coworkers, Wendy was the only one who made an impact on him. She often had a smile on her face and always asked how his latest project was coming along.

Although Rufus was nearly stumped by the task of coming up with five relationships, completing the questionnaire was easy for him. In fact, as Rufus went through the questions, his answers were unusually concrete. Most people worry a little over their answers and have the urge to fiddle with them, but Rufus didn't. I wondered whether he was unable to access his feelings well enough to form nuanced impressions of his relationships. Or perhaps he was merely decisive.

It was tempting to think of Rufus as a person who suffered from a straightforward case of addiction. Fix the addiction, problem solved. But the relational assessment showed us that unless Rufus attended to a few other areas, he'd have very little chance of beating his addiction in a permanent way.

RUFUS'S SAFETY GROUPS

High Safety: No one
Moderate Safety: No one
Low Safety: Drew, Kevin, Mom, Wendy, Angela

Given Rufus's self-definition as someone content to blend into life's scenery, doing his own thing, it was not surprising that his overall scores on his assessment show that he was deprived of growth-fostering relationships. There was little variation in how he scored each relationship (the scores stayed between 47 and 53, only a six-point difference), and each of them was in the lowest category of relational safety. This fit

Rufus's C.A.R.E. Relational Assessment Chart

Answer the questions on a 1-to-5 scale: 1=None or never 2=Rarely or minimal 3=Some of the time 4=More often than not; medium high 5=Usually; very high	#1 Drew	#2 Kevin	#3 Mom	#4 Wendy	#5 Angela	Total Statement Score	C.A.R.E. Code
1. I trust this person with my feelings.	2	2	2	2	2	10	Calm
2. This person trusts me with his feelings.	2	2	2	2	2	10	Calm
3. I feel safe being in conflict with this person.	3	2	2	2	2	11	Calm
4. This person treats me with respect.	3	2	3	4	3	15	Calm
5. In this relationship, I feel calm.	3	3	3	3	2	14	Calm Accepted
6. I can count on this person to help me out in an emergency.	3	2	4	4	4	17	Calm Accepted
7. In this relationship, it's safe to acknowledge our differences.	2	2	2	2	3	11	Calm Accepted
8. When I am with this person, I feel a sense of belonging.	3	3	4	2	4	16	Accepted
9. Despite our different roles, we treat each other as equals.	3	3	3	3	3	15	Accepted

Answer the questions on a 1-to-5 scale:	#1 Drew	#2 Kevin	#3 Mom	#4 Wendy	#5 Angela	Total Statement Score	C.A.R.E. Code
10. I feel valued in this relationship.	3	3	4	3	3	16	Accepted
11. There is give and take in this relationship.	2	2	3	3	2	12	Accepted
12. This person is able to sense how I feel.	2	2	3	2	3	12	Resonant
13. I am able to sense how this person feels.	2	2	3	2	3	12	Resonant
14. With this person I have more clarity about who I am.	2	2	2	2	2	10	Resonant
15. I feel that we "get" each other.	3	3	2	3	2	13	Resonant
16. I am able to see that my feelings impact this person.	2	2	2	2	2	10	Resonant
17. This relationship helps me be more productive in my life.	2	2	2	3	2	11	Energetic
18. I enjoy the time I spend with this person.	4	3	3	3	3	16	Energetic
19. Laughter is a part of this relationship.	3	3	2	3	2	13	Energetic
20. In this relationship, I feel more energetic.	3	2	2	2	2	11	Energetic
Safety Group Score	52	47	53	52	51		

with my sense that not only would Rufus have a hard time finding relationships to stretch in, but that he also had very little knowledge about how he might do this. The C.A.R.E. plan is *always* based on making small, unthreatening changes, but with Rufus, we'd have to be extra cautious in how we proceeded.

Rufus's C.A.R.E. Pathways
Calm: **88 (low)**
Accepted: **101 (moderate)**
Resonant: **57 (low)**
Energetic: **51 (low)**

There's a saying among physicians that the presenting problem—the problem that clients identify as their main issue—is never the *real* problem. That's not quite true. Porn addiction was definitely a real problem and a serious threat to Rufus's job and well-being. But although Rufus came in specifically for help with his addiction, it wasn't the whole story. He didn't have the exact words for it, but he seemed to want me to know about a curious flatness in his life. He claimed to like his routine, but he gave no sign that his life was satisfying. "Inert" was a better word. Porn gave him not just sexual gratification but a missing spark of energy. In fact, it was the hit of energy that brought him back to porn again and again. Until Rufus completed his assessment, this energy problem hovered in his peripheral vision, almost out of sight. When he looked at his numbers, he could see it clearly.

Remember, dopamine is what gives you good energy and motivation. When Rufus and I looked at his assessment, we saw that his Energetic score—which reveals the ability to get dopamine from relationships—was very low. No surprise there. Here's what was interesting: some people with low Energetic scores are in difficult, constantly frustrating relationships. Others have almost no relationships at all. That makes sense: bad relationships, or no relationships = low dopamine. But Rufus's relationships were actually okay. Not intimate or satisfying or truly safe, mind you, but okay. He liked hanging out with his buddies and his family. You'd think he would get at least a middling amount of energy from these contacts, but he was getting almost none. No wonder he didn't feel motivated to do any more at work or in life than he absolutely had to.

Was Rufus just a guy who didn't need people? No. Everyone is born with the capacity for getting dopamine from connections with people around them. Somewhere along the way, Rufus's dopamine system had become disconnected. His brain was like a toaster whose electrical cord had been unplugged from the socket. The socket can provide energy, but the signal can't travel down the cord to the toaster. The result: no toast. In Rufus's case, no mental energy, either.

The low Energetic score accounted for some of the flatness Rufus experienced, but not all of it. Look at the rest of his assessment. It describes a person who is not anxious or sad or irritable, which is a good sign. It also shows someone who does not have easy access to emotional information. For example, Rufus's Resonant score was also low, almost as low as his Energy. He had a hard time reading people or knowing when other people were accurately reading him. His Calm score, at 88, was also low; this was mostly due to the march of 2s across the statements about sharing feelings. At 101, his score for Accepted was in the moderate category (we celebrated this small victory), reflecting he felt safe and not overly stressed. He explained that he felt a definite sense of belonging with his mother and sister and that it never occurred to him that he might be ostracized with his friends or at work. I was glad that he was tight with his family; but in the rest of his relationships, he seemed to be missing something. Again, it wasn't that he had a bad feeling about his friends or colleagues; it was that he didn't have much of a feeling about them at all.

All in all, the relational flatness in Rufus's brain and body was a perfect setup for an addiction. Yes, he liked the porn itself, but he was really addicted to the feeling of finally having his dopamine system stimulated. As he said, he felt energized after viewing porn, in a way he'd never felt before.

Rufus needed a plan that would help him to do two things: reconnect his dopamine reward system to relationships (not porn), and develop more knowledge about how people interact. It was clear that Rufus would benefit from the entire program. But in his case, it made sense to rearrange the order of the steps.

ENERGETIC: Rufus's Energetic (dopamine) problem was the most urgent. He'd start with this step, which would help him disconnect his dopamine reward pathways from porn and reconnect them to healthy relationships.

RESONANT: By increasing the strength of his mirroring system, Rufus would make his connections to other people more satisfying. This would give him a larger supply of good feelings to send down the dopamine trail, resulting in more energy.

CALM: Although a low score here often results in anxiety or stress, Rufus seemed fairly placid. By increasing his vagal tone, he'd feel something richer than the blank dullness he was accustomed to. He'd feel content.

ACCEPTED: Rufus's dACC scores were decent, and he was not particularly concerned about having a sense of belonging. At this point, we decided not to focus on this step. I felt that as he developed a more textured sense of relationships, it was possible that he would begin to worry about inclusion or exclusion. If that happened, we could always go back and add this step.

We now had the outline of a plan. I didn't expect the plan to turn Rufus into Mr. Sensitivity, and I don't think he wanted the title. But I knew that if he could see life with a broader palette of relational colors, he would do more than end his addiction. He'd feel more animated and alive.

Ready to begin the C.A.R.E. program? The next step—strengthening the smart vagus to feel Calmer—begins on the next page.

Chapter 5

C IS FOR CALM

Make Your Smart Vagus Smarter

Signs that a relationship strengthens your Calm pathway:

I trust this person with my feelings.

This person trusts me with his feelings.

I feel safe being in conflict with this person.

This person treats me with respect.

In this relationship, I feel calm.

I can count on this person to help me out in an emergency.

In this relationship, it's safe to acknowledge our differences.

It feels terrible to be tense and irritable. Imagine what life was like for Juan, who felt tense and irritable *all the time*. On the Monday morning before I met Juan, he woke up feeling even worse than usual. He'd stayed up late watching football with a couple of friends the night before. They drank too much and ate too much, and his favorite team lost in overtime. The next morning, electric surges of rage shot through his body. He was angry about the game, and he was angry in general. Just the sound of toast crunching in his mouth threatened to push him over the edge. Juan considered calling in sick to his job as a computer programmer, but he was working on a new team project and the first meeting was scheduled for ten a.m. He showered and walked to the subway.

When he arrived at work, Juan could feel the tension building inside him. When he felt this way, the people around him seemed to become incredibly stupid. He didn't want to deal with their questions or hear stories about their weekends, so he sorted through his e-mail with earphones on, hoping no one would try to talk to him. But a new employee, Veronica, approached from behind and tapped him on the shoulder. He jolted from his chair, surprising them both. He sat down quickly and told her to leave him alone.

Juan hated meetings, particularly large team meetings intended to let everyone hear everyone else's thoughts about a new project. On a good day, Juan could barely sit through a meeting as people "threw out" their ideas. On a bad day, he rolled his eyes, snorted, or zoned out. In each of his evaluations at the company, Juan's boss praised him for his sharp analytic mind and computer skills but repeatedly told him he needed to change his attitude, his lack of interpersonal skills would prevent him from moving up. To Juan, this feedback felt like an attack, and another example of other people's annoying behavior.

Juan entered the meeting room ten minutes late, hoping to miss the opening chitchat. As his colleagues went around the table and described their thoughts about the project, Juan struggled to keep his patience. This felt like an unnecessary, self-indulgent step, aimed to please his touchy-feely boss. When Juan's turn came to "share," he gave a brief, monotone description of his role in the project, making eye contact with no one.

Midway through the meeting, Juan was asked how they might add new graphics to an existing demo product. His boss had told him that colleagues valued his skills; that's why they routinely turned to him with difficult problems. He enjoyed using his analytic mind to quickly break down even the most difficult problems and come up with plans that usually stunned his colleagues. But after Juan shared his ideas, a more junior member of the team spoke out, questioning the advice Juan had just given and suggesting an alternative approach. The electricity surged again, and Juan snapped. Furious, he stood up at the table and berated the young man. When Juan stopped yelling, the room was deathly quiet—until his boss asked him to leave the meeting. Juan stormed out of the room, slamming the door behind him. Later that morning his boss suggested Juan leave for the day and return to meet with him the next morning. Juan left the building, afraid he had gone too far this time and was likely to lose his job. But he didn't lose his job, as he found out the next day: he was referred to me for counseling.

. . .

When I met Juan, I was struck by his inability to sit still. Some part of his body was always in motion. For most of our meeting, his right leg bounced rhythmically. He picked at his fingers. He chewed gum, too—not a slow, relaxed chew but the kind of intense chewing you see in baseball players during a game. I could see the muscles of his jaw tighten over and over again. Despite this activity, Juan didn't look animated. He looked exhausted.

Juan knew that family members and coworkers described him as a hothead and that he reacted to many interpersonal exchanges with impatience. He appreciated that his job allowed him to spend hours interacting with his computer and not with people. He did occasionally have lunch with a colleague, but more often than not he ate at his desk, working comfortably between bites.

As we talked, Juan groaned and shook his head, looking at the floor.

"You groaned," I said. "What was that about?"

"I really don't want to be *that guy*," he said. "The Computer Guy with Anger Issues."

In truth, a lot of people suffer from jumpiness and irritability, and they work in all kinds of professions. Some are able to make it through the workday without exploding; these people often save up their tension for the unfortunate family members who wait for them at home. Some people aren't hostile at all, but they find interpersonal interactions so stressful that they want to jump into bed and pull up the covers after a trip to the grocery store. Some drink. A lot. (These are the people who need to "take the edge off.") I've always suspected that all these folks are underrepresented in therapy offices, in part because therapy sounds like fifty long minutes of irritating interaction, but also because they fear labels. *Something is terribly wrong with you*, they imagine me saying. *Here, let me show you this textbook that explains the word for people who can't handle being around others.*

But every person who's come to my office has been endlessly complex and interesting—and shorthand labels, even diagnoses, can never capture a soul's complexity. There's no judgment here: people with chronic interpersonal stress are usually relieved to know that their tension is not a character flaw or a personal failure. It's simply a problem with the Calm neural pathway. Specifically, this kind of constant relational stress is related to low tone in the smart vagus. Low vagal tone makes it hard to feel relaxed in the presence of others.

The autonomic nervous system contains three branches that help you react appropriately to threats: the sympathetic nervous system, which stimulates the fight-or-flight response when you are in danger; the parasympathetic nervous system, which brings on the freeze response when your life is threatened; and the smart vagus, which has the power to block the fight, flight, and freeze responses when you are feeling safe. At one end, the smart vagus feeds directly into the muscles of facial expression, vocalization, and swallowing, as well as the tiny muscles of your inner ear. At the other end, the smart vagus innervates the heart and lungs. When the smart vagus is working the way it should, it can "see" friendly expressions on the faces of people around you and "hear" warm voices. At these signals, the heart and lungs slow down into a relaxed pattern. In effect, the smart vagus has the power to tell the sympathetic and parasympathetic nervous systems: *I've surveyed the territory and things are okay. Your stress responses are not needed right now; it's safe to relax.* If the smart vagus doesn't get that input, it sends a different message: *The world looks pretty dangerous out there. Probably a good idea for you to mobilize, in case something bad goes down.*

I've mentioned that although the neural pathways for connection are constantly shaping themselves through your relationships, it's during childhood when these pathways are most malleable. The smart vagus needs stimulation from caring faces and voices in order to wire together with networks of nerves that associate that visual and audio input with safety. It needs to experience the relational qualities, like trust and the ability to feel safe during conflict, that strengthen the Calm pathway. Most important, the smart vagus—like a muscle—needs to be used to develop good tone. When that doesn't happen, the smart vagus doesn't grow strong, and it doesn't learn to associate relationships with serenity and safety. A person with low vagal tone may intellectually understand that he is surrounded by supportive, encouraging people and still feel terribly threatened *around those same people*, because his smart vagus isn't able to tell his stress-response systems to stand down. When vagal tone is very low, all relationships feel threatening.

Juan's smart vagus pathway was still under construction when, at age six, his mother died in a fiery car crash. His father, who was busy trying to keep his auto-body business afloat, had little time to nurture and care for his six children. Although Juan's sister, Blanca, tried to raise him, she was young herself—only twelve years old—when their mother died. And neither was able to protect themselves from their father, who yelled at them and sometimes hurt them. Instead of being exposed to soothing parental expressions, Juan became skilled at reading a different set of emotions. When his father came home with his eyes narrowed and his mouth pressed into a line, Juan knew to tread lightly and stay out of his father's way. When his father started yelling before even entering the house, Juan understood that it was time to take cover. On those nights, Juan wasn't sure he would live to see the morning. Juan's nervous system developed in a manner that was appropriate to this environment. His sympathetic nervous system was on almost all the time, its nerve pathways becoming muscular and efficient, while his smart vagus withered from disuse.

There was one reliable way Juan could relax and feel safe, and that was when he was alone. Studying computers was a godsend: the intricacies fascinated his detail-oriented brain, and there was little interpersonal interaction. When someone did approach him, even if just for a conversation, his body reacted with a surge of adrenaline, followed by anger or fear.

Early in life, he learned the route to staying safe and to minimizing those unsettling surges of stress: avoid people whenever possible.

As Juan became an adult, he had more control over the safety of his immediate world. But he still had an overprotective nervous system with a powerful fear response, and it was a significant barrier to healthy relationships. Nevertheless, Juan did have a social life. He still spent time with his family, even his father, and felt close to Blanca. He had a best friend, Bob, and they hung out with a small circle of friends. Juan dated quite a bit, though he'd had only one long-term relationship. That ended when his girlfriend decided she could no longer take Juan's reprimands and lectures.

You can see Juan's C.A.R.E. assessment on the following pages. Below, we'll look at how the different relational safety groups relate to the Calm pathway. We'll also see how Juan's safety groups shaped up.

Relational Safety Groups and the Calm Pathway

There are some patterns that tend to appear in people with weak Calm pathways, and some of these can be described within the three relational safety groups:

High safety (75–100 points): Low vagal tone means that it's hard for you to feel safe around other people. Given that Juan showed the classic signs of low vagal tone (irritability, anxiety, anger), it's not surprising that he had no relationships that helped him feel safe.

Moderate safety (60–74 points): If you have a weak Calm pathway, your closest relationships might be found here, in the moderately safe group. This may reflect a fear of trusting people, or it might mean that you don't have anyone in your life right now who is truly safe. I thought it was pretty good news, actually, that both Juan's sister, Blanca, and his friend Bob scored between 60 and 75 points, meaning that they felt at least somewhat safe to him. It was likely that as Juan learned skills to manage his overactive sympathetic nervous system, those relationships would improve. In turn, having safer and more rewarding relationships would help strengthen Juan's vagal tone.

Low safety (less than 60 points): Three of the relationships that took up major time and space in Juan's life scored below 60. These were relationships that were making his life worse, not better, because they exercised his sympathetic nervous system so frequently. Two of these people were from the office: his boss and a coworker. When they were around, Juan felt out of sync, as if everyone expected him to be as sociable as they were. This feeling of not quite measuring up could leave him irritated and then enraged. It didn't matter that when Juan described these guys to me, they actually sounded pretty friendly; his weak smart vagus kept him from feeling safe in these relationships. I didn't think Juan benefited from having his stress pathways constantly stimulated. But I wondered if, eventually, there would be potential for these work relationships to improve.

Juan's father was a different story. Juan's father had given

Juan's C.A.R.E. Relational Assessment Chart

Answer the questions on a 1-to-5 scale: 1=None or never 2=Rarely or minimal 3=Some of the time 4=More often than not; medium high 5=Usually; very high	#1 Blanca	#2 Dan (boss)	#3 Bob	#4 Sam (coworker)	#5 Father	Total Statement Score	C.A.R.E. Code
1. I trust this person with my feelings.	3	2	2	2	1	10	Calm
2. This person trusts me with his feelings.	2	2	2	2	2	10	Calm
3. I feel safe being in conflict with this person.	2	2	2	2	1	9	Calm
4. This person treats me with respect.	4	3	2	2	1	12	Calm
5. In this relationship, I feel calm.	3	2	2	2	1	10	Calm Accepted
6. I can count on this person to help me out in an emergency.	4	3	2	3	2	14	Calm Accepted
7. In this relationship, it's safe to acknowledge our differences.	3	3	3	2	2	13	Calm Accepted
8. When I am with this person, I feel a sense of belonging.	4	3	3	3	3	16	Accepted
9. Despite our different roles, we treat each other as equals.	3	4	4	3	2	16	Accepted

Answer the questions on a 1-to-5 scale:	#1 Blanca	#2 Dan (boss)	#3 Bob	#4 Sam (coworker)	#5 Father	Total Statement Score	C.A.R.E. Code
10. I feel valued in this relationship.	3	4	3	4	3	17	Accepted
11. There is give and take in this relationship.	3	3	3	3	2	14	Accepted
12. This person is able to sense how I feel.	5	3	3	2	2	15	Resonant
13. I am able to sense how this person feels.	3	2	3	2	3	13	Resonant
14. With this person I have more clarity about who I am.	4	3	3	2	1	13	Resonant
15. I feel that we "get" each other.	4	3	3	2	2	14	Resonant
16. I am able to see that my feelings impact this person.	3	4	3	3	2	15	Resonant
17. This relationship helps me be more productive in my life.	3	3	3	2	2	13	Energetic
18. I enjoy the time I spend with this person.	4	2	5	2	2	15	Energetic
19. Laughter is a part of this relationship.	4	2	5	2	2	15	Energetic
20. In this relationship, I feel more energetic.	3	2	4	2	2	13	Energetic
Safety Group Score	67	55	60	47	38		

up drinking years ago, but he was still a harsh and critical man. Though Juan was no longer an abused child, this relationship continued to weaken his Calm pathway and build up his sympathetic nervous system. This situation had to change.

Irritable . . . or Introverted?

Don't confuse irritability with introversion. Introversion is a normal, inborn personality trait. Introverts tend to be quieter and more reserved than extroverts. Being quiet and solitary is crucial for introverts, because it helps them feel refreshed. But introverts with healthy nervous systems definitely enjoy relationships. It's just that they prefer to be with a few close friends rather than go out with a big group of casual friends to a loud party. Their intimate friendships give their C.A.R.E. pathways plenty of stimulation and help them stay in good relational shape.

Introverts may be sensitive, and they're not at their best during large gatherings. But as a general rule, person-to-person interactions aren't likely to make them anxious and angry. They aren't exhausted by having to talk to a cashier at the convenience store. They can listen to a coworker's request without blowing a fuse. Whether you're an introvert or an outgoing extrovert, feeling irritable, anxious, and angry in your relationships is a sign that something is wrong—possibly that you're suffering from poor vagal tone.

Understanding Your Own Calm Score

Add up your scores for the statements whose C.A.R.E. Code includes the word "Calm." (That's statements 1 through 7.) Here's what the total number tells you:

When your C score is between 135 and 175: You've got healthy vagal tone, which means your Calm pathway is strong. Your smart vagus is robust and networked into neural pathways that can recall plenty of calming faces and voices; it's experienced at detecting when new people are friendly and when they're not. When you're around supportive people, your smart vagus transmits a calming message to your sympathetic and parasympathetic nervous systems. Being around your close friends helps you wind down and relax.

When your Calm score is between 100 and 134: Your close relationships don't always help you feel relaxed and comfortable. There can be a few reasons for this. One is that the people you spend most of your time with aren't trustworthy. The other is that your smart vagus isn't as strong as it could be, which means that even when you're with people you trust, your brain doesn't get the message to relax. Actually, both these reasons could come into play, because when you spend lots of time with people you can't trust, your smart vagus doesn't get exercised as frequently. As a result, your vagal tone gets weaker. A look at your relational safety groups can help you figure out whether you're spending too much time in low-safety relationships.

When your Calm score is lower than 100: Any Calm score below 100 is a low number. This is where Juan's score fell. The scores for all four of Juan's pathways were on the low side, but at 78, his Calm score stuck out. Given his chronic irritability and abusive upbringing, this was not a surprise. It wouldn't have made sense for his smart vagus to have good tone, because his smart vagus pathway was shaping itself at a time when his world was the opposite of safe and trustworthy. A very low Calm score usually describes a person who feels hyperalert and jumpy around people, and that fit my impression of Juan.

A low Calm score is a bad news/good news situation. Of course it's bad news that it's so hard to be around people—but you probably already know that you've been suffering. The good news is that a few therapies can help you feel a lot better, quickly.

Most people with low Calm scores have very few relationships that feel safe. Some have no safe relationships at all. There may be people on your list who are emotionally abusive (like Juan's father) or physically dangerous. There may also be others who are quite decent—it's just that you may be unable to pick up the messages of safety that their expressions and words are sending. As your reactive stress responses settles down, some of those relationships may feel more rewarding.

Strengthen Your Calm Pathway:
Ways to Feel Calmer and Less Stressed

For everyone with a weak Calm pathway, the first step in feeling better is education. Juan in particular was not used to thinking about his feelings and reactions to the world. When I asked him about friends and romantic relationships, he shrugged the question off by saying the words I hear so often: "I'm not good at relationships." He, like so many other people, believed he had been born like this.

Of course, he hadn't been born "like this"—he was born with the reflexes to connect with people, but he needed healthier relationships to build flourishing neural pathways for connection. Using a computer metaphor, I talked with him about the neural pathways for connection that are downloaded into each of us at birth. He was interested in this idea and became engaged in the neuroscience—a very good sign. We talked about how his nervous system had been formed in an environment of both traumatic loss (his mother's death) and constant threat (his father's emotional and physical violence). His neural pathways for healthy connection had not been stimulated enough to grow well. It was clear to both of us that until we could turn the volume down on his overactive sympathetic nervous system, he could not move out of the deep isolation he felt. In a self-protective move born out of experience, his brain was telling him to be angry and scared.

For anyone struggling with chronic irritability and

anxiety, learning to feel calmer and more trusting means strengthening your smart vagus so that it can tell your sympathetic and parasympathetic nervous systems when it's okay to calm down.

You can improve vagal tone by working on one, two, or three of these goals:

1. Starve some of the pathways to your sympathetic nervous system. An overactive sympathetic nervous system hogs all the stimulation, leaving the smart vagus with fewer opportunities to develop.
2. Strengthen the smart vagus directly.
3. If necessary, reduce stimulation to the parasympathetic nervous system. In rare cases, people equate social interaction with life-threatening danger, and the parasympathetic nervous system tells the body to shut down and play dead.

Ready for some ideas? You'll find plenty, below.

Ways to Starve Your Sympathetic Nervous System Stress Pathways

Many of us suffer from overdeveloped stress pathways. This can be the result of trauma, but it doesn't have to be. An overactive stress response is a byproduct of our culture. From our earliest days, we're taught to be independent above all else, and that the only safe place in the world is at the top of the heap, with the competition crushed at the bottom. This is the perfect environment for activating your stress system. By the time we're adults, most of us have spent two decades building up our sympathetic nervous system and ignoring smart vagus skills, like learning to soak up the calming effects of a trustworthy relationship. Adulthood brings a whole new bucket of stresses: paying the rent or mortgage, surviving life in the cubicle, raising children . . . not to mention worrying about terrorist bombings or anthrax in the mail. If you're living a typically hectic contemporary life with little time for relaxation and play, you probably feel chronically stressed. You're not sick, though, not any more than Juan was. Like him, you're having a normal response to a cold world.

And there was no doubt that Juan suffered from an overactive sympathetic nervous system. In fact, his sympathetic nervous system was stuck in the On position; he practically lived in fight-or-flight mode. That's one reason he was so prickly. Lots of people who frequently feel anxious are living with a noisy sympathetic nervous system.

If you feel so chronically tense that, like Juan, you are revved up and worn down, your most important job is to reduce how often your sympathetic nervous system kicks in. Remember the first rule of brain change: **Use it or lose it.** Use your sympathetic nervous system's stress pathways often enough and they bulk up. To reduce chronic jumpiness, you need to weaken those stress pathways by starving them of stimulation. Here's how to do it.

Reduce Exposure to Unsafe Relationships

Take a look at your relational safety groups. If there are any in the lowest safety range, examine these relationships more closely. Are you being physically or emotionally damaged by any of them? The first step to starving the sympathetic nervous system stress pathways is to end or reduce contact with people who are dangerous, who give your alarm system a very good reason to start ringing.

In Juan's case, this meant cutting back on time he spent with his father. I didn't think Juan needed to cut off the relationship completely, but together we decided that he could reduce the number and length of his visits. When Juan did see his father, he could bring Blanca along; he felt safer in her presence (that safe feeling was good for his smart vagus), and he wondered if maybe they could help each other by coming up with a plan to leave if their father turned nasty.

When a relationship is very stressful, it's not always easy to know what to do.

You should *always, always, always* leave a relationship that is physically or sexually abusive. If you are in a relationship that is emotionally disrespectful, the decision to leave can be weighed against the level of harm, the importance of the relationship to you, and whether you have other safe relationships to balance the emotional destruction. If the person who feels emotionally unsafe is a parent, the choice to leave can be extremely painful. You're biologically wired to connect with your parents. Cutting off a relationship with either one is like cutting off a leg: something you'd do to save your life, but only when there are no other options.

When staying is painful but leaving is too brutal, I suggest a couple of alternative approaches. Recruit a supportive mental health professional to help you with these. The first is to reduce your exposure to the emotionally unsafe person. Cut as far back as you can on the time you spend with him or her in person, on the phone, or online. Work with your therapist or counselor to help you identify how, when, and why you interact with this person. Those interactions are probably based mostly on the unsafe person's needs, but with some good help you may be able to change those terms. You can also start noticing when the unsafe person is getting worked up—and at that point you can end the exchange. As you get clearer about the ways that a person is being demeaning, and as you build other, safer relationships, you will be able to see the behavior and the damage it causes more clearly. This insight will help you make decisions that you can live with, including a decision to spend even less time with the person or, perhaps, to finally end the relationship.

While you're working to reduce your exposure to difficult relationships, you should also increase the amount of time you spend in your safest relationships. Every minute you spend with your most trusted friends helps heal the neural pathways that are being damaged by the low-safety relationship.

Consider Medication to Quiet the Stress Response

Aside from getting out of high-alarm situations, a smart move for calming an overactive sympathetic nervous system is to consider medication. Not everyone needs this step. But as Juan and I talked about how hard it was for him to sit still, he explained that he had once tried meditation. When he sat quietly for even a few minutes, his mind would spin, filled with traumatic images he could barely identify or remember. At this point, it was clear that he needed stronger help. He started fluoxetine, which is a serotonin reuptake inhibitor antidepressant, or SSRI. This class of drugs increases the availability of serotonin in the brain. You'll need to work with a doctor to get an antidepressant, obviously, and you should be aware that antidepressants come in different categories. Some, like bupropion (the brand name is Wellbutrin), can actually stimulate your sympathetic nervous system—which is counterproductive. I chose fluoxetine for Juan because not only does it treat symptoms of depression, it also buffers the stress response systems.

It can take between two weeks and two months for an antidepressant to start working, but when the effects did take hold in Juan's brain, they were very helpful. Juan felt a quieting in his body that he had never known—it felt like he finally had access to the ability to pause and reflect on his behavior. Juan reported that the effect was good but also so new that it was slightly unnerving. Now that he was a little less reactive, he could also sit still and even meditate—at first for just two five-minute periods each week, and then for fifteen-minute sessions four or five times weekly. When I saw him, he was visibly less jittery, and he looked less worn out. It was too soon to tell how long Juan would need to stay on antidepressants. Some people take them as a short-term strategy, sometimes for only six to twelve months; others need them for the long haul. No matter what, Juan had accomplished the first task: soothing his chronically overactive sympathetic nervous system.

Defuse Yourself Before You Blow Up

Do you tend to explode in anger? Many people with low vagal tone are on a short fuse. Juan frequently blew up at co-workers, girlfriends . . . anyone who happened to be in his sights when he felt stressed. But some people are like the husband of one of my clients: when he's frustrated, he loses his temper with himself. He doesn't lash out at his wife or anyone else, but his self-criticism is so vitriolic that it negatively affects everyone in the house.

Try monitoring your level of agitation on a scale of one to ten, with ten being a full-scale screaming, venting tantrum. The idea is to pull yourself out of a seriously irritating situation before it's too late. If you find yourself reaching a five, excuse yourself from the interaction. Leave the room if you can.

By keeping yourself from going over the edge, you decrease how many times your sympathetic nervous system goes into full-out war mode. Eventually, it will become less irritable and less likely to sound the alarm at relatively small problems. And, of course, the less you snap at people, the safer they will feel around *you*.

Relabel and Refocus

When your sympathetic nervous system is overactive, you feel more stress than other people. This leads to even more stress! Here's a way to step in and break the cycle. When you feel overwhelmed by stress, try the "relabel and refocus" approach. This method was created by Jeffrey Schwartz, a psychiatrist at UCLA who specializes in neuroplasticity, especially as it applies to obsessive-compulsive disorder (another problem with roots in neural pathways that have wired together and become strong from consistent use).[1]

First, for the "relabel" part, pause and take ten deep breaths. Stress causes us to take short, quick breaths, which reduce the oxygen levels in the brain. With less oxygen, brain cells can't work as well, and your brain becomes more irritable, which worsens the stressed feeling. So take those breaths—and then relabel your body's stress reaction. Instead of saying to yourself, *I can't take this!* or *My girlfriend is driving me crazy!* say, *This feeling is just my overactive sympathetic ner-*

vous system sending me a wrong message. This relabeling can feel stiff at first, or even ridiculous, but it helps you separate yourself from the experience of stress. This allows the cognitive part of your brain to come online and begin to modulate the agitation.

Then "refocus" your attention. Move it away from whatever is driving you nuts and think about something different, something that's pleasing. This is what Sally, the woman who lied to her boyfriend, did when she purposefully moved her thoughts away from how exciting it would be to tell a lie and on to how good she felt when she and her boyfriend were getting along on honest terms.

A particularly powerful kind of refocusing is what I call a PRM: a *positive relational moment.* A PRM is a time you remember feeling safe and happy in another person's presence. For me, a favorite PRM is the time I was walking with my then-thirteen-year-old twins toward Old Faithful at Yellowstone National Park. It's a gorgeous day and we're heading down the path, with me in the middle and each child holding one of my hands. Thirteen-year-old kids, willing to hold hands with their mother! When I bring this PRM into my mind, I always smile, and my smart vagus helps me feel less stressed. I also feel a fullness in my chest—it's like I'm brimming up with happiness—thanks to a little hit of relational dopamine. When I'm up against a stressful work deadline or stuck in Boston traffic, I think of this PRM. I know that instantly I'm activating healthy neural pathways and shrinking the ones that cause unnecessary stress.

(Of course, if you're stressed because you're in real danger, don't bother with relabeling and refocusing. Go ahead and let the stress response do its work—and escape, fight back, call 911, or do whatever you need to do.)

Relabel and refocus takes advantage of all three rules of brain change. First is the **Use it or lose it** rule. When you can lift your mind out of its stress, you *use* the stress response less; eventually you will begin to *lose* it. (Well, you'll lose its overactive, unnecessary aspects.) And there's the second rule: **Neurons that fire together, wire together.** When you are consistently overwhelmed by stress in particular situations, the neural pathways for stress link up with the neural pathways that pick up the sights, sounds, and other sensations of those situations. If you can keep these neurons from firing at the same times, they won't wire together as tightly. Finally, this exercise takes advantage of the third rule of brain change: **Repetition, repetition, dopamine.** You'll have to repeat the exercise to see results, but those results will happen faster if you add in the power of dopamine. By thinking of something positive, the way Sally did when she thought about genuinely intimate moments, you'll stimulate dopamine and help melt away the unwanted neural pathways. When you use a PRM, you're getting dopamine in an even bigger way, because a PRM generates dopamine from healthy relationships.

Try a Neurofeedback App

I've referred people with jittery sympathetic nervous systems to neurofeedback for years, but I didn't really understand the dramatic difference it can make in a person's life and relationships until a member of my own family decided to try it.

Ben was a highly competent man, admired by friends and colleagues for his keen intellect and easy way with people. However, his family and friends—and especially his partner, Aaron, knew him to be riddled with worry. Ben's sympathetic nervous system would fire, making him think that something dangerous was happening. He began to compile a mental list of dangerous things that could happen or that have happened—and the next time his body alarm went off, the items from the list popped into his head, and he immediately had ten things to worry about. Nighttime was a silent hell for Ben; he'd wake up with his heart pounding and his mind grabbing on to the nearest negative thought as an explanation. Unfortunately, every once in a while, something bad did happen, which was just the intermittent reinforcement his body needed to convince itself to remain on high alert all the time.

Aaron had mostly grown accustomed to the way Ben's anxiety could hijack their lives. When they traveled, he knew to expect an extra fifteen minutes before they left a hotel room, because Ben obsessively double- and triple-checked under the beds and in the drawers for forgotten items. Aaron barely registered the way Ben followed the weather forecast before a trip and constantly predicted that an impending storm would prevent their departure. Most days, Aaron could also screen out Ben's repeated attempts to feel safe and in control of his emotions. At least once a week, however, Ben's anxiety would surge unpredictably—and it seemed to suck the air out of the room. Aaron felt himself "catching" the feeling. As Ben panicked, Aaron could feel his own chest tighten and his breath become shallow. In those moments, the only way for him to manage was to leave for an hour or so to clear his thoughts and feelings. Ben understood Aaron's reaction cognitively, but each time Aaron walked away, Ben felt abandoned and judged. This chronic anxiety put them both in a no-win situation and undermined the relationship.

After his first neurofeedback treatment, Ben noticed a bounce in his step, and the rest of us, including Aaron, noticed that he was more communicative. After two weeks, his nighttime worrying had stopped, and even the daytime fears had greatly subsided. He radiated a brighter energy—and now Aaron "caught" this better mood instead of Ben's anxiety. The impact was so profound that he and Aaron decided to rent a neurofeedback unit so Ben could hook himself up throughout the week.

Neurofeedback takes advantage of the rules of brain change to rewire the brain.

Your central nervous system communicates by electrical current; individual brain cells send messages throughout your brain and body by electrochemical reactions. With a highly sensitive meter, the amount of electrical current sent through your brain cells can be measured and monitored. In an EEG, electrodes are placed on your scalp to produce a general picture of the electrical current running through your entire brain. The electrical signals emanating from your brain will vary, depending on where you are picking up the signals, and the frequency of current is divided into categories based on the wavelength and amplitude. It's the healthy integration of all the different kinds of brain waves that creates a sense of equilibrium or peace. For example, if you have too many alpha waves in the frontal part of your brain, you may find that attention is difficult. If you are having lots of anxiety, you may need to increase both alpha and alpha-theta waves.

Neurofeedback uses a reward system to help you pull your brain waves back into balance. What is so remarkable about this modality is that it bypasses cognition: you can't just think your way through a session. I was once hooked up to a neurofeedback machine at a conference in Texas many years before it became more popular. Electrodes were placed on my head in three locations, and at the other end they were hooked up to a computer system. On the computer screen was a game that looked like a simpler version of Pacman, one of my favorite old video games. When the electrical current in my brain gave off the desired brain waves, the Pacman unit began to munch up little dots. When my brain wandered off to another frequency, the munching slowed down. Miraculously, my brain knew that it should try to stay in the frequency that provided the dopamine-producing "reward" of the Pacman munching. After just a few moments, the munching was steady, the desired pathway was activated repeatedly, gaining strength and recruiting other neurons into its bulk. Neurofeedback is now more sophisticated, with dopamine rewards that appeal to a wider audience, such as watching a favorite DVD. When your brain waves are in the desired range, the video plays, and when they drift out of the desired range, the video fades out.

You can receive neurofeedback at a therapist or doctor's office, or, like Ben, you can rent a neurofeedback machine for your home. (If you rent a home device, you'll still need to work with a clinician to determine the appropriate settings, both at the beginning and as your brain changes over time.) But there's also an app for that: Xwave makes a headset plus app that you can use via your phone. The headset has only two settings: one that helps you grow the beta waves necessary for focused attention, and one for the alpha waves that you need to relax. The headset is a less sophisticated option than a full neurofeedback machine, but it can be useful if you want to focus on either of these two issues. Jennifer, the woman who felt a constant agitated buzz in her body, bought the Xwave app and headset to decrease her sympathetic activation. She often used it for fifteen minutes of relaxation at lunchtime—a smart scheduling decision in an office full of low-safety relationships.

More Ways to Treat Chronic Tension, Irritability, and Jumpiness

Sometimes doing psychological work is hard. But teaching your nervous system to calm down can be like a day at a spa—wonderfully indulgent and relaxing. Even if these strategies drive you crazy at first (for example, you might find it hard to be still), keep with them. You will come to love what they do for you. Jennifer, for example, downloaded a relaxation CD. By following the soothing voice at night, she was able to focus on each part of her body, first consciously tensing and then releasing it. By the end of the CD, she was usually asleep.

Here are nine soothing suggestions for managing a jumpy sympathetic nervous system:

1. Increase the time you spend with people who feel safe to you.
2. Work out. Moderate to intense cardiovascular exercise is best.
3. Use a relaxation CD. Some good choices include Dr. Alice D. Domar's *Breathe: Managing Stress* and Rod Stryker's *Relax into Greatness.*
4. Try the Emotional Freedom Technique. My clients report that EFT has a seemingly magical ability to

reduce the intensity of an overwhelming emotional state. EFT works by tapping gently on the endpoints of meridians (in Eastern medicine, meridians are your body's energy pathways) as you focus on the emotion that's been troubling you. For more information, visit the website www.emofree.com.

5. Meditate.

6. Play with a pet.

7. Take a hot bath.

8. Get a massage.

9. Ask a safe person for a cuddle or a hug.

Choose the ones that sound most appealing and see what happens. If you don't notice a difference after a few weeks, try a different set. Don't let these treatments go to the bottom of your daily to-do list just because they feel great. They're also vitally important to the health of your Calm pathway.

Strengthen Your Smart Vagus

Once you've calmed your stress pathways and you feel a little less reactive, you can start building up your smart vagus pathways. The benefit: you'll develop a better sense of when to trust people and enjoy them, and your brain will be able to send "relax" messages to the sympathetic and parasympathetic nervous systems.

Exchange Short Smiles

If you don't give your smart vagus regular exercise by exchanging caring expressions with people, it weakens. To help the smart vagus bulk up, trade short smiles with the people you like best. Not a huge fake grin, just a garden-variety smile that communicates a quick and friendly hello. Look the other person in the eye, and make an effort to notice the facial expression the other person delivers in return.

This exercise seemed like a perfect fit for Juan, who often avoided eye contact. When he did look at people directly, he often misinterpreted their expressions. A smile seemed like a smirk; a laugh might come across as sarcastic. In fact, when Juan and I went over what had happened when he blew up during the meeting, we pieced together the possibility that the junior colleague hadn't been trying to take Juan down a notch. He may have been more like a puppy, eager to share his ideas.

My instructions to Juan were simple: when you're interacting with someone, look at his or her face. Notice if the person is smiling or engaged in the conversation, and if they are, smile back and note what that feels like. This step meant that not only would Juan need to register the expression on the face of the other person, he would also begin to be mindful of the ways his brain and body immediately filtered facial expressions through his most prominent relational template—the one he had with his father. In that template, there was no kindness or respect. Juan could make a quick mental note that the person he was interacting with was not his father and that the smile was probably one of engagement, not rejection. This very basic process would activate his smart vagus and eventually improve its tone.

Juan began doing this with just Blanca and Bob, his safest relationships, but soon he moved on to his coworkers, too. Juan was surprised to find that exchanging a quick smile with colleagues gave him a momentary lift. Before long, he was able to hold longer conversations with people at work, and we moved our focus to helping him actively listen to their words. Engaging in facial communication and in active listening made him feel different—less alone and even a little calmer. This happened partly because he was enjoying the interaction, but it was also because he was, little by little, rewiring his autonomic nervous system.

In a workshop I did with a group of teenagers from the Bronx last year, we all took out our smartphones and looked at photos of smiling friends. I asked everyone to pay attention to what they were feeling in their bodies, and every single person reported feeling calmer, happier, or less stressed. It's amazing that such a quick relational intervention makes an immediately noticeable difference. So build a photo gallery on your desk or phone, with pictures of your safest people looking happy or goofy. Make a point of looking at them a few times each day to buff up your smart vagus and to feel better.

This is one of those exercises that can sound incredibly silly—*if* you have been told all your life that other people are judgmental, frightening, and competitive with you. Try it anyway. This is neuroscience, people; our brains are wired to work better when our faces engage and connect with the faces of others.

Listen Yourself into Safety

When a soothing sound wave enters your inner ear, the vibrations move the bones and muscles, and the smart vagus fires, helping you feel less stressed. So one way to grow the smart vagus is to listen to the voice of someone you love. You can also listen to music that reminds you of being with that person. (No breakup songs allowed!) The more you stimulate the smart vagus, the stronger it will get.

Another way to stimulate the smart vagus is to actively listen to another person. The next time you're feeling anxious in a social situation, use this technique:

First, scan your body and determine your stress level. If you pick up on a lot of stress, remind yourself not to talk mindlessly, space out, or walk away. Those are all stress reactions. Instead, try actively listening to a specific conversation.

In power-over cultures like ours, inserting your point of view into a conversation is seen as more valuable than listening to others, so it's normal to feel pressure to talk. But real dialogue means speaking *and* listening. It is essential to practice and value both skills equally. Take the pressure to speak off yourself, and head into the conversation focused on listening.

However, even when you no longer feel pressure to talk, listening can be hard work, especially when you're anxious. Your body could be screaming at you to *do something*, and listening means staying pretty still. It helps to give yourself tasks to focus on, so remind yourself to look at the speaker and mentally repeat her words (just in your head). If you catch yourself preparing what you'll say next while she's talking, gently move your mind from your own thoughts and place them back on the speaker. Ask questions, too, but just for clarification. Then run a quick repeat scan of your stress level. You should notice a difference; if not, go back to your active listening.

Ironically, actively listening makes you feel less stressed, and this means you'll have better access to the thinking part of your brain. When you do speak, you'll contribute more meaningfully to the conversation. None of us is particularly fluent when we're anxious.

Relational Mindfulness

Relational mindfulness is a two-person exercise developed by Janet Surrey and Natalie Eldridge, faculty members at the Jean Baker Miller Institute. It is a form of Insight Dialogue Meditation, and it is a powerful way to stimulate your smart vagus nerve by combining relationships with the known calming benefits of meditation.

Most meditation exercises involve sitting alone or in a

group, focusing on your breathing and attempting to escort random thoughts out of consciousness. Some types of meditation use mantras or chanting. The goal of these practices is to settle down your sympathetic nervous system by tapping into your parasympathetic nervous system. (Yes, some people have a freeze response caused by the parasympathetic nervous system. But for most of us, stimulating the parasympathetic nervous system in appropriate amounts and at appropriate times simply leads to a calm, centered feeling.) Studies have shown that regular meditation actually changes brain structure and creates more activity in the prefrontal cortex, an area that feeds back to the limbic system, causing you to feel less stressed.

Relational mindfulness uses the same techniques as meditation: breathing and ushering thoughts from the mind. But Jan and Natalie ask people to meditate by sitting across from each another, eyes open.

I bet this sounds overstimulating, and in some cases it can be. There's some evidence that when people hold eye contact for more than three seconds, they either fight or make love. Either of these activities will disturb your meditation! But glaring, unbroken eye contact is not the point. This is not a stare-me-down contest. A gentle, respectful gaze works much better, and you're always free to look away and take a break. Sometimes I have people ease into this exercise by practicing a few minutes of compassion meditation, which you can learn about on page 206.

Choose one of your safest friends to invite into a relational mindfulness practice. The first five or ten minutes can produce intense feeling; expect to temporarily Ping-Pong back and forth between activating your smart vagus (and feeling relaxed) and activating your sympathetic nervous system (and feeling like you want to jump up and run away). You may get a case of the giggles, too. But if you stay with it for just ten minutes, the stress of the interaction will give way to a safe sense of being intentionally held deeply and respectfully in a human relationship. The result can be a profound stimulation and reworking of the smart vagus, especially if you practice on a regular basis.

This exercise can be particularly moving and intense if you try it with a romantic partner—but do this only if the relationship is a safe one. Over time, a relational mindfulness practice can help couples bypass their usual squabbles. It also helps create even more safety inside the relationship, because the exercise trains the smart vagus nerves to fire at the sight of a partner's face. This leads to a calm, balanced feeling.

Starve the "Freeze" Response

People with a supersensitive parasympathetic nervous system feel so threatened by social interactions that they feel like they might die. I'm not exaggerating. Of course, they *know* they're not going to die, but their brains don't. Their brains remember an old equation: people = terror. It reacts by telling the body to shut down. This is different, really different, from the fight-or-flight response. It's a completely different branch of the nervous system that's activated. Instead of feeling a rush of adrenaline, you feel numb, quiet, and sleepy. You may not be able to speak if you feel this way. You may instinctively wander away and even feel like curling up into a ball. What you're experiencing is the human equivalent of playing dead, meant to persuade the threatening person to move away from you. You can't even talk to anyone to tell them how frightened you are, so people might react to your behavior by raising their voices or stomping around in bewilderment—which only increases your fear.

To recover from the effects of a parasympathetic nervous system response, you'll have to dig deep. Your body may order you to shut down, but you have to reach a compromise with your instincts. Go ahead and remove yourself from the situation that is scaring you, but try not to lie down or curl up. This is a time when you actually need to stimulate your sympathetic nervous system; studies show that mild to moderate stimulation of your fight-or-flight response can be energizing and focusing. But you need to stimulate it *gently*, just enough to feel alive and to warm you out of your frozen state. Physical movement is ideal—nothing very strenuous, just a walk, some flowing yoga postures, or even a slow jog.

A parasympathetic nervous system freeze response is a sign that you feel extremely threatened. No matter what the circumstances, if you experience a parasympathetic nervous system freeze response, you need more help and support than you're getting. Call on your safest friends and find a caring therapist who can help you gently address the source of your fears.

Take the Next Step

A feeling of calm is the cornerstone of a relationship. Without the experience of trusting each other, facing each other respectfully, looking at each other's facial expressions, finding the words to explain your relational experience, and having the patience and ability to actively listen to the other's point of view, the relationship can't feel safe. As you work on your Calm pathway, expect the positive effects to spill over into all your relationships—and into your other pathways for connection.

If you've practiced the exercises here and are noticing a change in how you feel around people, that's wonderful. Before you move on with the program, retake the C.A.R.E. relational assessment. Your scores may be different now, and you can adjust your next steps accordingly. Just don't stop! You've taken some relational hits in your life, but now you can feel even better by working on the next step. If you're following the program the way I've laid it out here, you'll move on to the Accepted pathway. But—of course—feel free to use whatever part of the program calls out to you. Always, the C.A.R.E. plan is all about *you*—and your relationships.

Chapter 6

A IS FOR ACCEPTED

Soothe the Dorsal Anterior Cingulate Cortex

Here's how you feel when a relationship soothes the Accepted
   pathway:
In this relationship, I feel calm.
I can count on this person to help me out in an emergency.
In this relationship, it's safe to acknowledge our differences.
When I am with this person, I feel a sense of belonging.
Despite our different roles, we treat each other as equals.
I feel valued in this relationship.
There is give and take in this relationship.

A few years ago, one of my fire alarms started going off at random. I'd be in the kitchen or just walking down the hall when the alarm would sound; each time, my body reacted with a jolt of adrenaline and I'd rush through the house, looking for smoke. When I found nothing burning, I'd worry that an electrical fire was smoldering within a wall. Then one day I was so frustrated by the beeping alarm that I took the little box down from the ceiling and opened it up. Inside, I discovered a bug, cooked to a crisp. It had crawled into the alarm and caused a short circuit.

Having an overactive dACC is like having a bug crawl into your fire alarm. Remember the dACC? It's that small strip of brain tissue that activates when you're in pain. The Cyberball study at UCLA, the one where volunteers were gradually left out of an online game of catch, showed that the dACC fires when you're physically hurt but also when you're socially left out. As a species, we seem to be incredibly sensitive to being left out. Later studies using Cyberball showed that even when the volunteer subjects believed that the other players were part of a group they didn't respect, such as the Ku Klux Klan, or when they were told that the other "players" were actually a computer program, research subjects still smarted from the rejection. It's as if your nervous system understands that belonging to a group is crucial to your well-being; when you don't feel a sense of belonging, your nervous system wants you to feel uncomfortable, even wounded, so that you can recognize that you have a problem and do something about it.

But if your dACC has become highly sensitized, it sends distress signals at inappropriate times, just like my fire alarm did. With an overactive dACC, you're always worried about or running from social "fires," never feeling safe in a relationship. The process leaves you feeling alone and abandoned. These feelings of estrangement feed back into the dACC, causing it to be even more active in sensing social rejection.

It took a while before I understood that my fire alarm wasn't telling me that I had a fire; it was trying to tell me there was a bug in the circuit. It's the same for people with highly reactive dACCs. It can be hard to identify what's really causing your feeling of distress. Is it that people are excluding you? It could be. We live in a society based on social competition and on identifying the people who are "in" and people who are "out." Both children and adults get rejected, judged, and jostled out of groups all the time. It hurts to be excluded, even if we pretend that it doesn't. Just to make things harder for all of us, however, a feeling of social pain can also be caused by a bug in the system. It's easier to identify this bug if you know what to look for.

I traced the feeling of a "bug in the system" with my patient Kara, but it was a long time before either of us could figure out what was going on. She didn't talk about alarms or fear or pain (or bugs) at all. When Kara and I first met, she described feeling like a black hole was inside her. Sometimes the black hole churned like an active volcano; other times it felt like a dead, stagnant space. Always the black hole was with her, like a negative energy that drained her. Kara had spent much of her life in therapy, trying to extricate, reshape, and even befriend this deep, dark energy. Nothing had helped.

Kara understood from her years in therapy that this black hole had probably been formed in childhood, when she had experienced losses that were sudden and frequent. Her parents had been doctors who worked for a medical relief organization; they moved around so often that all friendships stayed fairly superficial. She could remember longing to be close with her parents, but for years the Vietnam War got in the way. Her parents were preoccupied by their relief work, the number of soldiers and civilians dying every month, and by their opposition to both the draft and the war itself. In Kara's mind, her early years were a swirl of tension, grief, and being on the move, although nobody really talked about these issues with her. Then, when Kara was in elementary school, her much older sister died in a car accident in a foreign country. Her parents pulled away from their remaining children, emotionally out of reach, where they stayed.

Kara grew into a woman whose life looked pretty darn good, at least from the outside. For starters, she was the vice president of a real estate investment firm. She had married and divorced amicably, raising a son and two daughters on her own. She talked with her children frequently and was proud of their growing maturity and independence. Despite her stressful upbringing, Kara had stayed in regular, though not close, contact with her two younger siblings; in fact, she often organized vacations with them for the express purpose of fostering connections. She had a vast network of friends and dated occasionally. Despite Kara's success and her connections, the black hole remained, and it ate away at her. She instinctively turned to her friends to give her relief from the bad feeling—and this worked, but only temporarily. Within an hour after she returned home from socializing, the black hole would reemerge.

"Relationships are like drinking salt water," she told me. When I looked puzzled, she explained that she could drink and drink, but her thirst was never quenched.

Kara's nerves were so frayed that we agreed to work on her Calm pathway to soothe her hypersensitive sympathetic nervous system. After a while, she felt brighter—but even a steady program of antidepressants, neurofeedback, and other exercises did not seem to change some deep, broken place inside her. The black hole was a useful metaphor for her pain, but I wondered what specifically in her neurological wiring kept this black hole perpetually intact.

Then something surprising happened. Kara was standing in the foyer of her center-entry Colonial, a house nestled in a neighborhood that had been home to centuries of American patriots, politicians, and business leaders. Waiters passed roast beef on toast points; from another room, she heard a pop and then a cheer as someone opened a bottle of Champagne. She was having a party for her colleagues and important clients. There, in her sparkling home, surrounded by history, celebrating with some of her favorite people, Kara understood for the first time that *she did not feel that she belonged here.* This feeling was familiar, but it puzzled her, because she knew that her own credentials were rock solid and that her friendships were real. Why would she feel this way? Moreover, she asked, *why would this feeling bother her so much?*

In an attempt to help her understand the particular pain she was feeling, I described the Cyberball research that tells us why it hurts to be left out. Naomi Eisenberger and Matthew Lieberman, who conducted the original Cyberball research, used the results of their experiments as the basis for SPOT, or *social pain overlap theory.* SPOT describes the "overlap" between the pain of being physically hurt and the pain of being left out. In our bodies, there is literally no distinction between the two. For people, being part of a group is essential, and being excluded is dangerous.

Kara's insight at the party grew into a transformative concept that finally gave the black hole a definition. The black hole was, in fact, a deep sense of never belonging. She'd never felt that she truly belonged to any group. In her childhood, Kara's family was disorganized at best and then, after the death of her sister, emotionally incoherent. Then she'd entered a mostly male profession, where she never felt that she belonged, and when she was married she never felt like part of her husband's extended family. She moved to the East Coast but never quite assimilated into its clubby culture. She had always protected her children from knowing about the black hole; she was unable to share her full experience with them. On it went, this feeling of exclusion.

The next surprise happened when we talked about whether this view was accurate. Did she always feel left out, or was there anywhere in her life now where she felt comforted and like she belonged? Her answer was quick and clear. Kara's two Burmese cats, Wellington and Sealy, were constant, warm, loving creatures who made her feel far better than people ever could. As she described her cats, she could feel the dark hole getting smaller and smaller.

There was another time when Kara felt like she belonged: whenever she was with her brother, Max. The two of them shared a familiar style of wit and good-natured teasing that was "home" to her. Her relationship with her sister, Charlene, was sometimes strained by their different life choices, but their time together also had this "home" feeling. Kara explained this realization of belonging with her brother and sister like this: "There's a feeling of 'Oh, I really do belong with these people.' There's an illusion that I don't belong with my brother or my family, but I do."

Kara suffered from a bug in her neurological alarm system. Her early childhood experiences of being left out had caused her dACC to become oversensitive. Even when she was included, her brain zapped her with painful messages of social exclusion. Understanding that her black hole had a name—it was the feeling of not belonging—and that it had a neurological cause gave her tremendous relief.

All her life, Kara had suffered from a social catch-22. She needed healthy connections to heal her sense of not belonging, but when she reached out to friends, her overactive dACC would give her another zap of pain. In effect, Kara's brain would say, "See? Here's *another* person who doesn't really accept or like you." *Zap!* Her attempts to shrink the black hole were actually feeding it. The fact that her friends actually did like and accept her didn't matter to Kara's dACC.

For Kara, the solution was to identify where she already felt accepted and to go there whenever the black hole made itself known. Instead of calling friends or making dinner plans when she felt bad, Kara would curl up on the couch with Wellington and Sealy. She'd pet them and they would flip over onto their backs so that she could rub their bellies. Or she called her brother. This was not necessarily an obvious set of solutions, because cats, however warm and wonderful, don't have the same potential for conversational intimacy that people have. And Kara was not as close with her brother as she was with some of her friends. But when it came to healing the black hole, none of that mattered. What mattered was that in these relationships, the feeling of belonging was unquestionable. It was simply there. The relationships calmed her Accepted pathway—for Kara, it was like putting an ice pack on her red-hot dACC.

How a "Bug" Gets into Your dACC Cortex

I've been talking about a "bug in the system" of people with overactive dACCs, but of course it's not a real bug. What's more, the so-called bug doesn't crawl into your brain at random. Something happens to create this effect of an alarm system that's yelling out the message *I'm being left out!*, even when people want to welcome you in.

For most of us, that something happens in childhood. In Kara's case, her nervous system was formed at a time when her parents were unable to give her warm emotional acceptance. Children desperately need to be accepted and loved by their parents. The sights, smells, and feelings of a parent's loving gaze and comforting hugs inhibit the firing of the child's dACC, and the more often this happens, the more that the second rule of brain change—**Neurons that fire together, wire together**—can shape the neural pathways to make this effect even stronger. But when Kara would look into her parents' faces, she didn't see a loving, accepting expression. Instead, she got a preoccupied or vacant look. This is not as obviously cruel as neglect or abuse, but let's be clear: it's still a form of rejection. Worse, it was rejection by the people she most depended on.

Young Kara didn't have the words for this painful experience, but over time she simply stopped expecting to feel anything other than left out. In effect, she learned that she was unworthy of loving relationships. As her therapy continued and the adult Kara thought further about the issue of belonging, she realized that whenever she started to feel a desire for more closeness to another person, she felt one of those zaps of pain. The pain carried a message: *What are you thinking, Kara?*

You don't get to feel close to other people! You know you don't deserve it. What was this zap? You guessed it: a pain message that began in her overactive dACC.

The Relational Paradox

When Kara "heard" her dACC telling her that she didn't deserve to be in relationships, she naturally pulled away from the other person. This meant that although Kara had plenty of friends, she wasn't really close to any of them. Kara's behavior with her friends fits into a pattern that relational-cultural therapists call the *relational paradox.* This happens when you're convinced that your friends won't tolerate who you really are, so you decide that the best way to be accepted is to leave a part of yourself out of those relationships. You think, *If they knew about my insecurities* [or past history, secret habits, or anything you believe would keep you from fitting in], *I'd lose the relationship.* Kara's thoughts ran along the line of, *If they knew that I don't deserve to be in relationships, they would leave me.* So, ironically, Kara tried to save her relationships by withholding her fears.

Of course, by hiding yourself you may preserve the friendship, but at a cost of feeling that you don't legitimately belong, that if your friends could see who you truly are, they would cut you loose. The more you participate in the relational paradox, the more pain you feel, and the more sensitive your dACC becomes—which makes you want to hide and protect yourself even more.

You can start to dissolve the relational paradox little by little. I suggest you start by simply becoming aware of the times you hide yourself or pull back from relationships because you think you're unworthy. This can take practice! Then you can send a soothing message to the place in your mind that feels vulnerable. You can do this by revisiting a positive relational moment, which I explain in detail on page 157. If you have a reactive dACC, it's useful to build a library of positive relational moments that involve a close and clearly accepting connection. Kara would say to herself, *Hmm, I hear my dACC telling me I'm unworthy.* Then she'd play a funny conversation with her brother over in her head.

Eventually, you'll be able to see your current relationships with less bias. You can even try sharing some of your hidden self with the people who feel safest to you.

Relational Problems: A Package Deal

Kara's relational assessment chart is interesting because it shows how one problem—in her case, an oversensitive Acceptance pathway—usually shows up in the company of other problems.

Kara's C.A.R.E. Relational Assessment Chart

Answer the questions on a 1-to-5 scale: 1=None or never 2=Rarely or minimal 3=Some of the time 4=More often than not; medium high 5=Usually; very high	#1 Max (brother)	#2 Suzanne (daughter)	#3 Charlene (sister)	#4 Nina (friend)	#5 Alex (coworker)	Total Statement Score	C.A.R.E. Code
1. I trust this person with my feelings.	3	2	3	3	2	13	Calm
2. This person trusts me with his feelings.	3	2	3	4	2	14	Calm
3. I feel safe being in conflict with this person.	3	2	3	3	2	13	Calm
4. This person treats me with respect.	4	3	2	4	3	16	Calm
5. In this relationship, I feel calm.	3	2	2	3	2	12	Calm Accepted
6. I can count on this person to help me out in an emergency.	4	3	2	3	3	15	Calm Accepted
7. In this relationship, it's safe to acknowledge our differences.	3	2	2	2	2	11	Calm Accepted
8. When I am with this person, I feel a sense of belonging.	3	2	3	3	2	13	Accepted
9. Despite our different roles, we treat each other as equals.	4	3	2	3	3	15	Accepted

Answer the questions on a 1-to-5 scale:	#1 Max (brother)	#2 Suzanne (daughter)	#3 Charlene (sister)	#4 Nina (friend)	#5 Alex (coworker)	Total Statement Score	C.A.R.E. Code
10. I feel valued in this relationship.	3	2	2	2	2	11	Accepted
11. There is give and take in this relationship.	3	2	2	3	2	12	Accepted
12. This person is able to sense how I feel.	3	2	3	3	2	13	Resonant
13. I am able to sense how this person feels.	3	3	4	4	3	17	Resonant
14. With this person I have more clarity about who I am.	3	2	2	3	2	12	Resonant
15. I feel that we "get" each other.	2	2	3	3	2	12	Resonant
16. I am able to see that my feelings impact this person.	2	2	3	3	2	12	Resonant
17. This relationship helps me be more productive in my life.	3	2	2	3	3	13	Energetic
18. I enjoy the time I spend with this person.	2	2	3	3	3	13	Energetic
19. Laughter is a part of this relationship.	4	3	3	4	2	16	Energetic
20. In this relationship, I feel more energetic.	3	3	2	3	3	14	Energetic
Safety Group Score	61	46	51	62	47		

Here's how Kara scores on the C.A.R.E. pathways:

Calm (add up scores for statements 1 through 7;
    maximum total score is 175): **94 (low)**

Accepted (add up scores for statements 5 through 11;
    maximum total score is 175): **89 (low)**

Resonant (statements 12 through 16; maximum total
    score is 125): **66 (low)**

Energetic (statements 17 through 20; maximum total
    score is 100): **56 (moderate)**

Kara's Accepted score is her lowest number relative to the scoring range for each category. But her other numbers don't look so great, either. She's only a few points higher for Calm—and that score reflects the improvement she saw after using antidepressants and trying neurofeedback. She had some trouble reading other people, and this went hand in hand with a low Resonant score. She wasn't able to perceive that others really liked her and wanted her to be part of their group. Her energy level was okay, but she tended to feel drained after social interactions, mostly because she felt rejected. It makes sense. Would you feel like dancing if your brain was telling you that you're unwanted?

These kinds of chart results—with low to moderate scores across the board—are typical for people whose neurological wiring is dysregulated. One problem leads to another problem that makes the first problem worse, and so on. It's almost impossible to know precisely where one issue begins and the other ends. If you head into a relationship with your guard up, certain that you won't be accepted, it's hard to feel calm or to project yourself in a such way that others can see the real you, and vice versa. Eventually, all your neurological pathways can suffer.

Fortunately, the reverse is also true. By improving one relational pathway, the others have a head start on getting better, too.

Safety Groups: A Warning for People with Low Acceptance Scores

I want to alert you to a danger for people with low Acceptance scores: if you don't feel like you belong anywhere, assessing your safety groups might be a painful exercise. If your groups don't include anyone in the safest category, you might be tempted to think: *Oh, look—here's proof that I really don't belong anywhere and there's nobody who really likes me.*

If you catch yourself thinking this way, stop!—and relabel this depressing idea as an inaccurate message from your overactive dACC. It may be true that you spend most of your time with people who are critical, judgmental, and unaccepting. You need to identify these relationships so that you can understand the damaging effects that they are having on your dACC and so you can start to repair the damage that's already been done to it.

It can also be true that past experiences with feeling outside and outcast may have shaped your dACC so that it's hard for you to feel like part of any group, even when people want to welcome you in.

Both issues—that the people you hang out with are judgmental *and* that your brain has trouble understanding that you are safe and welcome—can be true at the very same time. This is why sorting your relationships into safety groups is so illuminating. It can help you figure out which relationships deliver a lot of exclusion pain, and which relationships are more promising.

Like Kara, you might be surprised to find that the relationships you turn to in a time of crisis are the ones that actually make you feel the worst. This doesn't necessarily mean that these friends or family members are cruel and excluding (although they might be). In Kara's case, it simply meant that she had a fundamental, instinctive feeling of belonging with her cats and with her brother—and that these were the relationships that she could rely on to help her feel a healing sense of belonging.

Here's how Kara's safety groups shaped up, with a look at how she used the insight:

High relational safety group (75–100 points): None. This helped Kara further identify the cause of her "black hole" as a feeling of exclusion.

Moderate relational safety group (60–74 points): Her brother, Max, had the highest score and was the safest of all of Kara's human relationships. Her friend Nina also made it into the moderate category, but Kara's gut feeling was that she just didn't have quite the same sense of belonging with Nina. This was a relationship that she could improve when she felt ready to share more of herself.

Low relational safety group (less than 60 points): Kara's sister, Charlene; adult daughter, Suzanne; and her co-worker Alex scored in the lowest group. Kara tried not to dump her problems onto her daughter, who suffered from bipolar disorder and was often extremely reactive herself. Kara loved Suzanne, but the relationship struggled. Kara could instinctively feel a sense of belonging with her sister—but she realized she had to proceed carefully. Charlene wasn't entirely safe for Kara.

Alex was a tech wiz who ran the IT department at the bank. He often seemed emotionally cool. Kara wondered if he might even be on the autism spectrum. Kara concluded that her relationship with Alex did not hold much potential for acceptance and belonging, and furthermore she decided that this was okay with her. She didn't need to feel a sense of belonging with everyone. When she was with Alex, she knew how to identify the discomfort she felt, and she could immediately say to herself, "Oh, well. I don't feel accepted by him. Thank goodness I've got my kitties to go home to." Eventually, she decided to focus on accepting *Alex* as he was, instead of wishing he could be different. As you'll see, the judgments you make about other people can boomerang back in a way that heightens your own feelings of being judged. One way to calm your dACC is to let some of those judgments go.

Our Judgmental Culture Leads
to Social Pain

Kara's dACC had become overactive in response to her early childhood losses. But there are other ways that you can develop an overactive dACC. When a culture dictates that normal human development is measured by how separate people are from one another, everyone's relational templates are distorted, and everyone's dACC is reactive to some degree. To make matters worse for the dACC, we live in a hypercompetitive society that's always asking the questions: Who's prettier? Who's more popular? Who's a member of the "best" race, gender, religion, class, or sexual orientation? Who's more competent? Who has achieved the most? Who's got the best stuff? *Who's better?*

To a large extent, our social groups are created around the answers to these questions. This happens so unconsciously that most of the time we're hardly aware of it. Yet it has the effect of putting us all on constant high alert. A part of us is always scanning our surroundings, wondering where we rank against the people we see. Are we better? Are we worse? Imagine what it does to the dACC to know that we could be kicked out of our social group if we buy the wrong handbag or don't get the right kind of job, or if we tell our friends that we're gay or that we don't agree with their politics. In this atmosphere, the dACC is constantly stimulated— and then it becomes more sensitive in response. The result:

this primitive part of the brain is trapped in a vicious circle. The world looks dangerous; every encounter could potentially result in social peril. Then, in self-protection, the brain says, "Withhold yourself. Don't expose who you really are. Take the other person down first if that's what you have to do to stay safe." And then the world *does* become more hostile in response to you.

This is exactly what happened to my client Nancy, a fifty-something woman with stylishly tousled hair and a wardrobe of casual but expensive-looking clothes. Nancy wanted to be in therapy to talk about her relationships. She was worried that she was becoming more distant from her children and losing many of her friends. As we talked, she salted her conversation with judgments about the people she knew:

"Everyone can see that my friend's son isn't very smart. That's why he has to go to the state school."

"My daughter wants a promotion, but that's hard to imagine. She's so lazy!"

"Well, *someone* had to tell my aunt that she's annoying."

I have to admit: I wondered what Nancy would say about *me* when she left my office.

Nancy's harsh comments were the effects of a lifetime of living with a highly stimulated dACC. Nancy did not have a traumatic childhood like Kara's. But throughout her life, she and her family looked to "in" groups to satisfy a desire for belonging. Her mother in particular was highly attuned to how her children appeared to the outside world, especially to the people she wanted to impress. When she thought Nancy had gained too much weight or wasn't doing well enough in school, she could be bitingly critical. By college, Nancy was so accustomed to criticism that a relentless chorus of judgment sounded in her mind: she was too fat, too dumb, not sweet enough. Then Nancy fell in love with a slightly older guy who was studying for his Ph.D. He was ambitious and handsome and from an educated family. Here was a desirable man, valued by the kind of people her family had always admired. The fact that such a man could love her quieted the critical voices in her head.

Nancy married this man and started a family. They were happy at first, but under the pressures of new parenthood, Nancy's husband lashed out at her. She bought a new dress, and he told her she looked ugly in it. He fumed that she was a lazy mother who kept the children in diapers all day, when other wives were out working and contributing to house expenses. If Nancy tried to bring up a complaint about the way he acted, he turned it back onto her: "*I* don't ignore the children. *You're* the one who lets them watch TV while you pretend to get stuff done!" His attacks resonated with the words she had heard repeatedly as a child from her mother. Instead of making her angry, they confirmed her biggest fear: that she was unlovable. Her dACC pain pathways were being chronically stimulated and growing more and more reactive.

Plenty of people suffer damage to their dACC pain pathway as a couples relationship develops—whether the partnership takes on an abrasive tone or not. Falling in love is great for the dACC, as the two people pay extra-close, tender attention to each other. Although it's definitely not healthy for a partner to be as spiteful as Nancy's husband was, it *is* normal for the intense feelings of this initial phase to fade. If one of the partners has even a little bit of reactivity in the dACC, this normal pulling away may not seem just like a change in the relationship. It can feel as if the other person doesn't love him or her at all. The dACC becomes even more stimulated, and feelings of judgment and abandonment cloud the relational picture. It becomes harder to see the other person more clearly. All relationships take work, but the ones that are really close can be the most difficult, because there are so many opportunities for distortion to occur.

Nancy coped with her feelings of inadequacy by trying to fit in with the best social groups in town. She always put forth what she considered to be the best version of herself and her family and hid what she believed were faults. This was the relational paradox at work: in an effort to belong, Nancy was hiding parts of herself. Only the perfect parts could show. Unfortunately, her only other strategy for lifting herself up was to put others down. It was typical for her to "honestly" describe their flaws: her friends were told when they were being ignorant, unstylish, or just irritating. Everyone who Nancy knew was subject to this judgment—even her children, whom she constantly compared to one another.

When I would point out that a statement she'd made sounded overly judgmental, Nancy's face went blank, as if she could not imagine any other way to be. It was all she knew. Of course, her relationships suffered as friends, hurt by her insults, showed her the door. Eventually, Nancy's relationships started to feel like land mines in a field to her, ready to blow any minute. And when they did, she felt hurt and judged and rejected . . . again. But she had trouble understanding the role of her own judgments in the explosions. There was no template in her mind for nonjudgmental acceptance, no alternative to piercing criticism.

From a distance, it might be tempting to wonder what on earth Nancy could be thinking. How could she believe that a constant drumbeat of criticism would draw her closer to her friends or her children? But that's what can happen when the dACC soaks in an atmosphere of judgment. Judgment becomes the way it protects itself. Judgment becomes all that it knows.

Exercises to Soothe Your Acceptance Pathway

Social disconnection isn't just painful. It can have serious health consequences. Science has long known that physical pain stimulates our stress response systems, and now we know that social pain is equal to physical pain. This means that chronic social pain leads to chronic stress, too—and there is an overwhelming amount of research documenting the negative effect of chronic stress on our minds and bodies. Stress dampens the immune system and increases the risk of cardiovascular disease, depression, headaches, diabetes, anxiety, asthma, and other conditions. People who live with chronic physical pain are at significant risk for health problems like these. So are people who live with chronic social pain.

Despite the link between social exclusion and devastating health problems, it's hard *not* to keep the vicious cycle going. Like Nancy, many of us are unable to see an alternative to constant judgment. Or, like Kara, we've turned the judgment onto ourselves, and the message that we're *not good enough* is so deeply written into our psyches that we don't even realize it's there.

The key to breaking the cycle is to become more aware of the cycle. It's so easy to pretend that social pain doesn't exist—that it doesn't hurt to be left out, that we're too grown up to feel bad when people are cold or rejecting. Both Kara and Nancy were perplexed by their suffering. They hardly had the words to describe what was hurting. That's why I'm devoting lots of space here to something I call SPOT removal, a series of steps designed to increase your awareness of social pain. I'm also sharing a few other activities that I use for increasing self-acceptance and acceptance of the people who are your friends.

SPOT Removal

SPOT removal is a set of exercises I developed in response to what researchers call SPOT—social pain overlap theory, meaning that social pain overlaps with physical pain in the same brain region. These exercises will help you identify how strongly your brain reacts to social exclusion. They'll also help you extricate yourself from the cycle of inclusion and exclusion that's constantly being played out in our stratified, power-based society.

First, think of a time when you were excluded from a group or uninvited to a social event:

- What were your feelings and thoughts about being excluded?
- What did you do in response to being left out?
- As you remember this time, what sensations do you notice in your body?
- What story did you tell yourself to explain why you were excluded?
- How did the experience affect your connections to people other than the ones who excluded you?

Then put yourself on the other side of the table. Think of a time when you, or a group you were a part of, knowingly excluded someone else. Ask yourself the same questions.

The goal of these first two steps is for you to become more aware of the impact of exclusion on your body and on your relationships. When you exclude others, or when you judge others, you are perpetuating a system of inclusion and exclusion—the same system that feels so threatening to your brain. This game of "in" and "out" is damaging to everyone who plays it. Even if you are currently "in," you feel, perhaps unconsciously, a sense of threat. On some deep level, you know that at any time *your* name could be called, and you could be the one who's "out."

I learned this lesson early in my career, when I was working in the psychiatric unit of a hospital where a clinician was being targeted by other staff members. The staff had some legitimate criticisms about the clinician's skill. That was fine. Being able to review someone's performance is critical to running an organization. But instead of giving her direct feedback, the staff turned on her. They made her the brunt of behind-the-scenes jokes and cut her out of the group. I'm ashamed to say that I participated. I was new and loved my status as one of the "included" doctors. A few short years later, though, I found myself on the "out" list. I was judged unfairly—just as I had unfairly judged my colleague earlier. Anyone participating in social inclusion and exclusion is in an emotionally precarious situation. Even now, when I think back to both those experiences as a young psychiatrist, my throat tightens and I want to hide. The experiences of excluding and being excluded are ones that can stay with you.

Repeating these two steps with a few different experiences of inclusion or exclusion will give you a better perspective on the revolving-door quality of this human dynamic. In, out, in, out. *Zap, zap, zap, zap.* Feel that? As you temporarily relive the stress of being left out, or the transient relief of being included when someone else is pushed aside, focus on all the feelings that arise. You may be surprised at their complexity.

Next, pick a time when you'll be out in the world for at least thirty minutes. Bring a notebook or your phone and make a small notation every time you make a judgment about someone else or judge yourself in comparison to someone else. When you're done, think about the messages that have been running through your head. Do you constantly think others are managing their lives better than you are? Or do you judge yourself as smarter and better than everyone else? Do you notice the weight of everyone around you, or their height, or the clothes they wear?

Judging immediately disconnects you from other people. In that moment, you can't see what does or could exist between you; you can only see where you rank in the power structure. If you've ever had a highly critical, micromanaging boss, the kind who thinks he's the only one with the "right" answers, you know what I mean. Every interaction leaves you feeling helpless, diminished, and angry! On the other extreme is the coworker who repeatedly apologizes for the work he's done, always sure that he's not good enough. He makes little eye contact in meetings; you can feel the shame he carries. The person who chronically judges others and the person who chronically judges himself base their interactions on old relational patterns and controlling images from the past. When you are in an interaction with someone like this, you may feel "unseen." Judgments are like a thick layer of fog settling between you and the other person, making it nearly impossible for you to see each other clearly. Some of these old relational images come from childhood experiences, but others are absorbed from the fabric of society's values. These are the "isms": racism, sexism, heterosexism, able-bodyism . . . in a stratified society, there is an infinite number of ways to judge others. Not only do we learn to judge individuals as a way for us to get ahead, but we also learn to judge entire groups of people and even whole cultures in order to justify an unequal division of power. By noticing how often you make mental criticisms of yourself and others, you'll become more conscious of the default program of judgment that runs in your head.

A way to decrease a chronically overactive dACC is to stop feeding it judgments. **So again, find thirty minutes when you will be out in the world with others.** When judgments pop into your mind, simply notice them—and then relabel them. Don't judge yourself for having judgments! Just say, "Oh, that's just my judging mind," and then actively lift your thoughts up out of their neural groove and move them to a new, more positive track. Try thinking something more generous about the person you were judging, even if that person is you. Or think about a happier moment, like your child's face during her birthday party or a relaxing afternoon you spent searching for stones on the beach.

When you take this step, you stop the revolving door of judgment in your mind. Active nonjudgments starve the neural pathways in your brain devoted to judging yourself and others.

This step is simple but not easy. The judging pathway isn't going to simply concede defeat and step out of the way to let the new thoughts take hold. The judging mind is an agile foe, and the judging pathways are robust from years of development. Expect some of the other neural pathways that the judging path has recruited to jump in and tell you things like, "But really, that person's hair is too long!" or "This SPOT removal thing is overly simplistic and a waste of time." It is essential to continue to notice, relabel, and refocus. Only then will you distance yourself from judgment enough to see that it isn't reality. Try this step for thirty minutes a day for two weeks, and you will begin to see the judging pathways diminish.

Challenge yourself to apply this technique in more complicated situations. Choose an environment that really pushes your hot buttons, like a political debate. There may be no place in American culture more judgmental than the field of politics (with the possible exception of fashion and beauty). Over the last couple of decades, opinions and judgments have become hair-triggered and hardened. This makes politics a great place to practice nonjudgmental acceptance. So regardless of your political beliefs, try watching a debate, or follow a political issue being argued through the media. When you feel a judgment coming on ("He's an ignorant idiot!" or "She's an elitist!"), see if you can notice it, name it—and then relabel it as the product of a judging mind.

Another challenging environment for most people is holiday dinner with the in-laws, whether or not politics comes up. So try to name and relabel your judgments next time you're sharing a turkey dinner with relatives who drive you crazy. To paraphrase Frank Sinatra: if you can practice active nonjudgment there, you can practice active nonjudgment anywhere.

The goal of this more challenging exercise is not to strip you of your belief systems. Having well-developed opinions is essential to a full life. The goal here is to create a healthier dACC by cutting back on how often you feed it the unhealthy food of demeaning judgments. And by starving the dACC in this particular way, you take advantage of the first rule of brain change: **Use it or lose it.** If your dACC isn't stimulated by judgments as often, it will lose some of its reactivity.

There's another way that toning down judgments can heal your brain. Judging is the domain of the emotional right brain, which is trying to protect you from something it perceives as a threat. This is a well-meaning activity on the part of your right brain, but it is an ineffective relational strategy. When you're judging, you're not listening. And if you're not listening, you're missing out on one of the best ways to stimulate your smart vagus pathway and turn down the volume of your stress-response system. But if you're not judging, you can listen more and feel calmer, and this, in turn, will make interacting with others much easier and judging others less necessary. As you listen, you may learn

something new. Or maybe not; there is always the possibility that you will hear things that you don't agree with. Fine.
Honest disagreements happen in even the best relationships.
If you can have a passionate argument without pathologiz-
ing the other side as sick or malicious, your relationships
will be more durable.

Sometimes people question the steps of SPOT removal,
wondering whether giving up judgment means that they
cannot give or receive feedback about interpersonal actions
and behaviors. Actually, feedback is absolutely critical to
growth-fostering relationships. How can you grow without
feedback? It's instrumental in helping people see each other
clearly and correcting behavior that undermines the relationship. But snap judgments and dismissive comments are very
different from respectful conversation about what needs to be
improved in a relationship. While both can be hard to handle,
judgments are usually mean-spirited and designed to enhance
your distance from the other person. Respectful conversation
is in the service of the relationship. These conversations are
in the category of growing pains; they are not fun to experience, but they are easier to bear because the pain isn't
being held by just one person. It's being held within the
relationship.

Judgments versus Feedback

What's the difference between making a snap judgment and offering helpful feedback? It's all about their intended effect on the relationship. Judgments set you and the other person further apart; feedback will, ideally, bring you closer. Here are some examples of both:

Judgments	Feedback
I can never get things right with you. You're never happy!	I try to consider your experience of things, but I am often confused by your reaction. Can we talk about how each of us can become more responsive in the relationship?
You're an undependable jerk for canceling our date last night.	Can I tell you something? We've been out on a few dates, and I like you a lot. But when you cancel on short notice, it feels as if you're sending me a message that your schedule is more important than mine.
You're lazy.	I've noticed that you tend to leave the room when it's time to put the kids to bed. I really wish you would stay and help me.
Your political opinions are crazy! You've been brainwashed by the media.	We have different political opinions. Why don't you tell me yours—and I'll promise not to interrupt or try to change your mind. Then I'll tell you about mine, if you promise to do the same for me.

What Are You Hiding?

Most people are hiding at least a few things—usually personal characteristics or beliefs or past experiences—from the people closest to them. Hiding who you are can make you feel safer, but only temporarily, because hiding produces follow-up thinking that goes, *If they knew the real me, they would reject me.* This is the relational paradox at work. In the hopes of being accepted, you don't share who you are—and then you feel as if you're always on the verge of being discovered and then rejected. You feel chronically unseen. What seems like a good, safe strategy for building relationships ends up activating your dACC pain pathways.

Ending this stimulation of your dACC requires some courage and at least one reasonably safe relationship. Begin by making a list of things you are hiding. Then choose your safest relationship and invite that person to perform an exercise in mutual sharing: you will both divulge one thing you've been hiding from others. The thing you are hiding is likely much more embarrassing or shameful to you than to the friend you are telling.

Here are some of the secrets, big and small, my patients have hidden from their partners, family, and closest friends:

- I lied and told my boss I got into a car accident because I didn't want to go to work.
- My family is from Germany.
- I took a year off from school after flunking out of college.
- I had an abortion when I was seventeen.
- I was sexually abused as a child.
- I hate camping.

- I give lots of speeches, but I throw up in the
  bathroom before each one because I am so anxious.
- Some days I'm so depressed and anxious that I can't
  get out of bed.
- Some days I really wish I didn't have kids.
- When I was a little boy, the older kids chased me
  all over the football field and I was scared to death.
- My wife earns more money than I do.

The relationship will probably be closer after you've been more honest with each other. Unpacking old secrets can significantly decrease the pain of life.

Root Chakra Work

In the Hindu and yogic traditions, the seven chakras are the body's energy centers, each located at a different point on the body and each governing a different psychological or emotional state. The root chakra, which sits at the base of your spine, right at your tailbone, helps you feel grounded and connected—to know that you belong in the world. You can try a very simple method of balancing this chakra by placing one palm over its area and another hand over your heart (the location of the heart chakra, which influences our sense of inner peace). You can do this while watching TV, meditating, or simply sitting and thinking. Over time, the bad feeling of exclusion will lift.

Compassion Meditation

Barbara Fredrickson, the director of the Positive Emotions and Psychophysiology Laboratory at the University of North Carolina at Chapel Hill, has spent her career researching love and acceptance. In her book *Love 2.0*, she describes what she calls "loving-kindness meditation" or "compassion meditation," a practice that her lab has shown to increase self-acceptance, decrease depression, and improve relationships.

To practice compassion meditation, find a quiet and comfortable spot. Breathe in and out, finding a slow, deep rhythm. Say these phrases to yourself:

> *May I live in safety.*
> *May I be happy.*
> *May I be healthy.*
> *May I live in ease.*

Then send the same wishes to a friend:

> *May he/she live in safety.*
> *May he/she be happy.*
> *May he/she be healthy.*
> *May he/she live in ease.*

Using the same script, send the wishes to a neutral person, and then to someone you dislike. Finally, send the wishes to the world:

May we live in safety.

May we be happy.

May we be healthy.

May we live in ease.

As you sit quietly, breathing deeply, you are decreasing your nervous system's level of arousal. You become calmer. When you send compassion to yourself and the world, you add a sense of warm-heartedness to that feeling of calm. You're teaching the brain to pair these two states of being—to use the second rule of brain change by wiring the two sets of neural pathways together. If your brain has been wired for snap judgments, this exercise will show it how to find pleasure in good wishes.

When you meditate on oneness and on compassion toward yourself and other people, you're enlarging—in a psychological and neurological sense—the knowledge that we're all one. It's remarkable to witness the change in people as they make a regular practice of compassion meditation. Over the weeks, its message begins to compete with the well-worn neurological pathways that insist *I don't belong*. A different pathway, one that has been weak for a long time, begins to remind you that you do belong, and that we are imprinted on one another. We can hurt and heal one another. And one of the best ways for us to grow is within our relationships.

Chapter 7

R IS FOR RESONANT

Strengthen Your Brain's Mirroring System

*Signs that a relationship is **Resonant**:*
This person is able to sense how I feel.
I am able to sense how this person feels.
With this person I have more clarity about who I am.
I feel that we "get" each other.
I am able to see that my feelings impact this person.

In a classic scene from the movie *Jaws*, chief of police Martin Brody sits at the dinner table, polishing off a bottle of wine. He rubs his face and his shoulders droop. There is no voice-over to tell me explicitly how Brody feels, but none is necessary. My brain has a mirroring system that takes in the information on the screen; it creates activity in my prefrontal cortex and somatosensory cortex that helps the neurons there internally copy his body movements and messages. The neural input passes through my insula, the little strip of brain tissue that helps connect context with emotions. This system of circuits from across the brain tells me Brody is exhausted and troubled. More than that, he is haunted by his decision to keep the beaches of Amity Island open after the first couple of shark attacks.

I'm not the only one who is mirroring Brody. While Brody is lost in thought, his young son sits at the table next to him, watching. Brody's son spontaneously imitates his father, rubbing his face as if he, too, were exhausted; he carefully raises his cup for a sip of juice the same way his father sips his wine. After a moment, Brody notices and plays along. He clasps his hands in front of him and then pops his fingers straight out, and his son follows along, pleased to have gotten his father's attention. The scene ends with a mutual, playful sneer and a loving kiss. Throughout the scene, Brody's son follows the actions of his pensive dad perfectly and mirrors his glum mood to a T. When they finally make eye contact, it's clear that Brody has been rescued from the brink of despair, drawn out of isolation into the loving connection with his son. That is the power of relationship and the beauty of an active mirroring system: one healthy connection can stave off the despair of shark-infested waters.

We are built to imitate people. Not because we are unoriginal copycats, but because we are blessed with a neurological system that automatically uses imitation as a crucial component of reading other people's behaviors, intentions, and feelings. The mirroring system can manifest itself in obvious ways, as when two people in conversation will start to copy each other's posture. You've seen this: one person crosses his legs and then the other crosses his. One leans forward, his chin in hand; the other copies the gesture almost instantly. I once had the strange experience of unintentionally copying George W. Bush. Just after he became president, his face was everywhere—on the cover of magazines, on the TV news, when I opened my Web browser. In most of the photographs, he was wearing that expression in which he appears to be in on a practical joke, like he's just put a whoopee cushion on his best friend's chair. For weeks, possibly even months after his inauguration, I would catch myself making the same face. And whenever my face transformed into a likeness of President Bush, his image would pop into my consciousness. The more I mimicked him, the more empathy I felt with him. The mirroring system is what allows us to resonate with other people without having to focus deliberately on the task.

I opened this book by claiming that boundaries are overrated. Resonance is the ultimate anti-boundary; it happens when one person's actions, intentions, and feelings are instantly, unconsciously replicated in a fainter way inside another person's brain. This replication is a good thing, because resonance is an important relational skill that lets us feel a deep-in-the-bones connection with others. Unfortunately, the mirroring pathway is the one that's most neglected when we're in a culture that emphasizes boundaries and separation.

Like the other C.A.R.E. pathways, the mirroring system is shaped by your relationships. It's well known that early, attuned relationships between mother and child lead to children who spend more time in social engagement, are able to better regulate their emotions, and are able to interpret and comment on their feelings and internal experiences.[1] The discovery that neuroplasticity exists throughout the life span suggests that pathways for connection, including the mirroring system, continue to shift and change in response to relationships. Healthy relationships nurture our neural capacity for resonance. Damaging relationships, especially ones with people who don't really understand you or see you for who you are, can weaken the neural circuits that are involved in the mirroring process. Those circuits may wither from disuse; they may not get the chance to build a rich neural network that allows for shared information; they may not receive the relational dopamine and other neurochemicals that solidify its pathways.

When that happens, it can be harder for the shared neural circuits that are involved in the mirroring process to imitate other people's feelings. As a result, you may find other people puzzling. You may think that everyone is blithely content when they are actually trying to send up flares of distress. Or you may be so sensitized to "dangerous" emotions that you *over*read people as being angrier or more distressed than they really are.

This oversensitization is what happened to Pauline. When I first met Pauline, she was waiting on a bench in the hallway outside my office, looking around nervously. Actually, she was looking for me. I was a few minutes late, and I immediately felt sorry that my tardiness had apparently increased her anxiety.

Most clients feel at least a little normal anxiety when they first see a psychiatrist. Truth be told, first meetings often make me a little nervous, too. I never know what I'm going to hear and learn. But Pauline's anxiety level was remarkable. When she saw I was ready for her, she turned her head down so that she was looking at the floor. I put out my hand and she extended hers limply, still without looking directly at me. As I said, her case is remarkable. I share her story here because it takes the garden-variety problems many of us have with resonance and magnifies them by a few factors, letting us see our own difficulties with greater accuracy.

As we went into my office and talked about the basics—where she lived, with whom, where she worked—Pauline relaxed a little. I tried not to look directly at her for very long, thinking that I didn't want to exacerbate her discomfort. When Pauline did look up, I made a point to smile and nod in my most outwardly interested way. Despite my best efforts to be welcoming, when Pauline spoke she often apologized about something she had said. "I'm not giving you the right answers, am I?" she asked. "I think you want more detail than I just gave. I'm sorry."

The interaction was confusing to me as we stuttered our way through the first thirty minutes. I'm an experienced psychiatrist who can usually get a lifetime's worth of information from a new client in sixty short minutes, but at this point in the session I felt like an unskilled dancer who kept stepping on her partner's toes. Pauline talked of feeling anxious much of the time, worried that others were angry or disappointed with her. Her fear with me and the way she described her disappointing and sometimes frightening interactions with other people made me wonder whether Pauline was unable to read friendliness on a face, or if people became frustrated by her inability to stay connected, make eye contact, and stop apologizing.

An answer arrived when we discussed her family history, and that answer loops back to the theme of early relationships that shape the brain. Pauline grew up with a father who'd gone to Vietnam when she was five and came home a brittle, angry man. I don't intend to point a blaming finger at Pauline's dad, because his behaviors as described by Pauline are in line with post-traumatic stress disorder—and this was a time when PTSD was barely understood, let alone treated. The mirroring system that helps you automatically connect with others does not necessarily turn off in the heat of battle and produce an emotionally disconnected solider. In fact, I often wonder if one of the reasons so many soldiers develop PTSD is that, despite the adrenaline rush of combat, their mirroring circuitry reads the pain of everyone around them, friend and foe alike. That pain is stamped onto the soldier's nervous system. When the solider goes home, the pain comes along, too.

Life with Pauline's father was unpredictable. It was hard to know what would set him off—one night it was being served leftovers for dinner; another night it was the neighbor's dogs barking, or his discovery that the garbage cans were still out on the curb a few hours after trash pickup was over. When her father's anger began to build, Pauline's mother advised her to lie low, to take herself out of the tornado path of his rage. Just as meteorologists learn to read cloud patterns, air pressure, and wind speed for signs that a storm is brewing, Pauline learned to read her father's face for the earliest hint of anger. If his eyebrows drew together, or if his lips narrowed, Pauline turned and quietly fled to her room. I wondered if what had started out as a smart protective strategy—the ability to tune in to the physical minutiae of her father's expressions—had grown over the years into a hyperawareness of *everyone's* expressions, and the generalization that all of us were just a second or two away from exploding into anger at her.

I smiled at Pauline, and then asked her if she could see that I was smiling at her, and that I was happy that she was here, sharing her concerns with me. Pauline looked up and into my face. After about fifty minutes of talking about five feet away from me, I think this was the first time she felt comfortable enough to see me. She smiled back.

"I'm sorry," she said. (Apologizing again!) "I don't think I know how to do this right. The therapists I've seen before have always been so critical."

Certainly, I know a number of psychiatrists who would fit that bill. But I also suspected that Pauline had not been able to see her therapists and read any kindness on their faces. I mean "see" both in the metaphorical sense of understanding another person and in the literal sense of being able to look into another person's face. I paused two times before our session ended and playfully asked Pauline to look me in the eye for just a moment—which she did, followed by a deep red blush of shame. When I paused and asked her to look at me a third time, she giggled. This was a good sign and an important first step. This was not simply a woman with anxiety. This was a woman with a deep sense of relational fear programmed into her nervous system. Every uncomfortable interaction only made the fear stronger. Unfortunately for Pauline, every interaction was uncomfortable.

Let's take a look at Pauline's C.A.R.E. scores:
Calm (add up scores for statements 1 through 7;
    maximum total score is 175): **82 (low)**
Accepted (add up scores for statements 5 through 11;
    maximum total score is 175): **94 (low)**
Resonant (statements 12 through 16; maximum total
    score is 125): **71 (moderate)**
Energetic (statements 17 through 20; maximum total
    score is 100): **54 (low)**

Two things immediately struck me about Pauline's relational assessment. First, only one of her relationships felt even moderately safe. This was her relationship with her outspoken and ambitious sister, Maureen. Pauline wasn't 100 percent comfortable in Maureen's company, but she did sense

Pauline's C.A.R.E. Relational Assessment Chart

Answer the questions on a 1-to-5 scale: 1=None or never 2=Rarely or minimal 3=Some of the time 4=More often than not; medium high 5=Usually; very high	#1 brother	#2 Maureen (sister)	#3 Dr. French (boss)	#4 Leslie (secretary)	#5 Sandy (research assistant)	Total Statement Score	C.A.R.E. Code
1. I trust this person with my feelings.	2	3	1	2	2	**10**	Calm
2. This person trusts me with his feelings.	3	4	1	3	3	**14**	Calm
3. I feel safe being in conflict with this person.	3	3	2	2	3	**13**	Calm
4. This person treats me with respect.	1	2	1	2	2	**8**	Calm
5. In this relationship, I feel calm.	2	3	2	3	2	**12**	Calm Accepted
6. I can count on this person to help me out in an emergency.	2	3	2	3	3	**13**	Calm Accepted
7. In this relationship, it's safe to acknowledge our differences.	2	3	2	2	3	**12**	Calm Accepted
8. When I am with this person, I feel a sense of belonging.	4	4	2	3	3	**16**	Accepted
9. Despite our different roles, we treat each other as equals.	2	3	2	3	3	**13**	Accepted

Answer the questions on a 1-to-5 scale:	#1 brother	#2 Maureen (sister)	#3 Dr. French (boss)	#4 Leslie (secretary)	#5 Sandy (research assistant)	Total Statement Score	C.A.R.E. Code
10. I feel valued in this relationship.	3	4	2	3	3	15	Accepted
11. There is give and take in this relationship.	2	3	2	3	3	13	Accepted
12. This person is able to sense how I feel.	2	3	2	3	3	13	Resonant
13. I am able to sense how this person feels.	5	4	4	3	4	20	Resonant
14. With this person I have more clarity about who I am.	3	3	2	2	3	13	Resonant
15. I feel that we "get" each other.	2	3	2	3	3	13	Resonant
16. I am able to see that my feelings impact this person.	2	3	2	2	3	12	Resonant
17. This relationship helps me be more productive in my life.	3	3	3	3	3	15	Energetic
18. I enjoy the time I spend with this person.	3	3	2	2	3	13	Energetic
19. Laughter is a part of this relationship.	3	3	2	3	3	14	Energetic
20. In this relationship, I feel more energetic.	2	3	2	2	3	12	Energetic
Safety Group Score	51	63	40	52	58		

that her sister felt protective of her, and she mostly liked that feeling.

Not surprisingly, Pauline had been drawn to a quiet life, one without a partner or even any close, intimate friendships. She felt so uneasy in any interpersonal interaction that sustained relationships simply stressed her out. Pauline had chosen a career in science that suited her desire for quiet, focused attention, and for years, she'd worked as a research assistant in a lab. She loved plating bacteria on an agar plate and returning the next day to see what had blossomed. There was no reading between the lines; either the bacteria grew or they didn't. She found this work refreshingly clear, and she was devoted to it—she was usually the person who volunteered to stay at the lab after hours to complete a timed experiment or to finish cleaning up from a long day of work. So it was in the lab where most of her relational time was spent.

Her steadiest work relationship was with Sandy, another research assistant who seemed appreciative of Pauline's work ethic. Pauline also had regular contact with an older secretary, Leslie, who worked in the lab across the hall, but Pauline found her penchant for doling out grandmotherly advice "too much." It felt like criticism. There was also her boss, Dr. French. Dr. French was pleasant enough, but Pauline had felt that someone with power must be dealt with cautiously. She paid very close attention to Dr. French and could anticipate things that she wanted or needed. Occasionally, Pauline would curiously watch how Dr. French and Sandy interacted.

They were casual together; they even talked about their weekends.

The only other person Pauline spent time with was her brother, who could be a difficult guy. He was opinionated and bossy, and though Pauline felt loyal to her family, she also hated the feeling that he was always annoyed at something she'd done—even when she knew she'd done nothing.

The second thing I noticed about Pauline's relational assessment was that all her C.A.R.E. pathways were on the low side. In fact, her Resonant score was actually higher than her others. This was a measure of just how anxious, left out, and drained she felt. But it also reflected a few other things. First, Pauline's ability to read people wasn't completely off; it was mixed. She could study someone like her boss and learn how to please her. But she also saw anger even when anger wasn't there. In fact, her highest Resonant scores came from statements about being able to read other people. Pauline wasn't aware that she was *mis*reading them.

In order to unwind the relational knot Pauline was in, she needed to follow all the steps of the C.A.R.E. program in order. When the Calm and Accepted pathways are weak, people naturally become so preoccupied with their own internal fear systems, and by the relational alarm bells that are constantly sounding, that they are too distracted to see others accurately. After she felt calmer and more trusting (I thought compassion meditation would be particularly good for her— see page 206), we'd tackle the Resonant pathway. With luck, these steps would improve at least a few of her relationships and spark some good relational energy.

Not everyone with a weak Resonant pathway is convinced that land mines are buried inside every person she meets. Take my friend Dan, who's got a short fuse. When someone is distant or distracted, he believes that they are intentionally trying to hurt him, so he jumps all over them. Or take Darcy, who imagined—with pleasure and pride—that her employees and family lived in awe of her. She had a rude shove out of that illusion when she was passed over for a promotion and her husband threatened to leave her, saying that she had no idea what he thought or felt.

Ways to Tune up Your Emotional Resonance

What about you? Do you find it hard to know what other people are thinking? Are you often convinced that other people at work hate your proposals, only to find out later that they've endorsed your ideas? Do you often feel blindsided by other people's anger, which seems to come at you out of nowhere? Or have you noticed a subtler pattern of relational drift, of the warmth draining out of relationships that were once cozy and close?

Remember, if you have difficulty reading other people, it's not because there is something inherently wrong with you. It's a result of how your brain has been shaped in relationship with others. For example, if you live with a person like Darcy—the woman who liked to think of her husband as an admiring underling—you will eventually suffer the effects. When other people refuse to see your anger or your sadness, it becomes harder for you to see those emotions in yourself. In the vicious circle that by now should be all too familiar, you will then struggle to read anger or sadness in others.

Although your brain is inevitably affected by relationships, you're not powerless. You can take your neural pathways and reshape them. The exercises below suggest that you begin by spending more time with people who are sensitive to your feelings, and that you reduce the proportion of time you spend with people who can't see who you are.

From there, learn to label your own emotional landscape and then practice by trying to read the emotions of fictional characters you see on TV or in the movies. Other "safe distance" suggestions include limiting your exposure to violent images, which can overwhelm and confuse your mirroring system, and using the rules of brain change to starve the pathways that devalue particular emotions. When you're ready, there are several one-on-one exercises you can try within the context of relationships that already feel comfortable.

Spend More Time in Resonant Relationships

A while ago, I introduced the idea of relative relational time— that we have a certain amount of time we spend in contact with other people, and that it's useful to know which relationships occupy the highest percentage of that time.

Pauline's relational time was spent like this:

Person	Percentage of Relational Time
Brother	25
Maureen (sister)	20
Dr. French (boss)	20
Leslie (secretary)	20
Sandy (research assistant)	15

If Pauline could spend more time with her sister, who felt fairly safe, and less time with her brother, who felt scary, she would leverage the power of good relationships to help her grow. We agreed that Sandy was another promising friendship, and that maybe she could try spending just a touch more time with her. Pauline started simply, by agreeing to make more eye contact when she and Sandy were talking. Locking eyes and holding the contact was too much, but Pauline could briefly look into Sandy's eyes and then look away again. She also used her observational habits to notice the kind of coffee Sandy liked and left a cup on her desk with a short, friendly note. Even Pauline could see that Sandy was touched, not angered, by this gesture.

If you are in a relationship with someone who can't or won't see you, reduce the damage to your mirroring system by rethinking how much time you spend with this person. Darcy's husband, for example, wasn't sure he was strong enough to stand up to his wife until he consciously reapportioned his relational time. He started playing tennis with a friend a few nights a week, and he began taking their children for frequent weekend trips to his parents' house. This was not done in the spirit of running from his difficulties. Instead, it helped him spend time with people who "got" his emotions, quirks, and personality tics. Eventually, he could remember what anger feels and looks like—and he realized that he was angry enough to have a healthy confrontation with Darcy about their problems.

Sometimes there's another solution: you can take small steps to improve a relationship that lacks resonance. I once worked with a recently retired woman who had become depressed and numb. Why? This woman had been an office manager, the bright hub of a busy medical practice. Everyone looked to her—literally—for guidance. Her mirroring system received constant positive stimulation. When she retired, it was as if someone had pulled the plug on this part of her nervous system. Her husband, who'd retired a few months earlier, had happily begun several painting projects. He was so absorbed in his new work that he didn't even look up when she entered the room. At night, he was tired and remote. My client began to ask her husband to say hello to her in the morning, to insist on conversational niceties that he thought were no longer necessary after so many years. After an awkward period in which their "Hello, how are you doing?" phrases sounded artificial, some of the neural pathways for their older, more affectionate habits reawakened. The person she spent most of her time with was now a person who could stimulate her mirroring system, not weaken it.

Identify the Physical Life of Emotions

Researchers have identified six basic human emotions that exist across all cultures:

Happiness
Sadness
Anger
Fear
Disgust
Surprise

These emotions don't just live in our heads. They have a life in our bodies, too, and even when an emotion is too distasteful to think about consciously, the body expresses it. Anger often lives as a pounding heart and rising blood pressure; fear can surface as chilly hands and feet. People who attend to these body signals and learn to interpret their meaning are better able to read emotions in themselves and in others.

You can cultivate your awareness of emotions in your body. It's best to do this in a safe and quiet place. Choose the emotion that you're most comfortable with, and then, with your eyes gently closed, let your mind drift to a time you experienced this feeling.

When I practice this exercise, I can easily generate a list of happy images involving my children. My son and daughter seem to live deep within my bones! One image that particularly captures a sense of happiness for me occurred when I coached my daughter's softball team. We made it to the championship, and my daughter pitched half the game. She struck out the last girl and the game was won. In the midst of a wild celebration with her teammates, we made eye contact. It was sheer pleasure. When I focus on this image with my eyes closed, I first notice that my chest feels full and that there is a direct connection between the full feeling in my chest and a smile that has formed on my face. I can't help myself: the feeling of joy travels throughout my body. My hands tingle a bit and I can feel my whole body energized by the memory.

Try on a couple of memories that call up the emotion you're thinking of. See if the feeling is experienced in the same location and in the same way—and if not, notice the differences. This simple exercise is one you can practice over and over again. The more you do it, the more easily identifiable your feelings will be to you.

Once you've practiced with an easy emotion, try a different one, something that feels less comfortable. For many of us, that emotion is anger. For some, it's fear. A sign that you're uncomfortable with an emotion is that you often read it in others. If people often seem angry with you or afraid of you, or if they seem so happy it strikes you as ridiculous . . . bingo. You have a valuable clue.

Jennifer, the young woman whose family gave her the

silent treatment, had learned over the years to squish her anger far, far, out of reach. So I asked her to let her mind drift to a time when she could remember feeling mad, really mad. And it was a time she was angry on behalf of someone else— when she first heard about the sexual abuse of young boys at Penn State. She was driving in her car, listening to a sports radio channel, when the news broke in. "The anger exploded in my body like a volcano," she said. "There was a bandlike feeling around the top of my head. My throat was so full that I wanted to scream."

When you try this exercise, you might notice that some-times feelings are more complex and overlapping. When Jennifer lingered on the anger she felt, she noticed a deep heaviness low in her chest, close to her abdomen. It was a profound sense of sadness for the children. Jennifer didn't enjoy reliving this moment. But it was helpful for her to lo-cate the feeling in her body and to know how to describe it. That way, she'll be less likely to be angry, or angry/sad, with-out even realizing it.

As you work on this particular kind of emotional intelli-gence, be patient with yourself. It took Rufus, who was ad-dicted to Internet porn, about six months before he could identify the basic emotions in his body—and to notice that when something made him angry or hurt, he immediately zoned out so that he was no longer connected to anyone around him. As he got pretty good at noticing feelings in himself, I invited him to notice what I might be feeling. This was difficult for Rufus: first he had to actually look at me and then he had to notice my body language and facial expressions. We passed a milestone one week when I came to work slightly distracted by something happening at my daughter's school. Without being prompted, Rufus asked if I was angry with him. Instead of jumping to that therapy kickback, "Why do you think I'm angry with you?" I paused and said that I was more distant but that I was definitely not mad at him—just a little concerned about something at home. I appreciated that he pointed this out. It allowed me to refocus on the work he and I were doing together. In fact, we had a great session and I was so absorbed that I was able to put my troubles on the back burner.

Name the Emotional Spectrum

There are six basic emotions, but each of those six has almost infinite grades of intensity. Here are just a few of the words available to describe those grades, ranging from mildest to strongest:

Happiness
> Contentment, gladness, happiness, serenity, joy, elation, bliss, euphoria

Sadness
> Disappointment, hurt, melancholy, sadness, gloom, despair

Anger

> Annoyance, irritation, frustration, anger, rage,
> fury

Fear

> Worry, nervousness, anxiety, helplessness, fear,
> alarm, panic, terror

Disgust

> Contempt, disgust, revulsion, loathing

Surprise

> Surprise, shock, amazement, astonishment

People who live in an environment that dismisses the importance of emotions may have an intellectual grasp of each of these words, but it is hard for them to distinguish among these complex states in their own minds and bodies. Annoyance, irritation, frustration, anger, rage, and fury may all blur into one unnamable emotion. Overwhelmed, the person may express the feeling in an impulsive, out-of-control way—or stifle it.

Trying to interact with others when you don't have the full repertoire of feelings at your fingertips is like trying to run a retail store with nothing but one-hundred-dollar bills. With no variability in the denominations, everything you sell must cost the same regardless of its actual value. A pair of boots and a candy bar would both cost one hundred dollars. The boots may actually be worth that amount, but spending one hundred dollars on a candy bar is never a good idea! (And you're talking to a candy lover here.) If you have a narrow range of feelings, you may express an intense fury in an interaction when irritation would be more relationally useful. Juan, the computer programmer who raged at his coworkers when they commented on his ideas, comes to mind.

To sharpen your emotional vocabulary, try this exercise, which you can do in private. Identify one of your safest relationships, and then choose one of the six basic emotions and sit quietly while you imagine feeling the mildest version of that emotion toward the other person. Move up the scale of intensity. As you do, notice where you feel the variations of emotion in your body and how those physical feelings change. If you can't notice a difference yet, that's fine. As you pay more attention to where feelings arise in your body, and start to think about the words you use to label them, this important relational skill will come more naturally.

Next, recall what happened when you felt each of the emotional shades. Could you express them accurately? If you did, what happened next? In healthy relationships, the expression of emotions usually deepens the relationship—even if the emotion is anger with the other person. Jean Baker Miller said that one of the defining aspects of a growth-fostering relationship is that it produces a clearer sense of yourself, of others, and of the relationship. When your emotions are respected within the relationship, your capacity to form and express your experience grows stronger. So does your ability to hear the other person's experience.

You might try the same exercise and imagine feeling emotional shades within a riskier relationship. What are the differences? For bonus points, track a character's emotions in all their grades of intensity as you watch a movie or show.

As you repeat this exercise with other emotions, you connect your cognitive understanding of a feeling with a more differentiated sense of it in your body. Eventually, this will translate into clearer communication in your relationships.

Of course, the ultimate goal is to move this exercise into the real world. When you're with one of your safest friends, try saying something like, "You seem irritated/joyful/worried today. Does that sound right?" Naming the emotion and then checking in are essential. So many problems come from our failure to confirm that we're reading people accurately. Then we travel full-speed in the wrong direction, piling up misunderstanding after misunderstanding until the relationship crashes.

All relationships have a rhythm of connection and disconnection. It's impossible to resonate with another person all the time. The point is not to be perfect in your reading of the relationship but to be more aware of how you're reading them, and to check out what you're sensing. This is the **Use it or lose it** rule of brain change working its magic. The more you stimulate the mirroring pathways, the stronger they become, so they can help you safely span the enormous differences we all encounter in daily life.

Starve Neural Pathways That Separate
Feelings from Thoughts

Back in 1976, before anyone was thinking about relational pathways in the brain, Jean Baker Miller introduced the concept of *feeling-thoughts*—the integration of intellectual and emotional experience that's necessary for participating in healthy relationships. But in a culture that promotes separation as the goal of healthy human development, we're not taught to respect feelings. We learn that *thoughts* are the sign of a mature brain and that *feelings* are somewhat distasteful and immature. Unfortunately, splitting feelings from thoughts puts you at a relational disadvantage. Your experience of a relationship is largely based on how you feel about it. If you deny or misread those feelings, you can end up communicating in a way that is confusing.

For example, in my psychotherapy practice I often ask clients what they are feeling. Instead, they'll share with me what they are thinking: "I feel like I do not want to be with my husband anymore" or "I feel like I am done with therapy." The emotion that is paired with the thought is missing. One of the important tasks of therapy is to reunite emotions with thoughts so that the client can make statements that are more accurate. The statements become more understandable, too: "When I am with my husband I feel lonely and hurt; I do not want to be married to him anymore" or "When I am in therapy, I feel annoyed and angry at the focus on my drinking. I think I will stop therapy."

Improving your emotional literacy is a way to get better at communicating feeling-thoughts. The exercises I've already described can help you do that. You may also need to starve the neural pathways that are telling you to associate maturity with thinking and immaturity with emotions. Watch for these messages in your day-to-day life:

- Do you live in a family that says feelings are for children only (and preferably just girls)?
- If you talk about the way something makes you feel, are you teased or ignored?
- Are you in a relationship with a partner who criticizes you when you mention feelings, rather than just "focusing on the facts"?

When you are expressing strong feelings with someone who has difficulty forming feeling-thoughts, he or she may experience an uncomfortable mirroring of your emotions. The other person may even be flooded with emotions that feel unmanageable—and that's why the person may become rigidly fixed on keeping emotions out of your conversation.

Your resource against these messages of "thought superiority" is our old method of brain change, relabel and refocus (page 156). When you're in a family interaction and are criticized for mentioning your emotions, relabel the criticism as "simply a family belief." Refocus on a time when you brought feelings into a relationship and enjoyed the connection that followed. Or rely on one of your positive relational moments (page 157); I often refocus on my PRMs of rich conversations I've had with my children and when I do, I can almost feel the old pathways melting away.

Practice In-Person Contact

Are you in a relationship that's based mostly on technological interfaces, not in-person interactions? Person-to-person contact is essential for exercising mirror neurons. Taking in the sensory input from another person's expressions and actions will directly stimulate the mirroring system. The more interpersonal context you have, the stronger the neural firing along the mirroring system. If we're Skyping, you can see my face, and maybe you can see my upper arm moving. But you won't be able to see that I'm reaching for a cup of coffee on my desk. When we're not interacting in person, your mirroring system doesn't get as much information and won't fire as well.

Please don't give up on texting, Skyping, FaceTime, and the like—technology has become a basic tool for communication and keeping up friendships. But if you don't practice in-person interactions, communicating via technology will actually become harder. Why? Because when you have well-connected, robust C.A.R.E. pathways, you are able to read a few words from another person or see just his or her face and be reminded, both mentally and physically, of everything you know about that person. You have a context for understanding the limited information you're getting via the tech interface. But if you don't have the body experience of the relationship, you have to rely on *other* body relationships to help you decode the words or sights. It's like getting a message from your best friend but reading it as if it came from your mother—which leaves lots of room for misunderstanding.

Reduce Your Exposure to Violent Imagery

Violent imagery is ubiquitous—in games, the news, movies, and television shows. What's damaging about this imagery is that it rarely shows the effects of the violence on the victims. When we have hurt someone, our brains and bodies need to see the impact of that pain on the other person. Seeing the impact of violence and aggression on the victims directly stimulates your mirror neurons, leading to empathy for the person who has been hurt. In fact, standing in another person's shoes, or imagining what their experience is like, is an essential part of violence prevention and is the core part of most programs that treat male perpetrators of violence. But disembodied violence is unrealistic and does a disservice to us all. Marco Iacoboni says that

taken together, the findings from laboratory studies, correlation studies, and longitudinal studies all support the hypothesis that media violence induces imitative violence. In fact, the statistical "effect size"—a measure of the strength of the relationship between two variables—for media violence and aggression far exceeds the effect size of passive smoking and lung cancer, or calcium intake and bone mass or asbestos exposure and cancer.[2]

Being exposed to large-scale violence can alter the adult nervous system, but for children the effect is even worse. They are in the critical period of learning and neural shaping, and they absorb excessive violence without adult filters. The combination of the two factors means that violence becomes built into their mental constructs of relationships.

For these reasons, limit your exposure to violent images. Even I admit that some of the most violent films and movies are also some of the most entertaining—but for the sake of your mental and relational health, watch some comedies instead. If you're a gamer who is drawn to simulations of war or crime, try some games that are a little more playful or that emphasize collaborative activity. If you find it challenging to make this switch, remember that each episode of violence that you see is mirrored in your body and brain as if *you* are being violent or being victimized. If you reduce or eliminate that exposure, you'll feel better.

Know Your Relational Templates

Have you ever begun a romantic relationship with someone you thought was completely different from your parents—and felt relieved that, *this time*, you wouldn't spend your time together replaying the most frustrating parts of your childhood? Things go blissfully for a week, a month, maybe even a year . . . until one day, you wake up and *poof!*—your perfect partner is telling you how to dress and wear your hair. Last week she taught you the correct way to load the dishwasher, and finally, this morning, as you were hurrying to work, she made a suggestion about how to roll the toothpaste tube. You lost it. You had a full-blown, eight-year-old tantrum, the kind you used to have whenever your controlling mother bossed you around. In that moment, standing at the bathroom sink, it finally happened: your sweet partner, chosen for her laid-back demeanor, had become your critical parent.

There is nothing more disheartening than traveling on these old relational loops over and over. But playing those loops is what almost always happens—because of the way we all learn to read each other's behavior. If you want to stop repeating old relational patterns, and if you're ready for some advanced work in reading other people, you need to become familiar with what are called *relational templates*.

At the place where your mirror system passes through your insula, there is a lifetime's worth of relational images, which are also known in relational-cultural therapy as relational templates. These are the ideas about relationships that you've held for so long you don't even recognize them. Relational templates are the molds for your ideas about how relationships are supposed to work, what you're entitled to within a relationship, and what particular actions and expressions signify. When two people misinterpret each other, it's often because their relational templates are drastically different.

Because early relationships and experiences sculpt our brains, and because our nervous system is drawn to the familiar for safety (even when it isn't safe!), we all repeat relational templates constantly. These templates become the unconscious rules that dictate how you act in relationships and how you expect others to behave. If much of your experience as a child was positive, with rich, respectful, and responsive people around you, people who were able to listen to others and to speak their voice, who could negotiate and compromise, you are probably in pretty good shape relationally. The skills of healthy relating will be built into your brain and body: you are more likely to have a calm dorsal anterior cingulate cortex, a robust smart vagus nerve to help modulate stress, and plenty of dopamine from family and friends. And you are much more likely to have a well-oiled mirror neuron system, with the ability to see people clearly.

In a culture that values separation, however, it is common to form a relational template that undermines your ability to read others and to be in a healthy relationship. An example is the close friendship between my friends Rob and Mary. They met in college, and as they realized they shared similar interests, values, and life goals, they became inseparable. Everyone thought they should get married, but Rob and Mary agreed that having the other for a spouse would be like marrying a sibling. The friendship survived graduation, cross-country moves, first jobs, and Mary's marriage. Even though they were on opposite coasts, they talked weekly and texted or e-mailed daily. Until Mary had a child. Rob flew east for the christening, and it was during that visit that a long-standing impasse began.

In Rob's mind, Mary was over-the-top obsessed with her child. She couldn't talk about anything else. *You can put her down for just one minute!* Rob would think as Mary tried to carry on conversations with Rob about her baby—all the while tending to her baby. Rob knew that babies are adorable and that they require hard work, but wasn't this a little much? He was surprised to feel divorced from Mary's world. *Am I really jealous of a baby?* he wondered.

Mary picked up on Rob's distraction, but she assumed he was just consumed by a job he'd recently started. But over the months, Rob grew frustrated by how long it took Mary to respond to his messages and how often she had to end their phone calls because of some need of the baby's. And talk about the baby was a colossal bore to Rob. He grew more and more distant. Their communication faded. Both felt an enormous loss but had no idea what to do about it.

Neither realized that deep-seated relational templates were playing out in the way they related to each other. Mary had grown up as an only child and had loved every minute of it. Her mother had doted on her and still did. Every month or so, she'd send Mary a care package filled with all her favorite treats—this made Mary feel seven years old again, in the best way possible—and they enjoyed long, chatty conversations. Mary always expected that she'd be the same kind of mother to her own child. Who wouldn't make a baby the center of the family universe?

Rob also enjoyed attentive parents—until his brother was born with cerebral palsy. Rob's mother and brother nearly died during the birth, and although both survived, little Jonathan was disabled for life. The house was transformed into a medical ward filled with wheelchairs, special beds, oxygen, and medications to keep Jonathan alive. Everything about their lives needed to fit around his schedule. Rob knew that his parents still loved him, but they were so overwhelmed and tired from taking care of his brother that he couldn't help feeling left out.

In print, it's not hard to see how Rob's and Mary's experiences have formed two very different relational templates. But the nature of relational templates is that they're our only reference point for how relationships should work. They feel like an instinctive list of the things all people are just supposed to know about how we relate with others. So to Mary, it felt like "everyone knows" that a new baby is supposed to be the center of everyone's attention. To Rob, it seemed that "everyone knows" that when you stop paying close attention to your best friend, you're sending a clear message to that friend: bye-bye. Rob and Mary didn't realize that they were reading from two different scripts, so they were both confused and hurt.

The tension broke one evening when Mary reached out to Rob in tears. Despite their distance, he was the only person she wanted to talk to about how isolating and tiring it can be to take care of a child full time. Rob was so relieved that Mary still saw him as a confidant that he was able to step out of his anger and feel compassion. They had a long talk that night, each explaining what they'd been thinking and feeling. Rob was finally able to make sense of his anger as he described the pain of being pushed out of his mother's arms by a sick little brother. Mary realized that not everyone shared her mother/baby ideal. By identifying elements of their relational templates, they were able to see each other more clearly and compassionately. This is how a good relationship can shape your brain for the better. In this case, Rob's and Mary's mirror neuron systems were strengthened when they learned more about how to "read" each other.

Relational templates are a major reason we misread people. Rob's relational template told him that a mother can love only one person at a time. Pauline's template told her that everyone teeters on a knife's-edge of anger. Jennifer's template framed low expectations of how other people would act toward her; she hardly knew when she was being mistreated. If you build an awareness of these deeply grooved mental pathways, you can more easily find your way to clarity when things in the relationship become confusing or fuzzy. It's like knowing to put on your prescription glasses to correct your out-of-focus vision. And we *all* need these "glasses" to help us see others, because we've all internalized different relational templates.

Use Your C.A.R.E. Relational Assessment to Spot Patterns

One way to spot some of your relational templates is to review the results of your C.A.R.E. Relational Assessment Chart. Look for patterns that carry over from one relationship to another. For example, Jennifer noticed that she had only one relationship in which she felt clear about herself most of the time. Eventually she decided that when she entered into most relationships she would feel confused—not just about how to express her needs but what those needs actually were. She hadn't quite felt the pain of this confusion before, because her family life had taught her it was normal to not be seen, heard, or understood. One client, who'd just realized that she played the emotional caretaker for her group of friends, arched her eyebrows and said, "Well, *that* sounds familiar. And by familiar, I mean familial." Of course, relationships are not simply replays of past relational experiences; each has its own tempo and color. So each relationship you evaluate will look a little different from the others. Nevertheless, you'll probably spy some general patterns.

Let Friends Help You "See" Your Template

Minds can get caught in perpetual self-deceptive loops. ("It's not that I imagine that other people are angry," Pauline said to me, "it's just that nobody else but me can see how angry they are.") That's why you'll want to collect some information about your relational patterns that comes from outside yourself. Invite someone from your relational safety group to give you honest feedback about how he or she sees you in your relational world. (If you don't have anyone in that group yet, wait until you do. If you ask someone who doesn't see you clearly to perform this work, you could end up with a distorted view of yourself.) Most people are hesitant to offer criticism of their friends, so here's a list of questions to get the conversation started:

1. Am I always the one doing the caretaking?
2. When other people have strong opinions, do I defer to them?
3. Do I have a hard time listening to others?
4. Do I get angry when other people challenge me?
5. When there is a conflict, do I get hurt easily and withdraw?
6. Am I aggressive when I don't get my way?
7. Do I act differently with men than with women?
8. Am I controlling?

9. Am I often too scattered and distracted to engage with people?

10. Do I say things impulsively that hurt people's feelings?

Unlock Implicit Memories

Explicit memories are the visual, often narrative memories that you can picture in your mind. You can't start saving explicit memories until the hippocampus, the memory storage in your brain, forms sometime between the ages of three and six. When people ask you about your very first memory, they're really asking about your first *explicit* memory. Your implicit memory, on the other hand, is formed in your first couple years of life, before the hippocampus is up and running. Memories that are stored implicitly are thought to be related to the action of the amygdala, which is associated with emotions and stress; these memories come up not on visual tracks but as feelings and bodily sensations.

You may not be able to "remember," in the traditional sense, the times your mother pushed you away when you were scared, or the times in nursery school when other children made fun of your lisp, or even the moments of absolute peace and comfort when you nestled into your grandmother's soft lap. Implicit memories are not visual; they're more like subliminal background noise stored in the cells of your body, constantly feeding you information about what to expect in the world. They may emerge as feelings or bodily sensations, as when you find yourself flooded with a strong dislike for someone with no apparent cause, or when a stranger seems familiar to you. Because these implicit memories don't *feel* like memories, they become the "truths" we fail to question, our biases, and source of any rigidity we feel in relationships. They also feel like the essence of your nature, so changing them or even identifying them as having the potential for change can feel downright scary.

I can't give you a way to track your implicit memories to an external event in the world. But there's a way to track some of the "truths" that are triggered by powerful implicit memories, and to help you realize how relative these truths can be. Begin by recalling a time when you were in a seemingly unresolvable conflict with someone. What was the truth you carried into the conflict—the idea that you knew, deep down, was correct and just? When you can identify this truth, you can be pretty sure you're touching the tip of an implicit memory.

Now try to identify the truth you believe the other person brought into the conflict. And then—here's the hard part—imagine a bridging truth that would allow both realities to exist. For example, Rob and Mary were each eventually able to identify the truths they brought into their conflict about how people should treat each other. A bridging truth was that a mother's tight bond with her baby could be healthy, but that the time she devoted to creating that bond could cause the mother's friend to feel lonely. Another bridging truth was that Rob and Mary missed each other and wanted the relationship to continue.

The point of this exercise is not to change all your core beliefs but to bring you an awareness of how relative and experiential they are. Sane people can and will differ on some pretty critical life issues, and having the brain flexibility to imagine the outlines of another person's relational template is a key relational skill.

Starve Unwanted Relational Images

So far, I've described how to reduce the power of your relational template by becoming more aware of it. In this final step, you can use the rules of brain change to actually change some of the relational images within your template. Make a mental list of the relational ideas that form your individual template; note how you feel when a relationship bumps up against one of those ideas. Decide which memories, images, and ideas you want to hold on to and which ones you'd like to move further into the background. You can't delete your memories, but you can move them further into the background of your mind. They will still be part of your life, but they can be a part that has little relevance to your relationships today.

And it's back to the relabel and refocus technique to starve the unwanted relational images. When an unwanted implicit or explicit memory makes itself known, simply label it as an old relational image. By giving it a name, you're separating the image from absolute reality. Then call on the third rule of brain change: **Repetition, repetition, dopamine.** Every time you relabel the image, refocus your mind on an especially pleasant PRM. With time (that's the repetition part), the old relational images will fade. (For more about relabeling, refocusing, and PRMs, see page 156.)

Rob, who realized how close he'd come to drifting away from his friend Mary forever, tried this technique. His template had been formed by the feeling that people he loved would push him aside, that he'd get bumped out by someone who was needier and more important. His head told him that his little brother was sick and vulnerable—of course he needed most of his parents' attention—but the memories stored in his body told a different story. When he imagined that time period, he could feel his heart beating faster, his chest growing tight, and his whole body coursing with a feeling of irritability. He could also feel, just below the anxiety, a profound sadness. When he paid attention to this feeling, forgotten images emerged: before his brother was born, he'd been excited. He was going to be a big brother! He was going to show this little guy his favorite toys; they were going to share a bedroom; and when they were supposed to go to sleep they would stay awake and have fun together. The grief of that loss was profound.

This loss—which was a controlling relational image for Rob—had influenced his adult interactions. Whenever he would become interested in a woman, he would immediately say to himself, *Don't get your hopes up.* He didn't like to let himself look forward to anything; he tried not to put himself in a position where he could be disappointed. In fact, that's why his relationship with Mary worked so well. She was a friend, with no pressure for anything more to develop. He loved that. It felt safe. But this impulse toward safety above all else had almost ruined his friendship with Mary, and it had ended other relationships before they could get off the ground.

Slowly, Rob began to starve the neural pathway, the one that told him not to get his hopes up. When he met a new person at work or a woman he liked, warnings poured into his head—and Rob reminded himself, "These are the ghosts of old memories from when my brother was born; they do not apply today." Then he focused on how he and Mary had reconnected. As his relational images became more explicit to him, they released their grip; and as he devoted more neural space to the memory of diving deeper into his friendship with Mary, he grew more confident. There is nothing more powerful than realizing you've rewired your brain for more hope and happiness.

Chapter 8

E IS FOR ENERGETIC

Reconnect Your Dopamine Reward System to Healthy Relationships

How do you know if a relationship stimulates your Energetic
  pathway? It feels like this:
This relationship helps me be more productive in my life.
I enjoy the time I spend with this person.
Laughter is a part of this relationship.
In this relationship, I feel more energetic.

Take a look at this couple in trouble, and think about how you'd describe their problems:

Melissa and Maggie sat on the couch in my office. Unlike many couples who come in for therapy, they were sitting together, holding hands. But something was clearly wrong.

They looked more like tired colleagues at the end of a long shift than partners in love.

The complaints tumbled out. Melissa had started drinking. First one glass of wine every now and then; then a glass every night; and soon she was buying a couple of bottles of pinot at the grocery store on Saturdays, just to see her through the week. Maggie didn't drink. "I'm too busy," she said, a bit primly.

Melissa arched an eyebrow. "Not too busy to watch hours of TV at a time," she noted. "And it's *stupid* TV."

A backstory emerged. Melissa and Maggie began seeing each other in college, where each was hundreds of miles from her family. As the romance progressed, they started to spend most weekends together. Melissa was aware that Maggie was close to her family, but it wasn't until their senior year, when Melissa and Maggie moved in together, that it became clear Maggie called or texted them multiple times a day.

> Which elective sounds better: Kinesiology or Intro to Theater?
>
> Remind me what kind of tomato sauce Mom buys.
>
> How did the twins' basketball practice go today?

Maggie rarely made a move without discussing it first with her family. Melissa found this odd, but not terribly troubling. The Melissa she knew was strong and capable, a woman who'd majored in electrical engineering and who had once told off the track coach for intimidating a freshman at practice.

The summer after graduation, Melissa and Maggie were

married. When Melissa found herself at the altar of a large, progressive church, she paused . . . and then she panicked. Glancing out at the church pews, she saw plenty of people but few familiar faces. Maggie's guests outnumbered hers by at least five to one.

"Hundreds of people," Melissa said to me, when the two of them came in for couples therapy a few years later. "And almost all were members of her family!"

"Well, who was I supposed to leave out?" Maggie asked. "You don't exclude family!" She turned to me for confirmation. "Right?"

It was an argument they'd had several times over. Melissa marked the ceremony as the point when her life became overrun by weddings, funerals, christenings, football games, and weekly Sunday dinners with her very large and very committed clan of in-laws. Melissa had agreed to move back to Maggie's hometown after they married, imagining that it would help them save money and give Maggie the emotional support she needed as Melissa started a career in finance with long hours. Within a couple months, though, Melissa realized she was leading her in-laws' life, not her own. The weekends that Maggie and Melissa used to enjoy together as a couple changed dramatically. Sundays in particular were all-day family events. After church—where everyone went together and sat in the same pews every week—they all gathered at the parents' house for lunch. They would eat a big meal that was served in the midafternoon, often with several courses. Then they sat around and talked and watched TV until night fell. Spending the day in a different manner was out of the question. In a broader sense, Melissa felt that Maggie's family was trying to suck them into their groupthink. At college, Melissa had enjoyed debating issues with Maggie, who'd held her own opinions. But now Maggie, her brothers and sisters, and her mother planned events together, painted their family rooms the same colors, consulted each other about what to eat for dinner, and were similarly critical of their spouses as a group—as if all the loves in their lives were an identical lump. The day that Melissa's sister-in-law came over to suggest some improvements to their front yard, Melissa broke.

"My God, your family can't let us alone! They expect us to be with them, all together, all of the time. It's like we've been absorbed by a giant amoeba."

Maggie lobbed back. "Oh, would you rather live the way your family does? They've only come to visit us once! And your mother didn't even give you a *hug* when she got off the plane."

"At least my family loves me enough to let me go and live my life!"

Since the landscaping incident, Melissa had refused to attend any of family gatherings. Melissa suspected that she'd become a scapegoat, with Maggie and her family bonding behind her back by talking about how different and strange Melissa was. It was about this time that the drinking had started.

Maggie treasured her family bond. When they were all together, she felt cozy and cherished. She could admit to some problems, though. Having expanded her beliefs, her likes, and dislikes during the four years away from home, she occasionally bristled at the way her mother tried to run her life. Often her mother would announce plans and simply assume that the "children" (all fully grown adults) would go along with them. Maggie had loved the independence she had in college, not to mention the togetherness she'd felt with Melissa. As they talked, a wave of missing Melissa swept over her.

"But there's the drinking . . ." Maggie said.

"There's your lack of interest in my *entire life*," Melissa said simply.

Maggie and Melissa are clearly at a crisis point, both in their marriage and in their lives as new adults.

What's gone wrong? What should Maggie and Melissa do?

This chapter is called "E Is for Energetic," so it's probably obvious that I'm thinking of Maggie and Melissa's problems in terms of their Energetic pathways, which transmits the feel-good, animating neurochemical, dopamine. But first let's look at their marriage in the same way that popular culture views couples' issues. Let's look at it through the lens of separation and individuation.

In this view, a few aspects of Maggie and Melissa's problem are clear. The first is that Maggie's family is pathologically unwilling to let her separate. If Maggie wants to do the essential work of growing up and forming a family of her own with Melissa, she will have to understand that her parents and siblings have been stunting her emotional growth with their demands for closeness. Their desire to have Maggie with them may look like love, but it's not: it's a desire to prevent her from growing into her own person, from developing boundaries between herself and them. If Maggie wants to survive as an individual, she will have to kick at her family, much the way a rebellious teenager would do, and push them away in order to recapture the independent self she forged in college. Only then will she be a mature person, ready to pull her weight in her marriage.

In this scenario, Maggie will have to forfeit the closeness and warmth she feels with her family. Would she be willing to do this? She might. If a trusted therapist tells Maggie that her family has deprived her of something that is essential for her growth, she might be so angry at her family that she'll *want* to push them away. If she feels she's been wronged, the loss of her family closeness won't sting as much as it otherwise might. One likely outcome is that Maggie will develop a kind of angry, amused tolerance of her needy family members. Instead of joking about Melissa with her family members, it's the family members who will become a sort of shared joke between Maggie and Melissa, one that helps the couple forge their own bond more securely.

A separation-individuation therapist would have some clear advice for Melissa, too. Melissa is not drinking a tremendous amount—not enough to affect her functioning—but she is definitely leaning on her nightly glasses of wine. And in separation-individuation theory, dependence is always a bad thing. Melissa's task is to grow strong enough that she doesn't need the wine. Or anything, or anyone, else.

At this point in the book, you might not see their problems in terms of the need to separate. You might see their problems differently. I certainly do. Right off the bat I notice that this relationship lacks sparkle. They're not bringing out the worst in each other—no one is uttering curses or breaking furniture—but they don't exactly come to life in each other's company, either. Trying desperately to feel better, Melissa has turned to wine. Maggie is hoping that a busy schedule, family time, and a whopping dose of television will produce good feelings.

These are classic signs of trouble with the Energetic pathway, which begins deep in your brain stem and travels a winding road until it ends in your orbitomedial prefrontal cortex, a part of your brain that helps you make decisions. Dopamine is a neurochemical that zips along this path and helps you feel simultaneously fulfilled and motivated. When dopamine is flowing, you don't feel like you've become a different person. That's what makes it so great. When you've got a steady supply of dopamine, you still feel like yourself, except that you feel like yourself on a really great day.

The human brain has evolved to get a burst of dopamine when it does something life-sustaining. Eating, drinking water, exercise, sex, and healthy relationships are all supposed to trigger feel-good sensations, to make us want to do the things that are good for us. But the brain loves to get dopamine, and if it can't get dopamine the ideal way, it will turn to other, less healthy, methods. Drugs and alcohol are common dopamine sources, but so are shopping, gaming, and obsessive eating. And, in Maggie's case, tight bonding with both one's family and one's television.

Problems that run along the Energetic pathway often look a lot like Maggie and Melissa's, in the sense that there is a basically loving relationship in which the fizziness has gone flat. I'm not speaking solely of romantic relationships here; dopamine is present in healthy friendships and family relationships, too. When the dopamine trickles out of one of those relationships, things don't feel fun anymore. You may try to accustom yourself to the drab, lackluster days. You may tell yourself that adult life isn't supposed to be fun. But eventually your brain will beg for some excitement. And, frankly, your brain is doing what it's built to do. It's telling you that it wants to claim its birthright; it wants to feel energized by its relationships. We are supposed to feel a sense of motivating satisfaction when we're with the people we love. Maybe not every minute, but most of the time. Moreover, we are capable of feeling that pop of good energy even in long-term relationships. In fact, our permanent relationships can be the most rewarding.

When a basically good relationship loses its sparkle, it's the Energetic pathway that is most obviously affected. Just look at Maggie and Melissa. Not only are they drinking and watching junk TV, they're so depleted they barely have the energy to snipe at each other. But often these Energetic symptoms are just the tip of the iceberg. To understand why the dopamine isn't flowing, you need to look at what's going on with *all* the C.A.R.E. pathways. Both women filled out the C.A.R.E. Relational Assessment, but I think you'll get a good sense of what was happening to them by looking at just Maggie's:

Here are Maggie's C.A.R.E. pathway scores:
Calm (add up scores for statements 1 through 7;
    maximum total score is 175): **128 (moderate)**
Accepted (add up scores for statements 5 through 11;
    maximum total score is 175): **144 (high)**
Resonant (statements 12 through 16; maximum total
    score is 125): **84 (moderate)**
Energetic (statements 17 through 20; maximum total
    score is 100): **64 (moderate)**

Energy and Resonance: A Synergistic Pair

The Resonant and Energetic pathways tend to go up and down together—not always, but often. Maggie's low Resonant scores underscore what happens when your family doesn't want to see your full personality—and your partner can't see how much you need your family. No wonder she didn't feel so energetic. Imagine trying to squeeze good energy out of a relationship where you feel stifled. With these scores, Maggie is still highly functional, able to work and go

Maggie's C.A.R.E. Relational Assessment Chart

Answer the questions on a 1-to-5 scale: 1=None or never 2=Rarely or minimal 3=Some of the time 4=More often than not; medium high 5=Usually; very high	#1 Melissa	#2 Mom	#3 Jane (sister)	#4 Ken (brother)	#5 Karen (sister)	Total Statement Score	C.A.R.E. Code
1. I trust this person with my feelings.	4	3	4	4	3	18	Calm
2. This person trusts me with her feelings.	4	3	4	4	4	19	Calm
3. I feel safe being in conflict with this person.	3	3	3	3	3	15	Calm
4. This person treats me with respect.	4	4	4	4	3	19	Calm
5. In this relationship, I feel calm.	5	3	4	3	3	18	Calm Accepted
6. I can count on this person to help me out in an emergency.	4	5	5	4	4	22	Calm Accepted
7. In this relationship, it's safe to acknowledge our differences.	4	3	4	3	3	17	Calm Accepted
8. When I am with this person, I feel a sense of belonging.	5	5	5	5	5	25	Accepted
9. Despite our different roles, we treat each other as equals.	5	4	4	4	4	21	Accepted

Answer the questions on a 1-to-5 scale:	#1 Melissa	#2 Mom	#3 Jane (sister)	#4 Ken (brother)	#5 Karen (sister)	Total Statement Score	C.A.R.E. Code
10. I feel valued in this relationship.	4	5	5	4	4	22	Accepted
11. There is give and take in this relationship.	4	3	5	3	4	19	Accepted
12. This person is able to sense how I feel.	3	3	4	3	3	16	Resonant
13. I am able to sense how this person feels.	4	4	4	3	4	19	Resonant
14. With this person I have more clarity about who I am.	3	3	4	3	3	16	Resonant
15. I feel that we "get" each other.	3	3	4	4	3	17	Resonant
16. I am able to see that my feelings impact this person.	3	3	4	3	3	16	Resonant
17. This relationship helps me be more productive in my life.	4	3	3	3	3	16	Energetic
18. I enjoy the time I spend with this person.	3	3	4	3	3	16	Energetic
19. Laughter is a part of this relationship.	3	3	4	3	3	16	Energetic
20. In this relationship, I feel more energetic.	3	3	4	3	3	16	Energetic
Safety Group Score	75	69	82	69	68		

through the motions of the day. But don't most of us hope for more out of life than just going through the motions?

We agreed to try boosting their energy by attacking some of the resonance issues.

We also talked about how to see their marriage and their extended families in terms other than the "individuality versus sameness" debate. If Maggie wanted to feel good again, if she wanted to feel more emotional resonance with her family, she'd have to be her real self in front of her family and (this is the hard part) negotiate the awkwardness and conflict that would almost inevitably occur. Maggie's task would be to help her family see that her maturity was not a threat—it wasn't a sign of rejection, just a difference.

After several conversations about the best place to begin their efforts, Maggie and Melissa decided to take on the all-day Sundays at Maggie's parents' house. Maggie and Melissa decided that they would meet the family at church, but that they would go back to her mother's only once a month; they explained kindly to her family that this was one of the only days they got time alone, and they needed to spend it on their many projects and to simply catch up on their relationship.

If you can't imagine how an innocuous little announcement like this could have caused a problem, you've never lived in a family like Maggie's. Her mother immediately wondered aloud if Maggie and Melissa's marriage was in danger. Her sisters suggested that Maggie and Melissa were being snooty. Her brother felt generally angry and betrayed. For a couple of months, this new plan was the family's favored topic of conversation. Melissa felt embarrassed and excluded, and Maggie was surprised by the intensity of the pushback they'd received. But instead of returning to the either/or options that they once felt they had, they decided to ride out the discomfort. They stuck to their guns by staying away most Sundays—and they kept their promise by coming once a month. They showed the family that they were committed to being both independent and close. The time away allowed Maggie and Melissa to come to the gatherings once a month in a more refreshed state, in which they could be more appreciative of the group. It wasn't perfect. They missed the threads of many inside jokes, and for a while, they were mildly punished by being treated as outsiders. But after a while, everyone adjusted to the new normal. Miraculously, even Melissa started to enjoy visiting her in-laws.

You don't have to wait for relationship nirvana to get more dopamine, though. Early in the therapy process, I asked Maggie and Melissa to tell me about the beginning of their relationship. I often ask couples this question, and I do it for several reasons. When people first fall in love, their neural circuits are flooded with dopamine, in the same way that alcohol and drugs can flood the brain with dopamine. If the couple can revisit that blissful time together, they can wake up some of the good energy that's gone dormant. Maggie immediately remembered how thrilling it was to find someone like Melissa, so solid and well defined. So different from her family! At this point, both women started telling the story of their early relationship, sometimes finishing each other's sentences. It was as if they had transported back to a time when they could see each other clearly. Our goal, I told them, was to get that energy and clarity back into the relationship.

What if you can't remember the good times? This is a clue, telling you that the relationship is suffering from serious disconnection. You may still be able to plug back into each other, so if the relationship is important to you, please don't give up on it. For a few couples, the relationship has never gone through those initial heady days; these are usually relationships that were built around responsibility or guilt or some other compulsive feeling. These couples have a harder road ahead.

Ways to Reconnect the Dopamine Reward System to Healthy Relationships

Melissa and Maggie were enjoying each other more, but they found it difficult to give up their substitute sources of dopamine: wine and TV. I explained that during their year or two of crisis, their Energetic pathways had become rewired. Melissa's dopamine reward system was still connected to wine, Maggie's to TV. Now that they could feel some pleasure in their relationship again, it was an ideal time to step in and break this unwanted neural connection.

How Are You Stimulating Your Dopamine
Reward System?

This exercise helps you get in touch with the primary ways you stimulate your dopamine pathways. You can pose the question like this:

How do I make myself feel better?

There is an endless number of things in the world that can supply dopamine, and that you can become addicted to. Here are some suggestions to get you thinking:

Relationships

Food

Drugs

Alcohol

Risk-taking activities

Shopping

Gambling

Sex

Working

Exercise

Internet surfing

Watching pornography

Check off any categories that apply to your life. If there are other behaviors that apply to you, add them. Then make a

rough assessment of what percentage of your feel-good time
is spent with each activity.

Source of Dopamine	Percentage of Feel-Good Time
Hanging out with my friends	10%
Shopping	20%
Exercising	15%
Eating	50%
Bungee jumping	5%

This exercise can unmask all sorts of interesting facts.
Like, hmmm, you often turn to food, sweets and carbohydrates particularly, when you need a lift. Exercise makes you
feel good but you don't do it that often. You don't call friends
when you're glum because you think that makes you "too
needy." Shopping always makes you feel better, at least until
you've spent too much money, and you run to the mall or shop
online more often than you realized. Bungee jumping is not a
frequent source of happiness, but you have done it a couple of
times and had to put it on the list because the euphoria afterward lifts your spirits for days.

When Rufus, the office worker who was addicted to Internet porn, did this exercise, he was shocked:

Source of Dopamine	Percentage of Feel-Good Time
Surfing porn sites	90%
Being with friends and family	5%
Ice cream	5%

As Rufus reflected on these results, he could easily see that over the course of the last few years he had become consumed with looking at pornography. His life had gotten very, very small.

For her part, Maggie's assessment helped her see she was spending more time with the TV than she'd realized. This unleashed some complicated feelings. For one thing, she didn't feel that the TV was "stupid." She described the relief she felt at the end of the day, when she'd jump into her pajamas, pour a cup of tea, and tune in to shows that were well-written dramas with intelligent character development. Some days, Maggie joked, she started to believe these characters were people in her actual life. In fact, this was Melissa's fear—that was she being elbowed aside by fictional people.

Identify Relationships That Are High in Zest

The next step is to identify your strongest sources of relational dopamine; these form your best shot at reconnecting your reward system. When Jean Baker Miller described growth-fostering relationships as producing a feeling of energy or zest, she was not thinking of dopamine. That zest is a palpable increase in energy, however, generated in part by elevated levels of dopamine, created by both of you. So go back to the C.A.R.E. Relational Assessment Chart and see which relationships produced the highest Energetic scores. Consciously stirring up good experiences with these people will exercise the neural circuitry between dopamine and relationships, making the Energetic pathway stronger.

Rufus liked his guy friends, but in a placid, passive way. His most obvious source of relational zest was his sister. He thought she was sweet and kind and really cared about him. He asked her to dinner, and she was psyched; Rufus noticed that he felt a little lift in his chest when he realized she wanted to spend time with him. It was not the buzzing excitement and arousal of porn, but it was a sensation worth his attention. The more time he could spend in relationships that created this feeling—and the more he paid attention to that feeling—the better. One day his friend Drew announced that he was getting married. Rufus was shocked: he thought that all his guy friends were bachelors for life. He found that he was curious to hear about Drew's experience with this woman, how excited and unembarrassed Drew was when he described her. Rufus felt a longing, halfway between his chest and belly, for a relationship with a real woman.

Melissa felt that drinking wine wasn't a big problem; it was a pleasant way to relax after a long, intense day at work. But she acknowledged that wine was taking focus and energy away from her relationships. She and Melissa agreed that two evenings a week, they'd make an extra effort to connect. Melissa suggested that they make dinner together and sit down to eat it without any distractions. This ended up being a pleasant and engaging way to spend time together. Melissa still had her glass of wine or even two, and sometimes Maggie joined her. On those evenings, drinking felt different—

not a way to numb out or escape, but simply a fun part of the meal.

Melissa also surprised herself by discovering that her parents—who were emotionally and physically distant—nevertheless scored high on her Energetic pathways. A few times a week, she called them at the end of the day. At first, they begged off the phone, saying that they knew she'd rather be with Maggie. Then, alarmed by the increased communication, they instructed Melissa to get off the phone and go take care of her marriage instead of calling them. But—and this is important—Melissa didn't let this awkwardness put her off. She kept up the phone calls, and kept asking questions about their lives, and as time went on, her parents were sharing funny stories about their day and their stresses at work. There were no big reveals, but there was enough connection to produce a nice shot of happiness.

Relabel and Refocus

Now it's time to make concrete change. First, recognize your habitual patterns. Do you turn to your addictions or bad habits when you have emotions that are uncomfortable? Twelve-step programs like Alcoholics Anonymous talk how about the urge to drink predictably comes on when you are hungry, angry, lonely, or tired. Those emotional and physical states form the acronym HALT, which perfectly describes what you should do when your feel the urge to participate in your bad habit. But in a culture that values logic over emotion, it can be hard to interpret what your body and mind are trying to tell you. If you have the urge to "use" something to feel better, try to pause and look inward to see if there is some emotion attached to the urge. For help identifying a full range of emotions, see pages 224–230.

If you're able to identify and label the feeling, see if you can watch it move by. Although a feeling can seem incredibly dangerous, it will not kill you. Feeling states are like the clouds; with time they simply dissipate.

If the feeling does not move on and your craving continues to be strong, relabel the craving. It's defeating to think of a troublesome habit as a failure of character or something that you just can't stop yourself from doing. Instead, label it for what it is: a neural pathway that's grown stronger with repeated use. I told Melissa that it would probably be too much for her to give up wine right away—her default neural pathways for wine were so strong that she would probably end up giving in. In a classic cycle, she'd feel bad about giving in . . . and then turn to more wine to help her feel better.

Instead, Melissa could say to herself, "Hmmm. I notice I really want to wind down with some wine. Okay. That's interesting. That neural pathway is *very* strong." Identifying the pathway for what it is—a series of neurons and not an inborn character flaw—is a first step toward releasing its hold over you. Recognize that whatever craving you have is just a desire to feel better, to get more dopamine. You can acknowledge that there are many other ways to stimulate dopamine that are healthier for you.

At this point, it's time to refocus your attention on one of those zestful relationships. Call up a positive relational moment with that person, one that is full of joy and humor—the more good energy, the better. (For an explanation of PRMs, see page 157.) If you're in a romantic relationship that's lost its energy, try mining your earliest days together. Chances are you'll find moments that are rich in dopamine.

If you feel comfortable, you could invite one or two of these people to participate in the refocusing process with you. They may have some dopamine-stimulating strategies they'd like to change, too. Agree that when you have a craving, you'll reach out to each other. If you can meet in person, great: you'll have the complete physiology of connection working for you and against the self-destructive craving. But if that's not possible, a phone call or text will help to break the immediate craving and ground you in healthier coping strategies.

I asked Rufus if he would call his sister in the evenings, just to catch up on the day, and see if that helped dislodge his habit a little. He disliked the idea but tried it twice—and on one of those two evenings, he found that calling his sister helped him avoid porn. He wondered aloud if this was cheating, because it wasn't the quality of the conversation that helped him; rather, he thought it was creepy to watch porn after speaking with his little sister.

"I'll take that," I said. "Talking to your sister allows you to pause and think." Rufus wasn't cheating. It was the brain-less drifting to porn that was so problematic for him. When he could interrupt that drifting, it was possible for him to make better choices . . . including reconnecting healthy rela-tionships to his dopamine reward system.

By lifting your thoughts up out of their well-worn neural track and moving them toward a healthy relationship, you're putting all three rules of brain change in motion. And by pairing your neural pathway for craving dopamine with your neural pathway for feeling connected to a friend, you'll even-tually wire those two pathways back together. You'll begin to crave relationship, not wine or ice cream or even bungee jumping, when you want a lift.

Starve Neural Pathways That Say, "You Should Learn to Feel Better on Your Own"

How many times have you been encouraged to self-regulate your emotions, deal with pain on your own, work out your troubles independently? This strategy is endemic in societies that see separation as a sign of maturity. This value is stored in your mind and in every cell in your body, so that when you are hungry, angry, lonely, or tired you learn that you are to take care of those needs on your own. That's what adults do! In fact, if you regularly turn to others for comfort, you can be called *codependent*. A whole self-help industry has built up around battling codependence in people—mostly women.

The truth, though, is that when humans successfully manage their emotions, they *never* do it alone. In fact, being completely alone is so toxic to the human brain and body that in most prison systems the last-ditch disciplinary tool is solitary confinement. If our brains were truly meant to self-regulate, solitary confinement would be a piece of cake and a pleasure. Instead, it's considered radical punishment and, according to some, a form of torture.

The goal of this exercise is the opposite of self-regulation. It's to learn how to regulate your emotions within growth-fostering relationships. Give this one some time; this is perhaps the most difficult relational skill to master when you've been steeped in a world that undermines relationships. Mutual regulation means that you and another person are invested and engaged in your growth and development. As we mutually grow, we each develop rich positive relational images tied to our pathways for connection—deep, strong body and mind memories stored in our cells of what human connection feels like. Intentionally or not, we refer to these images constantly to help us manage our stress levels. They're like a soft blanket to protect our psyches.

We'll call again on the first rule of brain change: **Use it or lose it.** Neural pathways compete for brain space, so if you want these good relational images to flourish, you must starve the pathways that are vying for real estate in your head. These are the pathways that carry the social messages that it is better to do things on your own, or that you are weak if you turn to others with your sadness or anger. Spend an afternoon or a day watching how often these messages float through your brain. Whenever you catch one, simply relabel it as a cultural message that sabotages your goal of reclaiming your connected brain. Immediately move your mind to a PRM, or to a stored image of a time you were supported and how good that felt. With practice, the world can transform in front of your eyes from one filled with competitors to one filled with helpers.

With this step, you've reached the end of the C.A.R.E. program. People who take the C.A.R.E. workshops often comment that the program works directly on the relational issues that have troubled them the most. For all its transparency, they say that the C.A.R.E. program is also rich, textured, and surprising—just like the best relationships. As you continue to grow within your relationships, a word of caution: whatever struggles you encounter, don't judge yourself harshly. Judging yourself will only throw your sympathetic nervous system into hyperdrive, making it harder for you to create the kind of change you're looking for.

As I see it, the C.A.R.E. program is a bridge that leads from isolation to connection. Exactly how far that bridge extends is up to you. Does the bridge arc toward a better relationship with your spouse? Your entire family? Your workplace, neighborhood, or community? Once you experience relationships that feel Calmer, more Accepting, Resonant, Energetic, and you may be surprised at how far you decide to travel.

Chapter 9

MAINTAIN YOUR BRAIN

As I write this chapter, there is a trend toward reality TV shows featuring people who demonstrate how to survive by yourself in the wild. You can learn some pretty interesting things from these shows: how to make a meal from frozen yak eyeballs, and how to use your pants as a flotation device. Most of all, the hosts impress on us, is the importance of physical fitness and adaptability. You've got to be able to leap over boulders. You've got to be strong enough to build a snow cave. Sometimes you'll have to run from wild pigs.

I love these shows. They're fun. But I can also see that the trend toward survival TV reflects our attitudes about separation, that surviving on your own is the truest, most elemental human situation, and the ultimate test of your maturity. Physical survival is an extension of how we see the social waters:

menacing, competitive, best navigated with a knife clenched between your teeth and a wary eye out for crocodiles.

Throughout this book I've tried to demonstrate an alternate way of thinking about our capacity for psychological maturity and growth. How our brains are designed to use relationships to help them grow and stretch and change. How those same brains contain neural pathways that can flourish only when given input from healthy relationships. How we mature, not by stepping away from other people but by moving into greater relational complexity. So maybe it won't be surprising that I'm offering a different way to think of fitness as well. I want you to begin thinking about a brain that is physically fit—a brain that, like a survivalist's body, can remain strong and flexible, and can adapt to changing conditions. Maybe not the conditions of an active volcano in a Pacific archipelago, but the relational terrain that changes as you meet new people, as technology creates different ways of interacting, as your own growth changes the nature of your relationships. At the beginning of this book, I compared relationships to a magician's interlocking rings. The acts of coming together, overlapping, moving away, and integrating what you've learned, require you to stay light on your feet, mentally speaking. For this, your brain needs relationships—but it also needs to stay physically fit. It needs to conduct electrical impulses with efficiency. It needs to grow new blood vessels and neurons. It needs to rest and recover.

Below are nine ways to keep your brain in shape for great relationships.

1. Drink Water.

At my neighborhood pool, there is a rule that if you hear thunder or see lightning, everyone must immediately get out of the water and remain out for thirty minutes. Every summer, the neighborhood children complain that their happy pool time is interrupted for what to them appears to be no good reason. They don't realize that this rule is lifesaving. The free ions, salts, and other minerals and metals that are found in water are highly efficient conductors of electricity. If lightning hits the water, its current travels almost instantaneously through the pool.

The same principle operates in your brain, which uses electrical currents to send its signals from one nerve to another. These signals include the impulses that zip from neuron to neuron along the smart vagus and eventually to the sympathetic and parasympathetic nervous systems, sending your autonomic nervous system accurate data about whether to stand up and fight or sit down and relax. Signals along the mirroring system let you have the imitative responses that produce an almost instant reading of another person. To do this and other complex, fast relational computation, your neurons need to be plump and well hydrated.

The Institute of Medicine of the National Academy of Sciences recommends that women have a total intake of 91 ounces of water per day; men should get 125 ounces daily. We get about 20 percent of these water needs through food, however, and most of us will do just fine by drinking whenever we're thirsty, or by drinking enough to produce clear or pale yellow urine. Caffeine and alcohol are diuretics, so if you consume these, you'll need to drink extra water to compensate. Also drink extra water if you exercise for more than an hour in a day.

2. Exercise Your Brain as Well as Your Body.

If you currently exercise to improve your stamina, shape your body, or save your heart, you are already ahead in the brain game. It's been known for a while that exercise gives you the so-called runner's high by increasing your endorphins, the natural morphine produced in your brain. But exercise does far more. Regular exercise increases key neurotransmitters like serotonin, dopamine, and norepinephrine, all of which support your mood and energy level. It also increases a recently discovered neurochemical called *brain-derived neurotrophic factor*, or BDNF, which improves your rate of learning. In his book *Spark: The Revolutionary New Science of Exercise and the Brain*, John Ratey, a clinical professor of psychiatry at Harvard Medical School, documents a novel physical education program called Zero Hour. Created in the Naperville, Illinois, school system seventeen years ago, Zero Hour has kids perform aerobic exercise at 80 to 90 percent of their maximum heart rate before the day's classes begin. The effects on learning have been dramatic. The district consistently ranks in the state's top ten for academics, despite spending significantly less per student than the state's other top-performing districts. One reason for these results could be that there is more electrical activity in the brains of fit children than in sedentary kids. Another is BDNF. Ratey writes, "BDNF gives the synapses the tools they need to take in information, process it, remember it, and put it in context."[1] Exercise also increases an important chemical, *vascular endothelial growth factor*, that supports the growth of blood vessels in organs and tissues throughout your body and brain. More blood vessels means more blood flow and more blood flow means more oxygen and nutrients sent to your brain cells. In Ratey's words, "exercise prepares neurons to connect, while mental stimulation allows your brain to capitalize on that readiness."[2]

To stimulate neurotransmitters, BDNF, and vascular endothelial growth factor—and to sharpen mental acuity in general—it is better to partake of cardiovascular exercise than to lift weights or do yoga. It appears that the crucial factor is getting your heart rate up and keeping it there. Ratey suggests performing cardiovascular exercise at these levels:

Two days each week, exercise at 70 to 75 percent of your maximum heart rate (so that you are sweaty and somewhat breathless) for 30 to 60 minutes; *and*

Four days each week, exercise at 60 to 65 percent of your max heart rate (you're still sweaty at this level, but you can talk fairly easily) for 30 to 60 minutes.[3]

I know. It's a lot of exercise, more than the amount recommended by the Centers for Disease Control to maintain physical health. If you struggle to get going, leverage the benefits of human interaction. A Stanford University study found that when people received a phone call about their workouts every two weeks, subjects increased their exercise amounts by 78 percent.[4] And the department of kinesiology at Indiana University discovered that couples who worked out separately had a 43 percent dropout rate in an exercise program, while only about 7 percent of couples who exercised together dropped out.[5] Remember that relational dopamine is a great way to melt old neural pathways and create ones that lead to new, better habits.

3. Get Omega-3 Fatty Acids Through Food or Supplements.

Some people call the brain "gray matter," but if you look at a picture of your brain, you'll see that it actually looks whitish. The source of that white color is fat—and a fatty brain is a very good thing, because it speeds the transmission of electrical signals. Omega-3 fatty acids in particular are an essential component of cell membranes. They also help replace damaged brain cells by promoting the growth of new neurons, and they may be protective against anxiety and mood disorders.[6]

There are three types of omega-3 fatty acids: EPA, DHA,

and ALA. While all three are good for your body, only EPA and DHA can cross the blood–brain barrier and nourish your brain cells. Perhaps the easiest way to get EPA or DHA is from natural sources such as salmon, herring, or tuna. Eating these fish two or three times per week will boost your brain functioning. For the non-fish-eater, taking a daily supplement of EPA or DHA is a great alternative and can be found in most local pharmacies and grocery stores.

You'll also need antioxidants. When your body metabolizes fatty acids, the by-products include free radicals, which can build up and disrupt protein and lipid development—and damage your DNA. The buildup of free radicals is referred to as having a high load of *oxidative stress*. Antioxidants like vitamins C and E can bind to the free radicals and lower this stress. It's best to get your antioxidants from brightly colored fruits and vegetables, but you can also take a supplement if necessary.

4. Wear a Helmet When Putting Your Brain at Risk.

Daniel Amen, a psychiatrist who has pioneered the use of brain imaging with single photon emission computed tomography (SPECT) to help diagnose and treat mental illness and brain injury, describes the texture of the human brain as similar to medium-firm tofu. If you have ever cooked with tofu, you will realize that this comparison is *not* reassuring. Even

MAINTAIN YOUR BRAIN   279

though this tofu sits within the hard human skull, the skull has a number of peaks and valleys that form sharp edges. When your head is hit with something—whether a soccer ball or the windshield of a car—and the tofu is jostled within the skull even a small amount, it can sustain significant injuries. The resulting brain bruise, usually referred to as a *concussion*, can have detrimental effects months and even years after the initial injury.

As a mom and a psychiatrist, I am thrilled that my son did not want to play football, a game that puts your brain at risk during every play. Additionally, I frown on bouncing the ball off the front part of the skull in soccer. The prefrontal cortex is simply too precious and too important in regulating executive functioning and impulse control to have it hit over and over again. For this same reason, I recommend helmets for anyone participating in contact sports; motorcycle and bicycle riding; skateboarding, skiing, and snowboarding; and under any condition where it is possible for you to bang your head.

5. Spend Time in the Sun.

One of the easiest things you can do for your brain is to spend time in the sun. The sun's rays don't simply bounce off your skin (or fry it). They actually have an integral role in supporting your health. Those long summer days we all look forward to after a dark winter actually improve blood flow in your brain and help regulate key neurotransmitters, serotonin and melatonin. Serotonin helps to maintain a positive mood and a focused, calm outlook on life. It's also a precursor to melatonin, which—aside from physical benefits like helping the body counter infection, inflammation, autoimmune responses, and even cancer—assists with the onset of sleep. Sleep, as you'll see in a moment, is critical to healthy brain functioning. Sunlight also increases vitamin D levels, which affect both your mood and memory.

In the sun-crazy days of my youth, people set up tinfoil boxes and slathered themselves with oil in an effort to bake themselves like potatoes in an oven. This practice ignored one of the eternal rules of health—moderation—and decades later, these men and women were developing skin cancers at an alarming rate. Suntan lotions and oils were developed to filter some of the more aggressive sun rays and protect the skin; then sunscreens gave way to sunblocks that can offer more than one hundred times your natural protection against the sun. Now we have a generation of people who aren't getting enough sun, and who suffer from low levels of vitamin D. Once again, it all goes back to moderation. Try to get a little sunshine every day if you can. If you live in an area where that's not possible, the recommended dose for people without a clear vitamin D deficiency is 600 to 800 IUs daily. People with a vitamin D deficiency should supplement with 2,000 units a day until the deficiency has been remedied. Your doctor should evaluate your blood levels of vitamin D during your regular checkup.

6. Get Enough Sleep.

Like getting an adequate amount of sunlight, getting enough sleep is a freebie—sort of. It's awfully easy to stay up an extra hour to watch a show because, finally, the kids are asleep and this is "your" time. When I was in medical school, there was a clear improvement in status for the person who could stay awake the longest and still perform on a high level. I have vivid memories (or maybe flashbacks) of spending nights in the emergency room seeing patient after patient and guzzling Diet Coke after Diet Coke to stay awake.

Yet even small amounts of sleep deprivation can cause multiple problems in the brain and body, including poor concentration, drowsiness, impaired memory, impaired physical performance, a decrease in ability to do math calculations, and mood swings. "Your time" at the end of the night is much better spent sleeping. You might notice that when you actually get enough sleep, you have more energy and focus to get through the list of things in the day that are usually left to the end. Research also shows that even though you might get used to functioning with a sleep debt, your reaction time and judgment can still be significantly impaired. That's because less sleep will create more irritable brain pathways.

Sleep needs depend on your age and, of course, on your own specific brain and body, but in general, adults need seven to eight hours of sleep a night (though a few people need as little as five or as much as ten), teenagers need roughly nine hours of sleep, and infants need a whopping sixteen hours of sleep per day. Remember, too little sleep creates a sleep debt that eventually has to be repaid!

7. Eat Brain Foods.

There is a connection between your gastrointestinal tract and your nervous system, and what you eat has a major impact on how your brain functions. The proteins, carbohydrates, and fats you eat become the building blocks for cells and neurotransmitters in your brain. Micronutrients, like vitamins and cofactors, are needed to run the little factories in your cells and produce energy. A balanced diet, including all of the essential food groups and plenty of fruits and vegetables, will make your body healthier and your brain work more efficiently.

But you can and should go beyond the traditional balanced diet when you're focusing on brain health. The brain foods listed here have specific benefits to mental and psychological functioning. Blueberries help prevent oxidative stress; in rats, they've been shown to enhance learning. Avocados and whole grains help preserve blood flow to the entire brain, including its C.A.R.E. pathways. Beans deliver a regular stream of glucose to the brain, providing a steady (not wild or erratic) supply of energy. Freshly brewed tea is an ideal drink, because it contains the ideal amount of caffeine to improve focus, mood, and memory. Tea also contains small amounts of catechin, which helps regulate blood flow. Nuts and seeds contain vitamin E, which helps stave off cognitive decline. Dark chocolate pulls off a hat trick with endorphins to calm the body and brain, caffeine for focus, and antioxidants to fight free radicals. The final brain food is any fish that contains the omega-3 fatty acids I've talked about: wild salmon, herring, and tuna.

8. Use a Brain Training Program.

Most of us know to keep our brains stimulated with games and activities, but not all stimulation expands overall brain functioning. If you are routinely doing crossword puzzles to keep your brain alive and active, it is likely that what is increasing for you is . . . your capacity to do crossword puzzles. Posit Science, a company founded by neuroscientist Michael Merzenich, has designed the SAAGE protocol to describe the benefits that brain games should include:

S is for *speed*. As your brain ages, the speed of electrical transmission slows. A good brain activity should improve the speed of your thinking.

A is for *accuracy*. Brain games should improve how well you classify pieces of information.

A is for *adaptivity*. Brain games need to adapt to your specific and current level of functioning. If you are having an off day, the tasks should get a little easier. The last thing your brain needs is to play a game at which you are constantly failing; it's not helpful for your C.A.R.E. pathways or your learning to stimulate the sympathetic nervous system unnecessarily.

G stands for *generalizability*, which refers to the ability for the program to improve real-life activities, not just the activity in the game (e.g., crossword puzzles).

E is for *engagement*. For adults to turn on their learning machinery, the nucleus basalis, novelty and attention are required; the reward system stimulates dopamine to help solidify new pathways. A game should engage the brain's attention, reward, and novelty systems hundreds of times per training hour. These systems must be engaged for long-lasting brain change.[7]

For a list of brain-change programs that fit all the SAAGE requirements, visit www.sharpbrains.com.

9. Find Stress-Reduction Techniques You Love.

Stress, and the stress chemicals it produces, can be remarkably toxic to your brain. But like most things in your body, there is a continuum of toxicity. Studies have shown that at mild levels, stress can actually help you improve your cognitive capacity. The release of adrenaline wakes up nerve pathways, allowing you to focus and concentrate better. As the stress level increases, however, the system turns on you—and the same chemicals that just a minute ago allowed you to focus more closely now cause you to feel anxious and panicky.

From an evolutionary perspective, the system makes sense. Imagine you are a caveperson, scanning the environment for danger. Being just stressed enough to stay alert and avoid spacing out is crucial to your survival. Off in the distance, you see a mountain lion on the prowl. The adrenaline simmers in your body and you remain attentive, but not reactive. After ten minutes, you notice the mountain lion seems to be stalking closer and closer to your cave. More adrenaline pumps through your nervous system and now your heart is starting to beat faster, your breaths are becoming shorter, your body is making the switch from scanning and evaluation to preparation for battle. If you are a cavewoman, a combination of adrenaline and the hormone oxytocin gives you the energy, focus, and wisdom to gather the other members of the clan and their children into a protective huddle. If you are a caveman, your testosterone and vasopressin rise, and you are thinking of tearing the mountain lion apart in order to defend your tribe.

Your stress response can be your friend and ally, helping you navigate a complicated and occasionally dangerous world.

However, when we socialize humans to be autonomous and not turn to others to help buffer stress, we actively undermine the development of the neural pathways for connection. These neural pathways are an essential balance to the sympathetic nervous system and help keep it in check so that you are not in a state of high arousal all the time.

People who develop post-traumatic stress disorder from childhood abuse, domestic violence, or war live with a sympathetic nervous system that is running full blast much of the time, and this response is incredibly destructive. The cortisol released in an effort to counter the high levels of adrenaline can be toxic to the hippocampus, the area of the brain that stores memories. It can also help create a cascade of physical destruction, leading to the development of chronic health problems, from diabetes to autoimmune disorders. And of course, having an overactive stress response system makes it even harder to build healthy relationships.

For all these reasons, if you are spending much of your life in a culture that actively cuts off your C.A.R.E. pathways, it is essential that you balance the excessive stress response with some activity that reduces stress. Start by simply focusing on your breath throughout the day. When you are stressed, your breathing becomes more superficial and rapid, which leads to less oxygen to your brain . . . which can lead to more irritable neurons and ultimately more stress. So throughout the day, pause every now and then and focus on taking ten deep breaths. You will quickly feel the impact of increased oxygen to your brain. The beauty of this technique is that you can do it anytime, on the subway or at your desk, even in an annoy-ing meeting with a colleague—and no one will notice.

Anything that reduces your stress can be a stress-reduction activity; on page 163, you'll find a list of suggestions for soothing a jumpy sympathetic nervous system. These are tried-and-true stress busters. The important thing is for you to pick something you can commit to, because balancing your autonomic nervous system is like everything else you are try-ing to change in your brain: it takes practice. Many people use meditation, yoga, and other forms of mindfulness, but if these aren't for you, think of what does decrease your stress. If playing with your children at the end of the day allows you to feel safe and out of the stressful world, then build this ac-tivity into your day. If going for a run at lunch allows you to dispel the neurochemicals of distress, then make time for it. The goal is to counteract the ongoing stress that comes from spending much of your time in a culture that under-mines your primary way to reduce stress: growth-fostering relationships.

C.A.R.E. FOR LIFE

As I've just noted, balancing your autonomic nervous system takes practice. So does strengthening all four of your C.A.R.E. pathways. Not only does it take practice to heal your con-nected brain, it *is* a practice, in the same sense that yoga or meditation is a practice. At first, learning to nourish your neural pathways for feeling Calm, Accepted, Resonant, and

Energetic will feel awkward. It may feel as if you're working against everything your culture has taught you about relationships—and, in fact, that's exactly what you're doing. But work on the C.A.R.E. pathways often enough and they will thrive. Soon, growing and sustaining healthy relationships will feel more natural.

It is time to send parents a new instruction manual for raising their children; it is time to send our children a new set of rules for interacting with friends and enemies; it is time to make our business leaders a new template for helping employees work cooperatively; and it is time to teach our world leaders how to guide their communities to fulfill their capacities to connect. We need an approach to human relationships that accurately reflects how interconnected we all are and nourishes our ability to use healthy relationships for richer, healthier lives.

It's often said that a culture changes one person at a time, and that the only person you can change is yourself. But when you realize that we are not separated by strict boundaries, and that our relationships have a neurological life that unfolds inside the brains and minds of everyone we encounter, those statements seem too limiting. The minute you make a change in the way you relate to people—when you become less judgmental, more curious, less fearful, more accepting—you also make a shift in the places where you and other people overlap. When you improve your pathways for connection, the artificial walls that support the separation mentality melt away;

those boundaries transform into rich areas of human interface, abuzz with growth and energy.

In other words, when a relationship changes, it quite literally changes the minds of everyone in that relationship. Your own transformation isn't limited to yourself alone, because you are not alone. We live within one another.

ACKNOWLEDGMENTS

I have heard authors say, "It takes a village to write a book," but if you have Leigh Ann Hirschman on your team, you can do it with a small neighborhood. Leigh Ann and I took a leap of faith in writing a book that challenges the deep-seated cultural belief in autonomy. It was a leap best done in tandem. Leigh Ann wore many hats—beginning as a consultant and wise editor, shifting to the role of brilliant writer, and ending as a trusted friend. Her integrity, good humor, and attention to detail far surpassed my expectations. By the end of the project, Leigh Ann had clarified and accentuated my thoughts and ideas, saying what I wanted to say far better than I could have said it. Thank you, Leigh Ann.

I am grateful to my agents, Kathryn Beaumont and Katherine Flynn from Kneerim, Williams & Bloom, who believed in this book and helped it find both a home and an enthusiastic editor, Sara Carder at Tarcher.

Christina Robb was instrumental in birthing this book.

As my writing coach, she gently read early drafts of the manuscript and convinced me that every writer struggles to find her voice. When I coughed up a twenty-page hairball, she calmly and kindly pointed out that I was clearing my throat for the first fifteen pages.

Mike Miller has been relentless in his support for the work done at the Jean Baker Miller Training Institute. His message has been clear and consistent: take yourselves seriously, write books, and promote the message of the centrality of relationships to health and well-being. Mike's ongoing support and culturally relevant clippings that arrive by snail mail continue to remind me there is a broader context to this work.

Roseann Adams, a friend and colleague, used the early C.A.R.E. Relational Assessment with her clients and provided me with invaluable feedback on the structure and impact of the tool. Through the years, I have gotten both support and helpful feedback from generous participants attending our annual intensive summer institute. This community of relational-cultural practitioners remains central to the creation and dissemination of the work associated with JBMTI. I am especially appreciative of Dr. Constance Gunderson and her colleagues at St. Scholastica, who are working with me on a research project focused on the effectiveness of the C.A.R.E. program in social work students. Mary Vicario has been exceedingly clever at taking relational neuroscience and creating activities for parents and children. Her enthusiasm for the work is contagious.

I have had the privilege of working with and learning from my two friends and colleagues at JBMTI, Maureen Walker and Judith Jordan. Maureen has the mind of a scholar, the heart of an activist, and the soul of a theologian. Listening to Maureen is a religious experience. Her thoughts and ideas have shaped my thinking and writing on the cultural context of relationships. Judith Jordan's prolific writings, intense intellectual curiosity, and Buddhist energy infuse relational-cultural theory (or RCT) with heart and soul.

Dan Siegel's work on the neurobiology of relationships continues to shape my own. His support for this project and endorsement of my work are deeply appreciated. It has been a pleasure becoming a "mwe" ("me" plus "we") with him.

I spend most of my days connecting with clients in my private practice. It is not always easy, but it is always interesting. In each of these relationships, I have grown, and I feel lucky that so many have trusted me with their most intimate feelings and life experiences.

My life and neural pathways have been deeply shaped by Melissa Coco, Angel Seibring, and Frank Anderson, who have supported the creation of this book directly and indirectly by reading early drafts and by providing friendship and distraction when I needed to recharge. I am indebted to Pamela Peck, a supervisor and friend who introduced me to RCT early in my residency. I clicked with the theory immediately, and it has been a guiding light in my personal and professional life.

For the past twenty-five years, I have been working with

Cindy Kettyle to reshape my own relational templates. Although she knows I hate that psychoanalytic couch in her home office (it looks like she dragged it from Vienna), Cindy has been the perfect therapist and confidant for me. In this relationship, I have laughed my way to health.

The revolutionary and courageous work of Jean Baker Miller, Irene Stiver, Judith Jordan, and Jan Surrey, who were the founding scholars at the Stone Center (which eventually was called the Jean Baker Miller Training Institute). They paved the way for my generation of clinicians and scholars to promote connection with very little shame. Their prophetic theory feeds a movement that continues to reshape Western culture.

My brother, Philip Banks, is the only person I know who could learn an entire computer language in one evening. Your love and support is greatly appreciated.

My older sister, Kate Banks, is a writer and healer who has been a role model for me in following the path less traveled, no matter where it has taken me.

My younger sister, Nancy Banks, is a fellow teacher and cultural critic. Her presence in my life has been equal parts love and laughter.

Finally, my deceased parents, Dr. Ronald F. Banks and Helena Poland Banks, both educators, gave me two invaluable gifts: the appreciation of teaching and learning, and the acceptance of my quirky differences.

NOTES

CHAPTER 1: BOUNDARIES ARE OVERRATED:
A NEW WAY OF LOOKING AT RELATIONSHIPS

1   Giacomo Rizzolatti, Luciano Fadiga, Vittorio Gallese, and Leonardo Fogassi, "Premotor Cortex and the Recognition of Motor Actions," *Cognitive Brain Research* 3 (1996): 131–41.

2   Lea Winerman, "The Mind's Mirror," *Monitor on Psychology* 36, no. 9 (2005): 48.

3   Marco Iacoboni, *Mirroring People: The New Science of How We Connect with Others* (New York: Farrar, Straus, and Giroux, 2008), 267.

4   Judith Jordan, in discussion with the author, May 2014.

5   Sigmund Freud, *Beyond the Pleasure Principle*, The International Psycho-Analytic Library (London: The International Psychoanalytical Press, 1922), chapter IV.

6   D. G. Blazer, "Social Support and Mortality in an Elderly Community Population," *American Journal of Epidemiology* 155, no. 5 (1982): 684–94.

7   T. E. Seeman and S. L. Syme, "Social Networks and Coronary Artery Disease: A Comparison of Structure and Function of Social Relations as Predictors of Disease," *Psychosomatic Medicine* 49, no. 4 (1987): 341–54.

8   P. L. Graves, C. B. Thomas, and L. A. Mead, "Familial and

Psychological Predictors of Cancer," *Cancer Detection & Prevention* 15, no. 1 (1991): 59–64.

9   L. G. Russek and G. E. Schwartz, "Narrative Descriptions of Parental Love and Caring Predict Health Status in Midlife: A 35-Year Follow-up of the Harvard Mastery of Stress Study," *Alternative Therapies in Health and Medicine* 2 (1996): 55–62.

CHAPTER 2: THE FOUR NEURAL PATHWAYS FOR HEALTHY RELATIONSHIPS

1   N. I. Eisenberger and M. Lieberman, "Why It Hurts to Be Left Out: The Neurocognitive Overlap between Physical and Social Pain," in K. D. Williams, J. P. Forgas, and W. von Hippel (eds.), *The Social Outcast: Ostracism, Social Exclusion, Rejection, and Bullying* (New York: Cambridge University Press, 2005), 109–27.

2   P. M. Niedenthal, L. W. Barsalou, P. Winkielman, S. Krauth-Gruber, and F. Ric, "Embodiment in Attitudes, Social Perception, and Emotion," *Personality and Social Psychology Review* 9 (2005): 184–211.

3   S. M. Wilson, A. P. Saygin, M. I. Sereno, and M. Iacoboni, "Listening to Speech Activates Motor Areas Involved in Speech Production," *Nature Neuroscience* 7 (2004): 701–702.

4   I. Meister, S. M. Wilson, C. Deblieck, A. D. Wu, and M. Iacoboni, "The Essential Role of Premotor Cortex in Speech Perception," *Current Biology* 17 (2007): 1692–96.

5   D. Neal and T. Chartrand, "Embodied Emotion Perception, Amplifying and Dampening Facial Feedback Modulates Emotion Perception Accuracy," *Social Psychological and Personality Science* 2, no. 6 (2011): 673–78.

6   Diana Martinez, Daria Orlowska, Rajesh Narendran, Mark Slifstein, Fei Liu, Dileep Kumar, Allegra Broft, Ronald Van Heertum, and Herbert D. Kleber, "Dopamine Type 2/3 Receptor Availability in the Striatum and Social Status in Human Volunteers," *Biological Psychiatry* 67, no. 3 (2010): 275–78.

7   Louis Cozolino, *The Neuroscience of Human Relationships* (New York: W. W. Norton, 2014).

CHAPTER 3: THE THREE RULES OF BRAIN CHANGE

1   Antonio M. Battro, *Half a Brain Is Enough: The Story of Nico* (Cambridge, Mass.: Cambridge University Press, 2001).
2   Norman Doidge, *The Brain That Changes Itself* (New York: Penguin, 2006).
3   Martha Burns, "Dopamine and Learning: What the Brain's Reward System Can Teach Educators," *Scientific Learning*, http://www.scilearn.com/blog/dopamine-learning-brains-reward-center-teach-educators.php#.U3LnkwjDs3s.gmail (accessed May 13, 2014).

CHAPTER 5: C IS FOR CALM: MAKE YOUR SMART VAGUS SMARTER

1   Jeffrey Schwartz, *Brain Lock: Free Yourself from Obsessive-Compulsive Behavior* (New York: Harper Perennial, 1997).

CHAPTER 7: R IS FOR RESONANT: STRENGTHEN YOUR BRAIN'S MIRRORING SYSTEM

1   Cozolino, *The Neuroscience of Human Relationships*, 202.
2   Iacoboni, *Mirroring People*, 204–209.

CHAPTER 9: MAINTAIN YOUR BRAIN

1   John Ratey, *Spark: The Revolutionary New Science of Exercise and the Brain* (New York: Little, Brown, 2008), 45.
2   Ibid., 207.
3   Ibid., 242.
4   A. C. King, R. Friedman, B. Marcus, C. Castro, M. Napolitano, D. Alm, and L. Baker, "Ongoing Physical Activity Advice by Humans versus Computers: The Community Health Advice by Telephone (CHAT) Trial," *Health Psychology* 26, no. 6 (2007): 718–27.
5   J. P. Wallace, J. S. Raglin, and C. A. Jastremski, "Twelve Month Adherence of Adults Who Joined a Fitness Program with a Spouse vs. Without a Spouse," *Journal of Sports Medicine and Physical Fitness* 35, no. 3 (1995): 206–13.
6   Stuart Wolpert, "Scientists Learn How What You Eat Affects

Your Brain—And Those of Your Kids," *UCLA Newsroom*, http://
newsroom.ucla.edu/releases/scientists-learn-how-food-affects-
52668 (accessed May 14, 2014).

7   Posit Science, "Company FAQ," http://www.brainhq.com/about/
company-faq (accessed May 14, 2014).

INDEX

Page numbers in **bold** indicate charts.

If you enjoyed this book, visit

www.tarcherbooks.com

and sign up for Tarcher's e-newsletter to receive special offers, giveaway promotions, and information on hot upcoming releases.

Great Lives Begin with Great Ideas

Connect with the Tarcher Community

• • •

Stay in touch with favorite authors!
Enter weekly contests!
Read exclusive excerpts!
Voice your opinions!

Follow us

 Tarcher Books
 @TarcherBooks

If you would like to place a bulk order
of this book, call 1-800-847-5515.

"A groundbreaking book that redefines what it means to be in a relationship."
—John Gray, Ph.D., bestselling author of *Men Are from Mars, Women Are from Venus*

978-1-58542-913-4

$15.95

The bestselling authors of *Energy Medicine* and *Energy Medicine for Women* present a complete program for using energy medicine to heal and strengthen romantic relationships.

978-1-58542-949-3

$27.95

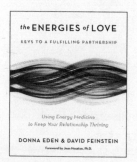

"The most crucial relationship advice book since *Men Are from Mars*."
—Erin Meanley, Glamour.com

978-0-39916-200-8

$17.95